The Power of the Dog

Don Winslow has worked as a movie theatre manager, a production assistant, and as a private investigator. In addition to being a novelist, he now works as an independent consultant in issues involving litigation arising from criminal behavioiur. His novels include *The Kings of Cool, The Death and Life of Bobby Z, California Fire and Life, The Winter of Frankie Machine* and *The Dawn Patrol.* In 2012, *Savages* was released as a blockbuster film.

Also by Don Winslow

THE

POWER OF THE DOG

Don Winslow

arrow books

27 29 30 28

Arrow Books
20 Vauxhall Bridge Road
London SW1V 2SA

Arrow Books is part of the Penguin Random House group of companies
whose addresses can be found at global.penguinrandomhouse.com

First published in Great Britain in 2005 by William Heinemann
Published by Arrow Books 2006

www.penguin.co.uk

A CIP catalogue record for this book is available from the British Library.

ISBN 9780099464983

Typeset by Palimpsest Book Production Ltd., Falkirk, UK

Printed and bound in Great Britain by Clays Ltd, Elcograf S.p.A.

Penguin Random House is committed to a sustainable future
for our business, our readers and our planet. This book is made from
Forest Stewardship Council® certified paper.

In memory of Sue Rubinsky,
who always wanted to learn the truth

Deliver my soul from the sword; my love from the power of the dog.

Psalms 22:20

THE POWER OF THE DOG

Prologue

El Sauzal
State of Baja California
Mexico
1997

The baby is dead in his mother's arms.

Art Keller can tell from the way the bodies lie—her on top, the baby beneath her—that she tried to shield her child. She must have known, Art thinks, that her own soft body could not have stopped bullets—not from automatic rifles, not from that range—but the move must have been instinctive. A mother puts her own body between her child and harm. So she turned, twisted as the bullets hit her, then fell on top of her son.

Did she really think that she could save the child? Maybe she didn't, Art thinks. Maybe she just didn't want the baby to see death blaze out from the barrel of the gun. Maybe she wanted her child's last sensation in this world to be that of her bosom. Enfolded in love.

Art is a Catholic. At forty-seven years of age, he's seen a lot of madonnas. But nothing like this one.

"Cuernos de chivo," he hears someone say.

Quietly, almost whispered, as if they were in church.

Cuernos de chivo.

Horns of the goat: AK-47s.

Art already knows that—hundreds of 7.62-mm shell casings lie on the patio's concrete floor, along with some .12-gauge shotgun shells and some 5.56s, probably, Art thinks, from AR-15s. But most of the casings are from the *cuernos de chivo,* the favored weapon of the Mexican *narcotraficantes.*

Nineteen bodies.

Nineteen more casualties in the War on Drugs, Art thinks.

He's used to looking at the bodies from his fourteen-year war with Adán Barrera—he's looked at many. But not nineteen. Not women, children, babies. Not this.

Ten men, three women, six children.

Lined up against the patio wall and shot.

Blasted is more the word, Art thinks. Blasted to pieces in an incontinent rush of bullets. The amount of blood is unreal. A pool the size of a large car, an inch thick with black, dried blood. Blood splattered on the walls, blood splattered on the manicured lawn, where it glistens black-red on the tips of the grass. The blades of which look to him like tiny, bloody swords.

They must have put up a fight as they realized what was about to happen. Pulled from their beds in the middle of the night, dragged out to the patio, lined up against the wall—someone had finally offered a struggle, because furniture is tipped over. Heavy wrought-iron patio furniture. Glass shattered on the concrete.

Art looks down and sees . . . Christ, it's a doll—its brown glass eyes staring up at him—lying in the blood. A doll, and a small cuddly animal, and a beautifully rendered pinto horse in plastic, all lying in blood by the execution wall.

Children, Art thinks, pulled out of sleep, grab their toys and hold on to them. Even as, especially as, the guns roar.

An irrational image comes to him: a stuffed elephant. A childhood toy he always slept with. It had one button eye. It was stained with vomit, with urine, with all the various childhood effluvia, and it smelled of all of them. His mother had sneaked it away in his sleep and replaced it with a new elephant with two eyes and a pristine aroma, and when Art woke up he thanked her for the new elephant and then found and retrieved the old one from the trash.

Arthur Keller hears his own heart break.

He switches his gaze to the adult victims.

Some are in pajamas—expensive silk pajamas and negligees—some in T-shirts. Two of them, a man and a woman, are naked—as if they had been grabbed from a postcoital sleeping embrace. What once had been love, Art thinks, is now naked obscenity.

One body lies alone along the opposite wall. An old man, the head of the family. Probably shot last, Art thinks. Forced to watch his family killed, and then dispatched himself. Mercifully? Art wonders. Was it some sort of sick mercy? But then he sees the old man's hands. His fingernails have been ripped out, then the fingers chopped off. His mouth is still open in a frozen scream and Art can see the fingers sticking to his tongue.

Meaning that they thought someone in his family was a *dedo,* a finger—an informer.

Because I led them to believe that.

God forgive me.

He searches through the bodies until he finds the one he's looking for.

When he does, his stomach lurches and he has to fight back the vomit in his throat because the young man's face has been peeled like a banana; the strips of flesh hang obscenely from his neck. Art hopes that they did this *after* they shot him, but he knows better.

The bottom half of his skull has been blown off.

They shot him in the mouth.

Traitors get shot in the back of the head, informers in the mouth.

They thought it was him.

Which was exactly what you wanted them to think, Art tells himself. Face it—it worked just the way you planned.

But I never envisioned this, he thinks. I never thought they'd do this.

"There must have been servants," Art says. "Workers."

The police have already checked the workers' quarters.

"Gone," one of the cops says.

Disappeared. Vanished.

He forces himself to look at the bodies again.

It's my fault, Art thinks.

I brought this on these people.

I'm sorry, Art thinks. I am so, so sorry. Bending over the mother and child, Art makes the sign of the cross and whispers, *"In nomine Patris et Filii et Spiritus Sancti."*

"El poder del perro," he hears one of the Mexican cops murmur.

The power of the dog.

PART ONE

Original Sins

1

The Men from Sinaloa

Seest thou yon dreary plain, forlorn and wild,
The seat of desolation, void of light,
Save what the glimmering of these livid flames
Casts pale and dreadful?

—John Milton, *Paradise Lost*

Badiraguato District
State of Sinaloa
Mexico
1975

The poppies burn.

Red blossoms, red flames.

Only in hell, Art Keller thinks, do flowers bloom fire.

Art sits on a ridge above the burning valley. Looking down is like peering into a steaming soup bowl—he can't see clearly through the smoke, but what he can make out is a scene from hell.

Hieronymus Bosch does the War on Drugs.

Campesinos—Mexican peasant farmers—trot in front of the flames, clutching the few possessions they could grab before the soldiers put the torch to their village. Pushing their children in front of them, the *campesinos* carry sacks of food, family photographs bought at great price, some blankets, some clothes. Their white shirts and straw hats—stained yellow with sweat—make them ghost-like in the haze of smoke.

Except for the clothes, Art thinks, it could be Vietnam.

He's half-surprised, glancing at the sleeve of his own shirt, to see blue denim instead of army green. Reminds himself that this isn't Operation

Phoenix but Operation Condor, and these aren't the bamboo-thick mountains of I Corps, but the poppy-rich mountain valleys of Sinaloa.

And the crop isn't rice, it's opium.

Art hears the dull bass *whop-whop-whop* of helicopter rotors and looks up. Like a lot of guys who were in Vietnam, he finds the sound evocative. Yeah, but evocative of what? he asks himself, then decides that some memories are better left buried.

Choppers and fixed-wing planes circle overhead like vultures. The airplanes do the actual spraying; the choppers are there to help protect the planes from the sporadic AK-47 rounds fired by the remaining *gomeros*—opium growers—who still want to make a fight of it. Art knows too well that an accurate burst from an AK can bring down a chopper. Hit it in the tail rotor and it will spiral down like a broken toy at a kid's birthday party. Hit the pilot, and, well . . . So far they've been lucky and no choppers have been hit. Either the *gomeros* are just bad shots, or they're not used to firing on helicopters.

Technically, all the aircraft are Mexican—officially, Condor is a Mexican show, a joint operation between the Ninth Army Corps and the State of Sinaloa—but the planes were bought and paid for by the DEA and are flown by DEA contract pilots, most of them former CIA employees from the old Southeast Asia crew. Now there's a tasty irony, Keller thinks—Air America boys who once flew heroin for Thai warlords now spray defoliants on Mexican opium.

The DEA wanted to use Agent Orange, but the Mexicans had balked at that. So instead they are using a new compound, 24-D, which the Mexicans feel comfortable with, mostly, Keller chuckles, because the *gomeros* were already using it to kill the weeds around the poppy fields.

So there was a ready supply.

Yeah, Art thinks, it's a Mexican operation. We Americans are just down here as "advisers."

Like Vietnam.

Just with different ball caps.

The American War on Drugs has opened a front in Mexico. Now ten thousand Mexican army troops are pushing through this valley near the town of Badiraguato, assisting squadrons of the Municipal Judicial Federal Police, better known as the *federales,* and a dozen or so DEA advisers like Art. Most of the soldiers are on foot; others are on horseback, like *vaqueros* driving cattle in front of them. Their orders are simple: Poison the poppy fields and burn the remnants, scatter the *gomeros* like dry leaves in a hurricane. Destroy the source of heroin here in the Sinaloan mountains of western Mexico.

The Sierra Occidental has the best combination of altitude, rainfall and soil acidity in the Western Hemisphere to grow *Papaver somniferum,* the poppy that produces the opium that is eventually converted to Mexican Mud, the cheap, brown, potent heroin that has been flooding the streets of American cities.

Operation Condor, Art thinks.

There hasn't been an actual condor seen in Mexican skies in over sixty years, longer in the States. But every operation has to have a name or we don't believe it's real, so Condor it is.

Art's done a little reading on the bird. It is (was) the largest bird of prey, although the term is a little misleading, as it preferred scavenging over hunting. A big condor, Art learned, could take out a small deer; but what it really liked was when something else killed the deer first so the bird could just swoop down and take it.

We prey on the dead.

Operation Condor.

Another Vietnam flashback.

Death from the Sky.

And here I am, crouched in the brush again, shivering in the damp mountain cold again, setting up ambushes.

Again.

Except the target now isn't some VC cadre on his way back to his village, but old Don Pedro Áviles, the drug lord of Sinaloa, El Patrón himself. Don Pedro's been running opium out of these mountains for half a century, even before Bugsy Siegel himself came here, with Virginia Hill in tow, to nail down a steady source of heroin for the West Coast Mafia.

Siegel made the deal with a young Don Pedro Áviles, who used that leverage to make himself *patrón,* the boss, a status he's maintained to this day. But the old man's power has been slipping a little lately as some young up-and-comers have started to challenge his authority. The law of nature, Art supposes—the young lions eventually take on the old. Art has been kept awake more than one night in his Culiacán hotel room by the sound of machine-gun fire in the streets, so common lately that the city has gained the nickname Little Chicago.

Well, after today, maybe they won't have anything to fight about.

Arrest old Don Pedro and you put an end to it.

And make yourself a star, he thinks, feeling a little guilty.

Art is a true believer in the War on Drugs. Growing up in San Diego's Barrio Logan, he saw firsthand what heroin does to a neighborhood, particularly a poor one. So this is supposed to be about getting drugs off the streets, he reminds himself, not advancing your career.

But the truth of it is that being the guy to bring down old Don Pedro Áviles would make your career.

Which, truth be told, could use a boost.

The DEA is a new organization, barely two years old. When Richard Nixon declared a War on Drugs, he needed soldiers to fight it. Most of the new recruits came from the old Bureau of Narcotics and Dangerous Drugs; a lot of them came from various police departments around the country, but not a few of the early start-up draft into the DEA came from the Company.

Art was one of these Company Cowboys.

That's what the police types call any of the guys who came in from the CIA. There's a lot of resentment and mistrust of the covert types by the law enforcement types.

Shouldn't be, Art thinks. It's basically the same function—intelligence gathering. You find your assets, cultivate them, run them and act on the intelligence they give you. The big difference between his new work and his old work is that in the former you arrest your targets, and in the latter you just kill them.

Operation Phoenix, the programmed assassination of the Vietcong infrastructure.

Art hadn't done too much of the actual "wet work." His job back in Vietnam was to collect raw data and analyze it. Other guys, mostly Special Forces on loan to the Company, went out and acted on Art's information.

They usually went out at night, Art recalls. Sometimes they'd be gone for days, then reappear back at the base in the small hours of the morning, cranked up on Dexedrine. Then they'd disappear into their hooches and sleep for days at a time, then go out and do it again.

Art had gone out with them only a few times, when his sources had produced info about a large group of cadres concentrated in the area. Then he'd accompany the Special Forces guys to set up a night ambush.

He hadn't liked it much. Most of the time he was scared shitless, but he did his job, he pulled the trigger, he took his buddies' backs, he got out alive with all his limbs attached and his mind intact. He saw a lot of shit he wishes he could forget.

I just have to live with the fact, Art thinks, that I wrote men's names down on paper and, in the act of doing so, signed their death warrants. After that, it's a matter of finding a way to live decently in an indecent world.

But that fucking war.

That goddamn motherfucking war.

Like a lot of people, he watched the last helicopters taking off from Saigon rooftops on television. Like a lot of vets, he went out and got good and stinking drunk that night, and when the offer came to move over to the new DEA, he jumped at it.

He talked it over with Althie first.

"Maybe this is a war worth fighting," he told his wife. "Maybe this is a war we can actually win."

And now, Art thinks as he sits and waits for Don Pedro to show up, we might be close to doing it.

His legs ache from sitting still but he doesn't move. His stint in Vietnam taught him that. The Mexicans spaced in the brush around him are likewise disciplined—twenty special agents from the DFS, armed with Uzis, dressed in camouflage.

Tío Barrera is wearing a suit.

Even up here in the high brush, the governor's special assistant is wearing his trademark black suit, white button-down shirt, skinny black tie. He looks comfortable and serene, the image of Latino male dignity.

He reminds you of one of those matinee idols from an old '40s movie, Art thinks. Black hair slicked back, pencil mustache, thin, handsome face with cheekbones that look like they're cut from granite.

Eyes as black as a moonless night.

Officially, Miguel Ángel Barrera is a cop, a Sinaloa state policeman, the bodyguard to the state governor, Manuel Sánchez Cerro. Unofficially, Barrera is a fixer, the governor's point man. And seeing how Condor is technically a Sinaloa state operation, Barrera is the guy who's really running the show.

And me, Art thinks. If I really want to be honest about it, Tío Barrera is running me.

The twelve weeks of DEA training weren't that hard. The PT was a breeze— Art could easily run the three-mile course and play basketball, and the self-defense component was unsophisticated compared with Langley. The instructors just had them wrestle and box, and Art had finished third in the San Diego Golden Gloves as a kid.

He was a mediocre middleweight with good technique but slow hands. He found out the hard truth that you can't learn speed. He was just good enough to get into the upper ranks, where he could really get beat up. But he showed he could take it, and that was his ticket as a mixed-race kid in the barrio. Mexican fight fans have more respect for what a fighter can take than for what he can dish out.

And Art could take it.

After he started boxing, the Mexican kids pretty much left him alone. Even the gangs backed off him.

In the DEA training sessions he made it a point to take it easy on his opponents in the ring, though. There was no point in beating someone up and making an enemy just to show off.

The law enforcement–procedure classes were tougher, but he got through them all right, and the drug training was pretty easy, questions like, Can you identify marijuana? Can you identify heroin? Art resisted the impulse to answer that he always could at home.

The other temptation he resisted was to finish first in his class. He could have, knew he could have, but decided to fly under the radar. The law enforcement guys already felt that the Company types were trespassing on their turf, so it was better to walk lightly.

So he took it a little easy in the physical training, kept quiet in class, punted a few questions on the tests. He did enough to do well, to pass, but not enough to shine. It was a little harder to be cool in the field training. Surveillance practice? Old hat. Hidden cameras, mikes, bugs? He could install them in his sleep. Clandestine meetings, dead drops, live drops, cultivating a source, interrogating a suspect, gathering intelligence, analyzing data? He could have taught the course.

He kept his mouth shut, graduated, and was declared a Special Agent of the DEA. They gave him a two-week vacation and sent him straight to Mexico.

Right to Culiacán.

The capital of the Western Hemisphere drug trade.

Opium's market town.

The belly of the beast.

His new boss gave him a friendly greeting. Tim Taylor, the Culiacán RAC (Resident Agent in Charge) had already perused Art's shield and seen through the transparent screen. He didn't even look up from the file. Art was sitting across from his desk and the guy said, "Vietnam?"

"Yup."

" 'Accelerated Pacification Program' . . ."

"Yup." Accelerated Pacification Program, aka Operation Phoenix. The old joke being that a lot of guys got peaceful in a hurry.

"CIA," Taylor said, and it wasn't a question, it was a statement.

Question or statement, Art didn't answer it. He knew the book on Taylor—he was an old BNDD guy who'd lived through the low-budget bad days. Now that drugs were a fat priority, he didn't intend to lose his hard-earned gains to a bunch of new kids on the block.

"You know what I don't like about you Company Cowboys?" Taylor asked.

"No, what?"

"You aren't cops," Taylor said. "You're killers."

And fuck you, too, Art thought. But he kept his mouth shut. Kept it firmly clamped while Taylor launched into a lecture about how he didn't want any cowboy shit from Art. How they're a "team" here and Art better be a "team player" and "play by the rules."

Art would have been happy to be a team player if they would have let him on the team. Not that Art cared one hell of a lot. You grow up in the barrio as the son of an Anglo father and a Mexican mother, you're not on anybody's team.

Art's father was a San Diego businessman who seduced a Mexican girl while on vacation in Mazatlán. (Art often thought it was funny that he was conceived, albeit not born, in Sinaloa.) Art Senior decided to do the right thing and marry the girl—not too painful an option, as she was a raving beauty; Art gets his good looks from his mother's side. His father brings her back to the States, only to decide that she's like a lot of things you get in Mexico on vacation—she looked a lot better on a moonlit beach in Mazatlán than in the cold, Anglo light of the American day-to-day.

Art Senior dumped her when Art was about a year old. She didn't want to throw away the one advantage her son had in life—U.S. citizenship—so she moved in with some distant relations in Barrio Logan. Art knew who his father was—sometimes he'd sit in the little park on Crosby Street and look at the tall glass buildings downtown and imagine going into one of them to see his father.

But he didn't.

Art Senior sent checks—faithfully at first and then sporadically—and he'd get occasional bouts of paternal urges or guilt and show up to take Art to dinner or maybe a Padres game. But their father-son time was awkward and forced, and by the time Art was in junior high the visits had stopped altogether.

Ditto the money.

So it was no easy thing when the seventeen-year-old Art finally made the trip downtown, marched into one of those tall glass buildings, strode into his father's office, laid his killer SAT scores and UCLA acceptance letter on his desk and said, "Don't freak out. All I want from you is a check."

He got it.

Once a year for four years.

He got the lesson, too: YOYO.

You're On Your Own.

Which was a good lesson to learn because the DEA just chucked him into Culiacán, virtually on his own. "Just get the lay of the land" is what Taylor told him at the start of a cliché-fest that also included "Get your feet wet," "Easy does it" and, honest to God, "Failing to prepare is preparing to fail."

It should have included "And go fuck yourself," because that was the thrust of it. Taylor and the cop types totally isolated him, kept info from him, wouldn't introduce him to contacts, froze him out on meetings with the local Mexican cops, didn't include him in the morning coffee-and-doughnut bull-shit or the sundown beer sessions where the real information was passed.

He was fucked from jump street.

The local Mexicans weren't going to talk to him because as a Yanqui in Culiacán he could only be one of two things—a drug dealer or a narc. He wasn't a drug dealer because he wasn't buying anything (Taylor wouldn't free up any money; he didn't want Art fucking up anything they already had going), so he had to be a narc.

The Culiacán police wouldn't have anything to do with him because he was a Yanqui narc who should stay home and mind his own business, and besides, most of them were on Don Pedro Áviles's payroll anyway. The Sinaloa state cops wouldn't deal with him for the same reasons, with the additional rationale that if Keller's own DEA wouldn't work with him, why should they?

Not that the team was doing much better.

The DEA had been hammering on the Mexican government for two years, trying to get them to move against the *gomeros*. The agents brought evidence—photos, tapes, witnesses—only to have the *federales* promise to move right away and then not move, only to hear, "This is Mexico, señores. These things take time."

While the evidence grew stale, the witnesses got scared and the *federales* rotated posts so that the Americans had to start all over again with a different federal cop, who told them to bring him solid evidence, bring him witnesses. Who, when they did, looked at them with perfect condescension and told them, "Señores, this is Mexico. These things take time."

While the heroin flowed down from the hills into Culiacán like mud in a spring thaw, the young *gomeros* slugged it out with Don Pedro's forces on a nightly basis until the city sounded to Art like Danang or Saigon, only with a lot more gunfire.

Night after night, Art would lie on the bed in his hotel room, drinking cheap scotch, maybe watching a soccer game or boxing match on TV, pissed off and feeling sorry for himself.

And missing Althie.

God, how he missed Althie.

He had met Althea Patterson on Bruin Walk in his senior year, introducing himself with a lame line: "Aren't we in the same Poli Sci section?"

Tall, thin and blond, Althea was more angular than curvy; her nose was long and hooked, her mouth a little too wide, and her green eyes set a little too deep to be considered classically pretty, but Althea was beautiful.

And *smart*—they actually were in the same Poli Sci section, and he'd listened to her talk in class. She argued her viewpoint (a little to the left of Emma Goldman) ferociously, and that turned him on, too.

So they went out for pizza and then they went to her apartment in Westwood. She made espresso and they talked and he found out that she was a rich girl from Santa Barbara, her family Old California Money and her father a very big deal in the state Democratic Party.

To her, he was madly handsome, with that shock of black hair that fell over his forehead, that rugged broken nose that saved him from being a pretty boy, and the quiet intelligence that had brought a kid from the barrio to UCLA. There was something else, too—a loneliness, a vulnerability, a hurt, an edge of anger—that made him irresistible.

They ended up in bed, and in the postcoital darkness he asked, "So, can you cross that off your liberal checklist now?"

"What?"

"Sleeping with a spic."

She thought about this for a few seconds, then answered, "See, I always thought that *spic* referred to a Puerto Rican. What I can cross off is sleeping with a *beaner*."

"Actually," he said, "I'm only *half* a beaner."

"Well then, Jesus, Art," she said. "What good are *you*?"

Althea was the exception to Art's Doctrine of YOYO, an insidious infiltrator into the self-sufficiency that was already well ingrained in him by the time he met her. Secrecy was already a habit, a protective wall he had carefully constructed around himself as a kid. By the time he fell in love with Althie, he'd had the added advantage of professional instruction in the discipline of mental compartmentalization.

The Company's talent-spotters had lamped him in his sophomore year, picked him like low-hanging fruit.

His International Relations professor, a Cuban expatriate, took him out for coffee, then started advising him on what classes to take, what languages to study. Professor Osuna brought him home to dinner, taught him which fork to use when, which wine to select with what, even which women to date. (Professor Osuna loved Althea. "She's perfect for you," he said. "She gives you sophistication.")

It was more of a seduction than a recruitment.

Not that Art was hard to seduce.

They have a nose for guys like me, Art thought later. The lost, the lonely, the bicultural misfits with a foot in two worlds and a place in neither. And you were perfect for them—smart, street-tough, ambitious. You looked white but you fought brown. All you needed was the polish, and they gave you that.

Then came the small errands: "Arturo, there's a Bolivian professor visiting. Could you escort him around the city?" A few more of those, then, "Arturo, what does Dr. Echeverría like to do in his leisure time? Does he drink? Does he like the girls? No? Perhaps the boys?" Then, "Arturo, if Professor Méndez wanted some marijuana, could you get it for him?" "Arturo, could you tell me who our distinguished poet friend is speaking to on the telephone?" "Arturo, this is a listening device. If you could perhaps insinuate it into his room . . ."

Art did it all without blinking, and did it all well.

They handed him his diploma and a ticket to Langley practically at the same time. Explaining this to Althie was an interesting exercise. "I can sort of tell you, but I can't really," was about the best he could manage. She wasn't stupid; she got it.

"Boxing," she told him, "is the perfect metaphor for you."

"What do you mean?"

"The art of keeping things out," she said. "You're so skilled at it. Nothing touches you."

That's not true, Art thought. *You* touch me.

They got married a few weeks before he shipped out to Vietnam. He'd write her long, passionate letters that never included anything about what he actually did. He was changed when he got home, she thought; of course he was, why wouldn't he be? But the insularity that had always been there was intensified. He could suddenly put oceans of emotional distance between them and deny that he was doing it. Then he would revert to being that sweet, intensely affectionate man with whom she had fallen in love.

She was relieved when he said he was thinking about changing jobs. He was enthused about the new DEA; he thought he could really do some good there. She encouraged him to take the job, even though it meant he was going to leave for another three months, even when he came home just long enough to get her pregnant and left again, this time for Mexico.

He wrote her long, passionate letters from Mexico that never included anything about what he actually did. Because I don't do anything, he wrote her.

Not a goddamn thing except feel sorry for myself.

So get off your ass and do something, she wrote back. Or quit and come home to me. I know Daddy could get you a job on a senator's staff in no time, just say the word.

Art didn't say the word.

What he did was get off his ass and go see a saint.

Everyone in Sinaloa knows the legend of Santo Jesús Malverde. He was a bandito, a daring robber, a man of the poor who gave back to the poor, a Sinaloan Robin Hood. His luck ran out in 1909 and the *federales* hanged him on a gallows just across the street from where his shrine now stands.

The shrine was spontaneous. First some flowers, then a picture, then a small building of rough-hewn planks, put up by the poor at night. Even the police were afraid to tear it down because the legend grew that the soul of Malverde lived in the shrine. That if you came here and prayed, and lit a candle and made a *manda*—a devotional promise—Jesús Malverde could and would grant favors.

Bring you a good crop, protect you from your enemies, heal your illnesses.

Notes of gratitude detailing the favors that Malverde has bestowed are stuck into the walls: a sick child cured, rent money magically appeared, an arrest evaded, a conviction overturned, a *mojado* returned safely from El Norte, a murder avoided, a murder avenged.

Art went to the shrine. Figured it was a good place to start. He walked down from his hotel, waited patiently in line with the other pilgrims and finally got inside.

He was used to saints. His mother had faithfully dragged him to Our Lady of Guadalupe in Barrio Logan, where he took catechism classes, made his First Communion, was confirmed. He had prayed to saints, lit candles at the statues of saints, sat as a child and looked at paintings of saints.

Actually, Art was a pretty faithful Catholic even during college. He was a regular communicant in Vietnam at first, but his devotion waned and he stopped going to confession. It was like, Forgive me, Father, for I have sinned, Forgive me, Father, for I have sinned, Forgive me, Father, for I have— Oh, fuck it, what's the point? Every day I mark men for death, every other week I kill them myself. I'm not going to come in here and tell you that I'm not going to do it again, when it's on the schedule, regular as Mass.

Sal Scachi, one of the Special Forces guys, used to go to Mass every Sunday he wasn't out killing people. Art used to marvel how the perceived hypocrisy didn't faze him. They even talked about it one drunken night, Art and this very Italian guy from New York.

"It don't bother me," Scachi said. "Shouldn't bother you. The VC don't believe in God, anyway, so fuck 'em."

They got into a ferocious debate, Art appalled that Scachi actually thought they were "doing God's work" by assassinating Vietcong. Communists are atheists, Scachi repeated, who want to destroy the Church. So what we're doing, he explained, is defending the Church, and that isn't a sin, it's a duty.

He reached under his shirt and showed Art the Saint Anthony's medal he kept around his neck on a chain.

"The saint keeps me safe," he explained. "You should get one."

Art didn't.

Now, in Culiacán, he stood and stared into the obsidian eyes of Santo Jesús Malverde. The saint's plaster skin was stark white and his mustache a sable black, and a garish circle of red had been painted around his neck to remind the pilgrim that the saint had, like all the best saints, been martyred.

Santo Jesús died for our sins.

"Well," Art said to the statue, "whatever you're doing, it's working, and whatever I'm doing, it's not, so . . ."

Art made a *manda*. Knelt, lit a candle, and left a twenty-dollar bill. What the hell.

"Help me bring you down, Santo Jesús," he whispered in Spanish, "and there's more where that came from. I'll give money to the poor."

Walking back to the hotel from the shrine, Art met Adán Barrera.

Art had walked past this gym a dozen times. He had been tempted to check it out and never had, but on this particular evening a fairly large crowd was inside, so he walked in and stood at the edge.

Adán was barely twenty then. Short, almost diminutive, with a thin build. Long black hair combed straight back, designer jeans, Nike running shoes, and a purple polo shirt. Expensive clothes for this barrio. Smart clothes, smart kid—Art could see that right away. Adán Barrera just had a look like he always knew what was going on.

Art put him at about 5'5", maybe 5'6", but the kid standing beside him had to go 6'3" easy. And built. Big chest, sloping shoulders, lanky. You wouldn't make them for brothers except for their faces. Same face on two different bodies—deep brown eyes, light coffee–colored skin, more Spanish-looking than Indian.

They were standing on the edge of the ring looking down at an unconscious boxer. Another fighter stood in the ring. A kid, really, certainly not out of his teens, but with a body that looked like it had been chiseled out of living stone. And he had those eyes—Art had seen them before in the ring—that had the look of a natural killer. Except now he seemed confused and a little guilty.

Art got it right away. The fighter had just knocked out a sparring partner and now had no one to work out with. The two brothers were his managers. It was a common enough scene in any Mexican barrio. For poor kids from the barrio, there were two routes up and out—drugs or boxing. The kid was an up-and-comer, hence the crowd, and the two middle-class Mutt-and-Jeff brothers were his managers.

Now the short one was looking around the crowd to find someone who could step into the ring and go a few rounds. A lot of guys in the crowd suddenly found something very interesting on the tops of their shoes.

Art didn't.

He caught the short guy's eye.

"Who are you?" the kid asked.

His brother took one look at Art and said, "Yanqui narc." Then he looked over the crowd, straight at Art, and said, *"¡Vete al demonio, picaflor!"*

Basically, "Get the hell out of here, faggot."

Art instantly answered, *"Pela las nalgas, perra."*

Shove it up your ass, bitch.

Which was a surprise coming out of the mouth of a guy who looked very white. The lanky brother started to push his way through the crowd to get at Art, but the smaller brother grabbed him by the elbow and whispered something to him. Tall brother smiled, then the smaller one said to Art, in English, "You're about the right size. You want to go a few rounds with him?"

"He's a kid," Art answered.

"He can take care of himself," the short brother said. "In fact, he can take care of you."

Art laughed.

"You box?" the kid pressed.

"Used to," Art said. "A little bit."

"Well, come on in, Yanqui," the kid said. "We'll find you some gloves."

It wasn't machismo that made Art accept the challenge. He could have laughed it off. But boxing is sacred in Mexico, and when people you've been trying to get close to for months invite you into their church, you go.

"So who am I fighting?" he asked one of the crowd as they were taping his hands and getting him into gloves.

"El Leoncito de Culiacán," the man answered proudly. "The Little Lion of Culiacán. He'll be champion of the world one day."

Art walked into the center of the ring.

"Take it easy on me," he said. "I'm an old man."

They touched gloves.

Don't try to win, Art told himself. Take it easy on the kid. You're here to make friends.

Ten seconds later, Art was laughing at his own pretensions. Between taking punches, that is. You couldn't be much less effective, he told himself, if you were wrapped in telephone wire. I don't think you have to worry about winning.

Worry about surviving, maybe, he told himself ten seconds later. The kid's hand speed was awesome. Art couldn't even see the punches coming, never mind block them, never mind counterpunch.

But you have to try.

It's about respect.

So he launched a straight right behind a left jab and collected a wicked three-punch combination in return. *Boom-boom-boom*. It's like living inside a fucking timpani drum, Art thought, backing away.

Bad idea.

The kid came rushing in, threw two lightning jabs and then a straight shot to the face, and if Art's nose wasn't broken, it was doing a damn good imitation. He swiped the blood off his nose, covered up, and took most of the subsequent drubbing on his gloves until the kid switched tactics and went downstairs, digging rights and lefts into Art's ribs.

It seemed like an hour later when the bell rang and Art went back to his stool.

Big Brother was right there. "You had enough, *picaflor*?"

Except this time the "faggot" wasn't quite so hostile.

Art answered in a friendly tone, "I'm just getting my wind, bitch."

He got the wind knocked out of him about five seconds into round two. A wicked left hook to the liver dropped Art right to one knee. He had his head down, and blood and sweat dripped off his nose. He was gasping for air, and out of the corners of his teary eyes he could see men in the crowd exchanging money, and he could just hear the smaller brother counting to ten with a tone of foregone conclusion.

Fuck you all, Art thought.

He got up.

Heard cursing from some in the crowd, cheers from a few.

Come on, Art, he told himself. Just getting the shit beat out of you isn't going to get you anywhere. You have to put up some kind of a fight. Neutralize this kid's hand speed, don't let him get off punches so easy.

He charged forward.

Took three hard shots for his trouble but kept going forward and worked the kid into the ropes. Stayed toe to toe with him and started throwing short, chopping punches, not hard enough to really hurt, but enough to make the kid cover up. Then Art ducked down, hit him twice in the ribs, and then leaned forward and tied him up.

Take a few seconds off the round, Art thought, get a blow. Lean on the kid, maybe wear him out a little. But even before Little Brother could come in and break the clinch, the kid slipped under Art's arms, spun out, and hit him with two punches in the side of the head.

Art kept coming forward.

Absorbing punches the whole time, but it was Art who was the aggressor, and that was the point. The kid was backing off, dancing, hitting him at will, but nevertheless going backwards. He dropped his hands and Art hit him with a hard left jab in the chest, driving him back. The kid looked surprised, so Art did it again.

Between rounds, the two brothers were too busy giving their boxer hell to give Art any shit. He was grateful for the rest. One more round, he thought. Just let me get through one more round.

The bell rang.

A lot of *dinero* changed hands when Art got off his stool.

He touched gloves with the kid for the last round, looked into his eyes and instantly saw that he'd wounded the kid's pride. Shit, Art thought, I didn't mean to do that. Rein in your ego, asshole, and don't take a chance on winning this thing.

He needn't have worried.

Whatever the brothers had told the kid between rounds, the kid made the adjustment, constantly moving to his left, in the direction of his own jab, keeping his hands high, pretty much hitting Art at will, then getting out of the way.

Art was moving forward, hitting at air.

He stopped.

Stood in the center of the ring, shook his head, laughed and waved the kid to come on in.

The crowd loved it.

The kid loved it.

He shuffled into the center of the ring and started raining punches down on Art, who blocked them the best he could and covered up. Art would shoot a jab or counterpunch back every few seconds, and the kid would fire over it and nail him again.

The kid wasn't going for knockout punches now. There was no anger in him anymore. He was truly sparring, just getting in his workout and showing that he could hit Art anytime he wanted, playing to the crowd, giving them the show they'd come to see. By the end, Art was down on one knee with his gloves tight to his head and his elbows tucked into his ribs, so he was taking most of the shots on his gloves and arms.

The final bell rang.

The kid picked Art up and they embraced.

"You are going to be champ one day," Art said to him.

"You did okay," the kid said. "Thank you for the match."

"You got yourself a good fighter," Art said as Little Brother was taking his gloves off.

"We're going all the way," Little Brother said. He stuck out his hand, "My name is Adán. That's my brother, Raúl."

Raúl looked down at Art and nodded. "You didn't quit, Yanqui. I thought you'd quit."

No "faggot" this time, Art noted.

"If I had any brains, I'd have quit," he said.

"You fight like a Mexican," Raúl said.

Ultimate praise.

Actually, I fight like half a Mexican, Art thought, but he kept it to himself. But he knew what Raúl meant. It was the same in Barrio Logan—it isn't so much what you can dish out as what you can take.

Well, I took plenty tonight, Art thought. All I want to do now is go back to the hotel, take a long, hot shower and spend the rest of the night with an ice pack.

Okay, several ice packs.

"We're going out for some beers," Adán said. "You want to come?"

Yeah, Art thought. Yeah, I do.

So he spent the night downing beers in a *cafetín* with Adán.

Years later, Art would have given anything in the world to have just killed Adán Barrera on the spot.

Tim Taylor called him into the office the next morning.

Art looked like shit, which was an accurate external reflection of his internal reality. His head was pounding from the beers and the *yerba* he'd ended up smoking in the after-hours club Adán had hauled him to. His eyes were black and there were still traces of dark, dried blood under his nose. He'd showered but hadn't shaved because one, he hadn't had time; and two, the thought of dragging anything across his swollen jaw was just unacceptable. And even though he lowered himself into the chair slowly, his bruised ribs screamed at him for the offense.

Taylor looked at him with undisguised disgust. "You had quite a night for yourself."

Art smiled sheepishly. Even that hurt. "You know about that."

"You know how I heard?" Taylor said. "I had a meeting this morning with Miguel Barrera. You know who that is, Keller? He's a Sinaloan state cop, the special assistant to the governor, *the* man in this area. We've been trying to get him to work with us for two years. And I have to hear from him that one of my agents is brawling with the locals—"

"It was a sparring match."

"Whatever," Taylor said. "Look, these people are not our pals or our drinking buddies. They're our targets, and—"

"Maybe that's the problem," Art heard himself say. Some disembodied voice that he couldn't control. He'd meant to keep his mouth shut, but he was just too fucked-up to maintain the discipline.

"*What's* the problem?"

Fuck it, Art thought. Too late now. So he answered, "That we look at 'these people' like 'targets.' "

And anyway, it pissed him off. People as targets? Been there, done that. Besides that, I learned more about how things work down here last night than I did in the last three months.

"Look, you're not in an undercover role here," Taylor said. "Work with the local law enforcement people—"

"Can't, Tim," Art said. "You did a good job of queering me with them."

"I'm going to get you out of here," Tim said. "I want you off my team."

"Start the paperwork," Art said. He was sick of this shit.

"Don't worry, I will," Taylor said. "In the meantime, Keller, try to conduct yourself like a professional?"

Art nodded and got up out of the chair.

Slowly.

While the Damoclean sword of bureaucracy was dangling, Art thought he might as well keep working.

What's the saying, he asked himself. They can kill you but they can't eat you? Which isn't true—they can kill you *and* eat you—but that doesn't mean you go easy. The thought of going to work on a senatorial staff depressed the hell out of him. It wasn't so much the work as it was Althie's father setting it up, Art having a somewhat ambivalent attitude toward father figures.

It was the idea of failure.

You don't let them knock you out, you *make* them knock you out. You make them break their fucking hands knocking you out, you let them know that they've been in a fight, you give them something to remember you by every time they look in a mirror.

He went right back to the gym.

"*¡Qué noche bruta!*" he said to Adán. "*Me mata la cabeza.*"

"*Pero gozamos.*"

We enjoyed ourselves all right, Art thought. My head is splitting, anyway. "How's the Little Lion?"

"Cesar? Better than you," Adán said. "Better than me."

"Where's Raúl?"

"Probably out getting laid," Adán said. "*Es el coño, ése.* You want a beer?"

"Hell, yes."

Damn, it tasted good going down. Art took a long, wonderful swig, then laid the ice-cold bottle against his swollen cheek.

"You look like shit," Adán said.

"That good?"

"Almost."

Adán signaled the waiter and ordered a plate of cold meats. The two men sat at the outdoor table and watched the world go by.

"So you're a narc," Adán said.

"That's me."

"My uncle is a cop."

"You didn't go into the family business?"

Adán said, "I'm a smuggler."

Art raised an eyebrow. It actually hurt.

"Blue jeans," Adán said, laughing. "My brother and I go up to San Diego, buy blue jeans and sneak them back across the border. Sell them duty-free off the back of a truck. You'd be surprised how much money there is in it."

"I thought you were in college. What was it, accounting?"

"You have to have something to count," Adán said.

"Does your uncle know what you do for beer money?"

"Tío knows everything," Adán said. "He thinks it's frivolous. He wants me to get 'serious.' But the jeans business is good. It brings in some cash until the boxing thing takes off. Cesar will be a champion. We'll make millions."

"You ever try boxing yourself?" Art asked.

Adán shook his head. "I'm small, but I'm slow. Raúl, he's the fighter in the family."

"Well, I think I fought my last match."

"I think that's a good idea."

They both laughed.

It's a funny thing, how friendships are formed.

Art would think about that years later. A sparring match, a drunken night, an afternoon at a sidewalk café. Conversation, ambitions shared over shared dishes, bottles and hours. Bullshit tossed back and forth. Laughs.

Art would think about that, the realization that until Adán Barrera, he'd never really had a friend.

He had Althie, but that was different.

You can describe your wife, truthfully, as your best friend, but it's not the same thing. It's not that male thing, that brother-you-never-had, guy-you-hang-out-with thing.

Cuates, amigos, almost *hermanos.*

Hard to know how that happens.

Maybe what Adán saw in Art was what he didn't find in his own brother—an intelligence, a seriousness, a maturity he didn't have himself but wanted. Maybe what Art saw in Adán . . . Christ, later he'd try for *years* to explain it, even to himself. It was just that, back in those days, Adán Barrera was *a good guy.* He really was, or at least it seemed that way. Whatever it was that was lying dormant inside him . . .

Maybe it lies in all of us, Art would later think.

It sure as hell did in me.

The power of the dog.

It was Adán, inevitably, who introduced him to Tío.

Six weeks later, Art was lying on his bed in his hotel room, watching a soccer match on TV, feeling shitty because Tim Taylor had just received the okay to reassign him. Probably send me to Iowa to check if drugstores are complying with regulations on prescribing cough medicine or something, Art thought.

Career over.

There was a knock at the door.

Art opened it to see a man in a black suit, white shirt and skinny black tie. Hair slicked back in the old-fashioned style, pencil mustache, eyes black as midnight.

Maybe forty years old, with an Old World gravitas.

"Señor Keller, forgive me for disturbing your privacy," he said. "My name is Miguel Ángel Barrera. Sinaloa State Police. I wonder if I might have a few moments of your time."

No shit you can, Art thought, and asked him in. Luckily, Art had most of a fifth of scotch left over from a bunch of lonely nights, so he could at least offer the man a drink. Barrera accepted it and offered Art a thin black Cuban cigar in return.

"I quit," Art said.

"Do you mind, then?"

"I'll live vicariously through you," Art answered. He looked around for an ashtray and found one, then the two men sat down at the small table next to the window. Barrera looked at Art for a few seconds, as if considering something, then said, "My nephew asked if I'd stop in and see you."

"Your nephew?"

"Adán Barrera."

"Right."

My uncle is a cop, Art thought. So this is "Tío."

Art said, "Adán conned me into getting in the ring with one of the best fighters I've ever seen."

"Adán fancies himself a manager," Tío said. "Raúl thinks *he's* a trainer."

"They do all right," Art said. "Cesar could take them a long way."

"I own Cesar," Barrera said. "I'm an indulgent uncle, I let my nephews play. But soon I will have to hire a real manager and a real trainer for Cesar. He deserves no less. He'll be a champion."

"Adán will be disappointed."

"Learning to deal with disappointment is part of becoming a man," Barrera said.

Well, that's no shit.

"Adán relates that you are in some sort of professional difficulty?"

Now, how do I answer that? Art wondered. Taylor would no doubt employ a cliché about "not washing our dirty laundry in public," but he'd be right. He'd shit jagged glass anyway if he knew that Barrera was even here, going under his head, as it were, to talk with a junior officer.

"My boss and I don't always see eye to eye."

Barrera nodded. "Señor Taylor's vision can be somewhat narrow. All he can see is Pedro Áviles. The trouble with your DEA is that it is, forgive me, so very American. Your colleagues do not understand our culture, how things work, how things *have* to work."

The man isn't wrong, Art thought. Our approach down here has been clumsy and heavy-handed, to say the least. That fucked-up American attitude of "We know how to get things done," "Just get out of our way and let us do the job." And why not? It worked so well in 'Nam.

Art answered in Spanish, "What we lack in subtlety, we make up for with a lack of subtlety."

Barrera asked, "Are you Mexican, Señor Keller?"

"Half," Art said. "On my mother's side. As a matter of fact, she's from Sinaloa. Mazatlán."

Because, Art thought, I'm not above playing that card.

"But you were raised in the barrio," Barrera said. "In San Diego?"

This isn't a conversation, Art thought, it's a job interview.

"You know San Diego?" he asked. "I lived on Thirtieth Street."

"But you stayed out of the gangs?"

"I boxed."

Barrera nodded, and then started speaking in Spanish.

"You want to take down the *gomeros*," Barrera said. "So do we."

"Sin falta."

"But as a boxer," Barrera said, "you know that you just can't go for the knockout right away. You have to set your opponent up, take his legs away from him with body punches, cut the ring off. You do not go for the knockout until the time is right."

Well, I didn't have a lot of knockouts, Art thought, but the theory is right. We Yanquis want to swing for the knockout right away, and the man is telling me that it isn't set up yet.

Fair enough.

"What you're saying makes great sense to me," Art said. "It's wisdom. But patience is not a particularly American virtue. I think if my superiors could just see some progress, some motion—"

"Your superiors," Barrera said, "are difficult to work with. They are . . ."

He searches for a word.

Art finishes it for him. *"Falta gracia."*

"Ill-mannered," Barrera agrees. "Exactly. If, on the other hand, we could work with someone *símpático, un compañero,* someone like yourself . . ."

So, Art thinks, Adán asked him to save my ass, and now he's decided it's worth doing. He's an indulgent uncle, he lets his nephews play; but he's also a serious man with a definite objective in mind, and I might be useful in achieving that objective.

Again, fair enough. But this is a slippery slope. An unreported relationship outside the agency? Strictly verboten. A partnership with one of the most important men in Sinaloa and I keep it in my pocket? A time bomb. It could get me fired from the DEA altogether.

Then again, what do I have to lose?

Art poured them each another drink, then said, "I'd love to work with you, but there's a problem."

Barrera shrugged. "¿Y qué?"

"I won't be here," Art said. "They're reassigning me."

Barrera sipped his whiskey with a polite pretense of enjoyment, as if it were good whiskey, when they both knew that it was cheap shit. Then he asked, "Do you know the real difference between America and Mexico?"

Art shook his head.

"In America, everything is about systems," Barrera said. "In Mexico, everything is about personal relationships."

And you're offering me one, Art thought. A personal relationship of the symbiotic nature.

"Señor Barrera—"

"My given names are Miguel Ángel," Barrera said, "but my friends call me Tío."

Tío, Art thought.

"Uncle."

That's the literal translation, but the word implies a lot more in Mexican Spanish. *Tío* could be a parent's brother, but he could also be any relative who takes an interest in a kid's life. It goes beyond that; a *Tío* can be any man who takes you under his wing, an older-brother type, even a paternal figure.

Sort of a godfather.

"Tío . . ." Art began.

Barrera smiled and accepted the tribute with a slight bow of his head. Then he said, "*Arturo, mi sobrino . . .*"

Arthur, my nephew . . .

You're not going anywhere.

Except up.

Art's reassignment was canceled the next afternoon. He was called back into Taylor's office.

"Who the fuck do you know?" Taylor asked him.

Art shrugged.

"I just had my leash jerked all the way from Washington," Taylor said. "Is this some CIA shit? Are you still on their payroll? Who do you work for, Keller—them or us?"

Me, Art thought. I work for myself. But he didn't say it. He just ate his ration of shit and said, "I work for you, Tim. Say the word, I'll have 'DEA' tattooed on my ass. If you want, it can be a heart with your name across it."

Taylor stared across the desk at him, obviously unsure of whether Art was fucking with him or not, and of how to respond. He settled on a tone of bureaucratic neutrality and said, "I have instructions to let you alone to do your own thing. Do you know how I choose to view this, Keller?"

"As giving me enough rope to hang myself?"

"Exactly."

How did I know?

"I'll produce for you, Tim," Art said, getting up to leave the room. "I'll produce for the team."

But on the way out he couldn't help singing, albeit softly, *"I'm an old cowhand, from the Rio Grande. But I can't poke a cow, 'cuz I don't know how . . ."*

A partnership made in hell.

This is how Art would later describe it.

Art Keller and Tío Barrera.

They met rarely and secretly. Tío chose his targets carefully. Art could see it building—or, more accurately, deconstructing, as Barrera used Art and the DEA to remove one brick after another from Don Pedro's structure. A valuable poppy field, then a cookery, then a lab, then two junior *gomeros,* three crooked state policeman, a *federale* who was taking the *mordida*—the bite, the bribe—from Don Pedro.

Barrera stayed aloof from it all, never getting directly involved, never taking any credit, just using Art as his knife hand to gut the Áviles organization. Art wasn't just a puppet in all this, either. He used the sources Barrera gave him to work other sources, to establish leverage, to create assets in the metastasizing algebra of intelligence gathering. One source gets you two, two gets you five, five gets you . . .

Well, among the good things, it also gets endless servings of shit from the cop types in the DEA. Tim Taylor had Art on the carpet a half-dozen times. *Where are you getting your info, Art? Who's your source? You got a snitch? We're a team, Art. There's no I in team.*

Yeah, but there is in *win,* Art thought, and that's what we're finally doing—winning. Creating leverage, playing one rival *gomero* against another, showing the Sinaloan *campesinos* that the days of the *gomero* over-lords are really coming to an end. So he told Taylor nothing.

He had to admit there was an element of Fuck you, Tim, and your team.

While Tío Barrera maneuvered like a master technician in the ring. Always pressing forward, but always with his guard up. Setting up his punches and throwing them only when there was minimal risk to himself. Knocking the wind and the legs out from under Don Pedro, cutting off the ring, then—

The knockout punch.

Operation Condor.

The mass sweep of troops and supporting aircraft, with bombing and defoliants, but still it was Art Keller who could direct them where to hit, almost as if he had a personal map of every poppy field, cookery and lab in the province, which was almost literally true.

Now Art crouches in the brush, waiting for the big prize.

With all the success of Condor, the DEA is still focused on one goal: Get Don Pedro. It's all Art has heard about: Where is Don Pedro? Get Don Pedro. We *have* to get El Patrón.

As if we have to hang that trophy head on the wall, or the whole operation is a failure. Hundred of thousands of acres of poppies destroyed, the entire infrastructure of the Sinaloan *gomeros* devastated, but we still need that one old man as a symbol of our success.

They're out there, running around like crazy, chasing every rumor and tidbit of intelligence; but always a step behind, or, as Taylor might say, a day late and a dollar short. Art can't decide what Taylor wants more—to get Don Pedro or for Art *not* to get Don Pedro.

Art was out in a Jeep, inspecting the charred ruins of a major heroin lab, when Tío Barrera came rolling up out of the smoke with a small convoy of DFS troops.

The fucking DFS? Art wondered. The Dirección Federal de Seguridad— Federal Security Directorate—is like the FBI and CIA rolled into one, except more powerful. The DFS boys virtually have carte blanche for whatever they do in Mexico. Now, Tío is a Jalisco state cop—what the hell is he doing with a squad of the elite DFS, and in command, no less? Tío leaned out of his open Jeep Cherokee and simply said, with a sigh, "I suppose we had better go pick up old Don Pedro."

Handing Art the biggest prize in the War on Drugs as if it were a bag of groceries.

"You know where he is?" Art asked.

"Better," Tío said. "I know where he's going to be."

· · ·

So now Art sits crouched in the brush, waiting for the old man to walk into the ambush. He can feel Tío's eyes on him. He looks over to see Tío pointedly looking at his watch.

Art gets the message.

Anytime now.

Don Pedro Áviles sits in the front seat of his Mercedes convertible as it slowly rumbles over the dirt back road. They've driven out of the burning valley, up onto the mountain. If he gets down the other side, he'll be safe.

"Be careful," he tells young Güero, who's driving. "Watch the holes. It's an expensive car."

"We have to get you out of here, *patrón*," Güero tells him.

"I know that," Don Pedro snaps. "But did we have to take this road? The car will be ruined."

"There will be no soldiers on this road," Güero tells him. "No *federales*, no state police."

"You know this for a fact?" Áviles asks.

Again.

"I have it straight from Barrera," Güero says. "He has cleared this route."

"He *should* clear a route," Áviles says. "The money I pay them."

Money to Governor Cerro, money to General Hernández. Barrera comes as regular as a woman's curse to collect the money. Always, the money to the politicians, to the generals. It has always been this way, since Don Pedro was a boy, learning the business from his father.

And there will always be these periodic sweeps, these ritual cleansings coming down from Mexico City at the behest of the Yanquis. This time it's in exchange for higher oil prices, and Governor Cerro sent Barrera to give Don Pedro the word: *Invest in oil, Don Pedro. Sell off opium and put the money in oil. It's going up soon. And the opium* . . .

So I let the young fools buy into my poppy fields. Took their money and put it into the oil. And Cerro let the Yanquis burn the poppy fields. Doing work that the sun would do for them.

For that's the great joke: Operation Condor timed to happen just before the drought years come. He has seen it in the sky the past two years. Seen it in the trees, the grass, the birds. The drought years are coming. Five years of bad crops before the rains come back.

"If the Yanquis did not burn the fields," Don Pedro tells Güero, "I would have. Refresh the soil."

So it is a farce, this Operation Condor; a play, a joke.

But still he has to get out of Sinaloa.

Áviles has not stayed alive for seventy-three years by being careless. So he has Güero driving and five of his most trusted *sicarios*—gunmen—in a car behind. Men whose families all live in Don Pedro's compound in Culiacán, who would all be killed if anything should happen to Don Pedro.

And Güero—his apprentice, his assistant. An orphan whom he took off the streets of Culiacán as a *manda* to Santo Jesús Malverde, the patron saint of all Sinaloan *gomeros*. Güero, whom he raised in the business, to whom he taught everything. A young man now, his right-hand man, cat smart, who can do monumental figures in his head in a flash, who is nevertheless driving the Mercedes too fast on this rough road.

"Slow down," Áviles orders.

Güero—"Blondie," because of his light hair—chuckles. The old man has millions and millions, but he will cluck like an old hen over a repair bill. He could throw this Mercedes away and not miss it, but will complain about the few *pesos* it will cost to wash the dust off.

It doesn't bother Güero; he's used to it.

He slows down.

"We should make a *manda* to Malverde when we get to Culiacán," Don Pedro says.

"We can't stay in Culiacán, *patrón*," Güero says. "The Americans will be there."

"To hell with the Americans."

"Barrera advised us to go to Guadalajara."

"I don't like Guadalajara," Don Pedro says.

"It's only for a little while."

They come to a junction, and Güero starts to turn left.

"To the right," Don Pedro says.

"To the left, *patrón*," Güero says.

Don Pedro laughs. "I have been smuggling opium out of these hills since your father's father was tugging at your grandmother's pants. Turn right."

Güero shrugs and turns right.

The road narrows and the dirt gets soft and deep.

"Keep going, slowly," Don Pedro says. "Go slow but keep going."

They come to a sharp right curve through thick brush and Güero takes his foot off the gas.

"*¿Qué coño te pasa?*" Don Pedro asks.

What the hell's the matter with you?

Rifle barrels peak out from the brush.

Eight, nine, ten of them.

Ten more behind.

Then Don Pedro sees Barrera, in his black suit, and knows that everything is all right. The "arrest" will be a show for the Americans. If he goes to jail at all, he will be out in a day.

He slowly stands up and raises his arms.

Orders his men to do the same.

Güero Méndez slowly sinks to the floor of the car.

Art starts to get up.

He looks at Don Pedro, standing in his car with his hands in the air, quivering in the cold.

The old man looks so frail, Art thinks, like a strong wind could blow him over. White stubble on his unshaven face, his eyes sunken with obvious fatigue. Just a weak old man near the end of the road.

It seems almost cruel to arrest him, but . . .

Tío nods.

His men open fire.

The bullets shake Don Pedro like a thin tree.

"What are you doing?!" Art yells. "He's trying to—"

His voice goes unheard under the roar of the guns.

Güero crouches deep on the car's floor, his hands over his ears because the noise is incredible. The old man's blood falls like soft rain on his hands, the side of his face, his back. Even over the roar of the rifles he can hear Don Pedro's screams.

Like an old woman chasing a dog from the chicken coop.

A sound from his early childhood.

Finally it stops.

Güero waits for ten long moments of silence before he dares to get up.

When he does he sees the police emerge from the cover of the thick green brush. Behind him, Don Pedro's five *sicarios* are slumped dead, blood running from the bullet holes in the side of their car like water from a downspout.

And beside him, Don Pedro.

The *patrón*'s mouth and one eye are open.

The other eye is gone.

His body looks like one of those cheap puzzles where you try to roll the little balls into the holes, except there are many, many more holes. And the old man is coated with shattered glass from the windshield, like spun sugar coating the groom on an expensive wedding cake.

Foolishly, Güero thinks of how angry Don Pedro would be at the damage to the Mercedes.

The car is ruined.

Art opens the car door, and the old man's body falls out.

He's amazed to see that the old man's chest is still heaving with breath. If we can air-evac him out, Art thinks, there's just a chance that—

Tío walks over, looks down at the body and says, "Stop, or I'll shoot."

He draws a .45 from his holster, points it at the back of the old *patrón*'s head, and pulls the trigger.

Don Pedro's neck jerks off the ground, then drops again.

Tío looks at Art and says, "He reached for his gun."

Art doesn't answer.

"He reached for his gun," Tío repeats. "They all did."

Art looks around at the corpses strewn on the ground. The DFS troops are picking up the dead men's weapons and firing into the air. Red flashes burst from the gun barrels.

This wasn't an arrest, Art thinks, it was an execution.

The skinny blond driver crawls out of the car, kneels on the blood-soaked ground and puts his hands up. He's trembling—Art can't tell if it's fear, or cold, or both. You'd be shaking, too, he tells himself, if you knew you were about to be executed.

Enough is fucking enough.

Art starts to step between Tío and the kneeling kid. "Tío—"

Tío says, *"Levántate, Güero."*

The kid shakily gets to his feet. *"Dios le bendiga, patrón."*

God bless you.

Patrón.

Boss.

Then Art gets it—this wasn't an arrest *or* an execution.

It was an assassination.

He looks at Tío, who has holstered his pistol and is now lighting one of his skinny black cigars. Tío looks up to see Art staring at him, nods his chin toward Don Pedro's body and says, "You got what you wanted."

"So did you."

"Pues . . ." Tío shrugs. "Take your trophy."

Art walks back to his Jeep and hauls out his rain poncho. He comes back and carefully rolls Don Pedro's body up in it, then hefts the dead man in his arms. The old man feels like he weighs practically nothing.

Art carries him to the Jeep and lays him across the backseat.
Drives off to take the trophy back to base camp.
Condor, Phoenix, what's the difference?
Hell is hell, whatever you name it.

A nightmare wakes Adán Barrera.

A booming, rhythmic bass.

He runs out of the hut to see giant dragonflies hovering in the sky. He blinks and they turn into helicopters.

Swooping down like vultures.

Then he hears shouting and the sounds of trucks and horses. Soldiers running, guns firing. He grabs a *campesino* and orders "Hide me!" and the man takes him into a hut, where Adán hides under the bed until the thatched roof bursts into flames and he runs out to face the bayonets of the soldiers.

A disaster—what the fuck is going on?

And his uncle—his uncle will be furious. He had told them to stay away this week—to stay in Tijuana or even San Diego, to be anyplace but here. But his brother Raúl *had* to see this Badiraguato girl he was lusting after, and there was going to be a party, and Adán had to go with him. And now Raúl is God knows where, Adán thinks, and I have bayonets pointed at my chest.

Tío has basically raised the two boys since their father died, when Adán was four. Tío Ángel was barely a man himself then, but he took on a man's responsibility, bringing money to the household, talking to the boys like a father, seeing that they did the right thing.

The family's standard of living rose with Tío's progress in the force, and by the time Adán was a young teen he had a solidly middle-class lifestyle. Unlike the rural *gomeros,* the Barrera brothers were city kids—they lived in Culiacán, went to school there, to pool parties in town, to beach parties in Mazatlán. They spent parts of the hot summers at Tío's hacienda in the cool mountain air of Badiraguato, playing with the children of the *campesinos*.

The boyhood days in Badiraguato were idyllic, riding bikes to mountain lakes, diving from quarry rock faces into the deep emerald water of the granite quarries, lazing on the broad porch of the house while a dozen *tías*—aunties—fussed over them and made them tortillas, and *albóndigas,* and, Adán's favorite—fresh, homemade flan blanketed with thick caramel.

Adán came to love *los campesinos.*

They became a large, loving family to him. His mother had been distant since his father's death, his uncle all business and seriousness. But the *campesinos* had all the warmth of the summer sun.

It was as his childhood priest, Father Juan, endlessly preached: "Christ is with the poor."

They work so hard, young Adán observed—in the fields, in the kitchens and the laundry rooms, and they have so many kids, but when the adults come back from work they always seem to have time to hold the children, bounce them on knees, play games and jokes.

Adán loved the summer evenings more than anything, when the families were together and the women cooked and the kids ran around in mad giggling swarms and the men drank cold beer and joked and talked about the crops, the weather, the livestock. Then they all sat down and ate together at large tables under ancient oak trees, and it got quiet as people first settled into the serious business of eating. Then, as hunger faded, the chatter started again—the jokes, the familiar teasing, the laughter. After the meal, as the long summer day eased into night and the air cooled, Adán would sit down as close as he could get to the empty chairs that would be filled when the men came back with their guitars. Then he sat literally at the feet of the men as they sang the *tambora,* listened rapt as they sang of the *gomeros* and *bandidos* and *revolucionarios,* the Sinaloan heroes who made up the legends of his boyhood.

And after a while the men tired, and talked about how the sun would be up early, and the *tías* shooed Adán and Raúl back to the hacienda, where they slept on cots on the screened-in balcony, on the sheets the *tías* had sprinkled with cool water.

And on most nights, the *abuelas*—the old women, the grandmothers—would tell them stories of the *brujas*—witches—stories of ghosts and spirits that took the forms of owls, of hawks and eagles, snakes, lizards, foxes and wolves. Stories of naïve men enchanted by *amor brujo*—bewitchment—crazed, obsessive love, and how the men fought battles with pumas and wolves, with giants and ghosts, all for the love of beautiful young women, only to find out too late that their beloved was really a hideous old hag, or an owl, or a fox.

Adán fell asleep to these stories and slept like the dead until the sun struck him in the eyes and the whole long, wonderful summer day started again with the smell of fresh tortillas, *machaca,* chorizo, and fat, sweet oranges.

Now the morning smells of ash and poison.

Soldiers are storming through the village, lighting thatched roofs on fire and smashing adobe walls with their rifle butts.

Federale Lieutenant Navarres is in a very bad mood. The American DEA agents are unhappy—they are tired of busting the "little guys"; they want to go up the chain and they're giving him a hard time about it, implying that he knows where the "big guys" are and that he's deliberately leading them away.

They've captured a lot of small-fry, but not the big fish. Now they want García Abrego, Chalino Guzmán, aka El Verde, Jaime Herrera and Rafael Caro, all of whom have so far slipped the net.

Mostly they want Don Pedro.

El Patrón.

"We're not on a 'search-and-avoid' mission here, are we?" one of the DEA men in his blue baseball cap actually asked him. It made Navarres furious, this endless Yanqui slander that every Mexican cop takes *la mordida,* the bribe, or, as the Americans say, is "on the arm."

So Navarres is angry, and humiliated, and that makes a proud man a dangerous man.

Then he sees Adán.

One look at the designer jeans and Nike running shoes tells the lieutenant that the short young man, with his city haircut and his fancy clothes, is no *campesino.* He looks exactly like some mid-level young *gomero* punk from Culiacán.

The lieutenant strides over and looks down at Adán.

"I am Lieutenant Navarres," the officer says, "of the Municipal Judicial Federal Police. Where is Don Pedro Áviles?"

"I don't know anything about that," Adán says, trying to keep his voice from shaking. "I'm a college student."

Navarres smirks. "What do you study?"

"Business," Adán answers. "Accounting."

"An accountant," Navarres is saying. "And what do you count? Kilos?"

"No," Adán says.

"You just happen to be here."

"My brother and I came up for a party," Adán says. "Look, this is all a mistake. If you will talk to my uncle, he will—"

Navarres draws his pistol and backhands Adán across the face. The *federales* toss the unconscious Adán and the *campesino* who hid him into the back of a truck and drive away.

This time Adán wakes to darkness.

He realizes that it's not night, but that a black hood is tied over his head. It's hard to breathe and he starts to panic. His hands are tied tightly behind his back and he can hear sounds—motors running, helicopter rotors. We must be at some kind of base, Adán thinks. Then he hears something worse—a man's moans, the solid thunks of rubber and the sharp crack of metal on flesh and bone. He can smell the man's piss, his shit, his blood, and he can smell the disgusting stink of his own fear.

He hears Navarres's smooth, aristocratic voice say, "Tell me where Don Pedro is."

Navarres looks down at the peasant, a sweating, bleeding, quivering mess curled up on the tent floor, lying between the feet of two large *federale* troopers, one holding a length of heavy rubber hose, the other clutching a short iron rod. The DEA men are sitting outside, waiting for him to produce. They just want their information; they don't want to know the process that produces it.

The Americans, Navarres thinks, do not like to see how sausages are made.

He nods to one of his *federales.*

Adán hears the *whoosh* of the rubber hose and a scream.

"Stop beating him!" Adán yells.

"Ah, you've joined us," Navarres says to Adán. He stoops over, and Adán can smell his breath. It smells like mint. "So *you* tell me, where is Don Pedro?"

The *campesino* yells, "Don't tell them!"

"Break his leg," Navarres says.

A terrible sound as the *federale* smashes the bar down on the *campesino*'s shin.

Like an ax on wood.

Then screaming.

Adán can hear the man moaning, choking, puking, praying but saying nothing.

"*Now* I believe," Navarres says, "that he doesn't know."

Adán feels the *comandante* coming close. Can smell the coffee and tobacco on the man's breath as the *federale* says, "But I believe you do."

The hood is jerked from Adán's head, and before he can see anything, it's replaced with a tight blindfold. Then he feels his chair being tipped backward so that he's almost upside down, his feet at a forty-five-degree angle toward the ceiling.

"Where is Don Pedro?"

"I don't know."

He doesn't. That's the problem. Adán has no idea where Don Pedro is, although he profoundly wishes that he did. And he's confronted with a harsh truth—if he did know, he would tell. I am not as tough as the *campesino,* he thinks, not as brave, not as loyal. Before I let them break my leg, before I heard that awful sound on *my* bones, felt that unimaginable pain, I would tell them anything.

But he doesn't know, so he says, "Honestly. I have no idea . . . I am not a *gomero*—"

"Hm-mmm."

This little hum of incredulity from Navarres.

Then Adán smells something.

Gasoline.

They jam a rag into Adán's mouth.

Adán struggles, but large hands hold him down as they pour the gasoline up his nostrils. He feels as if he's drowning and, in fact, he is. He wants to cough, to gag, but the rag in his mouth won't let him. He feels the vomit rising in his throat and wonders if he's going to suffocate in a mixture of puke and gasoline as the hands let him go and his head thrashes violently from side to side, and then they pull the rag out and tip the chair back up.

When Adán stops vomiting, Navarres asks him the question again.

"Where is Don Pedro?"

"I don't know," Adán gasps. He feels the panic rise in his throat. It makes him say a stupid thing. "I have cash in my pockets."

The chair is tilted back, the rag shoved back in his mouth. A flood of gas goes up his nose, fills his sinuses, feels like it's flooding his brain. He hopes it does, hopes it kills him, because this is unbearable. Just when he thinks he's going to black out, they tilt the chair back up and take out the rag and he vomits on himself.

As Navarres screams, "Who do you think I am?! Some traffic cop who stops you for speeding?! You offer me a *tip*?!"

"I'm sorry," Adán gasps. "Let me go. I will contact you, pay you what you want. Name the price."

Back down again. The rag, the gasoline. The awful, horrible feeling of the fumes penetrating his sinuses, his brain, his lungs. Feeling his head thrashing, his torso twisting, his feet kicking uncontrollably. When it finally stops, Navarres lifts Adán's chin between his thumb and forefinger.

"You little *traficante* garbage," Navarres says. "You think everyone is for sale, don't you? Well, let me tell you something, you little shit—you can't buy me. I'm not for sale. There's no bargaining here—there's no deal. You will simply give me what I want."

Then Adán hears himself say something very stupid.

"Comemierda."

Navarres loses it. Screams, "I should eat shit? *I should eat shit?!* Bring him."

Adán is yanked to his feet and dragged out of the tent to a latrine, a filthy hole with an old toilet seat thrown across. Filled almost to the top with shit, bits of toilet paper, piss, flies.

The *federales* lift the struggling Adán and hold his head over the hole.

"*I* should eat shit?!" Navarres is screaming. "*You* eat shit!"

They lower Adán until his head is completely immersed in the filth.

He tries to hold his breath. He twists, squirms, struggles, again tries to hold his breath, but finally has to breathe in the shit. They lift him out.

Adán coughs the shit out of his mouth.

He gulps for air as they lower him again.

Closes his eyes and mouth tightly, vowing to die before he swallows shit again, but soon he's thrashing, his lungs demanding air, his brain threatening to explode, and he opens his mouth again and then he's drowning in filth and they lift him out and toss him on the ground.

"*Now* who eats shit?"

"I do."

"Hose him off."

The blast of water stings, but Adán is grateful. He's on all fours, gagging and vomiting, but the water feels wonderful.

Navarres's pride restored, he's fatherly now as he leans over Adán and asks, "Now . . . where is Don Pedro?"

Adán cries, "I . . . don't . . . know."

Navarres shakes his head.

"Get the other one," he orders his men. A few moments later the *federales* come out of the tent dragging the *campesino*. His white pants are bloody and torn. His left leg drags at an odd, broken angle and a jagged piece of bone sticks through the flesh.

Adán sees it and pukes on the spot.

He feels even sicker when they start to drag him toward a helicopter.

Art pulls a kerchief tightly over his nose.

The smoke and ash are getting to him, stinging his eyes, settling in his mouth. And God knows, Art thinks, what toxic shit I'm sucking into my lungs.

He comes to a small village perched on a curve in the road. The *campesinos* stand on the other side of the road and watch as soldiers get ready to put the torch to the thatched roofs of their *casitas*. Young soldiers nervously hold them back from trying to get their belongings out of the burning houses.

Then Art sees a lunatic.

A tall, stout man with a full head of white hair, his unshaven face rough with white stubble, wearing an untucked denim shirt over blue jeans and tennis shoes, holds a wooden crucifix in front of him like a bad actor in a B-level vampire movie. He pushes his way through the crowd of *campesinos* and brushes right past the soldiers.

The soldiers must think he's crazy, too, because they stand back and let him pass. Art watches as the man strides across the road and gets between two torch-bearing soldiers and a house.

"In the name of your Lord and Savior, Jesus Christ," the man yells, "I forbid you to do this!"

He's like somebody's dotty uncle, Art thinks, who's usually kept in the house but got out in the chaos and is now wandering around with his messiah complex unleashed. The two soldiers just stand there looking at the man, unsure of what to do.

Their sergeant tells them; he walks over and screams at them to quit staring like two *fregados* and set fire to the *chingada* house. The soldiers try to move around the crazy man but he slides over to block them.

Quick feet for a fat man, Art thinks.

The sergeant takes his rifle and raises its butt toward the crazy man as though he's going to crack the man's skull if he doesn't move.

The lunatic doesn't move. He just stands there invoking the name of God.

Art sighs, stops the Jeep, and gets out.

He knows he has no business interfering, but he just can't let a crazy guy get his melon smashed without at least trying to stop it. He walks over to the sergeant, tells him that he'll take care of it, then grabs the lunatic by the elbow and tries to walk him away.

"Come on, *viejo*," Art says. "Jesus told me he wants to see you across the road."

"Really?" the man answers. "Because Jesus told *me* to tell *you* to go fuck yourself."

The man looks at him with amazing gray eyes. Art sees them and knows right away that this guy is no nut job, but something altogether different. Sometimes you see a person's eyes and you know, you just *know,* that the bullshit hour is over.

These eyes have *seen* things, and not flinched or looked away.

Now the man looks at the DEA on Art's cap.

"Proud of yourself?" he asks.

"I'm just doing my job."

"And I'm just doing mine." He turns back to the soldiers and once again orders them to cease and desist.

"Look," Art says, "I don't want to see you get hurt."

"Then close your eyes." Then the man sees the concerned look on Art's face and adds, "Don't worry, they won't touch me. I'm a priest. A bishop, actually."

A priest?! Art thinks. Go fuck yourself? What the hell kind of priest—excuse me, *bishop*—uses that kind of . . .

The thought is interrupted by gunfire.

Art hears the dull *pop-pop-pop* of AK-47 fire and throws himself to the ground, hugging the dirt as tightly as he can. He looks up to see the priest still standing there—like a lone tree on a prairie now, everyone else having hit the deck—still holding his cross up, shouting at the hills, telling them to stop shooting.

It's one of the most incredibly brave things Art has ever seen.

Or foolish, or just crazy.

Shit, Art thinks.

He gets to his knees, and then lunges for the priest's legs, knocks him over and holds him down.

"Bullets don't know you're a priest," Art says to him.

"God will call me when he calls me," the priest answers.

Well, God damn-near just reached for the phone, Art thinks. He lies in the dirt next to the priest until the shooting stops, then risks another look up and sees the soldiers starting to move away from the village, toward the source of the gunfire.

"Would you happen to have an extra cigarette?" the priest asks.

"I don't smoke."

"Puritan."

"It'll kill you," Art says.

"*Everything* I like will kill me," the priest answers. "I smoke, I drink, I eat too much. Sexual sublimation, I suppose. I'm Bishop Parada. You can call me Father Juan."

"You're a madman, Father Juan."

"Christ needs madmen," Parada says, standing up and dusting himself off. He looks around and smiles. "And the village is still here, isn't it?"

Yeah, Art thinks, because the *gomeros* started shooting.

"Do you have a name?" the priest asks.

"Art Keller."

He offers his hand. Parada takes it, asking, "Why are you down here burning my country, Art Keller?"

"Like I said, it's—"

"Your job," Parada says. "Shitty job, Arturo."

He sees Art react to the "Arturo."

"Well, you're part Mexican, aren't you?" Parada asks. "Ethnically?"

"On my mother's side."

"I'm part American," Parada says. "I was born in Texas. My parents were *mojados,* migrant workers. They took me back to Mexico when I was still a baby. Technically, though, that makes me an American citizen. A Texan, no less."

"Yee-haw."

"Hook 'em, Horns."

A woman runs up and starts talking to Parada. She's crying, and speaking so quickly Art has a hard time understanding her. He does pick up a few words, though: *Padre Juan* and *federales* and *tortura*—torture.

Parada turns to Art. "They're torturing people at a camp near here. Can you put a stop to it?"

Probably not, Art thinks. It's SOP in Condor. The *federales* tune them up, and then they sing for us. "Father, I'm not allowed to interfere in the internal matters of—"

"Don't treat me like an idiot," the priest says. He has a tone of authority that makes even Art Keller listen. "Let's get going."

He walks over and gets into Art's Jeep. "Come on, get your ass in gear."

Art gets in, starts the motor and rips it into gear.

When they get to the base camp, Art sees Adán sitting in the back of an open chopper with his hands tied behind his back. A *campesino* with a hideous greenstick fracture lies beside him.

The chopper is about to take off. The rotors are spinning, kicking dust and pebbles in Art's face. He jumps out of the Jeep, ducks below the rotors and runs up to the pilot, Phil Hansen.

"Phil, what the hell?!" Art shouts.

Phil grins at him. "Two birds!"

Art recognizes the reference: You take two birds up. One flies, the other sings.

"No!" Art says. He jabs a thumb toward Adán. "That guy is mine!"

"Fuck you, Keller!"

Yeah, fuck me, Art thinks. He looks in the back of the chopper, where Parada is already tending to the *campesino* with the broken leg. The priest turns to Art with a look that is both question and demand.

Art shakes his head, then pulls his .45, cocks it and sticks it in Hansen's face. "You're not taking off, Phil."

Art can hear *federales* lift their rifles and chamber rounds.

DEA guys come running out of the mess tent.

Taylor yells, "Keller, what the hell you think you're doing?!"

"This what we do now, Tim?" Art asks. "We toss people out of choppers?"

"You're no virgin, Keller," Taylor says. "You've jumped into the backseat lots of times."

I can't say anything to that, Art thinks. It's the truth.

"You're done now, Keller," Taylor says. "You're *finished* this time. I'll have your goddamn job. I'll have you thrown in jail."

He sounds happy.

Art keeps his pistol trained on Hansen's face.

"This is a Mexican matter," Navarres says. "Stay out of it. This is not your country."

"It's *my* country!" Parada yells. "And I'll excommunicate your ass so fast—"

"Such language, Father," Navarres says.

"You'll hear worse in a minute."

"We are trying to find Don Pedro Áviles," Navarres explains to Art. He points to Adán. "This little piece of shit knows where he is, and he's going to tell us."

"You want Don Pedro?" Art asks. He walks back to his Jeep and unrolls the poncho. Don Pedro's body spills onto the ground, raising little puffs of dust. "You got him."

Taylor looks down at the bullet-riddled corpse.

"What happened?"

"We tried to arrest him and five of his men," Art says. "They resisted. They're all dead."

"*All* of them," Taylor says, staring at Art.

"Yeah."

"No wounded?"

"No."

Taylor smirks. But he's pissed, and Art knows it. Art has just brought in the Big Trophy and now there's nothing Taylor can do to him. Nothing at fucking all. Still, it's time to make a peace offering. Art nods his chin toward Adán and the injured *campesino* and says softly, "I guess we *both* have things to keep quiet about, Tim."

"Yeah."

Art climbs into the back of the helicopter and starts to untie Adán. "I'm sorry about this."

"Not as sorry as I am," Adán says. He turns to Parada. "How's his leg, Father Juan?"

"You know each other?" Art asks.

"I christened him," Parada says. "Gave him his First Communion. And this man will be fine."

But he gives Adán and Art a look that says something different.

Art yells to the front, "You can take off now, Phil! Culiacán hospital, and step on it!"

The chopper lifts off.

"Arturo," Parada says.

"Yeah?"

The priest is smiling at him.

"Congratulations," Parada says. "You're a madman."

Art looks down at the ruined fields, the burned villages, the refugees already forming a line on the dirt road out.

The landscape is scorched and charred as far as he can see.

Fields of black flowers.

Yeah, Art thinks, I'm a madman.

Ninety minutes later, Adán lies between the clean white sheets of Culiacán's best hospital. The wound on his face from Navarres's pistol barrel has been cleaned and treated and he's been shot up with antibiotics, but he's refused the proffered painkillers.

Adán wants to feel the pain.

He gets out of bed and walks the corridors until he finds the room where, at his insistence, they have taken Manuel Sánchez.

The *campesino* opens his eyes and sees Adán.

"My leg . . ."

"It's still there."

"Don't let them—"

"I won't, " Adán says. "Get some sleep."

Adán seeks out the doctor.

"Can you save the leg?"

"I think so," the doctor says. "But it will be expensive."

"Do you know who I am?"

"I know who you are."

Adán doesn't miss the slight look or the slighter inflection: I know who your *uncle* is.

"Save his leg," Adán says, "and you will be chief of a new wing of this hospital. Lose the leg, you'll spend the rest of your life doing abortions in a Tijuana brothel. Lose the patient, you will be in a grave before he is. And it won't be my uncle who will put you there, it will be me. Do you understand?"

The doctor understands.

And Adán understands that life has changed.

Childhood is over.

Life is serious now.

Tío slowly inhales a Cuban cigar and watches the smoke ring float across the room.

Operation Condor could not have gone any better. With the Sinaloan fields burned, the ground poisoned, the *gomeros* scattered and Áviles in the dirt, the Americans believe they have destroyed the source of all evil, and will go back to sleep as far as Mexico is concerned.

Their complacency will give me the time and freedom to create an organization that, by the time the Americans wake up, they will be powerless to touch.

A *federación.*

There's a soft knock on the door.

A black-clad DFS agent, Uzi slung over his shoulder, enters. "Someone here to see you, Don Miguel. He says he's your nephew."

"Let him in."

Adán stands in the doorway.

Miguel Ángel Barrera already knows all about what happened to his nephew—the beating, the torture, his threat to the doctor, his visit to Parada's clinic. In one day, the boy has become a man.

And the man gets right to the point.

"You knew about the raid," Adán says.

"In fact, I helped to plan it."

Indeed, the targets had been carefully chosen to eliminate enemies, rivals and the old dinosaurs who would be incapable of understanding the new world. They wouldn't have survived anyway, and would only have been in the way.

Now they're not.

"It was an atrocity," Adán says.

"It was necessary," Tío says. "It was going to happen anyway, so we might as well take advantage. That's business, Adán."

"Well . . ." Adán says.

And now, Tío thinks, we will see what kind of man the boy has become. He waits for Adán to continue.

"Well," Adán says. "I want in the business."

Tío Barrera rises at the head of the table.

The restaurant has been closed for the night—private party. I'll say it is, Adán thinks; the place is surrounded by DFS men armed with Uzis. All the guests have been patted down and relieved of firearms.

The guest list would be a veritable wish list for the Yanquis. Every major *gomero* whom Tío selected to survive Operation Condor is here. Adán sits beside Raúl and scans the faces at the table.

García Abrego, at fifty years old an ancient man in this trade. Silver hair and a silver mustache, he looks like a wise old cat. Which he is. He sits and watches Barrera impassively, and Adán can't read his reaction from his face. "Which," Tío has told Adán, "is how he got to be fifty years old in this trade. Take a lesson from him."

Sitting next to Abrego is the man Adán knows as El Verde, "The Green," so called because of the green ostrich-skin boots he always wears. Besides that conceit, Chalino Guzmán looks like a farmer—denim shirt and jeans, straw hat.

Sitting next to Guzmán is Güero Méndez.

Even in this urbane restaurant Güero is wearing his Sinaloa cowboy out-fit: black shirt with mother-of-pearl snap buttons, tight black jeans with huge silver and turquoise belt buckle, pointed-toe boots and a large white cowboy hat, even inside.

And Güero cannot shut up about his miraculous survival of the *federale* ambush that killed his boss, Don Pedro. "Santo Jesús Malverde shielded me from the bullets," Güero was saying. "I tell you, brothers, I walked through the rain. For hours afterward I didn't know I was alive. I thought I was a ghost." On and on and fucking on about how he emptied his *pistola* at the *federales,* then jumped from the car and ran—"between the bullets, brothers"—into the brush from where he made his escape. And how he worked his way back to the city, "thinking every moment was my last, brothers."

Adán lets his eyes move over the rest of the guests: Jaime Herrera, Rafael Caro, Chapo Montana, all Sinaloa *gomeros,* all wanted men now, all on the run. Lost and windblown ships that Tío has brought into safe harbor.

Tío has called this meeting, and in the very act of calling it has estab-lished his superiority. He's made them all sit down together over huge buckets of chilled shrimp, platters of thinly sliced *carne* and cases of the ice-cold beer that real Sinaloans prefer over wine.

In the next room, young Sinaloan musicians are warming up to sing *bandas*—songs praising the exploits of famous *traficantes,* many of them sitting at the table. In a private room farther in the back are gathered a dozen high-priced call girls who have been called in from Haley Saxon's exclusive brothel in San Diego.

"The blood that has been spilled has dried," Tío says. "Now is the time to put away all grudges, to wash the bitter taste of *venganza* from our mouths. These things are gone, like the water of yesterday's river."

He takes a swallow of beer into his mouth, swills it around, then spits it on the floor.

He pauses to see if anyone objects.

No one does.

He says, "Gone also is the life we led. Gone in poison and flame. Our old lives are like the fragile dreams we dream in the waking hours, floating away from us like a wisp of smoke in the wind. We might like to call the dream back, to go on sweetly sleeping, but that is not life, that is a dream.

"The Americans wanted to scatter us Sinaloans. Burn us off our land and scatter us to the winds. But the fire that consumes also makes way for new growth. The wind that destroys also spreads the seeds to new ground. I say if they want us to scatter, so be it. Good. We will scatter like the seeds of the *manzanita,* which grow in any soil. Grow and spread. I say we spread out like the fingers of a single hand. I say if they will not let us have our Sinaloa, we take the whole country.

"There are three critical territories from which to conduct *la pista secreta:* Sonora, bordering Texas and Arizona; the Gulf, just across from Texas, Louisiana and Florida; and Baja, next door to San Diego, Los Angeles and the West Coast. I ask Abrego to take the Gulf as his *plaza,* to have as his markets Houston, New Orleans, Tampa and Miami. I ask El Verde, Don Chalino, to take the Sonoran *plaza,* to base himself in Juárez, to have New Mexico, Arizona and the rest of Texas for his market."

Adán tries without success to read their reactions: the Gulf *plaza* is potentially rich, but fraught with difficulties as American law enforcement finishes with Mexico and concentrates on the eastern Caribbean. But Abrego should make millions—no, billions—if he can find a source for the product to sell.

He glances at El Verde, whose *campesino* face is impenetrable. The Sonoran *plaza* should be lucrative. El Verde should be able to move tons of drugs into Phoenix, El Paso and Dallas, not to mention the route going north from those cities to Chicago, Minneapolis and especially Detroit.

But everyone is waiting for the other shoe to fall, and Adán watches their eyes as they realize that Tío has saved the plum for himself.

Baja.

Tijuana provides access to the enormous markets of San Diego, Los Angeles, San Francisco, San Jose. And to the transportation systems able to move product to the even richer markets of the northeast United States: Philadelphia, Boston and the gem of gems—New York City.

So there is a Gulf Plaza and a Sonora Plaza, but Baja is *the* Plaza.

La Plaza.

So no one's real thrilled, and no one is real surprised, when Barrera says, "Myself, I propose to . . .

". . . move to Guadalajara."

Now they're surprised.

None more so than Adán, who can't believe that Tío is giving up the most potentially lucrative piece of real estate in the Western world. If the Plaza isn't going to the family, then who—

"I ask," Barrera says, "Güero Méndez to take the Baja Plaza."

Adán watches Güero's face break into a grin. Then he gets it. Has an epiphany that explains the miracle of Güero's survival in the ambush that killed Don Pedro. Knows now that the Plaza is not a surprise gift but a promise fulfilled.

But why? Adán wonders. What is Tío up to?

And where is my place?

He knows better than to open his mouth and ask. Tío will tell him in private, when he's ready.

García Abrego leans forward and smiles. His mouth is small under his white mustache. Like a cat's mouth, Adán thinks. Abrego says, "Barrera divides the world into three pieces, then takes a fourth for himself. I cannot help but wonder why."

"Abrego, what crops grow in Guadalajara?" Barrera asks. "What border does Jalisco sit on? None. It is a place to be, that's all. A safe place from which to serve our Federación."

It's the first time he's put a word to it, Adán thinks. The Federation. With himself as its head. Not by title, but by positioning.

"If you accept this arrangement," Barrera says, "I will share what is mine. My friends will be your friends, my protection your protection."

"How much will we pay for this protection?" Abrego asks.

"A modest fee," Barrera says. "Protection is expensive."

"How expensive?"

"Fifteen percent."

"Barrera," Abrego says. "You divide the country into *plazas*. All very well and good. Abrego will accept the Gulf. But you have forgotten something—in slicing up the fruit, you slice up nothing. There is nothing left. Our fields are burned and poisoned. Our mountains are overrun with *policía* and Yanquis. So you give us markets—there is no opium for us to sell in these new markets of ours."

"Forget opium," Barrera says.

"And the *yerba*—" Güero begins.

"Forget the marijuana, too," Barrera says. "It's small stuff."

Abrego holds his arms out and says, "So, Miguel Ángel, El Ángel Negro, you tell us to forget *la mapola* and *la yerba.* What would you have us grow?"

"Stop thinking like a farmer."

"I am a farmer."

"We have a two-thousand-mile land border with the United States," Barrera says. "Another thousand miles by sea. That's the only crop we need."

"What are you talking about?" Abrego snaps.

"Will you join the Federación?"

"Sure, yes," Abrego says. "I accept this Federation of Nothing. What choice do I have?"

None, Adán thinks. Tío owns the Jalisco State Police and is partners with the DFS. He's staged an overnight revolution through Operation Condor and come out on top. But—and Abrego is also right about this—on top of what?

"El Verde?" Barrera asks.

"Sí."

"Méndez?"

"Sí, Don Miguel."

"Then, *hermanos,*" Barrera says. "Let me show you the future."

They repair to a heavily guarded room in the hotel that Barrera owns next door.

Ramón Mette Ballasteros is waiting for them.

Mette is a Honduran, Adán knows, usually connected with the Colombians in Medellín, and the Colombians do little if any business through Mexico. Adán watches him dissolve powder cocaine into a beaker containing a mixture of water and bicarbonate of soda.

He watches as Mette fixes the beaker over a burner and turns the flame up high.

"It's cocaine," Abrego says. "So what?"

"Watch," Barrera says.

Adán watches as the solution starts to boil and listens as the coke makes a funny crackling sound. Then the powder starts to come together into a solid. Mette carefully removes it and sets it out to dry. When it does, it forms a ball that looks like a small rock.

Barrera says, "Gentlemen, meet the future."

Art stands in front of Santo Jesús Malverde.

"I made you a *manda*," Art says. "You kept your part of the deal, I'll keep mine."

He leaves the shrine and takes a taxi to the edge of the city.

Already the shantytown is going up.

The refugees from Badiraguato are turning cardboard boxes, packing crates and blankets into the makings of new homes. The lucky and the early have found sheets of corrugated tin. Art even sees an old movie billboard—*True Grit*—being raised as a roof. A sun-faded John Wayne looks down at the group of families building walls from old sheets, odd bits of plywood, broken cinder blocks.

Parada has found some old tents—Art wonders, Did he browbeat the army?—and has set up a soup kitchen and a makeshift clinic. Some boards laid on sawhorses make a serving table. A tank of propane feeds a flame that heats a thin sheet of tin on which a priest and some nuns are heating soup. Some women are making tortillas on a grill set over an open fire a few feet away.

Art goes into a tent where nurses are washing children, swabbing their arms in preparation for the tetanus shots the doctor is administering for small cuts and wounds. From another part of the big tent, Art hears kids screaming. He moves closer and sees Parada cooing softly to a little girl with burns on her arms. The girl's eyes are wide with fear and pain.

"The richest opium soil in the Western world," says Parada, "and we have nothing to ease a child's pain."

"I'd change places with her if I could," Art says.

Parada studies him for a long moment. "I believe you. It's a pity that you can't." He kisses the girl's cheek. "Jesus loves you."

A little girl in pain, Parada thinks, and that's all I have to say to her. There are worse injuries as well. We have men beaten so badly the doctors have had to amputate arms, legs. All because the Americans can't control their own appetite for drugs. They come to burn the poppies, and they burn children. Let me tell you, Jesus, we could use you in person right now.

Art follows him through the tent.

" 'Jesus loves you,' " Parada mutters. "Nights like this make me wonder if that's just crap. What brings you here? Guilt?"

"Something like that."

Art takes money from his pocket and offers it to Parada. It's his last month's salary.

"It will buy medicine," Art says.

"God bless you."

"I don't believe in God," Art says.

"Doesn't matter," Parada says. "He believes in you."

Then He, Art thinks, is a sucker.

2

Wild Irish

Where e'er we go, we celebrate
The land that makes us refugees,
From fear of priests with empty plates
From guilt and weeping effigies.

—Shane MacGowan, "Thousands Are Sailing"

Hell's Kitchen
New York City
1977

Callan grows up on bloody fables.

Cuchulain, Edward Fitzgerald, Wolfe Tone, Roddy McCorley, Pádraic Pearse, James Connelly, Sean South, Sean Barry, John Kennedy, Bobby Kennedy, Bloody Sunday, Jesus Christ.

The rich red stew of Irish Nationalism and Catholicism, or Irish Catholic Nationalism, or Irish National Catholicism. Doesn't matter. The walls of the small West Side walk-up and the walls of St. Bridget's Elementary are decorated, if that's the word, with bad pictures of martyrdom: McCorley dangling from the Bridge of Toome; Connelly tied to his chair, facing the British firing party; Saint Timothy with all them arrows sticking out of him; poor, hopeless Wolfe Tone slicing his own neck with a razor but fucking it up and severing his windpipe instead of his jugular—anyway, he manages to die before they manage to hang him; poor John and poor Bobby looking down from heaven; Christ on the Cross.

Of course there are the Twelve Stations of the Cross in St. Bridget's itself. Christ being whipped, the Crown of Thorns, Christ staggering through the streets of Jerusalem with the Cross on his back. The nails going in his blessed hands and feet. (A very young Callan asks the sister if Christ was Irish, and she sighs and tells him, No, but he might as well have been.)

He's seventeen years old and he's slamming beers in the Liffey Pub on Forty-seventh and Twelfth with his buddy O-Bop.

Only other guy in the bar besides Billy Shields the bartender is Little Mickey Haggerty. Little Mickey's sitting at the far end of the bar doing some serious drinking behind an upcoming date with a judge who's a lock to put him eight-to-twelve from his next Bushmills. Little Mickey came in with a roll of quarters, all of which he fed into the jukebox while pressing the same button. E-5. So Andy Williams has been crooning "Moon River" for the past hour, but the boys don't say nothing because they know all about Little Mickey's hijacking beef.

It's one of those killer New York August afternoons—one of those "It's not the heat, it's the humidity" afternoons—when shirts stick to backs and grudges just plain stick.

Which is what O-Bop's talking about to Callan.

They're sitting at the bar drinking beers, and O-Bop just can't let it go.

What they did to Michael Murphy.

"What they did to Michael Murphy was wrong," O-Bop says. "It was a wrong thing."

"It was," Callan agrees.

What happened with Michael Murphy is that he'd shot and killed his best friend, Kenny Maher. It was one of them things; they was both stoned at the time, flat ripped on Mexican Mud, the brown-opium heroin that was making the rounds of the neighborhood at the time, and it was just one of them things. A quarrel between two junkies that gets out of hand, and Kenny whacks Michael around a little and Michael stays pissed off and he goes out and gets a little .25-caliber target pistol and follows Kenny home and puts one in his head.

Then he sits down in the middle of fucking Forty-ninth Street, sobbing because he killed his best friend. It's O-Bop that comes along and gets him out of there before the cops come, and Hell's Kitchen being what it is, the cops never find out who canceled Kenny's reservation.

Except the cops are the only people in the neighborhood who don't know who killed Kenny Maher. Everyone else gets the word, including Eddie Friel, which is bad news for Murphy. Eddie "The Butcher" Friel collects money for Big Matt Sheehan.

Big Matt runs the neighborhood, he runs the West Side Longshoreman's Union, he runs the local teamsters, he runs the gambling, the loan-sharking, the whores, you name it—except Matt Sheehan won't let any drugs in the neighborhood.

That's a point of pride with Sheehan, and a reason he's so popular with the Kitchen's older residents.

"Say what you will about Matt," they'll say. "He's kept our kids off of dope."

Except for Michael Murphy and Kenny Maher and a few dozen others, but that don't seem to make no difference to Matt Sheehan's rep. And a big part of Matt's rep is due to Eddie the Butcher, because the whole neighborhood is scared to death of him. When Eddie the Butcher comes to collect, you pay. Preferably, you pay in money, but if not, you pay in blood and broken bones. And then you still owe the money.

At any given point in time, roughly half of Hell's Kitchen owes money to Big Matt Sheehan.

Which is another reason they all got to pretend to like him.

But O-Bop, he hears Eddie talking about how someone should take care of that fucking junkie Murphy, and he goes to Murphy and tells him he should go away for a while. So does Callan. Callan tells him this because not only does Eddie have a reputation for backing up his bad words, but Matty's put the word out that junkies killing each other is bad for the neighborhood and bad for his reputation.

So O-Bop and Callan tell Murphy he should split, but Murphy says fuck it, he's staying where he is, and they guess he's suicidal over having killed Kenny. But a few weeks later they suddenly don't see him around anymore so they figure he got smart and took off, and this is what they figure until one morning Eddie the Butcher shows up in the Shamrock Cafe with a big grin and a milk carton.

He's like showing it around, and he comes over to where Callan and O-Bop are trying to have a quiet cup of coffee to work on a hangover and he tilts the carton down so O-Bop can see and he says, "Hey, look in here."

O-Bop looks in the carton and then he throws up right on the table, which Eddie thinks is hysterical, and he calls O-Bop a pussy and walks away laughing. And the talk in the neighborhood for the next few weeks is how Eddie and his asshole buddy Larry Moretti go to Michael's apartment, drag him into the shower and stab him about a hundred and forty-seven times and then cut him up.

The story is that Eddie the Butcher goes to work on Michael Murphy's body and cuts him up like he's a piece of pork and takes the different pieces out in garbage bags and scatters them around the city.

Except for Michael's cock, which he puts in the milk carton to show around the neighborhood lest there be any doubt about what happens to you when you fuck with one of Eddie's buddies.

And no one can do anything about it, because Eddie is so connected with Matt Sheehan and Sheehan has an arrangement with the Cimino Family, so he's like untouchable.

Except six months later, O-Bop's still brooding about it.

Saying it's wrong what they did to Murphy.

"Okay, maybe they had to kill him," O-Bop is saying. "*Maybe*. But to do him that way? Then do what they did, showing that part of him around? No, that is wrong. That is so wrong."

The bartender, Billy Shields, is wiping the bar—which is like the first time maybe ever—and he's getting real nervous listening to this kid bad-mouth Eddie the Butcher. He's wiping the bar like he's going to perform surgery on it later.

O-Bop sees the bartender eyeing him, but it doesn't slow him down. O-Bop and Callan have been at it all day, walking along the Hudson toking on a joint and drinking beer from brown paper bags, so while they're not exactly wasted they're not exactly all there, either.

So O-Bop keeps it up.

Actually, it was Kenny Maher that gave him the name O-Bop. They're all in the park playing street hockey and they're taking a break when Stevie O'Leary, as he was still known back then, comes walking up and Kenny Maher, he looks at Stevie and he says, "We should call you 'Bop.'"

Stevie's not displeased. He's what, fifteen? And getting tagged by a couple of older guys is cool, so he smiles and says, " 'Bop'? Why 'Bop'?"

"Because of the way you walk," Kenny says. "You bounce on every step. You sort of *bop*."

"Bop," Callan says. "I like that."

"Who cares what you like?" Kenny says.

Then Murphy busts in, "What the fuck kind of a name is 'Bop' for an Irishman? Fuckin' look at him with that red hair. He's standing on the corner, cars stop. Look at the fuckin' white skin and the freckles, for Christ's sake. How can you call him 'Bop'? Sounds like a black guy. This is the whitest guy I ever seen in my life."

Kenny thinks about this.

"Has to be Irish, huh?"

"Fuck yes."

"Okay," Kenny says. "How about O'Bop?"

Except he says it with the stress on the O, so it becomes O-Bop.

And it sticks.

Anyway, O-Bop keeps it up about Eddie the Butcher.

"I mean, fuck that guy," he says. "So he's hooked up with Matty Sheehan, he can do anything he wants? Who the fuck is Matty Sheehan? Some lace-curtain old drunk Harp still crying in his beer about Jack Kennedy? I gotta respect this guy? Fuck him. Fuck the both of them."

"Steady," Callan says.

"Steady my ass," O-Bop says. "What they did to Michael Murphy was wrong."

He hunches over the bar and goes back to drinking his beer. Turns sullen, like the afternoon.

It's maybe ten minutes later when Eddie Friel walks in.

Eddie Friel is a big fucking guy.

He walks in and sees O-Bop and says, real loud, "Hey, pubic hair."

O-Bop doesn't sit up or turn around.

"Hey!" Eddie yells. "I'm talking to you. That *is* pubic hair on your head, isn't it? All curly and red?"

Callan watches O-Bop turn around.

"What do you want?"

He's trying to sound tough, but Callan can hear he's scared.

Why not? So is Callan.

"I hear you have a problem with me," Friel says.

"No, I got no problem," O-Bop says.

Which Callan thinks is the smart thing to say, except Friel isn't satisfied.

"Because if you got a problem with me, I'm standing right here."

"No, I don't got a problem."

"That's not what I heard," Friel says. "I heard you was going around the neighborhood running your mouth about you have a problem with something I may have did."

"No."

If it wasn't one of them murderous New York August afternoons it would probably end right there. Shit, if the Liffey was air-conditioned, it would probably end right there. But it ain't, it's just got a couple of ceiling fans giving a bunch of dust and dead flies a lazy merry-go-round ride, so anyway, it doesn't end right there where it should.

Because O-Bop has totally backed down. His balls are like lying on the floor, and there's no need to push this any further except that Eddie is a sadistic prick, so he says, "You lying little cocksucker."

Down at the end of the bar, Mickey Haggerty finally glances up from his Bushmills and says, "Eddie, the boy told you he don't have no problem."

"Anyone ask you, Mickey?" Friel says.

Mickey says, "He's just a boy, for Christ's sake."

"Then he shouldn't be running his mouth like a man," Friel says. "He shouldn't be going around talking about how certain people got no right to be running the neighborhood."

"I'm sorry," O-Bop whines.

His voice is shaking.

"Yeah, you're sorry," Friel says. "You're a sorry little motherfucker. Look at him, he's crying like a little girl, and this is the big man who thinks certain other people got no right to run the neighborhood."

"Look, I said I was sorry," O-Bop whines.

"Yeah, I hear what you say to my face," Friel says. "But what are you going to say behind my back, huh?"

"Nothing."

"Nothing?" Friel pulls a .38 from under his shirt. "Get down on your knees."

"What?"

" 'What?' " Friel mimics. "Get down on your fucking knees, you little cocksucker."

O-Bop is pale anyway, but now Callan sees he is like *white*. He looks dead already, and maybe he is, because it looks for all the world like Friel's going to execute him right here.

O-Bop is shaking as he lowers himself off the stool. He has to lower his hands to the floor first so he doesn't just topple over as he gets to his knees. And he's crying—big tears spilling out of his eyes and streaming down his face.

Eddie's got this shit-eating grin on his face.

"Come on," Callan says to Friel.

Friel turns on him.

"You want part of this, kid?" Eddie asks. "You need to decide who you're with, us or him."

Staring Callan down.

"Him," Callan says as he pulls a .22 from under his shirt and shoots Eddie the Butcher twice in the forehead.

Eddie looks like he can't fucking believe what just happened. He just looks at Callan like *What the fuck?* and then folds up. He's lying on his back on the dirty floor when O-Bop takes the .38 from his hand, sticks it in Eddie's mouth, and starts jerking on the trigger.

O-Bop's crying and shrieking obscenities.

Billy Shields has his hands up.

"I got no problem," he says.

Little Mickey looks up from his Bushmills and tells Callan, "You might want to think about leaving."

Callan asks, "Should I leave the gun?"

"No," Mickey says. "Give it to the Hudson."

Mickey knows the Hudson River between Thirty-eighth and Fifty-seventh streets has more hardware at the bottom than, say, Pearl Harbor. And the cops ain't exactly going to drag the bottom to find the weapon that rained on Eddie the Butcher. The reaction at Manhattan South is going to go something like *Someone blanked Eddie Friel? Oh. Anyone want this last chocolate glazed?*

No, these kids' problem is not the law, these kids' problem is Matt Sheehan. Not that it's going to be Mickey that goes running to Big Matt to tell him who popped Eddie. Matt could have reached out one ham-fisted hand to the judge and lifted some of the weight off Mickey on this hijacking beef, but he couldn't be bothered, so Mickey doesn't figure he owes any loyalty to Sheehan.

But Billy Shields the bartender will trip all over himself to get a marker with Big Matt, so these two kids might as well go hang themselves up on meat hooks and save Matt the aggravation. Unless they can take out Big Matt first, which they can't. So these kids are pretty much dead, but they shouldn't ought to stand around and wait for it.

"Go now," Mickey says to them. "Get out of town."

Callan tucks the .22 back under his shirt and gets an arm under O-Bop's elbow and lifts him up from where he's crouching over Eddie the Butcher's body.

"Come on," he says.

"Hold on a second."

O-Bop digs into Friel's pockets and comes out with a wad of crumpled bills. Rolls him on his side and takes something out of his back pocket.

A black notebook.

"Okay," O-Bop says.

They walk out the door.

Cops come in around ten minutes later.

The Homicide guy, he steps over the pool of blood forming a big, wet, red halo around Friel's head, then he looks at Mickey Haggerty. Homicide guy is just up from Safes and Lofts, so he knows Mickey. Looks at Mickey and shrugs like *What happened?*

"Slipped in the shower," Mickey says.

They never get out of town.

What happens is they walk out of the Liffey Pub and follow Mickey Haggerty's suggestion and walk right over to the river and toss in the guns.

Then they stand out there and count Eddie's roll.

"Three hundred and eighty-seven bucks," O-Bop says.

Which is disappointing.

They ain't gonna get very far on three hundred and eighty-seven bucks.

And anyway, they don't know where to go.

They're neighborhood guys, they never been anywhere else, they wouldn't know what to do, what not to do, how to act, how to function. They oughta get on a bus to somewhere, but where?

They go into a corner store and buy a couple quart bottles of beer and then get under an abutment under the West Side Highway to think it over.

"Jersey?" O-Bop says.

This is about the limit of his geographical imagination.

"You know anyone in Jersey?" Callan asks.

"No. Do you?"

"No."

Where they know people is in Hell's Kitchen, so they end up slamming a couple more beers and waiting until it's dark, and then they slip back into the neighborhood. Break into an abandoned warehouse and sleep there. Early in the morning they go to Bobby Remington's sister's apartment on Fiftieth Street.

Bobby's there, having had another fight with his old man.

He comes to the door, sees Callan and O-Bop standing there and pulls them inside.

"Jesus Christ," Bobby says, "what'd you guys *do*?"

"He was going to shoot Stevie," Callan explains.

Bobby shakes his head, "He wasn't going to shoot him. He was going to piss in his mouth, is all. That's the word out."

Callan shrugs. "Anyway."

"Are they looking for us?" O-Bop asks.

Bobby doesn't answer. He's too busy pulling down blinds.

"Bobby, do you have any coffee?" Callan asks.

"Yeah, I'll make some."

Beth Remington comes out of her bedroom. She's wearing a Rangers jersey that comes down over her thighs. Her red hair is all tangled and droops down around her shoulders. She looks at Callan and says, "Shit."

"Hi, Beth."

"You gotta get outta here."

"I'm just going to get 'em some coffee, Beth."

"Hey, Bobby," Beth says. She flicks a cigarette out of a pack on the kitchen counter, slips it into her mouth and lights it. "Bad enough I got you crashing on my couch, I don't need these guys. No offense."

O-Bop says, "Bobby, we need some hardware."

"Oh, great," Beth says. She flops down on the couch next to Callan. "Why the fuck did you come here?"

"Nowhere else to go."

"I'm honored." She gets drunk a couple times and does the dirty with him and now he thinks he can come over here, now he's in trouble. "Bobby, make them toast or something."

"Thank you," says Callan.

"You're *not* staying here."

"So, Bobby," O-Bop says, "can you hook us up?"

"They find out, I'm fucked."

"You could go to Burke, tell him it's for you," O-Bop says.

"What are you guys still doing in the neighborhood?" Beth asks. "You should be in like Buffalo by now."

"Buffalo?" O-Bop says, smiling. "What's in Buffalo?"

Beth shrugs. "Niagara Falls. I dunno."

They drink their coffee and eat their toast.

"I'll go see Burke," Bobby says.

"Yeah, that's what you need," Beth says, "to get sideways with Matty Sheehan."

"Fuck Sheehan," Bobby says.

"Yeah, go tell him that," says Beth. She turns to Callan. "You don't need guns, what you need is bus tickets. I got some money . . ."

Beth is a cashier at Loews Forty-second Street. Occasionally she sells one of the theater's tickets along with her own. So she has a little cash tucked away.

"We have money," Callan says.

"Then go."

They go. They go all the way up to the Upper West Side, hang around in Riverside Park, up by Grant's Tomb. Then they come back downtown; Beth lets them into Loews and they sit in the back of the balcony all day, watching *Star Wars*.

Fucking Death Star's about to blow for like the sixth time when Bobby shows up with a paper bag and leaves it by Callan's feet.

"Good movie, huh?" he says, and takes off as fast as he came in.

Callan eases his ankle over to the bag and feels the metal.

They go into the men's room and open the bag.

An old .25 and an equally ancient .38 police special.

"What?" O-Bop says. "He didn't have flintlocks?"

"Beggars can't be choosers."

Callan feels a lot better with a little hardware at his waist. Funny how quick you miss not having it there. You just feel light, he thinks. Like you might float up off the ground. The metal keeps you on the earth.

They sit in the theater until just before it closes, then carefully work their way back to the warehouse.

A Polish sausage saves their lives.

Tim Healey, he's been sitting up there half the fucking night and he's hungrier than shit waiting for these two kids, so he gets Jimmy Boylan to go out for a Polish sausage.

"What you want on it?" Boylan asks.

"Sauerkraut, hot mustard, the works," Tim says.

So Boylan goes out and comes back and Tim wolfs down that Polish sausage like he's spent the war in a Japanese prison camp, and that solid sausage is converting itself to gas in his intestines just when Callan and O-Bop are coming in. They're in a stairwell on the other side of a closed metal door when they hear Healey cut loose.

They freeze.

"Jesus Christ," they hear Boylan say. "Anybody *hurt*?"

Callan looks at O-Bop.

"Bobby gave us up?" O-Bop whispers.

Callan shrugs.

"I'm gonna open the door, get some air," Boylan says. "Christ, Tim."

"Sorry."

Boylan opens the door and sees the boys standing there. He yells, "Shit!" as he raises his shotgun, but all Callan can hear is the explosion of guns echoing in the stairwell as he and O-Bop let loose.

The tinfoil slides off Healey's lap as he gets up from the wooden folding chair and goes for his gun. But he sees Jimmy Boylan staggering backwards as chunks of him are flying out the back of him and loses his nerve. Drops his .45 to the ground and throws his hands up.

"Do him!" O-Bop yells.

"No, no, no, no, no!" Healey yells.

They've known Fat Tim Healey all their lives. He used to give them quarters to buy comic books. One time they're playing hockey in the street and Callan's backswing breaks Tim Healey's right headlight and Healey comes out of the Liffey and just laughs and says it's okay. "You'll get me tickets when you're playing for the Rangers, okay?" is all Tim Healey says.

Now Callan stops O-Bop from shooting Healey.

"Just get his gun!" he hollers.

He's yelling because his ears are ringing. His voice sounds like it's at the other end of a tunnel, and his head hurts like a bastard.

Healey's got mustard on his chin.

He's saying something about being too old for this shit.

Like there's a *right* age for this shit? Callan thinks.

They take Healey's .45 and Boylan's 12-gauge and hit the street.

Running.

Big Matty freaks when he hears about Eddie the Butcher.

Especially when he gets the word that it was two kids practically with shit in their diapers. He's wondering what the world is coming to—what kind of world it's going to be—when you have a generation coming up that has no respect for authority. What also concerns Big Matty is how many people approach him to plead mercy for the two kids.

"They have to be punished," Big Matt tells them, but he's disturbed when they question his decision.

"Punished, sure," they tell him. "Maybe break their legs or their wrists, send them out of the neighborhood, but they don't deserve to get killed for this."

Big Matt ain't used to being challenged like this. He don't like it all. He also don't like that the pipeline don't seem to be working. He should have had his hands on these two young animals within hours, but they've been down for days now and the rumor's going around that they're still in the neighborhood—which is shoving it in his face—but no one seems to know exactly where.

Even people who should know don't know.

Big Matt even considers this idea of punishment. Decides that maybe the just thing to do is just to take the hands that pulled the triggers. The more he considers it, the more he likes the idea. Leave these two kids walking around Hell's Kitchen with a couple of stumps as reminder of what happens when you don't show the proper respect for authority.

So he'll have their hands cut off and leave it at that.

Show them that Big Matt Sheehan can be magnanimous.

Then he remembers he don't have Eddie the Butcher anymore to do the cutting.

A day later he also don't have Jimmy Boylan or Fat Tim Healey, because Boylan is dead and Healey has just disappeared. And Kevin Kelly has found it convenient to take care of some business in Albany. Marty Stone has a sick aunt in Far Rockaway. And Tommy Dugan is on a bender.

All of which leads Big Matt to suspect that there's maybe a coup—a downright revolution—in the works.

So he makes a reservation to fly down to his other home in Florida.

Which would be very good news for Callan and O-Bop, except that it looks like before Matty got on the plane, he reached out to Big Paulie Calabrese, the new *representante*—the boss—of the Cimino Family, and called in a marker.

"What do you think he gave him?" Callan asks O-Bop.

"Piece of the Javits Center?" O-Bop says.

Big Matt controls the construction unions and the teamsters' unions working on the huge convention center being planned on the West Side. The Italians have been slavering after a piece of that business for a year or more. The skim off the cement contract alone is worth millions. Now Matt's in no real position to say no, but he could reasonably expect a little favor for saying yes.

Professional courtesy.

Callan and O-Bop are holed up in a second-floor apartment on Fortyninth between Tenth and Eleventh. They don't get a lot of sleep. Lie there looking at the sky. Or what you can see of it from a rooftop in New York.

"We've killed two guys," O-Bop says.

"Yeah."

"Self-defense, though," O-Bop says. "I mean, we had to, right?"

"Sure."

A while later O-Bop says, "I wonder if Mickey Haggerty's gonna trade us in."

"You think?"

"He's looking at eight-to-twelve on a robbery," O-Bop says. "He could trade up."

"No," Callan says. "Mickey is old-school."

"Mickey could be old-school," O-Bop says, "but he also could be tired of doing time. This is his second bit."

Callan knows that Mickey will do his time and come back to the neighborhood and want to hold his head up. And Mickey knows he won't be able to get as much as a bowl of peanuts in any bar in the Kitchen if he rolls over to the cops.

Mickey Haggerty's the least of their worries.

. . .

Which is what Callan's thinking as he looks out the window at the Lincoln Continental parked across the street.

"So we might as well get it over with," he says to O-Bop.

O-Bop's got his head of kinky red hair under the kitchen tap, trying to get cool. Yeah, that's gonna work—it's a hundred and four out and they're in a two-room apartment on the fifth floor with a fan the size of a propeller on a toy boat and the water pressure is zero because the little neighborhood bastards have opened up every fire hydrant on the street and if all that wasn't bad enough there's a crew from the Cimino Family out there looking to whack them.

And will whack them, soon as it's late enough for darkness to provide a curtain of decency.

"What do you wanna do?" O-Bop asks. "You want to go out there blasting? Gunfight at the OK Corral?"

"It would be better than baking to death up here."

"No it wouldn't," O-Bop says. "Up here sucks to be sure, but down there we'd be gunned down in the street like dogs."

"We have to go down sometime," Callan says.

"No we don't," O-Bop says. He takes his head out from under the tap and shakes the water off. "As long as they still deliver pizza, we never have to go down."

He comes over to the window and looks at the long black Lincoln parked across the street.

"Fucking Italians never change," O-Bop says. "You think they'd maybe mix in a Mercedes, a BMW, I dunno, a fuckin' Volvo or something. Anything but these fucking Lincolns and Caddies. I'm tellin' ya, it must be some kind of goombah rule or something."

"Who's *in* the car, Stevie?"

There are four guys in the car. Three more guys standing around outside. Real casual like. Smoking cigs, drinking coffee, shooting the shit. Like a mob announcement to the neighborhood—we're going to whack somebody here so you might want to be someplace else.

O-Bop refocuses.

"Piccone's sub-crew of Johnny Boy Cozzo's crew," O-Bop says. "Demonte wing of the Cimino Family."

"How do you know?"

"The guy in the passenger seat is eating a can of peaches," O-Bop says. "So it's Jimmy Piccone—Jimmy Peaches. He's got this thing for canned peaches."

O-Bop is the Paul's Peerage of mobdom. He follows them like some guys follow baseball teams. He has the whole Five Families organizational chart in his head.

So O-Bop is hipped to the fact that since Carlo Cimino died last year, the family's been in a state of flux. Most of the hard-core guys were sure Cimino would pick Neill Demonte to be his successor, but he went for his brother-in-law Paulie Calabrese instead.

It was an unpopular choice, especially among the old guard, who think that Calabrese is too white-collar, too soft. Too focused on turning the money into legitimate businesses. The hard guys—the loan sharks, extortion artists and flat-out plain robbers—don't like it.

Jimmy "Big Peaches" Piccone is one of these guys. In fact, he's sitting in the Lincoln holding forth on it.

"We're the Cimino *Crime* Family," Peaches is saying to his brother, Little Peaches. Joey "Little Peaches" Piccone is actually bigger than his older brother, Big Peaches, but no one is going to say that, so the nicknames stick. "Even the fuckin' *New York Times* calls us the Cimino *Crime* Family. We do crime. If I wanted to be a businessman I would've joined—what—IBM."

Peaches also doesn't like that Demonte was overlooked as boss. "He's an old man, what's the harm of letting him have his few years in the sun? He's earned it. What the Old Man should have done is, he should have made Mister Neill boss and Johnny Boy the underboss. Then we would have had 'our thing,' our cosa nostra."

For a young guy—Peaches is twenty-six—he's a throwback, a conservative, a mafioso William F. Buckley without the tie. He likes the old ways, the old traditions.

"In the old days," Peaches says, like he was even around in the old days, "we would have just *taken* a piece of the Javits Center. We wouldn't have to suck ass to some old Harp like Matty Sheehan. Not like Paulie's gonna give us a taste anyway. He don't care if we fuckin' starve."

"Hey," Little Peaches says.

"Hey what."

"Hey, Paulie gives this job to Mister Neill, who gives it to Johnny Boy, who gives it to us," Little Peaches says. "All I need to know: Johnny Boy gives us a job, we do the job."

"We're gonna do the fuckin' job," Peaches says. He don't need his little brother giving him lectures about how it works. Peaches *knows* how it works, *likes* how it works, especially in the Demonte wing of the family, where it works like it did in the old days.

Another thing, Peaches fucking worships Johnny Boy.

Johnny Boy is everything the Mafia used to be.

What it oughta be again, Peaches thinks.

"Soon as it gets really dark," Peaches says, "we'll go up there and punch their tickets."

Callan's sitting there flipping through the black notebook.

"Your dad's in here," he says.

"There's a surprise," O-Bop says sarcastically. "For how much?"

"Two large."

"Probably bet on the Budweiser Clydesdales to show at Aqueduct," O-Bop says. "Hey, here comes the pizza. Hey, what the fuck is this? They're taking our pizza!"

O-Bop is genuinely pissed. He's not especially angry that these guys are here to kill him—that's to be expected, that's just business—but he takes the pizza hijacking as a personal affront.

"They don't got to do that!" he wails. "That's just wrong!"

Which, Callan recalls, is how this whole thing started in the first place.

He glances up from the black book to see this fat guinea with a big grin on his face, holding a slice of pizza up at him.

"Hey!" O-Bop yells.

"It's good!" Peaches yells back.

"They've got our pizza!" O-Bop says to Callan.

"It's no big deal," Callan says.

O-Bop whines, "I'm hungry!"

"Then go down and take it from them," Callan says.

"I might."

"Take a shotgun."

"Fuck!"

Callan can hear the guys out in the street laughing at them. He doesn't care. It doesn't get to him the way it gets to O-Bop. O-Bop hates to be laughed at. It's always been an instant fight with him. Callan, he can just walk away.

"Stevie?"

"What."

"What did you say was the name of that guy down there?"

"Which guy?"

"Guy they sent to whack us."

"Jimmy Peaches."

"He's in here."

"Say what?"

O-Bop comes away from the window. "For how much?"

"A hundred thousand."

They look at each other and start to laugh.

"Callan," O-Bop says, "we got us a whole new ball game here."

Because Peaches Piccone owes Matty Sheehan $100,000. And that's just the principal—the vigorish has to be piling up faster than stink in a garbage strike, so Piccone is in serious trouble here. He's in to Matt Sheehan deep. Which would be bad news—all the more motivation for him to do Sheehan a solid—except that Callan and O-Bop have the book.

Which gives them an angle.

If they can live long enough to play it.

Because it's getting dark, fast.

"You got any ideas?" O-Bop asks.

"Yes, I do."

It's one of them desperate fourth-and-long plays, but shit, it's fourth and long.

O-Bop walks out onto the fire escape with a milk bottle in his hand.

Yells, "Hey, you guinea bastards!"

The boys look up from the Continental.

Just as O-Bop lights the rag stuck in the bottle, yells, "Eat this!" and launches it in a long, lazy arc at the Lincoln.

"What the fuck—"

This is from Peaches, who presses the button to roll the window down and sees this freaking torch coming out of the sky straight at him, so he scrambles to get the door open and get his ass out of the backseat of the Lincoln, and he does it just in time because O-Bop's aim is perfect and the bottle crashes onto the top of the car and flames spread across the roof.

Peaches yells up at the fire escape, "That's a new fucking car!"

And he's really pissed because he don't even have a chance to shoot at nobody because a crowd gathers, and then there's sirens and all that shit and it's just a couple of minutes before the whole block is full of Irish cops and Irish firemen, who start hosing down what's left of the Lincoln.

Irish cops and Irish firemen and about fifteen thousand fucking drag queens from Ninth Avenue, and they're standing around Peaches screaming and screeching and dancing and shit. He sends Little Peaches down to the phone on the corner to make a call and get a new fucking vehicle, and then he feels metal pressed against his left fucking kidney and someone whispers, "Mr. Piccone, turn around very slowly, please."

Respectful like, though, which Peaches appreciates.

He turns around and here's this Irish kid—not the red Brillo-pad asshole with the bottle but a tall, dark kid—standing there with a pistol in a brown paper bag and holding something up in his other hand.

The fuck is it? Peaches wonders.

Then he gets it.

Matty Sheehan's little black book.

"We should talk," the kid says.

"We should," says Peaches.

So they're in the basement of Paddy Hoyle's ptomaine palace way the fuck over on Twelfth and you could call it a Mexican standoff, except there ain't no Mexicans involved.

What you got is, you got this Italo-Irish get-together, and what it looks like is Callan and O-Bop are standing at one end with their backs literally to the wall, and Callan he looks like some freaking desperado with a pistol in each hand, and O-Bop he's holding the shotgun leveled at his waist. And by the door, you got the two Piccone brothers. The Italians, they don't got their guns pulled, they're just standing there in their nice clothes looking very cool and very tough.

O-Bop, he respects this. He totally gets it. Like they've already been embarrassed once tonight—never mind losing a Lincoln—they're not going to embarrass themselves further by looking like they're even concerned with two punks openly holding an arsenal on them. It's mob chic, and O-Bop gets it. In fact, he likes it.

Callan could give a rat's ass.

If this thing starts to go wrong, he's going to start pulling triggers and just see what happens.

"How old are you guys anyway?" Peaches asks.

"Twenty," O-Bop lies.

"Twenty-one," Callan says.

"You're two tough little humps, I'll tell you that," Peaches says. "Anyway, we gotta deal with this Eddie Friel thing."

Here it comes, Callan thinks. He's one slow-muscle-fiber twitch away from touching it all off.

"I hated that sick twist," says Peaches. "Pissing in guy's mouths? What's that about? How many times did you fucking shoot him anyway? Like eight? You guys wanted to get the job done, didn't you?"

He laughs. Little Peaches laughs with him.

So does O-Bop.

Not Callan. He's just ready, is all.

"Sorry about your car," O-Bop says.

"Yeah," Peaches says. "Next time you want to talk, use the fucking phone, all right?"

Everyone except Callan laughs.

"It's what I try to tell Johnny Boy," says Peaches. "I tell him you got me over here on the West Side with the Zulus and the PRs and the Wild Irish. What the fuck am I supposed to do? I'm going to tell him they're fucking flinging fire from the sky, now I gotta get a new car. Wild fucking Irish. You look inside that little black book?"

"What do you think?" O-Bop asks.

"I think you did. I definitely think you did. What did you see?"

"Depends."

"On?"

"What happens here."

"Tell me what should happen here."

Callan hears O-Bop swallow. Knows that O-Bop is scared to death, but he's going to go for it anyway. Callan thinks, Do it, Stevie, make the play.

"First thing is," O-Bop says, "we ain't got the book with us."

"Hey, Brillo," Peaches says. "We start going to work on you, you'll tell us where the book is. That is not an ace you're holding. Ease up on that trigger there, we're still talking."

Looking now at Callan.

O-Bop says, "We know where every penny is that Sheehan has on the street."

"No kidding—he's sweating bricks to get that book back."

"Fuck him," says O-Bop. "He don't get his book back, you don't owe him shit."

"Is that right?"

"As far as we're concerned," O-Bop says. "And Eddie Friel ain't gonna say different."

O-Bop sees the relief on Peaches' face, so he presses it.

"There's cops in that book," he says. "Union guys. Councilmen. Couple of million dollars in money out on the street."

"Matty Sheehan's a rich man," Peaches says.

"Why should he be?" O-Bop says. "Why not us? Why not you?"

They watch Peaches think. Watch him weigh the risks versus rewards. After a minute he says, "Sheehan's doing some favors for my boss."

O-Bop says, "You got that book, you could deliver the same favors."

Callan realizes he's made a mistake, having the guns out. His arms are getting tired, shaky. He'd like to lower the gun but he doesn't want to send any messages. Still, he's afraid that if Peaches decides the wrong way, his own hands will be too shaky to shoot straight, even at this range.

Finally, Peaches asks, "Have you told anyone else about seeing my name in that book?"

O-Bop says no so quickly that Callan realizes it's a very important question. Makes him wonder why Peaches borrowed the money, what he was using it for.

"Wild Irish," Peaches says to himself. Then to them, "Keep your fucking heads down. Try not to kill anyone for a day or so, all right? I'll get back to you on this."

Then he turns around and walks back up the stairs, his brother right behind him.

"Jesus," Callan says. He sits down on the floor.

His hands start shaking like crazy.

Peaches rings the doorbell of Matt Sheehan's building.

Some big fucking Harp answers the door. Peaches hears Sheehan inside, asking, "Who is it?"

His voice sounds scared.

"It's Jimmy Peaches," the guy says, letting him in. "He's in the den."

"Thanks."

Peaches goes down the hallway, takes a left into the den.

Room has green fucking wallpaper. Shamrocks and shit all over the place. Big picture of John Kennedy. Another one of Bobby. Picture of the Pope. Guy's got everything in here except a fucking leprechaun perched on a stool.

Big Matt's got the Yankees game on.

He gets out of his chair, though—Peaches likes the respect—and gives Peaches one of these big Irish-politician smiles and says, "James, it's good to see you. Did you have any luck with that little difficulty while I was gone?"

"Yeah."

"You found those two animals."

"Yeah."

"And?"

Jimmy's got the knife in him before Matty can say "Gosh and begorra." Sticks the blade in under the left pectoral and shoves it upward. Rolls the blade around a little to make sure there'll be no difficult ethical decisions at the hospital.

Fucking knife gets stuck in Sheehan's ribs, so Jimmy has to put his foot into the man's broad chest and shove to get the blade out. Sheehan hits the floor so hard the pictures on the walls shake.

Fat guy who let him in is standing in the doorway.

Not looking like he wants to do anything.

"How much *you* owe him?" Peaches asks.

"Seven-five."

"You don't owe him nothing," Peaches says, "if he disappears."

They cut Matty up and take him out to Wards Island, dump him into the sewage disposal.

On the way back, Peaches is singing,

> *"Anybody here seen my old friend Matty . . .*
> *Can you tell me where he's go-o-o-one?"*

A month after what has come to be known in Irish Hell's Kitchen as the "Rising of the Moon River," Callan's life has changed a little. Not only is he still living it, which is a surprise to him, he's become a neighborhood hero.

Because while Peaches was flushing Sheehan, he and O-Bop were taking a black felt-tip pen to Matty's little black book and literally settling some debts. They had a great goddamn time—eliminating some entries, reducing others, maintaining the ones they figured would give them the most swag.

It's fat times in the Kitchen.

Callan and O-Bop set themselves up in the Liffey Pub like they own it, which if you look carefully at the black book, they sort of do. People come in and practically kiss their rings, either they're so grateful they're off the hook with Matty or they're so scared they're still on the hook with the boys who took down Eddie Friel, Jimmy Boylan and very probably Matty Sheehan himself.

Someone else, too.

Larry Moretti.

It's the only killing Callan will feel bad about. Eddie the Butcher was necessary. So was Jimmy Boylan. So, especially, was Matty Sheehan. But Larry Moretti is just revenge—for helping Eddie cut up Michael Murphy.

"It's expected of us," O-Bop says. "It's a respect thing."

Moretti knows it's coming. He's holed up in his place on 104th, off Broadway, and he's been drinking on it. Hasn't made a meeting in a couple of weeks—he just stays drunk—so he's an easy mark when Callan and O-Bop come through the door.

Moretti's lying on the floor with a bottle. Got his head between the stereo speakers and he's listening to some fucked-up disco shit with the bass booming like distant artillery. He opens his eyes for a second and looks at Callan and O-Bop standing there with their guns pointed at him, and then he shuts his eyes and O-Bop yells, "This is for Mikey!" and starts shooting. Callan feels bad about it but he joins in, and it's weird, blasting a guy who's already down.

Then they got the body to deal with, but O-Bop's come prepared and they roll Moretti onto a sheet of heavy plastic and Callan now realizes how strong Eddie Friel had to be to cut meat up like that. It's hard fucking work and Callan goes into the bathroom a couple of times to throw up, but they finally get Moretti into enough pieces to get him into garbage bags and then they take the bags out to Wards Island. O-Bop thinks they should put Moretti's thing into a milk carton and walk it around the neighborhood, but Callan says no.

They don't need that shit. The word gets out and a lot of people come into the Liffey to pay tribute.

One guy who doesn't come in is Bobby Remington. Callan knows Bobby is scared that they think he gave them up to Matty, and he knows that Bobby didn't.

Beth did.

"You were just trying to protect your brother," Callan tells her when she shows up at his new apartment. "I understand that."

She looks down at the floor. She's come looking good; her long hair is brushed and shiny and she's wearing a dress. A black dress cut just low enough in front to show the tops of her white breasts.

Callan gets it. She's come over prepared to give it up to save her life, her brother's.

"Does Stevie understand?" she asks.

"I'll make him understand," Callan says.

"Bobby feels awful," she says.

"No, Bobby's good."

"He needs a job," she says. "He can't get a union card . . ."

Callan feels weird hearing this addressed to him. It's the sort of favor people used to ask of Matty.

"Yeah, we can do that," Callan says. He's holding paper from union officers in teamsters, construction, whatever. "Tell him to come around. I mean, we're friends."

"How about me?" she asks. "Are we friends?"

He'd like to make her. Shit, he'd *love* to make her. But it would be different, it would be like he was taking her just because he can, because she owes him. Because he has power now and she doesn't.

So he says, "Yeah, we're *friends*."

To let her know it's all right, it's cool, she doesn't have to put out for him.

"And that's all we are?"

"Yeah, Beth. That's all."

He feels kind of bad because she's dressed up and put on makeup and everything, but he doesn't want to go to bed with her anymore.

It's kind of sad.

Anyway, Bobby comes around and they hook him up with a job that his new boss assumes is a no-show—and Bobby doesn't disappoint him in this regard—and other people come in to pay their vig or look for a favor, and for about a month Callan and O-Bop are playing junior godfathers from a booth in the Liffey Pub.

Until the real godfather calls.

Big Paulie Calabrese reaches a hand out and demands that they come to Queens to explain to him personally why (a) they are not dead, and (b) his friend and associate Matt Sheehan is.

"I told them it was you guys whacked Sheehan," Peaches explains. They're sitting in a booth at the Landmark Tavern, and Peaches is trying to eat some fucking lamb shit with potatoes and greasy brown gravy poured all over it. At least at the sitdown with Big Paulie, they'll get a decent fucking meal.

It might be their last, but it'll be decent.

"Why did you do that?" Callan asks.

"He has his reasons," O-Bop says.

"Good," says Callan. "What are they?"

"Because," Peaches carefully explains, "if I told him I did it, he'd have me killed, no question."

"This is a great reason," Callan says to O-Bop. He turns back to Peaches. "So now he'll just have *us* whacked."

"Not necessarily," Peaches says.

"Not *necessarily*?"

"No," Peaches explains. "You guys aren't in the family. You're not made guys. You're not subject to the same discipline. See, if I were going to kill Matt Sheehan, I'd have to get Calabrese's permission, which he would never give. So if I went ahead and did it anyway, I'm in serious trouble."

"Oh, this is good news," Callan says.

"But you guys don't need permission," Peaches says. "All you need is a good reason. And the right attitude."

"What kind of attitude?"

"Toward the future," Peaches says. "An attitude of friendship. Cooperation."

O-Bop gets seriously geeked. This is like a dream come true.

"Calabrese wants to hook us up?" he asks. He's practically coming out of his seat.

"I don't know if I want to be hooked up," Callan says.

O-Bop says, "This is our shot! This is the fucking Cimino Family! They want to work with us!"

"There's another thing," Peaches says.

"That's good," says Callan. "I was hoping that wasn't, you know, everything."

"The book," Peaches says.

"What about it?"

"My entry," Peaches says. "The hundred grand? Calabrese can't ever know about that. If he does, I'm dead."

"Why?" Callan asks.

"It's his money," Peaches says. "Sheehan laid off a couple hundred from Paulie. I borrowed it from Matt."

"So you're ripping off Paul Calabrese," Callan says.

"We," Peaches corrects him.

"Jesus God," says Callan.

Even O-Bop doesn't look so enthusiastic now. Says, "I dunno, Jimmy."

"What the fuck?" Peaches says. "You don't know? I was supposed to whack you guys. Those were my orders, and I didn't obey them. They could kill me just for that. I saved your fucking lives. Twice. First I didn't kill you, then I took out Matty Sheehan for you. And you don't *know*?"

Callan stares at him. Then he says, "So this meeting. It's gonna make us rich, or it's gonna make us dead."

"That's pretty much it," Peaches says.

"What the fuck," Callan says.

Rich or dead.

There's worse choices.

The meeting is set for the back room of a restaurant in Bensonhurst.

"Goombah Central," Callan says.

Very convenient. If Calabrese decides to kill us, all he has to do is walk out and shut the door behind him. He goes out the front, our bodies go out the service entry.

Or exit, or whatever.

He's thinking this as he's looking in the mirror trying to knot his tie.

"Haven't you ever worn a tie before?" O-Bop asks. His voice is high, nervous.

"Sure I have," says Callan, "at my First Communion."

"Shit." O-Bop comes over and starts to tie the tie for him. Then says, "Turn around, I can't tie it backwards like this."

"Your hands are shaking."

"Fuck yes, they're shaking."

They got to go to this sitdown naked. No hardware of any kind. No one carries a gun around the boss except the boss's people. Which is going to make it even easier to take them out.

Not that they intend to go out unaccompanied. They got Bobby Remington and Fat Tim Healey and another kid from the neighborhood, Billy Bohun, going to cruise in a car outside the restaurant.

O-Bop's instructions are very clear.

"Anyone other than us comes out the front door," he tells them, "kill them."

And another precaution: Beth and her girlfriend Moira are going to be having lunch in the public part of the restaurant. Beth and Moira are also going to be having a .22 and a .44 in their respective handbags, just in case things go sick and the boys have a chance to get out of the back room.

As O-Bop says, "If I'm going to hell, it's going to be on a crowded bus."

They take a subway to Queens because O-Bop says he doesn't want to come out of a happy, successful meeting and get into his car and have it go *boom.*

"Italians don't do bombs," Peaches tries to tell him. "That's Irish shit."

O-Bop reminds him he's Irish and takes the subway. They get off in Bensonhurst, and him and Callan are walking down the street toward the restaurant and turn the corner and O-Bop says, "Oh, fucking shit."

"What, oh, fucking shit? What?"

There's four or five wise guys standing out front of the restaurant. Callan's like, So what, there are always four or five wise guys standing out front of wise-guy restaurants—it's what they *do.*

"That's Sal Scachi," O-Bop says.

Big, thick guy, early forties, with Sinatra-blue eyes and silver hair, which is razor-cut short for a goombah. He looks like a wise guy, Callan thinks, but then again he *don't* look like a wise guy. And he's wearing these real square black shoes, which are polished so they shine like black marble.

This is a serious fucking guy, Callan thinks.

"What's his story?" he asks O-Bop.

"He's a fucking colonel in the Green Berets," O-Bop says.

"You're shittin' me."

"I shit you not," O-Bop says. "Tons of medals from 'Nam, *and* he's a made guy. If they decide to take us off the count, it's Scachi who'll do the subtraction."

Now Scachi turns and sees them coming. Steps away from his group, walks up to O-Bop and Callan, smiles and says, "Gentlemen, welcome to the first or last day of the rest of your lives. No offense, but I have to make sure you're not carrying sidearms."

Callan nods and lifts his arms. Scachi pats him down with a few smooth moves, all the way to his ankles, then does the same with O-Bop. "Good," he says. "Now shall we go get some lunch?"

He takes them into the back room of the restaurant. Callan's seen it before, in about forty-eight freaking mob movies. Murals on the walls depict happy scenes from sunny Sicily. There's a long table with a red-and-white-checkered tablecloth. Wineglasses, espresso cups, little pats of butter sitting on iced plates.

Bottles of red, bottles of white.

Even though they're exactly on time, there's guys already there. Peaches nervously introduces them to Johnny Boy Cozzo and Demonte and a couple of others. Then the door opens and two hitters come in, chests like butcher's blocks, and then Calabrese comes in.

Callan gets a glance in at Johnny Boy, who has a smile on his face that's dangerously close to a smirk. But they all do that Sicilian hugging and kissing shit and then Calabrese sits down at the head of the table and Peaches makes the necessary introductions.

Callan doesn't like it that Peaches looks scared.

Peaches gets their names out, then Calabrese holds up a hand and says, "First we eat, *then* business."

Even Callan has to admit that the food is out of this world. It's the best meal Callan's had in his whole life. It starts with a big antipasto with provolone and prosciutto and sweet red peppers. Thin rolls of ham and tiny little tomatoes that Callan's never seen before.

Waiters are coming in and out like they're nuns waiting on the Pope.

They finish the appetizer and the pasta course comes in. Nothing fancy, just small bowls of spaghetti in a red sauce. Then there's a chicken piccata— thin slices of chicken breast in white wine, lemon and capers and then a baked fish. Then there's another salad, then dessert—a sweet white cake soaked with anisette.

All this and the wines coming in and out, and by the time the waiters set the espressos down Callan's about half in the bag. He watches Calabrese take a long sip from an espresso cup. Then the boss says, "Tell me why I shouldn't kill you."

One motherfuck of an essay question.

Part of Callan wants to scream, You shouldn't kill us because *Jimmy Piccone stole a hundred grand from you and we can prove it!* but he keeps his mouth shut, trying to think of a different answer.

Then he hears Peaches say, "They're good boys, Paul."

Calabrese smiles. "But *you're* not a good boy, Jimmy. If you were a good boy, I'd be having lunch with Matt Sheehan today."

He turns and looks at O-Bop and Callan.

"I'm still waiting for your answer."

So is Callan. He's trying to think whether he's going to hear one, or whether he should try to bust through the two slabs of meat guarding the door, make it into the dining room to grab the guns from Beth and come back in blasting.

But even if I make it out and make it back, Callan thinks, O-Bop will be dead by then. Yeah, but I can send him out on his crowded bus.

He tries to slide to the edge of his chair without anyone noticing. Inch to the edge of his seat and get his legs under him so he can burst off that chair. Maybe go straight for Calabrese and get a hold around his neck and back out the door . . .

And go where? he thinks. The freaking moon? Where can we go that the Cimino Family can't find us?

Fuck it, he thinks. Go for the guns, go out like men.

Across the table, Sal Scachi shakes his head at him. It's an almost imperceptible gesture, but it's there, telling him that if he keeps moving, he's dead.

Callan doesn't move.

All this thinking seems to take about an hour, but it actually takes only a few seconds in the, shall we say, tense atmosphere of the room, and Callan is actually surprised when he hears O-Bop's thin voice pipe up with, "You shouldn't kill us because . . ."

Because, uhhhhhhhhh . . .

". . . because we can do more for you than Sheehan ever could," Callan says. "We can deliver you a piece of the Javits Center, teamsters' local, construction local. Not a chunk of concrete moves or goes in you don't own a piece of. You get ten percent of every shylock dollar we move on the street, and we take care of all of this for you. You don't have to lift a finger or get involved."

Callan watches Calabrese consider this.

And take his sweet freaking time about it.

Which starts to piss Callan off. Like he's almost hoping Calabrese says *Fuck you guys* so they can cut this diplomatic crap and just get down to it.

But instead, Big Paulie says, "There are some conditions and some rules. First, we'll take thirty—not ten—percent of your book. Second, we'll take fifty percent of any monies arising from union and construction activities, and thirty percent of any monies emanating from any other activities. In exchange, I offer you my friendship and protection.

"While you cannot become members of the family because you are not Sicilian, you can become associates. You will work under the supervision of Jimmy Peaches. I will hold him personally responsible for your activities. If you have a need, you go to Jimmy. If you have a problem, you go to Jimmy. This Wild West nonsense must stop. Our business functions best in an atmosphere of quietude. Do you understand?"

"Yes, Mr. Calabrese."

Calabrese nods. "From time to time I might have need of your assistance. I will communicate that to Jimmy, who will communicate it to you. My expectation is that, in return for the friendship and protection I afford you, you will not turn your faces when I reach out to you. If your enemies are to be my enemies, then mine must be yours."

"Yes, Mr. Calabrese."

Callan wonders if this is when they kiss his ring.

"One last thing," Calabrese says. "Attend to your business. Make money. Prosper. Do what you need to do, except—no drugs. This was the rule that Carlo handed down, and it is still the rule now. It's too dangerous. I do not intend to spend my old age in prison, so the rule is absolute: You deal, you die."

Calabrese gets up from his chair. Everyone else gets up from theirs.

Callan's standing there when Calabrese gives a brief good-bye and the two slabs open the door for him.

And Callan is like, What is wrong with this picture?

He says, "Stevie, the man is leaving."

O-Bop looks at him like, Good.

"Stevie, the man is headed out the door."

Everything stops. Peaches is appalled by this faux pas, and he says as graciously as he can, "The don always leaves first."

"Is there a problem?" Scachi asks.

"There is," Callan says. "There is a problem."

O-Bop turns absolutely white. Peaches has his jaw clenched so tight it's going to take an Allen wrench to loosen it. Demonte's looking at them like he's watching something on a *National Geographic* special. Johnny Boy just thinks it's kind of funny.

Scachi doesn't. He snaps, "What's the problem?"

Callan gulps and says, "The problem is, we got people out in the street we told to kill the first person comes out the door, if it's not us."

A tense moment.

Calabrese's two guards have their hands on their guns. So does Scachi, except his .45 service revolver is pointed squarely at Callan's head.

Calabrese is looking at Callan and O-Bop, shaking his head.

Jimmy Peaches is trying to remember the exact wording of the Act of Contrition.

Then Calabrese laughs.

Laughs so hard he has to pull a white handkerchief out of his jacket pocket and dab his eyes. That doesn't even do it—he has to sit back down. Finishes laughing and looks at Scachi and says, "What are you standing there for? Shoot 'em."

Then, just as quickly, he says, "I'm kidding, I'm kidding. You two boys, thinking I was going to walk out that door and World War Three was going to start. Aww, that's funny."

He waves them toward the door.

"*This* time," he says.

They go out the door and it shuts behind them. From the restaurant's dining room they can still hear them in there laughing. They walk past Beth and her friend Moira, out onto the street.

No sign of Bobby Remington and fat Tim Healey.

Just a bunch of black Lincolns from corner to corner.

Mob guys standing around them.

"Jesus Christ," O-Bop says. "They couldn't get a parking spot."

Later, an apologetic Bobby will tell them that he just drove around and around until some of the mob guys stopped the car and told them to get the fuck out of there. So they did.

But that will be later.

Right now, O-Bop stands out on the street and looks up at the blue sky and says, "You know what this means, don't you?"

"No, Stevie, what does it mean?"

"It means," O-Bop says, throwing his arm around Callan, "we're the kings of the West Side."

Kings of the West Side.

That's the good news.

The bad news is what Jimmy Peaches has done with the hundred grand he now has free and clear from the last will and testament of Matty Sheehan. What he's done is he's bought dope with it.

Not the usual heroin from the usual Turkey-to-Sicily connection. Not from the Marseilles connection. Not even from the new Laotian connection that Santo Trafficante set up. No—if he buys from any of those sources, Calabrese hears about it about fifteen seconds later, and about a week after that Jimmy Peaches' bloated body shocks tourists on the Circle Line.

No, he has to find a new source.

Mexico.

3

California Girls

I wish they all could be California girls.

—Brian Wilson, "California Girls"

La Jolla, California
1981

Nora Hayden's fourteen the first time one of her dad's friends hits on her.
He's driving her home from baby-sitting his boy brat and all of a sudden he takes her hand and sets it on his bulge. She's going to take it off except she's fascinated by the look on his face.

And how it makes her feel.

Powerful.

So she keeps her hand there. Doesn't move it around or anything, but it seems to be enough and she can hear his rough breathing and see his eyes get all intense and funny and she wants to laugh except she doesn't want to, you know, break the spell.

Next time he does it he keeps his own hand on top of hers and moves it around in circles. She can feel him grow under her palm. Feels him twitch. His face looks ridiculous.

Time after that he pulls the car over and asks her to take it out.

And she, like, hates this guy, right?

He utterly grosses her out, but she does it the way he shows her, but it feels like she's the boss, not him. Like she can jerk him and *jerk* him, just by stopping and then starting again.

"It's not a penis," she'll tell her friend Elizabeth. "It's a leash."

"No, it's the whole puppy," Elizabeth says. "You pet it, stroke it, kiss it, give it a warm place to sleep and it'll go fetch things for you."

She's fourteen and looks seventeen. Her mom sees it, but what can she do? Nora's splitting time between her mom's and her dad's and never has the term *joint custody* had quite such piquant meaning. Because every time she goes to her dad's place, that what he's doing—a joint.

Dad's like some sort of white Rastafarian without the dreadlocks or the religious convictions. Dad couldn't find Ethiopia on a map of Ethiopia; he just likes his herb. *That* part of it, he totally gets.

Mom's over all that, and it's the big reason they divorced. She outgrew her hippie phase with a vengeance, like hippie to yuppie, zero to sixty in five seconds flat. He's stuck in the Birkenstocks like they're clamped onto his feet, but she's moving on.

In fact, she gets a real good job in Atlanta and wants Nora to go with her, but Nora is like, Nah, unless you can show me where the beach is in Atlanta I'm not going. Eventually it comes down to a judge asking Nora which parent she'd like to live with and she almost says, "Neither," but what she actually says is, "My dad," so by the time she's fifteen she's going to Atlanta for major holidays and one month in the summer.

Which is just bearable if, like, she has enough good weed.

The kids at school call her "Nora the Whora," but she doesn't care and neither, really, do they. It's not really so much a term of contempt as it is an acknowledgment of reality. What do you say about a classmate who gets picked up from school in Porsches, Mercedeses and limos, none of which belong to her parents?

Nora is stoned one afternoon, filling out some stupid questionnaire for the guidance counselor, and under "After School Activities" she puts down "Blow Jobs." Before she erases it, she shows the form to her friend Elizabeth and they both laugh.

And don't be pulling that limo into the drive-thru at Mickey D's, either. Ditto Burger King, Taco Bell and Jack in the Box. Nora has the face and the body to command Las Brisas, the Inn at Laguna, El Adobe.

You want Nora, you provide her with good food, good wine, good dope.

Jerry the Doof always has good coke.

He wants her to go to Cabo with him.

Of course he does. He's a forty-four-year-old coke dealer with more memories than possibilities; she's sixteen with a body like springtime. Why shouldn't he want to take her for a dirty weekend in Mexico?

Nora's cool with it.

She's sixteen but not sweet.

She knows dude isn't, like, in *love* with her. She sure as shit knows she isn't in love with him. In fact, she thinks he's more or less a doof, with his black silk jacket and his black ball cap to cover his thinning hair. His bleached jeans, his Nikes with no socks. No, Nora gets it—dude is just terrified of getting old.

No fear, dude, she thinks. Nothing to fret about.

You *are* old.

Jerry the Doof has only two things going for him.

But they're two good things.

Money and coke.

The same thing, really. Because, Nora knows, if you have money, you have coke. And if you have coke, you have money.

She sucks him off.

It takes longer because of the coke, but she doesn't mind, she's got nothing better to do. And melting Jerry's popsicle is better than having to talk to him, or worse, listen to him. She doesn't want to hear any more about his ex-wives, his kids—shit, she knows two of his kids better than he does; she goes to school with them—or how he hit that game-winning triple in his league softball game.

When she's finished he asks, "So, you want to go?"

"Go where?"

"Cabo."

"Okay."

"So when do you want to go?" Jerry the Doof asks.

She shrugs. "Whenever."

She's about out of the car when Jerry hands her a Baggie full of fine herb.

"Hey," her dad says when she comes in. He's stretched out on the couch watching a rerun of *Eight Is Enough.* "How was your day?"

"Fine." She tosses the Baggie onto the coffee table. "Jerry sent this for you."

"For me? Cool."

So cool he actually sits up. All of a sudden he's like Mr. Initiative, rolling himself a nice tight joint.

Nora goes into her room and closes the door.

Wonders what to think about a father who'll pimp his own daughter for dope.

Nora has a life-changing experience in Cabo.

She meets Haley.

Nora's lying by the pool next to Jerry the Doofus, and this chick on a chaise across the pool is clearly checking her out.

A very-cool-lady type of chick.

Late twenties, dark brown hair cut short under a black sun visor. Small, thin body cut in the gym, shown off under a next-to-nothing black two-piece. Nice jewelry—spare, gold, expensive. Every time Nora glances up, this chick is looking at her.

With this know-it-all smile, just shy of a smirk.

And she's always there.

Nora looks up from her chaise—she's there. Walking on the beach—she's there.

Having dinner in the hotel dining room—she's there. Nora shies from the eye contact; it's always Nora who looks away first. Finally she can't handle it anymore. She waits for Jerry to lapse into one of his postcoital siestas and goes out to the pool and sits on the chaise next to the woman and says, "You've been checking me out."

"I have."

"I'm not interested."

The woman laughs. "You don't even know what it is that you're not interested in."

"I'm not a lesbian," Nora says.

Like, she's not into guys, but she's not into chicks, either. Which leaves cats and dogs, but she's not that crazy about cats.

"Neither am I," the woman says.

"So?"

"Let me ask you this," the woman says. "Are you making any money?"

"Huh?"

"Being a coke bunny," the woman says. "Are you making any money?"

"No."

The woman shakes her head, says, "Kiddo, with your face and body, you could be an earner."

An earner. Nora likes the sound of that.

"How?" she asks.

The woman reaches into her bag and hands Nora a business card.

Haley Saxon—with a San Diego phone number.

"What are you in, like, sales?" Nora asks.

"In a manner of speaking."

"Huh?"

" 'Huh?' " Haley mocks. "See, that's what I mean. If you want to be an earner, you have to stop saying things like 'huh.' "

"Well, maybe I don't want to be an earner."

"In which case, have a nice weekend," Haley says. She picks her magazine back up and goes back to reading. But Nora doesn't go anywhere, just sits there feeling stupid. It's like five full minutes before she finds the nerve to say, "Okay, maybe I want to be an earner."

"Okay."

"So what do you sell?"

"You. I sell you."

Nora starts to say "Huh," then checks herself and says, "I'm not sure what you mean."

Haley smiles. Lays an elegant hand on top of Nora's hand and says, "It's as simple as it sounds. I sell women to men. For money."

Nora's quick on the uptake. "So this is about sex," she says.

"Kiddo," Haley says, "everything is about sex."

Haley gives her a whole speech, but basically it boils down to this: The whole world is—all the time—looking to get off.

She wraps up the spiel by saying, "You want to give it away, or sell it cheap, that's your business. If you want to sell it for big bucks, that's my business. How old are you, anyway?"

"Sixteen," Nora says.

"Jesus," Haley says. She shakes her head.

"What?"

Haley sighs. "The potential."

First the voice.

"If you want to keep doing backseat blow jobs for trinkets you can talk like a beach girl," Haley tells her a couple of weeks after they meet in Cabo. "If you want to move up in the world . . ."

Haley puts Nora to work with some alcoholic refugee from the Royal Shakespeare Company who drops Nora's voice about an octave. ("That's important," Haley says. "A deep voice makes a dick sit up and listen.") The dipso tutor rounds out Nora's vowels, punches up her consonants. Makes her do monologues: Portia, Rosalind, Viola, Paulina . . .

> *"What studied torments, tyrant, hast for me?*
> *What wheels? racks? fires? what flaying? boiling?"*

So her voice becomes cultured. Deeper, fuller, lower. It's all part of the package. Like the clothes Haley takes her shopping for. The books Haley makes her read. The daily newspaper. "And not the fashion page, kiddo, or the arts," Haley says. "A courtesan reads the sports section first, then the financial pages, then maybe the news."

So she starts showing up at school with the morning paper. Her friends are out in the parking lot having that last-minute bong hit before the bell rings, and Nora's sitting there checking out the scores, the Dow Jones, the editorial page. She's reading the *National Review, The Wall Street Journal,* the freaking *Christian Science Monitor.*

And that's about the only time she spends in the backseat.

Nora the Whora goes to Cabo and comes back Nora the Ice Maiden.

"She's a virgin again," is how Elizabeth explains it to their bewildered friends. She doesn't mean it unkindly; it just seems to be true. "She went to Cabo and had her hymen reattached."

"I didn't know you could do that," their friend Raven says.

Elizabeth just sighs.

Raven asks her for the name of the doctor.

Nora becomes a gym fiend, spending hours on the stationary cycle, more hours on the treadmill. Haley hires her a personal trainer, a fascist health-freak chick named Sherry whom Nora dubs her "physical terrorist." This nazi has a body like a greyhound, and she starts whipping Nora's body into the tight little package that Haley wants to market. Gets her doing push-ups, sit-ups, crunches, and starts her on weights.

The interesting thing is that Nora starts to dig it.

All of it—the rigorous mental and physical training. Nora is, like, into it. She gets up one morning and goes to wash her face (with the special cleanser Haley buys her), looks in the mirror, and she's like, "Wow, who is this woman?" She goes to class, she hears herself discoursing about current affairs and she's like, "Wow, who *is* this woman?"

Whoever she is, Nora likes her.

Her dad doesn't notice the change. How could he? Nora thinks. I don't come in a Baggie.

Haley takes her on a drive up to the Sunset Strip in L.A. to show her the crack whores. Crack cocaine has hit the country like a virus, and the whores have caught it. Big time. They're on their knees in alleys, on their backs in cars. Some of them are young, some old—Nora is shocked that they all *look* so old. And so sick.

"I could never be one of these women," Nora says.

"Yes, you could," Haley says. "If you don't stay straight. Keep off dope, don't let your head get fucked-up. Most of all, put the money away. You'll have ten to twelve peak earning years, if you take care of yourself. Tops. After that, it's all downhill. So you want to have stocks, bonds, mutual funds. Real estate. I'll hook you up with my financial planner."

Because the girl is going to need one, Haley thinks.

Nora is the package.

When she turns eighteen, she's ready to go to the White House.

White walls, white carpet, white furniture. A pain in the ass to clean and maintain, but worth it because it quiets the men the moment they walk in. (There's not one of them who wasn't as a boy scared shitless of spilling something on his mother's white whatever.) And when Haley is in attendance, she always wears white: The house is me, I am the house. I'm untouchable, my house is likewise untouchable.

Her women always wear black.

Nothing else, always stark black.

Haley wants her women to stand out.

And they're always fully dressed. Never in lingerie or robes—Haley's not running some cheap Nevada mustang ranch. She's been known to costume the women in turtlenecks, in business suits, in basic little black frocks, in gowns. She dresses her women in clothes that the men can imagine removing. And she makes them wait to do that.

They have to jump through hoops, even at the White House.

On the walls hang black-and-white renditions of goddesses: Aphrodite, Nike, Venus, Hedy Lamarr, Sally Rand, Marilyn Monroe. Nora finds the pictures intriguing, especially the one of Monroe, because they look a little alike.

No kidding, they do, Haley thinks.

She's billing Nora as a young Monroe without the body fat.

Nora's nervous. She's staring into a video monitor of the sitting room, looking at this party of clients, one of whom is going to be her first professional lay. She hasn't had sex in a year and a half anyway, and she's not even sure she remembers how to do it, never mind do it five hundred bucks' worth. So she's hoping she gets this one, the tall, dark, shy one, and it does seem that Haley is trying to steer things in that direction.

"Nervous?" Joyce asks her. Joyce is her polar opposite, a flat-chested gamine in a 1950s Paris outfit—Gigi as whore—who's been helping with her makeup and clothes, an open-neck black blouse over a black skirt.

"Yes."

"Everyone is the first time," Joyce says. "Then it gets to be routine."

Nora keeps looking at the four men sitting awkwardly on the big sofa. They look young, only in their mid-twenties, but they don't look like rich spoiled college kids, and she wonders how they got the money to come here. How they got here at all.

Callan wonders the same thing.

Like, what the hell are we doing here?

Big Paulie Calabrese would shit blood if he knew Jimmy Peaches was out here connecting the pipeline that will suck cocaine like a giant straw from Colombia through Mexico and on to the West Side.

"Will you relax?" Peaches says. "I set a place for you at the table, will you fucking sit down and eat?"

" 'You deal, you die,' " Callan reminds him. "That's what Calabrese said."

"Yeah, 'You deal, you die,' " Jimmy says. "But if we don't deal, we starve. Is fuckin' Paulie giving us a taste of the unions? No. The kickbacks? No. Trucking? Construction? No. Fuck him. Let him give me a taste of those businesses and *then* he can tell me don't deal. In the meantime, I deal."

The doors haven't shut on the bellhops' behinds and Peaches says he wants to go to this cathouse he's heard about.

Callan's not into it.

"We flew three thousand miles to get laid?" he asks. "We can get laid at home."

"Not like this we can't," Peaches says. "They say they got the best pussy in the world at this place."

"Sex is sex," Callan says.

"What do you know about it?" Peaches asks. "You're Irish."

It's not like Callan ain't tempted here, it's just that this was supposed to be a business trip, and when it comes to business Callan is just that— business. Tough enough keeping the Brothers Piccone from stepping on their own dicks on the job, never mind when they're dogging women.

So he says, "I thought this was a business trip."

"Jesus, will you lighten up?" Peaches says. "You're gonna die, on your headstone it's gonna say you never had no fun. We'll get laid, we'll do business. We might even take a minute to get a meal if that's okay with you. I hear they got great seafood here."

Yeah, this is real smart of Peaches, Callan thinks. Looking out the window at nothing but ocean, he figures someone out here might have figured out how to cook a fish.

"You're a grim bastard, you know that?" Peaches adds.

Yeah, I'm a grim bastard, Callan thinks. I've punched what, five guys' tickets for the Ciminos, Peaches tells me I'm a grim bastard.

"Who gave you the number?" Callan asks. He doesn't like it. Peaches calls this number, some bimbo tells him, Sure, come over, they get to some warehouse where all that's waiting for them is a shit storm.

"Sal Scachi gave me the number, all right?" Peaches says. "You know Sal."

"I don't know," Callan says. If Calabrese's gonna hit them over this drug deal, it *would* be Scachi who'd set it up.

"Will you relax?" Peaches says. "You're starting to make me nervous."

"Good."

" 'Good.' He wants me to be nervous."

"I want you to be alive."

"I appreciate the sentiment, Callan, I do." Peaches reaches over, grabs Callan by the back of the head and kisses him on the cheek. "There, now you can go tell the priest you committed a homosexual act with a guinea. I love ya, ya mick bastard. I'm telling you, tonight's strictly pleasure."

Nevertheless, Callan straps on his silenced .22 before they go out. They pull up to the White House and a minute later they're all standing in the foyer just gawking.

Callan figures to drink a beer, then stand back and keep an eye on things. If anyone's scheming to take Peaches off the count they'll wait until Jimmy's humping away and then put one in the back of his head. So Callan's going to drink his beer, grab O-Bop and set up some kind of security. Of course, O-Bop will tell him to fuck off, he wants to get laid, so security is going to be pretty much Callan's job. So he sips on his beer as Haley sets several black three-ring binders on the glass coffee table.

"We have a number of ladies here tonight," she says, opening a binder. Each page has an 8×10 black-and-white glossy photograph in a plastic sleeve, with smaller, full-body poses on the reverse side. Haley's not about to parade her women out like a livestock auction. No, this is classy, dignified, and it serves to fire the men's imaginations.

"Knowing these ladies as I do," she says, "I'll be happy to assist you in making an appropriate match."

After the other men have made their selections, she sits next to Callan, notices that he's fixated on Nora's head shot and whispers in his ear, "Her eyes could make you come." Callan blushes to his toes.

"Would you like to meet her?" Haley asks.

He manages a nod.

Turns out that he would.

And he falls instantly in love.

Nora comes into the room, looks at him with those eyes. He feels a charge that goes from his heart to his groin and back again, and by the time it does he's a goner. He's never seen anything so beautiful in his life. The thought that something—someone—so lovely could be his even for a little while is something he didn't think was possible in his life. Now it's imminent.

He swallows hard.

For her part, she's relieved it's him.

He's not bad-looking, and he doesn't look mean.

She puts out her hand and smiles.

"I'm Nora."

"Callan."

"Do you have a first name, Callan?" she asks.

"Sean."

"Hello, Sean."

Haley's beaming at them like a yenta. She wanted the shy one for Nora's first time out, so she manipulated the others to select the more experienced women. Now everyone's paired off into the couples she wanted, standing and chatting, getting ready to go to the rooms. She slips out back to her office so she can phone Adán and tell him his customers are having a good time.

"I'll take care of the bill," Adán tells her.

It's nothing. It's tip money compared to the business the Piccone brothers could bring him. Adán can sell a lot of cocaine in California. He has plenty of customers in San Diego and L.A. But the New York market would be enormous. To put his product onto the streets of New York through the Cimino distribution network . . . well, Jimmy Peaches can have all the whores he wants, on the house.

Adán doesn't come to the White House anymore. Not as a customer, anyway. Bedding even high-class call girls doesn't fit his persona as a serious businessman.

Besides, he's in love.

Lucía Vivanca is the daughter of a middle-class family. Born in the USA, she's "won the Daily Double," as Raúl puts it; that is, she has dual U.S. and Mexican citizenship. Only recently graduated from Our Lady of Peace High School in San Diego, she's living with an older sister and taking classes at San Diego State.

And she's a beauty.

Petite, with natural blond hair against striking dark eyes, and a trim little figure that Raúl obscenely comments upon at every opportunity.

"Those *chupas,* brother," he says, "poking out of that blouse. You could cut yourself on them. Too bad she's a *chiflona.*"

She's not a cocktease, Adán thinks, she's a lady. Well-bred, cultured, educated by nuns. Still, he has to admit that he's frustrated after countless wrestling matches in the front seat of his parked car, or on the sofa of her sister's apartment the rare times the watchful *bruja* gives them a few minutes alone.

Lucía will just not give it up, not until they're married.

And I don't have the money to get married yet, Adán thinks. Not to a lady like Lucía.

"You'd be doing her a favor," Raúl argues, "by going with a whore. Not putting all that pressure on her. In fact, you *owe* it to Lucía to go to the White House. Your morality is a selfish indulgence."

Raúl certainly isn't selfish in that regard, Adán thinks. His generosity is more than abundant. My brother, Adán thinks, hits the White House the way a restaurant cook raids the pantry and eats up all the profits.

"It's my giving nature," Raúl says. "What can I say? I'm a people person."

"Keep your giving nature in your pants tonight," Adán says to him now. "Tonight is about business."

He hopes things are going well at the White House.

"Would you like a drink?" Callan asks Nora.

"A grapefruit juice?"

"That's all?"

"I don't drink," Nora says.

He has no clue what to do or say, so he just stands there, staring at her.

She stares back at him, surprised. Not so much by what she feels, but by what she doesn't feel.

Contempt.

She can't seem to work up any contempt.

"Sean?"

"Yeah?"

"I have a room here. Would you like to go?"

He's grateful to her for cutting through the bullshit. Keep him from standing there feeling like a jerk.

Hell yes I want to go, he thinks. I want to go up there and take off your clothes and touch you everywhere and be inside you and then I want to take you home. Take you back to the Kitchen and treat you like the Queen of the West Side and have you be the first thing I see when I get up in the morning and the last thing I see at night.

"Yeah. Yeah, I would."

She smiles and takes his hand and they are turning to go upstairs when Peaches' voice comes across the room.

"Yo, Callan!"

Callan turns to see him standing in the corner beside a small woman with short black hair.

"Yeah?"

"I wanna trade."

"What?" Callan asks.

Nora says, "I don't think—"

"Good. Keep on don't thinking," Peaches says. He looks at Callan. "So?"

Peaches is pissed. He spotted Nora when she came into the room. Maybe the most beautiful piece of ass he's ever seen in his life. If he'd been shown her first, he'd have picked her.

"No," Callan says.

"C'mon, be a sport."

Everything in the room stops.

O-Bop and Little Peaches stop scoping the women they're with and start checking out the situation.

Which is dangerous, is what O-Bop's thinking.

Because while Jimmy Peaches is clearly not the craziest of the Piccone brothers—that honor goes to Little Peaches, hands down—Jimmy's got a temper on him. It's sudden, it comes from nowhere and you never know what Jimmy Peaches is going to do—or worse, order *you* to do—on the spur of the moment.

And Jimmy's *irritated* right now, thinking about Callan, because Callan has gotten—what?—moody, quiet, since they got out to California. And this makes Jimmy nervous because he needs Callan. And now Callan's about to go upstairs to fuck the woman Peaches wants to fuck and that's just not right because Peaches is the boss here.

There's something else, though, that makes this argument dangerous, and they all know it, although no one in Piccone's crew is ever going to utter the words out loud: Peaches is afraid of Callan.

Flat out, there it is. They all know that Peaches is good. He's tough, smart and mean.

He's stone.

But Callan.

Callan is the best.

Callan is the stone-coldest killer there's ever been.

And Jimmy Peaches needs him and is scared of him, and that's a volatile combination. That is nitro on a bumpy road, is what that is, O-Bop thinks. He doesn't like this shit at all. He's busted his ass putting them together with the Ciminos, they're all making money and now it's all going to go to shit over some gash?

"What the fuck, guys," O-Bop says.

"No, *what* the fuck?" Peaches asks.

"I said no," Callan repeats.

Peaches knows that Callan can whip that little .22 out and put one between his eyes before any of them can blink. But he also knows that Callan can't gun down the whole freaking Cimino Family, which is what he'll have to do if he kills Peaches.

So that's what Peaches has going for him.

Which really pisses Callan off.

He's sick of being the guineas' attack dog.

To hell with Jimmy Peaches.

To hell with him, Johnny Boy, Sal Scachi and Paulie Calabrese. Without taking his eyes off Peaches, he asks O-Bop, "You got my back?"

"I got your back."

So there it is.

They got a situation here.

Which don't look like it's gonna end happy for him or anyone else, until Nora says, "Why don't *I* decide?"

Peaches smiles. "That's fair. Is that fair, Callan?"

"It's fair."

Thinking that it ain't fair. That you get so close to beauty you can't breathe and then it slips away. But what the fuck has fair ever had to do with it?

"Go ahead," Peaches says. "Choose."

Callan feels like his heart's outside of him. Out there beating away where everyone can see it.

She looks up at him and says, "You'll like Joyce. She's beautiful."

Callan nods.

"I'm sorry," she whispers.

She is, too. She wanted to go with Callan. But Haley, now back in the room and doing her best to defuse the situation, has given her the eye, and Nora's smart enough to understand she's supposed to choose the gross guy.

Haley's relieved. Tonight has to go well. Adán's made it very clear that tonight is not about her business, it's about *his*. And seeing as how Tío Barrera set her up with the money to open the place, she is going to take care of the Barrera family business.

"Don't be sorry," Callan says to Nora.

He doesn't go with Joyce. Tells her, "No offense, but no thanks," and goes and stands by the car. Pulls his .22 and holds it behind his back a few minutes later when a car pulls up and Sal Scachi gets out.

He's dressed California casual but he's still got them polished army shoes on. Guineas and their shoes, Callan thinks. He tells Scachi to stop right there and keep his hands where he can see them.

"Hey, it's the shooter," Scachi says. "Don't worry, Shooter, Jimmy Peaches got nothing to worry about from me. What Paulie don't know . . ."

He gives Callan a little punch under the chin and goes into the house. He's happy as hell to be there, because he's spent the past few months in his green suit working on some CIA op called Cerberus. Scachi with a crew of other Forces guys putting up three radio towers in the fucking Colombian jungle, then keeping an eye on them to make sure the Communist guerrillas don't knock them down.

Now he has to make sure Peaches gets hooked up with Adán Barrera. Which reminds him . . .

He turns around and calls to Callan.

"Hey, kid! There's a couple of Mexican guys coming," Scachi says. "Do me a favor—don't shoot them."

He laughs and goes into the house.

Callan looks up again at the light in the window.

Peaches does her hard.

Nora tries to slow him down, soften him, show him the sweet, slow things that Haley taught her, but the man isn't having it. He's hard already, from his victory downstairs. He throws her facedown on the bed, yanks her skirt and panties down and shoves himself inside her.

"You *feel* that, huh?" he says.

She feels it.

It hurts.

He's big and she's not nearly wet enough and he's pounding at her, so she definitely feels it. Feels his hands reach under her and rip her bra off and start to squeeze her breasts hard and at first she tries to talk to him, to tell him that, but then she feels the anger and contempt come over her and she's like, *Knock yourself out, asshole,* so she lets her pain out in cries he mistakes for pleasure so he rams her harder and she remembers to squeeze him so he'll come but he pulls out.

"Don't give me any of your fucking whore's tricks."

He turns her over and straddles her. Pushes her breasts together, then lays his cock between them and pushes it up toward her mouth.

"Suck it."

She does.

She does it the best he'll let her as he pistons in and out because she wants this *over*. He's doing his own porno flick anyway, so it is over soon, as he grabs his cock and pumps it and lets himself loose on her face.

She knows what he wants.

She's seen the movies, too.

So she takes some on her finger, swirls it into her mouth and looks him in the eyes as she moans, *"Mmmmmmm."*

And sees him smile.

When Peaches leaves she goes into the bathroom, brushes her teeth until her gums bleed and swishes Listerine around her mouth for a full minute until she spits it out. She takes a long, almost scalding shower, then puts on a robe, goes to the window and looks out.

She sees the nice one, the shy one, leaning against the car, and wishes he could have been her boyfriend.

PART TWO

Cerberus

4

The Mexican Trampoline

Who has the boats? Who has the planes?

—Malcolm X

Guadalajara
Mexico
1984

Art Keller watches the DC-4 land.

He and Ernie Hidalgo sit in a car on a bluff overlooking the Guadalajara airport. Art continues to watch as Mexican *federales* help off-load the cargo.

"They don't even bother to change out of their uniforms," Ernie says.

"Why should they?" Art answers. "They're on the job, aren't they?"

Art has his night-vision binoculars trained on a cargo airstrip that juts sideways from the main runway. On the near side of the strip a number of cargo hangars and a few small shacks serve as offices for the airfreight companies. Now trucks are parked outside the hangars and the *federales* carry crates from the plane into the backs of the trucks.

He says to Ernie, "You getting this?"

"Say cheese," Ernie answers. The electric motor of his camera whirs. Ernie grew up among the gangs in El Paso, saw what dope did to his barrio and wanted to do something about it. So when Art offered him the Guadalajara job, he jumped at it. Now he asks, "And what do we think might be in the crates?"

"Oreo cookies?" Art suggests.

"Bunny slippers?"

"One thing we know it isn't," Art says. "It isn't cocaine, because . . ."

They both finish the line, *". . . there is no coke in Mexico!"*

They laugh at this shared joke, a ritual chant, a sarcastic rendering of the official line given to them by their bosses at the DEA. According to the suits in Washington, the planes full of coke that've been coming in more regularly and more often than United Airlines are a figment of Art Keller's imagination.

The received wisdom is that the Mexican drug trade was destroyed back in the Operation Condor days. The official reports say so, the DEA says so, the State Department says so, and the attorney general says so—and none of the aforementioned needs Art Keller to create fantasies about Mexican drug "cartels."

Art knows what they say about him. That he's becoming a genuine pain in the ass, firing off monthly memos, trying to create a Federación from a gaggle of Sinaloan hillbillies who were chased out of the mountains nine years ago. Bugging everyone with a bunch of Frito Banditos who are running a little marijuana and maybe a little heroin, when what he needs to realize is that there's a freaking crack *epidemic* ripping through the streets of America, and the cocaine is coming from Colombia, not goddamn Mexico.

They even sent Tim Taylor over from Mexico City to tell him to shut the fuck up. The man in charge of the whole DEA operation in Mexico gathered Art, Ernie Hidalgo and Shag Wallace in the back room of the DEA office in Guadalajara and said, "We're not where the action is. You guys need to face that instead of inventing—"

"We're not inventing anything," Art said.

"Where's the proof?"

"We're working on it."

"No," Taylor said. "You're *not* working on it. There is nothing for you to work *on*. The attorney general of the United States has announced to Congress—"

"I read the speech."

"—that the Mexican drug problem is all but over. Are you trying to make the AG look like an asshole?"

"I think he can manage that without any help from me."

"I'll be sure to tell him you said that, Arthur," Taylor said. "You are not, I repeat *not*, to go running around Mexico chasing snow that doesn't exist. Do we have an understanding here?"

"Sure," said Art. "If anyone tries to sell me Mexican cocaine, I should just say no."

Now, three months later, he's watching nonexistent *federales* loading nonexistent cocaine into nonexistent trucks that will deliver the cocaine to nonexistent members of the nonexistent Federación.

It's the Law of Unintended Consequences, Art thinks as he watches the *federales*. Operation Condor was intended to cut the Sinaloan cancer out of Mexico, but what it did instead was spread it through the entire body. And you have to give the Sinaloans credit—their response to their little diaspora was pure genius. Somewhere along the line they figured out that their real product isn't drugs, it's the two-thousand-mile border they share with the United States, and their ability to move contraband across it. Land can be burned, crops can be poisoned, people can be displaced, but that border— that border isn't going anywhere. A product that might be worth a few cents one inch on their side of the border is worth thousands just one inch on the other side.

The product—DEA, State, and Mexican government notwithstanding— is cocaine.

The Federación made a very simple and profitable deal with the Medellín and Cali cartels: The Colombians pay $1,000 for every kilo of cocaine the Mexicans can safely deliver to them inside the United States. So, basically, the Federación got out of the drug-growing business and into the transportation business. The Mexicans take delivery of the coke from the Colombians, transport it to staging areas along the border, move it across into safe houses in the States and then give it back to the Colombians and get their thousand bucks per kilo. The Colombians move it to their labs and process it into crack, and the shit is on the streets weeks—sometimes just days—after leaving Colombia.

Not through Florida—the DEA has been pounding those routes like a rented mule—but through the neglected Mexican "back door."

The Federación, Art thinks—when it absolutely, positively has to be there overnight.

But how? he wonders. Even he has to admit there are some problems with his theory. How do you fly a plane under the radar from Colombia to Guadalajara, across a Central American terrain that is swarming not only with DEA but, thanks to the presence of the Communist Sandinista regime in Nicaragua, with CIA as well? Spy satellites, AWACS—none of them is picking up these flights.

And then there's the fuel problem. A DC-4, like the one he's looking at right now, doesn't have the fuel capacity to make that flight in one shot. It would have to stop and refuel. But where? It doesn't seem possible, as his bosses have cheerfully pointed out to him.

Yeah, well, it may not be possible, Art thinks. But the plane is sitting there, fat with cocaine. Just as real as the crack epidemic that's causing so much pain in the American ghettos. So I know you're doing it, Art thinks, looking at the plane. I just don't know *how* you're doing it.

But I'm going find out.

And then I'm going to prove it.

"What's this?" Ernie asks.

A black Mercedes pulls up to the office shack. Some *federales* trot up and open the back door of the car and a tall, thin man in a black suit gets out. Art can see the glow from a cigar as the man walks through the cordon of *federales* into the office.

"I wonder if that's him," Ernie asks.

"Who?"

"The mythical M-1 himself," Ernie says.

"M-1" is the Mexican sobriquet for the nonexistent head of the non-existent Federación.

The intelligence that Art has managed to gather over the past year is that M-1's Federación, like Caesar's Gaul, is divided into three parts: the Gulf States, Sonora, and Baja. Together they cover the border with the United States. Each of these three territories is run by a Sinaloan who was forced out of the home province by Operation Condor, and Art has managed to put a name to all three.

The Gulf: García Abrego.

Sonora: Chalino Guzmán, aka El Verde, "The Green."

Baja: Güero Méndez.

At the top of this triangle, based in Guadalajara: M-1.

But they can't put a name or a face to him.

But you can, can't you, Art? he asks himself. You know in your gut who's the patron of the Federación. You helped put him in office.

Art peers through his night scope into the little office, focuses on the man who now sits down behind a desk. He wears a conservative black business suit, a white button-down shirt open at the neck, no tie. His black hair, flicked with a little silver, is combed straight back. His thin, dark face sports a pencil mustache, and he smokes a thin, brown cigar.

"Look at them," Ernie is saying. "They're acting like this is a papal visit. I mean, I haven't seen this guy before, have you?"

"No," Art says, setting the binoculars down, "I haven't."

Not for nine years, anyway.

But Tío hasn't changed much.

. . .

Althea's asleep when Art gets home to their rented house in the Tlaque-paque district, a leafy suburb of single-family homes, boutiques and trendy restaurants.

Why shouldn't she be asleep, Art thinks. It's three o'clock in the morning. He's spent the last two hours in the charade of tailing M-1 to find out his identity. Well, it was skillfully done, anyway, Art thinks. He and Ernie had laid way off the black Mercedes as it pulled out onto the highway that led back into downtown Guadalajara. They tailed the car through the old Centro Histórico district and past the Cross of Squares—Plaza de Armas, Plaza de la Liberación, Plaza de la Rotonda de los Hombres and Plaza Tapatía—that has the cathedral at its center. Then into the modern business district and back out toward the suburbs, where the black Mercedes finally pulled off at a car dealership.

German imports. Luxury cars.

They'd stayed a block away and waited while Tío let himself into the office, then came out a few minutes later with a set of keys and got into a new Mercedes 510—no driver this time, no guards. They followed him out to the wealthy garden district, where Tío pulled into a driveway, got out of the car and went into his house.

Just another businessman coming home after a late night's work.

So, Art thinks, in the morning I'll go through another charade, entering the car dealership and the home address into the system to come up with the identity of our alleged M-1.

Miguel Ángel Barrera.

Tío Ángel.

Art goes into the dining room, opens the liquor cabinet and pours himself a Johnnie Walker Black. He takes his drink and walks down the hallway and looks in on his kids. Cassie is five and looks, thank God, like her mother. Michael is three and also favors Althea, although he has Art's thicker build. Althea is thrilled that, due to a Mexican housekeeper and a Mexican nanny, both kids are on their way to being bilingual. Michael doesn't ask for bread anymore, he asks for *pan;* water has become *agua.*

Art sneaks into each of their rooms, kisses them softly on the cheeks and then goes back down the long hallway, through the master bedroom and into the attached bathroom, where he takes a long shower.

If Althie was a crack in Art's Doctrine of YOYO, the kids were a hydrogen bomb. The moment he saw his daughter born, and then lying in Althie's arms, he knew his shell of "himself alone" had been blown to bits. When his son came along, it wasn't better, it was just different, looking down at that little version of himself. And an epiphany—the only redemption for having a bad father is being a good one.

And he's been a good one. A warm, loving father to his kids; a faithful, warm husband to his wife. So much of the anger and bitterness of his youth has faded away, leaving only this—this thing with Tío Barrera.

Because Tío used me, back in the Condor days. Used me to take out his rivals so he could set up his Federación. Played me for a sucker, let me think I was destroying the drug network, when all I was doing was helping him set up a bigger and better one.

Face it, he thinks as he lets the hot spray hit his tired shoulders, it's why you came here.

It had seemed an odd assignment request, a backwater like Guadalajara, especially for the hero of Operation Condor. Bringing down Don Pedro put his career on a bullet. He went from Sinaloa to Washington, then to Miami, then to San Diego. Art Keller, the Boy Wonder, was about to be, at thirty-three, the youngest RAC—Resident Agent in Charge—in the agency. He could pick his spot.

Everyone was stunned when he picked Guadalajara.

Took his career off the fast track and derailed it.

Colleagues, friends, ambitious rivals asked why.

Art wouldn't say.

Even to himself, really.

That he had unfinished business.

And maybe I should leave it that way, he thinks as he gets out of the shower, grabs a towel from the rack and dries off.

It would be so easy to back off and toe the company line. Just take the small-time marijuana dealers the Mexicans want to give you, dutifully file reports that the Mexican anti-drug effort is going swimmingly (which would be a good joke, given that the U.S.-funded Mexican defoliation planes are dropping mostly water—they're actually *watering* the marijuana and poppy crops) and sit back and enjoy your tour here.

No investigation of M-1, no revelations about Miguel Ángel Barrera.

It's in the past, he thinks. Leave it there.

You don't *have* to kiss the cobra.

Yes, you do.

It's been eating away at you for nine years. All the destruction, all the suffering, all the death brought by Operation Condor, all so Tío could set up his Federación with himself as its head. The Law of Unintended Consequences, bull*shit*. It was exactly what Tío intended, what he planned, what he set up.

He *used* you, set you like a dog on his enemies, and you did it.

Then you kept your mouth shut about it.

While they lauded you as a hero, slapped you on the back, finally let you on the team. You pathetic son of a bitch, that's what it's been about, hasn't it? Your desperation to finally belong.

You sold your soul for it.

Now you think you can buy it back.

Let it go—you have a family to take care of.

He slips into bed, trying not to wake Althea, but it doesn't work.

"Time is it?" she asks.

"Almost four."

"In the morning?"

"Go back to sleep."

"What time're you getting up?" she asks.

"Seven."

"Wake me," she says. "I have to go to the library."

She has a reader's ticket at the University of Guadalajara, where she's working on a post-doc thesis: "The Agricultural Labor Force in Pre-Revolutionary Mexico—A Statistical Model."

Then she says, "You want to mess around?"

"It's four in the morning."

"I didn't ask for time and temperature," she says. "I asked you to do me. C'mon."

She reaches for him. Her hand feels warm and in a few seconds he's inside her. It always feels like coming home to him. When she climaxes she grabs his ass and pushes him in tight. "That was beautiful, baby," she says. "Now let me sleep."

He lies awake.

In the morning, Art looks at the pictures of the airplane, of the *federales* off-loading the coke, then opening the car door for Tío, then Tío sitting at the desk in the office.

Then he listens to Ernie brief him on what he already knows.

"I got on EPIC," Ernie says, referring to the El Paso Intelligence Center, a computer databank that coordinates DEA, Customs and Immigration information. "Miguel Ángel Barrera was a former Sinaloa state policeman, in fact, the bodyguard to the governor himself. Heavy connections with the Mexican DFS. Now get this: He played on *our* team—he was one of the state cops who *ran* Operation Condor back in '77. Some EPIC reports credit Barrera with single-handedly dismantling the old Sinaloan heroin operation. He left the force and disappeared off the EPIC radar after that."

"No hits post-'75?" Art asks.

"Nada," Ernie answers. "You pick up his story here in Guadalajara. He's a very successful businessman. He owns the car dealership, four restaurants, two apartment buildings and considerable real-estate holdings. He sits on the boards of two banks and has powerful connections in the Jalisco state government and in Mexico City."

"Not exactly the profile of a drug lord," Shag says.

Shag is a good old boy out of Tucson, a Vietnam vet who found his way from military intelligence into the DEA, and is in his own quiet way as much of a hard-ass as Ernie is. He uses his "aw-shucks" cowboy persona to disguise his smarts, and a number of drug dealers are now in prison because they underestimated Shag Wallace.

"Until you see him supervising a shipment of coke," Ernie says, pointing at the photographs.

"Could he be M-1?"

Art says, "Only one way to find out."

Taking, he thinks, one more step toward the edge of the cliff.

"There will be no investigation of the Barrera cocaine connection," he says. "Is that clear?"

Ernie and Shag look a little stunned, but they both nod.

"I want to see nothing on your logs, no paperwork of any kind," he says. "We're just chasing marijuana. In that connection: Ernie, work your Mexican sources, see if the Barrera name rings any alarms. Shag, work the airplane."

"What about surveillance on Barrera?" Ernie asks.

Art shakes his head. "I don't want to stir him up before we're ready. We'll bracket him. Work on the street, work on the plane, work in toward him. If that's where it leads."

But shit, Art thinks. You know it does.

The DC-4's serial number is N-3423VX.

Shag works through the tangled paper chase of holding corporations, shell companies and DBAs. The trail ends at an airfreight company called Servicios Turísticos—SETCO—operating out of Aguacate Airport in Tegucigalpa, Honduras.

Someone running drugs out of Honduras is about as surprising as someone selling hot dogs in Yankee Stadium. Honduras, the original "banana republic," has an old and distinguished history in the drug trade, dating back to the turn of the twentieth century when the country was out-and-out owned by the Standard Fruit and United Fruit companies. The fruit companies were based in New Orleans, and the city's docks were out-and-out owned by the

New Orleans Mafia through its control of the dockworkers' union, so if the fruit companies wanted their Honduran bananas off-loaded, the boats had better be carrying something else under those bananas.

So much dope came into the country in those banana boats that Mafia slang for heroin became *banana*. The Honduran registry isn't surprising, Art thinks, and it answers the question of where the DC-4s are refueling.

The ownership of SETCO is likewise enlightening.

Two partners—David Núñez and Ramón Mette Ballasteros.

Núñez is a Cuban ex-pat now living in Miami. Nothing extraordinary there. What is extraordinary is that Núñez was with Operation 40, a CIA op in which Cuban expatriates were trained to go in and take political control after the successful Bay of Pigs invasion. Except the Bay of Pigs was, conspicuously, not a success. Some of the Operation 40 guys ended up dead on the beach, others went to firing squads. The lucky ones made it back to Miami.

Núñez was one of the lucky.

Art doesn't really need to read the file on Ramón Mette Ballasteros. He already knows the book. Mette was a chemist for the *gomeros* back in the heroin heyday. Got out just before Condor and went back to his native Honduras and into the cocaine business. The word is that Mette personally financed the coup that recently overthrew the Honduran president.

Okay, Art thinks, the two profiles actually walk the company line. A major coke dealer owns an airline that he's using to fly coke to Miami. But at least one of SETCO's planes is flying to Guadalajara, and that doesn't conform to the official line.

The next normal step would be to call the DEA office in Tegucigalpa, Honduras, but he can't do that because it was closed last year due to "lack of business." Honduras and El Salvador are now both being handled out of Guatemala, so Art gets on the horn to Warren Farrar, the RAC in Guatemala City.

"SETCO," Art says.

"What about it?" Farrar asks.

"I was hoping you'd tell me," Art says.

There's a pause that Art is tempted to describe as "pregnant," then Farrar says, "I can't come out and play with you on this, Art."

Really? Art wonders. Why the hell not? We only have about eight thousand conferences a year, just so we *can* come out and play with each other, on things exactly like this.

So he takes a shot. "Why was the Honduras office closed, Warren?"

"What are you fucking around with, Art?"

"I don't know. That's why I'm asking."

Because I'm wondering if the quid pro quo for Mette financing a presidential coup was the new government tossing out the DEA.

In response, Farrar hangs up.

Well, thanks a bunch, Warren. What's got you so nervous?

Next, Art phones the State Department's Drug Assist Desk, a title so pungent with irony it makes him want to weep, because they tell him in polite bureaucratese to please go fuck himself.

Next Art calls the CIA Liaison Desk, puts in his request and gets a call back that same afternoon. What he doesn't expect is a call back from John Hobbs.

Himself.

Back in the day, Hobbs was the head of Operation Phoenix. Art had briefed him a few times. Hobbs had even offered him a job after his year in-country, but by that time the DEA had beckoned and Art went.

Now Hobbs is the CIA's station chief for Central America.

Makes sense to me, Art thinks. A cold warrior goes where there's a cold war.

They make small talk for a few minutes (How are Althea and the kids? How do you like Guadalajara?), then Hobbs asks, "What can we do to be of assistance, Arthur?"

"I was wondering if you could help me get a handle on an airfreight company called SETCO," Art says. "It's owned by Ramón Mette."

"Yes, my people passed along your request," Hobbs says. "That has to be a negative, I'm afraid."

"A negative."

"Yes," Hobbs says. "A no."

Yes, we have no bananas, Art thinks. We have no bananas today.

Hobbs continues, "We don't have anything on SETCO."

"Well, thanks for giving me the call."

Then Hobbs asks, "What have you got going on down there, Arthur?"

"I'm just getting some radar pings," Art lies, "that SETCO might be moving some marijuana around."

"Marijuana."

"Sure," Art says. "That's about all that's left in Mexico these days."

"Well, good luck with that, Arthur," Hobbs says. "Sorry we couldn't be of any help."

"I appreciate the effort," Art says.

He hangs up wondering why the Company's chief of Latin American operations would take time out from his busy day of trying to overthrow the Sandinistas to call him personally and lie to him.

Nobody wants to talk about SETCO, Art thinks, not my colleagues in the DEA, not the State Department, not even CIA.

The whole inter-agency alphabet soup just spells out YOYO.

You're On Your Own.

Ernie reports pretty much the same thing.

You put the name Barrera out to any of the usual sources and they clam up. Even the most loquacious snitches develop a case of lockjaw. Barrera's one of the most prominent businessmen in town, except no one ever heard of him.

So drop it, Art tells himself. This is your chance.

Can't.

Why not?

Just can't.

At least be honest.

Okay. Maybe because I just can't let him win. Maybe because I owe him a beating. Yeah, except he's beating you. And he's not even showing up. You can't lay a glove on him.

It's true—they can't get near Tío.

Then the damnedest thing happens.

Tío comes to them.

Colonel Vega, the ranking *federale* in Jalisco and the man whom Art is supposed to be liaising with, comes into Art's office, sits down and says sadly, "Señor Keller, I will be frank. I have come here to ask you politely but firmly—please cease your harassment of Don Miguel Ángel Barrera."

He and Art stare at each other, then Art says, "As much as I'd like to help you, Colonel, this office isn't conducting an investigation of Señor Barrera. Not that I know about, anyway."

He yells out into the main office, "Shag, are you investigating Señor Barrera?"

"No, sir."

"Ernie?"

"No."

Art raises his arms in a shrug.

"Señor Keller," Vega says, glancing out the door at Ernie, "your man is tossing Don Miguel's name about in a very irresponsible fashion. Señor Barrera is a respected businessman with many friends in government."

"And, apparently, in the Municipal Judicial Federal Police."

"You're Mexican, aren't you?" Vega asks.

"I'm American." But where are you going with this?

"But you speak Spanish?"

Art nods.

"Then you're familiar with the word *intocable*," Vega says, getting up to leave. "Señor Keller, Don Miguel is *intocable*."

Untouchable.

With that concept imparted, Vega leaves.

Ernie and Shag come into Art's office. Shag starts to speak, but Art signals for him to shut up and gestures for them all to go outside. They follow him for about a block before he says, "How did Vega know we're running an op on Barrera?"

Back inside, it takes them just a few minutes to find the little mike under Art's desk. Ernie goes to rip it out but Art grabs his wrist and stops him. "I could use a beer," Art says. "How about you guys?"

They go to a bar downtown.

"That's beautiful," Ernie says. "In the States, the cops bug the bad guys. Here, the bad guys bug the cops."

Shag shakes his head. "So they know everything we know."

Well, Art thinks, they know we suspect Tío is M-1. They know that we've tracked the plane to Núñez and Mette. And they know we can't get shit after that. So what's making them nervous? Why send in Vega to shut down an investigation that's going nowhere?

And why now?

"Okay," Art says. "We'll broadcast to them. Let them think they've backed us off. You guys stand down for a while."

"What are you going to do, boss?"

Me? I'm going to touch the untouchable.

Back in the office, he regretfully tells Ernie and Shag that they're going to have to shut down the Barrera investigation. Then he goes to a phone booth and calls Althea. "I'm not going to make it home for dinner."

"I'm sorry."

"Me, too," he says. "Kiss the kids good night for me."

"I will. Love you."

"Love you, too."

Every man has a weakness, Art thinks, a secret that could drag him down. I should know. I know mine, but what's yours, Tío?

. . .

Art doesn't make it home that night, or the next five.

I'm like an alcoholic, Art thinks. He's heard reformed drunks talk about how they would drive to the liquor store, all the time swearing they weren't going to go, then go in swearing they weren't going to buy, then buy swearing they weren't going to drink the booze they'd just bought.

Then they'd drink it.

I'm that guy, Art thinks, drawn toward Tío like a drunk to the bottle.

So instead of going home at night he sits in his car on the broad boulevard, parked a block and a half from Tío's car dealership, and watches the office through the rearview mirror. Tío must be selling a lot of cars, because he's there until eight or eight-thirty in the evening, and then he gets into his car and drives home. Art sits at the bottom of his road, the only way in or out of the housing development, until midnight or one, but Tío doesn't come out.

Finally, on the sixth night, Art gets lucky.

Tío leaves the office at six-thirty and drives not to the suburbs but back downtown. Art stays back in the rush-hour traffic but manages to stay with the Mercedes as it drives through the Centro Histórico and pulls up beside a *tapas* restaurant.

Three *federales,* two Jalisco state policemen and a couple of guys that look like DFS agents are on guard outside, and the sign on the restaurant door reads CERRADO—closed. One of the *federales* opens Tío's door. Tío gets out and the *federale* drives the Mercedes away like a parking valet. A Jalisco state cop opens the closed restaurant door and Tío walks in. Another Jalisco cop waves to Art to keep his car moving.

Art rolls his window down. "I want to grab a bite."

"Private party."

Yeah, I guess, Art thinks.

He parks the car two blocks away, takes his Nikon camera with the 70-300 lens and sticks it under his coat. He crosses the street and walks half a block up, then takes a left into the alley and walks until he figures he's at the back of the building across the street from the restaurant, then hops the fire-escape ladder and pulls it down. He climbs up the metal ladder, bolted to the bricks, until he makes it the three stories up to the roof.

DEA RACs aren't supposed to be doing this kind of work—they're supposed to be office creatures, liaising with their Mexican counterparts. But seeing as how my Mexican counterparts are across the street guarding my target, Art thinks, the liaison thing isn't going to work out.

He ducks and crosses the roof, then lies down behind the low parapet that edges the building. Surveillance work is hell on the dry-cleaning bill, he thinks as he stretches out on the dirty roof, rests the lens on the parapet and focuses on the restaurant. And you can't turn it in on your expense account, either.

He settles down to wait but he doesn't have to wait long before a parade of cars pulls up alongside Talavera's *tapas* place. The drill is the same—the Jalisco police stand guard while the *federales* play valet, and a major player in the Mexican drug trade gets out and goes into the restaurant.

It's like a Hollywood opening for drug stars.

García Abrego, head of the Gulf cartel, gets out of his Mercedes. The older man looks distinguished with his silver hair, trim mustache and businessman's gray suit. Güero Méndez, Baja cartel, looks like the narco-cowboy he is. His blond hair—hence the nickname Güero, "Blondie"—hangs long under his white cowboy hat. He wears a black silk shirt, open to the waist, black silk pants and black cowboy boots with pointed toes capped with silver. Chalino Guzmán looks more like the peasant he is in an ill-fitting old suit jacket, mismatched pants and green boots.

Jesus, Art thinks, it's a fucking Apalachin meeting, except these guys don't look too worried about police interference. It would be like the god-fathers of the Cimino, Genovese and Colombo families getting together for a sit-down guarded by the FBI. Except if this was the Sicilian Mafia, I'd never get this close. But these guys are complacent. They think they're safe.

And they're probably not wrong.

What's curious, though, Art wonders, is, Why *this* restaurant? Tío owns half a dozen places in Guadalajara, but Talavera's isn't one of them. Why wouldn't he hold this summit meeting in one of his own joints?

But I guess this dispels any doubt about Tío being M-1.

The traffic stops out front and Art settles in for the long wait. There is no such thing as a quick Mexican dinner, and these boys probably have an agenda. Jesus, what I wouldn't give to have a microphone in there.

He pulls a Kit Kat bar out of his pants pocket, unwraps it, breaks off two sections and puts the rest back, not knowing when he'll get a chance to grab more food. Then he rolls onto his back, crosses his arms over his chest for warmth and takes a nap, bagging a couple of hours of uneasy sleep before car doors and voices wake him up.

Showtime.

He rolls back over and sees them all coming out on the sidewalk. If there's no such thing as a Federación, he thinks, they're doing a damn good imitation of one. They're absolutely brazen, all standing out on the sidewalk, laughing, shaking hands and lighting each other's Cuban cigars as they wait for the *federale* valets to bring their cars around.

Shit, Art thinks, you can practically smell the smoke and the testosterone overload.

The atmosphere changes suddenly when the girl comes out.

She's stunning, Art thinks. A young Liz Taylor, but with olive skin and black eyes. And long lashes, which she's batting at all the men while an older man who has to be her father stands in the doorway, smiling nervously and waving *adiós* to the *gomeros*.

But they're not leaving.

Güero Méndez is all over the girl. He even takes off his cowboy hat, Art notices. Maybe not your best move, Güero, at least until you wash your hair. But Güero bows—actually *bows*—sweeps his hat along the sidewalk and smiles up at the girl.

His silver teeth flash in the streetlights.

Yeah, Güero, that'll get her, Art thinks.

Tío rescues the girl. Comes over, puts an almost paternal arm around Güero's shoulders and smoothly walks him back toward his car, which has just pulled up. They hug and do their good-bye thing, and Güero looks over Tío's shoulder at the girl before he gets into his car.

Must be true love, Art thinks. Or at least true lust.

Then Abrego leaves, with a dignified handshake instead of an embrace, and Art watches as Tío walks back to the girl, bends over, and kisses her hand.

Latin chivalry? Art wonders.

Or . . .

No . . .

But Art eats lunch at Talavera's the next day.

The girl's name is Pilar, and sure enough, she's Talavera's daughter.

She sits in a booth in the back, pretending to study a textbook, every now and again performing a self-conscious turn of the hip as she looks up from under those long lashes to see who might be checking her out.

Every guy in the place, Art thinks.

She doesn't look fifteen except for a remaining trace of baby fat and the perfected adolescent pout on her precociously full lips. And even though it makes him feel a little like a child molester, Art can't help but notice that she has a figure that is definitely very post-adolescent. The only thing that tells Art she's fifteen is the ongoing argument she's having with her mother, who sits down in the booth and loudly reminds her several times that she's only fifteen.

And Papa glances up anxiously every time the door opens. The hell is he so nervous about? Art wonders.

Then he finds out.

Tío walks through the door.

Art has his back to the door and Tío walks right past him. Doesn't even notice his long-lost nephew, Art thinks, he's so focused on the girl. And he has flowers in his hand—honest to God, he has flowers clutched in his long, thin fingers—and honest to God has a box of candy under his other arm.

Tío has come courting.

Now Art gets why Talavera's so freaked out. He knows that Miguel Ángel Barrera is accustomed to the droit de seigneur of rural Sinaloa, in which girls her age and younger are routinely deflowered by the dominant *gomeros*.

And that's their concern. That this powerful man, this married man, is going to turn their precious, beautiful, virginal daughter into his *segundera*, his mistress. To use her and then throw her aside, her reputation ruined, her chances for a good marriage destroyed.

And there's not a goddamn thing they can do about it.

Tío won't rape the girl, Art knows. He won't take her by force. That might happen up in the hills of Sinaloa, but it won't happen here. But if she accepts him, if she goes with him willingly, the parents are helpless. And what fifteen-year-old's head wouldn't be turned by attention from a rich and powerful man? This kid isn't stupid—she knows it's flowers and candy now, but it could be jewelry and clothes, trips and vacations. She's at the base of an arc, but she can't see the downside from where she's standing—that one day the jewelry and clothes will slide back to flowers and candy, and then it won't even be that anymore.

Tío's back is turned to Art, who leaves some *pesos* on the table, gets up as quietly as he can, goes to the counter and pays the check.

Thinking, She may look like a young piece of strange to you, Tío.

To me she looks like a Trojan horse.

Nine o'clock that night, Art climbs into a pair of jeans and a sweater and goes into the bathroom where Althea is taking a shower. "Babe, I gotta go out."

"Now?"

"Yeah."

She's too smart to ask where he's going. She's a cop's wife, she's been in the DEA with him for the past eight years, she knows the drill. But knowing doesn't stop her from worrying. She slides the glass door open and kisses him good-bye. "I'm guessing I shouldn't wait up?"

"Good guess."

What are you doing? he asks himself as he drives toward the Talaveras' house in the suburbs.

Nothing. I'm not going to drink.

He finds the address and pulls over a half-block away on the other side of the street. It's a quiet neighborhood, solidly upper-middle-class, just enough streetlights to make it safe, not enough to be obtrusive.

He sits in his dark spot and waits.

That night, and the next three.

He's there each night as the Talavera family comes home from the restaurant. As a light goes on in a room upstairs, then goes off a little while later when Pilar turns in for the night. Art gives it another half-hour and then goes home.

Maybe you're wrong, he thinks.

No, you're not. Tío gets what he wants.

Art's about to go home on the fourth night when a Mercedes comes down the street, kills its headlights and pulls up in front of the Talavera house.

Ever gallant, Art thinks, Tío sends a car and driver. No taxicab for this underage piece of ass. It's fucking pathetic, he thinks as he watches Pilar come out the front door and scurry into the backseat of the car.

Art gives it a good head start, then pulls out.

The car pulls up in front of a condo on a little knoll in the west suburbs. It's in a nice, quiet neighborhood, fairly new, individual units nestled among the city's trademark jacaranda trees. The address is new to Art, not any of the properties he's traced to Tío. How sweet, Art thinks—a brand-new love nest for a brand-new love.

Tío's car is already there. The driver gets out and opens the door for Pilar. Tío meets her at the door and ushers her in. They're in each other's arms before the door is even shut.

Jesus, Art thinks, if I were fucking a fifteen-year-old girl, I'd at least pull the curtains.

But you think you're safe, don't you, Tío?

And the most dangerous place on earth—

Is where you're safe.

He's back at La Casa del Amor (as he styles it) late that morning, when he knows that Tío will be at the office and Pilar in, well, *ahem,* school. He's wearing the overalls he uses to work in his own garden and he carries a pair of clippers. In fact, he does trim a couple of unruly jacaranda branches as he makes his reconnaissance, noting the color of the exterior paint and plaster, the location of the phone lines, the windows, the pool, the spa, any outbuildings.

A week later, after visits to a hardware store and a model-supply shop and a call to a mail-order techno warehouse in San Diego, he goes back, wearing the same outfit, and clips a few more branches on his way to ducking behind the shrubs that have been thoughtfully planted outside the bedroom wall. He likes this location not for prurient reasons—he'd actually rather *not* hear that part of it—but because the telephone lines go into the bedroom. He pulls a small flathead screwdriver from his pocket and, delicate as a surgeon, pries a minuscule opening behind the aluminum windowsill. He inserts the tiny FX-101 bug into the opening, removes a small tube of caulking from his pocket and reseals the opening, then takes the little bottle of green paint that closely matches the original color and, with a tiny brush meant for painting model airplanes, paints over the caulk. He blows gently on the paint to dry it, then leans back to assess his work.

The bug, illegal and unauthorized, is also undetectable.

The FX-101 can pick up any sound within ten yards and throw it for another sixty, so Art has some flexibility. He goes outside the complex to the sewer opening. He takes the unit that contains the receiver and a voice-activated tape recorder and duct-tapes it to the top of the sewer. Now it will be a simple matter of swinging by, taking out one cassette and replacing it with a fresh one.

He knows it's going to be hit-and-miss, but he needs only a few hits. Tío will use La Casa del Amor mostly as a spot for his assignations with Pilar, but he'll also use the phone. He might even use the condo for meetings. Even the most cautious criminal, Art knows, can't separate his business from his personal life.

Of course, he admits, neither can you.

He lies to Ernie and Shag.

They take jogs together now. Ostensibly, it's Art's mandate for his team to stay in shape, but in reality it's a cover for them to have the conversations they can't have in the office. It's hard to listen in on a moving target, particularly in the open *plazas* of downtown Guadalajara, so every day before lunch they change into sweats and Nikes and go out for their run.

"I have a CI," he tells them. A Confidential Informant.

He feels bad about lying to them, but it's for their own protection. If this goes sick and wrong, as it almost has to, he wants to take it all on his own shoulders. If his guys know that he's running an illegal tap, they're obliged by regulations to inform their superiors. Otherwise, they're concealing "guilty knowledge," which would ruin their careers. He knows that they would never rat him out, so he makes up a confidential informant.

An imaginary friend, Art thinks. At least it's consistent—a nonexistent source for nonexistent coke, et cetera . . .

"That's great, boss," Ernie says. "Who—"

"Sorry," Art says. "It's early. We're just dating."

They get it. A relationship with a snitch is like a relationship with the opposite sex. You flirt, you seduce, you tempt. You buy them presents, you tell them how much you need them, you can't live without them. And if they do get in bed with you, you don't tell, even—especially—the boys in the locker room.

At least not until it's a done deal, and by the time it becomes common knowledge, it's usually about over anyway.

So this becomes Art's day: He puts in his hours at the office, goes home, leaves the house late at night to retrieve his daily tape, then comes home and listens to it in his study.

This goes on for two useless weeks.

What he hears is mostly love talk, sex talk, as Tío woos his young inamorata and gradually instructs her in the finer points of lovemaking. Art fast-forwards through most of this, but he gets the idea.

Pilar Talavera is growing up fast as Tío starts introducing some interesting grace notes into the music of love. Well, interesting if you're into that sort of thing, which Art is decidedly not. In fact, it makes him want to puke.

You've been a bad girl.

Have I?

Yes, and you need to be punished.

It's a commonplace of surveillance—you hear so much shit that you never wanted to hear.

Then, albeit rarely, the rose in the manure pile.

One night Art brings his tape home, makes himself a scotch and sips on it while he goes through that evening's sick tedium, and hears Tío confirm the delivery of "three hundred wedding gowns" to an address in Chula Vista, a neighborhood that sits between San Diego and Tijuana.

Now that you've got it, Art thinks, what do you do with it?

The SOP requires that you turn the info over to your Mexican colleagues, and simultaneously to the DEA office in Mexico City, for transferral to the San Diego office. Well, if I turn it over to my Mexican counterpart it goes straight to Tío, and if I turn it in to Tim Taylor he'll just repeat the official line that there are no "wedding gowns" moving through Mexico. And he'll demand to know who my source is.

Which I ain't about to give him.

They talk it over on the morning jog.

"We're fucked," Ernie says.

"No, we're not," Art answers.

Time to take the next step toward the cliff.

He leaves the office after lunch and goes to a phone booth. In the States, he thinks, it's the criminals who have to sneak around and use pay phones. Here, it's the cops.

He phones a guy he knows on the San Diego Police narco squad. He met Russ Dantzler at some inter-agency conference a few months ago. Seemed like a decent guy, a player.

Yeah, and what I need now is a definite player.

With a set of stones.

"Russ? Art Keller, DEA. We had a couple of beers together, what was it, last July?"

Dantzler remembers him. "What's up, Art?"

Art tells him.

"This might be bullshit," he finishes, "but I don't think so. You might want to hit it."

Hell yes, he might want to hit it. And there's nothing the attorney general of the United States or the State Department or the entire federal government can do about it. The Feds come down on San Diego PD, San Diego PD is just going to tell them to go fuck themselves sideways with something jagged.

With a proper regard to cop etiquette, Dantzler asks, "What do you want from me?"

"You keep me out of it and you keep me in it," Art answers. "You forget I gave you the tip, and you remember to share any intel you get with me."

"Deal," Dantzler says. "But I need a warrant, Art. Just in case you've forgotten how things work in a democracy that scrupulously protects the rights of its citizens."

"I have a CI," he lies.

"Gotcha."

They don't need to say anything more. Dantzler will take the info to one of his own guys, who will tell it to one of *his* CIs, who'll then turn around and tell it to Dantzler, who will take it to a judge and presto—probable cause.

The next day Dantzler calls Art back at the phone booth at a prearranged time and screams, "Three hundred pounds of cocaine! That's six million dollars in street value! Art, I'll make sure you get a lot of the credit!"

"Forget I gave you anything," Art says. " Just remember you owe me."

Two weeks later, the El Paso police also owe Art for the seizure of a trailer-truck full of cocaine. A month after that, Art goes back to Russ Dantzler with another tip, about a house in Lemon Grove.

The subsequent raid yields a paltry fifty pounds of cocaine.

Plus $4 million in cash, three money-counting machines, and stacks of interesting documents that include bank deposit slips. The deposit slips are so interesting that when Dantzler takes them into federal court the judge freezes an additional $15 million in assets deposited under several names in five San Diego County banks. Although none of the names is Miguel Ángel Barrera, every penny of the money belongs either to him or to cartel members who are paying him a fee to keep their assets safe.

And Art can hear from the phone traffic that none of them is very happy.

Neither is Tim Taylor.

The DEA boss is looking at a faxed copy of *The San Diego Union-Tribune,* its headline screaming MASSIVE DRUG BUST IN LEMON GROVE, with references to a *"federación,"* and at another fax, from the AG's office, screaming, *Just what the fuck is going on?* He gets on the horn to Art.

"Just what the fuck is going on?!" he yells.

"What do you mean?"

"Goddammit, I know what you're doing!"

"Then I wish you'd share it with me."

"You have a CI! And you're running it through other agencies and goddamn it, Arthur, you'd better not be the one leaking this shit to the press!"

"I'm not," Art answers truthfully. I'm leaking it to other agencies so *they* can leak it to the press.

"Who's the CI?!"

"There is no CI," Art answers. "I have nothing to do with this."

Yeah, except three weeks later he gives the LAPD a 200-pound bust in Hacienda Heights. The Arizona state cops get a trailer-truck with 350 pounds rolling up I-10. Anaheim PD pops a house for cash and prizes totaling ten mil.

They all deny getting anything from him, but they all speak his gospel:

La Federación, La Federación, La Federación, forever and ever, world without end, amen.

Even the RAC Bogotá comes to the altar.

Shag answers the phone one day and holds it into his chest as he tells Art, "It's the Big Man himself. Straight from the front lines of the War on Drugs."

Even two months ago, Chris Conti, the RAC in Colombia, wouldn't have touched his old friend Art Keller with the proverbial ten-foot pole. But now even Conti has apparently gotten religion.

"Art," he says, "I ran across something I think you might be interested in."

"You coming up here?" Art asks. "Or do you want me to come down there?"

"Why don't we split the difference? You been to Costa Rica lately?"

What he means is that he doesn't want Tim Taylor or anyone else to know he's sitting down with Art Keller. They meet in Quepos. Sit in a palm-frond cabana on the beach. Conti comes bearing gifts: He spreads a series of deposit slips out on the rough table. The slips match up with the cashier-check receipts from the Bank of America in San Diego that were captured in the last raid. Documentary proof linking the Barrera organization with Colombian cocaine.

"Where'd you get these?" Art asks.

"Small-town banks in the Medellín area."

"Well, thanks, Chris."

"You didn't get them from me."

"Of course not."

Conti lays a grainy photograph on the table.

An airstrip in the jungle, a bunch of guys standing around a DC-4 with the serial numbers N-3423VX. Art recognizes Ramón Mette right away, but one of the other men rings a fainter bell. Middle-aged, he has a short, military haircut and wears fatigues over highly polished black jump boots.

Been a long time.

A *long* time.

Vietnam. Operation Phoenix.

Even then, Sal Scachi liked polished boots.

"You thinking what I'm thinking?" Conti asks.

Well, if you're thinking the man looks Company, you're thinking right. Last time I heard, Scachi had been a bird colonel in Special Forces, then pulled the pin. Which is a Company résumé all the way.

"Look," Conti says. "I've heard some rumors."

"I trade in rumors. Go ahead."

"Three radio towers in the jungles north of Bogotá," Conti says. "I can't get near the area to check it out."

"The Medellín people are easily capable of that kind of technology," Art says. And it would explain the mystery of how the SETCO planes are flying under the radar. Three radio towers emitting VOR signals could guide them out and back.

"The Medellín cartel has the technology to build them," Conti says. "But does it have the technology to make them disappear?"

"What do you mean?"

"Satellite photos."

"Okay."

"They don't show up," Conti says. "Not three radio towers, not two, not one. We can read license plates off those photos, Art. A VOR tower's not going to show up? And what about the planes, Art? I get the AWACS gen, and they don't show up. Any plane flying from Colombia to Honduras has to go over Nicaragua, Sandinista Land, and *that,* my friend, we definitely have the Eye in the Sky on."

That's no shit, Art thinks. Nicaragua is the bull's-eye in the Reagan administration's Central American scope, a Communist regime right in the heart of the Monroe Doctrine. The administration was sponsoring the Contra forces that surround Nicaragua from Honduras to the north and from right here in Costa Rica on the south, but then the U.S. Congress passed the Boland Amendment, banning military aid to the Contras.

Now you have a former Special Forces guy and ardent anti-Communist (They're atheists, aren't they? Fuck 'em) in the company of Ramón Mette Ballasteros and a SETCO plane.

Art leaves Costa Rica more freaked out than when he got there.

Back in Guadalajara, Art sends Shag to the States on a mission. The cowboy huddles up with every narco squad and DEA office in the Southwest and in his soft cowboy drawl tells them, "This Mexican thing is for real. It's going to blow up, and when it does, you don't want to be caught with your pants down trying to explain why you didn't see it coming. Shit, you can toe the company line in public, but in private, you might want to be playing ball with us because when the trumpets blow, *amigos,* we're gonna remember who are the sheep and who are the goats."

There's nothing that the boys in Washington can do about it. What are they going to do—tell American cops not to make drug busts on American soil? The Justice Department wants to crucify Art. They suspect that he's disseminating this shit, but they can't touch him, even when the State Department calls up screaming about "irreparable damage to our relationship with an important neighbor."

The AG's office would like to flog Art Keller up Pennsylvania Avenue then nail him to a pole on Capitol Hill, except he hasn't done anything they can prove. And they can't transfer him out of Guadalajara because the media has picked up on La Federación, so how would *that* look?

So they have to sit by in mounting frustration as Art Keller builds an empire based on pronouncements from the invisible, unknowable, nonexistent CI-D0243.

"CI-D0243 is kind of impersonal, isn't it?" Shag asks one day. "I mean, for a guy who's contributing as much as he is."

"What do you want to call him?" Art asks.

"Deep Throat," suggests Ernie.

"It's been done," Art says. "But he is sort of a Mexican Deep Throat."

"Chupar," Ernie says. "Let's call him Source Chupar."

Blow job.

Source Chupar gives Art a bank account with every other law enforcement agency on the border. They deny getting anything from the guy, but they all owe him. Owe him? Shit, they *love* him. The DEA can't function without local cooperation, and if they want that cooperation, they better not fuck with Art Keller.

No, Art Keller is fast becoming *intocable.*

Except he's not.

It's wearing him down, running an op against Tío while pretending that he's not. Leaving his family late at night, keeping his activities secret, keeping his past secret, waiting for Tío to track it back to him and then come to remind him that they have a past relationship.

Tío to *sobrino.*

Art's not eating, he's not sleeping.

He and Althea rarely make love anymore. She chides him for being irritable, secretive, closed.

Untouchable.

Art thinks, as he sits on the edge of his bathtub at four in the morning. He's just thrown up the leftover chicken *mole* that Althea left in the fridge for him and that he ate at three-thirty. No, the past isn't catching up with you, you're marching toward it. Resolutely, step by step, walking toward the abyss.

. . .

Tío's lying awake nights trying to figure out who the *soplón*—the informer—is. The Federación *patrónes*—Abrego, Méndez, El Verde—have taken serious shots, and they're putting enormous pressure on him to *do something*.

Because it's obvious that the problem is right here in Guadalajara. Because all three *plazas* have been hit. Abrego, Méndez, El Verde all insist that there must be a *soplón* in M-1's organization.

Find him, they are saying. Kill him. Do something.

Or we will.

Pilar Talavera lies beside him, breathing evenly and easily in the deep, untroubled sleep of youth. He looks down at her shiny black hair, her long black eyelashes, now closed, her full upper lip moist with sweat. He loves the fresh, young smell of her.

He reaches out to the night table, grabs a cigar and lights it. The smoke won't wake her. Neither will the smell. He's gotten her used to it. Besides, he thinks, nothing could wake the girl after such a session as we have had. How odd, to have found love at this age. How odd and how wonderful. She is my happiness, he thinks, *la sonrisa de mi corazón*—the smile of my heart. I will make her my wife within a year. A quick divorce, then a quicker marriage.

And the Church? The Church can be bought. I will go to the cardinal himself and offer him a hospital, a school, an orphanage. We will marry in the cathedral.

No, the Church will be no problem.

The problem is the *soplón*.

Condenado "Source Chupar."

Costing me millions.

Worse, making me vulnerable.

I can just hear Abrego now, the jealous *zorro viejo*, the old fox, whispering against me, *M-1 is losing it. He's charging us fortunes for protection he can't deliver. There is a* soplón *in his organization.*

Abrego wants to be *patrón* of the Federación anyway. How long before he thinks he's strong enough to act? Will he come at me directly, or will he use one of the others?

No, he thinks, they'll all act together if I can't find the *soplón*.

It starts at Christmas.

The kids have been bugging Art to take them to see the big Christmas tree in the Cross of Squares downtown. He had hoped they'd be satisfied with the *posadas,* the nightly parades of children who go house to house through the Tlaquepaque neighborhood dressed as Mary and Joseph looking for a place to stay. But the little processions only fired the kids up to go see the tree and the *pastorelas,* the funny, slapstick plays about the birth of Christ that are performed outside the cathedral.

It isn't the time for funny plays. Art has just listened in on one of Tío's conversations about *sixteen hundred pounds* of cocaine in eight hundred boxes, all brightly wrapped in Christmas paper, with ribbons and bows and the whole holiday nine yards.

Thirty million dollars' worth of Christmas cheer at a safe house in Arizona, and Art hasn't decided yet whom he's going to take it to.

But he knows he's been neglecting his family, so on the Saturday before Christmas he takes Althea, the kids and the extended household of the cook, Josefina, and the maid, Guadalupe, shopping in the open market in the old district.

He has to admit that he's having a wonderful time. They go Christmas shopping for each other and buy little handcrafted ornaments for the tree back at the house. They have a long, wonderful lunch of freshly sliced *carnitas* and black-bean soup, then sweet, honied *sopaipillas* for dessert.

Then Cassie spots one of the fancy horse-drawn carriages, enamel-black with red velvet cushions, and she has to have a ride, *Please, Daddy, please,* and Art negotiates a price with the driver in his bright gaucho suit and they all get under a blanket in the back and Michael sits on Art's lap and falls asleep to the steady *clop-clop* of the horses' hooves on the cobblestones of the *plaza.* Not Cassie; she's beside herself with excitement, looking at the white caparisoned horses with the red plumes in their harnesses, and then at the sixty-foot tree with its bright lights, and as Art feels his son's deep breathing against his chest he knows that he's happier than it's possible to be.

It's dark by the time the ride ends, and he gently wakes Michael and hands him down to Josefina and they walk through the Plaza Tapatía toward the cathedral, where a small stage has been set up and a play is about to start.

Then he sees Adán.

His old *cuate* wears a rumpled business suit. He looks tired, like he's been traveling. He sees Art and walks into a public rest room at the edge of the *plaza.*

"I need to use the bathroom," Art says. "Michael, do you need to go?"

Say no, kid, say no.

"I went in the restaurant."

"Go see the show," Art says. "I'll catch up with you."

Adán's leaning against the wall when Art comes in. Art starts to check the stalls to make sure they're empty, but Adán says, "I already did that. And no one will be coming in. Long time no see, Arturo."

"What do you want?"

"We know it's you."

"What are you talking about?"

"Don't play games with me," Adán says. "Just answer me a question—what do you think you're doing?"

"My job," Art says. "It's nothing personal."

"It's very personal," Adán says. "When a man turns on his friends it is *very fucking personal.*"

"We're not friends anymore."

"My uncle is very unhappy about this."

Art shrugs.

"You called him Tío," Adán says. "Just like I do."

"That was then," Art says. "Things change."

"That *doesn't* change," Adán says. "That's forever. You accepted his patronage, his counsel, his help. He made you what you are."

"We made each other."

Adán shakes his head. "So much for an appeal to loyalty. Or gratitude."

He reaches into his lapel pocket and Art takes a step toward him to check him from pulling the gun.

"Easy," Adán says. He takes out an envelope, sets it on the edge of a sink. "That's a hundred thousand U.S. dollars, cash. But if you prefer, we can make deposits for you in the Caymans, Costa Rica . . ."

"I'm not for sale."

"Really? What's changed?"

Art grabs him, pushes him against the wall and starts to pat him down. "You wearing a wire, Adán? Huh? You setting me up? Where are the fucking cameras?"

Art lets him go and starts searching the room. In the top corners, the stalls, under the sinks. He doesn't find anything. He stops searching and, exhausted, leans against the wall.

"A hundred thousand right now for good faith," Adán says. "Another hundred for the name of your *soplón.* Then twenty a month just for doing nothing."

Art shakes his head.

"I told Tío you wouldn't take it," Adán says. "You prefer a different kind of coin. Okay, we'll give you enough marijuana busts to make you a star again. That's Plan A."

"What's Plan B?"

Adán walks over, wraps his arms around Art and holds him tightly. Says quietly into his ear, "Arturo, you're an ungrateful, inflexible, *güero*-wannabe prick. But you're still my friend and I love you. So take the money, or don't take the money, but *back off.* You don't know what you're fucking around with here."

Adán leans back so he's face-to-face with Art. Their noses are practically touching as he looks him in the eyes and repeats, *"You don't know what you're fucking around with here."*

He steps back, takes the envelope and holds it up. "No?"

Art shakes his head. Adán shrugs and puts the envelope back into his pocket. "Arturo?" he says. "You don't even want to know about Plan B."

Then he walks out.

Art steps to the sink, runs the tap and splashes cold water on his face. Then he dries himself off and goes outside to meet his family.

They're standing on the edge of a small crowd in front of the stage, the kids hopping up and down in delight to the antics of two actors dressed as the Ángel Gabriel and Lucifer, banging each other on the head with sticks, fighting for the soul of the Christ Child.

When they leave the parking garage that night, a Ford Bronco pulls off the curb and follows them. The kids don't notice, of course—they're sound asleep—and neither do Althea, Josefina and Guadalupe, but Art keeps track of him in the rearview mirror. Art plays with him for a while through the traffic, but the car stays with him. Not even trying to disguise himself, Art thinks, so he's trying to make a point, send a message.

When Art pulls into the driveway, the car passes, then turns around, then parks across the street a half-block away.

Art gets his family inside, then makes an excuse about forgetting something in the car. He goes out, walks over to the Bronco and knocks on the window. When the window slides down, Art leans in, pins the man to the seat, reaches into his left lapel pocket and hauls out his wallet.

He tosses the wallet with the Jalisco State Police badge back onto the cop's lap.

"That's my *family* in there," Art says. "If you scare them, if you frighten them, if they even get the idea you're out here, I'm going to come back, take that *pistola* you have on your hip and shove it so far up your ass it'll come out your mouth. Do you understand me, brother?"

"I'm just doing my job, *brother.*"

"Then do it better."

But Tío's message has been delivered, Art thinks as he walks back into the house—you don't fuck your friends.

After a mostly sleepless night, Art gets up, makes himself a cup of coffee and sips at it until his family wakes up. Then he fixes the kids' breakfast, kisses Althea good-bye and drives toward the office.

On the way he stops at a phone booth to commit professional suicide—he calls the Pierce County, Arizona, Sheriff's Department. "Merry Christmas," he says, and tells them about the eight hundred boxes of cocaine.

Then he goes to the office and waits for a phone call of his own.

Althea's driving back from the grocery store the next morning when a strange car starts to follow her. Not even being subtle about it, just getting on her tail and staying there. She doesn't know what to do. She's afraid to drive home and get out of the car, and she's afraid to go anywhere else, so she heads for the DEA office. She's absolutely terrified—her two kids are in car seats in the back—and she's three full blocks from the office when the car forces her over and four men with guns get out.

The leader flashes a Jalisco State Police badge.

"Identification, Señora Keller?" he asks.

Her hand shakes as she fumbles for her driver's license. As she does, he leans through the window, looks in the back and says, "Nice children."

She feels stupid as she hears herself say, "Thank you."

She hands him the license.

"Passport?"

"It's at home."

"You're supposed to have it on you."

"I know, but we've been here a long time and—"

"Maybe you've been here *too* long," the cop says. "I'm afraid you'll have to come with me."

"But I have my children with me."

"I can see that, Señora, but you must come with me."

Althea finds herself near tears. "But what am I supposed to do with my *children*?"

The cop excuses himself for a moment and goes back to his car. Althea sits, trying to get herself under control, for long minutes. She fights off the temptation to look in the rearview mirror to see what's going on, likewise fights the urge to just get out of the car with the kids and start walking. Finally, the cop comes back. Leans through the window and with elaborate courtesy says, "In Mexico we appreciate the meaning of family. Good afternoon."

Art gets his phone call.

Tim Taylor, phoning to say he's heard something disturbing and they need to talk about it.

Taylor's still yapping at him when the shooting starts.

Plan B.

First they hear the roar of a speeding car, then the cacophony of AK-47s going off, then they are all on the floor, crouching behind desks. Art, Ernie and Shag wait for a few minutes after the shooting stops and then go out to look at Art's car. The Ford Taurus's windows are all blown out, the tires flat and a few dozen large bullet holes punched into its sides.

Shag says, "I don't think you're going to get Blue Book on this, boss."

The *federales* are there within moments.

If they weren't here already, Art thinks.

They take him to the station, where Colonel Vega looks at him with deep concern.

"Thank God you were not in the vehicle," he says. "Whoever could have done such a thing? Do you have any enemies in the city, Señor Keller?"

"You know goddamn well who did this," Art snaps. "Your boy, Barrera."

Vega gives him a look of wide-eyed incredulity. "Miguel Ángel Barrera? But why would he want to do such a thing? You yourself told me you are not investigating Don Miguel."

Vega keeps him in the interview room for three and a half hours, basically interrogating him about his investigations, on the pretext of trying to determine who might have had a motive for the attack.

Ernie's half-afraid he's not coming out. He parks himself in the lobby and refuses to leave until his boss comes back out those doors. While Ernie's camped there, Shag drives over to the Kellers' house and tells Althea, "Art's fine, but . . ."

When Art gets home, Althea is in their bedroom packing.

"I got us on a flight to San Diego tonight," she says. "We'll stay with my parents for a while."

"What are you talking about?"

"I was *scared* today, Art," she says. She tells him about the interaction with the Jalisco cop, about what it felt like to hear that his car had been shot up and that he was being taken to the *federale* station. "I've never been really scared before, Art. I want out of Mexico."

"There's nothing to be scared of."

She looks at him like he's nuts. "They shot your car up, Art."

"They knew I wasn't in it."

"So when they bomb the house," she says, "are they going to know that me and the kids aren't in it?!"

"They won't hurt families."

"What is that," she asks, "some sort of rule?"

"Yes, it is," he says. "Anyway, it's me they're after. It's personal."

"What do you mean, 'it's personal'?"

When he hasn't answered after about thirty seconds she says, *"Art, what do you mean?!"*

He sits her down and tells her about his prior relationship with Tío and Adán Barrera. Tells her about the ambush in Badiraguato, the execution of six prisoners and how he kept his mouth shut about it. How it helped Tío form his Federación, which is now flooding the streets of America with crack, and how it's up to him to do something about it.

She looks at him incredulously. "You have all that on your shoulders."

He nods.

"You must be a pretty powerful guy, Art," she says. "What were you supposed to have done back then? It wasn't your fault. You couldn't have known what Barrera was up to."

"I think," Art says, "maybe a part of me knew. And just didn't want to admit it."

"So you feel you have to atone for this in some way?" she asks. "By bringing the Barreras down? Even if it costs your life."

"Something like that."

She gets up and goes into the bathroom. It seems to him as if she's in there forever, but it's really only a few minutes later when she comes out, goes into the closet, grabs his suitcase and tosses it onto the bed. "Come with us."

"I can't do that."

"This crusade of yours is more important to you than your family?" she asks.

"Nothing is more important to me than my family."

"Prove it," she says. "Come with us."

"Althea—"

"You want to stay here and play *High Noon,* fine," she says. "If you want to keep your family together, start packing. Just enough for a few days.

Tim Taylor said he'd arrange to have the rest of our things packed and shipped."

"You talked to Tim Taylor about this?!"

"He called," she says. "Which is more than you did, by the way."

"I was in an interrogation room!"

"Which is supposed to make me feel better?!"

"Goddamn it, Althie! What do you want from me?!"

"I want you to come with us!"

"I can't!"

He sits on the bed, his empty suitcase beside him like a piece of evidence that he doesn't love his family. He does love them—deeply and profoundly—but he just can't bring himself to do what she's asking.

Why not? he asks himself. Is Althea right? Do I love this crusade more than my own family?

"Don't you get it?" she asks. "This isn't about the Barreras. It's about you. It's about you not being able to forgive yourself. It's not them you're obsessed with punishing, it's yourself."

"Thanks for the dime-store psychotherapy."

"Fuck you, Art." She snaps her suitcase shut. "I called a taxi."

"At least let me take you to the airport."

"Not unless you're getting on the plane. It's too hard on the kids."

He picks up her bag and carries it downstairs. Stands there with her bag in his hand as she and Josefina exchange hugs and tears. He squats down to hug Cassie and Michael. Michael doesn't really understand. Cassie's tears are warm on Art's cheek.

"Why aren't you coming, Daddy?" she asks.

"I have some work I have to do," Art says. "I'll be along in just a little bit."

"But I want you to come with us!"

"You'll have so much fun with Grandpa and Grandma," he says.

A horn beeps and he carries their bags outside.

The street is crowded with a *posada,* the local kids dressed as Joseph and Mary and kings and shepherds. The latter bang their staffs, decked out with ribbons and flowers, in time with the music of a little band that follows the procession down the street. Art has to hand the bags over the children to the cab driver.

"*Aeropuerto,*" Art says.

"*Yo sé,*" the cabbie says.

As the driver puts the luggage in the trunk, Art gets the kids into the backseat. He hugs and kisses them again and keeps a smile on his face as he says good-bye. Althea is standing awkwardly by the front passenger door. Art hugs her and goes to kiss her but she turns to take it on her cheek.

"I love you," he says.

"Take care of yourself, Art."

She gets in. Art watches until the cab's red taillights disappear in the night. Then he turns and makes his way through the *posada,* hears the singing in the background—

> *"Come in, you holy pilgrims—*
> *Into this humble house—*
> *It is a poor lodging—*
> *But it is a gift from the heart—"*

He sees the white Bronco still parked down the street and heads for it, bumping into a little boy who asks the ritual question: "A place to stay tonight, Señor? Do you have a room for us?"

"What?"

"A place to stay—"

"No, not tonight."

He makes it over to the Bronco and knocks on the window. When it slides down, he grabs the cop, pulls him out of the window and hits him with three straight, hard rights before slamming him onto the street. Holding him by the shirtfront, he hits him over and over again, yelling, "I *told* you not to fuck with my family! I *told* you not to fuck with my family!"

Two of the local parents pull him off.

He shucks himself out of their grip and starts to walk back to his house. As he does, he sees the cop, still lying on the ground, reach around and pull the pistol from his hip holster.

"Do it," Art says. "Do it, motherfucker."

The cop lowers his gun.

Art makes his way through the shocked crowd and goes into his house. He kills two strong scotches, then goes to bed.

Art spends Christmas Day with Ernie and Teresa Hidalgo, at their insistence and over his objections. He gets there late, not wanting to watch Ernesto Jr. and Hugo open their presents, but he arrives with toys in his hands and the boys, already crazed with overstimulation, jump around, screaming, "Tío Arturo! Tío Arturo!"

He feigns an appetite. Teresa has gone to great trouble to make a traditional turkey dinner (traditional for him, not for a Hispanic household), so he forces himself to down a great quantity of turkey and mashed potatoes, which he really doesn't want. He insists on clearing the table, and it's in the kitchen that Ernie says to him, "Boss, I've been offered a transfer to El Paso."

"Oh?"

"I'm going to take it."

"Okay."

Ernie has tears in his eyes. "It's Teresa. She's scared here. For me, for the boys."

"You don't owe me any explanations."

"Yeah, I do."

"Look, I don't blame you."

Tío has unleashed his *federale* dogs to harass the DEA agents in Guadalajara. The *federales* have come to the office, searching for guns, illegal wiretapping equipment, even drugs. They've stopped the agents in their cars two or three times a day on the flimsiest of pretexts. And Tío's *sicarios* drive past their houses at night, or park across the street, wave to them in the morning when they come out to get their newspapers.

So Art doesn't blame Ernie for bugging out. Just because I've lost my family, he thinks, doesn't mean he should lose his. He says, "I think you're doing the right thing, Ernie."

"Sorry, boss."

"Don't be."

They share an awkward hug.

When it breaks up, Ernie says, "It'll be a month or so before the new job opens up, so . . ."

"Sure. We'll do some damage before you go."

Art excuses himself shortly after dessert. He can't stand the thought of going back to his empty house, so he drives around until he finds an open bar. Sits on a stool and has two drinks that don't numb him enough to face going home, so instead he drives to the airport.

Sits in his car on the ridge over the airfield and watches the SETCO flight come in. "On Dancer, on Prancer," he says to himself. "On Donner, on Blitzen." Santa's sleigh coming in with goodies for all the good children.

We could seize enough snow to cover a Minnesota winter, he thinks, and the snow would just keep coming. We could seize enough cash to pay off the national debt, and the cash would just keep rolling in. As long as the Mexican Trampoline is still in operation it doesn't matter. The coke just bounces from Colombia to Honduras to Mexico and then into the States. Gets turned into crack and bounces merrily onto the street.

The white DC-4 sits on the runway.

This coke isn't meant to be snorted by stockbrokers or starlets. This coke is going to be smoked as crack—sold at ten bucks a rock to the poor, mostly black and Hispanic. This coke ain't going to Wall Street or Hollywood; it's going to Harlem and Watts, to South Chicago and East L.A., to Roxbury and Barrio Logan.

Art sits up on the ridge and watches the *federales* finish loading the coke into trucks. The usual SETCO drill, he thinks, smooth and *intocable,* and he's about to go home when something new happens.

The *federales* start loading something *on* to the plane. Art watches as they lift crate after crate into the DC-4's cargo hold.

What the hell? he thinks.

He swings his binocs around and sees Tío supervising the load-in.

What the hell? What could they be loading *on* to the plane?

He considers it on the drive home.

Okay, he thinks, you have airplanes flying coke out of Colombia. The planes aren't guided by any radio signals, and they fly under the radar. They stop and refuel in Honduras under the protection of Ramón Mette, whose partner is an old Operation 40 Cuban ex-pat.

The planes then fly to Guadalajara, where they're off-loaded under Tío's protection and distributed to one of the three cartels—Gulf, Sonora or Baja. The cartels take the coke across the border to safe houses, then deliver it back to the Colombians at $1,000 a kilo. Then the Mexican cartels pay Tío a percentage of that fee.

It's the Mexican Trampoline, Art thinks, cocaine bouncing from Medellín to Honduras to Mexico to the States. And the Honduran DEA office is closed, Mexico doesn't want do anything about it, and the DEA, the Justice Department and the State Department don't want to know. See no evil, hear no evil, and for God's sake *speak* no evil.

Okay, that's old news.

What's different?

What's different is two-way traffic. Now you have something going back the other way.

But what?

He's thinking about this as he unlocks the door and goes into his empty house and feels a gun barrel shoved into the back of his head.

"Don't turn around."

"I won't." Fuckin' A, I won't. I'm scared enough just feeling the gun. I don't need to see it.

"See how fucking easy it is, Art?" the man says. "To get to you?"

It's an American voice, Art thinks. East Coast. New York. He risks a look down, but all he can see are the tips of the man's shoes.

Black, shined to a mirror-like gloss.

"I get that, Sal," Art says.

The subsequent moment of silence tell him he's right.

"That was really fucking stupid, Art," Sal says.

He pulls the trigger.

Art hears the dry, metallic click.

"Jesus God," he says. His knees feel weak, like water, like he's going to fall down. His heart is racing, his body hot. He feels like he can't breathe.

"The next chamber ain't empty, Art."

"Okay."

"Knock this shit off," Sal says. "You don't know what you're fucking with."

Same thing Adán told me, Art thinks. Same words.

"Did Barrera send you?" he asks.

"When you got a gun at *my* head, you can ask the questions," Sal says. "I'm telling you, stay away from the airport. Next time—and there'd better not be a next time, Arthur—we won't be having a 'dialogue.' You'll just be alive, and then you won't. Got it?"

"Yeah."

"Good," Sal says. "I'm going to be leaving now. Don't turn around. And Arthur?"

"Yeah?"

"Cerberus."

"What?"

"Nothing," the man says. "Don't turn around."

Art doesn't turn around as he hears Sal walk away. He stands where he is for a full minute, until he hears a car on the street pull away.

Then he sits down and starts shaking. It takes a few minutes and a heavy scotch to get it together, but he tries to think it through.

Stay away from the airport.

So whatever it is they were loading on that plane, Art thinks, they're very sensitive about it.

And what the hell is Cerberus?

He looks out the window, and there's another Jalisco cop out there on surveillance. He goes into his study and calls Ernie at home. "I need you to bring a car over here. Come in the other way, and park it two blocks south. Take a cab home."

He lets himself out the back way, through the kitchen door, then climbs over the back fence into his neighbor's yard and out onto the back street. He finds Ernie's car where it's supposed to be, but there's a problem.

Ernie's still in it.

"I told you to take a cab home," Art says as he slides in.

"I guess I didn't hear that part."

"Go home," Art says. When Ernie doesn't move, he says, "Look, I don't want to fuck up *your* life, too."

"When are you going to let me in on this?" Ernie asks as he gets out of the car.

"When I know what I'm doing," Art says.

Like, maybe never.

He gets into Ernie's car and drives to La Casa del Amor.

What if they're waiting for me? he thinks as he makes his way over to the wall to retrieve the tape.

You'll just be alive, and then you won't.

Click.

Out.

He shakes off his fear and makes his way through the shrubbery to the wall. Takes a quick glance over the top and sees that Tío's bedroom light is on. Crouching by the wall, he taps his earpiece into the tape recorder so he can listen live.

They say eavesdroppers never hear anything nice about themselves, Art thinks as he listens.

"Did it work?" Tío asks.

"I don't know." Sal's Spanish is pretty good, Art thinks, but it's definitely the same voice. *"I think so, though. The guy seemed pretty scared."*

Yeah, no shit, Art thinks. Let me stick a gun in your neck and see how cool you are.

"Did he know anything about Cerberus?"

"I don't think so. He didn't respond at all."

Relax, Art thinks. I don't know shit about it. Whatever it is.

Then he hears Tío say, *"We can't take the chance. The next exchange . . ."*

Exchange? Art thinks. What exchange?

". . . we'll do El Norte."

El Norte, Art thinks.

THE POWER OF THE DOG

In the States.
Yeah, Art thinks. Do it, Tío.
Fly it across the border.
Because as soon as you do?
I'm going to reach up and grab that plane right out of the sky.

Borrego Springs, California
January 1985

The plane, any plane really, flies toward a VOR signal. A VOR (Variable Oscillation Radio) signal is kind of like the radio version of a lighthouse, but instead of a beam of light it emits sound waves that register as *beeps* on a plane's radio or a pulsing light on its instrument panel. All airports, even small ones, have a VOR.

But a plane full of dope isn't going to land at an airport in the United States, not even a small one. What it's going to do is land on a private airstrip bulldozed out of a remote part of the desert. The VOR signals are still crucial because the pilot is going to locate the landing strip by triangulating the location between three VOR signals, in this case, the VORs at Borrego Springs, Ocotillo Wells and Blythe. What happens is that the people on the ground are going to get on the ADF radio and give him that location, cross-referencing it by distance and compass points—called "vectors" in air navigation—from the three known locations of the VORs.

Then they're going to park at the end of that landing strip, and when they see the plane, they'll become their own landing tower, if you will, by flashing their headlights. The pilot will line his plane up toward the headlights and bring down the plane, with its valuable cargo.

For security reasons, the guys on the ground aren't going to give that pilot the landing location until he's in the air, because once he's in the air, what could happen?

Well, lots, because the F in ADF stands for "frequency," and that's what Art has from listening in on Tío's conversations, and he's tuned in on it so he's going to know the landing location just as soon as the pilot does. But that's not good enough—Art's crew can't wait for him to land and then bust everyone, because they can't get close enough without being spotted long before the plane gets there.

Once you get out of the little town of Borrego Springs, California, the

Anza-Borrego Desert is a million acres of nothing, and if you turn on so much as a flashlight, it's going to stand out like a spotlight. And it's quiet out there, so a jeep sounds like an armored column. You're not going to get close even if you can get there in time once you learn the location.

This is why Art is going in a different direction—instead of trying to chase the plane down and then sneak up on it, he's just going to land it at his own airstrip.

It's outrageous, his plan. It's so out there, so totally crazed, that no one's going to expect it.

First he needs an airstrip.

Turns out that Shag knows a rancher out there where it takes about a hundred acres to feed a single cow. So Shag's old buddy has him a few thousand acres and, yes, he has a landing strip because, as Shag explains to Art, "old Wayne flies to Ocotillo to buy his groceries," and he ain't kidding. And as old Wayne's opinion of drug dealers is about the same as his opinion of the federal government, he's happy to host this little ambush, and even happier to keep his mouth shut about it.

Next thing Art needs is a co-conspirator, because the aforementioned Washington, D.C., would be somewhat less than thrilled to have the Guadalajara RAC conduct a stunt like this several hundred miles away from his assigned territory. What Art needs is someone who can make the necessary arrests and seizures, get it in the press and then start to track the airplane back without any interference from the DEA or the State Department. So that's why he has Russ Dantzler sitting next to him.

Another thing Art needs to do is jam the pilot's ADF, switch him over to a new frequency and then talk him down to the party at old Wayne's ranch.

So the most important thing Art needs is, as old Wayne might put it, one big old shitload of luck.

Adán's sitting in the front of a Land Rover in the middle of the *chingada* desert with a few million dollars' worth of coke in the air and his future in his hands.

And now the *chingada* radio won't work.

"What's wrong with it?" he snaps again.

"I don't know," the young technician repeats, fiddling with knobs, dials and switches, trying to get the signal back. "Electrical storm, something on the plane . . . I'm trying."

The kid sounds scared. He should—Raúl takes out a .44 and points it at the kid's head. "Try harder."

"Put that away," Adán snaps. "That's not going to help."

Raúl shrugs and tucks the pistol back into his belt.

But the radio-geek kid's hand is shaking on the dials now. This isn't the way it was supposed to go down—he was just supposed to do a little easy work for a little easy coke, and now they're threatening to blow his brains out if he can't get the plane on the ADF.

And he can't.

All he can get is a Led Zeppelin–on–acid kind of guitar-feedback squeal. And his hand is rattling on the dials.

"Relax," Adán says. "Just get the plane in."

"I'm trying," the kid repeats, looking like he's going to cry.

Adán looks at Raúl like, See what you did?

Raúl frowns.

Especially when Jimmy Peaches walks over and taps on the window. "The fuck is going on?"

"We're trying to get the plane on the radio," Adán says.

"How hard is that?" Peaches asks.

"Harder if you keep bothering us," Raúl says. "Go back, hang in your truck, everything's cool."

No, everything isn't cool, Peaches thinks as he walks back to the truck. First thing that isn't cool is I'm out here playing Lawrence of Arabia in East Bumfuck, second thing is I'm sitting in a truck chock-fulla felony, third thing is I got major non-returnable investment in the truck that I leveraged with other people's money, fourth thing is them other people is Johnny Boy Cozzo, Johnny's brother Gene, and Sal Scachi, none of which is exactly known for his forgiving nature, which brings me to the fifth thing, which is that if Big Paulie ever gets wind we're dealing dope he's gonna have us whacked—the "us" starting with "me"—which leads me to the sixth thing, which is that all the coke is now in an airplane somewhere in the sky and these beaners can't seem to *find* it.

"Now they can't find the fucking plane," he says to Little Peaches as he climbs back into the truck.

"What do you mean?" Little Peaches asks.

"Which word didn't you fucking understand?"

"Irritable."

"Fucking A, I'm irritable."

Drive all the way out to California with a truck full of guns, and not just a few pistols but major freaking weaponry—M-16s, AR-15s, ammo, they even got a couple of LAWs back there, and what the fucking Mexicans need rocket launchers for I'll never know. But that was the deal—the beaners wanted to get paid in weapons this time, so I get the money from the Cozzos and Sal, add a little secret surcharge to cover my end and haul ass all over the East Coast hustling up this freaking arsenal. Then I drive it all the way across the country, shitting my pants every time I see a state trooper because I got Life in Lewisburg in the back.

Peaches is also irritable because things in the Cimino Family ain't going so well.

First of all, Big Paulie has his panties in a wad about the Commission Case, what with New York Eastern District D.A. Giuliani threatening to lay about a century each on the heads of the other four families. So Paulie ain't letting them do nothing to earn a living. No robberies, no hits and, of course, no dope. And when they kick it up the chain that they're fucking starving here, the answer comes back down that they should have invested their money.

They should have legitimate businesses to fall back on.

Which is bullshit, Peaches thinks. All the fucking hoops you gotta jump through to get made—for what? Sell shoes?

Fuck that.

Fucking Paulie is such a fucking woman.

Peaches has even started calling him the Godmother.

Just the other day on the phone, him and Little Peaches were talking about it.

"Hey," Peaches says, "you know that maid the Godmother is pronging? You ready for this? I hear he's got this pump-up dick he uses."

"How does that work?" Little Peaches asks.

"Nothin' I want to think about," Peaches says. "I guess it's like a flat tire, and you pump it up to get it hard."

"He's got, what, like an inner tube in his dick?"

"I guess so," Peaches says. "Anyway, it's wrong what he's doing, tappin' the maid right there in the house where his wife is living. It's disrespectful. Thank God Carlo ain't alive to see it."

"If Carlo was alive, there'd be nothing to see," Little Peaches says. "Paulie wouldn't have the balls, never mind the inflatable dick, to fuck some whore in the house right in front of Carlo's sister. What Paulie would be is dead, is what."

"Your lips to God's ears," says Peaches. "You want some strange, fine—go get yourself some strange. You want a little something on the side, get it on the side, not in the house. The house is the wife's home. You respect that. That's our way."

"That's right."

"It's all so fuckin' bad right now," Big Peaches says. "And when Mr. Neill finally passes . . . I'm telling you, the underboss job better go to Johnny Boy."

"Paulie ain't gonna make John underboss," Little Peaches says. "He's too scared of him. The job's going to Bellavia, you watch."

"Tommy Bellavia is Paulie's chauffeur," Big Peaches snorts. "He's a cabbie, for chrissakes. I'm not reporting to no fucking chauffeur. I'm telling you, it better be John."

Little Peaches says, "Anyway, we can't take no chances on this shipment. We gotta get it and put it out on the street and get some fuckin' money in here."

"I hear that."

Callan's thinking pretty much the same thing as he sits in the back of the truck in the middle of a cold desert night. Wishes he had more than just his old leather jacket.

"Who knew," O-Bop says to him, "that it would be *cold* in the fucking *desert*?"

"What's going on?" Callan asks.

He doesn't like this shit. Doesn't like being out of New York, doesn't like being out in the middle of nowhere, doesn't even like what they're doing here. He sees what's going on in the streets, what crack is doing to the neighborhood, to the whole city. He feels bad—it's not a right way to make a living. The union shit is one thing, the construction shit, the loan-sharking, the gambling—even the contracts—but he don't really like helping Peaches put crack on the street.

"What are we gonna do?" O-Bop had said when it came up. "Say no?"

"Yeah."

"This thing fucks up, it's our ass, too."

"I know."

So here they are, sitting in the back of a truck on top of enough weaponry to take a small banana republic, waiting for the plane to come down so they can make the exchange and go home.

Unless the Mexicans get cute, in which case Callan has ten .22 rounds in the clip and another in the chamber.

"You got an arsenal in here," O-Bop asks. "What you want with a .22?"

"It's enough."

Fuck yes it is, O-Bop thinks, remembering Eddie Friel.

Fuck yes it is.

"Find out what's going on," Callan says.

O-Bop bangs on the wall. "What's going on?!"

"They can't find the fucking plane!"

"You're kidding!"

"Yeah, I'm kidding!" Peaches yells back. "The plane landed, we made the switch and we're all sitting at Rocco's eating linguini with clam sauce!"

"How do you lose a whole airplane?" Callan asks.

There's nothing out here.

That's the problem. The pilot is eight thousand feet over the desert, looking at nothing but dark down there. He can find Borrego Springs, he can find Ocotillo Wells or Blythe, but unless someone gets on the horn and gives him the landing location, he has as much chance of finding that airstrip as he does of seeing the Cubs win the World Series.

Zip.

It's a problem because he has only so much fuel, and pretty soon he's going to have to think about turning around and flying back to El Salvador. He tries the radio again and gets the same metallic squeal. Then he turns it up one half-frequency and hears—

"Come in, come in."

"Where the hell you been?" the pilot asks. "You're on the wrong frequency."

Says you, Art thinks.

Saint Anthony is the patron saint of hopeless causes, and Art makes a mental note to thank him with a candle and a twenty-dollar bill as Shag says into the radio mike, "You want to bitch or you want to land?"

"I want to land."

The small knot of men huddled around the radio on this freezing night look at one another and flat-out grin. It warms them up considerably because they're within moments of landing, literally, a SETCO flight full of cocaine.

Unless it all goes sick and wrong.

As it very well could.

Shag doesn't care. "My career's fucked anyway."

He gives the pilot the landing coordinates.

"Ten minutes," the pilot says.

"I copy. Out."

"Ten minutes," Art says.

"A long ten minutes," says Dantzler.

A lot can happen in ten minutes. In ten minutes the pilot might get hinky, change his mind and turn the plane around. In ten minutes, the real airstrip might break through Dantzler's radio jam and make contact with the plane, guiding it to the correct location. In ten minutes, Art thinks, there could be an earthquake that sends a crack down the middle of this airstrip and swallows us all. In ten minutes . . .

He lets out a long sigh.

"No shit," Dantzler says.

Shag smiles at him.

Adán Barrera isn't smiling.

His stomach is churning, his jaw is clamped tight. This is the deal that can't be allowed to go wrong, Tío had warned him. This one has to happen.

For a lot of reasons, Adán thinks.

He's a married man now. He and Lucía were married in Guadalajara with Father Juan performing the ceremony himself. It had been a wonderful day, and a more wonderful night, after years of frustration finally getting inside Lucía. She had been a surprise in bed, a more-than-willing partner, enthusiastically wriggling and writhing, calling his name, her blond hair splayed on the pillow in unconscious symmetry with her open legs.

So married life is great, but with marriage comes responsibility, especially now that Lucía is pregnant. That, Adán thinks as he sits out in the desert, changes everything. Now you're playing for keeps. Now you're about to be a *papá,* with a family to support, their future in your hands. He's not unhappy about this—on the contrary, he's thrilled, he's excited to be taking on a man's responsibility, delighted beyond measure by the thought of having a child—but it means that more than ever, this deal cannot be allowed to go wrong.

"Try another frequency," he tells the technician.

"I've tried every—"

He sees Raúl touch the butt of the pistol in his belt.

"I'll try them again," he says, even though he's now convinced it's not the frequency. It's the equipment, the radio itself. Who knows what might have gotten jarred loose, bouncing around out here? People are always the same, he thinks. They have millions of dollars of coke floating around somewhere up there, but they aren't willing to spend an extra couple hundred bucks on a radio to bring it in. Instead I have to work with this cheap shit.

He doesn't offer this critique to his employers, though.

He just keeps twirling the knobs.

Adán stares up into the night sky.

The stars seem so low and so bright he feels like he can almost reach up and pull one down. He wishes he could do the same thing with the airplane.

So does Art.

Because there's nothing up there, nothing but the stars and a sliver of moon.

He checks his watch.

Heads turn as if he's pulled a gun.

It's been ten minutes.

You've had your ten minutes, he thinks. You've had your endless, nerve-rattling, stomach-turning, heart-pounding ten minutes, so stop playing with us. Stop the torture.

He looks into the sky again.

It's what they're all doing, standing in the cold, staring at the sky like some prehistoric tribe, trying to figure out what it all means.

"It's over," Art says a minute later. "He must have figured it out."

"Shiiit," says Shag.

"Sorry, Art," Dantzler says.

"Sorry, boss."

"It's all right," Art says. "We gave it a shot."

But it isn't all right. They probably won't ever get another chance to land physical proof that the Mexican Trampoline is real.

And they'll close the Guadalajara office and bust us up and that will be it.

"We'll give it another five minutes and then—"

"Shut up," Shag says.

They all stare at him—it's uncharacteristically brusque of the cowboy.

"Listen," he says.

Then they can just make it out.

The sound of an engine.

An airplane engine.

Shag sprints to the truck, fires up the engine and blinks the lights.

The plane's running lights blink back. In two minutes Art watches the plane come down from the blackness and land smoothly.

The pilot breathes a sigh of relief as he sees a man trot over.

Then the man sticks a gun in his face.

"Surprise, asshole," Russ Dantzler says. "You have the right to remain silent . . ."

Silent?

The guy is motherfucking *speechless*.

· · ·

Shag isn't. He's in the car with Art, doing a cowboy Bundini Brown. "You are the greatest, boss! You have the arms of an orangutan! You are King Kong! You reach into the sky and pull down airplanes!"

Art laughs. Then he sees Dantzler walk over to the car. The San Diego narc is shaking his head, and even in the faint light looks pale.

Shaken.

"Art," Dantzler begins. "The guy . . . the pilot . . . he says . . ."

"What?"

"That he's working for us."

Art opens the door to where they have the pilot sitting in the back.

Phil Hansen should be a very nervous guy, but he isn't. He's leaning back as if he's waiting out a traffic ticket that's going to get fixed anyway. Art would like to slap the smirk off his face.

"Long time no see, Keller," he says casually, like this is all one big joke.

"What the hell is this about you working for us?"

Hansen looks at him serenely. "Cerberus."

"What?"

"C'mon. Cerberus? Ilopongo? Hangar Four?"

"What the fuck are you talking about?"

The smile fades from Hansen's face. Now he looks alarmed.

"You thought what, you got a pass?" Art asks. "You fly a couple hundred Ks of coke into the United States and you think you get a pass? What makes you think that, asshole?"

"They said you were—"

"They said I was what?"

"Nothing."

Hansen turns his head and looks out the window.

Art says, "If you have a Get Out of Jail Free card, now is the time to lay it down. Give me a name, Phil. Who do I call?"

"You know who to call."

"No, I don't. Tell me."

"I'm done here."

He stares out the window.

"Someone fucked you, Phil," Art says. "I don't know who told you what, but if you think we're playing for the same team you're mistaken. We got you carrying thirty-to-life weight, Phil. You're going to *do* fifteen, minimum.

But it's not too late to get on the right side of this. Cooperate with me and if it works out, I'll see that you get a deal."

When Hansen turns back to him there are tears in his eyes. He says, "I have a wife and kids in Honduras."

Ramón Mette, Art thinks. The guy is scared shitless that Mette will retaliate against his family. Tough shit—you should have thought of that before you started flying coke around. "You want to see them before they have kids of their own? Talk to me."

Art's seen the look before—he calls it the Skell Scale, the guilty guy weighing his options, realizing to his horror that there is no good option, just a less bad one. He waits for Hansen to work it out.

Hansen shakes his head.

Art slams the car door and walks out into the desert for a minute. He could bust the plane now, but what good would it do? It would prove that SETCO is flying drugs, but he already knows that. And it wouldn't tell him what's going back as cargo on the return trip, and to whom.

No, it's time to take another big chance.

He walks back over to Dantzler. "Let's play this one different. Let the plane go through."

"What?!"

"Then we can track it three ways," Art says. "See where the coke goes, see where the money goes, see what's on the plane going back."

Dantzler gets on board with it. What the hell is he going to do? It's Art fucking Keller asking.

Art nods and gets back into the car.

"Just testing," he tells Hansen. "You passed. Get going."

Art watches the plane take off again.

Then he gets on the radio to tell Ernie to expect the return SETCO flight, to photograph it and let it go.

But Ernie doesn't answer.

Ernie Hidalgo has gone off the radar.

5

Narcosantos

There are two things the American people don't want: another Cuba on the mainland of Central America, and another Vietnam.

—Ronald Reagan

Mexico
January 1985

Six hours after Ernie goes off the screen, Art storms into Colonel Vega's office.

"One of my men is missing," he says. "I want this city turned upside down and inside out. I want you to arrest Miguel Ángel Barrera, and I don't want to hear any of your shit—"

"Señor Keller—"

"—your *shit* about not knowing where he is, and anyways, he's innocent. I want you to pick up all of them—Barrera, his nephews, Abrego, Méndez, every goddamn one of the drug-pushing cocksuckers—and I—"

"You don't know that he's been kidnapped," Vega says. "He might be having an affair, he might be drunk somewhere. You certainly don't know that Barrera has anything to do with—"

Art comes across the man's desk, right in the colonel's face.

"If I have to," Art says, "I'll start a fucking war."

He means it. He'll call in every favor, threaten to go to the press, go there, threaten to go to certain congressmen, go to them—he'll bring a division of Marines down from Camp Pendleton and start a real goddamn shooting war if that's what it takes to rescue Ernie Hidalgo.

If—please, God, please, Jesus and Mary, the mother of God—Ernie's still alive.

A second later he adds, "Now, why are you still sitting there?"

They hit the streets.

All of a sudden, like magic, Vega knows where the *gomeros* are. It's a miracle, Art thinks. Vega knows where every low- and middle-level *narcotraficante* in the city lives, hangs out or does business. They roust them all—Vega's *federales* bust through the city like the Gestapo, only they don't find Miguel Ángel, or Adán or Raúl, or Méndez, or Abrego. It's the same old dye test, Art thinks, the same old search-and-avoid mission. They know where these guys were, they just can't seem to find where they *are*.

Vega even leads a raid on Barrera's condominium, the address of which he suddenly acknowledges, but when they get there they find that Miguel Ángel is gone. They also find something else that makes Art go absolutely berserk.

A photograph of Ernie Hidalgo.

An ID photo taken in the Guadalajara MJFP office.

Art grabs it and waves it in Vega's face.

"Look at this!" he yells. "Did your guys give him this picture?! Did your fucking guys do that?!"

"Certainly not."

"My ass," Art says.

He goes back to the office and calls Tim Taylor in Mexico City.

"I heard," Taylor says.

"So what are you doing?"

"I've been at the ambassador's office," Taylor says. "He's going to see the president personally. Did you get Teresa and the kids out?"

"She didn't want to go, but—"

"Shit, Arthur."

"But I had Shag take her to the airport," Art says. "They should be in San Diego now."

"What about Shag?"

"He's working the streets."

"I'm pulling you guys out."

"The hell you are," Art says.

There's a brief silence, then Taylor asks, "What do you need, Art?"

"An honest cop," Art says. He tells Taylor about the photo he found in Barrera's condo, then says, "I don't want any more of these MJFP assholes. Send me someone clean, someone with some weight."

Antonio Ramos arrives in Guadalajara that afternoon.

· · ·

Adán listens to the man scream.

And to the quiet voice patiently asking the same question over and over again.

Who is Chupar? Who is Chupar? Who is Chupar?

Ernie tells them again that he doesn't know. His interrogator doesn't believe him and pushes the ice pick in again, scraping it against Ernie's shinbone.

The question starts again.

You do *know. Tell us who he is. Who is Source Chupar?*

Ernie gives them names. Any names he can think of. Minor dealers, major dealers, *federales,* Jalisco State Police—any *gomero* or dirty cop, he doesn't care. Anything to make them stop.

They don't. They don't buy a single name he gives them. The Doctor—the others actually call the man "Doctor"—just keeps it up with the ice pick, slowly, patiently, meticulously, unshaken by Ernie's shouts. Unhurried.

Who is Chupar? Who is Chupar? Who is Chupar?

"I don't knoooooowwww . . ."

The ice pick finds a new angle to a fresh piece of bone, and scrapes.

Güero Méndez comes out of the room, shaken.

"I don't think he knows," Güero says.

"He knows," Raúl says. "He's macho—a tough son of a bitch."

Let's hope he's not *too* tough, Adán thinks. If he'll just give us the name of the *soplón* we can let him go before all this gets too far out of hand. I know the Americans, Adán had told his uncle, better than you do. They can bomb, burn and poison other peoples, but let one of their own be harmed and they'll react with self-righteous savagery.

Hours after the agent was reported missing, an army of DEA agents busted Adán's safe house in Rancho Santa Fe.

It was the biggest drug bust in history.

Two thousand pounds of cocaine worth $37.5 million, two tons of sinsemilla worth another $5 million, plus another $27 million in cash, plus money-counting machines, scales and other miscellaneous office equipment of the drug trade. Not to mention fifteen illegal Mexican workers who were employed in weighing and packaging the coke.

But it cost far more than that, Adán thinks as he tries to shut out the moans of pain coming from the other room. It cost far more than that. Drugs and money you can always replace, but a child . . .

"A lymphatic malformation," the doctors had called it. "Cystic lymph-angioma." They said it had nothing to do with the stress of their sudden flight from their home in San Diego, steps ahead of the DEA, nothing to do with the jostling of the high-speed run across the border into Tijuana, nothing to do with the flight to Guadalajara. The doctors said the condition develops in the early months of pregnancy, not late, and they don't really know what causes it, only that somehow Adán and Lucía's daughter's lymph channels failed to develop properly and because of that her face and neck are deformed, distorted, and there is no treatment or cure. And while the lifespan is *usually* normal, there are risks of infection or stroke, sometimes difficulty with breathing . . .

Lucía blames him.

Not him directly, but their lifestyle, the business, the *pista secreta.* If they had been able to stay in the States, with the excellent prenatal care, if perhaps the baby had been born at Scripps Clinic as planned, if perhaps in those first moments when they saw that something was terribly wrong, if they'd had access to the best doctors in the world . . . perhaps, just perhaps . . . even though the doctors in Guadalajara assured her it wouldn't have made any difference.

Lucía wanted to go back to the States to have the baby, but she wouldn't go without him, and he couldn't go. There was a warrant out for him and Tío forbade it.

But if I had known, he thinks now, if I'd had the slightest thought that anything might have been wrong with the baby, I would have taken the chance. And with it, the consequences.

Goddamn the Americans.

And goddamn Art Keller.

Adán had called Father Juan in those first few terrible hours. Lucía was in agony, they all were, and Father Juan had hurried to the hospital right away. Came and held the baby, baptized her on the spot just in case, and then held Lucía's hand and talked with her, prayed with her, told her that she would be a wonderful mother to a special, wonderful child who would need her. Then, when Lucía finally yielded to the tranquilizers and fell asleep, Father Juan and Adán went out to the parking lot so the bishop could smoke a cigarette.

"Tell me what you're thinking," Father Juan said.

"That God is punishing me."

"God doesn't punish innocent children for the sins of their fathers," Parada answered. The Bible, he thought, notwithstanding.

"Then explain this to me," Adán said. "Is this the way God loves children?"

"Do you love your child, despite her condition?"

"Of course."

"Then God loves through you."

"That's not a good enough answer."

"It's the only one I have."

And it's not good enough, Adán thought, and thinks it now. And this Hidalgo kidnapping is going to destroy us all, if it hasn't already.

Grabbing Hidalgo had been the easy part. Christ, the police had done it for them. Three cops picked Hidalgo up in La Plaza de Armas and delivered him to Raúl and Güero, who drugged him, blindfolded him and brought him here to this house.

Where the Doctor had revived him and started his ministrations.

Which, so far, have produced no results.

He hears the Doctor's soft, patient voice from inside the room.

"Tell me the names," the Doctor says, "of the government officials who are on Miguel Ángel Barrera's payroll."

"I don't have any names."

"Did Chupar give you those names? You said that he did. Tell them to me."

"I was lying. Making it up. I don't know."

"Then tell me the name of Chupar," the Doctor says. "So we can ask him instead of you. So we can do this to him instead of you."

"I don't know who he is."

Is it possible, Adán wonders, that the man really *doesn't* know? He hears echoes of his own scared voice eight years ago during Operation Condor, when the DEA and the *federales* beat and tortured him for information that he didn't have. Told him that they had to be *sure* that he didn't know, so kept up the torture after he told them, again and again, *I don't know.*

"Christ," he says. "What if he doesn't know?"

"What if he doesn't?" Raúl shrugs. "The fucking Americans need to be taught a lesson anyway."

Adán hears the lesson being conducted in the other room. Hidalgo's moans as the metal of the ice pick grinds against his shinbone. And the Doctor's gently insistent voice: "You want to see your wife again. Your children. Surely you owe them more than you owe this informant. Think: Why have we blindfolded you? If we intended to kill you we wouldn't have bothered. But we intend to let you go. Back to your family. To Teresa and Ernesto and Hugo. Think of them. How worried they are. How scared your little sons must be. How they want their *papá* back. You don't want them to have to grow up without a father, do you? Who is Chupar? What did he tell you? Whose names did he give you?"

And Hidalgo's response, punctuated by sobs.

"I . . . don't . . . know . . . who . . . he . . . is."

"Pues..."

It starts again.

Antonio Ramos grew up on the garbage dumps of Tijuana.

Literally.

He lived in a shack outside the dump and picked through garbage for his meals, clothes, even his shelter. When they built a school nearby, Ramos went, every day, and if some other kid teased him for smelling like garbage, Ramos beat the kid up. Ramos was a big kid—skinny from lack of food, but tall and with quick hands.

After a while, he wasn't teased.

He made it all the way through high school, and when the Tijuana police accepted him, it was like going to heaven. Good pay, good food, clean clothes. He lost that skinny look and filled out, and his superiors found out something new about him. They knew he was tough; they didn't know he was *smart*.

The DFS, Mexico's intelligence service, found it out, too, and recruited him.

Now if there's an important assignment that requires smart and tough, Ramos usually gets the call.

He gets the call to bring back this American DEA agent, Hidalgo, at all or any cost.

Art meets him at the airport.

Ramos' nose and several knuckles are crooked and broken. He has thick black hair, a shock of which hangs over his forehead despite his occasional attempts to control it. Jammed into his mouth is his trademark black cigar.

"Every cop needs a trademark," he tells his men. "What you want the bad boys saying is, 'Look out for the macho with the black cigar.' "

They do.

They say it and they watch out and they're scared of him because Ramos has a well-earned reputation for his own brand of rough justice. Guys rousted by Ramos have been known to yell for the police. The police won't come—they don't want any of Ramos, either.

There's an alley near Avenida Revolución in TJ nicknamed La Universidad de Ramos. It's littered with cigar stubs and snuffed-out bad attitudes, and it's where Ramos, when he was a TJ street cop, taught lessons to the boys who thought they were bad.

"You're not bad," he told them. "*I'm* bad."

Then he showed them what bad was. If they needed a reminder, they could usually find one in the mirror for years afterward.

Six bad hombres have tried to kill Ramos. Ramos went to all six funerals, just in case any of the bereaved wanted to take a shot at revenge. None of them did. He calls his Uzi "Mi Esposa"—my wife. He's thirty-two years old.

Within hours he has in custody the three policemen who picked up Ernie Hidalgo. One of them is the chief of the Jalisco State Police.

Ramos tells Art, "We can do this the fast way or the slow way."

Ramos takes two cigars from his shirt pocket, offers one to Art and shrugs when he refuses it. He takes a long time to light the cigar, rolling it so that the tip lights evenly, then takes a long pull and raises his black eyebrows at Art.

The theologians are right, Art thinks—we become what we hate.

Then he says, "The fast way."

Ramos says. "Come back in a little while."

"No," Art says. "I'll do my part."

"That's a man's answer," Ramos says. "But I don't want a witness."

Ramos leads the Jalisco police chief and two *federales* into a basement cell.

"I don't have time to fuck around with you guys," Ramos says. "Here's the problem: Right now, you're more afraid of Miguel Ángel Barrera than you are of me. We need to turn that around."

"Please," the chief says, "we are all policemen."

"No, *I'm* a policeman," Ramos says, slipping on black, weighted gloves. "The man you kidnapped is a policeman. You're a piece of shit."

He holds the gloves up for them all to see.

"I don't like to bruise my hands," Ramos says.

The chief says, "Surely we can work something out."

"No," Ramos says, "we can't."

He turns to the bigger, younger *federale*.

"Put your hands up. Defend yourself."

The *federale*'s eyes are wide, scared. He shakes his head, doesn't raise his hands.

Ramos shrugs, "As you wish."

He feints with a right to the face and then puts all his weight behind three ripping left hooks to the ribs. The weighted gloves smash bone and cartilage. The cop starts to fall, but Ramos holds him up with his left hand and hits him with three more shots with his right. Then he throws him against the wall, turns him around and drives rights and lefts into his kidneys. Holds him against the wall by the back of the neck as he says, "You embarrassed your country. Worse, you embarrassed *my* country," and holds him with one hand by the neck and the other by the belt and runs him full speed across the room into the opposite wall. The *federale*'s head hits the concrete with a dull thud. His neck snaps back. Ramos repeats the process several times before he finally lets the man slide to the floor.

Ramos sits down on a wooden three-legged stool and lights his cigar as the two other cops stare at their unconscious friend, who lies facedown, his legs jerking spasmodically.

The walls are splotched with blood.

"Now," Ramos says, "you're more afraid of me than of Barrera, so we can get started. Where is the American policeman?"

They tell him everything they know.

"They delivered him to Güero Méndez and Raúl Barrera," Ramos tells Art. "And a Doctor Álvarez, which is why I think your friend might still be alive."

"Why is that?"

"Álvarez used to work for DFS," Ramos says. "As an interrogator. Hidalgo must have information they want, *sí*?"

"No," Art says. "He doesn't have the information."

Art's stomach sinks. They're torturing Ernie for the identity of Chupar.

And there is no Chupar.

"Tell me," Tío says.

Ernie moans, "I don't know."

Tío nods to Doctor Álvarez. The Doctor uses oven mitts to pick up a white-hot iron rod, which he inserts—

"Oh my God!" Ernie shouts. Then his eyes widen and his head collapses on the table where they have strapped him down. His eyes are closed, he's unconscious, and his heartbeat, which was racing a moment ago, is now dangerously slow.

The Doctor sets down the oven mitts and grabs a syringe full of lidocaine, which he injects into Ernie's arm. The drug will keep him conscious to feel the pain. It will keep his heart from stopping. A moment later, the American's head snaps up and his eyes pop open.

"We won't let you die," Tío says. "Now talk to me. Tell me, who is Chupar?"

I know Art's looking for me, Ernie thinks.

Moving heaven and earth.

"I don't know," he gasps, "who Chupar is."

The Doctor picks up the iron bar again.

A moment later Ernie shouts, *"Oh my Godddddddd!"*

Art watches the flame ignite, then flicker, then reach up toward heaven.

He kneels in front of the bank of votive candles and says a prayer for Ernie. To the Virgin Mary, to Saint Anthony, to Christ himself.

A tall, fat man comes down the center aisle of the cathedral.

"Father Juan."

The priest has changed little in nine years. His white hair is a little thinner, his stomach somewhat thicker, but the intense gray eyes still have their light.

"You're praying," Parada says. "I thought you didn't believe in God."

"I'll do anything."

Parada nods. "How can I help?"

"You know the Barreras."

"I baptized them," Parada answers. "Gave them their First Communion. Confirmed them." Married Adán to his wife, Parada thinks. Held their malformed, beautiful baby in my arms.

"Reach out to them," Art is saying.

"I don't know where they are."

"I was thinking of radio," Art says. "Television. They respect you, they'll listen to you."

"I don't know," Parada says. "Certainly I can try."

"Right now?"

"Of course," Parada says, then adds, "I can hear your confession."

"There isn't time."

So they drive to the radio station and Parada broadcasts his message to "those who have kidnapped the American policeman." Pleads with them, in the name of God the Father and Jesus Christ and Mother Mary and all the saints to release the man unharmed. Urges them to consult their souls, and then, to even Art's surprise, pulls the ultimate card—threatens excommunication if they harm the man.

Condemns them with all his power and authority to eternal hell.

Then repeats the hope of salvation.

Release the man and come back to God.

His freedom is your freedom.

". . . gave me an address," Ramos is saying.

"What?" Art asks. He's been listening to Parada's broadcast on the office radio.

"I said they gave me an address," Ramos says. He loops the Uzi over his shoulder. "Mi Esposa. Let's go."

The house is in a nondescript suburb. Ramos' two Ford Broncos, overflowing with his special DFS troops, roar up, and the men jump out. Gunfire—long, undisciplined AK bursts—comes out of the windows. Ramos' men drop to the ground and return the fire in short bursts. The shooting stops. Covered by his men, Ramos and two others run to the door with a battering ram and knock it in.

Art goes in just behind Ramos.

He doesn't see Ernie. He runs to every room of the small house but all he finds are two dead *gomeros,* a neat hole in each forehead, lying by the windows. A wounded man sits propped against the wall. Another sits with his hands high above his head.

Ramos pulls his pistol and puts it to the head of the wounded man.

"*¿Dónde?*" Ramos asks. Where?

"*No sé.*"

Art flinches as Ramos pulls the trigger and the man's brains splatter against the wall.

"Jesus!" Art shouts.

Ramos doesn't hear this. He puts the pistol against the other *gomero*'s temple.

"*¿Dónde?*"

"*¡Sinaloa!*"

"*¿Dónde?*"

"*¡Un rancho de Güero Méndez!*"

"*¿Cómo lo encuentro?*"

The *gomero* shouts, "*¡No sé! ¡No sé! ¡No sé! ¡Por favor! ¡Por el amor de Dios!*"

Art grabs Ramos by the wrist.

"No."

Ramos looks for a second like he might shoot Art. Then he lowers his pistol and says, "We have to find that farm before they move him again. You should let me shoot this bastard so he doesn't talk."

The *gomero* breaks down into sobs. "*¡Por el amor de Dios!*"

"You have no god, you motherless fuck," Ramos says, cuffing him along the side of the head. "*¡Te voy a mandar pa'l carajo!*"

I'm going to send you to hell.

"No," Art says.

"If the *federales* find out we know about Sinaloa," Ramos says, "they'll just move Hidalgo again before we can find him."

If we can find him, Art thinks. Sinaloa is a large, rural state. Locating a single farm there is like finding a specific farm in Iowa. But killing this guy won't help.

"Put him in isolation," Art says.

"*¡Ay, Dios! ¡Qué chingón que eres!*" Ramos yells. "God, you're a pain in the ass!"

But Ramos orders one of his men to take the *gomero* and keep him somewhere and find out what else he knows, and says, "For God's sake, don't let him talk to anyone or it will be *your* balls I stuff in his mouth."

Then Ramos looks at the bodies on the floor.

"And throw out the garbage," he says.

Adán Barrera hears Parada's radio message.

The bishop's familiar voice comes softly over the background chords of Hidalgo's rhythmic moans.

Then thunders the threat of excommunication.

"Superstitious shit," Güero says.

"This was a mistake," Adán says.

A blunder. An enormous miscalculation. The Americans have reacted even more extremely than he had feared, bringing all their enormous economic and political pressure to bear on Mexico City. The fucking Americans closed the border, leaving thousands of trucks stranded on the road, their loads of produce rotting in the sun, the economic cost staggering. And the Americans are threatening to call in loans, screwing Mexico with the IMF, launching a debt and currency crisis that could literally destroy the *peso*. So even our bought-and-paid-for friends in Mexico City are turning against us, and why not? The MJFP and DFS and the army are responding to the Americans' threats, rounding up every cartel member they can find, raiding houses and ranches . . . there's rumor that a DFS colonel beat a suspect to death and shot three others, so there's four Mexican lives already lost for this one American, but no one seems to care because they're only Mexicans.

So the kidnapping was an enormous mistake, compounded by the fact that, for all the cost, they haven't even learned the identity of Chupar.

The American clearly doesn't know.

He would have told. He could not have stood the bone-tickling, the electrodes, the iron bar. If he'd known, he would have told. And now he lies moaning in the bedroom that has become a torture chamber and even the Doctor has thrown his hands up and said he cannot get anything more, and the Yanquis and their *lambiosos* are tracking me down and even my old priest is sending me to hell.

Release the man and come back to God.

His freedom is your freedom.
Perhaps, Adán thinks.
You might be right.

Ernie Hidalgo exists now in a bipolar world.

There is pain, and there is the absence of pain, and that is all there is.

If life means pain, it's bad.

If death mean the absence of pain, it's good.

He tries to die. They keep him alive with saline drips. He tries to sleep. They keep him awake with injections of lidocaine. They monitor his heart, his pulse, his temperature, careful not to let him die and end the pain.

Always with the same questions: *Who is Chupar? What did he tell you? Whose names did he give you? Who in the government? Who is Chupar?*

Always the same answers: *I don't know. He didn't tell me anything I haven't told you. Nobody. I don't know.*

Followed by more pain, then careful nursing, then more pain.

Then a new question.

Out of the blue, a new question and a new word.

What is Cerberus? Have you heard of Cerberus? Did Chupar ever talk to you about Cerberus? What did he tell you?

I don't know. No, I haven't. No, he didn't. He didn't tell me anything. I swear to God. I swear to God. I swear to God.

What about Art? Did he ever talk to you about Cerberus? Did he ever mention Cerberus? Did you ever overhear him talking to anyone about Cerberus?

Cerberus, Cerberus, Cerberus . . .

You know the word, then.

No. I swear to God. I swear to God. God help me. God help me. Please, God, help me.

The Doctor leaves the room, leaves him alone with his pain. Leaves him wondering, Where is God, where is Arthur? Where are Jesus, Mother Mary and the Holy Ghost? Mary, bring me mercy.

Mercy comes, oddly enough, in the form of the Doctor.

It's Raúl who suggests it.

"Shit, that moaning is driving me fucking crazy," he says to the Doctor. "Can't you shut him up?"

"I could give him something."

"Give him something," Adán says. The moans are bothering him, too. And if they're planning to release him, as he wants to do, it would be better to deliver him in the best shape possible. Which isn't very good, but is better than dead. And Adán has an idea how to give the cop back and get what they want in return.

Reach out again to Arturo.

"Heroin?" the Doctor asks.

"You're the doctor," Raúl says.

Heroin, Adán thinks. Homegrown Mexican Mud. The irony is deft.

"Fix him up," he tells the Doctor.

Ernie feels the needle go into his arm. The familiar prick and burn, then something different—blessed relief.

The absence of pain.

Maybe not absence; say, detachment, as if he's floating on a cumulus cloud high above the pain. The observed and the observer. The pain is still there, but it's distant.

Eloi, eloi, thank you.

Mother Mary Mexican Mud.

Mmmmmmm . . .

Art's in the office with Ramos, poring over maps of Sinaloa and comparing them with intelligence reports on marijuana fields and Güero Méndez. Trying to somehow narrow down the grid. On television, an official from the Mexican attorney general's office is solemnly pronouncing, "In Mexico, the category of major drug gang does not exist."

"He could work for us," Art says.

Maybe the category of major drug gang doesn't exist in Mexico, Art thinks, but it sure as hell does in the United States. The second they got the news about Ernie's disappearance, Dantzler busted the cocaine shipment in two directions.

His sweep just missed Adán at his safe house in San Diego, but the bust was epic.

On the East Coast he hit pay dirt again, arresting one Jimmy "Big Peaches" Piccone, a *capo* in the Cimino Family. The FBI in New York passed along every surveillance photo of the crew they had, and Art's looking through them when he sees something that freezes his balls.

The photo is obviously taken outside some wise-guy hangout, and there's fat Jimmy Piccone and his equally obese little brother, and a few other goombahs, and then there's someone else standing there.

Sal Scachi.

Art gets on the phone to Dantzler.

"Yeah, that's Salvatore Scachi," Dantzler tells him. "A made man in the Cimino Family."

"In the Piccone crew?"

"Apparently, Scachi isn't in a crew," Dantzler says. "He's sort of a wise guy without a portfolio. He reports directly to Calabrese himself. And get this, Art—the guy was a full colonel in the U.S. Army."

God*damn,* Art thinks.

"There's something else, Art," Dantzler says. "This Piccone guy, Jimmy Peaches? FBI has had a tap on him for months. He's Chatty-fucking-Cathy. Been running his mouth about a lot of stuff."

"Coke?"

"Yup," Dantzler says. "And guns. Seems like his crew is heavy into selling off hijacked weapons."

Art is taking this in when another line rings and Shag jumps on it.

Then, sharply, "Art."

Art hangs up from Dantzler and gets on the other line.

"We need to talk," Adán says.

"How do I know you have him?"

"Inside his wedding ring. It's inscribed, *'Eres toda mi vida.' "*

You're my whole life.

"How do I know he's still alive?" Art asks.

"You want us to make him scream for you?"

"No!" Art says. "Name the place."

"The cathedral," Adán says. "Father Juan will guarantee safety for both of us. Art, I see one cop, your man is dead."

In the background, along with Ernie's groans, he hears something that gives him, if possible, worse chills.

"What do you know about Cerberus?"

Art kneels in the confessional.

The screen slides back. Art can't make out the face behind the screen, which, he supposes, is the point of this sacrilegious charade.

"We warned you and warned you and warned you," Adán says, "and you wouldn't listen."

"Is he alive?"

"He's alive," Adán says. "Now it's up to you to keep him alive."

"If he dies, I'll find you and kill you."

"Who is Chupar?"

Art's already thought this through—if he tells Adán that there is no Chupar, it's tantamount to putting a bullet in Ernie's head. He has to string it out. So he says, "You give me Hidalgo first."

"That's not going to happen."

Art's heart practically stops as he says, "I guess we have nothing to talk about, then."

He starts to get up. Then he hears Adán say, "You have to give me something, Art. Something I can take back."

Art kneels back down. Forgive me, Father, I'm about to sin.

"I'll shut down all operations against the Federación," he says. "I'll leave the country, resign from the DEA."

Because, what the hell, right? It's what everyone's been wanting him to do anyway—his bosses, his government, his own wife. If I can trade this vicious, stupid cycle for Ernie's life . . .

Adán asks, "You'll leave Mexico?"

"Yes."

"And leave our family alone?"

Now that you've crippled my daughter.

"Yes."

"How do I know you'll keep your word?"

"I swear to God."

"Not good enough."

No, it's not.

"I'll take the money," Arthur says. "You open an account for me, I'll make a withdrawal. Then you release Ernie. When he shows up, I'll give you the identity of Chupar."

"And leave."

"Not a second later than I need to, Adán."

Art waits for an eternity while Adán thinks it over. While he waits, he prays silently for both God and the devil to take this deal.

"A hundred thousand," Adán says, "will be wired to a numbered account in First Georgetown Bank, Grand Cayman. I'll phone you with the numbers. You will withdraw seventy by wire. As soon as we see the transaction, we'll let your man go. You will both be out of Mexico on the next flight. And Art, don't you *ever* come back."

The window slides shut.

The waves rise ominously, then break and crash on his body.

Waves of pain, larger with each set.

Ernie wants more drugs.

He hears the door open.

Are they coming with more drugs?

Or more pain?

Güero looks down at the American cop. The dozens of puncture wounds where the ice pick was inserted are pussy and infected. His face is bruised and swollen from the beatings. His wrists, feet and genitals are burned from the electrodes, his ass . . . The stench is horrendous—the infected wounds, the piss, the shit, the rancid sweat.

Clean him, Adán had ordered. And who is Adán Barrera to give orders? When I was killing men, he was selling blue jeans to teenyboppers. And now he comes back, having made a deal—without M-1's knowledge or permission—to release this man, in exchange for what? Empty promises from another American cop? Who is going to do what, Güero wonders, after he sees his tortured, mutilated comrade? Who is Adán kidding? Hidalgo will be lucky to survive the car ride. Even so, he will probably lose his legs, maybe his arms. What kind of peace does Adán think he will buy with this bleeding, stinking, rotting piece of flesh?

He squats beside Hidalgo and says, "We're going to take you home."

"Home?"

"*Sí,*" Güero says, "you can go home now. Go to sleep. When you wake up, you will be home."

He sticks the needle into Ernie's vein and pushes the plunger.

The Mexican Mud takes only a second to hit.

Ernie's body jerks and his legs kick back.

They say that a jolt of heroin is like kissing God.

Art looks at Ernie's naked corpse.

Lying fetal inside a sheet of black plastic in a ditch off a dirt road in Badiraguato. His dried blood is caked flat black against the shiny black plastic. The black blindfold is still around his eyes. Otherwise he's naked, and Art can see the open wounds where they jammed an ice pick through his flesh and scraped his bones, the electrode burns, the signs of anal rape, the needle marks from the lidocaine and heroin injections up and down his arms.

What have I done? Art asks himself. Why did someone else have to pay for my obsession?

I'm sorry, Ernie. I'm so goddamn sorry.

And I'll pay them back for you, so help me God.

There are cops—*federales* and Sinaloa State Police—everywhere. The state police arrived first and effectively trampled the scene, obscuring tire prints, footprints, fingerprints, any evidence that might tie anyone to the murder. Now the *federales* have assumed control and are going over everything again, making sure that not a shred of evidence has been neglected.

The *comandante* comes over to Art and says, "Don't worry, Señor, we will never rest until we find out who did this terrible thing."

"We know who did it," Art answers. "Miguel Ángel Barrera."

Shag Wallace loses it. "Goddamnit, three of your fucking guys kidnapped him!"

Art pulls him away. He's holding him up against the car when a jeep comes roaring up and Ramos hops out and trots over to Art.

Ramos says, "We found him."

"Who?"

"Barrera," says Ramos. "We have to go *now*."

"Where is he?"

"El Salvador."

"How did—"

"Apparently, M-1's little girlfriend is homesick," Ramos says. "She called Mommy and Daddy."

El Salvador
February 1985

El Salvador, "The Savior," is a little country about the size of Massachusetts located on the Pacific coast of the Central American isthmus. It's not, Art knows, a banana republic like its eastern neighbor Honduras, but a coffee republic, whose workers have such a reputation for industriousness that they were nicknamed "the Germans of Central America."

The hard work hasn't done them much good. The so-called Forty Families, about 2 percent of the current population of three and a half million, have always owned almost all the fertile land, mostly in the form of large coffee *fincas*—plantations. The more land that was devoted to growing coffee meant less land devoted to growing food, and by the mid–nineteenth century most of the hardworking Salvadoran *campesinos* were basically starving.

Art looks at the green countryside. It looks so peaceful—pretty, really—from the air, but he knows that it's a killing ground.

The serious slaughter started in the 1980s as *campesinos* started to flock into the FLMN, the Martí National Liberation Front, or into workers' unions, while students and priests led the movement for labor and land reform. The Forty Families responded by forming a right-wing militia called ORDEN—

the Spanish acronym means "order"—and the order they had in mind was the same old order.

ORDEN, most of its members active-duty Salvadoran army officers, got right to work. *Campesinos,* workers, students and priests started disappearing, their bodies finally turning up on roadsides or their heads left in school playgrounds as a civics lesson.

The United States, pursuing its Cold War agenda, pitched in. Many of the ORDEN officers were trained at the U.S. School of the Americas. To hunt down FLMN guerrillas and farmers, students and priests, the Salvadoran army had the help of American-donated Bell helicopters, C-47 transport planes, M-16 rifles and M-60 machine guns. They killed a lot of the guerrillas, but also hundreds of students, teachers, farmers, factory workers and priests.

Nor were the FLMN exactly angels, Art thinks. They committed their own murders, and funded themselves through kidnappings. But their efforts paled in comparison to the well-organized, amply funded Salvadoran army and its ORDEN doppelgänger.

Seventy-five thousand deaths, Art thinks as his plane lands in a country that has become its own mass grave. A million refugees, another million homeless. Out of a population of only five and a half million.

The Sheraton lobby is gleaming and clean.

The well-dressed and the well-heeled relax in its air-conditioned lounge or sit in the cool, dark bar. Everyone is so clean and so nicely dressed—in cool linens and the white dresses and jackets of the tropics.

It's all so *nice* in here, Art thinks. And so American.

There are Americans everywhere, drinking beer at the bar, sipping Cokes in the coffee shop, and most of them are military advisers. They're in civvies, but the military look is unmistakable—the short sidewall haircuts, the short-sleeved polo shirts, the jeans over tennis shoes or highly polished brown army-issue.

Ever since the Sandinistas took over Nicaragua, just to the south, El Salvador has become an American military ghetto. Ostensibly, the Americans are there to advise the Salvadoran army in their war against the FLMN guerrillas, but they're also there to make sure that El Salvador doesn't become the next domino to topple in Central America. So you have American soldiers advising the Salvadorans and American soldiers advising the Contras, and then you have the spooks.

The Company types are as obvious in their own way as the off-duty soldiers are in theirs. They dress better, for one thing—they wear tailored suits with open shirts and no ties instead of sports clothes that came off the rack at the base commissary. Their haircuts are stylish—even a little long, in the current Latin American fashion—and their shoes are expensive Churchills and Bancrofts. If you see a spook wearing tennis shoes, Art thinks, he's playing tennis.

So there are the soldiers and the spooks and then there are the embassy types—who might be neither, either or both. There are the actual diplomats and the consular officials who deal with the daily, mundane issues of visas and lost passports and American retro-hippie kids arrested for vagrancy and/or drug use. Then there are the cultural attachés, and the secretaries and the typists; and then there are the military attachés, who look just like the military advisers except that they dress better; and then there are the embassy employees, who wear fictional job descriptions as transparent veils of decency, and who are really spooks. They sit in the embassy and monitor radio broadcasts out of Managua, their ears keenly pitched for the sound of a Cuban accent or, better yet, Russian. Or they work "the street," as they say, meeting their sources in exactly such places as the Sheraton bar, trying to suss out which colonel is on the way up, which is on the way out, which might be planning the next *golpe*—coup—and whether this would be a good thing or a bad thing.

So you have your soldiers, your spooks, your embassy types and your embassy spooks, and then you have your businessmen.

Coffee buyers, cotton buyers, sugar buyers.

The coffee buyers look like they belong. They should, Art thinks. Their families have been down here for generations. They have the easy air of ownership of the place—this is their bar, theirs and the Salvadoran growers with whom they're having lunch on the broad patio. The cotton and sugar buyers look more classically American corporate—these are more recent crops on the Salvadoran landscape—and the American buyers have yet to blend in. They look uncomfortable, incomplete without ties.

So you have a lot of Americans, and you have a lot of wealthy Salvadorans, and the only other Salvadorans you see are either hotel workers or secret police.

Secret police, Art thinks. Now there's an oxymoron. The only thing secret about the secret police is how they manage to stand out so much. Art stands in the lobby and picks them out like bulbs on a Christmas tree. It's simple—their cheap suits are bad imitations of the expensive tailored look of the upper class. And while they try to look like businessmen, they still have the brown, weathered faces of *campesinos*. No *ladino* from the Forty Families is going to enroll in the ranks of the police, secret or otherwise, so these guys assigned to monitor the comings and goings at the Sheraton still look like farmers attending a city cousin's wedding.

But, Art knows, the role of the secret police in a society like this isn't to blend in but to be seen. To be noticed. To let everyone know that Big Brother *is* watching.

And taking notes.

Ramos finds the cop he's looking for. They repair to a room and start the negotiations. An hour later he and Art are on their way to the compound where Tío is holed up with his Lolita.

The drive out of San Salvador is long, frightening and sad. El Salvador has the highest population density in Central America, growing every day, and Art sees the evidence everywhere. Little shanty villages seem to occupy every wide spot in the road—jerry-rigged stalls made of cardboard, corrugated tin, plywood, or just plain chopped brush offer everything for sale to people who have little or nothing with which to buy. Their owners rush the jeep when they see the gringo in the front seat. The kids push up against the jeep, asking for food, money, anything.

Art keeps driving.

He has to get to the compound before Tío disappears again.

People disappear in El Salvador all the time.

Sometimes at the rate of a couple hundred a week. Snatched by right-wing death squads, and then they're just gone. And if anyone asks too many questions about it, he disappears, too.

All Third World slums are the same, Art thinks—the same mud or dust, depending on the climate and the season, the same smells of charcoal stoves and open sewers, the same heartbreakingly monotonous scenery of malnourished kids with distended bellies and big eyes.

It's sure as hell not Guadalajara, where a large and generally prosperous middle class softens the slope between rich and poor. Not in San Salvador, he thinks, where the shanty slums press against gleaming high-rises like the thatched huts of medieval peasants pressed against castle walls. Except these castle walls are patrolled by private security guards wielding automatic rifles and machine pistols. And at night, the guards venture out from the castle walls and ride through the villages—in jeeps instead of on horseback—and slaughter the peasants, leaving their bodies at crossroads and in the middle of village squares, and rape and kill women and execute children in front of their parents.

So the survivors will know their place.

It's a killing ground, Art thinks.

El Salvador.

The Savior, my ass.

. . .

The compound sits in a grove of palm trees a hundred yards from the beach.

A stone wall topped by barbed wire surrounds the main house, the garage and the servants' quarters. A thick wooden gate and a guard shack block the driveway from the private road.

Art and Ramos crouch behind the wall thirty yards from the gate.

Hiding from the full moon.

A dozen Salvadoran commandos are posted at intervals around the wall's perimeter.

It's taken frantic hours of negotiation to procure Salvadoran cooperation, but now the deal is in place: They can go in and get Barrera, whisk him to the U.S. Embassy, fly him out on a State Department jet to New Orleans and charge him there with first-degree murder and conspiracy to distribute narcotics.

A cowed real-estate agent has been hauled out of bed and taken to his office, where he gives the commando team a diagram of the compound. The shaken man is being held incommunicado until the raid is over. Art and Ramos pore over the diagram and come up with an operational plan. But it all has to be done quickly, before Barrera's protectors in the Mexican government can get wind of it and interfere; and it has to be done cleanly—no fuss, no muss and above all no Salvadoran casualties.

Art checks his watch—4:57 a.m.

Three minutes until H hour.

A breeze wafts the scent of jacaranda from the compound, reminding Art of Guadalajara. He can see the tops of the trees over the wall, their purple leaves shimmering silver in the bright moonlight. On the other side, he hears the waves lap softly on the beach.

A perfect lovers' idyll, he thinks.

A perfumed garden.

Paradise.

Well, let's hope Paradise is about to be lost for good this time, he thinks. Let's hope Tío is sleeping soundly, sexually drugged into a postcoital stupor from which he can be rudely awakened. Art has an admittedly vulgar image of Tío being dragged bare-assed into the waiting van. The more humiliation the better.

He hears footsteps, then sees one of the compound's private security guards headed toward him, casually flashing a light along the wall, looking for any lurking burglars. Art slowly scrunches his body closer to the wall.

The flashlight beam hits him square in the eyes.

The guard reaches for his holstered pistol, then a cloth garrote slips around his neck and Ramos is lifting him off the ground. The guard's eyes bulge and his tongue comes out of his mouth, and then Ramos eases the unconscious man to the ground.

"He'll be okay," Ramos says.

Thank God, Art thinks, because a dead civilian would screw up the whole delicate deal. He looks at his watch as it hits five, and the commandos must be a crack unit because at that precise second Art hears a dull *whomp* as an explosive charge blows the gate of the wall.

Ramos looks at Art. "Your gun."

"What?"

"Better to have your gun in your hand."

Art had forgotten he even had the damn thing. He pulls it from his shoulder holster and now he's running behind Ramos, through the blown gate and into the garden. Past the servants' quarters, where the frightened workers lie on the ground, a commando pointing an M-16 at them. As Art runs toward the main house he tries to remember the diagram, but as the adrenaline flows in, his memory flows out, and then he thinks, Screw it, and just follows Ramos, who trots at a quick but easy pace in front of him, Esposa swinging on his hip.

Art glances up at the wall, where black-clad commando snipers perch like crows, their rifles trained on the compound's grounds, ready to mow down anyone who tries to run out. Then, suddenly, he's at the front of the main house and Ramos grabs him and shoves him down as there's another bass thump, and the sound of wood splintering as the front door flies off.

Ramos looses half a clip into the empty space.

Then he steps in.

Art enters behind him.

Trying to remember—the bedroom, where is the bedroom?

Pilar sits up and shouts as they come through the door.

Pulls the sheet up over her breasts and screams again.

Tío—and Art can't quite believe this, it's all too surreal—is actually hiding under the covers. He's pulled the sheets up over his head like a small child who thinks, *If I can't see them they can't see me,* but Art can most definitely see him. Art is all adrenaline—he yanks off the sheet, grabs Tío by the back of the neck, jerks him up like a barbell and then slams him face-first onto the parquet wood floor.

Tío isn't bare-assed, but wearing black silk boxer shorts, which Art can feel slide along his leg as he plants his knee into the small of Tío's back, grabs his chin and lifts his head back far enough so that his neck threatens to snap, then jams the pistol barrel into his right temple.

"Don't hurt him!" Pilar screams. "I didn't want you to *hurt* him!"

Tío wrenches his chin from Art's hold and cranes his neck to stare at the girl. Pure hatred as he pronounces a single word: *"Chocho."*

Cunt.

The girl turns pale and looks terrified.

Art pushes Tío's face to the floor. Blood from Tío's broken nose flows across the polished wood.

Ramos says, "Come on, we have to hurry."

Art starts to pull the handcuffs from his belt.

"Don't cuff him," Ramos says with undisguised irritation.

Art blinks.

Then he gets it—you don't shoot a man who's trying to escape if the man is handcuffed.

Ramos asks, "Do you want to do him in here or out there?"

That's what he expects me to do, Art thinks, shoot Barrera. That's why he thinks I insisted on coming along on the raid, so I could do just that. His head whirls as he realizes that maybe everybody expects him to do that. All the DEA guys, Shag—especially Shag—expect him to enforce the old code that you don't bring a cop killer back to the house, that a cop killer always dies trying to escape.

Christ, do they expect that?

Tío sure does. Says smoothly, calmly, tauntingly, *"Me maravilla que todavía estoy vivo."*

I'm amazed I'm still alive.

Well, don't be too amazed, Art thinks as he pulls the hammer back.

"Date prisa," Ramos says.

Hurry up.

Art looks up at him—Ramos is lighting a cigar. Two commandos are looking down at him, waiting impatiently, wondering why the soft gringo hasn't already done what should be done.

So the whole plan to bring Tío back to the embassy was a sham, Art thinks. A charade to satisfy the diplomats. I can pull the trigger and everyone will swear that Barrera resisted arrest. He was pulling a gun. I had to shoot him. And nobody's going to look too closely at the forensics, either.

"Date prisa."

Except this time, it's Tío saying it, and he sounds annoyed, almost bored.

"Date prisa, sobrino."

Hurry up, nephew.

Art grabs him by the hair and yanks his head up.

Art remembers Ernie's mutilated body lying in the ditch bearing the marks of his torture.

He lowers his mouth to Tío's ear and whispers, *"Vete al demonio, Tío."*

Go to hell, Uncle.

"I'll meet you there," Tío answers. "It was supposed to have been *you,* Arturo. But I talked them into taking Hidalgo instead, for old times' sake. Unlike you, I honor relationships. Ernie Hidalgo died for you. Now do it. Be a man."

Art squeezes the trigger. It's hard, it takes more pressure than he remembers.

Tío grins at him.

Art feels the presence of pure evil.

The power of the dog.

He jerks Tío to his feet.

Barrera smiles at him with utter contempt.

"What are you doing?" Ramos asks.

"What we planned." He holsters his pistol, then cuffs Tío's hands behind his back. "Let's get going."

"I'll do it," Ramos says. "If you're squeamish."

"I'm not," Art says. *"Vámonos."*

One of the commandos starts to slip a black hood over Tío's head. Art stops him, then gets into Tío's face and says, "Lethal injection or the gas chamber, Tío. Be thinking about it."

Tío just smiles at him.

Smiles at him.

"Hood him," Art orders.

The commando pulls the black hood over Tío's head and ties it at the bottom. Art grabs his pinioned arms and marches him outside.

Through the perfumed garden.

Where, Art thinks, the jacarandas have never smelled so sweet. Sweet and sickly, Art thinks to himself, like the incense he remembers from church as a kid. The first scent of it was pleasant; the next would make him feel a little sick.

That's how he feels now as he frog-marches Tío through the compound toward the van waiting in the street, except the van isn't waiting anymore, and about twenty rifle barrels are pointed at him.

Not at Tío.

At Art Keller.

They're Salvadoran regular army troops, and, with them, a Yanqui in civilian clothes and shiny black shoes.

Sal Scachi.

"Keller, I told you the next time I'd just shoot."

Art looks around and sees snipers perched on the walls.

"There was a little difference of opinion within the Salvadoran government," Scachi says. "We got it worked out. Sorry, kid, but we can't let you have him."

As Art wonders who "we" are, Scachi nods and two Salvadoran soldiers take the hood off Tío's head. No wonder he was fucking smiling, Art thinks. He knew the cavalry couldn't be far off.

Some other soldiers bring Pilar out. She wears a negligee now, but it accents more than it hides and the soldiers gape at her openly. As they walk her past Tío, she sobs, "I'm sorry!"

Tío spits in her face. The soldiers have her hands behind her back and she can't wipe it off, so the saliva runs down her cheek.

"I won't forget this," Tío says.

The soldiers march Pilar to a waiting van.

Tío turns to Art. "I won't forget you, either."

"All right, all right," Scachi says. "Nobody's forgetting anybody. Don Miguel, let's get you into some real clothes and out of here. As for you, Keller, and you, Ramos, the local police would like to throw you both in prison, but we talked them into deportation instead. There are military flights waiting. So, if this little pajama party is over . . ."

"Cerberus," Art says.

Scachi grabs him and hauls him off to the side.

"The fuck did you say?"

"Cerberus," Art answers. He thinks he's figured it all out now. "Ilopongo Airport, Sal? Hangar Four?"

Scachi stares at him, then says, "Keller, you just earned first-ballot entry into the Asshole Hall of Fame."

Five minutes later Art's in the front seat of a jeep.

"I swear to Christ," Scachi says as he drives, "if it was up to me, I'd put one in the back of your head right now."

Ilopongo's a busy airfield. Military aircraft, helicopters and transport planes are everywhere, along with the personnel needed to maintain them.

Sal steers the jeep to a series of large Quonset-hut-type hangars, with signs on the front designating them numbers 1 through 10. The door of Hangar 4 slides open and Sal drives inside.

The door closes behind him.

The hangar is bustling. A couple dozen men, some in fatigues, some in cammies, all armed, are unloading cargo from a SETCO plane. Three other men are standing around talking. It's been Art's experience that any time you see a bunch of men working and other men standing around talking, the ones talking are the ones in charge.

He can see one of their faces.

David Núñez. Ramón Mette's partner in SETCO, Cuban expatriate, Operation 40 veteran.

Núñez breaks off the conversation and walks over to where the crates are being stacked. He barks an order and one of the worker bees opens a crate. Art watches Núñez lift a grenade launcher out of the crate like it's a religious idol. Bitter men handle weapons differently than the rest of us, he thinks. The guns seem connected to them in a visceral way, as if a wire runs from the trigger through their dicks and to their hearts. And Núñez has *that* look in his eye—he's in love with the weapon. He left his balls and his heart on the beach in the Bay of Pigs, and the weapon represents his hope of retribution.

It's the old Cuba–Miami–Mafia drug connection, Art realizes, hooked up again and flying coke from Colombia to Central America to Mexico to Mafia dealers in the United States. And the Mafia pays in armaments, which go to the Contras.

The Mexican Trampoline.

Sal hops out of the jeep and goes up to a young American who has to be a military officer in mufti.

I know that guy, Art thinks. But from where? Who is he?

Then the memory comes back. Shit, I *should* know that guy—I did night ambushes with him in Vietnam, Operation Phoenix. What the hell is his name? He was Special Forces back then, a captain . . . Craig, that's it.

Scott Craig.

Shit, Hobbs has the old team here.

Art watches Scachi and Craig talking, pointing to him. He smiles and waves. Craig gets on the radio and there's another confab. Behind him, Art can see packages of cocaine stacked to the ceiling.

Scachi and Craig walk over to him.

"This what you wanted to see, Art?" Scachi asks. "You happy now?"

"Yeah, I'm fucking thrilled to death."

"You shouldn't joke," Scachi says.

Craig's giving him the bad look.

It isn't working. He looks like a Boy Scout, Art thinks. Boyish face, short hair, clean-cut good looks. An Eagle Scout going for his Dope for Guns Badge.

"The question is," Craig says to Art, "are you going to be a team player?"

Well, it would be the first time, wouldn't it? Art thinks.

Scachi's apparently thinking the same thing. "Keller's got a reputation as a cowboy," he says. "Out on the lone prairieee . . ."

"Bad place to be," Craig says.

"Lonely, shallow grave," Scachi adds.

"I've left a full account of everything I know in a safe-deposit box," Art lies. "Anything happens to me, it goes to *The Washington Post*."

"You're bluffing, Art," Scachi says.

"You want to find out?"

Scachi walks away and gets on the radio. Comes back a little later and snaps an order: "Hood the motherfucker."

Art knows he's in the back of an open car, probably a jeep, from the bouncy action. He knows he's moving. He knows that wherever they're taking him, it's a long way away because it feels like they've been traveling for hours. It feels like that, anyway, but he doesn't really know because he can't see his watch, or anything else, and now he understands the terrifying, disorienting effect of being hooded. The floating, fearful sensation of not being able to see but being able to hear, and each sound a stimulus for a progressively frightened imagination.

The jeep stops and Art waits to hear the metallic scrape of a rifle bolt or the click of a pistol hammer being pulled back or, worse, the *whoosh* of a machete slicing first through the air and then—

He feels the gears shift and the jeep lurches forward again and now he starts to tremble. His legs twitch uncontrollably and he can't stop them, nor can he stop his mind from producing images of Ernie's tortured corpse. He can't stop the thought Don't let them do to me what they did to Ernie, or its logical corollary, Better him than me.

He feels ashamed, wretched, coming to the realization that when push comes to shove, when the terrible reality is at hand, he really would have them do it to someone else rather than himself—he *wouldn't* take Ernie's place if he could.

He tries to remember the Act of Contrition, recalling what the nuns taught him in elementary school—if you're about to die and there's no priest to give you absolution, if you say a sincere Act of Contrition you can still go to heaven. He remembers that; what he can't remember is the goddamn prayer itself.

The jeep stops.

The motor idles.

Hands grab Art above the elbows and lift him out of the jeep. He can feel leaves under his feet; he trips over a vine but the arms won't let him fall. He realizes that they're taking him into the jungle. Then the hands push him down to his knees. It doesn't take much force—his legs feel like water.

"Take off the hood."

Art knows the voice giving the crisp order. John Hobbs, the CIA station chief.

They're at some kind of military base, a training camp by the looks of it, deep in the jungle. To his right, young soldiers in cammies are running an obstacle course—badly. To his left he sees a small airstrip that has been carved out of the jungle. Straight ahead of him, Hobbs's small, tidy face comes into focus—the thick white hair, the bright blue eyes, the disdainful smile.

"And take off the handcuffs."

Art feels the circulation come back into his wrists. Then the burning pins-and-needles sensation as it does. Hobbs gestures for him to follow and they go into a tent with a couple of canvas chairs, a table and a cot.

"Sit down, Arthur."

"I'd like to stand for a while."

Hobbs shrugs. "Arthur, you need to understand that if you weren't 'family,' you would have been disposed of already. Now, what's this nonsense about a safe-deposit box?"

Now Art knows he was right, that his last-gasp Hail Mary had hit the target—if the cocaine-running out of Hangar 4 was just the work of renegades, they would have capped him back on the road. He repeats the threat he made to Scachi.

Hobbs stares at him, then asks, "What do you know about Red Mist?"

What the hell is Red Mist? Art wonders.

Art says, "Look, I only know about Cerberus. And what I know is enough to sink you."

"I agree with your analysis," Hobbs says. "Now, where does that leave us?"

"With our jaws clamped on each other's throats," Art says. "And neither of us can let go."

"Let's go for a walk."

They hike through the camp, past the obstacle course, the shooting range, the clearings in the jungle where cammie-clad soldiers sit on the ground and listen to instructors teach ambush tactics.

"Everything in the training camp," Hobbs says, "was paid for by Miguel Ángel Barrera."

"Jesus."

"Barrera understands."

"Understands what?"

Hobbs leads him up a steep trail to the top of a hill. Hobbs points out over the vast jungle stretching below.

"What does that look like to you?" he asks.

Art shrugs. "Rain forest."

"To me," Hobbs says, "it looks like a camel's nose. You know the old Arab proverb: Once the camel gets his nose inside the tent, the camel will be inside the tent. That's Nicaragua down there, the Communist camel's nose in the tent of the Central American isthmus. Not an island like Cuba, that we can isolate with our navy, but part of the American mainland. How's your geography?"

"Passable."

"Then you'll know," Hobbs says, "that Nicaragua's southern border—which we're looking at—is a scant three hundred miles from the Panama Canal. It shares a northern border with an unstable Honduras and a less-stable El Salvador, both of which are struggling against Communist insurgencies. So is Guatemala, which would be the next domino to fall. If you're up on your geography, you'll know that there is very little but mountainous jungle and rain forest between Guatemala and the southern Mexican states of Yucatán, Quintana Roo and Chiapas. Those states are overwhelmingly rural and poor, populated by landless helots who are perfect victims for a Communist insurgency. What if Mexico falls to the Communists, Arthur? Cuba is dangerous enough—now imagine a two-thousand-mile border with a Russian satellite country. Imagine Soviet missiles based in hardened silos in Jalisco, Durango, Baja."

"So what, they take Texas next?"

"No, they take Western Europe," Hobbs says, "because they know—and it's the truth—that even the United States doesn't have the military or financial resources to defend a two-thousand-mile border with Mexico and the Fulda Gap at the same time."

"This is crazy."

"Is it?" Hobbs asks. "The Nicaraguans are already exporting arms across the border to the FLMN in El Salvador. But don't even take it that far. Just consider Nicaragua, a Soviet client state that straddles Central America. Imagine Soviet subs based on the Pacific side from the Gulf of Fonseca, or on the Atlantic side along the Gulf of Mexico. They could turn the Gulf and the Caribbean into a Soviet lake. Consider this: If you think it was hard for us to spot missile silos in Cuba, try detecting them in those mountains, over there in the Cordillera Isabelia. Intermediate-range missiles could easily reach Miami, New Orleans or Houston with very little response time available to us. That's not to mention the threat of submarine-launched missiles striking from somewhere in the Gulf or the Caribbean. We cannot allow a Soviet client state to remain in Nicaragua. It's that simple. The Contras are willing to do the job, or would you rather see American boys fighting and dying in that jungle, Arthur? Those are your choices."

"That's what you want me to choose? Dope-pushing Contras? Cuban terrorists? Salvadoran death squads that murder women, kids, priests and nuns?"

"They're brutal, vicious and evil," Hobbs says. "The only worse people I can think of are the Communists.

"Look at the globe," Hobbs continues. "We ran away in Vietnam, and the Communists learned exactly the right lesson from that. They took Cambodia in the blink of an eye. We did nothing. They marched on Afghanistan, and we did nothing except pull some athletes out of a track meet. So it's Afghanistan, next it's Pakistan and then it's India. And then it's *done,* Arthur—the entire Asian landmass is red. You have Soviet client states in Mozambique, Angola, Ethiopia, Iraq and Syria. And we do nothing and nothing and nothing, so they think, *Fine, let's see if they do nothing in Central America.* So they take Nicaragua, and how do we respond? The Boland Amendment."

"It's the law."

"It's suicide," Hobbs says. "Only a fool or Congress couldn't see the folly of allowing a Soviet puppet to remain in the heart of Central America. The stupidity beggars description. We had to do something, Arthur."

"So the CIA takes it upon itself to—"

"The CIA took nothing on itself," Hobbs says. "This is what I'm trying to tell you, Arthur. Cerberus comes from the highest possible authority in the land."

"Ronald Reagan—"

"—is Churchill," Hobbs says. "At a critical moment in history, he has seen the truth for what it is and has had the resolve to act."

"Are you telling me—"

"He doesn't know any of the details, of course," Hobbs says. "He simply ordered us to reverse the tide in Central America and overthrow the Sandinistas by *whatever means necessary.* I'll read chapter and verse to you, Arthur—National Security Department Directive Number Three authorizes the vice president to take charge of activities against Communist terrorists operating anywhere in Latin America. In response, the vice president formed TIWG—the Terrorist Incident Working Group—based in El Salvador, Honduras and Costa Rica, which in turn instituted the NHAO—the National Humanitarian Assistance Operation—which, in accordance with the Boland Amendment, is meant to provide nonlethal 'humanitarian' aid to Nicaraguan refugees, aka the Contras. Operation Cerberus doesn't run through the Company—that's where you're wrong—but through the VP's office. Scachi reports directly to me, and I report to the VP."

"Why are you telling me this?"

"I'm appealing to your patriotism," Hobbs says.

"The country I love doesn't get in bed with people who torture its own agents to death."

"Then to your pragmatism," Hobbs says. He takes some documents out of his pocket. "Bank records. Deposits made to your accounts in the Caymans, Costa Rica, Panama . . . all from Miguel Ángel Barrera."

"I don't know anything about that."

"Withdrawal slips," Hobbs says, "with your signature."

"It was a deal I had to make."

"The lesser of two evils. Exactly," Hobbs says. "I understand the dilemma completely. Now I'm asking you to understand ours. You keep our secrets, we keep yours."

"Fuck you."

Art turns and starts to walk back down the trail.

"Keller, if you think we're just going to let you walk out of here—"

Art holds up his middle finger and keeps walking away.

"There must be some sort of arrangement—"

Art shakes his head. They can take their domino theory, he thinks, and shove it sideways. What could Hobbs offer me that would make up for Ernie?

Nothing.

There is nothing in this world. Nothing you can offer a man who's lost everything—his family, his work, his friend, his hope, his trust, his belief in his own country. There's nothing you can offer that man that means anything.

But it turns out there is.

Then Art understands—Cerberus isn't a guard, he's an usher. A panting, grinning, tongue-lolling doorman who eagerly invites you into the underworld.

And you can't resist.

6

The Lowest
Bottom Shook

. . . and every bolt and bar
Of massy iron or solid rock with ease
Unfastens: on a sudden open fly,
With impetuous recoil and jarring sound,
Th' infernal doors, and on their hinges grate
Harsh thunder, that the lowest bottom shook
Of Erebus.

—John Milton, *Paradise Lost*

Mexico City
September 19, 1985

The bed shakes.

The shaking merges into her dream, then her waking thoughts: The bed is shaking.

Nora sits up in bed and looks at the clock but has a hard time focusing on the digital numbers because they seem to be vibrating, almost liquefying, in front of her eyes. She reaches over to steady the clock—it's 8:18 in the morning. Then she realizes that it's the side table that's shaking, that everything is—the table, the lamps, the chair, the bed.

She's in a room on the seventh floor of the Regis Hotel, the gracious old landmark on Avenida Juárez near La Alameda Park in the heart of the city. The guest of a cabinet minister, she was brought down to help him celebrate Independence Day, and she's still here three days later. The minister goes home to his wife in the evenings. In the afternoons he comes to the Regis to celebrate his independence.

Nora thinks she might still be asleep, still dreaming, because now the walls are pulsing.

Am I sick? she wonders. She does feels dizzy, nauseated, all the more so when she gets out of bed and can't walk or even stand, as the floor seems to be rolling beneath her.

She looks over to the large wall mirror across from the bed, but her face doesn't look pale. It's just that her head keeps moving around in the mirror, and then the mirror bows and shatters.

She throws her arm up in front of her eyes and feels little shards of glass hit her. Then she hears the sound of a hard rain, but it isn't rain—it's debris falling from the higher floors. Then the floor seems to slide like one of those metal plates in a funhouse, but this isn't fun—it's terrifying.

She'd be more terrified if she could see outside the building. See it literally waving, see the top of the hotel bend and sway and actually smack the top of the building next door. She hears it, though. Hears the wicked, dull crack, then the wall behind the bed falls in and she opens the door and runs into the hallway.

Outside, Mexico City is shaking to death.

The city is built on an old lake bed, soft soil, which in turns sits on the large Cocos Tectonic Plate, which is constantly shifting under the Mexican landmass. The city and its soft, loose foundation sit just two hundred miles from the edge of the plate, and one of the world's largest faults, the giant Middle American Trench, which runs under the Pacific Ocean from the Mexican resort town of Puerto Vallarta all the way to Panama.

For years there have been small quakes along the northern and southern edges of this plate, but not near the center, not near Mexico City, which the scientists refer to as a "seismic gap." The geologists compare it to a string of firecrackers that have exploded along both ends but not in the center. They say that sooner or later, the center has to catch fire and explode.

The trouble starts about thirty kilometers beneath the earth's surface. For countless eons the Cocos Plate has been trying to sink, to slide under the plate to the east of it, and on this morning it succeeds. Forty miles off the coast, 240 miles west of Mexico City, the earth cracks, sending a giant quake through the lithosphere.

If the city had been closer to this epicenter, it might have held up better. The high-rise buildings might have survived the high-frequency, rapid jolting that happens near the actual quake. The buildings might have jumped and landed and cracked, but held up.

But as the quake moves from the center its energy dissipates, which, counterintuitively, makes it more dangerous because of that soft soil. The quake fades into long, slow rolling motions—a set of giant waves, if you will, that get under that soft lake bed, that bowl of Jell-O the city is built on—and that Jell-O just rolls, rolling the buildings with it, shaking the buildings not so much vertically as horizontally, and that's the problem.

Each floor of the high-rises moves farther sideways than the floor below. The now top-heavy buildings literally slide out into the air, knock heads and slide back again. For two long minutes the tops of these buildings slide sideways, back and forth in the air, and then they just break.

Concrete blocks fall off and tumble down onto the street. Windows burst; huge, jagged pieces of glass fly into the air like missiles. Interior walls collapse, support beams with them. Rooftop swimming pools crack, sending tons of water to collapse the roofs beneath them.

Some buildings just snap off at the fourth or fifth floors, sending two, three, eight, *twelve* stories of stone, concrete and steel slamming into the street below, thousands of people falling with them, buried under them.

Building after building—250 of them in four minutes—collapses in the quake. The government literally falls—the Secretariat of the Navy, the Secretariat of Commerce and the Secretariat of Communications all topple. The city's tourist center reads like a roll of casualties, name after name—the Hotel Monte Carlo, the Hotel Romano, the Hotel Versailles, the Roma, the Bristol, the Ejecutivo, the Palacio, the Reforma, the Inter-Continental and the Regis all go down. The top half of the Hotel Caribe snaps off like a stick, dumping mattresses, luggage, curtains and guests through the crack and onto the street. Whole neighborhoods virtually disappear—Colonia Roma, Colonia Doctores, Unidad Aragón and the Tlatelolco Housing Project, where a twenty-story apartment tower collapses on its occupants. In a particularly cruel twist, the quake destroys the General Hospital of Mexico and the Juárez Hospital, killing and trapping patients and desperately needed doctors and nurses.

Nora doesn't know any of this. She runs into the hallway, where room doors that have fallen in look like cards in a sophisticated house of cards that has started to collapse. A woman runs ahead of her and presses for the elevator.

"No!" Nora yells.

The woman turns and looks at her, wide-eyed with fear.

"Don't take the elevator," Nora says. "Take the stairs."

The woman stares at her.

Nora tries to remember the words in Spanish, but can't.

Then the elevator doors slide open and water pours out, like a scene from a bad, grotesque horror film. The woman turns around, looks at Nora, laughs and says, *"Agua."*

"Vámos," Nora says. *"Vámonos,* whatever. Let's go. Come on."

She grabs the woman by the hand to try to pull her down the hall but the woman won't budge. She yanks her hand back and starts to press the elevator's Down button again and again.

Nora leaves her and finds the exit door to the stairwell. The floor ripples and rolls under her feet. She gets into the stairway and it's like being in a long, swaying box. The force knocks her from side to side as she runs down the stairs. There are people in front of her now, and behind; the stairwell is getting crowded. Sounds, horrible sounds, echo in the confined space: cracking, breaking, the noises of a building tearing itself apart—and screams—women's screams and, worse, the shrill keening of children. She grabs on to the handrail to steady herself, but it's moving, too.

One floor, two, she tries to count by the landings, then gives up. Is it three floors, four, five? She knows she has to go seven. Idiotically, she can't remember how they number their floors in Mexico. Do they start on ground and go first, second? Or is the ground floor the first, then second, third, fourth . . . ?

What does it matter? Just keep moving, she tells herself, then an awful lurch, like a ship rolling, slams her into the left wall. She keeps her balance, gets her feet under her again. Just keep moving, just keep moving, get out of this building before it comes down on top of you. Just keep going down these stairs.

She thinks, oddly, of the steep stairs going down from Montmartre through the Place Willette, how some people take the cable car but she always takes the steps because it's good for her calves but also because she just enjoys it, and if she walks instead of rides it justifies a *chocolat chaud* at that pretty café at the bottom. And I want to go back there again, she thinks, I want to sit at a sidewalk table again and have the waiter smile at me and watch the people, see the funny cathedral, the Basilique du Sacré Coeur at the top, the one that looks like it was made from spun sugar.

Think about that, think about that, don't think about dying in this trap, this crowded, swaying, rolling deathtrap. God, it's getting hot in here, God, stop screaming, it doesn't do any good, *shut up,* there's a breath of air, now people are jammed in front of her and then the jam breaks up and she moves behind the people in the lobby.

Chandeliers drop from the ceiling like rotten fruit from a shaken tree, falling and shattering on the old tile floor. She steps over the broken glass toward the revolving doors. So jammed—she waits her turn—she gets in. No need to push, it's being more than pushed from behind. She gets a scent of air—wonderful air, she sees dim sunlight, she's almost out—

Then the building comes down on her.

He's saying Mass when it hits.

Ten miles from the epicenter, in the Cathedral of Ciudad Guzmán, Archbishop Parada holds the host above his head and offers a prayer to God. It's one of the perks and privileges of being archbishop of the Guadalajara Archdiocese, that he gets to come out here to say the occasional Mass in the little town. He loves the cathedral's classic churrigueresque architecture, Mexico's unique adaptation of the European Gothic into the pagan Aztec and Mayan. The cathedral's two Gothic towers are rounded into pre-Columbian polyforms, flanking a dome decorated with a panoply of multicolored tiles. Even now, as he faces the *retablo* behind the altar, he can see the gilded wood carvings—European cherubs and human heads, but also native scrolls of fruit and flowers and birds.

The love of color, of nature, the joy of life—this is what makes him revel in the Mexican brand of Christianity, the seamless blending of indigenous paganism with an emotional, unshakable faith in Jesus. It is not the dry, spare religion of European intellectualism, with its hatred of the natural world. No, the Mexicans have the innate wisdom, the spiritual generosity—how shall he put this?—arms long enough to wrap themselves around this world and the next in a warm embrace.

That's pretty good, he thinks as he turns back toward the congregation. I should find a way to work that into a sermon.

The cathedral is crowded with worshippers this morning—even though it's a Thursday—because he is there to celebrate the Mass. I have, he thinks, enough of an ego to enjoy that fact. The truth is that he's an enormously popular archbishop—he gets out among the people, shares their concerns, their thoughts, their laughs, their meals. Oh, God, he thinks, how I share their meals. He knows that it's a village joke in whatever town he visits, and he visits all of them: "Widen the chair at the head of the table—Archbishop Juan is coming to dinner."

He takes a host and starts to place it on the tongue of the worshipper kneeling in front of him.

Then the floor bounces beneath him.

That's exactly what it feels like, a bounce. Then another and another until the bounces blend into one constant series of jolts.

He feels something wet on his sleeve.

Looks down to see wine hopping out of the cup held by the acolyte beside him. He puts his arm around the boy's shoulders.

"Move first under the arches," he says, "then outside. Everyone go now, calmly, quietly."

He gently pushes the altar boy. "Go on."

The boy steps down from the altar.

Parada waits. He will wait there until the rest of the crowd in the church has filed out. Be calm, he tells himself. If you are calm, they will be calm. If there's panic, people might crush one another to get out.

So he stays and looks around.

The carved animals come to life.

They hop and quiver.

The carved faces nod up and down.

A frenzied agreement, Parada thinks. On what, I wonder?

Outside, the two towers tremble.

They are made of old stone. Beautifully handcrafted by local artisans. So much love went into them, so much care. But they stand in the town of Ciudad Guzmán, in the province of Jalisco, a name that comes from the original Tarascan inhabitants and means "sandy place." The stones in the tower are fine, strong and level, but the mortar was made from that sandy soil.

It could hold firm against many things, wind and rain and time, but it was never meant to hold up against a 7.8 earthquake, thirty kilometers deep and just ten miles away.

So as the worshippers patiently file out, the towers quiver, the mortar holding them together shakes loose, and they collapse on top of the great-grandchildren of the men who carved them and set them in place. The towers crash through the tiled dome and come down on twenty-five worshippers.

Because the church is crowded this morning.

For the love of Bishop Juan.

Who stands on the altar, untouched, in shock and horror as the people in front of him just disappear in a cloud of yellow dust.

The host still in his hand.

The body of Christ.

Nora is pulled from the dead.

A steel support beam saved her life. It fell diagonally onto a broken piece of wall and stopped another column from crushing her. Left a crack of space, a little air, as she lay buried beneath the rubble of the Regis Hotel, so she could at least breathe.

Not that there's much *to* breathe, the air is filled with so much dust.

She chokes on it, she coughs, she can't see a thing, but she can hear. Is it minutes later, hours? She doesn't know, but in that time she wonders if she's dead. If this is what hell is—trapped in a small, hot space, unable to see, choking on dust. I'm dead, she thinks, dead and buried. She hears the sounds of moans, cries of pain, and wonders if this will last forever. If this is her eternity. Where a whore goes when she dies.

She has just enough space to lay her head on her arm. Maybe I can sleep through hell, she thinks, sleep through eternity. It hurts. She finds that her arm is caked with moist blood, then she remembers the mirror shattering and the glass flying into her arm. I'm not dead, she thinks, feeling the wet blood. Dead people don't bleed.

I'm not dead, she thinks.

I'm buried alive.

Then she starts to panic.

Starts to hyperventilate, knowing that she shouldn't, that she's only using up the small supply of oxygen more quickly, but she can't help it. The thought of being buried alive, in this coffin under the ground—she remembers some stupid Poe story they made her read in high school. The scratch marks on the top of the coffin . . .

She wants to scream.

No point in using up my air freaking out, she thinks. There's better things to do with it. She yells, simply, "Help!"

Over and over again. At the top of her lungs.

Then she hears sirens, footsteps, the sound of feet right above her.

"Help!!"

A beat, then, *"¿Dónde estás?"*

"Right here!" she yells. Then thinks, then yells, *"¡Aquí!"*

She hears and feels things being lifted above her. Orders being given, cautions issued. Then she reaches her hand up as far as it will go. A second later feels the incredible warmth of another hand grabbing hers. Then she feels herself being pulled, out and up, and then, miraculously, she's standing in open space. Well, sort of open. There's a ceiling of sorts above. Walls and columns slanting crazily. Like standing in a museum of ruins.

A rescue worker holds her by the arms, looks curiously at her.

Then she smells something. A sweet, sickly smell. God, what is that?

A spark hits the gas and sets it off.

Nora hears a sharp crack, then a bass boom that rattles her heart and she falls over the hole. When she looks up again, there's fire everywhere. It's like the freaking *air* is on fire.

And moving toward her.

The men yell, *"¡Vámonos! ¡Ahorita!"*

Let's go! Right now!

One of the men grabs Nora's arm again and pushes her, and they're running. Flames are all around them, and burning debris falls on their heads, and she hears a crackling sound, smells an acrid, sour smell, and a man is slapping at her head and she realizes that her hair is on fire, but she doesn't feel it. The man's sleeve catches on fire but he keeps pushing her, pushing her, and then suddenly they're in the open air and she wants to fall down but the man won't let her, he keeps pushing her and pushing her because, behind them, what's left of the Regis Hotel tumbles and burns.

The other two men don't make it. They join the other 128 heroes who will die trying to rescue people trapped in the earthquake.

Nora doesn't know this yet as she trots across Avenida Benito Juárez into the relative safety of the open space of La Alameda Park. She drops to her knees as a policewoman, a traffic warden, throws a coat over her head and pats out the fire.

Nora looks around her—the Regis Hotel is a pile of burning rubble. Next door, the Salinas y Rocha department store looks like it's been cut in half. Red, green and white streamers, decorations from Independence Day, are floating in the air above the truncated shell of the building. All around her, as far as she can see through the clouds of dust, buildings lie toppled or cut in half. Huge chunks of stone, concrete and twisted steel lie in the streets.

And the people. All over the park, people are on their knees praying.

The sky is dark from smoke and dust.

Blocking out the sun.

And over and over again, she hears the same muttered phrase: *"El fin del mundo."*

The end of the world.

The right side of Nora's hair is scorched black; her left arm is bloody and studded with tiny shards of glass. The shock and adrenaline are wearing off and the pain is starting to come in for real.

Parada kneels over the corpses.

Giving them, posthumously, the last rites.

A line of corpses awaits his attention. Twenty-five bodies wrapped in makeshift shrouds—in blankets, towels, tablecloths, anything that could be found. Lying in a neat line in the dirt outside the fallen cathedral while frantic townspeople comb the ruins for more. Search for their loved ones, missing, trapped under the old stone. Desperately, hopefully listening for any signs of life.

So his mouth mumbles the Latin words, but his heart . . .

Something has broken inside him, has cracked as surely and lethally as the earth has cracked. There is now a fault line between me and God, he thinks.

The God that is, the God that isn't.

He can't tell them that—it would be cruel. They're looking to him to send the souls of their dearly departed to heaven. He can't disappoint them, not at this time, maybe never. The people need hope and I can't take it away. I'm not as cruel as You, he thinks.

So he says the prayers. Anoints them with oil and goes on with the ritual.

Behind him a priest approaches.

"Padre Juan?"

"Can't you see I'm busy?"

"You're wanted in Mexico City."

"I'm needed here."

"They are orders, Padre Juan."

"Whose orders?"

"The papal nuncio," the priest says. "Everyone is being summoned, to organize the relief. You have done such work before, so—"

"I have dozens of dead here—"

"There are thousands dead in Mexico City," the priest says.

"Thousands?"

"No one knows how many," says the priest. "And tens of thousands homeless."

So, Parada thinks, there it is—the living must be served.

"As soon as I'm done here," Parada says.

He goes back to giving the last rites.

They can't get her to leave.

A lot of people try—police, rescue workers, paramedics—but Nora won't go to get medical help.

"Your arm, Señorita, your face—"

"Bullshit," she says. "There are a lot of people hurt a lot worse. I'm okay."

I'm in pain, she thinks, but I'm okay. It's funny, a day ago I would have thought that those two things couldn't go together, but now I know they can. So her arm hurts, her head hurts, her face, scorched from the fire like a very bad sunburn, *hurts,* but she feels okay.

In fact, she feels strong.

Pain?

Fuck pain—there are people dying.

She doesn't want help now—she wants *to* help.

So she sits down and carefully picks the glass out of her arm, then washes it in a broken water main. Rips a sleeve off the linen pajamas she's still wearing (glad that she's always opted for linen over some flimsy silk thing) and ties it around the wound. Then she tears the other sleeve and uses it as a kerchief over her nose and mouth because the dust and smoke are choking, and the smell . . .

It's the smell of death.

Unimaginable if you've never smelled it, unforgettable once you have.

She tightens the kerchief on her face and goes in search of something to put on her feet. Not hard to do, seeing as how the department store has basically exploded its contents onto the street. So she appropriates a pair of rubber flip-flops, doesn't consider it looting (there is no looting—despite the overwhelming poverty of many of the city's residents, there is no looting), and joins a volunteer rescue crew digging up the rubble of the hotel, searching for survivors. There are hundreds of these crews, thousands of volunteers digging through fallen buildings all over the city, working with shovels, picks, tire irons, broken rebar and bare hands to get to the people trapped underneath. Carrying the dead and wounded out in blankets, sheets, shower curtains, anything to help the hopelessly overextended emergency personnel. Other volunteer crews help remove the rubble from the streets to clear the way for ambulances and fire trucks. Fire department helicopters hover over burning buildings, lowering men on winches to pluck out people who can't be reached from the ground.

All the while, thousands of radios drone a litany, pierced by screams of grief or joy from the listeners as the announcer reads the names of the dead and the names of the survivors.

There are other sounds—moans, whimpers, prayers, screams, cries for help—all muffled, all from deep within the ruins. Voices of people trapped under tons of rubble.

So the workers keep working. Quietly, doggedly, the volunteers and professionals search for survivors. Digging beside Nora is a troop of Girl Scouts. They can't be more than nine years old, Nora thinks, looking at their serious, determined faces, already carrying, literally, the weight of the world. So there are Girl Scouts and Boy Scouts, soccer clubs, bridge clubs, and just individuals like Nora, who form themselves into teams.

Doctors and nurses, the few who are left after the collapse of the hospitals, comb the rubble with stethoscopes, lowering the instruments to the rocks to listen for any faint signs of life. When they do, the workers holler for quiet, the sirens stop, the vehicles turn off their motors and everyone remains perfectly still. And then a doctor might smile or nod, and the crews move in, carefully, gently but efficiently moving the rock and steel and concrete, and sometimes there's a happy ending with someone plucked from the rubble. Other times it is sadder—they just can't move the rubble fast enough; they are too late and find a lifeless body.

Either way, they keep working.

All that day and through the night.

Nora stops once during the night. Takes a break and gets a cup of tea and a slice of bread from a relief station set up in the park. The park is crowded with the newly homeless and with people afraid to stay in their houses and apartment buildings. So the park resembles a giant refugee center, which, Nora thinks, I guess it is.

What's different about it is the quiet. Radios are turned on low, people whisper prayers, talk quietly to their children. There's no arguing, no pushing or shoving for the small supply of food or water. People wait patiently in line, bring the spare meals to the old and the children, help one another carry water, set up makeshift tents and shelters, dig latrines. Those whose homes weren't damaged bring blankets, pots and pans, food, clothing.

A woman hands Nora a pair of jeans and a flannel shirt.

"Take these."

"I couldn't."

"It's getting cold."

Nora takes the clothing.

"Thank you. *Gracias.*"

Nora goes behind a tree to change. Clothes never felt so good. The flannel feels wonderful and warm on her skin. She has closets full of clothes at home, she thinks, most of which she's worn once or twice. She'd give a lot right now for a pair of socks. She's known that the elevation of the city is more than a mile high, but now she feels it as the night gets cold. She wonders about the people still trapped beneath the buildings, if they can stay warm.

She finishes her tea and bread, then ties her kerchief back on and walks back to the ruins of the hotel. Gets on her knees beside a middle-aged woman and starts to move more rubble.

Parada walks through hell.

Fires burn crazily, rampantly, from broken gas lines. Flames glow from inside the shells of ruined buildings, lighting the Stygian darkness outside. The acrid smoke stings his eyes. Dust fills his nose and mouth and makes him cough. He gags on the smell. The sickening stench of decomposing bodies, the stink of burned flesh. Underneath those sharp smells, the duller but still pungent scent of human feces, as the sewer systems have failed.

It gets worse as he moves along, encounters child after child, wandering, crying for their mothers and fathers. Some of them in just underwear or pajamas, others in full school uniforms. He gathers them up as he goes along. He has a little boy in one arm and he's holding the hand of a little girl with the other, and she's holding another child's hand, who is holding another . . .

By the time he gets to La Alameda Park he has over twenty children with him. He wanders until he finds where Catholic Relief has set up a tent.

Parada finds a monsignor and asks, "Have you seen Antonucci?"

Meaning Cardinal Antonucci, the papal nuncio, the Vatican's highest representative in Mexico.

"He's saying Mass at the cathedral."

"The city doesn't need a Mass," Parada says. "It needs power and water. Food, blood and plasma."

"The spiritual needs of the community—"

"*Sí, sí, sí, sí,*" Parada says, walking away. He needs to think, to get his head together. There's so much to be organized, so many people with so many needs. It's overwhelming. He pulls a pack of cigarettes from his pocket and starts to light one.

A voice—a woman's voice—bites out of the darkness. "Put that out. Are you nuts?"

He snuffs the match out. Shines his flashlight and finds the woman's face. An extraordinarily pretty face, even under all the dust and grime.

"Broken gas lines," she says. "Do you want to blow us all up?"

"There are fires all over," he says.

"Then I guess we don't need another one, huh?"

"No, I suppose not," Parada says. "You're American."

"Yeah."

"You got here quickly."

"I was here," Nora says, "when it happened."

"Ah."

He looks her over. Feels the faint ghost of a long-forgotten stirring. The woman is small, but there's something of the warrior about her. A real chip on her shoulder. She wants to fight, but she doesn't know what or how.

Like me, he thinks.

He puts a hand out.

"Juan Parada."

"Nora."

Just Nora, Parada observes. No last name.

"Do you live in Mexico City, Nora?"

"No, I came down on business."

"What kind of business are you in?" he asks.

She looks him square in the eye. "I'm a call girl."

"I'm afraid I don't—"

"A prostitute."

"Ah."

"What do *you* do?"

He smiles. "I'm a priest."

"You're not dressed like a priest."

"You're not dressed like a prostitute," he says. "Actually, I'm even worse than a priest, I'm a bishop. An *arch*bishop."

"Is that better than a bishop?"

"If you're judging solely by rank," he says. "I was happier as a priest."

"Then why don't you go back to being a priest?"

He smiles again, and nods, and says, "I'm going to wager that you're a very successful call girl."

"I am," Nora says. "I'll bet you're a very successful archbishop."

"As a matter of fact, I'm thinking of quitting."

"Why?"

"I'm not sure I believe anymore."

Nora shrugs and says, "Fake it."

"Fake it?"

"It's easy," she says. "I do it all the time."

"Oh. *Ohhhh,* I see." Parada feels himself blushing. "But why should I fake anything?"

"Power," Nora says. Seeing Parada's puzzled look, she goes on. "An archbishop must be pretty powerful, right?"

"In some ways."

Nora nods. "I sleep with a lot of powerful men. I know that when they want something done, it gets done."

"So?"

"So," she says, pointing her chin at the park around her, "there's a lot that needs to get done."

"Ah."

From the mouths of babes, Parada thinks. Not to mention prostitutes.

"Well, it's been nice talking to you," he says. "We should stay in touch."

"A whore and a bishop?" Nora says.

"Clearly, you've never read the Bible," Parada says. "The New Testament? Mary Magdalene? Ring a bell?"

"No."

"In any case, it would be all right for us to be friends," he says, then quickly adds, "I don't mean *that* kind of friends, of course. I took a vow . . . I simply mean . . . I would like it if we were friends."

"I think I'd like that, too."

He takes a card from his pocket. "When things calm down, would you call me?"

"Yeah, I will."

"Good. Well, I'd better get going. Things to do."

"Me, too."

He walks back to the Catholic Relief tent.

"Start getting these kids' names," he orders a priest, "then compare them with the roll of dead, missing, and survivors. Someone somewhere must be keeping a list of parents looking for children. Cross-index their names against that."

"Who are you?" the priest asks.

"I'm the Archbishop of Guadalajara," he says. "Now, get moving. And put someone else to getting these children food and blankets."

"Yes, Your Grace."

"And I'll need a car."

"Your Grace?"

"A car," Parada says. "I'll need a car to take me to the nunciate."

The papal nunciate, Antonucci's residence, is in the south of the city, far from the most damaged areas. The electricity will be running, the lights on. Most importantly, the phones will be working.

"Many of the streets are blocked, Your Grace."

"And many of them aren't," Parada says. "You're still standing there. Why?"

Two hours later, Papal Nuncio Cardinal Girolamo Antonucci returns to his residence to find an upset staff and Archbishop Parada in his office, his feet up on the desk, sucking on a cigarette, snapping orders into the telephone.

Parada looks up when Antonucci comes in.

"Can you get us some more coffee?" Parada asks. "It's going to be a long night."

And a longer day tomorrow.

. . .

Guilty pleasures.

Hot, strong coffee. Fresh warm bread.

And thank God Antonucci is Italian and smokes, Parada thinks as he draws into his lungs that guiltiest of all guilty pleasures, at least among the ones available to a priest.

He exhales the smoke and watches it rise to the ceiling, listening as Antonucci sets his cup down and says to the minister of the interior, "I have spoken to His Holiness personally, and he wishes me to assure the government of his beloved people of Mexico that the Vatican stands ready to offer whatever aid it can, despite the fact that we still do not enjoy formal diplomatic relations with the government of Mexico."

Antonucci looks like a bird, Parada thinks.

A tiny bird with a small, neat beak.

He was dispatched from Rome eight years ago with the mission of bringing Mexico formally back into the fold after over one hundred years of official government anti-clericism, since the Ley Lerdo of 1856 had seized the vast church-owned haciendas and other lands and sold them off. The revolutionary constitution of 1857 had stripped the power of the Church in Mexico, and the Vatican retaliated by excommunicating any Mexican who took the constitutional oath.

So for a century an uneasy truce has existed between the Vatican and the Mexican government. Formal relations have never been resumed, but not even the most rabid socialists of the PRI—the Partido Revolucionario Institucional, the Institutional Revolutionary Party that has ruled Mexico in a one-party, pseudo-democratic government since 1917—would try to totally abolish the Church in this land of faithful peasants. So there have been petty harassments such as the ban on clerical garb, but mostly there has been a grudging accommodation between the government and the Vatican.

But it has always been a goal of the Vatican to regain formal status in Mexico, and as a politician from the Church's arch-conservative wing, Antonucci has lectured Parada and the other bishops that "we must not lose the faithful of Mexico to godless Communism."

So it's natural, Parada thinks, that Antonucci would view the earthquake as an opportunity. See the deaths of ten thousand of the faithful as God's way of bringing the government to its knees.

Necessity will force the government to eat a lot of crow over the next few days; it has yet to humble itself by accepting aid from the Americans, but it will. And it has yet to crawl to the Church for help, but here it is.

And we'll give them the money.

Money that we've collected from the faithful, rich and poor, for centuries. The coin in the collection plate, untaxed, invested at great profit. So now, Parada thinks, we will extract a price from a prostrate country to give it back the money we took from it in the first place.

Christ would weep.

Money changers in the temple?

We *are* the money changers in the temple.

"You need money," Antonucci says to the minister. "You need it quickly, and you're going to have a hard time borrowing it, given your government's already precarious credit ratings."

"We'll issue bonds."

"Who'll buy them?" Antonucci asks, a hint of a satisfied sneer playing at the corners of his mouth. "You can't offer enough interest to tempt investors for that kind of money. You can't even service, never mind repay, the debts you already have. We should know; we already hold a stack of Mexican paper."

"Insurance," the minister says.

"You're underinsured," Antonucci says. "Your own Department of the Interior has turned a blind eye to all the hotels' practice of underinsurance, to encourage tourism. The stores, the apartment buildings—same thing. Even the government ministries that collapsed were grossly underinsured. Or self-insured, I should say, without the funds to back it up. It's a bit of a scandal, I'm afraid. So while your government might hold the Vatican in official disdain, the financial institutions have a somewhat better opinion of us. I believe it's referred to in the jargon as 'Triple A.' "

Machiavelli could only have been an Italian, Parada thinks.

If it weren't such a hideously cynical piece of extortion, you'd almost have to admire it.

But there's too much work to be done, and it's urgent, so Parada says, "Let's cut through the shit, shall we? We will gladly bring whatever aid we can, financial and material, on an informal basis. You, in return, will allow our clergy to wear the cross and clearly label any material aid as coming from the Holy Roman Catholic Church. You will guarantee that the next administration, within thirty days of taking office, will commence good-faith negotiations on establishing formal relations between the state and the Church."

"That's in 1988," Antonucci snaps. "Almost three years away."

"Yes, I did the math," Parada says. He turns back to the minister. "Do we have a deal?"

Yes, they do.

"Just who do you think you are?" Antonucci asks after the minister leaves. "Don't you ever supersede me in a negotiation again. I had him on the run."

"Is that our role now?" Parada asks. "To keep needy people on the run?"

"You do not have the authority to—"

"Am I being taken to the woodshed?" Parada asks. "If so, please be quick about it. I have work to do."

"You seem to forget that I am your direct superior."

"You can't forget what you don't acknowledge in the first place," Parada says. "You're not my superior. You're a politician sent by Rome to conduct politics."

Antonucci says, "The earthquake was an act of God—"

"I can't believe what I'm hearing."

"—which provides an opportunity to save the souls of millions of Mexicans."

"Don't save their *souls*!" Parada yells. "Save *them*!"

"That is sheer heresy!"

"Good!"

It isn't just the earthquake victims, Parada thinks. It's the millions living in poverty. The literally countless millions in the slums of Mexico City, the people living on garbage dumps in Tijuana, the landless peasants in Chiapas who are in reality little more than serfs.

"This 'liberation theology' doesn't fly with me, " Antonucci says.

"I don't care," Parada says. "I don't answer to you—I answer to God."

"I can pick up this phone and have you transferred to a chapel in Tierra del Fuego."

Parada grabs the phone and hands it to him.

"Do it," he says. "I'd be very happy being a parish priest at the ends of the earth. Why aren't you dialing? Shall I do it for you? I'm calling your bluff. I'll call Rome, and then I'll call the newspapers to tell them exactly why I'm being transferred."

He watches little red spots appear on Antonucci's cheeks. The bird is upset, Parada thinks. I have ruffled his smooth feathers. But Antonucci regains his calm, his placid exterior, even his self-satisfied smile, as he sets down the receiver.

"Good choice," Parada says with a confidence he doesn't feel. "I'll head up this relief effort, I'll launder the Church's money so as not to embarrass the government, and I'll help bring the Church back to Mexico."

"I'm waiting for the *quid*," Antonucci says, "in the *pro quo*."

"The Vatican will make me a cardinal."

Because the power to do good can come only with, well, power.

Antonucci says, "You have become something of a politician yourself."

It's true, Parada thinks.

Good.

Fine.

So be it.

"So we have an understanding," Parada says.

Suddenly he's become more of a cat than a bird, Parada thinks. Thinking he's swallowed the canary. That I've sold my soul to him for the sake of my ambition. A transaction that he can understand.

Good, let him think it.

Fake it, the lovely American prostitute had said.

She's right—it's easy.

Tijuana
1985

Adán Barrera contemplates the deal he just made with the PRI.

It was really quite simple, he thinks. You go into breakfast with a briefcase full of cash and you leave without it. It stays under the table by your feet, never mentioned but assumed, a tacit understanding: Despite American pressure to the contrary, Tío will be allowed to come home from his exile in Honduras.

And retire.

Tío will live quietly in Guadalajara and manage his legitimate businesses in peace. That's the upside of the arrangement.

The downside is that García Abrego will realize his longtime ambition of replacing Tío as El Patrón. And perhaps this is not such a bad thing. Tío's health is precarious and, face it, he's changed since that Talavera bitch betrayed him. God, he actually loved the little *segundera,* wanted to marry her, and he's not the same man he was.

So Abrego will assume the leadership of the Federación from his base in the Gulf states. El Verde will continue to run Sonora; Güero Méndez will still have the Baja Plaza.

And the Mexican federal government will look the other way.

Thanks to the earthquake.

The government needs cash to rebuild, and right now there are only two sources—the Vatican and the narcos. The Church has already kicked in, Adán knows, and so will we. But there will be a quid pro quo, and the government will honor it.

In addition, the Federación will also foot the bill to make certain that the ruling party, the PRI, wins the upcoming elections, as it has since the revolution. Even now, Adán is helping Abrego organize a $25 million–a–plate fund-raising dinner, to which every major narco and businessman in Mexico will be expected to contribute.

If, that is, they want to do business.

And do we ever need to do business, Adán thinks. The Hidalgo fiasco was a major disruption, and even with Arturo out of the country and things settling down, there is a lot of money to be made up. Now, with our relationship with Mexico City on firm footing again, we can get back to business as usual.

Which means stealing the Baja Plaza from Güero.

It had been Tío's idea for his nephews to infiltrate Tijuana.

Like cuckoo birds.

Because the long-term plan is to slowly grow rich in power and influence, and then throw Güero out of his nest. He's an absentee landlord anyway, trying to run the Baja Plaza from his ranch outside Culiacán. Güero relies on lieutenants to run the day-to-day in La Plaza, narcos loyal to him, like Juan Esparagoza and Tito Mical.

And Adán and Raúl Barrera.

It had been Tío's idea for Adán and Raúl to ingratiate themselves with the scions of the Tijuana establishment. "Become part of the fabric, so if they want to rip you out, they can't do it without ripping the whole blanket. And that, they will not do." Do it slowly, do it carefully, do it without Güero taking notice, but do it.

"Start with the kids," he'd advised. "Senior will do anything to protect Junior."

So Adán and Raúl had launched a charm offensive. Bought expensive homes in the exclusive Colonia Hipódromo, and suddenly they were just *there*. Actually, everywhere. Like one day there was no Raúl Barrera, and the next day he's everywhere you go. Go to a club, Raúl is there picking up the tab; go to the beach, Raúl is out there doing karate katas; go to the races, Raúl is there laying down piles of bills on long shots; go to a disco, Raúl is there flooding the place with Dom Pérignon. He starts to gather a following around him, the scions of Tijuana society, the nineteen- and twenty-year-old sons of bankers, lawyers, doctors and government officials, who like to park their cars alongside a wall by a huge, ancient oak tree and talk shit with Raúl.

Pretty soon, the tree becomes just "the tree"—and everyone who's anyone hangs out at El Arbol.

Like Fabián Martínez.

Fabián is movie-star handsome.

He doesn't resemble his namesake—some old singer/beach-movie guy—he looks like a young, Hispanic Tony Curtis. Fabián is a handsome kid and knows it. Everyone's been telling him this since he was six years old, and the mirror is just a confirmation. He's tall, with copper skin and a wide, sensuous mouth. His black hair is full and worn slicked straight back. He has bright, white teeth—created by years of expensive orthodontics—and a smile that is seductive.

He knows this because he's practiced it—a lot.

Fabián is hanging out one day when he overhears someone say, "Let's go kill somebody."

Fabián looks at his *cuate* Alejandro.

This is just too cool.

This is right out of *Scarface*.

Although Raúl Barrera doesn't look anything like Al Pacino. Raúl is tall and well-built, with big heavy shoulders and a neck that goes along with the karate moves he's always demonstrating. Today he's wearing a leather jacket and a San Diego Padres baseball cap. The jewelry, though—that's like Pacino. Raúl is dripping in it—thick gold chains around his neck, gold bracelets on his wrists, gold rings and the inevitable gold Rolex watch.

Actually, Fabián thinks, Raúl's older brother looks more like Al Pacino, but there the resemblance to *Scarface* ends. Fabián's met Adán Barrera only a few times: at a nightclub with Ramón, at a boxing match, another time at "El Big"—Ted's Big Boy hamburger joint on Avenida Revolución. But Adán looks more like an accountant than a *narcotraficante*. No mink coats, no jewelry, very quiet and soft-spoken. If nobody pointed him out to you, you wouldn't know he was there.

Raúl you know is there.

Today he's leaning against his bright red Porsche Targa, talking casually about killing somebody.

Anybody.

"Who has a grudge?" Raúl asks them. "Who do you want hosed off the street?"

Fabián and Alejandro exchange another glance.

They've been *cuates*—buddies—a long time, almost from birth, seeing as how they were born just a few weeks apart in the same hospital—Scripps in San Diego. This was a common practice among Tijuana's upper class back in the late '60s: They went across the border to have their children so that the kids would have the advantage of dual citizenship. So Fabián and Alejandro and most of their *cuates* were born in the States, went to kindergarten and preschool together in the exclusive Hipódromo neighborhood in the hills above downtown Tijuana. Around the time they were ready to go into the fifth or sixth grade, their mothers moved back to San Diego with the children so that the kids could attend middle and high school in the States, learn English, become totally bicultural and make the trans-national contacts that would become so important to success in later life. Their parents recognized that while Tijuana and San Diego might be in two different countries, they're in the same business community.

Fabián, Alejandro and all their buddies went to the Catholic all-boy Augustine High School in San Diego; their sisters went to Our Lady of Peace. (Their parents took a quick look at the San Diego public schools and decided they didn't want their children to be *that* bicultural.) They spent their weekdays with the priests and their weekends back in Tijuana, partying at the country club or hitting the beach resorts of Rosarito and Ensenada. Or sometimes they stayed in San Diego, doing the same shit that American teenagers do on the weekend—shopping for clothes in the mall, going to movies, heading out to Pacific Beach or La Jolla Shores, partying at the house of whichever friend's parents were away for the weekend (and they're away a lot—one of the bonuses of being a rich kid is that your parents have the money to travel), drinking, screwing, smoking dope.

These boys have cash in their pockets and dress well. They always did—junior high, high school. Fabián, Alejandro and their crowd wore the latest styles, shopped at the best stores. Even now, both of them in college back in Baja, they have the pocket money to put the best threads on their backs. A lot of the time they don't spend in discos and clubs or hanging out here under El Arbol they spend shopping. They spend a hell of a lot more time shopping than they do studying, that's for sure.

It's not that either of them is stupid.

They're not.

Particularly Fabián—he's one smart kid. He could ace a business course with his eyes closed—which they are in class about half the time. Fabián can figure compound interest in his head by the time you've punched the numbers into your calculator. He could be a terrific student.

But there's no need. It isn't part of the plan.

The plan is this: You go to high school in the States, you come back and get gentlemen's C's at college, your daddy puts you into business, and with all the connections you've made on both sides of the border, you make money.

That's the life plan.

But the plan didn't figure on the Barrera brothers moving into town. It wasn't anywhere on the chart that Adán and Raúl Barrera would move into Colonia Hipódromo and rent a big white mansion on the hill.

Fabián met Raúl at a disco. He's sitting at a table with a bunch of friends and this amazing guy walks in—full-length mink coat, bright green cowboy boots and a black cowboy hat, and Fabián looks at Alejandro and says, "Will you look at this?"

They think the dude is a joke, except the joke looks at them, shouts for a waiter and orders thirty bottles of champagne.

Thirty bottles of champagne.

And not some cheap shit, either—Dom.

For which he pays cash.

Then he asks, "Who's partying with me?"

Everybody, as it turns out.

The party is on Raúl Barrera.

The party is on, *period,* man.

Then one day he's not just there, he's *taking* you there.

Like, they're sitting around El Arbol one day, smoking a little weed and doing some karate, and Raúl starts talking about Felizardo.

"The boxer?" Fabián asks. Cesar Felizardo—only about the biggest hero in Mexico.

"No, the farmworker," Raúl answers. He finishes a spinning back kick, then looks at Fabián. "Yes, the boxer. He's fighting Pérez next week here in town."

"You can't get tickets," Fabián answers.

"No, *you* can't get tickets," Raúl says.

"You can?"

"He's from my town," Raúl says. "Culiacán. I used to manage him—he's my *viejo.* You guys want to go, I'll hook it up."

Yes, they want to go, and yes, Raúl hooks it up. Ringside seats. The fight doesn't last long—Felizardo knocks Pérez out in the third round—but still it's a kick. The bigger kick is that Raúl takes them into the dressing room afterward—they actually get to meet Felizardo. He stands around talking with them like they're old buddies.

Fabián notices something else here, too: Felizardo treats them like buddies, and Raúl he treats like a *cuate,* but the boxer treats Adán differently. There's an air of deference in the way he talks to Adán. And Adán doesn't stay long, just comes in and quietly congratulates the boxer and then leaves.

But everything stops for the few minutes he's in the room.

Yeah, Fabián gets the idea that the Barrera brothers can take you places, and not just grandstand seats at the soccer match (Raúl takes them there); or box seats at the Padres games (Raúl takes them there); or even to Vegas, where they all fly a month later, stay at the Mirage, lose all their fucking money, watch Felizardo pound the shit out of Rodolfo Aguilar for six rounds to retain his lightweight title, then party with a platoon of high-priced call girls in Raúl's suite and fly home—hungover, fucked-out and happy—the next afternoon.

No, he gets the idea that the Barreras can take you places in a hurry that you might not get in years, if ever, working fourteen-hour days in your daddy's office.

You hear things about the Barreras—the money they throw around comes from drugs (yeah, like, *duh*)—but you especially hear things about Raúl. One of the stories they've heard whispered about Raúl goes like this:

He's sitting in his ride outside the house, *bandera* music *blasting* on the speakers and the bass turned up to sonic-boom level, when one of the neighbors comes out and knocks on the car window.

Raúl lowers the window. "Yeah?"

"Could you turn it down?!" the guy screams over the music. "I can hear it inside! It's rattling the windows!"

Raúl decides to fuck with him a little.

"What?!" he yells. "I can't hear you!"

The man's in no mood to be messed with. He is macho, too. So he hollers, "The music! Turn it down! It's too fucking loud!"

Raúl takes his pistol from his jacket, sticks it in the man's chest and pulls the trigger.

"It's not too fucking loud *now*, is it, *pendejo*?"

The man's body disappears, and no one complains about Raúl's music after that.

Fabián and Alejandro have talked about that story and decided that it must be bullshit, right, it can't be true, it's too *Scarface* to be real, but now here is Raúl finishing up a roach and suggesting, "Let's go kill somebody," like he's suggesting going to Baskin-Robbins for an ice cream cone.

"Come on," Raúl says, "there must be somebody you want to get even with."

Fabián smiles at Alejandro and says, "All right . . ."

Fabián's dad had given him a Miata; Alejandro's parents had kicked forth with a Lexus. They were out racing the cars the other night, like they do a lot of nights. Except this one night Fabián goes to pass Alejandro on a two-lane road and there's another car coming the other way. Fabián just tucks it back into his lane, missing a head-on crash by a *pelo del chocho*. Turns out the other driver is a guy who works in his father's office building and recognizes the car. He calls Fabián's dad, who has a shit fit and jerks the Miata for six months, and now Fabián is without a ride.

Fabián tells this tale of woe to Raúl.

It's a joke, right? It's a goof, a laugh, stoner talk.

It is until a week later, when the man disappears.

One of those rare nights that Fabián's dad comes home for dinner, Fabián's there, and his dad starts talking about how a man in his building is missing, just dropped off the face of the earth, and Fabián excuses himself from the table and goes into the bathroom and splashes cold water on his face.

He meets Alejandro later at a club and they talk about it under the cover of the booming music. "Shit," Fabián says, "do you really think he did it?"

"I don't know," Alejandro says. Then he looks at Fabián, laughs and says, *"Noooooo."*

But the man never comes back. Raúl never says word one about it, but the man never comes back. And Fabián is, like, freaked out. It was just a joke, he was just testing, just bouncing off Raúl's bullshit, and now because of it a man is dead?

And how, as a school counselor might ask, does *that* make you feel?

Fabián's surprised by the answer.

He feels freaked, guilty and—

Good.

Powerful.

You point your finger and—

Adiós, motherfucker.

It's like sex, only better.

Two weeks later he works up the nerve to talk to Raúl about business. They get into the red Porsche and go for a drive.

"How do I get in?" Fabián asks.

"In what?"

"La pista secreta," Fabián says. "I don't have a lot of money. I mean, not a lot of my own money."

"You don't need money," Raúl says.

"I don't?"

"You have a green card?"

"Yeah."

"That's your starter kit."

Easy as that. Two weeks later Raúl gives Fabián a Ford Explorer and tells him to drive it across the border at Otay Mesa. Tells him what time to cross and what lane to use. Fabián's scared as shit, but it's a weird, good scared—it's a shot of adrenaline, a kick. He crosses the border like it doesn't exist; the man waves him right through. He drives to the address Raúl gives him, where two guys get into his Explorer and he gets into theirs and then drives back to TJ.

Raúl lays ten grand American on him.

Cash.

Fabián hooks Alejandro up, too.

They're *cuates,* dig, buddies.

Alejandro makes a couple of runs as his wingman and then he's in business for himself. It's all good, they're making money, but—

"We're not making real money," he tells Alejandro one afternoon.

"Feels real to me."

"But the real money is in moving coke."

He goes to Raúl and says he's ready to move up.

"That's cool, bro," Raúl says. "We're all about upward mobility."

He tells Fabián how it works and even sets him up with the Colombians. Sits with him while they make a pretty standard contract—Fabián will take delivery of fifty kilos of coke, dropped off a fishing boat at Rosarito. He'll take it across the border at a thousand a key. A hundred of that g, though, goes to Raúl for protection.

Bam.

Forty g's, just like that.

Fabián does two more contracts and buys himself a Mercedes.

Like, you can keep the Miata, Dad. Park that Japanese lawn mower, and keep it parked. And while you're at it, you can lay off busting my chops about grades because I've already aced Marketing 101. I am already a commodities broker, Dad. Don't worry about whether you can bring me into the firm because the last thing in this world I want is a J-O-B.

Couldn't afford the pay cut.

You think Fabián was pulling chicks before, you should see him now.

Fabián has M-O-N-E-Y.

He's twenty-one years old and living large.

The other guys see it, the other sons of doctors and lawyers and stockbrokers. They see it and they want it. Pretty soon, most of the guys who hang around Raúl's little circle at El Arbol—doing karate and blowing *yerba*—are in the business. They're driving the shit into the States, or they're making their own contracts and kicking up to Raúl.

They're in it—the next generation of the Tijuana power structure—up to their necks.

Pretty soon, the group gets a nickname.

The Juniors.

Fabián becomes, like, *the* Junior.

He's hanging loose down in Rosarito one night when he bumps into a boxer named Eric Casavales and his promoter, an older guy named José Miranda. Eric's a pretty good boxer, but tonight he's drunk and completely miscomprehends this soft yuppie pup he jostles in the street. Drinks are spilled, shirts are stained, words exchanged. Laughing, Casavales whips a pistol out of his waistband and waves it at Fabián before José can walk him away.

So Casavales staggers off, laughing at the scared look on rich boy's face when he saw the pistol barrel, and he's still laughing as Fabián goes to his Mercedes, takes his own pistol out of the glove box, finds Casavales and Miranda standing out in front of the boxer's car and shoots them both to death.

Fabián throws the pistol into the ocean, gets back into his Mercedes and drives back to TJ.

Feeling pretty good.

Pretty good about himself.

That's one version of the story. The other—popular at Ted's Big Boy—is that Martínez's confrontation with the boxer wasn't accidental at all, that Casavales's promoter was holding up a fight that Cesar Felizardo needed in order to move up and just wouldn't budge on it, even after Adán Barrera approached him personally with a very reasonable offer. Nobody knows what the real reason is, but Casavales and Miranda are dead, and later that year, Felizardo gets his fight for the lightweight championship and wins it.

Fabián denies killing anyone for *any* reason, but the more he denies it, the more the stories gain credence.

Raúl even gives him a nickname.

El Tiburón.

The Shark.

Because he moves like a shark through the water.

Adán doesn't work the kids—he works the grown-ups.

Lucía is an enormous help, with her pedigree and old-school style. She takes him to a good tailor, buys him conservative, expensive business suits and understated clothes. (Adán tries, but fails, to make Raúl undergo the same transformation. If anything, his brother becomes more flamboyant, adding to his Sinaloan narco-cowboy wardrobe, for instance, a full-length mink coat.) She takes him to the private power clubs, to the French restaurants in the Río district, to the private parties at the private homes in the Hipódromo, Chapultepec and Río neighborhoods.

And they go to church, of course. They're at Mass every Sunday morning. They leave large checks in the collection plate, make large contributions to the building fund, the orphans' fund, the fund for aged priests. They have Father Rivera to the house for dinner, they host backyard barbecues, they serve as godparents for an increasing number of the young couples just starting their families. They're like any other young upwardly mobile couple in Tijuana—he's a quiet, serious businessman with first one restaurant, then two, then five; she's a young businessman's wife.

Lucía goes to the gym, to lunch with the other young wives, to San Diego to shop at Fashion Valley and Horton Plaza. She understands this as her duty to her husband's business, but limits it to her duty. The other wives understand—poor Lucía must spend time with the poor child, she wants to be home, she is devoted to the Church.

She's a godmother now to half a dozen babies. It hurts her—she feels that she's doomed to stand with a stricken smile on her face, holding someone else's healthy child by the baptismal font.

Adán, when he's not at home, can be found in his office or in the back of one of his restaurants, sipping coffee and doing the numbers on a yellow manuscript pad. If you didn't know what business he was really in, you would never guess it. He looks like a young accountant, a numbers-cruncher. If you couldn't see the actual figures scratched in pencil on the manuscript pad, you would never think that they are calculations of x kilos of cocaine times the delivery fee from the Colombians, minus the transport costs, the protection costs, the employee wages and other overhead, Güero's 10 percent cut, Tío's ten points. There are more prosaic calculations as to the cost of beef tenderloin, linen napkins, cleaning supplies and the like for the five restaurants he now owns, but most of his time is taken up with the more complicated accounting of moving tons of Colombian cocaine as well as Güero's sinsemilla, and a small bit of heroin just to keep their hand in the market.

He rarely, if ever, sees the actual drugs, the suppliers or the customers. Adán just handles the money—charging it, counting it, cleaning it. But not collecting it—that's Raúl's business.

Raúl handles his business.

Take the case of the two money mules who take $200K of Barrera cash, drive it across the border and keep driving toward Monterrey instead of Tijuana. But Mexican highways can be long, and sure enough, these two *pendejos* get picked up near Chihuahua by the MJFP, who hold them long enough for Raúl to get there.

Raúl is not pleased.

He has one mule's hands stretched across a paper cutter, then asks him, "Didn't your mother ever teach you to keep your hands to yourself?"

"Yes!" the mule screams. His eyes are bulging out of his head.

"You should have listened to her," Raúl says. Then he leans all his weight on top of the blade, which crunches through the mule's wrists. The cops rush the guy to the hospital because Raúl has been quite clear that he wants the handless man alive and walking around as a human message board.

The other errant mule does make it to Monterrey, but he's chained and gagged in the trunk of a car that Raúl drives to a vacant lot, douses with gasoline and sets on fire. Then Raúl drives the cash to Tijuana himself, has lunch with Adán and goes to a soccer match.

No one tries to expropriate any Barrera cash for a long time.

Adán doesn't get involved with any of this messy stuff. He's a businessman; it's an export/import for him—export the drugs, import the cash. Then handle the cash, which is a problem. It's the sort of problem a businessman wants to have, of course—What do I do with all this money?—but it's still a problem. Adán can wash a certain amount of it through the restaurants, but five restaurants can't handle millions of dollars, so he's on a constant search for laundry facilities.

But it's all numbers to him.

He hasn't seen any drugs in years.

And no blood.

Adán Barrera has never killed anybody.

Never as much as thrown a fist in anger. No, all the tough-guy stuff, all the enforcement, goes Raúl's way. He doesn't seem to mind; quite the contrary. And this division of labor makes it easier for Adán to deny what really brings the money into the household.

And that's what he needs to get back to doing, bringing the money in.

7

Christmastime

> *And the tuberculosis old men*
> *At the Nelson wheeze and cough*
> *And someone will head south*
> *Until this whole thing cools off . . .*
>
> —Tom Waits, "Small Change"

New York City
December 1985

Callan planes a board.

In one long, smooth motion, he runs the plane from one end of the wood to the other, then steps back to examine his work.

It looks good.

He takes a piece of fine sandpaper, wraps it around a block of scrap wood and starts to smooth the edge he just created.

Things are good.

Mostly, Callan reflects, they're so good because they got so bad.

Take Peaches' big cocaine score: 0.

Actually, minus zero.

Callan got not one cent from that, seeing as how all the cocaine ended up in a Feebee storage locker before it could be put out on the street. The Feds must have had it up the whole time, because as soon as Peaches brought that coke into the jurisdiction of the Eastern District of New York, Giuliani's trained Feebees were on it like flies on shit.

And Peaches got indicted for possession with intent to distribute.

Heavy weight.

Peaches is looking at having his mid-life crisis in Ossining, if he lives that long, and he has to come up with Carl Sagan bail money, not to mention lawyer money, not to mention while all this is going on he isn't earning, so Peaches is like, *Ante up, boys, it's tax time,* so not only do Callan and O-Bop lose their coke investment, they got to kick in to the Big Peaches Defense Fund, which takes a chunk out of their kickback money, extortion money and loan-shark money.

But the good news is that they didn't get indicted on the coke. For all his faults, Peaches is a stand-up guy—so is Little Peaches—and although the Feds got Peaches on tape talking to and/or about every goombah in the Greater New York Metropolitan Area, they don't have O-Bop or Callan.

Which, Callan thinks, is a major fucking blessing.

That weight of coke puts you in for thirty-to-life, closer to life.

So, that's good.

That makes the air very sweet, just being able to smell it and know you're going to *keep* smelling it.

You're already ahead on your day.

But Peaches is up a pole, so is Little Peaches, and word is the Feds got Cozzo and Cozzo's brother and a couple of others and they're just waiting to try to flip Big Peaches to nail it down.

Yeah, good luck on that, Callan thinks.

Peaches is old-school.

Old-school don't roll over for nothing.

But hard time is the least of Peaches' problems, because the Feds have indicted Big Paulie Calabrese.

Not for the coke, but on a boatload of other RICO predicates, and Big Paulie's really sweating it because it's only been a few months since that major hard-on Giuliani got four other bosses a century each in the penitentiary, and Big Paulie's case is coming up next.

That Giuliani is a funny fuck, well aware of the old Italian toast *"Cent' anni"*—May you live a hundred years—except what he means is "May you live a hundred years in the hole." And Giuliani wants to hit for the cycle—he wants to punch out *all* the heads of the old Five Families, and it looks like Paulie is going down. Understandably, Paulie don't want to die in the joint, so he's a little tense.

He's looking to take a little of his *agita* out on Big Peaches.

You deal, you die.

Peaches, he's screaming that he's innocent, that the Feds set him up, that he wouldn't dream of defying his boss by dealing dope, but Calabrese keeps hearing rumors about tapes that have Peaches talking about the coke and saying a few inflammatory things about Paul Calabrese himself, but Peaches is like, Tapes? What tapes? And the Feds won't turn the tapes over to Paulie, because they don't intend to use them as evidence in Calabrese's case— yet—but Calabrese knows that they're sure as hell going to use them against Peaches in his case, so Peaches has them, and Paulie's demanding that he bring them around to the house at Todt Hill.

Which Peaches is desperate not to do, because he might as well just stick a grenade up his ass, reach around and pull the pin. Because he's on them tapes saying shit like, *Hey, you know that maid the Godmother is pronging? You ready for this? I hear he's got this pump-up dick he uses . . .*

And other choice tidbits about the Godmother and what a cheap, mean, limp-dick asshole he is, not to mention a verbal rundown of the whole Cimino batting order, so Peaches does not want Paulie getting an earful of them tapes.

What makes it even more tense is that the cancer is finally taking Neill Demonte, the old-school Cimino underboss and the only thing keeping the Cozzo wing of the family from open rebellion. So not only is that restraining influence gone, but the underboss position is going to be vacant, and the Cozzo wing has expectations.

That Johnny Boy, and not Tommy Bellavia, better be made the new underboss.

"I ain't reporting to no fucking chauffeur," Peaches grumbles like he isn't already skating on skinny ice. Like he's going to have a fucking chance to report to anybody other than the warden or Saint Peter.

Callan gets all this gossip from O-Bop, who just refuses to believe that Callan's getting out.

"You can't get out," O-Bop says.

"Why not?"

"What, you think you just walk away?" O-Bop asks. "You think there's an exit door?"

"That's what I was thinking," Callan says. "Why, are you gonna stand in it?"

"No," O-Bop says quickly, "but there are people out there who have, you know, *resentments*. You don't want to be out there alone."

"That's what I want."

Well, not exactly.

The truth is, Callan's in love.

He finishes planing the board and walks home, thinking about Siobhan.

He met her at the Glocca Mora pub on Twenty-sixth and Third. He is sitting at the bar having a beer, listening to Joe Burke play his Irish flute, and he sees her with a group of friends at a table in the front. It's her long black hair he notices first. Then she turns around and he sees her face and those gray eyes and he's done for.

He goes over to the table and sits down.

Turns out her name is Siobhan and she's just over from Belfast—grew up on Kashmir Road.

"My dad was from Clonnard," Callan says. "Kevin Callan."

"I heard of him," she says, then turns away.

"What?"

"I came here to get away from all that."

"Then why are you in *here*?" he asks. Shit, every other song they sing in the place is about all that—about the Troubles, past, present or future. Even now, Joe Burke puts down the flute, picks up the banjo and the band launches into "The Men Behind the Wire":

> *"Armoured cars and tanks and guns*
> *Came to take away our sons*
> *But every man will stand behind*
> *The men behind the wire."*

She says, "I don't know—it's where the Irish go, isn't it?"

"There are other places," he says. "Have you had dinner?"

"I'm here with friends."

"It'd be okay with them."

"But not with me."

Shot down in flames.

Then she says, "Another time, though."

"Is that 'another time,' like a polite blow-off?" Callan asks. "Or another time, we make a date?"

"I'm off Thursday night."

He takes her to an expensive place on Restaurant Row, just outside the Kitchen but well within his and O-Bop's sphere of influence. Not a piece of clean linen arrives in this place without him and O-Bop give it the pass, the fire inspector don't notice that the back door stays locked, a beat cop always finds it convenient to stroll past the place and show the colors, and sometimes a few cases of whiskey come straight off the truck without the hassle of an invoice, so Callan gets a prime table and attentive service.

"Jesus," Siobhan asks as she scans the menu. "Can you afford this?"

"Yeah."

"What do you do?" she asks. "For work?"

Which is an awkward question.

"This and that."

"This" being labor racketeering, loan-sharking and contract murder; "that" being dope.

"It must be lucrative," she says, "this and that."

He thinks she's maybe going to get up and walk out right then, but instead she orders the fillet of sole. Callan don't know shit about wine, but he stopped by the restaurant that afternoon and let it be known that whatever the girl orders, the wine steward should bring the right bottle.

He does.

Compliments of the house.

Siobhan gives Callan a funny look.

"I do some work for them," Callan explains.

"This and that."

"Yeah."

He gets up a few minutes later to go to the bathroom, finds the manager and says, "Look, I want the check, okay?"

"Sean, the owner would fucking kill me if I gave you a check."

Because this isn't the deal. The deal is, whenever Sean Callan and Stevie O'Leary come in they eat and no check appears and they leave a heavy cash tip for the waiter. That is just understood, just like it's understood that they don't come in too often, but spread their visits around the places on Restaurant Row.

He's nervous—he don't go out on a lot of dates, and when he does usually it's to the Gloc or the Liffey and if they eat at all it's a burger or maybe some lamb stew and they usually just get shit-faced and stagger back and screw and don't hardly remember it. He only comes into a place like this on business, to—as O-Bop puts it—show the flag.

"That," she says, wiping the final remnants of chocolate mousse off her lips, "was the best meal I've ever had in my entire life."

The bill comes and it's a fucking whopper.

When Callan looks at it he don't know how the average guy can afford to live. He pulls a wad of bills from his pocket and lays them on the tray. This gets him another curious look from Siobhan.

Still, he's surprised when she takes him to her apartment and leads him straight into the bedroom. She pulls her sweater over her head and shakes her hair out, then reaches behind herself to unsnap her bra. Then she kicks off her shoes, steps out of her jeans and gets under the covers.

"You still have your socks on," Callan says.

"My feet are still cold," she says. "Are you coming in?"

He strips down to his underwear and waits until he's under the sheets to take off his shorts. She guides him inside her. She comes quickly, and when he's about to come he tries to pull out, but she locks her legs around him and won't let him. "It's okay, I'm on the Pill. I want you to come in me."

Then she rolls her hips and that settles it.

In the morning she gets up to go to confession. Otherwise, she tells him, she can't take Communion on Sunday.

"Are you going to confess us?" he asks.

"Of course."

"Are you going to promise not to do it again?" he asks, half-afraid the answer will be yes.

"I wouldn't lie to a priest," she says. Then she's out the door. He falls back asleep. Wakes up when he feels her get back in bed with him. But when he reaches for her, she refuses him, telling him that he'll have to wait until after Mass tomorrow because her soul has to be clean to take Communion.

Catholic girls, Callan thinks.

He takes her to midnight Mass.

Pretty soon they're together most of the time.

Too much of the time, according to O-Bop.

Then they move in together. The actress Siobhan has been subletting from comes back from her tour, and Siobhan has to find a place to live, which is not easy in New York on what a waitress makes, so Callan suggests she just move in with him.

"I don't know," she says. "That's a big step."

"We sleep together almost every night anyway."

"*Almost* being the operative word there."

"You'll end up living in Brooklyn."

"Brooklyn's okay."

"It's okay, but it's a long subway ride."

"You *really* want me to move in with you."

"I really want you to move in with me."

The problem is, his place is a shit hole. A third-floor walk-up on Forty-sixth and Eleventh. One room and a bath. He's got a bed, a chair, a TV, an oven he's never turned on and a microwave.

"You make how much money?" Peaches asks. "And you live like this?"

"It's all I need."

Except now it isn't, so he starts looking for another place.

He's thinking about the Upper West Side.

O-Bop don't like it. "It wouldn't look good," he says, "you leaving the neighborhood."

"There's no good places left here," Callan says. "Everything's taken."

Turns out that's not true. O-Bop drops a word to a few building managers, some deposits get returned and four or five nice apartments become available for Callan to choose from. He picks a place on Fiftieth and Twelfth with a small balcony and a view of the Hudson.

He and Siobhan start playing house.

She starts buying stuff for the place—blankets and sheets and pillows and towels and all the female shit for the bathroom. And pots and pans and dishes and dishcloths and shit, which freaks him out at first but then he kind of likes it.

"We could eat at home more," she says, "and save a lot of money."

"Eat at home more?" he asks. "We don't eat at home at all."

"That's what I mean," she says. "It adds up. We spend a fortune we could be saving."

"Saving for what?"

He don't get it.

Peaches sets him straight. "Men live in the now. Eat now, drink now, get laid *now*. We're not thinking about the next meal, the next drink, the next fuck—we're just happy *now*. Women live in the future—and this you better learn, you dumb mick: The woman is always building the nest. Everything she does, what she's really doing is gathering twigs and leaves and shit for the nest. And the nest is not for you, *paisan*. The nest is not even for her. The nest is for the *bambino*."

So Siobhan starts cooking more and at first he don't like it—he misses the crowds and the noise and the chatter—but then he gets to liking it. Likes the quiet, likes looking at her as she eats and reads the paper, likes wiping the dishes.

"The hell you drying dishes for?" O-Bop asks him. "Get a dishwasher."

"They're expensive."

"No they're not," O-Bop says. "You go to Handrigan's, pick out a dishwasher, it comes off the back of the truck, Handrigan gets the insurance."

"I'll just wipe the dishes."

But a week later, him and O-Bop are out taking care of business and Siobhan's at home when the buzzer buzzes and two guys come up with a dishwasher in the box on a hand truck.

"What's this?" Siobhan asks.

"A dishwasher."

"We didn't order a dishwasher."

"Hey," one of the guys says, "we just humped this thing up here, we ain't humping it back down. And I ain't telling O-Bop I didn't do what he said for me to do, so why don't you just be a nice girl and let us hook up the dishwasher for you?"

She lets them put it in, but it's a topic of discussion when Callan gets home.

"What's this?" she asks.

"It's a dishwasher."

"I know what it is," she says. "I mean, what *is* it?"

I'm going to give fucking Stevie a beating is what it is, Callan thinks, but he says, "A housewarming present."

"It's a very generous housewarming present."

"O-Bop's a generous guy."

"It's stolen, isn't it?"

"Depends on what you mean by *stolen*."

"It's going back."

"That would be complicated."

"What's complicated about it?"

He don't want to explain to her that Handrigan has probably already put in a claim for it, and for three or four others just like it, which he's sold for half-price in a "soup-and-sandwich" scam. So he just says, "It's complicated is all."

"I'm not stupid, you know," she says.

No one's said anything to her, but she gets it. Just living in the neighborhood—going to the store, to the cleaner's, dealing with the cable guy, the plumber—she feels the deference with which she's treated. It's little things—a couple of extra pears tossed into the basket, the clothes done tomorrow instead of the day after, the uncharacteristic courtesy of a cabbie, the man at the newsstand, the construction guys who don't hoot or whistle.

That night in bed she says, "I left Belfast because I was tired of gangsters."

He knows what she means—the Provos have become little more than thugs, controlling in Belfast most of the things that, well, most of the things that he and O-Bop control in the Kitchen. He knows what she's telling him. He wants to beg her to stay, but instead says, "I'm trying to get out."

"Just get out."

"It's not that simple, Siobhan."

"It's complicated."

"That's right, it is."

The old myth about only leaving toes-up is just that—a myth. You can walk away, but it is complicated. You can't just up and stroll. You have to ease out, otherwise there are dangerous suspicions.

And what would I do? he thinks.

For money?

He hasn't put much away. His is the businessman's lament—a lot of money comes in, but a lot goes out, too. People don't understand—there's Calabrese's cut, and Peaches', right off the top. Then the bribes—to union officials, to cops. Then the crew gets taken care of. Then he and O-Bop cut up whatever's left, which is still a lot but not as much as you think. And now they have to kick into the Big Peaches Defense Fund . . . well, there ain't enough to retire on, not enough to open a legit business.

And anyway, he wonders, what would that be? What the hell am I qualified for? All I know about is extortion and strong-arm and—face it—turning the lights out on guys.

"What do you want me to do, Siobhan?"

"Anything."

"What? Wait tables? I don't see myself with a towel over my arm."

One of them long silences in the dark before she says, "Then I guess I don't see myself with you."

He gets up the next morning, she's sitting at the table drinking tea and smoking a cig. (You can take the girl out of Ireland, but . . . he thinks.) He sits down across the table and says, "I can't get out just like that. That's not how it works. I need a little more time."

She gets right down to it, one of the things he loves about her—she's bottom-line. "How much time?"

"A year, I dunno."

"That's too long."

"But it might take that long."

She nods several times, then says, "As long as you're headed toward the door."

"Okay."

"I mean steadily toward the door."

"Yeah, I get that."

So now, a couple of months later, he's trying to explain it to O-Bop. "Look, this is all fucked-up. You know, I don't even know how it all got started. I'm sitting in a bar one afternoon and Eddie Friel walks in and then it all just gets out of hand. I don't blame you, I don't blame anybody, all I know is this has got to end. I'm out."

As if to put a period on it he puts all his hardware into a brown-paper grocery bag and gives it to the river. Then goes home to have a talk with Siobhan. "I'm thinking of carpentry," he says. "You know, storefronts and apartments and shit like that. Maybe, eventually, I could build cabinets and desks and stuff. I was thinking of going to talk with Patrick McGuigan, maybe see if he'd take me on as an unpaid apprentice. We have enough money set aside to see us over until I can get real work."

"Sounds like a plan."

"We're gonna be poor."

"I've been poor," she says. "I'm good at it."

So the next morning he goes to McGuigan's loft on Eleventh and Forty-eighth.

They went to Sacred Heart together and talk about high school for a few minutes, and about hockey for a few more minutes, and then Callan asks if he can come to work for him.

"You're shitting me, right?" McGuigan says.

"No, I'm serious."

Hell yes he is—Callan works like a *mother* learning the trade.

Shows up at seven sharp every morning with a lunch bucket in his hand and a lunch-bucket attitude in his head. McGuigan wasn't sure what to expect, but what he really didn't expect was for Callan to be a workhorse. He figured him to be a drunk or a hungover druggie, maybe, but not the citizen who walks through the door on time every morning.

No, the guy came to work, and he came to learn.

Callan finds he likes working with his hands.

At first he's all thumbs—he feels like a jerk, a mook—but then it starts coming along. And McGuigan, once he sees that Callan is serious, is patient. Takes the time to teach him things, brings him along, gives him small jobs to screw up until he gets to the point where he can do them without screwing up.

Callan goes home at night *tired*.

End of the day, he's physically worn out—he's sore, his arms ache—but mentally he feels good. He's relaxed, he's not worried about anything. There's nothing he's done during the day he's going to have bad dreams about that night.

He stops going around to the bars and pubs where he and O-Bop used to hang out. He don't go around the Liffey or the Landmark no more. Mostly he comes home and he and Siobhan have a quick supper, watch some TV, go to bed.

One day O-Bop shows up at the carpentry studio.

He stands there in the doorway, looking stupid for a minute, but Callan ain't even looking at him, he's paying attention to his sanding, and then O-Bop turns around and leaves, and McGuigan thinks maybe he should say something but there don't seem to be nothing *to* say. It's like Callan just took care of it, that's all, and now McGuigan don't have to worry about the West Side boyos coming by.

But after work, Callan goes and searches out O-Bop. Finds him on the corner of Eleventh and Forty-third, and they walk over to the waterfront together.

"Fuck you," O-Bop says. "What was that?"

"That's me telling you that my work is my work."

"What, I can't come say hello?"

"Not when I'm working."

"We ain't, what, *friends* no more?" O-Bop asks.

"We're friends."

"I dunno," says O-Bop. "You don't come around, no one sees you. You could come have a pint sometimes, you know."

"I don't hang in the bars no more."

O-Bop laughs. "You're gettin' to be a regular fuckin' Boy Scout, aren't you?"

"Laugh if you want."

"Yeah, I will."

They stand there looking across the river. It's a cold evening. The water looks black and hard.

"Yeah, well, don't do me any favors," O-Bop says. "You're not any fuckin' fun anyway since you're on this working-class-hero, Joe-Lunchbucket thing. It's just that people are asking about you."

"Who's asking about me?"

"People."

"Peaches?"

"Look," O-Bop says. "There's a lot of heat right now, a lot of pressure. People getting edgy about other people maybe talking to grand juries."

"I'm not talking to anybody."

"Yeah, well, see that you don't."

Callan grabs Stevie by the lapels of his pea coat.

"Are you getting *heavy* with me, Stevie?"

"No."

A hint of a whine.

"Because you don't get heavy with *me,* Stevie."

"I'm just saying . . . you know."

Callan lets loose of him. "Yeah, I know."

He knows.

It's a lot harder to walk out than to walk in. But he's doing it, he's walking away, and every day he gets more distance. Every day he gets closer to getting this new life, and he likes this new life. He likes getting up and going to work, working hard and then coming home to Siobhan. Having dinner, going to bed early, getting up and doing it all over again.

He and Siobhan are getting along great. They even talk about getting married.

Then Neill Demonte dies.

"I *have* to go to the funeral," Callan says.

"Why?" Siobhan asks.

"To show respect."

"To some gangster?"

She's pissed off. She's angry and scared. That he'll slip back into all of it. Because he's struggling with all the old demons in his life and now it seems like's he just walking right back into it after he's worked so hard to walk away.

"I'll just go, pay my respects and come back," he says.

"How about paying *me* some respect?" she asks. "How about respecting our relationship?"

"I do respect it."

She throws up her hands.

He'd like to explain it to her but he doesn't want to scare her. That his absence would be misunderstood. That people who are already suspicious of him would get more suspicious, that it might cause them to panic and do something about their suspicions.

"Do you think I *want* to go?"

"You must, because that's what you're doing."

"You don't understand."

"That's right, I *don't* understand."

She walks away and slams the bedroom door behind her and he hears the click of the lock. He thinks about kicking the door in, then thinks better of it, so he just punches the wall and walks out.

Hard to find a place to park at the cemetery, what with every wise guy in the city there, not to mention the platoons of local, state and federal cops. One of whom snaps Callan's picture as he walks past, but Callan don't care.

Right now he's like, *Fuck everybody.*

And his hand hurts.

"Trouble in paradise?" O-Bop says when he sees the hand.

"Go fuck yourself."

"That's it," says O-Bop. "You're not getting your Funeral Etiquette Merit Badge now."

Then he shuts up because it's clear from the darkness on Callan's face that he ain't in the mood for humor.

It seems like every wise guy that Giuliani hasn't already put in the slammer is here. You got your Cozzo brothers, all razor-cut hair and tailored suits, you got the Piccones, you got Sammy Grillo and Frankie Lorenzo, and Little Nick Corotti and Leonard DiMarsa and Sal Scachi. You got the whole Cimino Family, plus some Genovese captains—Barney Bellomo and Dom Cirillo. And some Lucchese people—Tony Ducks and Little Al D'Arco. And what's left of the Colombo Family, now that Persico is doing his hundred, and even a few of the old Bonanno guys—Sonny Black and Lefty Ruggiero.

All here to pay respect to Aniello Demonte. All here to try to sniff out how things are going to go now that Demonte is dead. They all know it depends on who Calabrese picks to be the new underboss, because with the likelihood that Paulie's going away, the new underboss is going to be the next boss. If Paulie picks Cozzo, then there'll be peace in the family. But if he picks someone else . . . Look out. So all the goombahs are here to try to suss it out.

They're all here.

With one huge exception.

Big Paulie Calabrese.

Peaches just can't believe it. Everyone's waiting for his big black limo to pull up so they can start the service, but it doesn't arrive. The widow is appalled, she doesn't know what to do, and finally Johnny Cozzo steps up and says, "Let's get started."

"Guy doesn't go to his own underboss's funeral?" Peaches says after the service. "That is wrong. That is just wrong."

He turns to Callan. "I'm glad to see you here, anyway. Where the fuck you been?"

"Around."

"You ain't been around *me*."

Callan's not in the mood.

"You guineas don't own me," he says.

"You watch your fucking mouth."

"Come on, Jimmy," O-Bop says. "He's good people."

"So," Peaches says to Callan, "I hear you're supposed to be what, a carpenter, now?"

"Yeah."

Peaches says, "I knew a carpenter got nailed to a cross."

"When you come for me, Jimmy," Callan says, "come in a hearse—because that's how you're leaving."

Cozzo moves in between them.

"What the fuck?" he says. "You wanna make *more* tapes for the Feds?

What do you want now, the 'Jimmy Peaches Live Album'? I need you fucking guys to stick together now. Shake hands."

Peaches puts out his hand to Callan.

Callan takes it and Peaches wraps his other hand around the back of Callan's head and pulls him close. "Shit, kid, I'm sorry. It's the tension, it's the grief."

"I know. Me, too."

"I love you, you dumb fucking mick," Peaches whispers in his ear. "You want out, good for you. You're out. You go build your cabinets and desks and whatever and be happy, all right? Life is short, you gotta be happy while you can."

"Thank you, Jimmy."

Peaches releases Callan and says loudly, "I'll beat this drug thing, we'll have a party, okay?"

"Okay."

Callan's invited back to the Ravenite with the rest of them, but he doesn't go.

He goes home.

Finds a parking spot, walks up the stairs and waits outside the door for a minute, working up his nerve before he can turn the key and go in.

She's there.

Sitting in a chair by the window, reading a book.

Starts to cry when she sees him. "I didn't think you were going to come back."

"I didn't know if you were going to be here."

He bends over and hugs her.

She holds him very tightly. When she lets go he says, "I was thinking we could go get a Christmas tree."

They pick a pretty one. It's small and a little sparse. It isn't a perfect tree, but it suits them. They put some corny Christmas music on, and they're busy decorating their tree the rest of the night. They don't even know that Big Paulie Calabrese has named Tommy Bellavia as his new underboss.

They come for him the next night.

Callan's walking home from work, the front of his jeans and the tops of his shoes covered with sawdust. It's a cold night, so he has the collar of his coat pulled up around his neck and his watch cap pulled low over his ears.

So he doesn't see or hear the car until it pulls up beside him.

A window slides down.

"Get in."

There's no gun, nothing sticking out. It's not needed. Callan knows that sooner or later he's going to get in the car—if not this one, the next one—so he gets in. Slides into the front seat, lifts his arms and lets Sal Scachi unbutton his coat and feel under his arms, the small of his back, down his legs.

"So it's true," Scachi says when he's done. "You're a civilian now."

"Yeah."

"A citizen," Scachi says. "The fuck is this? Sawdust?"

"Yeah, sawdust."

"Shit, I got it on my coat."

A nice coat, Callan thinks. Has to be five bills.

Scachi pulls onto the West Side Highway, heads uptown and then pulls under a bridge and stops.

A good spot, Callan thinks, to put a bullet into somebody.

Conveniently near the water.

He hears his heart thumping.

So does Scachi.

"Nothing to be afraid of here, kid."

"What do you want from me, Sal?"

"One last job," Scachi says.

"I don't do that kind of work no more."

He looks across the river at the lights of Jersey, such as they are. Maybe me and Siobhan should move to Jersey, he thinks, get a little distance from this shit. And then we could walk along the river and look at the lights of New York.

"You don't have a choice, kid," Scachi says. "Either you're with us or you're against us. And you're too dangerous for us to let you be against us. You're Billy the Kid Callan. I mean, you've shown from day one you got a taste for revenge, right? Remember Eddie Friel?"

Yeah, I remember Eddie Friel, Callan thinks.

I remember I was scared for myself, and scared for Stevie, and the gun came out and up like something else was moving it and I remember the look in Eddie Friel's eyes as the bullets smacked into his face.

I remember I was seventeen years old.

And I'd give anything to have been anywhere but in that bar that afternoon.

"Some people gotta go, kid," Scachi's saying. "And it would be . . . impolitic . . . for anyone actually in the family to do it. You understand."

I understand, Callan thinks. Big Paulie wants to purge the Cozzo wing of the family—Johnny Boy, Jimmy Peaches, Little Peaches—but he also wants to be able to deny that he did it. Blame it on the Wild Irish. We have killing in our blood.

And I *do* have a choice, he thinks.

I can kill or I can die.

"No," he says.

"No what?"

"I'm not killing any more people."

"Look—"

"I'm not doing it," Callan repeats. "If you want to kill me, kill me."

He feels free all of a sudden, like his soul is already in the air, flying over this dirty old town. Cruising around the stars.

"You got a girl, right?"

Crash.

Back to earth.

"Her name's something funny," Scachi's saying. "Like it's not spelled the way it's pronounced. Something Irish, right? No, I remember—it's like old dress material girls used to wear. Chiffon? What is it?"

To this dirty world.

"You think," Scachi's saying, "something happens to you, they're just going to leave her to run to Giuliani, repeat pillow talk you guys maybe had?"

"She don't know anything."

"Yeah, but who's going to take the chance, huh?"

There ain't nothin' I can do about it, Callan thinks. Even if I grabbed Sal right here, took his gun and emptied it into his mouth—which I could do—Scachi's a made guy and they'd kill me and they'd still kill Siobhan, too.

"Who?" Callan asks.

Who do you want me to kill?

Nora's phone rings.

Wakes her up. She's sleepy, having been out on a late date.

"Do you want to work a party?" Haley asks.

"I don't think so," Nora says. She's surprised that Haley's asking her. She's a *long* way past working parties.

"This one's a little different," Haley says. "It is a party, they want several girls, but it's all going to be one-on-one. You've been specifically asked for."

"Some kind of corporate Christmas party?"

"In a manner of speaking."

Nora looks at the digital clock on her alarm radio. It's 10:35 in the morning. She needs to get up, have her coffee and grapefruit and get to the gym.

"Come on," Haley's saying. "It'll be fun. I'm even going."

"Where is it?"

"That's the other fun thing," Haley says.

The party's in New York.

"That's some tree all right," Nora says to Haley.

They're standing by the skating rink in Rockefeller Plaza, looking up at the enormous Christmas tree. The plaza is packed with tourists. Carols blare through loudspeakers, Salvation Army Santas ring bells, streetcart vendors hawk warm chestnuts.

"See?" Haley says. "I told you it'd be fun."

It has been, Nora admits to herself.

Six of them, five working girls and Haley, flew first-class on a red-eye, were picked up by two limos at La Guardia and driven to the Plaza Hotel. Nora had been there before, of course, but never at Christmastime, and it did seem different. Beautiful and old-fashioned with all the decorations up, and her room had a view of Central Park, where even the horse carriages were festooned with holly wreaths and poinsettia.

She took a nap and a shower, then she and Haley set out on a serious shopping expedition to Tiffany's and Bergdorf's and Saks—Haley buying, Nora mostly just looking.

"Spend a little," Haley said. "You're so cheap."

"I'm not cheap," Nora says. "I'm conservative."

Because a thousand dollars is not just a thousand dollars to her. It's the interest on a thousand dollars invested over the course of, say, twenty years. It's an apartment in Montparnasse and the ability to live there comfortably. So she doesn't spend money loosely because she wants her money out there, working for her. But she does buy two cashmere scarves—one for herself and one for Haley—because it is very cold and because she wants to give Haley a present.

"Here," she says when they step back out onto the street. She pulls the chalk-gray scarf from the bag. "Wrap up."

"For me?"

"I don't want you to catch cold."

"How sweet you are."

Nora wraps her own scarf around her neck, then adjusts her faux-fur hat and coat.

It's one of those clear, cold New York City days, when a breath of air is startling in its frigid intensity and the wind comes rushing down the canyons that are the avenues, to bite your face and make your eyes water.

So when Nora's eyes tear up as she looks at Haley, she tells herself it's the cold.

"Have you ever seen the tree?" Haley asks.

"What tree?"

"The Christmas tree in Rockefeller Center," Haley says.

"I guess not."

"Come on."

So now they're standing, gawking at the huge tree, and Nora has to admit that she's having fun.

The *last* Christmas.

This is the point Jimmy Peaches is making to Sal Scachi.

"It's my last freaking Christmas outside the joint," he's saying. Calling phone booth to phone booth to leave the Feds out of the conversation for once. "For a long freaking time. They got me dead to rights, Sally. I'm going away for thirty-to-life, this fucking Rockefeller Act. By the time I get pussy again I probably won't care."

"But—"

"But nothing," Peaches says. "It's my party. And I want a big fucking steak, I want to go to the Copa with a beautiful babe on my arm, I wanna hear Vic Damone sing and then I want to get the world's best piece of ass and fuck until my dick is sore."

"Think of how it will look, Jimmy."

"My *dick*?"

"The fact that you're bringing five hookers to the sit-down," Sal says. He's pissed, he's wondering when and if Jimmy Peaches will ever grow the fuck up. The guy is a loose fucking cannon. You bust your balls to get something set up right, then this fat, horny fuck does something like fly five working girls in from fucking California. Just what he needs—five people in the room who aren't supposed to be there. Five innocent fucking bystanders. "What does John think about this?"

"John thinks it's *my* party."

Fucking A, he does, Peaches thinks. John is old-school, John is class, not like that fucking old hump they got for a boss now. John is properly grateful that I'm going to go in like a man and take what's coming, without trying to cut a deal, without naming any names, especially his.

What does John think? John's footing the fucking bill.

Anything you want, Jimmy. Anything. It's your night. On me.

What Jimmy wants is Sparks Steak House, the Copa, and this chick Nora, the best-looking, most delectable piece he's ever had. Ass like a ripe peach. He's never gotten her out of his head. Putting her on all fours and slamming her from behind, watching those peaches quiver.

"Okay," Sal says. "How about meeting the women at the Copa, *after* Sparks?"

"Fuck that."

"Jimmy—"

"What?"

"This is *serious* business tonight."

"I know that."

"I mean, it doesn't *get* more serious."

"Which is why," Peaches says, "I'm going to do some serious partying."

"Look," Sal says, bringing the hammer down, "I'm in charge of security for this thing—"

"Then make sure I'm secure," Peaches says. "That's all you gotta do, Sal, then forget about it, okay?"

"I don't like it."

"*Don't* like it," Peaches says. "Fuck you. Merry Christmas."

Yeah, Sal thinks as he hangs up.

Merry Christmas to you, Jimmy.

I got your present all ready for you.

There are a few packages under the tree.

Good thing it's a small tree because there aren't many presents, money being tight and all. But he's gotten her a new watch, and a silver bracelet and some of those vanilla candles she likes. And there are a few packages for him—they look like clothes, which he needs. A new work shirt, maybe, some new jeans.

A nice little Christmas.

They were planning to go to midnight Mass.

Open presents in the morning, try to cook a turkey, hit an afternoon movie.

A nice, quiet little Christmas.

But that ain't gonna happen, Callan thinks.

Not now.

It was going to end anyway, but it ends quicker because she finds the other package, the one he shoved way under the bed. He comes home early from work that evening and she's sitting there with the long box at her feet.

She's turned the tree lights on. They blink red and green and white behind her.

"What's this?" she asks.

"How'd you get that?"

"I was dusting under the bed," she says. "What *is* it?"

It's a Swedish Model 45 Garl Gustaf 9-mm submachine gun. With a folding metal stock and a thirty-six-round magazine. More than enough to do the job. Numbers filed off, clean and untraceable. Only twenty-two inches long with the stock folded. Weighs eight pounds. He can carry the box like a Christmas present down to midtown. Drop the box and carry the gun under his pea coat.

Sal had it delivered.

He doesn't tell her all that. What he says is stupid and obvious: "You weren't supposed to see that."

She laughs. "I thought it was a present for me. I was feeling guilty for opening it."

"Siobhan—"

"You're back into it again, aren't you?" she says. Gray eyes hard as stone. "You're doing another job."

"I have to."

"*Why?*"

He wants to tell her, but he can't let her carry that weight around with her the rest of her life. So he says, "You wouldn't understand."

"Oh, I understand," she says. "I'm from Kashmir Road, remember? Belfast? I grew up watching my brothers and uncles leave the house with their little Christmas boxes, going out to kill people. I've seen machine guns under the bed before. It's why I left—I was sick of the killing. And the killers."

"Like me."

"I thought you'd changed."

"I have."

She gestures down to the box.

"I have to," he repeats.

"Why?" she asks. "What's so important it's worth killing for?"

You, he thinks.

You are.

But he stands there mute. A dumb witness against himself.

"I won't be here when you come back this time," she says.

"I'm not coming back," he says. "I have to go away for a while."

"Jesus," she says. "Were you planning on telling me? Or were you just going to go?"

"I was planning on asking you to come with me."

It's true. He has two passports, two sets of tickets. He digs them out from the bottom of the desk drawer and lays them on top of the box, at her feet. She doesn't pick them up. She doesn't even look at them.

"Just like that?" she asks.

A voice inside him is screaming, *Tell her. Tell her you're doing it for her, for the both of you. Beg her to come.* He starts to tell her, but then he can't. She would never forgive herself, being part of it. She'd never forgive you.

"I love you," he says. "I love you so much."

She gets up from the chair.

Comes close and says, "I don't love you. I did, but I don't now. I don't love what you are. A killer."

He nods. "You're right."

He walks past her, puts his ticket and passport into his pocket, closes the box and hefts it over his shoulder.

"You can live here if you want," he says. "The rent's paid."

"I can't live here."

This was a good place, though, he thinks, looking around the small apartment. The happiest, best place of his life. This place, this time, here with her. He stands there trying to think of the words to tell her that, but nothing comes out.

"Get out," she says. "Go murder somebody. That's what you do, isn't it?"

"Yeah."

He gets out in the street, it's raining like hell. A cold, icy rain. He pulls up his collar and looks back up at the apartment.

Sees her still sitting by the window.

Bent over, her face in her hands.

The tree lights blinking red and green and white behind her.

Her dress sparkles in the lights.

A sequined top of red and green.

Very Christmasy, Haley had said, very sexy.

Très décolleté.

In fact, Jimmy Peaches can't help looking down her dress.

Otherwise she has to admit that he's acting the gentleman. Cleans up surprisingly well in his steel gray Armani. Even the black shirt and tie don't seem horrible. A touch of goombah chic, perhaps, but not entirely gross.

Same with the restaurant. She expected some gaudy Sicilian horror show, but Sparks Steak House, despite the prosaic name, turns out to be done in understated good taste. Not *her* taste—the oak-paneled walls and hunting prints, basically the English look, are not her thing, but it's tasteful all the same and not at all what she expected from a mob hangout.

They arrived in several limos, and a doorman held an umbrella to cover the two feet between the car and the long green awning. They make quite an entrance, the wise guys with their dates on their arms. Diners sitting at tables in the big front room stop eating and openly stare, and why not, Nora thinks.

The girls are fantastic.

Haley's best, served to order.

Chosen by their hair color, their faces, their figures.

Cool, lovely, sophisticated women without a touch of the whore about them. Elegantly dressed, impeccably coiffed, beautifully mannered. The men practically blush with pride as they make their entrance. The women don't—they take the adulation as their birthright. They take no visible notice of it.

A properly obsequious headwaiter shows them to the private room in the back.

Everyone watches them go in.

Well, not everyone.

Not Callan.

He misses their entrance. He's around the corner, on Third Avenue, waiting for the word to move in closer. He sees the limos come, working their way through the thick rush-hour holiday traffic, then turning right onto Forty-sixth toward Sparks, so he figures that Johnny Boy and the Piccones and O-Bop have arrived for the sit-down.

He checks his watch.

It's 5:30—dead on time.

Scachi's there to greet them, all the wise guys and the girls in turn. He's the host, right, he set up the meeting. He even (sneaking a glance down her dress) kisses Nora's hand.

"A pleasure," he says. God, he can see why Peaches would want her for his last ride. An incredible beauty. They all are, but this one . . .

Johnny Boy takes Scachi by the arm.

"Sal," he says, " just wanted to take a minute to thank you for setting this up. I know it took a lot of diplomatic work, a lot of details. If we get the result we hope for tonight, maybe we can have peace in the family."

"That's all I want, Johnny."

"And a place for you at the table."

"I'm not looking for that," Scachi says. "I just love my family, Johnny. I love this thing of ours. I want to see it stay strong, unified."

"That's what we want, too, Sally."

"I gotta go out, check on things," Sal says.

"Sure," Johnny Boy says. "Now you can call and tell the king he can make his entrance, now that the peasants are here."

"See, that's just the kind of attitude—"

Johnny Boy laughs. "Merry Christmas, Sal."

They hug and exchange kisses on the cheeks.

"Merry Christmas, Johnny." Sal puts on his coat and starts to go. "Oh, and Johnny?"

"Yeah?"

"Happy fucking New Year."

Sal steps outside under the awning. *Miserable* fucking night. Sheets of rain coming down, threatening to turn into an ice storm. The drive back to Brooklyn's going to be a bitch and a half.

He takes the small walkie-talkie from his overcoat pocket and holds it under his collar and against his mouth.

"You there?"

"Yeah," Callan says.

"I'm calling the boss in," Sal says. "So the clock's on."

"Everything's good?"

"Just like we talked," Sal says. "You got ten minutes, kid."

Callan walks over to a trash can. Drops the box into it, slides the gun under his coat and starts to walk down Forty-sixth Street.

Into the rain.

The champagne flows over the glass.

To laughs and giggles.

"What the hell," Peaches announces. "Champagne we got."

He fills all the glasses.

Nora lifts hers. She won't really drink it, but she'll take a sip for the upcoming toast. Anyway, she likes the bubbles in her nose.

"A toast," Peaches says. "Hey, we got some bad stuff in our lives, but we got some good stuff, too. So don't nobody be sad this holiday. Life is beautiful. We have plenty to celebrate."

In this season of hope, Nora thinks.

Then all hell breaks loose.

Callan opens his coat and swings the gun out.

Pulls back the bolt as he aims through the driving rain.

Bellavia sees him first. He's just finished opening the car door for Mr. Calabrese and he looks over and sees Callan. There's a small glimmer first of recognition and then of alarm in the man's piggish eyes, and he starts to ask *What are you doing out here* but then he realizes the answer and goes for his own gun inside his coat.

Much too late.

His arm is blasted away as the 9-mm Parabellum rounds stitch across his chest. He falls back against the open door of the black Lincoln Continental, then slumps onto the sidewalk.

Callan turns the gun on Calabrese.

Their eyes meet for half a second before Callan pulls the trigger again. The old man staggers, then seems to melt into a puddle with the rain.

Callan steps in and stand above the two crumpled bodies. Holds the barrel near Bellavia's head and squeezes the trigger twice. Bellavia's head bounces off the wet concrete. Then Callan places the barrel to Calabrese's temple and pulls the trigger.

Callan drops the gun, turns around and walks east toward Second Avenue.

The blood flows down the gutter after him.

Nora hears the screams.

The door flies open.

The headwaiter comes in yelling that someone's been shot outside. Nora stands up, they all do, but they don't know why. Don't know whether to run outside or stay where they are.

Then Sal Scachi comes in to tell them.

"Everyone stay put," he orders. "Someone killed the boss."

Nora's like, What boss? Who?

Now the keening of sirens drowns out everything else, and she jumps as—

Pop.

Her heart is in her throat. Everyone startles as Johnny Boy, still sitting, pours the champagne into his glass.

A car's waiting at the corner.

The rear passenger door opens and Callan gets in. The car turns east on Forty-seventh, goes to the FDR and heads uptown. There are fresh clothes in the back. Callan takes his own clothes off and wriggles into the new ones.

All the while, the driver doesn't say nothing, just efficiently works his way through the brutal traffic.

So far, Callan thinks, it's gone just the way they'd planned it. Bellavia and Calabrese arrived expecting to find a crime scene, their colleagues brutally murdered and the stage set for their own weeping and gnashing of teeth and cries of *We came here to make peace in our family.*

Only that's not what Sal Scachi and the rest of the family had in mind.

You deal, you die, but if you don't deal you die anyway, because that's where the money and the power are. And if you let the other families get all the money and the power, you're just on a slow road to suicide. That was Scachi's reasoning, and it was correct.

So Calabrese had to go.

And Johnny Boy had to become king.

"It's a generational thing," Sal had explained on their long walk in Riverside Park. "Out with the old, in with the new."

Of course, it will take a while for it all to shake out.

Johnny Boy will deny any involvement because the heads of the other Four Families, or what's left of them, would never accept his doing this without their permission, which they would never have given. ("A king," Scachi had lectured him, "will never sanction the assassination of another king.") So Johnny Boy will swear that he'll track down the drug-dealing cocksuckers who killed his boss, and there'll be a few recalcitrant Calabrese loyalists who'll have to follow their boss to the next world, but it will all shake out in the end.

Johnny Boy will reluctantly allow himself to be chosen as the new boss.

The other bosses will accept him.

And the dope will flow again.

Uninterrupted from Colombia, to Honduras, to Mexico.

To New York.

Where it's going to be a White Christmas after all.

But I won't be here to see it, Callan thinks.

He opens the canvas bag on the floor.

As agreed, a hundred thousand dollars in cash, a passport, airline tickets. Sal Scachi set it all up. A ride to South America and a new gig.

The car makes it onto the Triborough Bridge.

Callan looks out the window and, even through the rain, can see the Manhattan skyline. Somewhere in there, he thinks, was my life. The Kitchen, Sacred Heart, the Liffey Pub, the Landmark, the Glocca Morra, the Hudson. Michael Murphy and Kenny Maher and Eddie Friel. And Jimmy Boylan, Larry Moretti and Matty Sheehan.

And now Tommy Bellavia and Paulie Calabrese.

And the living ghosts—

Jimmy Peaches.

And O-Bop.

Siobhan.

He looks back at Manhattan and what he sees is their apartment. Her coming to the table for breakfast on Saturday mornings. Her hair mussed, no makeup, so beautiful. Sitting there with her over a cup of coffee and the newspaper, mostly unread, and looking out over the gray Hudson with Jersey on the other side.

Callan grew up on fables.

Cuchulain, Edward Fitzgerald, Wolfe Tone, Roddy McCorley, Pádraic Pearse, James Connelly, Sean South, Sean Barry, John Kennedy, Bobby Kennedy, Bloody Sunday, Jesus Christ.

They all ended bloody.

PART THREE

NAFTA

8

Days of the Innocents

In Rama was there a voice heard, lamentation, and weeping,
and great mourning, Rachel weeping for her children, and
would not be comforted, for they are not.

—Matthew 2:18

Tegucigalpa, Honduras
San Diego, California
Guadalajara, Mexico
1992

A rt sits on a park bench in Tegucigalpa and watches a man in a maroon Adidas tracksuit leave his building across the street.

Ramón Mette has seven of the suits—one for each day of the week. Every day he puts on a fresh one and leaves his mansion in suburban Tegus for a three-mile jog, flanked by two security guards in matching outfits, except theirs are bulging in unusual places to allow for the Mac-10s they carry to keep him safe on his jogs.

So Mette goes out every morning. Runs a three-mile round-trip and returns to the mansion and takes a shower while one of the bodyguards whips up a fruit smoothie in the blender. Mango, papaya, grapefruit and, this being Honduras, bananas. Then he takes his drink out onto the patio and sips it while he reads the paper. Makes some phone calls, conducts a little business, then goes to his private gym to pump some iron.

That's his routine.

By the clock, every day.

For months.

Except this one morning, the bodyguard opens the door, a sweaty, puffing Mette goes in, and a pistol butt slams into the side of his head.

He slides onto his knees in front of Art Keller.

His bodyguard stands helplessly with his hands up as a black-clad Honduran secret-service trooper points an M-16 at his head. There have to be fifty troopers standing there. Which is odd, Mette thinks through a haze of pain and dizziness, because don't I own the secret service?

Apparently not, because none of them do shit as Art Keller kicks Mette square in the teeth. Stands over him and says, "I hope you enjoyed your jog because it's the last you're ever going to get."

So Mette's drinking his own blood instead of a fruit smoothie as Art slips the old black hood over his head, ties it tight and frog-marches him to a waiting van with tinted windows. And this time there's no one there to object as they haul him onto an Air Force plane for a flight to the Dominican Republic, where he's taken to the American embassy, arrested for the murder of Ernie Hidalgo, taken to another plane and flown to San Diego, where he's promptly arraigned, denied bail and put in a solitary cell in the federal holding facility.

All of this touches off riots in the streets of Tegucigalpa, where thousands of angry citizens, incited and paid for by Mette's lawyers, burn the American embassy in protest against Yanqui imperialism. They want to know where this American cop gets the *huevos* to come into their country and snatch one of their prominent citizens.

A lot of people in Washington are wondering the same thing. They would also like to know where Art Keller, the disgraced former RAC of the closed Guadalajara office, gets the balls to create an international incident. And not just the balls, but the package to pull it off.

How the hell did that happen?

Quito Fuentes is a small-time operator.

He is now, and he was in 1985 when he drove the tortured Ernie Hidalgo from the safe house in Guadalajara to the ranch in Sinaloa. Now he lives in Tijuana, where he does small-time dope deals with small-time Americans coming across the border for a quick score.

You do that kind of business, you don't want to show up light, in case one of the Yanqui kids decides he's a real bandito and tries to take your dope and make a run for the border. No, you want some weight on your hip, and Quito's current piece is, well, a piece of shit.

Quito needs a new gun.

Which, contrary to public image, is hard to come by in Mexico, where the *federales* and the state police like to have a monopoly on firepower. Lucky for Quito, living as he does in TJ, he's right next door to the world's biggest arms supermarket, Los Estados Unidos, so he's all ears when Paco Méndez calls from Chula Vista to tell him he's got a deal for him. A clean Mac-10 he just has to move.

All Quito has to do is come pick it up.

But Quito doesn't like to venture north of the border anymore.

Not since the thing with the Yanqui cop, Hidalgo.

Quito knows he's pretty safe from arrest on that thing in Mexico, but in the United States it might be a different story, so he tells Paco thanks but no thanks, and couldn't he just bring it down to TJ? It's more of a hopeful question than a realistic one, because you have to be either (a) very well connected or (b) some kind of fucking moron to try to smuggle any firearm, never mind a machine pistol, into Mexico. If you got caught, the *federales* would beat you like wet laundry on a dry line, then you'd catch a minimum two-year sentence in a Mexican prison. Paco knows that they don't feed you in Mexican prisons—that's your family's problem, and Paco doesn't have family in Mexico anymore. And as he's neither well connected nor a fucking moron, he tells Quito he doesn't think he can make that trip.

But as Paco has to turn this gun into some quick cash, he tells Quito, "Let me think about it. I'll call you back."

He hangs up and tells Art Keller, "He won't come over."

"Then you have a big problem," Art says.

No shit, a big problem—a cocaine *and* a gun charge, and just in case Paco isn't gripping hard enough already, Art adds, "I'll take it federal and I'll ask the judge for consecutive sentences."

"I'm trying!" Paco whines.

"You don't get points for effort," Art says.

"You're a real ball-buster, you know that?"

"I know that," Art says. "Do *you* know that?"

Paco slumps in his chair.

"Okay," Art says. "Just get him to the fence."

"Yeah?"

"We'll do the rest."

So Paco gets back on the horn and arranges to make the deal at the rickety chain-link border fence along Coyote Canyon.

No-man's-land.

You go into Coyote Canyon at night, you'd *better* bring a gun, and even that might not be enough, because a lot of God's children got guns in Coyote

Canyon, a big scar in the rolling hills of barren dirt that flank the ocean along the border. The Canyon runs from the north edge of TJ for about two miles into the United States, and it is bandit country. Late in the afternoon, thousands of would-be immigrants start forming up on either side of the canyon on a ridge above the dry aqueduct that is the actual border. When the sun goes down, they make a rush through the canyon, simply overwhelming the outmanned Border Patrol agents. It's the law of numbers—more get through than get caught. And even if you get caught, there's always tomorrow.

Maybe.

Because real banditos get into the canyon and lie in wait like predators for the herd of *mojados* to come through. Pick off the weak and the wounded. Rob, rape and murder. Take what little cash the illegals have, drag their women into the bushes and rape them, then maybe slit their throats.

So you want to come pick oranges in los Estados Unidos, you have to run the gauntlet of Coyote Canyon. And in that chaos, in the dust from a thousand running feet, in the darkness amid screams, gunfire and flashing blades, with the Border Patrol vehicles roaring up and down hills like cowboys trying to control a stampede (which they are; which it is), a lot of business gets done along the fence.

Deals for dope, for sex, for guns.

And that's what Quito's doing as he crouches by a hole cut in the fence.

"Gimme the gun."

"Gimme the money."

Quito can see the Mac-10 glittering in the moonlight, so he's pretty sure his old *cuate* Paco's not going to rip him off. So he reaches through the hole to hand Paco the cash and Paco grabs—

—not the money, but his wrist.

And holds on.

Quito tries to pull back, but now there are three Yanquis grabbing him, and one of them says, "You're under arrest for the murder of Ernie Hidalgo."

And Quito says, "You can't arrest me, I'm in Mexico."

"No problem," Art says.

Then starts to pull him into the United States, just starts yanking him through the hole in the fence, but one of the jagged pieces of the cut fence snags Quito's pants. But Art keeps pulling, and the sharp wire pierces Quito's butt, then pokes out the other side.

So he's lying there basically impaled through the left butt cheek, and he's screaming, "I'm stuck! I'm stuck!"

Art doesn't care—he braces his feet against the American side of the fence and just pulls. The wire rips through Quito's butt, and now he's really screaming because he's hurt and bleeding and in America and the Yanquis are punching the shit out of him, and then they stick a rag in his mouth to shut him up, and handcuff him, and they're carrying him toward a jeep, and Quito sees a Border Patrol agent and tries to scream for help, but the *migra* just turns his back like he don't see nothing.

Quito tells all this to the judge, who looks solemnly down at Art and asks him where the arrest took place.

"The defendant was arrested in the United States, Your Honor," Art says. "He was on American soil."

"The defendant claims you pulled him through the fence."

Then, as Quito's public defender literally hops up and down with indignation, Art answers, "There's not a word of truth to that, Your Honor. Mr. Fuentes came into the country of his own volition, to purchase an illegal firearm. We can offer a witness."

"Would that be Mr. Méndez?"

"Yes, Your Honor."

"Your Honor," the PD says, "Mr. Méndez obviously has made a deal with—"

"There was no deal," Art says. "My hand to God."

Next.

The Doctor's not going to be so easy.

Doctor Álvarez has a thriving gynecology practice in Guadalajara, and he isn't leaving. There's nothing on earth that's going to lure him across or even near the border. He knows the DEA is aware of his role in the Hidalgo murder, he knows how badly Keller wants him, so the good doctor is staying put in Guadalajara.

"Mexico City's already screaming about Quito Fuentes," Tim Taylor tells Art.

"Let them."

"Easy for you to say."

"Yeah, it is."

"I'm telling you, Art," Taylor says. "We can't just go in and grab the Doctor, and the Mexicans aren't going to do it. They're not going to extradite him, either. This isn't Honduras, this isn't Coyote Canyon. Case closed."

Maybe for you, Art thinks.

Not for me.

It will never be over until every person involved in Ernie's murder is dead or behind bars.

If we can't do it, and the Mexican cops won't do it, I just have to find someone who will.

Art goes to Tijuana.

Where Antonio Ramos owns a little restaurant.

He finds the big ex-cop sitting outside with his feet up on a table, his cigar clenched in his mouth and a cold Tecate at the ready. He sees Art walk up and says, "If you're on a search for the perfect *chile verde,* I can tell you this isn't the place."

"Not what I'm after," Art says, sitting down. He orders a *cerveza* from the waitress who comes over like a shot.

"What, then?" Ramos asks.

"Not what—who," Art says. "Doctor Humberto Álvarez."

Ramos shakes his head. "I retired."

"I remember."

"Anyway, they broke up the DFS," Ramos says. "I make one grand gesture in my life, and they render it inconsequential."

"I still could use your help."

Ramos swings his legs off the table and sits forward in his chair to bring his face closer to Art's. "You had my help, remember? I gave you fucking Barrera, and you wouldn't pull the trigger. You didn't want revenge, you wanted justice. You got neither."

"I haven't quit."

"You should," Ramos says. "Because there is no justice, and you're not serious about revenge. You're not Mexican. There aren't many things we take seriously, but vengeance is one of them."

"I'm serious."

"I don't think so."

"I'm a-hundred-thousand-dollars serious," Art says.

"You're offering me a hundred thousand dollars to kill Álvarez."

"Not kill him," Art says. "Kidnap him. Bag him, put him on a plane to the States, where I can bring him to trial."

"See, this is exactly what I mean," says Ramos. "You're soft. You want revenge, but you're not man enough to just take it. You have to mask it with this 'fair trial' *mierda.* It would be a lot easier just to shoot him."

"I'm not interested in easy," Art says. "I'm interested in hard, long suffering. I want to put him in some federal hellhole for the rest of his life and hope it's a long one. You're the one who's soft, wanting to put him out of his misery."

"I don't know . . ."

"Soft and bored," Art says. "Don't tell me you're not bored. Sitting here day after day, cranking out tamales for tourists. You've kept up with the news. You know I got Mette and Fuentes already. And next I'm going to get the Doctor, with or without you. And then I'm going to get Barrera. With or without you."

"A hundred grand."

"A hundred grand."

"I'll need a few men . . ."

"I have a hundred grand for the job," Art says. "Split it any way you want."

"Tough guy."

"You better believe it."

Ramos takes a long pull on his cigar, exhales in perfect smoke circles and watches them float into the air. Then says, "Shit, I'm not making any money here. Okay. *Acuérdate.*"

"I want him alive," Art says. "You bring me a corpse, you can whistle for your money."

"*Sí, sí, sí . . .*"

Doctor Humberto Álvarez Machain finishes with his last patient, gallantly sees her out the door, says good night to his receptionist and steps back into his private office to gather up some papers before going home. He doesn't hear the seven men come through the outer door. He doesn't hear anything until Ramos steps into his office, points a stun gun at his ankle and shoots.

Álvarez falls to the floor and rolls in pain.

"You've seen your last *funciete,* Doctor," Ramos says. "No *chocho* where you're going."

And shoots him again. Ramos says, "Hurts like a bastard, doesn't it?"

"Yes," Álvarez moans.

"If it were up to me I'd put a bullet in your head right now," Ramos says. "Lucky for you, it isn't up to me. Now, you're going to do everything I say, aren't you?"

"Yes."

"Good."

They blindfold him, wrap telephone ties around his wrists and take him out the back door to a car waiting in the alley and shove him into the back-seat, where they make him lie on the floor. Ramos gets in and sets his feet on Álvarez's neck, and they drive to a safe house in the suburbs.

They bring him into the darkened living room and take off the blindfold.

Álvarez starts to cry when he sees the tall man stretched out in the chair in front of him.

"Do you know who I am?" Art asks. "Ernie Hidalgo was my close friend. *Un hermano. Sangre de mi sangre.*"

Álvarez is trembling uncontrollably now.

"You were his torturer," Art says. "You scraped his bones with metal skewers, you shoved white-hot iron rods inside him. You gave him shots to keep him conscious and alive."

"No," Álvarez says.

"Don't lie to me," Art says. "It only makes me angrier. I have you on tape."

A stain emerges on the front of the doctor's pants and spreads down one leg.

"He's pissing himself," Ramos says.

"Strip him."

They pull his shirt off and leave it dangling around his bound wrists. Jerk his pants and his shorts down to his ankles. Álvarez's eyes widen in little orbs of terror. All the more so when Kleindeist says, "Take a whiff. What do you smell?"

Álvarez shakes his head.

"From the kitchen," Kleindeist says. "Think hard—you've smelled it before. No? Okay—metal heating. A piece of rebar, over the stove."

One of Ramos' men comes in, holding the red-hot, glowing metal in an oven mitt.

Álvarez faints.

"Wake him up," Art says.

Ramos shoots him in the calf.

Álvarez comes to and screams.

"Bend him over the couch."

They heave Álvarez over the arm of the couch. Two men hold his arms and spread them wide. Two others pin his feet to the floor. The other man brings over the hot iron and shows it to him.

"No, please . . . no."

"I want the names," Art says, "of everyone you saw in the house with Ernie Hidalgo. And I want them now."

No problema.

Álvarez starts talking like a comic speed-reader on crank.

"Adán Barrera, Raúl Barrera," he says. "Ángel Barrera, Güero Méndez."

"What?"

"Adán Barrera, Raúl Barrera—"

"No," Art snaps. "The last name."

"Güero Méndez."

"He was there?"

"*Sí, sí, sí.* He was the leader, Señor." Álvarez takes a gulp of air, then says, "He killed Hidalgo."

"How?"

"An overdose of heroin," Álvarez says. "An accident. We were going to free him. I swear. *La verdad.*"

"Pick him up."

Art looks at the sobbing doctor and says, "You're going to write out a statement. Telling all about your involvement. All about the Barreras and Méndez. *¿De acuerdo?*"

"*De acuerdo.*"

"Then you're going to write another statement," Art says, "affirming that you were not tortured or compelled to make this statement in any way. *¿De acuerdo?*"

"*Sí.*" Then, regaining his composure, he starts to deal. "Will you offer me some kind of consideration for my cooperation?"

"I'll put in a good word for you," Art says.

They sit him down at the kitchen table with paper and pen. An hour later, both statements are finished. Art reads them, puts them in his briefcase and says, "Now you're going for a little trip."

"No, Señor!" Álvarez screams. He knows all about little trips. They usually involve shovels and shallow graves.

"To the United States," Art says. "We have a plane waiting at the airport. You're going of your free will, I assume."

"Yes, of course."

Goddamn right, of course, Art thinks. The man just dropped a dime on the Barreras and Güero Méndez. His life expectancy in Mexico is approximately nil. Art hopes his longevity in Marion federal penitentiary will be of Old Testament proportions.

Two hours later they have Álvarez, cleaned up and with a fresh pair of pants, on a plane to El Paso, where he is arrested and arraigned in the torture murder of Ernie Hidalgo. At his jailing, he's photographed, naked, from his head to his knees to show that he hasn't been tortured.

And Art, faithful to his promise, puts in a good word for Álvarez. Through the federal prosecutors, he doesn't seek the death penalty.

He wants life in prison without the possibility of parole.

Life without hope.

The Mexican government protested and a squadron of American civil-liberties lawyers joined them, but both Mette and Álvarez are sitting in Marion federal maximum security prison awaiting their appeals, Quito Fuentes is in a San Diego jail cell, and no one has laid a restraining hand on Art Keller.

Those who would, can't.

And those who can, won't.

Because he lied.

Art lied his ass off to the Senate committee that investigated rumors that the CIA was somehow complicit with the Contras' arms-for-drugs dealings. Art still has a transcript of his testimony running in his head like the sound track of a movie you can't shut off.

Q: Have you ever heard of an air-freight company called SETCO?

A: Remotely.

Q: Are you now or were you ever of the belief that SETCO airplanes were being used to transport cocaine?

A: I have no knowledge on that subject.

Q: Did you ever hear of something called the "Mexican Trampoline"?

A: No.

Q: May I remind you that you're under oath?

A: Yes.

Q: Have ever heard of TIWG?

A: What's that?

Q: The Terrorist Incident Working Group.

A: Not until just now.

Q: How about NSD Directive #3?

A: No.

Q: The NHAO?

Art's lawyer leaned across and said into the microphone, "Counsel, if you just want to go fishing, may I suggest you charter a boat?"

Q: Have you ever heard of NHAO?

A: Only recently, in the newspapers.

Q: Did anyone at NHAO pressure you in regard to your testimony?

"I'm not going to let this go on much longer," Art's lawyer said.

Q: Did Colonel Craig, for instance, pressure you?

This question had the intended effect of waking up the press.

Colonel Scott Craig was shoving the American flag, pole and all, right up another committee's butt as it tried to pin him to the arms-for-hostages deal with the Iranians. In the process Craig was becoming an American folk hero, a media darling, a television patriot. The country focused in on the Iran–Contra sideshow, the shitty guns-for-hostages deal, and never caught on to the real scandal—that the administration had helped the Contras deal drugs for arms. So the suggestion that Colonel Craig, whom Art had last seen at Ilopongo off-loading cocaine, had pressured Keller into silence was a dramatic moment.

"That's outrageous, counselor," Art's lawyer said.

Q: I agree. Will your client answer the question?
A: I came here to answer your questions truthfully and accurately, and that's what I'm attempting to do.
Q: So would you answer the question?
A: I've never met nor had any conversations with Colonel Craig on any subject whatsoever.

The media went back to sleep.

Q: How about something called "Cerberus," Mr. Keller? Did you ever hear of that?
A: No.
Q: Did something called Cerberus have anything at all to do with the murder of Agent Hidalgo?
A: No.

Althea left the gallery at that answer. Later, at the Watergate, she told him, "Maybe a bunch of senators can't tell when you're lying, Art, but I can."

"Can we just go and have a nice dinner with the kids?" Art asked.

"How could you?"

"What?"

"Align yourself with a bunch of right-wing—"

"Stop."

He held his hand up and turned his back to her. He's tired of hearing it.

He's tired of hearing everything, Althea thought. If he was remote during their last few months in Guadalajara, that was a goddamn honeymoon compared to the man who came home from Mexico. Or *didn't* come home, not the man she recognized as her husband. He didn't want to talk, didn't want to listen. Spent most of his long "administrative leave" sitting alone out by her parents' pool or taking long, lone walks through Pacific Palisades or down on the beach. He'd sit at dinner barely speaking, or worse, launching into an angry diatribe about how politics is all bullshit, then excusing himself to go upstairs, alone, or out for a nocturnal stroll. Late nights he'd lie in bed, thumbing the TV remote like some kind of speed freak, switching from channel to channel, pronouncing everything crap and more crap. On the increasingly rare occasions that they would make love (if you wanted to call it that), he was aggressive and quick, as if he were trying to work out his anger rather than express his love or even his lust.

"I'm not a punching bag," she said one night as he lay on top of her in one of his spectacular postcoital depressions.

"I've never hit you."

"That's not what I meant."

He remained a dutiful, if wooden, father. He did all the daddy things he used to do, but now it was more like he was just going through the motions. Like a robot version of Art taking the kids to the park, robot Art showing Michael how to body-board, robot Art playing tennis with Cassie. The kids knew.

Althea tried to get him to see someone.

He laughed. "A shrink?"

"A shrink, a counselor, somebody."

"All they do is give you drugs," he said.

Christ, then *take* them, she thought.

It got worse when the subpoenas came.

The meetings with DEA bureaucrats, administration officials, congressional investigators. And lawyers—God, so many lawyers. She was worried that the legal fees would bankrupt them, but all he would say was not to worry, "It's taken care of." She never knew where the money was coming from, but it was coming because she never saw a legal bill, not one.

Art, of course, refused to discuss it.

"I'm your wife," she'd pleaded one night. "Why won't you open up to me?"

"There are things you can't know about," he said.

He *wanted* to talk to her, tell her everything, get close again, but he couldn't. It was like there was this invisible wall, this science-fiction force field—not between them but inside him—that he just couldn't break through. It was as if he spent all his time walking through water, *under*water, looking up at the light of the real world but seeing only the water-distorted faces of his wife and his kids. Unable to reach up, reach through and touch them. Unable to let them touch him.

Instead he dove deeper.

Retreated into silence, the slow poison of a marriage.

That day at the Watergate he looked at Althea and knew that she knew he'd taken a dive—lay down and lied for the administration, helped them cover up a shitty deal that had put crack out onto the streets of American ghettos.

What she didn't know was why.

This is why, Art thinks now as he peers through the window blinds across the way at 2718 Cosmos Street, where Tío Barrera is holed up.

"I got you now, motherfucker," Art says. "And no one's going to snatch you out of it this time."

Tío's been switching residences every few days, moving around between his dozen apartments and condos in Guadalajara. Whether it's a result of his fearing arrest or, as rumor has it, because he's been smoking his own product, Tío has become increasingly paranoid.

With good reason, Art thinks. He's been watching Tío in this place for three days now. That's a long time for Tío to be in any one place. He'll probably move again this afternoon.

Or thinks he will.

Art has his own plans for Tío's next move.

But it has to be done right.

His government has promised the Mexican government that it will be done with no fuss, no muss. Above all, with no collateral casualties. And Art has to disappear as soon as possible—this has to look like a Mexican operation all the way, a triumph for the *federales*.

Whatever, Art thinks.

I don't care, Tío, as long as it ends with you in a prison cell.

He crouches by the window and peeks out again. The reward for My Years in the Desert, as he came to call that god-awful stretch of '87, '88 and '89, when he maneuvered through the minefield of investigations, sweated out the perjury indictment that never came, watched as one president left office and his vice president—the same man who had run the secret war against the Sandinistas—came in. My Years in the Desert, Art recalls, transferred from one desk job to another as his marriage dried up, as he and Althea retreated into separate rooms and separate lives, as Althea finally demanded a divorce and he fought it every step of the way.

Even now, Art thinks, a fresh set of divorce papers sits unsigned on the kitchenette table of his barren little apartment in downtown San Diego.

"I will *never*," Art told his wife, "let you take my kids."

Eventually peace came.

Not to the Kellers, but to Nicaragua.

Elections were held, the Sandinistas were tossed out, the secret war came to end, and about five minutes later Art went to John Hobbs to claim his reward.

The destruction of every man involved in the murder of Ernie Hidalgo.

A laundry list: Ramón Mette, Quito Fuentes, Doctor Álvarez, Güero Méndez.

Raúl Barrera.

Adán Barrera.

And Miguel Ángel Barrera.

Tío.

Whatever Art might have thought about the president, John Hobbs, Colonel Scott Craig and Sal Scachi, they were men of their word. Art Keller was given a free hand and all possible cooperation. He went on his tear.

"As a result," Hobbs had said, "we have a burned embassy in Honduras and a raging civil-liberties battle, and our diplomatic relationship with Mexico is in ashes. To stretch the metaphor to the breaking point, State would like to host an auto-da-fé for you, to which Justice will bring the marshmallows."

"But I'm confident," Art says, "that I have the full support of the White House and the president."

Which was Art reminding Hobbs that before the current president occupied the White House he was busy funding the Contras with cocaine, so let's not hear any more bullshit about "State" and "Justice."

The extortion worked; Art got permission to go after Tío.

Not that this had been easy to arrange.

Negotiations at the highest level, and Art hadn't even been involved.

Hobbs went to Los Pinos, the president's residence, to make the deal: The arrest of Miguel Ángel Barrera would remove one stumbling block to the passage of NAFTA.

NAFTA is the key, the absolutely essential key, to Mexican modernization. With it in place, Mexico can move ahead into the next century. Without it, the economy will stagnate and collapse, and the country will remain a Third World backwater forever, mired in poverty.

So they'll trade Barrera as part of the deal for NAFTA.

But there's another, more troublesome condition: This is the last arrest. This closes the books on the Hidalgo murder. Art Keller won't even be allowed back in the country after this. So he'll get Barrera, but not Adán, Raúl, or Güero Méndez.

That's okay, Art thinks.

I have plans for them.

But first, Tío.

So now Art watches and waits.

The problem is Tío's three bodyguards (Cerberus again, Art thinks, the unavoidable three-headed guard dog), armed with 9-mm machine pistols, AK-47s and hand grenades. And willing to use them.

Not that it worries Art overmuch. His team has firepower, too. There are twenty-five special *federale* officers with M-16s, sniper rifles and the whole SWAT arsenal, not to mention Ramos and his crew of privateers. But the Mexican mandate was "We can absolutely not have a gun battle in the streets of Guadalajara, it just cannot happen," and Art is determined to live up to the deal.

So they're trying to find an opening.

It's the girl who gives it to them.

Barrera's latest stringy-haired mistress.

She won't cook.

Art has watched the past three mornings as the bodyguards have trooped out to a local *comida* to buy their breakfast. Listened through sound detectors at the arguments, her shouting, their grumbling as they go out and come back twenty minutes later, nourished and ready for a long day of guarding Miguel Ángel.

Not today, Art thinks.

Going to be a short day today.

"They should be coming out," he says to Ramos.

"Don't worry."

"I worry," Art says. "What if she gets a sudden attack of domesticity?"

"That pig?" Ramos asks. "Forget it. Now, if she were my woman, she'd cook breakfast. She'd wake up in the morning whistling and wanting to please me. The happiest woman in Mexico."

But he's edgy, too, Art sees. His jaws are clamped on the omnipresent cigar, and his fingers are drumming little tattoos on the stock of Esposa, his Uzi, as he adds, "They have to eat."

Let's hope so, Art thinks. If they don't, and we miss this opportunity, the whole fragile arrangement with the Mexican government could fall apart. They're already nervous, reluctant allies. The secretary of the interior and the governor of Jalisco have literally distanced themselves from the operation; they're miles out at sea on a three-day "diving excursion" so that they can plead non-involvement to both the nation and the surviving Barrera brothers. And there are so many moving pieces in this operation, all of which have to be coordinated, that the whole thing is extremely time-sensitive.

The team of *federales* from Mexico City is in place here, waiting to grab Barrera. At the same time, a special unit of army troops is perched on the edge of town, ready to move in and detain the entire Jalisco State Police force, its chief and the governor of the state until Barrera is flown to Mexico City, arraigned and jailed.

It's a state coup d'état, Art thinks, planned to the second, and if this moment passes, it will be impossible to maintain secrecy for another day. The Jalisco police will get their boy Barrera out, the governor will plead ignorance, and it will be over.

So it has to be now.

He watches the front door of the house.

Please, God, let them be hungry.

Let them go to breakfast.

He stares at the door of the house as if he could make it open.

Tío is a crackhead.

Hooked on the pipe.

It's tragic, Adán thinks as he looks at his uncle. What started as a pantomime of disability has become real, as if Tío acted his way into a role that he can't shake off. Always a slim man, he's thinner than ever, doesn't eat, chainsmokes one cigar after another. When he's not inhaling the smoke, he coughs it up. His once jet-black hair is now silver, and his skin has a yellowish tint. He's hooked up to a glucose IV on a rolling stand that he drags behind him everywhere like a pet dog.

He's fifty-three years old.

A young girl—Christ, what is this? the fifth or sixth since Pilar—comes in, plops her ample ass down on the easy chair and clicks the television on with the remote. Raúl is shocked at the disrespect, even more shocked when his uncle says meekly, "*Calor de mi vida,* we are talking business."

Warmth of my life, my ass, Adán thinks. The girl—he can't even think of her name—is yet another pale imitation of Pilar Talavera Méndez. Twenty pounds heavier, limp, greasy hair, a face that's many *carnitas* away from being pretty, but there is a faint resemblance. Adán could understand the obsession with Pilar—God, what a beauty—but with this *segundera,* he can't comprehend. Especially when the girl puts a pout on her gash of a fat mouth and mewls, "You're *always* talking business."

"Make us some lunch," Adán says.

"I don't cook." She sneers and waddles out. They can hear another television come on, loudly, from another room.

"She likes her soap operas," Tío explains.

Adán has been silent so far, sitting back in his chair and watching his uncle with growing concern. His obvious bad health, his weakness, his attempts to replace Pilar, attempts as persistent as they are disastrous. Tío Ángel is fast becoming a pathetic figure and yet he is still the *patrón* of the *pasador.*

Tío leans over and whispers, "Do you see her?"

"Who, Tío?"

"Her," Tío croaks. "Méndez's *mujer.* Pilar."

Güero had married the girl. Met her as she got off the plane from her Salvadoran "honeymoon" with Tío, and actually married a girl whom most Mexican men wouldn't have touched because not only was she not a virgin, she was Barrera's thing-on-the-side, his *segundera.*

That's how much Güero loves Pilar Talavera.

"*Sí*, Tío," Adán says. " I see her."

Tío nods. Looks quickly toward the living room to make sure the girl is still watching television, and then whispers, "Is she still beautiful?"

"No, Tío," Adán lies. "She is fat now. And ugly."

But she isn't.

She is, Adán thinks, exquisite. He goes to Méndez's Sinaloa ranch every month with their tribute and he sees her there. She's a young mother now, with a three-year-old daughter and an infant son, and she looks terrific. The adolescent baby fat is gone, and she's matured into a beautiful young woman.

And Tío is still in love with her.

Adán tries to get back on track. "What about Keller?"

"What about him?" Tío asks.

"He snatched Mette out of Honduras," Adán says, "and now he's kidnapped Álvarez right here from Guadalajara. Are you next?"

It's a real concern, Adán thinks.

Tío shrugs. "Mette got complacent, Álvarez was careless. I'm none of those things. I'm careful. I change houses every few days. The Jalisco police protect me. Besides, I have other friends."

"You mean the CIA?" Adán asks. "The Contra war is over. What use are you to them now?"

Because loyalty is not an American virtue, Adán thinks, nor is long memory. If you don't know that, just ask Manuel Noriega in Panama. He had also been a key partner in Cerberus, a touch point on the Mexican Trampoline, and where is he now? Same place as Mette and Álvarez, in an American prison, except it wasn't Art but Noriega's old friend George Bush who put him there. Invaded his country, grabbed him and put him away.

So if you're counting on the Americans to repay you with loyalty, Tío, count on the fingers of one hand. I watched Art's performance on CNN. There is a price for his silence, and the price might be you, might be all of us.

"Don't worry, *mi sobrino*," Tío is saying. "Los Pinos is a friend of ours."

Los Pinos, the residence of the president of Mexico.

"What makes him such a friend?" Adán asks.

"Twenty-five million of my dollars," Tío answers. "And that other thing."

Adán knows what "that other thing" is.

That the Federación had helped this president to steal the election. Four years ago, back in '88, it seemed certain that the opposition candidate, the leftist Cárdenas, was going to win the election and topple the PRI, which had been in power since the 1917 Revolution.

Then a funny thing happened.

The computers that counted the votes magically malfunctioned.

The election commissioner appeared on television to shrug and announce that the computers had broken down and that it would take several days to count the votes and determine the winner. And during those several days, the bodies of the two opposition watchdogs in charge of monitoring the computer votes—the two men who could have and would have asserted the truth, that Cárdenas had won 55 percent of the vote—were found in the river.

Facedown.

And the election commissioner had gone back on television to announce with a perfectly straight face that the PRI had won the election.

The current *presidente* took office and proceeded to nationalize the banks, the telecommunications industries, the oil fields, all of which were purchased at below-market prices by the same men who had come to his fund-raising dinner and left twenty-five million dollars apiece on the table as a tip.

Adán knows that Tío hadn't arranged the murders of the election officials—that had been García Abrego—but Tío would have known about it and given his okay. And while Abrego is thick as thieves with Los Pinos—partners, in fact, with El Bagman, the president's brother, who owns a third of all the cocaine shipments that Abrego runs through his Gulf cartel—Tío has good reason to believe that Los Pinos has every reason to be loyal to him.

Adán has his doubts.

Now he looks at his uncle and sees that he's anxious to end the meeting. Tío wants to smoke his crack and won't do it in front of Adán. It's sad, he thinks as he leaves, to see what the drug has done to this great man.

Adán takes a taxi to the Cross of Squares and walks toward the cathedral to request a miracle.

God and science, he thinks.

The sometimes cooperative, sometimes conflicting powers to whom Adán and Lucía go to try to help their daughter.

Lucía turns more to God.

She goes to church—prays, offers Masses and benedictions, kneels before a panoply of saints. She buys *milagros* outside the cathedral and offers them up, she burns candles, she gives money, she sacrifices.

Adán goes to church on Sundays, makes his offerings, says his prayers, takes Communion, but it's more of a gesture, a nod to Lucía. He doesn't believe, anymore, that help will come from that direction. So he genuflects, mumbles the words, goes through the motions, but they are empty gestures. On his regular trips to Culiacán to bring his regular offering to Güero Méndez, he stops at the shrine of Santo Jesús Malverde and makes his *manda*.

He prays to the *Narcosanto,* but puts more hope in the doctors.

Adán markets drugs; he *gets* biopharmacology.

Pediatric neurologists, neuropsychologists, psychoneurologists, endocrinologists, brain specialists, research chemists, herbal healers, native healers, charlatans, quacks. Doctors everywhere—in Mexico, Colombia, Costa Rica, England, France, Switzerland and even just across the border, in the USA.

Adán can't go on *those* visits.

Can't accompany his wife and daughter on their sad, futile trudges to specialists at Scripps in La Jolla or Mercy in Los Angeles. He sends Lucía with written notes, written questions, stacks of medical records, histories, tests results. Lucía takes Gloria by herself, crosses the border under her maiden name—she's still a citizen—and sometimes they are gone for weeks, sometimes months, when Adán *aches* for his daughter. They always return with the same old news.

That there is no news.

No new miracle has been discovered.

Or revealed.

Not by God or the doctor.

There is nothing more they can do.

Adán and Lucía comfort each other with hope and faith—which Lucía possesses and Adán feigns—and love.

Adán loves his wife and daughter deeply.

He's a good husband, a wonderful father.

Other men, Lucía knows, might have turned their backs on a deformed child, might have avoided the girl, avoided the home, made a thousand excuses to spend time away.

Not Adán.

He is home almost every night, almost every weekend. He's in Gloria's room the first thing every morning to kiss her and give her a hug; then he makes her breakfast before he goes off to work. When he comes home in the evening his first stop is to her room. He reads to her, tells her stories, plays games with her.

Nor does Adán hide his child like something shameful. He takes her for long strolls in the Río district. Takes her to the park, to lunch, to the circus, anywhere, everywhere. They are a common sight in the better neighborhoods of Tijuana—Adán, Lucía and Gloria. All the shopkeepers know the girl—they give her candy, flowers, small pieces of jewelry, hairpins, bracelets, pretty things.

When Adán has to go away on business—as he is now, on his regular junket to Guadalajara to visit with Tío, then to Culiacán with a briefcase of cash for Güero—he calls every day, several times a day, to speak with his daughter. He tells her jokes, funny things that he has seen. He brings her presents from Guadalajara, Culiacán, Badiraguato.

And those trips to the doctors that he can go on—all of them except in the United States—he goes. He's become an expert on cystic lymphangioma; he reads, he studies, he asks questions, he offers incentives and rewards. He makes large donations to research, quietly inveighs his business partners to do the same. He and Lucía have nice things, a nice home, but they could have much nicer things, a much bigger home, except for the money they spend on doctors. And donations and pledges and Masses and benedictions and playgrounds and clinics.

Lucía is glad for this. She doesn't need nicer things, a bigger home. She doesn't need—and wouldn't want—the lavish and, frankly, tasteless mansions that some of the other *narcotraficantes* have.

Lucía and Adán would give anything they have, any parent would, to any doctor or any god, every doctor and every god, who would cure their child.

The more science fails, the more Lucía turns to religion. She finds more hope in a divine miracle than in the hard numbers of the medical reports. A blessing from God, from the saints, from Our Lady of Guadalupe could reverse the tide of those numbers in the blink of an eye, in the flutter of a heart. She haunts the church, becomes a daily communicant, brings their parish priest, Father Rivera, home for dinners, for private prayer and counseling sessions, for Bible study. She questions the depth of her faith ("Perhaps it is my doubt that is blocking a *milagro*"), questions the sincerity of Adán's. She urges him to attend Mass more often, to pray harder, to give even more money to the Church, to talk with Father Rivera, to "tell him what's in your heart."

To make her feel better, he goes to see the priest.

Rivera's not a bad guy, if a bit of a fool. Adán sits in the priest's office, across the desk from him, and says, "I hope you're not encouraging Lucía to believe that it's her lack of faith that prevents a cure for our daughter."

"Of course not. I would never suggest or even think such a thing."

Adán nods.

"But let's talk about you," Rivera says. "How can I be of help to *you*, Adán?"

"Really, I'm fine."

"It can't be easy—"

"It isn't. It's life."

"And how are things between you and Lucía?"

"They're fine."

Rivera gets this clever look on his face, then asks, "And in the bedroom? May I ask? How are the connubial—"

Adán makes a successful effort to suppress a smirk. It always amuses him when priests, these self-castrated eunuchs, want to give advice on sexual matters. Rather like a vegetarian offering to barbecue your steak for you. Nevertheless, it's obvious that Lucía has been discussing their sex life with the priest; otherwise, the man would never have had the nerve to raise the subject.

The fact is that there's nothing to discuss.

There is no sex life. Lucía is terrified of getting pregnant. And because the Church forbids artificial contraception and she will do nothing that might indicate anything other than a total commitment to the laws of the Church . . .

He has told her a hundred times that the chances of having another baby with a birth defect are a thousand to one, a million to one, really, but logic has no traction with her. She knows he's right, but she tearfully confesses to him one night that she just can't bear the thought of that moment in the hospital, that moment when she was told, when she saw . . .

She can't bear the thought of reliving that moment.

She has tried to make love with him several times when the rhythms of natural contraception allowed, but she simply froze up. Terror and guilt, Adán observes, are not aphrodisiacs.

The truth, he would like to tell Rivera, is that it isn't important to him. That he's busy at work, busy at home, that all his energies are taken up with running a business (the specific nature of that business is *never* discussed), taking care of a very ill, severely handicapped child, and trying to find a cure for her. Compared with their daughter's suffering the lack of a sex life is insignificant.

"I love my wife," he tells Rivera.

"I have encouraged her to have more children," Rivera says. "To—"

Enough, Adán thinks. This is getting insulting. "Father," he says, "Gloria is all we can care for now."

He leaves a check on the desk.

Goes home and tells Lucía that he has spoken with Father Rivera, and the talk strengthened his faith.

But what Adán really believes in are numbers.

It hurts him to see this sad, futile faith of hers; he knows she is hurting herself more deeply every day, because the one thing Adán knows for certain is that numbers never lie. He deals with numbers all day, every day. He makes key decisions based on numbers, and he knows that arithmetic is the absolute law of the universe, that a mathematical proof is the only proof.

And the numbers say that their daughter will get worse, not better, as she gets older, that his wife's fervent prayers are unheard or unanswered.

So he puts his hopes in science, that someone somewhere will come up with (literally) the right formula, the miracle drug, the surgical procedure that will trump God and His useless entourage of saints.

In the meantime, there is nothing to do but keep putting one foot in front of the other in this futile marathon.

Neither God nor science can help his daughter.

Nora's skin is a warm pink, flushed from the bath's steaming water.

She has on a thick white terry-cloth bathrobe, and a towel wrapped in a turban around her hair, and she plops down on the sofa, puts her feet up on the coffee table and picks up the letter.

She asks, "Are you going to?"

"Am I going to what?" Parada asks as her question pulls him out of the sweet reverie of the Coltrane album playing on the stereo.

"Resign."

"I don't know," he says. "I suppose so. I mean, a letter from Il Papa himself . . ."

"But you said it was a request," Nora says. "He's asking, not ordering."

"That's just a courtesy," Parada answers. "It amounts to the same thing. One doesn't refuse a request of the Pope's."

Nora shrugs. "First time for everything."

Parada smiles. Ah, for the careless courage of youth. It is, he thinks, a simultaneous flaw and virtue of young people that they have so little regard for tradition, and even less for authority. A superior asks you to do something you don't wish to do? Easy—just refuse.

But it would be so easy to accede, he thinks. More than easy—tempting. Resign and become a mere parish priest again, or accept an assignment to a monastery—a "period of reflection," they would probably call it. A time for contemplation and prayer. It sounds wonderful, as opposed to the constant stress and responsibility. The endless political negotiations, the ceaseless efforts to acquire food, housing, medicine. Not to mention the chronic alcoholism, spousal abuse, unemployment and poverty, and the myriad tragedies that spring from them. It's a burden, he thinks with full realization of his own self-pity, and now Il Papa is not only willing to remove the cup from my hands, he's requesting that I give it up.

Will, in fact, forcibly rip it from me if I don't meekly hand it over.

This is what Nora doesn't understand.

One of the few things that Nora doesn't understand.

She's been coming to visit for years now. At first, it was short visits of a few days, helping out at the orphanage outside the city. Then it turned into longer visits, with her staying for a few weeks, and then the weeks turned into months. Then she would go back to the States to do what she does to make her money, and then return, and the stays at the orphanage became longer and longer.

Which is a good thing because she's invaluable there.

To her surprise, she's become quite good at doing whatever needs to be done. Some mornings it's looking after the preschool kids, others it's supervising repair of the seemingly endless plumbing problems or negotiating with contractors on prices for the new dormitory. Or driving into the big central market in Guadalajara to get the best deal on groceries for the week.

At first, each time a task came up she'd whine the same refrain—"I don't know anything *about* that"—just to get the same answer from Sister Camella: "You'll learn."

And she did; she has. She's become a veritable expert on the intricacies of Third World plumbing. The local contractors simultaneously love and hate to see her coming—she's so beautiful but so relentlessly ruthless, and they're both shocked and delighted to see a woman walk up to them and pronounce in butchered but effective Spanish the words *"No me quiebres el culo."*

Don't bust my ass.

Other times, she can be so charming and seductive that they give her what she wants at barely a profit. She leans over and looks up at them with those eyes and that smile and tells them that the roof *can't* really wait until they have the cash—the rains are coming, don't you see the sky?

No, they don't. What they see is her face and body and, let's be honest, her *soul,* and they go and fix the *condenada* roof. And they know she's good for the money, she'll get it, because who at the diocese is going to say no to her?

No one, that's who.

No one has the balls.

And at the market? *Dios mío,* she's a terror. Strolls through the vegetable stands like a queen, demanding the best of this, the freshest of that. Squeezing and smelling and asking for samples to test.

One morning a fed-up grocer asks her, "Who do you think you're buying for? The patrons of a luxury hotel?"

She answers, "My kids deserve as good or better. Or do you disagree?"

She gets them the best food at the best price.

The rumors about her abound. She's an actress—no, a whore—no . . . she is the cardinal's mistress. No, she was a high-priced courtesan, and she is dying of AIDS, she has come to the orphanage to do penance for her sins before she goes to meet God.

But that story loses credence as a year goes by—then two, then five, then seven—and still she comes to the orphanage and her health hasn't declined and her looks haven't faded and by that time the speculation on her past has pretty much ended anyway.

She does enjoy the meals on her visits to the city. She eats herself into a near stupor, then takes a glass of wine into the big bathroom with real tiles and soaks in hot water until her skin is a glowing pink. Then she dries herself with the big, fluffy towels (the ones at the orphanage are small and practically transparent), and a maid comes in with the clean clothes that were being washed while she was in the tub, and then she rejoins Father Juan for an evening of conversation, music or movies. She knows he's taken advantage of her bath to go outside in the garden and sneak cigarettes (the doctors have told him and told him and told him and his response is, "What if I give up the smokes and then get hit by a car? I will have sacrificed all that pleasure for nothing!"), and then he does this funny thing of sucking on a mint before she comes back, as if he's fooling anybody, as if he needs to fool her.

In fact, they've come to measure the length of her baths by cigarettes—"I'm going to have a five-cig bath," or, if she feels especially grimy and tired, "This is going to be an eight-cig bath"—but he still goes to the trouble to deny by silent implication that that's what he's doing, and he always sucks on the mint anyway.

This game has been going on now for almost seven years.

Seven years—she can't believe it.

On this particular visit she came, unusually, in the morning, having spent all night bringing a sick child into the city hospital and then sitting up with him. When the crisis had passed she'd taken a taxi over to Juan's residence and availed herself of a bath and a full breakfast. Now she sits in his den and listens to the music.

"Where has it gone?" she asks him as the Coltrane solo rises to a crescendo and then falls again.

"Where has what gone?"

"Seven years."

"Where it's always gone," he says. "Doing what there is to be done."

"I suppose."

She's worried about him.

He looks tired, worn down. And, even though they make a joke of it, he's lost weight lately, and he seems more susceptible to colds and bouts of flu.

But it's more than his health.

It's also his safety.

Nora's afraid they're going to kill him.

It's not only his constant political sermons and labor organizing; for the past few years he's been spending more and more time in the State of Chiapas, making the church down there a center for indigenous Indian movement, infuriating the local landowners. He's been increasingly outspoken on a range of social issues, always taking a dangerously left-wing position, even coming out against the NAFTA treaty, which, he argues, will only further dispossess the poor and the landless.

He's even railed against it from the pulpit, angering his superiors in the Church and the right wing in Mexico.

The writing is, literally, on the wall.

The first time she saw one of the posters she angrily went to tear it down, but he stopped her. He thought it was funny, the cartoonish drawing of him with the legend EL CARDENAL ROJO—The Red Cardinal—and the announcement DANGEROUS CRIMINAL—WANTED FOR BETRAYING HIS COUNTRY. He wanted to have one copied and framed.

It doesn't scare him—he assures her that even the right-wingers wouldn't kill a priest. But they murdered Oscar Romero in Guatemala, didn't they? His robes didn't deflect those bullets. A right-wing death squad marched into his church as he was saying Mass and gunned him down. So she's afraid of the Mexican Guardia Blanca, and of these posters that encourage some lone nut to make himself a hero by killing a traitor.

"They're just trying to intimidate me," Juan told her when they first saw the posters.

But that's just what scares her because she knows that he won't be intimidated. And when they see that he won't, what will they do? So maybe the "request" to resign is a good thing, she thinks. Which is why she floats the idea of his resigning. She's too smart to overtly bring up his health, his fatigue and the threats against him, but she wants to leave the door open for him to walk away.

Just walk away.

Alive.

"I don't know," she says casually. "Maybe it's not such a bad idea."

He told her about the argument when the papal nuncio had summoned him to Mexico City to explain his "grave pastoral and doctrinal errors" in Chiapas.

"This 'liberation theology,' " Antonucci had started.

"I don't care about liberation theology."

"I'm relieved to hear it."

"I only care about liberation."

Antonucci's little finch-like face darkened as he said, "Christ liberates our soul from hell and death, and I would think that would be sufficient liberation. That is the good news of the gospel, and that is what you are supposed to deliver to the faithful of your diocese. And that, not politics, should be your main concern."

"My main concern," Parada said, "is that the gospel becomes good news to the people now, and not after they starve to death."

"This political orientation was all the rage after Vatican Two," Antonucci said, "but perhaps it has escaped your notice that we have a different Pope now."

"Yes," Parada said, "and he sometimes gets things backwards: Everywhere he goes he kisses the ground and walks on the people."

Antonucci said, "This is no joke. They're investigating you."

"Who is?"

"The Latin Affairs Desk at the Vatican," Antonucci said. "Bishop Gantin. And he wants you removed."

"On what grounds?"

"Heresy."

"Oh, ridiculous!"

"Is it?" Antonucci picked up a file from his desk. "Did you celebrate Mass in a Chiapan village last May garbed in Mayan robes, replete with a feathered headdress?"

"Those are symbols that the indigenous people—"

"So the answer is yes," Antonucci said. "You were openly engaging in pagan idolatry."

"Do you think that God only arrived here with Columbus?"

"You're quoting yourself now," Antonucci said. "Yes, I have that little tidbit here. Let me see. Yes, here it is, 'God loves all humankind—' "

"Do you have an objection to that statement?"

" '—and therefore has revealed his "Godself" to all cultural and ethnic groups in the world. Before any missionary arrived to speak of Christ, a process of salvation was already there. We know in truth that Columbus did not bring God aboard his ships. No, God is already present in all these cultures, so missionary work has a whole different meaning—announcing the presence of a God who is already there.' Do you deny saying that?"

"No, I embrace it."

"They are saved *before* Christ?"

"Yes."

"Sheer heresy."

"No, it isn't." It's pure salvation. That one simple statement, Columbus did not bring God with him, did more than a thousand catechisms to launch a spiritual revival in Chiapas as the indigenous people began to search their own culture for signs of the revealed God. And found them—in their customs, their stewardship of the earth, their ancient laws on how to treat their brothers and sisters. It was only then, when they had found God in themselves, that they could truly receive the good news of Jesus Christ.

And the hope of redemption. From five hundred years of slavery. Half a millennium of oppression, humiliation and dire, desperate, murderous poverty. And if Christ didn't come to redeem that, then he didn't come at all.

"How about this, then?" Antonucci asked. " 'The mystery of the Trinity is not the mathematical riddle of Three in One. It is the manifestation of the Father in politics, the Son in economics, and the Holy Spirit in the culture.' Does this really reflect your thinking?"

"Yes."

Yes, it is, because it takes all of that—politics, economics and culture—for God to reveal himself in all his power. That's why we've spent the past seven years building cultural centers, clinics, farming co-ops and, yes, political organizations.

Antonucci said, "You would reduce God the Father to mere politics, and Jesus Christ His Son Our Savior to the level of a chair of Marxist Theoretics in some third-rate economics department?! And I won't even comment on your blasphemous connection of the Holy Spirit to local pagan culture, whatever that even means."

"The fact that you don't know what that means is the problem."

"No," Antonucci said, "the problem is the fact that you do."

"Do you know what an old Indian man asked me the other day?"

"Doubtless you're going to tell me."

"He asked me, 'Does this God of yours save just our souls? Or does he save our bodies, too?' "

"I tremble to think how you might have answered him."

"You should."

They sat there across a desk, staring at each other, then Parada let down a bit and tried to explain, "Look at what we're achieving in Chiapas: We have six thousand indigenous catechists now, spread through every village, teaching the gospel."

"Yes, let's look at what you've achieved in Chiapas," Antonucci said. "You have the highest percentage of converts to Protestantism in all of Mexico. Only a little more than half of your people are even Catholic anymore, the lowest percentage in Mexico."

"So that's what this is really about," Parada snapped. "Coke is worried about losing market share to Pepsi."

But Parada instantly regretted the quip. It was immature and prideful and killed any chance for a rapprochement.

And Antonucci's main contention is true, he thinks now.

I went to the countryside to convert the Indians.

Instead, they converted me.

And now this NAFTA horror would throw them off what little land they have left, to make room for the more "efficient" large ranches. To open the way for larger coffee *fincas,* mining, lumber operations and, of course, oil drilling.

Must everything, he wonders, be sacrificed on the altar of capitalism?

Now he gets up, turns the music down, and searches the room for his cigarettes. He always has to look for them, just like he has to look for his glasses. She doesn't help, even though she sees them sitting by a side table. He's smoking way too much. It can't be helping.

"The smoke really bothers me," she says.

"I'm not going to light it," he says, finding the pack. "I'm only going to suck on it."

"Try the gum."

"I don't like the gum."

He sits back down across from her and says, "You want me to get out."

She shakes her head. "I want you to do what you want to do."

"Stop handling me," he snaps. "Just tell me what you think."

"You asked," she says. "You deserve some kind of a life. You've earned it. If you decide to resign, no one will blame you. They'll blame the Vatican, and you can walk away from all this with your head up."

She gets up from the sofa, walks to the sidebar and pours herself a glass of wine. She wants the wine, but mostly she wants to avoid his eyes. Doesn't want him looking at her as she says, "I'm selfish, okay? I couldn't stand it if anything happened to you."

"Ah."

The shared, unspoken thought hangs heavily between them: If he were to resign not just the cardinalate, but the priesthood itself, then they could . . .

But he could never do that, she thinks, and I wouldn't really want him to.

And you're being an exceptionally foolish old man, he thinks. She's forty years your junior and you are, when all is said and done, a priest. So he says, "I'm afraid I'm the one who is being selfish. Perhaps our friendship is keeping you from seeking a relationship—"

"Don't."

"—that would meet more of your needs."

"You meet all my needs."

The expression on her face is so serious that he is taken aback for a moment. Those startling eyes so intense. He answers, "Certainly not all."

"All."

"Don't you want a husband?" he asks. "A family? Children?"

"No."

She wants to scream, *Don't leave me. Don't make me leave you.* I don't need a husband or a family or children. I don't need sex or money or comfort or safety.

I need you.

And there are probably a billion psychological reasons—indifferent father, sexual dysfunction, fear of committing to a man who's actually available; a shrink would have a fucking field day—but I don't care. You are the best man I've ever known. The smartest, kindest, funniest, *best* man I've ever known, and I don't know what I'd do if anything ever happened to you, so please don't go away. Don't make me go away.

"You're not going to resign, are you?" she asks.

"I can't."

"Okay."

"Is it?"

"Sure."

She never really thought he would resign.

A soft knock on the door, and his assistant murmurs that he has an unscheduled visitor who has been told—

"Who is it?" Parada asks.

"A Señor Barrera," the assistant answers. "I have told him—"

"I will see him."

Nora gets up. "I need to get going anyway."

They embrace and she goes to get dressed.

Parada goes into his private office to find Adán sitting there.

He's changed, Parada thinks.

He still has the boyish face, but it's a boy with cares. And little wonder, Parada thinks, what with the sick child. Parada offers his hand to shake. Adán takes it and, unexpectedly, kisses his ring.

"That's certainly unnecessary," Parada says. "It's been a long time, Adán."

"Almost six years."

"Then why—"

"Thank you for the gifts you send Gloria," Adán says.

"You're welcome," Parada says. "I also say Masses for her. And offer prayers."

"They're appreciated more than you know."

"How is Gloria?"

"The same."

Parada nods. "And Lucía?"

"Fine, thank you."

Parada goes behind his desk and sits down. Leans forward on the desk, clasps his fingers together and looks at Adán with a studied, pastoral expression. "Six years ago I reached out to you and asked for your mercy on a helpless man. You answered by killing him."

"It was an accident," Adán says. "It was out of my control."

"You can lie to yourself and to me," Parada says. "You cannot lie to God."

Why not? Adán thinks. He lies to us.

But he says, "On the lives of my wife and my child, I was going to release Hidalgo. One of my colleagues accidentally gave him an overdose, trying to reduce his pain."

"Which he required because he had been tortured."

"Not by me."

"Enough, Adán," Parada says, waving his hand as if to swat away the evasion. "Why are you here? How can I minister to you?"

"You can't."

"Then . . ."

"I'm asking you to be a pastor to my uncle."

"Jesus walked on water," Parada says. "I don't know that it's been done since."

"Meaning?"

"Meaning," Parada says as he takes a pack of cigarettes from the desktop, shakes one into his mouth and lights it, "that despite the official party line, I have to believe that some people are beyond redemption. What you are asking for is a miracle."

"I thought you were in the miracle business."

"I am," Parada answers. "For instance, right now I am trying to feed thousands of hungry people, provide them with clean water, decent homes, medicine, education and some hope for the future. Any one of these would be a miracle."

"If it's a matter of money—"

"Fuck your money," Parada says. "There, is that plain enough?"

Adán smiles, remembering why he loves this man. And why Father Juan is probably the only priest tough enough to help Tío. He says, "My uncle is in torment."

"Good. He should be."

When Adán raises an eyebrow, Parada says, "I'm not sure I believe in a fiery hell, Adán, but if there is one, your uncle is doubtless going there."

"He's addicted to crack."

"I will let the irony of that pass without comment," Parada says. "You are familiar with the concept of karma?"

"Vaguely," Adán says. "I know he needs help. And I know that you cannot refuse to help a soul in torment."

"A soul who comes in true repentance, seeking to change his ways," Parada says. "Does that describe your uncle?"

"No."

"Does it describe you?"

"No."

Parada stands up. "Then what do we have to talk about?"

"Please go see him," Adán says. He takes a notepad from his jacket pocket and scribbles Tío's address. "If you could persuade him to go to a clinic, a hospital . . ."

"There are hundreds in my diocese who *want* such treatment and can't afford it," Parada says.

"Send five of them with my uncle, and send their bills to me."

"As I said before—"

"Right, fuck my money," Adán says. "*Your* principles, *their* suffering."

"From the drugs you sell."

"He says with a cigarette in his mouth."

Adán drops his head, looks at the floor for a second then says, "I'm sorry. I came to ask you for a favor. I should have checked my attitude at the door. I meant to."

Parada takes a long pull on the cigarette, walks to the window and looks outside onto the *zócalo,* where the street vendors have spread their blankets and laid out their *milagros* to sell.

"I'll go see Miguel Ángel," he says. "I doubt it will do any good."

"Thank you, Father Juan."

Parada nods.

"Father Juan?"

"Yes?"

"There are a lot of people who want to know that address."

"I'm not a policeman," Parada says.

"I shouldn't have said anything," Adán says. He walks to the door. "Good-bye, Father Juan. Thank you."

"Change your life, Adán."

"It's too late."

"If you really believed that," Parada says, "you wouldn't have come here."

Parada walks Adán out the door into the small foyer, where a woman is standing with a small overnight bag over her shoulder.

"I should be going," Nora says to Parada. She looks at Adán and smiles.

"Nora Hayden," Parada says, "Adán Barrera."

"Mucho gusto," Adán says.

"Mucho gusto." She turns to Parada. "I'll be back in a few weeks."

"I'll look forward to it." She turns to leave.

"I'm just going now myself," Adán says. "May I carry your bag? Do you need a taxi?"

"That would be nice."

She kisses Parada on the cheek. *"Adiós."*

"Buen viaje."

Outside in the *zócalo* she says, "That sly smile on your face . . ."

"Is there a sly smile on my face?"

"—is misplaced. It's not what you think."

"You misunderstand," Adán says. "I love and respect the man. Any happiness he finds in this world, I would never begrudge him."

"We're just friends."

"As you wish."

"We are."

Adán looks across the square. "There's a good café over there. I was about to have breakfast, and I hate to eat alone. Do you have the time and inclination to join me?"

"I haven't eaten."

"Come on, then," Adán says. Crossing the square with her, he adds, "Look, I just have to make one phone call."

"Go ahead."

He gets his cell phone out and dials Gloria's number.

"Hola, sonrisa de mi alma," he says when she answers. She *is* the smile of his soul. Her voice is his dawn and his dusk. "How are you this morning?"

"Good, Papa. Where are you?"

"In Guadalajara," he says. "Visiting Tío."

"How is he?"

"He's good, too," Adán says. He looks out over the square where the street merchants have gathered in strength. *"Ensancho de mi corazón,* comfort of my heart, they sell songbirds here. Shall I bring one home to you?"

"What songs do they sing, Papa?"

"I don't know," he says. "I think you have to teach them songs. Do you know any?"

"Papa," she laughs, delighted, knowing she's being teased, "I sing to you all the time."

"I know you do." Your songs crack my heart.

"Yes, please, Papa," she says. "I would love to have a bird."

"What color?"

"Yellow?"

"I think I see a yellow one."

"Or green," she says. "Any color, Papa. When will you be home?"

"Tomorrow night," he says. "I have to go see Tío Güero, then I'll come home."

"I miss you."

"I miss you, too," he says. "I'll call you tonight."

"I love you."

"I love *you.*"

He ends the call.

"Your girlfriend?" Nora asks.

"The love of my life," Adán says. "My daughter."

"Ah."

They choose an outdoor table. Adán pulls the chair out for her, then sits down. He looks across the table at those remarkable blue eyes. She doesn't look away or flinch or blush. Just looks right back at him.

"And your wife?" she asks.

"What about her?"

"That's what I was going to ask," Nora says.

The door cracks like a gunshot.

Wood shattering on metal.

Ángel's *pito* slides out of the girl as he turns to see *federales* coming through the door.

Art thinks it's almost comical as Tío shuffles with his pants around his ankles into a grotesque imitation of a run, the rolling IV stand following him like a harried servant, trying to reach the guns that are stacked in the corner of the room. Then the stand topples over in a crash, pulling the needle out of his arm, and Tío falls in the corner, on top of the guns, and comes up with a hand grenade and sits there fumbling with the pin until a *federale* grabs him and jerks the grenade out of his hand.

There's still a fat, white ass sticking up from the kitchen table like a gigantic pile of dough. And the sound of a *thwack* as Ramos walks over and whacks it with the butt of his rifle.

She yelps an indignant "Ow."

"You should have cooked breakfast, you lazy slut."

He grabs her by the hair and pulls her up. "Get your pants on, no one wants to look at your *nalgas grandes*."

Your big ass.

"I'll give you five million dollars," Ángel is saying to the *federale*. "Five million dollars American to let me go." Then he sees Art standing there and knows that five mil isn't going to do it, that there isn't enough money. He starts crying. "Kill me. Please, kill me now."

And this is the face of evil, Art thinks.

A sad burlesque.

The man sitting there in the corner with his pants off, begging me to kill him.

Pathetic.

"Three minutes," Ramos says.

Before the guards get back.

"Let's get this piece of shit out of here, then," Art says. He kneels down so his mouth is right next to his uncle's ear and whispers, "Tío, let me tell you what you've always wanted to know."

"What?"

"Who Source Chupar was."

"Who?"

"Güero Méndez," Art lies.

Güero Méndez, motherfucker.

"He hated you," Art adds, "for taking that little bitch away from him and ruining her. He knew the only way of getting her back was to get rid of you."

Maybe I can't get to Adán, Raúl and Güero, Art thinks, so I'll settle for the next best thing.

I'll make them destroy each other.

Adán collapses on Nora's body. She holds his neck and strokes his hair.

"That was incredible," he says.

"You haven't had a woman in a long time," she says.

"Was it that obvious?"

They had left the café and gone directly to a nearby hotel. His fingers had trembled, unbuttoning her blouse.

"You didn't come," he says.

"I will," she says. "Next time."

"Next time?"

An hour later she braces her hands against the windowsill, her legs a muscular V as he pumps into her from behind. The breeze through the open window cools the sweat on her skin as she moans and whimpers a beautiful fake climax until he is satisfied and lets himself come.

Later, lying on the floor, he says, "I want to see you again."

"That can be arranged," Nora says.

It's just a matter of business.

Tío sits in a cell.

His arraignment didn't go well—not the way it should have gone at all.

"I don't know why they connect me with the cocaine business," he said from the dock. "I'm a car dealer. All I know about the drug trade is what I read in the newspapers."

And the people in the courtroom laughed.

Laughed, and the judge bound him over for trial. No bail—a dangerous criminal, the judge said. A definite risk of flight. Especially in Guadalajara, where the defendant is alleged to have considerable influence in the law enforcement community. So they had put him—shackled—on a military aircraft and flown him to Mexico City. Under a special canopy from the plane to a van with black-painted windows. Then to Almoloya prison and into solitary confinement.

Where the cold makes his bones ache.

And the screaming need for crack gnaws at his bones like a hungry dog. The dog chewing on him, chewing on him, wanting that cocaine.

But worse than any of that is the anger.

The rage of betrayal.

The betrayal of his allies—for there must have been a betrayal at the highest levels for him to be sitting in this cell.

That *hijo de puta* and his brother in Los Pinos. Whom we bought and paid for and put in office. The election that was stolen from Cárdenas using my money and the money I made the cartel give them—and they have betrayed me like this. The motherless whores, the *cabrones*, the *lambiosos*.

And the Americans, the Americans whom I helped in their war against the Communists, they have betrayed me, too.

And Güero Méndez, who stole my love. Méndez, who has the woman that should have been mine, and the children that should have been mine.

And Pilar, that cunt who betrayed me.

Tío sits on the floor of the cell, his arms around his legs, rocking back and forth with need and rage. It takes him a day to find a guard to sell him crack. He inhales the delicious smoke and holds it in his lungs. Lets it seep into his brain. Give him euphoria, then clarity.

Then he sees it all.

Revenge.

On Méndez.

On Pilar.

He falls asleep smiling.

Fabián Martínez—aka El Tiburón—is a stone killer.

The Junior has become one of Raúl's key *sicarios*, his most efficient gunman. That newspaper editor in Tijuana whose investigative journalism got a little too investigative—El Tiburón took him out like a target in a video game. That loser Californian surfer and dope dude who had three tons of *yerba* dropped off on the beach near Rosarita but didn't pay his landing fee—El Tiburón popped him like a balloon and then went out to party. And those three totally fucking idiotic *pendejos* from Durango who did a *tombe*, a robbery-murder, on a shipment of coke that the Barreras had guaranteed— well, El Tiburón took an AK and hosed them off the street like dogshit, then poured gasoline over their bodies, set them on fire and let them burn like *luminarias*. The local firemen were afraid, with good reason, to put them out, and the story goes that two of the guys were still breathing when El Tiburón dropped the match on them.

"That's bullshit," Fabián would say, denying the story. "I used my lighter."

Whatever.

He kills without feeling or conscience.

Which is what we need, Raúl thinks now as he sits in the car with the kid and asks him to do this favor for the Barrera *pasador*.

"We want you to take over making the cash deliveries to Güero Méndez," Raúl tells him. "Become the new courier."

"That's it?" Fabián asks.

He'd thought it would be something else, something wet, something that involved the sharp, sweet adrenaline high of killing.

Actually, there is something else.

Pilar's children are the loves of her life.

She's a young madonna, with a three-year-old daughter and an infant son, her face and body more mature, and there is character around her eyes that wasn't there before. She sits at the edge of the pool and dangles her bare feet in the water.

"The children are *la sonrisa de mi corazón*," she tells Fabián Martínez. Then adds pointedly, sadly, "Not my husband."

Fabián thinks that Güero Méndez's *estancia* is totally gross.

"*Traficante* chic" is how Pilar privately describes it to him, her tone not even attempting to hide her contempt. "I am trying to change it, but he has this image in his head . . ."

Narcovaquero, Fabián thinks.

Drug cowboy.

Instead of running from his rural roots, Güero flaunts them. Creates a grotesque, modern version of the great landowners of the past—the dons, the ranchers, the *vaqueros* who wore wide-brimmed hats and boots and chaps because they needed them out in the mesquite, herding cattle. Now the new *narcos* are turning the image on its head: black polyester cowboy shirts with fake mother-of-pearl buttons, polyester chaps in bright pastels—lime greens, canary yellows and coral pinks. And high-heeled boots. Not practical walking boots, but pointed-toe Yanqui cowboy boots, made from all kinds of materials, the more exotic the better—ostrich, alligator—dyed in bright reds and greens.

The old *vaqueros* would have laughed.

Or would spin in their graves.

And the house . . .

Pilar's embarrassed by it.

It's not the classic *estancia* style—one-floor, tile roof, gentle, gracious porch—but a three-story monstrosity of yellow brick, pillars and ironwork railing. And the interior—leather chairs with cattle horns as wings, and hooves for feet. Sofas made from red and white cattle hide. Barstools with saddles for seats.

"With all his money," she sighs, "what he could do . . ."

Speaking of money, Fabián has a briefcase of it in his hand. More money for Güero Méndez to commit to his war against taste. Fabián's the courier now, the pretext being that it's too dangerous for the Barrera brothers to move around, with all that's happened to Miguel Ángel.

They have to lie low.

So Fabián will make the monthly cash deliveries and report from the front.

They're having a weekend party at the ranch. Pilar is playing the gracious hostess, and Fabián is surprised to find himself thinking that she *is* gracious—lovely and charming and subtle. He'd expected some frumpy housewife, but she's not that. And at dinner that night, in the large formal dining room now crowded with guests, he sees her face in candlelight, and her face is exquisite.

She glances over and sees him looking.

This movie-star-handsome boy with the good, stylish clothes.

Pretty soon, he finds himself walking out by the pool with her, and then she tells him that she doesn't love her husband.

He doesn't know what to say, so he shuts his mouth. He's surprised when she continues, "I was so young. So was he, and *muy guapo, no*? And, forgive me, he was going to rescue me from Don Ángel. Which he did. Make me into a grand lady. Which he has. An unhappy grand lady."

Fabián says, stupidly, "You're unhappy?"

"I don't love him," she says. "Isn't that terrible of me? I am a terrible person. He treats me well, gives me everything. He has no other women, doesn't go with whores . . . I am the love of his life, and that's what makes me feel so guilty. Güero worships me, and I have contempt for him because of that. When he is *with* me, I don't feel . . . I don't feel. And then I start to make a list of the things I dislike about him: He's crass, he has no taste, he's a hick, a hillbilly. I *hate* it here. I want to go back to Guadalajara. Real restaurants, real shops. I want to go to museums, concerts, galleries. I want to travel—see Rome, Paris, Rio. I don't want to be bored—with my life, with my husband."

She smiles, then looks back at the guests gathered around the enormous bar at the other end of the pool. "They all think I'm a whore."

"They don't."

"Of course they do," she says evenly. "But none of them is brave enough to say it out loud."

Of course not, Fabián thinks—they all know the story of Rafael Barragos.

He wonders if she does.

"Rafi" had been at a barbecue at the ranch, shortly after Güero and Pilar were married, and was standing around with some *cuates* when Güero came out of the house with Pilar on his arm. And Rafi chuckled, and under his breath made a wisecrack about Güero hitching his cart to Barrera's *puta*. And one of his good buddies went to Güero and told him, and that night Rafi was grabbed from his guest room and the silver plate that he had given them for a wedding present was melted down in front of him and a funnel was stuck in his mouth and the molten silver poured into it.

As Güero watched.

That's how Rafi's body was found—hanging upside down from a telephone pole on a roadside twenty miles from the ranch, his eyes widened in agony, his open mouth filled with hardened silver. And no one dared to take the body down, not the police, not even the family, and for years the old man who herded goats by that place told about the strange sound the crows' beaks made as they pecked through Rafi's cheeks and struck silver.

And that spot along the road became known as *"Donde los Cuervos son Ricos"*—where crows are rich.

So yes, Fabián thinks as he looks at her, the reflected water from the pool glimmering gold on her skin, Everyone is afraid to call you a *puta*.

They're probably afraid to even think it.

And, Fabián thinks, if Güero did that to a man who merely insulted you, what would he do to the man who seduces you? He feels a stab of fear, but then feels it turn into excitement. It turns him on; it makes him proud of his own cool courage, his prowess as a lover.

Then she leans close to him and, to his shock and excitement, whispers, *"Yo quiero rabiar."*

I want to burn.

I want to rage.

I want to go crazy.

Adán screams his orgasm.

He collapses on Nora's soft breasts, and she holds him tightly with her arms and squeezes him rhythmically inside herself.

"My God," he gasps.

Nora smiles.

"Did you come?" he asks.

"Oh, yes," she lies. "It was beautiful."

She doesn't want to tell him that she never comes with a man, that later, alone, she will use her own fingers to give herself relief. It would be pointless to tell him, and she doesn't want to hurt his feelings. She actually likes him, feels a certain sort of affection for him, and besides, it's just not something you tell a man you're trying to please.

They've been meeting regularly for some months since their first encounter in Guadalajara. Now, like today, they usually take a hotel room in Tijuana, which is an easier commute for her from San Diego and, obviously, convenient for him. So once a week or so he disappears from one of his restaurants and meets her in a hotel room. It's the clichéd "love in the afternoon"; he's always home in the evening.

Adán made this clear from the very start.

"I love my wife."

She'd heard this a thousand times. They all love their wives. And most of them really do. This is about sex, not love.

"I don't want to hurt her," Adán stated as if he were laying out a business policy. Which, Nora thought, he was. "I don't want her to be embarrassed or humiliated in any way. She's a wonderful person. I will never leave her or my daughter."

"Good," Nora said.

Both of them businesspeople, they come to an arrangement quickly and without any emotional fuss. She never wants to see any actual money. He opens a bank account for her and deposits a certain amount every month. He chooses the dates and times for their assignations, and she will be there, but he has to provide a week's notice. If he wants to see her more than once a week, that's fine, but he still has to let her know in advance.

Once a month, the results of a blood test, certifying her sexual health, will discreetly arrive at his office. He'll do the same for her, and they can dispense with the annoying condom.

One other thing they agree on—Father Juan cannot know about them.

In a crazy way they each feel as if they're cheating on him—she on their platonic friendship, Adán on their former relationship.

"Does he know what you do for a living?" he'd asked her.

"Yes."

"And does he approve?"

"We're friends anyway," Nora said. "Does he know what *you* do for a living?"

"I'm a restaurateur."

"Uh-huh."

She didn't believe it then, and she certainly doesn't believe it now, after months of meeting with him. The name had rung a faint bell anyway, from a night almost ten years ago at the White House when Jimmy Piccone had so brutally inaugurated her into the trade. So when she returned from Guadalajara she called Haley, asked her about Adán Barrera and got the whole rundown.

"Be careful," Haley advised. "The Barreras are dangerous."

Maybe, Nora thinks now as Adán falls into a postcoital slumber. But she hasn't seen that side of Adán and doubts that it even exists. He's been only gentle to her, even sweet. She admires his loyalty to his sick daughter and his frigid wife. He has needs, is all, and he's trying to get them met in the most ethical way possible.

For a relatively sophisticated man he's remarkably unsophisticated in bed. She's had to ease him into certain practices, teach him positions and techniques; the man is startled by the depth of pleasure she can make him feel.

And he's unselfish, she thinks. He doesn't come to bed with the consumer mentality that so many johns have, the sense of entitlement that comes with their platinum cards. He wants to please her, wants her to be as satisfied as he is, wants her to feel the same joy.

He doesn't treat me, she thinks, like a vending machine. Put in your quarter, pull the knob and get the candy.

Goddamn it, she thinks, I like the man.

He's started to open up, sexually and personally. They spend the interstitial moments talking. Not about drug business, of course—he knows she knows what he does, and they leave it at that—but about the restaurant business, the multitude of problems associated with putting food in the mouths and smiles on the lips of the consuming public. They talk about sports—he's delighted to find that she can discuss boxing in depth and knows the difference between a slider and a curveball—and about the stock market; she's a shrewd investor who starts her day the same way he does, with *The Wall Street Journal* beside her morning coffee. They discuss menu items, debate the rankings of middleweights, dissect the relative strengths and weaknesses of mutual funds versus municipal bonds.

She knows it's another cliché, just as hackneyed as love in the afternoon, but men do come to hookers to *talk*. The wives of the world would take a chunk out of her business if they glanced at the sports pages, spent a few minutes watching ESPN or *Wall Street Week*. Their husbands would willingly spend a few hours discussing *feelings* if the wives were willing to just talk about *stuff* a little more.

So it's part of her job, but she really enjoys her conversations with Adán. She's interested in the topics and she likes talking about them with *him*. She's used to intelligent, successful men, but Adán is really *smart*. He's an unrelenting analyst; he thinks things through, performs intellectual surgery until he cuts to the bottom line.

And face it, she tells herself, you're attracted to his sorrow. To the sadness he carries with such quiet dignity. You think you can ease his pain, and you like that. It's not about the usual shallow satisfaction of leading a man around by the dick, but about taking a man who's in pain and making him forget his sadness for a little while.

Yeah, Nurse Nora, she thinks.

Florence Fucking Nightingale with a blow job instead of a lantern.

She leans over and gently touches his neck until his eyes pop open. "You have to get up," she says. "You have an appointment in an hour, remember?"

"Thanks," he says sleepily. He gets up and goes into the shower. Like most things he does, it's brisk and efficient—he doesn't luxuriate under the spray of hot water, but washes up, towels off, comes back into the room and starts to get dressed.

But today, as he buttons his shirt, he says, "I want us to be exclusive."

"Oh, Adán, that would be very expensive," she says, a little disconcerted, caught off-guard. "I mean, if you want all my time, you'd have to pay for all my time."

"I assumed as much."

"Can you afford that?"

"Money is not my problem in life."

"Adán," she says, "I don't want you taking money from your family."

She instantly regrets saying it because she can see he's offended. He looks up from his shirt, stares at her in a way she's never seen before and says, "I think you already know that is something I would never do."

"I know. I'm sorry."

"I'll get you a condo here in Tijuana," he says. "We can agree on annual compensation and renegotiate it at the end of every year. Other than that, we never have to discuss the money. You would simply be my—"

"Mistress."

"I was thinking more of the word 'lover,' " he says. "Nora, I do love you, I want you in my life, but there's only so much of my life to go around and most of it is already taken up."

"I understand."

"I know you do," he says. "And I appreciate that, more than you can know. I know you don't love me, but I think I'm more than just a customer to you. The arrangement I'm proposing isn't ideal, but I think it can give us the most we can have with each other."

He's prepared for this, she thinks. He thought it through, chose his exact words and practiced them.

I should probably think that's pathetic, she tells herself, but I'm actually touched.

That he took the time and the thought.

"Adán, I'm flattered," she says, "and tempted. It's a lovely offer. Can I take a little time to think about it?"

"Of course."

She thinks hard after he leaves.

Takes stock.

You're twenty-nine years old, she tells herself, a young twenty-nine, a good twenty-nine, but nevertheless, just on the edge of over-the-hill. The breasts are still firm, the ass is still tight, the stomach flat. None of that will change for a while, but every year it will be harder to maintain, even with the workout fanaticism. Time *will* take its toll.

And there are younger girls coming up, girls with long legs and high breasts, girls to whom gravity is still an ally. Girls who have the bodies without hours on the stationary bicycle and the treadmill, without the sit-ups and the weight lifting, without the diets. And increasingly, those are the girls the platinum johns are going to want.

So how many years do you have left?

Years at the top, because the middle is not where you want to be and the bottom is a place you don't want to go. How many years before Haley starts sending you out to the B-list clients, then stops sending you at all?

Two, three, five at the outside?

Then what?

Will you have banked enough money to retire?

Depends on the market, on the investments. In two or three or five years I might have enough money to live in Paris, or I might have to work, in which case, what's the work?

There are two broad streams in the sex industry.

Prostitution and porn.

Sure, there's stripping, but that's where most girls start, and they don't stay for long. They either get out or go into prostitution or porn. You skipped the dancing phase—thank you, Haley—and went straight to the top end of the prostitution business, but what happens next?

If you don't take Adán's offer and the market doesn't perform?

Porn?

God knows she's had offers. The money is good, if the work is hard. And she hears that they're careful about the health issues, but God . . . there's something about doing it in front of a camera that puts her off.

And again, how long could it last?

Six or seven years, tops.

Then it would be a steep slide to the low-budget video quickies. Fucking on a mattress in the backyard of some house in the Valley. Girl-girl scenes; orgy scenes; being the hot, horny housewife; the nympho mother-in-law; the sex-starved, cock-hungry, grateful, eager older woman.

You'd kill yourself in a year.

A razor along the wrists or a drug overdose.

Same with the inevitable slide as a call girl. You've seen it, cringed at it, pitied the women who stayed too long, didn't save their money, didn't get married, didn't hook up with a long-term john. You've watched as their faces became bed-worn, their bodies old, their spirits crushed, and pitied them.

Pity.

Self or otherwise, you couldn't stand that.

Take this man's offer.

He loves you, he treats you well.

Take his offer while you're still beautiful, while he still wants you, while you can still give him more pleasure than he ever dreamed possible. Take his money and put it away and then when he gets tired of you, when he starts looking harder at the younger girls, starts looking at them the way he looks at you now, then you can leave with your dignity intact and a decent life in front of you.

Retire from the business and just live.

She decides to tell Adán yes.

Guamuchilito, Sinaloa, Mexico
Tijuana, Mexico
Colombia
1992

Fabián burns.

With what Pilar had whispered to him.

"Yo quiero rabiar."

Was she telling me, he wonders, what I *think* she was telling me? Leads to other thoughts, about her mouth, her legs, her feet dangling in the water, the outline of her sex beneath the bathing suit. And fantasies—of reaching his hand beneath that suit and feeling her breasts, of stroking her *chocho,* of hearing her moan, of being inside her and . . .

And did she mean *rabiar*? Spanish is a subtle tongue, in which each word can take many meanings. *Rabiar* can mean to thirst, to burn, to rage, to go crazy, all of which he thinks she meant. And it can also refer specifically to S&M, and he wonders if she could have possibly meant that she wants to be tied up, whipped, fucked roughly—and that gives him yet more tantalizing fantasies. Surprising fantasies that he's never had before about anyone. He pictures himself tying her down with silk scarves, spanking her beautiful ass, whipping her. Sees himself behind her, she on her hands and knees, fucking her doggie-style and she yelling at him to pull her hair. And he grabs a handful of that thick, black, shiny hair and yanks it back like the reins of a horse, so her long neck arches and stretches and she screams with pain and pleasure.

"Yo quiero rabiar."

¡Ay, Dios mío!

The next time he goes to Rancho Méndez (weeks later—*endless* weeks later), he can barely breathe as he gets out of the car. There's a tightness in his chest and he feels light-headed. And guilty. Wonders, as Güero greets him with an embrace, if his wanton lust for the man's wife isn't visible on his face. And he's sure it must be when she comes out the door of the house and smiles at him. She is carrying the baby and has her arm around the little girl, to whom she says, *"Mira, Claudia, Tío Fabián está aquí."*

Uncle Fabián.

He feels a twinge of shame, like, Hello Claudia, Uncle Fabián wants to fuck Mommy.

Badly.

He kisses her that night.

Fucking Güero leaves them alone again in the living room to take a phone call, and they're standing by the fire and she smells like mimosa flowers and his heart feels like it's going to explode and they're looking at each other and then they're kissing.

Her lips are amazingly soft.

Like overripe peaches.

He feels dizzy.

The kiss ends and they step back from each other.

Amazed.

Scared.

Stimulated.

He walks to the other side of the room.

"I didn't mean for that to happen," she says.

"Neither did I."

But he did.

It's the plan.

The plan that Raúl told him, but Fabián is certain that it came from Adán. And perhaps from Miguel Ángel Barrera himself.

And Fabián is carrying out the plan.

So pretty soon they're sneaking kisses, embraces, brushes of the hands, significant glances. It's an insanely dangerous game, insanely exciting. Flirting with sex, and death, because Güero would surely kill them both if he ever found out.

"I don't think so," Pilar tells Fabián. "Oh, I think he would kill *you*, but then I think he would yell and cry and forgive me."

She says it almost sadly.

She doesn't want to be forgiven.

She wants to burn.

Nevertheless, she says, "Nothing can ever happen between us."

Fabián agrees. In his words. In his head, he is thinking, Yes, it can. Yes, it will. It's my job, my task, my assignment: *Seduce Güero's wife. Take her away with you.*

He starts with the magic words, *What if.*

The two most powerful words in any language.

What if we'd met each other first? *What if* we were free? *What if* we could travel together—Paris, Rio, Rome? *What if* we ran away? *What if* we took enough money with us to start a new life?

What if, what if, what if.

They're like two children playing a game. (*What if* these rocks were gold?) They start imagining the details of their escape—when they would go, how, what they would take with them. How could they get away without Güero knowing? What about his bodyguards? Where could they meet? What about her children? She wouldn't leave them behind. Could *never* leave them behind.

All this shared fantasy done in snatches of conversations, moments stolen from Güero—she's already unfaithful to Güero in her mind and her heart. And in the bedroom—when he's on top of her, she's thinking about Fabián. Güero is so pleased with himself when she screams out her orgasm (this is new, this is fresh), but she's thinking about Fabián. She's started stealing even that from him.

The infidelity is complete—all that remain are the physical details.

Possibility shifts to fantasy, fantasy becomes speculation, speculation turns to planning. It's delicious, planning this new life. They go after it in minute detail. Each of them a clotheshorse, they spend entire precious minutes discussing what they will pack, what they can buy there ("there" being, variously, Paris, Rome or Rio).

Or more serious details: Should we leave Güero a note? Or just disappear? Should we go together or meet somewhere? If we rendezvous, where? Or maybe we can go separately, on the same flight. Exchange meaningful looks across the aisle—a long, sexually torturous overnight flight, then put the children to bed and meet in his room in a Paris hotel.

Rabiar.

No, I couldn't wait, she tells him. I will go to the washroom on the plane. You will follow. The door will be unlocked. No, they will meet in a bar in Rio. Pretend they are strangers. He'll follow her into an alley, shove her against a fence.

Rabiar.

Will you hurt me?

If you want.

Yes.

Then I'll hurt you.

He's everything that Güero isn't: sophisticated, handsome, well dressed, stylish, sexy. And charming. So charming.

She's ready.

She asks him when.

"Soon," he says. "I want to run away with you, but . . ."

But.

The terrible counterweight to *What if.* The intrusion of reality. In this case . . .

"We'll need money," he says. "I have some money, but not enough to hide us for as long as we'll need to hide."

He knows this is delicate. This is the fragile moment in which the bubble could burst. It floats now on the light air of romance, but the mundane, gross financial details could pop it in a flash. He puts on his face a mask of sensitivity, mixed with a dash of shame, and looks down at the ground as he says, "We will have to wait until I can make more money."

"How long will that be?" she asks. She sounds hurt, disappointed, on the verge of tears.

He has to be careful. So careful. "Not long," he says. "A year. Maybe two."

"That's too long!"

"I'm sorry. What can I do?"

He leaves the question in the air as if there is no other answer. She provides the response that he wants and expects. "I have money."

"No," he says firmly. "Never."

"But two years—"

"It's out of the question."

Just as their flirting was once out of the question, just as their kissing was out of the question, just as their running away . . .

"How much would we need?" she asks.

"Millions," he says. "That's why it will take—"

"I can withdraw that much from the bank."

"I couldn't."

"You're just thinking of yourself," she says. "Your male pride. Your machismo. How could you be so selfish?"

And that's the key, Fabián thinks. It's a done deal now that he's flipped the equation. Now that his taking her money would be an act of generosity and unselfishness on his part. Now that he loves her so much he would sacrifice his pride, his machismo.

"You don't love me," she pouts.

"I love you more than life."

"You don't love me enough to—"

"Yes," he says. "I do."

She throws her arms around him.

When he goes back to Tijuana he finds Raúl and tells him it's a done deal. It's taken months, but the Shark's about to feed.

It's good timing, Raúl thinks.

Because it's time to start the war with Güero Méndez.

Pilar carefully folds and packs a little black dress.

Along with black brassieres and panties and other lingerie.

Fabián likes her in black.

She wants to please him. She wants it to be perfect, her first time with him. *Pues, a menos que la fantasía sea mejor que e acto*—well, unless the fantasy is better than the actual fuck. But she doesn't think it will be. No man can talk the way he does, use the words he uses, have the ideas he has, and not be able to back up at least some of them. He makes her wet talking to her—what will he do when he has her in his arms?

I'll let him do anything he wants to me, she thinks.

I want him to do anything he wants.

Will you hurt me?

If you want.

Yes.

Then I'll hurt you.

She hopes so, she hopes he means it, that he won't be intimidated by her beauty and lose his nerve.

About *any* of it—because she wants a new life, away from this Sinaloan backwater with her husband and his hillbilly friends. She wants a better life for her children—a good education, some culture, some sense that the world is wider and better than a grotesque fortress tucked away on the outskirts of an isolated mountain town.

And Fabián has that sense—they've talked about it. He's talked to her about making friendships outside the narrow circle of *narcotraficantes,* about creating relationships with bankers, investors, even artists and writers.

She wants that for herself.

She wants that for her children.

So when, at breakfast, Güero had excused himself and Fabián had leaned over and whispered, "Today," she'd felt a thrill that fluttered her heart. It was almost like a little orgasm.

"Today?" she whispered back.

"Güero is going out into the countryside," Fabián said, "to inspect his fields."

"Yes."

"So when I go to the airport, you will go with me. I've booked us a flight to Bogotá."

"And the children?"

"Of course," Fabián said. "Can you pack a few things? Quickly?"

Now she hears Güero coming down the hall. She slips the suitcase under the bed.

He sees the clothes scattered around. "What are you doing?"

"I'm thinking of getting rid of a few of these old things," she says. "I will bring them to the church."

"Then go shopping?" he asks, smiling, teasing her. He likes when she goes shopping. Likes it when she spends money. He encourages it.

"Probably."

"I'm going," he says. "I'll be gone all day. I might even stay overnight."

She kisses him warmly. "I will miss you."

"I will miss you," he says. "Maybe I will grab *una nena* to keep me warm."

I wish you would, she thinks. Then you wouldn't come to our bed with such desperation. But she says, "Not you. You are not one of those old *gomeros*."

"And I love my wife."

"And I love my husband."

"Has Fabián left yet?"

"No, I think he's packing."

"I'll go say good-bye to him."

"And kiss the children."

"Aren't they still asleep?"

"Of course," she says. "But they like to know that you kissed them before you left."

He reaches for her and kisses her again. *"Eres toda mi vida."*

You are all my life.

As soon as he goes out, she closes the door and gets the suitcase out from under the bed.

Adán says good-bye to his family.

Goes into Gloria's room and kisses her on the cheek.

The girl smiles.

Despite everything, she smiles, Adán thinks. She's so cheerful, so brave. In the background, the bird he brought her from Guadalajara chirps.

"Have you given the bird a name?" he asks her.

"Gloria."

"After yourself?"

"No," she giggles. "Gloria Trevi."

"Ah."

"You're going away, aren't you?" she asks.

"Yes."

"Papaaaa . . ."

"Only for a week or so," he says.

"Where?"

"A bunch of places," he says. "Costa Rica, maybe Colombia."

"Why?"

"To look at coffee to buy," he says. "For the restaurants."

"Can't you buy coffee here?"

"Not good enough for *our* restaurants."

"Couldn't I come with you?"

"Not this time," he says. "Maybe next time."

If there is a next time, he thinks. If everything goes right in Badiraguato, in Culiacán and on the bridge over the Río Magdalena, where he is going to meet the Orejuelas.

If everything goes well, my love.

If not, he has always made sure that Lucía knows where the life-insurance policies are, and how to access the bank accounts in the Caymans, the securities in safe-deposit boxes, the investment portfolios. If things go badly on this trip, if the Orejuelas toss his body off the bridge, then his wife and child will be taken care of for the rest of their lives.

So will Nora.

He's left a bank account and instructions with his private banker.

If he doesn't come back from this trip, Nora will have sufficient funds to start a small business, a new life.

"What can I bring back for you?" he asks his daughter.

"Just come back," she says.

The intuition of small children, he thinks. They read your mind and your heart with uncanny accuracy.

"I'll make it a surprise," he says. "Give Papa a kiss?"

He feels her dry lips on his cheek and then her thin arms around his neck in a lock that won't let go. It breaks his heart. He never wants to leave her, and for a moment he considers not going. Just getting out of the *pista secreta* and running the restaurants. But it's much too late for that—the war with Güero is coming, and if they don't kill him, Güero will kill them.

So he steels his heart, breaks her grip and straightens up.

"Good-bye, *mi alma*," he says. "I'll call you every day."

Turns quickly so she won't see the tears in his eyes. They would frighten her. He walks out of her room, and Lucía is waiting in the living room with his suitcase and a jacket.

"About a week," he says.

"We'll miss you."

"I'll miss you." He kisses her on the cheek, takes his jacket and walks to the door.

"Adán?"

"Yes?"

"Are you all right?"

"Fine," he says. "A little tired."

"Maybe you can sleep on the plane."

"Maybe." He goes to open the door, then turns around and says, "Lucía, you know I love you."

"I love you, too, Adán."

She says it like it's an apology. It sort of is. An apology for not making love to him, for making their bed a cold place, for her helplessness to make it any different. To tell him that it doesn't mean she doesn't still love him.

He smiles sadly and leaves.

On the way to the airport he phones Nora to tell her he won't be seeing her this week.

Maybe never, he thinks as he hangs up.

It depends on what's happening in Culiacán.

Where the banks have just opened.

Pilar withdraws seven million dollars.

From three different banks in Culiacán.

Two of the bank managers start to object and want to contact Señor Méndez first—to Fabián's horror, one even picks up the phone—but Pilar's insistent, informing the cowed managers that she's Señora Méndez, not some housewife overspending her allowance.

The receiver is replaced on the hook.

She gets her money.

Before they even get on the plane, Fabián has her wire-transfer two million to accounts set up in a dozen banks around the world. "Now we can live," Fabián tells her. "He can't find us, he can't find the money."

They bundle the kids into her car and drive toward the airport for a private flight to Mexico City.

"How did you arrange this?" Pilar asks Fabián.

"I have influential friends," Fabián answers.

She's impressed.

Güerito's too young to know what's happening, of course, but Claudia wants to know where Daddy is. "We're playing a game with Daddy," Pilar explains. "Like hide-and-go-seek." The girl accepts the explanation, but Pilar can see she's still concerned.

The drive to the airport is terrifying and exciting; they are always looking behind them, wondering if Güero and his *sicarios* are coming. Then they are at the airport itself, driving out onto the tarmac where the private plane is waiting. Sitting and waiting for permission to take off, Fabián looks out the window and sees Güero and a handful of men roll up in two jeeps.

The bank manager must have phoned after all.

Pilar is staring at him, her eyes wide with terror.

And excitement.

Güero jumps out of the jeep, and Pilar watches him argue with a security cop and then he's looking right at her through the little window of the plane, he's pointing at the plane, then Fabián coolly leans over and kisses her on the lips and then leans toward the cockpit and snaps, *"Vámonos."*

The plane starts rolling down the runway. Güero jumps back into the jeep and races down the runway after the jet, but Pilar feels the wheels lift off and they're airborne and Güero and the whole small world of Culiacán get smaller.

Pilar feels as if she could take Fabián into the little bathroom on the plane and fuck him right there, but the children are looking at her, so she has to wait, and the frustration and excitement only build.

They fly first to Guadalajara to refuel. Then they fly to Mexico City, where they leave the private plane and get on a tourist flight to Belize, where she thinks surely they will stop and go to some resort on the beach and then she will get some release, but in the small Belize airport they change planes again and take another flight to San José, Costa Rica, where she thinks *surely* they will stop for a day or so *at least,* but then they check in for a flight to Caracas but don't board it.

Instead, they get on another commercial flight, to Cali in Colombia.

With different passports and false names.

It's all so stimulating and exciting, and when they finally get to Cali, Fabián tells her that they are going to stay for a few days. They take a taxi to the Hotel Internacional, where Fabián gets them two adjoining rooms under yet different names and she feels as if she's going to explode as they all sit in one room until the exhausted children fall asleep.

He takes her by the wrist and leads her into his room.

"I want to take a shower," she says.

"No."

"No?"

Not a word she's used to hearing.

He says, "Get your clothes off. Now."

"But—"

He slaps her across the face. Then he sits in a chair in the corner and watches as she unbuttons her blouse and slides it off. She kicks off her shoes and slides her pants down and stands there in her black lingerie.

"Off."

God, his prick is pounding. Her white breasts against the black brassiere are tantalizing. He wants to touch them, caress her, but he knows it isn't what she wants, and he doesn't dare disappoint her.

She unhooks the bra and her breasts drop, but just a little. Then she takes the panties off and looks at him. She's blushing furiously as she asks, "Now what?"

"On the bed," he says. "On your hands and knees. Present yourself to me."

She's trembling as she climbs onto the bed and lowers her head to her hands.

"Are you wet for me?" he asks.

"Yes."

"You want me to fuck you?"

"Yes."

"Say 'Please.' "

"Please."

"Not yet."

He takes his belt off. Grabs her hands, lifts them—God, her breasts are beautiful as they quiver—wraps it around her wrists and then around the railing at the head of the bed.

Now he has a handful of her hair, jerking her head back, arching her neck. Riding her like a horse, whipping her rump, racing her to a finish. She loves the sharp sound of his slaps, the sting; she feels it deep inside her, a throb pushing her orgasm out.

It hurts.

Rabiar.

Pilar is burning. Her skin is burning, her ass is burning, her pussy is burning as he strokes her, spanks her, fucks her. She twists on the bed, on her knees, her wrists bound together, tied to the head of the bed.

It hurts so good because she's waited so long. Months, yes, of the flirting, then the fantasizing, then the planning, but also the excitement of the escape itself.

Ah. Ah. Ah. Ah.

He hits her in rhythm with her grunts.

Smack. Smack. Smack. Smack.

She moans, *"¡Voy a morir! ¡Voy a morir!"*

I'm going to come! I'm going to die!

And yells, *"¡Voy a volar!"*

I'm flying! Exploding!

Then she screams.

A long, inchoate, tremulous scream.

Pilar comes out of the bathroom and sits on the bed. Asks him to zip the back of her dress. He does. Her skin is beautiful. Her hair so beautiful. He strokes her hair with the back of his hand and kisses her neck.

"Later, *mi amor*," she purrs. "The children are waiting in the car."

He strokes her neck again. Reaches around with his other hand and brushes her nipple. She sighs and leans back. Soon she is on all fours again, presenting, waiting for him (he makes her wait; she loves him making her wait) to come inside her. He grabs her hair and pulls her head back.

Then she feels the pain.

Around her throat.

At first she thinks it's another S&M game, him choking her, but he doesn't stop and the pain is—

She twists.

She burns.

Rabiar.

She struggles and her legs kick out involuntarily.

Fabián hisses in her ear, "This is for Don Miguel Ángel, *bruja*. He sends you his love."

He squeezes and pulls until the wire slices through her throat, then her vertebrae, and then her head itself pops up before it falls face-first on the floor with a hollow *thump*.

Blood sprays the ceiling.

Fabián picks the head up by its shiny black hair. Her lifeless eyes stare at him. He puts it in a cooler, locks it, then puts the cooler inside a box that has already been addressed. He wraps the box tightly with several layers of packing tape.

Then he takes a shower.

Her blood dances on his feet before spiraling down the drain.

He dries off, puts on fresh clothes and carries the box out to the street, where a car is waiting.

The children sit in the backseat.

Fabián slides in with them and nods for Manuel to drive.

"Where is Mommy? Where is Mommy?" Claudia asks.

"She's going to meet us there."

"Where?" Claudia starts to cry.

"A special place," Fabián says. "A surprise."

"What is the surprise?" Claudia asks. Seduced, she stops crying.

"If I told you, it wouldn't be a surprise, would it?"

"Is the box a surprise, too?"

"What box?"

"The box you put in the trunk," Claudia says. "I saw you."

"No," Fabián says. "That's just something I have to mail."

He goes into the post office and hefts the box onto the counter. It's surprisingly heavy, he thinks, her head. He remembers the thickness of her hair, its heaviness in his hands as he would play with it, stroke it, part of his seduction. She was marvelous in bed, he thinks. Feeling—to his slight horror, considering what he has just done, what he's about to do—a frisson of sexual desire.

"How do you want this sent?" the postal clerk asks.

"Overnight."

The clerk puts it on a scale and asks, "Do you want it insured?"

"No."

"It's going to be expensive anyway," the clerk says. "Are you sure you don't want it sent priority? It will be there in two or three days."

"No, it has to be there tomorrow," Fabián says.

"A gift?"

"Yes, a gift."

"A surprise?"

"I hope so," Fabián says. He pays for the postage and goes back to the car.

Claudia has gotten scared again in the interval of waiting.

"I want Mommy."

"I am taking you to her," Fabián says.

The Santa Ysabel Bridge spans a gorge of the same name, through which, seven hundred feet below, the Río Magdalena rushes over jagged rocks on its long, tortured trip from its source in the Cordillera Occidental to the Caribbean Sea. On the way, it traverses most of central Colombia, passing near, but not through, the cities of Cali and Medellín.

Adán can see why the Orejuela brothers chose this place—it is isolated, and from either end of the bridge you could detect an ambush from hundreds of yards away. Or I hope so anyway, Adán thinks. The truth is that they could be cutting off the road behind me even now and I wouldn't know it. But it's a chance that has to be taken. Without a source of cocaine from the Orejuelas, the *pasador* can't hope to win a war against Güero and the rest of the Federación.

A war which, by now, ought to have been irrevocably declared.

El Tiburón should have already run off with Pilar Méndez, convinced her to steal millions of dollars from her husband. He should be showing up here anytime with the cash to seduce the Orejuelas away from the Federación. All part of Tío's plan to get his revenge on Méndez by making him a cuckold, then compounding the humiliation by having his wife provide the cash to wage the war against him.

Or maybe Fabián is hanging from a telephone pole with his mouth full of silver and the Orejuelas are coming to assassinate me.

He hears the sound of another car coming up from behind him on the road. Bullets in the back, he wonders, or Fabián with the money? He turns around to see—

Fabián Martínez with a driver and, in the backseat, Güero's children. What the hell is that about? Adán gets out of his car and walks over. Asks Fabián, "Do you have the money?"

Fabián smiles his movie-star smile. "With a bonus."

He hands Adán the suitcase with the five million.

"Where's Pilar?" Adán asks.

"On her way home," Fabián says with a twisted grin that gives Adán the creeps.

"She left without her children?" Adán asks. "What are they doing here? What—"

"I'm just following Raúl's instructions," Fabián says. "Adán—"

He points to the other side of the bridge, where a black Land Rover is slowly rolling up.

"Wait here," Adán says. He takes the suitcase and starts to walk across the bridge.

Fabián hears the little girl's voice ask, "Is this where Mommy's meeting us?"

"Yes," Fabián says.

"Where is she? Is she with those people?" Claudia asks, pointing to the car on the other side of the bridge, from which the Orejuelas are just now getting out.

"I think so, yes," Fabián says.

"I want to go there!"

"You have to wait a few minutes," Fabián says.

"I want to go *now*!"

"We have to talk with those men first."

Adán walks toward the center of the bridge, as agreed. His legs feel wooden from fear. If they have a sniper in the hills, I am dead, that's all, he tells himself. But they could have killed me anytime I was in Colombia, so they must want to hear what I have to say.

He gets to the middle of the bridge and waits as the Orejuelas walk toward him. Two brothers, Manuel and Gilberto, short, dark and squat. They all shake hands and then Adán asks, "Shall we get to business?"

"It's why we're here," Gilberto says.

"*You* asked for this meeting," says Manuel.

Brusquely, Adán thinks. Rudely. And he doesn't care. So the dynamic appears to be that Gilberto is leaning toward making the deal, and Manuel is resisting. All right, then. Let's get started.

"I will be taking our *pasador* out of the Federación," Adán says. "I want to ensure that we will nevertheless have a relationship here in Colombia."

"Our relationship is with Abrego," says Manuel, "and the Federación."

"Just so," Adán says, "but for every kilo of your cocaine the Federación handles, it handles *five* kilos from Medellín."

He can see he's hit a chord, especially with Gilberto. The brothers are jealous of their bigger Medellín rivals, and ambitious. And with the American DEA pounding so hard on the Medellín cartel and its Florida outlets, there is opportunity here for the Orejuelas to make a move.

Gilberto asks, "And you're offering us an exclusive arrangement?"

"If you agree to allow me to handle your cocaine," Adán says, "we would handle only product from Cali."

"That would be a very generous offer," Manuel says, "except that Don Abrego would resent our keeping you in business, and deny us his."

But Gilberto is looking for an answer to that, Adán thinks. He's tempted.

"Don Abrego is the past—we're the future," Adán says.

"That's hard to believe," says Manuel, "when the head of your *pasador* sits in prison. It would appear that the powers-that-be in Mexico think that Abrego is their future. And after him . . . Méndez."

"We'll beat Méndez."

"What makes you think you can?" asks Manuel. "You will have to fight Méndez for it, and Abrego will line up behind Méndez, as will all the other *pasadores*. And the *federales*. Truly, no offense, Adán Barrera, but I think I am looking at a dead man, standing here offering me an exclusive, if I dump my business with the living to do business with the dead. How much cocaine can you handle from your grave?"

"We are the Barrera *pasador*," Adán says. "We've won before, we will—"

"No," Manuel says. "Again, pardon me, but you are not the Barrera *pasador* anymore. Your uncle, I agree, could have beaten Abrego and Méndez and the whole Mexican government, but you are not your uncle. You are very smart, but brains alone are not enough. How *tough* are you? I will tell you the truth, Adán—you look soft to me. I do not think that you are a hard enough man to do what you say you will do, what you will have to do."

Adán nods, then asks permission to open the suitcase at his feet. He gets their okay, then bends over, flips open the lid, shows them the money inside and says, "Five million of Güero Méndez's money. We fucked his wife in the ass and made her give us his money. Now, if you still think we can't beat him, take this money, shoot me, toss my body off the bridge and keep collecting your tip money from the Federación. If you decide that we can beat Méndez, then please accept this as our goodwill gesture and a down payment on the many millions we're going to make together."

He puts a look of calm on his face, but he can tell from their expressions that this could go either way.

So can Fabián.

And El Tiburón's instructions in this case are clear. Orders from Raúl that came straight down from the legendary M-1.

"Vengan," Fabián says to the kids. "Come on."

"Are we going to see Mommy now?" Claudia asks.

"Sí." Fabián takes her hand and hefts Güerito to his shoulder and starts walking back to the middle of the bridge.

¡Mi esposa, mi esposa linda!

Güero's cries echo through the large, empty house.

The servants are hiding. The bodyguards outside are lying low, as Güero staggers through the house, throws furniture, smashes glass, throws himself on the cowhide sofa and buries his face in a pillow as he sobs.

He has found her simple note: I DON'T LOVE YOU ANYMORE. I HAVE LEFT WITH FABIÁN AND TAKEN THE CHILDREN. THEY ARE ALL RIGHT.

His heart is broken. He'd do anything to get her back. Would take her back, too, and make it up to her. He tells all this to the pillow. Then lifts his head and wails, *"¡Mi esposa, mi esposa linda!"*

The bodyguards, the dozen *sicarios* manning the *estancia* walls and gates, can hear him from outside. It spooks them, and they were already on edge, ever since the arrest of Don Miguel Ángel Barrera, knowing that a war might be coming. Certainly a shake-out, and that is usually accompanied by the shedding of blood.

And now the *jefe* is in his house bawling like a woman for everyone to hear.

It is *inquietante*—unsettling.

And it's been going on all day.

A FedEx truck comes down the road.

A dozen AK-47s train on it.

The guards stop the truck well short of the gate. One holds a machine gun on the driver as the other looks in the back of the truck. Asks the shaken driver, "What do you want?"

"A package for Señor Méndez."

"Who from?"

The driver points to the return address on the label. "His wife."

Now the guard is worried—Don Güero said he was not to be disturbed, but if this is from Señora Méndez he had better take it in.

"I'll take it to him," the guard says.

"I have to have his signature."

The guard points the gun barrel at the driver's face and says, "I can sign for him, yes?"

"Certainly. Of course."

The guard signs, carries the package to the house and rings the bell. A maid comes to the door. "Don Güero is not to be—"

"A package from the señora. Federal Express."

Güero appears behind the maid. His eyes are swollen, his face red, his nose running.

"What is it?" he snaps. "Goddamnit, I said—"

"A package from the señora."

Güero takes it and slams the door shut.

Güero tears the box open.

After all, it is from *her.*

So he rips the box open and inside is the little cooler. He unlatches it and flips the lid open and sees her shiny black hair.

Her dead eyes.

Mouth open.

And in her teeth, a card.

He screams and screams.

The panicked guards kick the door in.

Burst into the room, and there is *el jefe,* standing back from a box, screaming and screaming. The guard who brought the package looks inside the box, then leans over and vomits. Pilar's severed head sits on a bed of dried blood, her teeth clenched on a calling card.

Two other guards take Güero by the arms and try to pull him away, but he digs in his feet and just keeps screaming. The other guard wipes his mouth, recovers himself and takes the note from Pilar's mouth.

The message makes no sense:

HOLA, CHUPAR.

The other guards try to lead Güero to the sofa but he snatches the note, reads it, turns, if possible, even paler and then yells, *"¡Dios mío, mis nenes! ¡¿Dónde están mis nenes?!"*

Oh, my God, my children!

Where are my children?!

. . .

"¿Dónde está mi madre? ¡Yo quiero mi madre!"

"Where is my mommy? I want my mommy!" Claudia howls because she doesn't see her mother on the bridge, just a bunch of strange men staring at them. Güerito sees her panic and picks up her cry. And Claudia doesn't want to be held now. She twists and fights in Fabián's arms and cries, *"¡Mi madre! ¡Mi madre!"*

But Fabián keeps walking toward the center of the bridge.

Adán sees him coming.

Like a nightmare, a vision from hell.

Adán feels paralyzed, his feet nailed to the wood of the bridge, and he just stands there as Fabián smiles at the Orejuela brothers and says, "Don Miguel Ángel Barrera assures you that his blood flows through the veins of his nephew."

Adán believes in numbers, in science, in physics. It is at this precise moment that he understands the nature of evil, that evil has a momentum of its own, which, once started, is impossible to stop. It's the law of physics—a body at rest tends to stay at rest; a body set in motion tends to stay in motion.

Unless something stops it.

And Tío's plan is, as usual, brilliant. Even in its total, crack-inspired depravity it is deadly accurate in its perception of individual human nature. This is Tío's genius—he knows that a man who would never have the weakness to set a great evil into motion doesn't have the strength to stop it once it's moving. That the hardest thing in the world isn't to refrain from committing an evil, it's to stand up and stop one.

To put one's life in the way of a tidal wave.

Because that is what it is, Adán thinks, his mind whirling. If I put a stop to this now it will show weakness to the Orejuelas—a weakness that will immediately or eventually prove fatal. If I show the slightest disunity with Fabián, that, too, will guarantee our demise.

Tío's genius—putting me in exactly this position, knowing that I have no real choice.

"I want Mama!" Claudia screams.

"Shh," Fabián whispers, "I am taking you to her."

Fabián looks to Adán for a signal.

And Adán knows that he's going to give it to him.

Because I have a family to protect, Adán thinks, and there is no other choice. It's Méndez's family or mine.

Had Parada been there he would have phrased it differently. He would have said that in the absence of God there's only nature, and nature has its cruel laws. That the first thing the new leaders do is kill the offspring of the old. Without God, that's all there is: survival.

Well, there is no God, Adán thinks.

He nods.

Fabián throws the girl off the bridge. Her hair lofts up like futile wings and she plummets as Fabián grabs the little boy and in one easy swing tosses him over the railing.

Adán forces himself to look.

The children's bodies plunge seven hundred feet, then smash onto the rocks below.

Then he looks at the Orejuela brothers, whose faces are white with shock. Gilberto's hand shakes as he shuts the suitcase, picks it up and walks shakily back across the bridge.

Below, the Río Magdalena washes away the bodies and the blood.

9

Days of the Dead

Will no one rid me of this meddlesome priest?

—Henry II

San Diego
1994

It's the Day of the Dead.

Big day in Mexico.

The tradition goes back to Aztec times and honors the goddess Micte-cacihuatl, "Lady of the Dead," but the Spanish priests cleaned it up and moved it from midsummer to autumn to make it coincide with All Hallow's Eve and All Souls' Day. Yeah, okay, Art thinks, the Dominicans can call it what they want—it's still about La Muerte.

The Mexicans, they don't mind talking about death. They have lots of names for it—The Fancy Lady, The Skinny, The Bony, or just plain old La Muerte. They don't try to keep it at arm's length. They're tight with death, intimate with it. They keep their dead close to them. On El Día de los Muertos, the living go to visit the dead. They cook elaborate dishes and take them to the cemeteries and sit down and share a nice meal with their dearly departed.

Shit, Art thinks, I'd like to share a nice meal with my *living* family. They live in the same city, occupy the same physical space and time, and yet somehow we're all on separate planes of existence.

He'd signed the divorce papers shortly after getting word of the murders of Pilar Méndez and her two children. A simple acknowledgment of an inevitable reality, he wondered, or a form of penance? He knew that he shared some responsibility for the children's deaths, that he'd helped to set that hideous train in motion the moment he whispered into Tío's ear the false information that Güero Méndez was the imaginary Source Chupar. So when the word came through intelligence channels—the rumors that the Barreras had decapitated Pilar and thrown her children off a bridge in Colombia—Art finally picked up a pen and signed the divorce papers that been on his desk for months.

He gave full custody of the children to Althie.

"I'm grateful, Art," she said. "But why now?"

Punishment, he thought.

I lose two kids, too.

He hasn't lost them, of course. He gets them every other weekend and for a month in the summer. He goes to Cassie's volleyball matches and Michael's baseball games. He faithfully attends school assemblies, plays, ballet recitals, parent-teacher conferences.

But it's forced. By definition, the little spontaneous moments don't happen during scheduled time, and he misses the little things. Making them their breakfasts, reading stories, wrestling on the floor. The sad reality is that there's no such thing as "quality time"; there's only "time," and he misses it.

He misses Althie, too.

God, how he misses Althie.

But you threw her away, he thinks.

And for what?

To become "The Border Lord"? That's what they call him now in the DEA—behind his back, that is. Except for Shag, who says it to his face. Brings a cup of coffee into his office and asks, "How's the Border Lord this morning?"

Technically, he's the head of the Southwest Border Task Force and runs a coordinating group of all the agencies fighting the War on Drugs: DEA, FBI, Border Patrol, Customs and Immigration, local and state police—they all report to Art Keller. Based in San Diego, he has a huge office, with a staff to match.

It's a powerful position, exactly the one he demanded of John Hobbs.

He's also a member of the Vertical Committee. It's a small group—it consists of him and John Hobbs—that coordinates DEA and CIA activities in the Americas to ensure that they don't trip over each other's feet. That's the stated purpose; the unstated purpose is to make sure Art doesn't do anything to screw the Company's agenda.

That was the quid pro quo. Art got the Southwest Border Task Force so he could wage his war against the Barreras; in exchange, he slips his head into the leash.

Day of the Dead? he thinks as he sits in a parked car on a street in La Jolla. I might as well go put candy on my own grave.

Then he sees Nora Hayden come out of the boutique.

She's a creature of habit and has been for the months that he's had her under surveillance. She first came to his attention through sources he keeps in Tijuana. The word was that Adán Barrera had a girlfriend, a mistress, that he had rented an apartment in the Río district and went to see her there regularly.

Uncharacteristically careless of Adán, picking an American woman for his piece of strange, Art thinks as he watches the woman come down the sidewalk with shopping bags in both hands. Not like Adán at all, really, who had the reputation—at least until recently—of being a devoted family man.

But Art can understand the temptation as he looks at Nora.

She might be the most beautiful woman he's ever seen.

On the *outside,* anyway, he thinks, reminding himself that this cunt fucks Adán Barrera.

Professionally.

He'd had a tail put on her three months ago when she'd come back across the border. So he had a name and an address, and pretty soon he had something else.

Haley Saxon.

The DEA had had the madam up for years. So, it turned out, had the IRS. The San Diego PD knew all about the White House, of course, but nobody had moved on it because Haley Saxon's client list was a political hornet's nest that nobody had the balls to stir up.

And now it turns out that Adán's *segundera* is one of Haley's best earners. Shit, Art thinks, if Haley Saxon were Mary Kay, Nora Hayden would have her own fleet of pink Cadillacs by now.

He waits until she gets a little closer, then steps out of the car, shows her his badge. "Ms. Hayden, we need to talk."

"I don't think we do."

She has amazing blue eyes, and her voice is cultured and confident. He has to remind himself that she's just a whore.

"Why don't we sit in my car?" Art suggests.

"Why don't we not?"

She starts to walk away but he holds her by the elbow. "Why don't I have your friend Haley Saxon arrested for running a house of prostitution?" Art asks. "Why don't I shut her down for good?"

She lets him walk her to the car. He opens the front passenger door and she gets in. Then he walks around and sits in the driver's seat.

Nora looks pointedly at her watch. "I'm trying to make a one-fifteen movie."

Art says, "Let's talk about your boyfriend."

"My *boyfriend*?"

"Or is Barrera your 'client'?" Art asks. "Or your 'john'? Educate me on the jargon."

She doesn't blink. "He's my lover."

"Does he pay you for the privilege?"

"That's none of your business."

Art asks, "Do you know what your lover does for a living?"

"He's a restaurateur."

"Come on, Nora," Art says.

"Mr. Keller," she said, "let's just say I have some sympathy for dealing in pleasures that society deems illegal."

"Yeah, okay," Art said. "How about murder? Are you okay with that?"

"Adán's never killed anybody."

"Ask him about Ernie Hidalgo," Art says. "While you're at it, ask him about Pilar Méndez. He had her head cut off. And her children. Do you know what your boyfriend did with them? He threw them off a bridge."

"That is an old lie that Güero Méndez put out to—"

"Is that what Adán told you?"

"What do you want, Mr. Keller?"

She's a businesswoman, Art thinks. She's getting right down to it. Good. Time to make your pitch. Don't fuck it up.

"Your cooperation," Art says.

"You want me to inform on—"

"Let's just say you're in a unique position to—"

She opens the car door. "I'm going to be late for my movie."

He grabs her and stops her. "Go to a later show."

"You have no right to hold me against my will," Nora says. "I haven't committed any crime."

"Let me explain a few things to you," Art says. "We know that the Barreras are investors in Haley Saxon's business. That alone puts her on Queer Street. If they ever used the house to have a meeting, I'll RICO her into twenty-to-life, and it will be your fault. You'll have plenty of time to apologize to her, though, because I'll put you in the same cell. Can you explain all your income, Ms. Hayden? Can you account for the money that Adán is paying you now to be your 'lover'? Or is he laundering drug money along with the dirty sheets? You're in deep, hot water, Ms. Hayden. But you can save yourself. You can even save your pal Haley. I'm reaching out my hand. Take it."

She looks at him with pure loathing.

Which is fine, Art thinks. I don't need you to love me, I just need you to do what I want.

"If you could do what you say you can do to Haley," Nora says calmly, "you would already have done it. And as for what you can do to me—take your best shot."

She starts to get out again.

"How about Parada?" Art asks. "Are you doing him, too?"

Because they have her visiting the priest in Guadalajara, and even San Cristóbal, on numerous occasions.

She turns and glares at him.

"You're a piece of filth."

"You'd better believe it."

"For the record," she says, "Juan and I are friends."

"Yeah?" Art says. "Would he still be your friend if he knew you were a hooker?"

"He does know."

He loves me anyway, Nora thinks.

"Does he know you sell yourself to a murdering little piece of shit like Adán Barrera?" Art asks. "Would he still be your friend if he knew that? Should I pick up the phone and tell him? We go way back."

I know, Nora thinks. He's told me about you. What he didn't tell me is how awful you are.

"Do whatever you're going to do, Mr. Keller," Nora says. "I don't care. May I go?"

"For now."

She gets out of the car and walks back down the street, her skirt swinging against her beautiful, tanned legs.

Looking, Art thinks, as cool as if she'd just had tea with a friend.

You fucking asshole, he thinks, you totally blew it.

But I'd love to know, Nora, if you tell Adán about our little chat.

Mexico
1994

Adán has spent the whole day at cemeteries.

He had nine graves to visit, nine little shrines to build, nine elaborate meals to lay out. Nine family members killed by Güero Méndez on a single night barely one month ago. His men, dressed in the black uniforms of the *federales*, had taken them from their houses or kidnapped them off the streets, in Mexico City and Guadalajara, driven them to safe houses and tortured them, then dumped their bodies on busy corners for the morning street sweepers to find.

Two uncles, an aunt and six cousins—two of the latter women.

One of the female cousins was a lawyer working for the *pasador*, but the others were uninvolved with the drug end of the family business. Their only connection was being related to Miguel Ángel and Adán and Raúl, and that was enough. Well, it was enough for Pilar and Güerito and Claudia, wasn't it? Adán thinks. Méndez didn't start this thing of killing families.

We did.

So it was *expected*, Méndez's "Bloody September," by everyone in Mexico who knew anything about the drug trade. The local police barely investigated the murders. "What did they expect?" ran the general opinion. "They killed his wife and children." And not only killed them, but sent Méndez his wife's head and a videotape of his children plummeting off a bridge. It was too much, even for Mexico, even for the *narcotraficantes*—it put the Barrera *pasador* beyond the pale, as it were. And if Méndez retaliated by killing members of the Barrera family, well, it was *expected*.

So Adán had a busy day, starting early in the morning with the Mexico City graves, then flying to Guadalajara to attend to his duties there, then a quick flight here to Puerto Vallarta where his brother Raúl was, characteristically, throwing a party.

"Cheer up," Raúl tells Adán when he arrives at the club. "It's El Día de los Muertos."

Sure, they've taken some hits, but they've delivered some, too.

"Maybe we should bring food to their graves, too," Adán says.

"Shit, we'd go broke," Raúl says to him, "feeding all the guys we've sent to the devil. Fuck them—let their families feed them."

The Barreras v. the world.

Cali cocaine v. Medellín cocaine.

If Adán hadn't made the deal with the Orejuela brothers, the Barreras would be the recipients of the candy and flowers today. But with the steady supply of product from Cali, they have the men and the money to fight the war. And the battle for La Plaza has been bloody but simple. Raúl has presented the local dealers with a clean choice: Do you want to be a Coca-Cola distributor or a Pepsi distributor? You have to choose; you can't be both. Coke or Pepsi, Ford or Chevy, Hertz or Avis—it's either one or the other.

Alejandro Cazares, for instance, had chosen Coke. The San Diego real-estate investor, businessman and dope dealer had declared his loyalty to Güero Méndez, and his body was found in his car off a dusty dirt street in San Ysidro. And Billy Brennan, another San Diego dealer, was found with a bullet in his brain in a motel room in Pacific Beach.

The American cops were puzzled as to why each of these victims had a Pepsi can stuck in his mouth.

Güero Méndez struck back, of course. Eric Mendoza and Salvador Marechal went with Pepsi, and their charred bodies were found in their still-smoldering cars in a vacant lot in Chula Vista. The Barreras answered in kind, and for a few weeks Chula Vista became a virtual parking lot for burning cars with burned bodies inside.

But the Barreras were making their point: We're here, *pendejos*. Güero is trying to run La Plaza from Culiacán, but we are *here*. We're local. We can reach right out and touch somebody—in Baja or San Diego—and if Güero is so tough, why can't he reach out for us in his own territory in Tijuana? Why hasn't Güero had us killed? The answer is simple, my friends—because he can't. He's holed up in his mansion in Culiacán, and if you want to take his side go ahead, but brothers, he's there and we're here.

Güero's lack of action is a show of weakness, not strength, because the truth is that he is running out of resources. He may have a firm grip on Sinaloa, but their beloved home state is landlocked. Without use of La Plaza, Güero has to pay El Verde to move drugs through Sonora, or pay Abrego to move them through the Gulf, and you can bet those two greedy old bastards charge him plenty for every ounce of his product that passes through their territories.

No, Güero is almost finished, and his slaughter of Barrera uncles, aunt and cousins was just the flopping of a fish on the deck.

It's the Day of the Dead and Adán and Raúl are still alive, and that is something to celebrate.

Which they do at their new disco in Puerto Vallarta.

Güero Méndez makes the pilgrimage to the Jardines del Valle cemetery in Culiacán, to an unmarked crypt with carved marble columns, bas-relief sculptures and a dome decorated with frescoes of two little angels. Inside are the tombs of his wife and children. Colored photographs locked in glass cases hang from the wall.

Claudia and Güerito.

His two *angelitos*.

Pilar.

His *esposa* and *querida.*

Seduced, but still beloved.

Güero has brought with him *ofrenda a los muertos,* offerings to the dead.

For his *angelitos,* he has *papel picado,* tissue paper cut in the shapes of skeletons and skulls and little animals. And cookies, and candies shaped like skulls and inscribed with their names in frosting. And toys—little dolls for her, little soldiers for him.

For Pilar he has brought flowers—the traditional chrysanthemums, marigolds and coxcomb—formed into crosses and wreaths. And a coffin made from spun sugar. And the little cookies made with amaranth seeds that she liked so much.

He kneels in front of the tombs and lays down his offerings, then pours fresh water into three bowls so that they can wash their hands before the feast. Outside, a small *norteño* band plays cheerful music under the watchful eye of a platoon of *sicarios.* Güero lays a clean hand towel beside each bowl, then sets up an altar, carefully arranging the votive candles and the dishes of rice and beans, *pollo* in *mole* sauce, candied pumpkins and yams. Then he lights a stick of *campol* incense and sits on the floor.

Shares memories with them.

Good memories of picnics, swims in mountain lakes, family games of *fútbol.* He speaks out loud, hears their answers in his head. A sweeter music than they're playing outside.

Soon I will join you, he tells his wife and children.

Not soon enough, but soon.

First there is much work to be done.

First I must set a table for the Barreras.

And load it with bitter fruit.

And candy skulls with each of their names: Miguel Ángel, Raúl, Adán.

And send their souls to hell.

After all, it's the Day of the Dead.

The disco, Adán thinks, is a monument to vulgarity.

Raúl has done La Sirena up in an underwater theme. A grotesque neon mermaid (La Sirena herself) presides over the front entrance, and when you come inside, the interior walls are sculpted like coral reefs and underwater caves.

The entire left wall is one huge reef tank holding five hundred gallons of salt water. The price of the glass wall made Adán shudder, not to mention the cost of the exotic tropical fish—yellow, blue and purple tangs at $200 each;

a porcupine puffer fish at $300; a $500 clown trigger fish, with its admittedly beautiful yellow and black spots. Then there were the expensive corals, and of course Raúl had to have several kinds: open brain coral, mushroom coral, flower coral and pumping venicia coral, shaped like fingers, reaching up from underwater like a drowned sailor. And "live rocks" with calcified algae glowing purple in the lights. Eels—black-and-white snowflake eels and black-striped brown morays—peek their heads out from holes in the rock and the coral, and crabs crawl across the tops of the rocks and shrimp float in the electrically created current.

The right side of the club is dominated by an actual waterfall. ("That doesn't make any sense," Adán objected to his brother when it was under construction. "How can you have an underwater waterfall?" "I just wanted one," Raúl answered. Well, that answers that, Adán thought—he just wanted one.) And underneath the waterfall is a grotto with flat rocks that serve as beds for couples to lounge on, and Adán is just glad that, for hygienic purposes, the grotto is regularly sprayed by the waterfall.

The club's tables are all twisted, rusted metal, the surfaces done in mother-of-pearl with seashells encrusted on them. The dance floor is painted like an ocean bottom, and the expensive lighting creates a blue ripple effect, as if the dancers were swimming underwater.

The place cost a fortune.

"You can build it," Adán had warned Raúl, "but it had better make money."

"Haven't they all?" Raúl answered.

In all fairness, this is true, Adán had to admit. Raúl might have appalling taste, but he's a genius at creating trendy nightclubs and restaurants, profit centers in themselves and invaluable for laundering the narco-dollars that now flow south from El Norte like a deep green river.

The place is packed.

Not only because it is El Día de los Muertos but also because La Sirena is a smash, even in this highly competitive resort town. And during the annual drunken orgy known as spring break the American college kids will flock to the club, spending even more (clean) American dollars.

But tonight the crowd is mostly Mexican, mostly, in fact, friends and business associates of the Barrera brothers, here to celebrate with them. There are a few American tourists who have found their way in, and a hand-ful of Europeans as well, but that's all right. There will be no business con-ducted here tonight, or any night, for that matter—there is an unwritten rule that the legitimate businesses in the resort towns are strictly off limits for any narco activities. No drug deals, no meetings and above all, no violence. After narcotics, tourism is the country's biggest source of foreign currency, so no one wants to scare away the Americans, British, Germans and Japanese who leave their dollars, pounds, marks and yen in Mazatlán, Puerto Vallarta, Cabo San Lucas and Cozumel.

All the cartels own nightclubs, restaurants, discos and hotels in these towns, so they have an interest to protect, an interest that would be ill served by a tourist catching a stray bullet. No one wants to pick up a newspaper and see headlines of a bloody shoot-out with photos of corpses lying in the street. So the *pasadores* and the government all have a healthy agreement of the "Take it somewhere else, boys" variety. There's just too much money being made to mess with.

You can play in these towns, but you have to play nice.

And they are certainly playing tonight, Adán thinks as he watches Fabián Martínez dance with three or four blond German girls.

There is too much business to take care of, the unceasing cycle of product going north and money coming south. There are the constant business arrangements with the Orejuelas, then the actual movement of the cocaine from Colombia to Mexico, then the endless challenge of getting it safely into the States and converting it to crack, then selling it to the retailers, collecting the money, getting the cash back into Mexico and cleaning it.

Some of the money goes into fun, but a lot of the money goes into bribes.

Silver or lead.

Plata o plomo.

One of the Barrera lieutenants would simply go to the local police *comandante* or army commander with a bag full of cash and give him the choice in those exact words: *"¿Plata o plomo?"*

That's all that needed to be said. The meaning was clear—you can get rich or you can get dead. You choose.

If they chose rich, it was Adán's business. If they chose dead, that was Raúl's business.

Most people chose rich.

Coño, Adán thinks, most of the cops *planned* on getting rich. In fact, they had to buy their positions from their superiors, or pay a monthly share of their *mordida.* It was like a franchise operation. Burger King, Taco Bell, McBribes. Easiest money in the world. Money for nothing. Just look the other way, be someplace else, see no evil, hear no evil, speak no evil, and the monthly payment will be there in full and on time.

And the war, Adán reflects, watching the partiers dance in the shimmering blue light, has been a further boon for the cops and the army. Méndez pays his cops to bust our dope, we pay our guys to bust Méndez's dope. It's a good deal for everyone except the guy whose dope gets popped. Say the Baja State Police seize a million dollars of Güero's cocaine. We pay them a $100,000 "finder's fee," they get to be heroes in the papers and look like good guys to the Yanquis, and then after a decent interval they sell us that million bucks' worth of blow for $500,000.

It's a win-win deal.

And that's in Mexico alone.

There are also U.S. Customs agents to pay to look the other way when cars full of coke or grass or heroin come through their stations—$30,000 a carload, no matter what's in it. And still, there's no way to guarantee that your car is going to go through a "clean" checkpoint, even though you've bought condo buildings whose top floors overlook the crossing stations and you have lookouts up there who are in radio contact with your drivers and try to steer them toward the "right" lanes. But the Customs agents are switched often and arbitrarily, and other agents are monitoring radio bands, so if you send a dozen cars at a time through the border crossings at San Ysidro and Otay Mesa, you expect nine or ten of them to get through.

There are bribes to city cops in San Diego, Los Angeles, San Bernardino, you name it. And to state police, and sheriff's departments. And secretaries and typists in the DEA who can slip you info on what investigations are going on, with what technology. Or even to that rare, *rare,* DEA agent you could get on the arm, but they are few and far between, because between the DEA and the Mexican cartels there is a blood feud, *still,* from the killing of Ernie Hidalgo.

Art Keller sees to that.

And thank God for that, Adán thinks, because while Keller's revenge obsession might cost me money in the short run, in the long run it *makes* me money. And that is what the Americans simply cannot seem to understand— that all they do is drive up the price and make us rich. Without them, any *bobo* with an old truck or a leaky boat with an outboard motor could run drugs into El Norte. And then the price would not be worth the effort. But as it is, it takes millions of dollars to move the drugs, and the prices are accordingly sky-high. The Americans take a product that literally grows on trees and turn it into a valuable commodity. Without them, cocaine and marijuana would be like oranges, and instead of making billions smuggling it, I'd be making pennies doing stoop labor in some California field, picking it.

And the truly funny irony is that Keller is himself another product because I make millions selling protection against him, charging the independent contractors who want to move their product through La Plaza thousands of dollars for the use of our cops, soldiers, Customs agents, Coast

Guard, surveillance equipment, communications . . . This is what Mexican cops appreciate that American cops don't. We are partners, *mi hermano Arturo,* in the same enterprise.

Comrades in the War on Drugs.

We could not exist without each other.

Adán watches as two Nordic-looking young women stand under the waterfall, letting the spray soak their thin T-shirts to display their breasts to any and all admirers, of which there are quite a few. The disco music is pounding, the dancing frenetic, the drinking hard, fast and constant. It's El Día de los Muertos, and most of the people in the crowd here tonight are old friends from Culiacán or Badiraguato, and if you're a narco from Sinaloa you have a lot of dead to remember.

There are a lot of ghosts at this party.

It's been a bloody war.

But, Adán thinks, hopefully it is almost over, and we will get back to pure business.

Because Adán Barrera has reinvented the drug business.

The traditional shape of any of the Mexican *pasadores* was the pyramid. Similar to the Sicilian Mafia families, there was a godfather, a boss, then captains, then soldiers, and every level "kicked up" to the next. The lower levels made very little money unless they could build levels beneath them, who would in turn kick up, but make very little. Anybody but a fool could figure out the problem with the pyramid—if you get in early, you're gold; if you get in late, you're fucked. All it did, in Adán's analysis, was create motivation to go out and start a new pyramid.

The pyramid was also too vulnerable to aggressive law enforcement. All you had to do, Adán thought, was look at what had happened to the American Mafia to see that. All you needed was one *dedo,* one snitch, one dissatisfied soldier at the lower levels, and he could take the cops up and down the integrated pyramid structure. Every single one of the heads of New York's Five Families was now in prison, with their families going into serious and inevitable decline.

So Adán tore down the pyramid and replaced it with a horizontal structure. Well, almost horizontal. His new organization had only two levels: the Barrera brothers on top, everyone else underneath them.

But on the same level.

"We want entrepreneurs, not employees," Adán told Raúl. "Employees cost money, entrepreneurs make money."

The new structure created a growing pool of highly motivated, richly rewarded independent businessmen who paid 12 percent of their gross to the

Barreras and were happy to do it. There was now only one level to kick up to, and you ran your own business, took your own risks, reaped your own rewards.

And Adán saw to it that the potential rewards were greater for the emerging entrepreneurs. He rebuilt his Baja cartel on that principal, allowing—no, *encouraging*—his people to go into business for themselves: lowering their "taxes" to 12 percent, giving low-interest loans for start-up capital, providing them with access to financial services—i.e., money-laundering—all in exchange for simple loyalty to the cartel.

"Twelve percent from many," Adán had explained to Raúl when first proposing the drastic tax reduction, "will be more than thirty percent from a few." He had observed the lessons of the Reagan Revolution. They could make more money by lowering taxes than by raising them because the lower taxes allowed more entrepreneurs to come into the business and make more money and pay more taxes.

Raúl is of the opinion that lead, not a new business model, is winning the war against Méndez, and in a narrow sense he's right. But Adán is convinced that the more powerful factor was the pure force of economics—the Barreras simply undersold Güero Méndez. You can sell Coke with a 30 percent overhead, or Pepsi with a 20 percent overhead—you choose. An easy choice to make—you can sell Pepsi and make a lot of money, or Coke and make less money until Raúl kills you. Suddenly, there were a lot of Pepsi distributorships. You would have to be a fool to choose the lead Coke over the silver Pepsi.

Silver or lead.

The yin and yang of the new Baja cartel.

Deal with Adán and get the silver, or deal with Raúl and get the lead. A structure that tipped the scales in Baja against Güero Méndez. He was simply too slow catching up, and by the time he did, he couldn't afford to lower his prices because he couldn't get enough cocaine through La Plaza and had to pay out thirty points to move it through Sonora or the Gulf.

No, Raúl later had to admit, the 12 percent deal had been an act of sheer genius.

It's perfect for guys like Fabián Martínez and the rest of the Juniors.

The rules were simple.

You would tell the Barreras when you were bringing the product through, what it was (cocaine, marijuana or heroin), how much weight, and what your pre-arranged sale price was—usually somewhere between $14,000 and $16,000 per kilo—and what date you were planning on delivering it to the retailer in the States. You then had forty-eight hours after that date to pay the

Barreras 12 percent of the pre-arranged sale price. (The pre-arranged price was simply a guarantee on a bottom—if you sold it for less, you still owed the percentage on the quoted price; if you sold it for more, you owed the percentage on the higher price.) If you couldn't deliver the money within the two days, you had better sit down with Adán and arrange a payment plan, or sit down with Raúl and . . .

Silver or lead.

The 12 percent was just for bringing the drugs through La Plaza. If you wanted to make your own arrangement with the local police, *federales* or army *comandante* to guarantee the safety of your shipment, fine, but if it got busted, you still owed the twelve points. If you wanted the Barreras to make those security arrangements, that was also fine, but it would cost you—the price of the *mordida* plus a handling fee. But in that case, the Barreras guaranteed the safety of your shipment on the Mexican side of the border. If it was seized, they would reimburse you for the wholesale cost of the shipment. That is, if it was cocaine, for instance, the Barreras would pay you the purchase price you had negotiated with the Orejuela cartel in Cali, not the retail price you expected to get in the States. If you bought the Barrera security package, the safety of your shipment was absolutely guaranteed from the time it reached Baja until the time it hit the border. No other dealer would try to rip it off, no bandits would try to hijack it. Raúl and his *sicarios* saw to that—you would have to be seriously insane to try to steal a shipment the safety of which was spoken for by Raúl Barrera.

The Barreras also offered financial services. Adán wanted to make it as easy as possible for as many people as possible to get into the business, so the 12 percent never had to be fronted. You didn't have to pay it until after you had sold it. It was always done on the come. But the Barreras went the extra step—they would help you launder the money once you had sold your shipment, and this was an increasingly profitable product for the Barreras. The going rate for money cleansing was 6.5 percent, but bribed bankers would give the Barreras a volume price of 5 percent, so Adán was making an additional 1.5 percent on every customer's dollar. Again, you didn't have to launder your cash through the Barreras—you were an independent business-man, you could do whatever you wanted. But if you went somewhere else and got ripped off or cheated, or if your money got seized at U.S. Customs on the way back through the border, it was your own tough luck, whereas the Barreras guaranteed your money. Whatever you put in dirty, you got back clean—within three working days—minus the 6.5 percent.

And this has been Adán's "Baja Revolution"—catching the drug busi-ness up with times.

"Miguel Ángel Barrera dragged the drug business into the twentieth century," is how one *narcotraficante* put it. "Adán is leading it into the twenty-first."

And beating Güero Méndez while we're at it, Adán thinks. If he cannot move his cocaine, he cannot pay *mordida.* If he cannot pay *mordida,* he cannot move cocaine. In the meantime, we are building a network that is fast, efficient and entrepreneurial, using the newest and best technology and financial mechanisms.

Life is good, Adán thinks, on this Day of the Dead.

Day of the Dead, Callan thinks.

Big deal.

Like, ain't they *all* days of the dead?

He's knocking a few back at the bar of La Sirena. You want a challenge, try getting a straight-up whiskey at a Mexican beach bar. Tell the guy you want a drink without a goddamn umbrella in it, he looks at you like you ruined his fuckin' day.

Callan does it anyway. "Yo, *viejo,* is it raining in here?"

"No."

"Then I don't need *this,* do I?"

And if I wanted fruit juice, *amigó,* I'd *order* fruit juice. Only juice I want is the juice of the barley.

Irish Vitamin C.

The old waters of life.

Which is kind of funny, Callan thinks, when you consider what I do for a living, what I've *always* done, basically.

Cancel people's reservations.

Sorry, sir, you're checking out early.

Yeah, but—

Yeah, but nothin'. *Out of the pool.*

It ain't for the Cimino Family anymore, but Sal Scachi is still calling the shots, in a manner of speaking. Callan was chilling out down in Costa Rica, waiting for the shit storm in New York to blow itself out, when Scachi came to see him.

"How would you feel about going down to Colombia?" he'd asked Callan.

"To do what?"

To hook up with something called "MAS" was the answer.

Muerte a Secuestradores—Death to Kidnappers. Scachi explained that it started back in '81 when the left-wing insurgent group M-19 kidnapped the sister of Colombian drug lord Fabián Ochoa and held her for ransom.

Yeah, *that* was a good business plan, Callan thought, kidnapping a boss's sister.

Like Ochoa was going to pay, right?

What the cocaine magnate did instead, Scachi said, was he convened a meeting of 223 associates and made them each cough up $20,000 in cash and ten of their best gunmen. Do the math—that's a war chest of four and a half million bucks and an army of over two *thousand* button men.

"Dig this," Scachi said. "These guys actually flew over a soccer stadium in a helicopter and dropped leaflets *announcing* what they were going to do."

Which was basically rip through Cali and Medellín like rabid dogs on crack. Busted into homes, dragged college kids right out of their classrooms, shot some of them on the spot and took others away to safe houses for "questioning."

Ochoa's sister was released unharmed.

"What's all this to me?" Callan asked.

Scachi tells him. In '85 the Colombian government struck a truce with the various leftist groups that formed an above-ground alliance called the Unión Patriótica, which won fourteen seats in parliament in the '86 elections.

"Okay," Callan said.

"Not okay," Scachi answered. "These people are Communists, Sean."

Scachi launched into a fucking tirade, the gist of which was that we fought the Communists so the people could have democracy, then the ungrateful motherfuckers turn around and vote for Communists. So what Sal was saying, Callan guessed, is that the people should have democracy, just not *that much* democracy.

They got the absolute freedom to choose what we want them to.

"MAS is going to do something about it," Scachi was saying. "They could use a man with your talents."

Maybe they could, Callan thought, but they ain't *gettin'* a man with my talents. I don't know what Sal's connection is to this MAS, but it ain't nothin' to me.

"I think I'll just go back to New York," Callan said. After all, Johnny Boy was firmly in charge of the family, and Johnny Boy had no reason to give Callan anything but love and safe harbor.

"Yeah, you can do that," Scachi said. "Except for there are about three thousand federal indictments waiting for you."

"For what?!"

"For what?" Scachi said. "Cocaine dealing, extortion, racketeering. The word I get is they also like you for the Big Paulie thing."

"They like *you* for the Big Paulie thing, Sal?" Callan asks.

"What are you saying?"

"I mean, you put me there."

"Listen, kid, I can probably get this straightened out for you," Scachi says, "but it wouldn't hurt if you would, you know, help us out on this thing."

Callan didn't ask how Sal Scachi could straighten out a federal beef by getting him to go down to Colombia to hook up with a bunch of anti-Communist cocaine vigilantes, because there are some things you don't want to know. He just took the plane ticket and the fresh passport, flew to Medellín and reported for work with MAS.

Death to Kidnappers turned out to be Death to Winning Unión Patriótica Candidates. Six of them took bullets to the head instead of the oath of office. (Days of the Dead, Callan thinks now, working on his drink. Days of the Dead.)

After that, it was just *on,* he remembers. M-19 retaliated by seizing the Palace of Justice, and over a hundred people, including several Supreme Court judges, got killed in the fucked-up rescue attempt. Which is what you get, Callan thinks, for using the cops and the army instead of professionals.

They used professionals, though, to hit the leader of the Unión Patriótica. Callan didn't pull the trigger, but he rode shotgun when they whacked Jaime Pardo Leal. It was a good hit—clean, efficient, professional.

Turned out, though, that was just the warm-up.

The real killing started in '88.

The money behind a lot of it came from the Man himself, Medellín cocaine lord Pablo Escobar.

At first Callan couldn't figure why Escobar and the other coke lords gave a rat's ass about the politics. But then he tripped to the fact that the cartel boys had put a lot of their coke money into real estate, large cattle ranches that they didn't want to see broken up by some leftist land-distribution scheme.

Callan got to know one of these ranches real well.

In the spring of '87, MAS moved him out to Las Tangas, a large *finca* owned by a couple of brothers, Carlos and Fidel Cardona. When they were still teenagers their father had been kidnapped and murdered by Communist guerrillas. So as much as you want to talk about politics and all that shit, Callan thought when he met them at their ranch, it's personal. It's always personal.

Las Tangas wasn't as much a ranch as it was a fucking fort. Callan saw some cattle out there, but what he saw mostly were other killers like himself. There were a lot of Colombians, cartel soldiers on loan, but there were also South Africans and Rhodesians who had lost their own war and were looking to win this one. Then there were Israelis, Lebanese, Russians, Irish and Cubans. It was a fucking Olympic Village for button men.

They trained hard, too.

Some guy rumored to be an Israeli colonel came in with a bunch of fucking Brits who were all ex-SAS, or claimed to be anyway. As a good mick, Callan hated the Brits and the SAS, but he had to admit that these limeys knew what they were doing.

Callan was always pretty slick with a .22, but there was a lot more to this kind of work, and pretty soon Callan was getting instruction on the use and handling of the M-16, the AK-47, the M-60 machine gun and the Barrett-Model .90 sniper rifle.

He also trained in hand-to-hand combat—how to kill with a knife, a garrote, his hands and feet. Some of the permanent instructors were former U.S. Special Forces guys—some of them Operation Phoenix vets from Vietnam. A lot of them were Colombian army officers who spoke English like they were from Mayberry, USA.

It used to crack Callan up, whenever one of these upper-crust Colombians would open his mouth and sound like some cracker. Then he found out that most of these guys had gotten their training at Fort Benning in Georgia.

Something called the School of the Americas.

Yeah, what the fuck kind of school is that? Callan thought. Reading, writing and whacking. Whatever, they taught some nasty skills, which the Colombians were happy to pass on to the group that had become known as Los Tangueros.

There was a lot of OJT, too. On-the-Job Training.

One day a squad of Tangueros went out to ambush a group of guerrillas that had been operating in the area. A local army officer had delivered photos of the six intended targets, who lived in villages like your average *campesinos* when they weren't out doing guerrilla-type shit.

Fidel Cardona led the mission himself. Cardona had become kind of a kick, calling himself "Rambo" and pretty much dressing like the guy in the movie. Anyway, they went out and set up an ambush on a dirt road these guys were supposed to be using.

The Tangueros spread out in a perfect U-shaped formation, just the way they'd been taught. Callan didn't like it, lying in the brush, wearing cammies, sweating in the heat. I'm a city guy, he thinks. When did I join the fucking army?

Truth is, he was edgy. Not scared, really, more *apprehensive,* not knowing what to expect. He'd never gone up against guerrillas before. He thought that they'd probably be pretty good, well trained, know the terrain better and how to use it.

The guerrillas strolled right into the open top of the U.

They weren't what Callan was expecting, hardened fighters in camouflage gear with AKs. These guys looked like farmers, in old denim shirts and short *campesino* trousers. And they didn't move like soldiers, either—spread out, alert. They were just walking up the road.

Callan laid the sights of his Galil rifle on the guy farthest to the left. Aimed a little low, at the guy's stomach, in case the rifle kicked up. Also, he didn't want to look at the guy's face because the man had this baby face and he was talking to his friends and laughing, like a guy does with his buddies at the end of a day of work. So Callan kept his eyes on the blue of the man's shirt because then it was like shooting this *thing,* just like target shooting.

He waited for Fidel to take the first shot, and when he heard it, he squeezed the trigger twice.

His man went down.

They all did.

The poor fuckers never saw it coming, never knew what hit them. There was just a volley of fire from the bushes beside the road and then there were six guerrillas down, bleeding into the dirt.

They never even had time to pull their weapons.

Callan forced himself to walk over to the man he had shot. The guy was dead, lying facedown in the road. Callan nudged the body over with his foot. They had strict orders to pick up any guns, except Callan didn't find one. All the guy was carrying was a machete, the kind that the *campesinos* used to cut bananas off the trees.

Callan looked around and saw that none of the guerrillas had guns.

That didn't bother Fidel. He walked around, putting insurance shots into the backs of their heads, then radioed back to Las Tangas. Pretty soon a truck rolled up with a pile of clothes like the Communist guerrillas usually wore, and Fidel ordered his men to dress the corpses in the new clothes.

"You gotta be fuckin' kiddin' me," Callan said.

Rambo wasn't kidding. He told Callan to get busy.

Callan got busy sitting on the side of the road. "I ain't no fuckin' undertaker," is what he told Fidel. So Callan sat and watched as the other Tangueros changed the corpses' clothes, then snapped photos of the dead "guerrillas."

Fidel yapped at him all the way back. "I know what I'm doing," Fidel said. "I went to school."

Yeah, I went to school, too, Callan told him. They held the classes in

Hell's Kitchen. "But the guys *I* shot, Rambo?" Callan added. "They usually had *guns* in their hands."

Rambo must have bitched to Scachi about him because Sal showed up a few weeks later at the ranch to have a "counseling session" with Callan.

"What's your problem?" Scachi asked him.

"My problem is gunning down fuckin' farmers," Callan said. "Their hands were empty, Sal."

"We ain't making Westerns, here," Sal answered. "There's no 'code of honor.' What, you want to hit them when they're in the jungle with AKs in their hands? You feel better if you take casualties? This is a motherfuckin' *war,* Sparky."

"Yeah, I get it's a war."

Scachi said, "You're getting paid, aren't you?"

Yeah, Callan thought, I'm getting paid.

The eagle screams twice a month, in cash.

"And they're treating you well?" Scachi asked.

Like fucking kings, Callan had to admit. Steaks every night, if you wanted them. Free beer, free whiskey, free coke if that was your thing. Callan blew a little coke now and then, but it didn't do it for him like the booze did. A lot of the Tangueros would snort a pile of coke, then hit the whores that were brought in on weekends and fuck them all night.

Callan went with the whores a couple of times. A man has needs, but that's about all it was, just meeting a need. These weren't high-class call girls like at the White House, either—these were mostly Indian women brought in from the oil fields to the west. They weren't even women, if you wanted to be honest about it. They were mostly just girls in cheap dresses and heavy makeup.

First time he used one, Callan felt more sad than relieved afterward. He went into a little cubicle in the back of their barracks. Bare plywood walls and a bed with a bare mattress. She tried to talk sexy to him, saying things she thought he'd like to hear, but he finally asked her to shut up and just fuck.

He lay there afterward thinking about the blond woman back in San Diego.

Nora was her name.

She was beautiful.

But that was a different life.

After Scachi's pep talk Callan soldiered up and went on more missions. Los Tangueros bushwhacked another six unarmed "guerrillas" on the banks of a river, gunned down another half-dozen right in the town square of a local village.

Fidel had a word for their activities.

Limpieza, he called it.

Cleansing.

They were cleansing the area of guerrillas, Communists, labor leaders, agitators—all the fucking garbage. Callan heard talk they weren't the only ones doing the cleansing. There were lots of other groups, other ranches, other training centers, all over the country. All the groups had nicknames— Muerte a Revolucionarios, ALFA 13, Los Tinados. Inside two years they killed over three thousand activists, organizers, candidates and guerrillas. Most of these killings took place in isolated rural villages, especially in the Medellín stronghold area in the Magdalena Valley, where the entire male populations of villages would be herded together and machine-gunned. Or chopped to pieces with machetes, if bullets were deemed too expensive.

And there were a lot of people other than Communists getting cleansed—street kids, homosexuals, drug addicts, winos.

One day the Tangueros went out to cleanse some guerrillas who were on the move from one base of operation to another. So Callan and the others waited for this rural bus to come down the road, stopped it and took everybody but the driver off. Fidel went through the passengers, comparing their faces with photos he had in his hand, then pulled five men from the group and had them taken into the ditch.

Callan watched as the men dropped to their knees and started praying.

They didn't get much beyond *"Nuestro Padre"* before a bunch of Tangueros sprayed them with bullets. Callan turned away, only to see two of his other comrades chaining the bus driver to the steering wheel.

"What the fuck are you doing?!" Callan yelled.

They siphoned gasoline from the fuel tank of the bus into a plastic water jug and then poured it on the driver, and as he screamed for mercy Fidel turned to the passengers and announced, "This is what you get for transporting guerrillas!"

Two of the Tangueros held Callan back as Fidel tossed a match into the bus.

Callan saw the driver's eyes, heard his screams and watched the man's body twist and dance to the flames.

He never got the smell out of his nose.

(Sitting here now in this Puerto Vallarta bar, he can smell the burning flesh. Ain't enough scotch in the world to cleanse that smell.)

That night Callan hit the bottle hard. Got good and fuckin' drunk and thought about picking up the old .22 and putting a deuce into Fidel's face. Decided he wasn't ready to commit suicide and started packing instead.

One of the Rhodesians stopped him.

"You don't leave here on your feet," the guy told him. "They'll kill you before you walk a klik."

The guy's right, I wouldn't make it a kilometer.

"There's nothing you can do," the Rhodesian said. "It's Red Mist."

"What's Red Mist?" Callan asked.

The guy looked at him weird and then just shrugged.

Like, If you don't know . . .

"What's Red Mist?" Callan asked Scachi on Sal's next visit to Las Tangas to adjust Callan's ever-shittier attitude. The fucking mick was just sitting in the barracks having long conversations with Johnnie Walker.

"Where'd you hear of Red Mist?" Scachi asked.

"Don't matter."

"Yeah, well, *forget* you heard it."

"Fuck that, Sal," Callan said. "I'm a part of somethin', I want to know what it is."

No, you don't, Scachi thought.

And even if you did, I can't tell you.

Red Mist was the code name for the coordination of scores of operations to "neutralize" left-wing movements across Latin America. Basically, the Phoenix program for South and Central America. Half the time, the individual operations didn't even know they were being coordinated as part of Red Mist, but it was Scachi's role as John Hobbs's errand boy to make sure that intelligence was shared, assets were distributed, targets were hit and nobody stepped on anyone else's dick in the doing of it.

It wasn't an easy job, but Scachi was the perfect man for it. Green Beret, sometime CIA asset, made member of the Mafia, Sal would just disappear on "detached duty" from the army and work as Hobbs's waterboy. And there was a lot of water to be carried: Red Mist encompassed literally hundreds of right-wing militias and their drug-lord sponsors, a thousand army officers and a few hundred thousand troops, dozens of separate intelligence agencies and police forces.

And the Church.

Sal Scachi was a Knight of Malta and a member of Opus Dei, the fervently right-wing, anti-Communist secret organization of bishops, priests and committed laypeople such as Sal. The Catholic Church was at war with itself, its conservative leadership in the Vatican fighting the "liberation theologists"—left-wing, often Marxist, priests and bishops on the ground in the Third World—for the soul of Mother Church herself. The Knights of Malta and Opus Dei worked hand-in-glove with the right-wing militias, the army officers, even the drug cartels when necessary.

And the blood flowed like wine at Communion.

Most of it paid for, directly or indirectly, with American dollars. Directly from American aid to the countries' militaries, whose officers made up the bulk of the death squads; indirectly by Americans buying drugs, the dollars for which went to the cartels sponsoring the death squads.

Billions of dollars in economic aid, billions of dollars in dope money.

In El Salvador, right-wing death squads murdered left-wing politicians and labor organizers. In 1989, on the campus of Central American University in San Salvador, Salvadoran army officers gunned down six Jesuit priests, a maid and her little girl with sniper rifles. In that same year, the United States government sent half a billion dollars in aid to the Salvadoran government. By the end of the '80s, approximately 75,000 people had been killed.

Guatemala doubled that figure.

In the long war against the Marxist rebels, over 150,000 people were killed and another 40,000 were never found. Homeless kids were gunned down in the streets. College students were murdered. An American hotelier was beheaded. A university professor was stabbed in the hall of her classroom building. An American nun was raped, killed and thrown onto the corpses of her companions. Through it all, American soldiers provided training, advice and equipment, including the helicopters that flew the killers to the killing grounds. By the end of the '80s, U.S. president George Bush was so disgusted by the carnage that he finally cut off funds and armaments for the Guatemalan military.

Everywhere in Latin America it was the same—the long shadow war between the haves and the have-nots, between the right wing and the Marxists, with the liberals caught, deer-in-the-headlights, between them.

Always, Red Mist was there.

John Hobbs oversaw the operation.

Sal Scachi ran the day-by-day.

Liaising with army officers trained at the School of the Americas at Fort Benning, Georgia. Providing training, technical advice, equipment, intelligence. Lending assets to the Latin American armed forces and militias.

One of these assets was Sean Callan.

The man is a fucking mess, Scachi thought, looking at Callan—long, dirty hair, his skin yellow from days of hard drinking. Not exactly the specimen of a warrior, but looks are deceiving.

Whatever Callan isn't, Scachi thought, he is talent.

And talent's hard to come by, so . . .

"I'm taking you out of Las Tangas," Scachi said.

"Good."

"I got other work for you."

No shit he did, Callan remembers.

Luis Carlos Galán, the Liberal Party presidential candidate who was miles ahead in the polls, was taken off the count in the summer of '89. Bernardo Jaramillo Osa, the leader of the UP, was shot to death as he got off a plane in Bogotá the following spring. Carlos Pizarro, M-19's candidate for president, was gunned down just a few weeks later.

After that Colombia was too hot for Sean Callan.

But Guatemala wasn't. Neither was Honduras, nor was El Salvador.

Scachi moved him around like a knight in a chess set. Jumping him here, jumping him there, using him to take pieces off the board. Guadalupe Salcedo, Héctor Oqueli, Carlos Toledo—then a dozen others. Callan started to lose track of the names. He might not have known exactly what Red Mist really was, but he sure as hell knew what it was to him—blood, a red mist filling his head until that's all he could see.

Then Scachi moved him to Mexico.

"What for?" Callan asked.

"Chill you out for a while," Scachi answered. "Just help provide a little protection for some people. You remember the Barrera brothers?"

How couldn't he? It was the cocaine-for-guns deal that had started all the shit back in '85. Got Jimmy Peaches sideways with Big Paulie, which started his own strange trip.

Yeah, Callan remembered them.

What about them?

"They're friends of ours," Scachi said.

Friends of ours, Callan thought. Weird choice of words, a phrase that made guys use only to describe other made guys to each other. Well, I ain't a made guy, Callan thought, and a couple of Mexican coke dealers sure aren't, so what the fuck?

"They're good people," Scachi explained. "They contribute to the effort."

Yeah, that makes them fucking angels, Callan thought.

But he went to Mexico.

Because where else was he going to go?

So now he's here at this beach resort for a Day of the Dead party.

Decides to have a couple of pops because they're in a safe place on a holy day, so there ain't going to be no problems. Even if there are, he thinks, I'm better a little drunk these days than totally sober.

He throws back the last of his drink, then sees the big aquarium shatter and the water burst out and two people drop in that particular twisting way that people do only when they've been shot.

Callan drops behind the bar stool and pulls his .22.

There must be forty black-uniformed *federales* busting through the front door, firing M-16s from the hip. Bullets strike the fake rock walls of the cave, and it's a good thing they *are* fake, Callan thinks, because they're absorbing the bullets instead of deflecting them back into the crowd.

Then one of the *federales* unhooks a grenade from his shoulder strap.

Callan yells, "Get down!" as if anyone could hear or understand him, then he pops two rounds into the *federale*'s head, and the man drops before he can pull the pin and the grenade falls harmlessly to the floor, but another *federale* flings another grenade and it hits near the dance floor and explodes in a disco-pyrotechnic flash, and now several partyers go down, screaming with pain as the shrapnel rips into their legs.

Now people are ankle-deep in bloody water and flopping fish and Callan feels something hit his foot, but it isn't a bullet, it's a blue tang fish, pretty and electric indigo in the nightclub lights, and he loses himself in a peaceful moment watching the fish, and it is pandemonium now inside La Sirena as the partiers scream and cry and try to push their way out, but there *is* no way out because the *federales* are blocking the doors.

And shooting.

Callan's glad he's a little buzzed. He's on alcohol-Irish-hired-killer autopilot, his head is clear and cool, and he knows now that the shooters aren't *federales*. This isn't a bust, it's a *hit,* and if these guys are cops, they're off-duty and picking up a little extra money for the upcoming holidays. And he realizes quickly that no one is going to get out through the front door—not alive, anyway—and there must be a back exit, so he lowers himself into the water and starts to crawl toward the back of the club.

It's the wall of water that saves Adán's life.

It knocks him off his chair and sends him to the floor, so the first round of gunfire and shrapnel passes over his head. He starts to pick himself up, but then instinct takes over as he feels bullets zinging over him and he sits back down. Looks stupidly at the bullets chopping into the expensive coral, now dry and exposed behind the shattered aquarium, then jumps as an agitated moray eel twists beside him. He looks over to the other wall, where, behind the waterfall, Fabián Martínez is trying to twist himself back into his pants as one of the German girls sitting on the rock shelf does the same, and Raúl stands there with his pants around his ankles and a pistol in his hand and shoots back through the waterfall.

The faux *federales* can't see through the waterfall. That's what saves Raúl, who stands there blasting away with impunity until he runs out of ammo, drops the gun and reaches down and pulls up his pants. Then grabs Fabián by the shoulder and says, "Come on, we have to get out of here."

Because the *federales* are pushing their way through the crowd now, searching for the Barrera brothers. Adán sees them coming and gets up to head for the back, slips and falls, gets back up again and, when he does, a *federale* points a rifle in his face and smiles, and Adán is dead, except the *federale*'s smile disappears in a whirl of blood and Adán feels someone grab his wrist and pull him down and then he's in the water on the floor, face-to-face with a Yanqui who says, "Get down, asshole."

Then Callan starts shooting at the advancing *federales* with short, efficient bursts—*pop-pop, pop-pop*—knocking them down like floating ducks in a carnival game. Adán glances down at the dead *federale,* and, to his horror, sees that the crabs have already scuttled over to feed at the gaping hole where the cop's face used to be.

Callan crawls forward and takes two grenades from the guys he just shot, then quickly reloads, belly-crawls back, grabs Adán and, firing behind with the other hand, pushes him toward the back.

"My brother!" Adán yells. "I have to find my brother!"

"Down!" Callan yells as a fresh burst of fire explodes toward them. Adán does go down as bullets punch him in the back of his right calf and send him sprawling face-first into the water, where he stupidly lies watching his own blood flow past his nose.

He can't seem to move now.

His brain is trying to tell him to get up, but he's suddenly exhausted, much too tired to move.

Callan squats down, hefts Adán over his shoulder and staggers toward the door labeled BAÑOS. He's almost there when Raúl takes the weight off him.

"I got him," Raúl says.

Callan nods. Another Barrera shooter has their backs, firing behind him into the chaos of the club. Callan kicks the door open and finds himself in the relative quiet of a little hallway.

To the right is a door marked SIRENAS, with a little silhouette of a mermaid; the door to the left is marked POSEIDONES, with a silhouette of a man with long, curly hair and a beard. Directly in front is the SALIDA, and Raúl makes straight for this exit.

Callan screams, "NO!" and pulls him away by the collar. Just in time, because slugs come ripping through the open door just like he expected they would. Anyone who has the time and manpower to stage this kind of hit is going to place some shooters outside the back door.

So he yanks Raúl through the POSEIDONES door. The other shooter goes in behind him. Callan pulls the pin on one of the grenades and tosses it out the back door to discourage anyone from standing around there or coming in.

Then he jumps into the men's room and closes the door behind him.

Hears the grenade go off with a dull bass thump.

Raúl sits Adán down on the toilet and the other shooter guards the door while Callan examines Adán's wounded leg. The bullets have passed clean through, but there's no way of telling if they've broken any bones. Or hit the femoral artery, in which case Adán is going to bleed to death before they can get him help.

The truth is that none of them are going to make it, not if the shooters keep coming, because they're trapped. Fuck, he thinks, somehow I always knew I'd die in a shithouse, then he looks around, and there are no windows like you're supposed to have in American restrooms but there is, directly above him, a skylight.

A skylight in a men's room?

It had been another one of Raúl's style points.

"I want the bathrooms to look like cruise-liner cabins turned sideways," he'd explained to Adán when arguing for the skylights. "You know, as if the ship was sunk?"

So the skylight is in the shape of a porthole, and the bathrooms are ornate, and everything except the sink and the toilet is turned sideways. Which is just what you want, Callan thinks, if you've been pounding margaritas and go to take a piss—a seasick shitter. He wonders how many college kids have staggered in here in pretty good shape and then puked it all up once they got sideways, but he doesn't think about it for long because that fucking stupid porthole above them is the way out, so he climbs up on the sink counter and opens the skylight. He jumps, gets a grip then pulls himself up and through and then he's on the roof and the air is salty and warm and then he sticks his head back down through the porthole skylight and says, "Come on!"

Fabián jumps and pulls himself through the skylight, then Raúl lifts Adán up and Callan and Fabián pull him up onto the roof. Raúl has a hard time squeezing himself through the small porthole, but manages just in time as the *federales* kick open the door and spray the room with bullets.

Then they rush in, expecting to see dead bodies and screaming, twisting wounded. But they don't see any of that and they're puzzled until one of them looks up and sees the open skylight and then he gets it. But the next thing he sees is Callan's hand dropping a grenade and then the skylight closes, and now there *are* dead and screaming, twisting bodies in the men's room of La Sirena.

Callan leads the way across the roof to the back of the building. There's only one *federale* guarding the alley in back now, and Callan dispatches him with two quick shots to the back of the head. Then he and Raúl carefully lower Adán down to a waiting Fabián.

Then they take off trotting down the alley, Raúl with Adán slung over his shoulder, toward the back street, where Callan shoots the window out of a Ford Explorer, opens the door and takes about thirty seconds to hot-wire the ignition.

Ten minutes later they're in the emergency room of Our Lady of Guadalupe hospital, where the registration nurses hear the name Barrera and ask no questions.

Adán is lucky—the femur is chipped but not broken, and the femoral artery is untouched.

Raúl is giving blood with one arm, on the phone with the other, and in minutes his *sicarios* are either rushing to the hospital or searching the neighborhood of La Sirena for any of Güero's boys who might be lingering. They don't come back with any, only the news that six of the partyers were killed, and ten of the *"federales"* are either dead or wounded.

But Méndez's gunmen have failed to kill the Barrera brothers.

Thanks to Sean Callan.

"Whatever you want," Adán tells him.

On this Day of the Dead.

You have only to ask.

Whatever you want in this world.

The teenage girl makes him his own *pan de muerto*.

Bread of the Dead.

The traditional sugary sweet roll with a surprise hidden inside, a treat which she knows Don Miguel Ángel Barrera especially likes and looks forward to on this holiday. And as it's good luck for the person who takes the bite that has the surprise in it, she makes one roll just for him, to make sure that Don Miguel is the one who receives the surprise.

She wants everything just right for him on this special night.

So she dresses with special care: a simple but elegant black dress, black stockings and heels. She applies her makeup slowly, paying particular attention to the exact thickness of the mascara, then brushes her long black hair until it shines. She checks the effect in the mirror and what she sees pleases her—her skin is smooth and pale, her dark eyes are highlighted, her hair falls softly on her shoulders.

She goes into the kitchen and places the special *pan de muerto* on a silver tray, flanks it with amber candles, lights them and goes into his dining-room cell.

He looks regal, she thinks, in a maroon smoking jacket over silk pajamas. Don Miguel's nephews make sure that their uncle has all the luxuries that he requires to make his existence in prison bearable—good clothing, good food, good wines, and, well, her.

People whisper that Adán Barrera takes such good care of his uncle to assuage his own guilt because he prefers his uncle to linger in prison so the old man won't interfere with his leadership of the Barrera *pasador.* Sharper tongues wag that Adán actually set up his own uncle so that he could take over.

The girl doesn't know the truth behind any of this and doesn't care. All she knows is that Adán Barrera rescued her from a future of misery in a Mexico City brothel and chose her instead as his uncle's companion. The gossips would have it that she resembles a woman whom Don Miguel once loved.

Which is my good fortune, the girl thinks.

Don Miguel's demands aren't heavy. She cooks for him, launders his clothes, accommodates his needs as a man. True, he beats her, but not as often or as viciously as her own father, and his sexual demands are not as frequent. He beats her, then screws her, and if he cannot keep his *floto* hard he gets angry and beats her until he can do it.

There are worse lives, she thinks.

And the money that Adán Barrera sends her is generous.

But not as generous as . . .

She puts the thought out of her head and presents Don Miguel with the *pan de muerto*.

Her hands are shaking.

Tío notices.

Her small hands quiver as she lays the bread on the table in front of him, and when he looks into her eyes they're moist, on the verge of tears. Is it sorrow? He asks himself. Or fear? And as he looks closely into her eyes she glances down at the *pan de muerto* and then back up at him and then he knows.

"It is beautiful," he says, looking down at the sweet roll.

"Thank you."

Is there a crack in her voice? he wonders. Just the slightest hesitation?

"Please sit down," he says, standing and holding her chair out for her. She sits down, her hands gripping the edges of the chair.

"Please, you have the first bite," he says, sitting back down.

"Oh, no, it is for you."

"I insist."

"I couldn't."

"*I insist.*"

It's a command.

She can't disobey.

So she tears off a piece of the *pan* and lifts it to her lips. Or tries to, anyway—her hand shakes so badly that it has a hard time finding her mouth. And try as she might to hold them back, tears fill her eyes and then spill over, and her mascara runs down her cheeks, leaving black streaks on her face.

She looks up at him and sniffles, "I can't."

"And yet you would have fed it to me."

She sniffs, but little bubbles of snot run out of her nose.

He hands her a linen napkin.

"Wipe your nose," he says.

She does.

Then he says, "Now you must eat the bread that you baked for me."

She blurts out, "Please."

Then she looks down.

Are my nephews already dead? Tío wonders. Güero wouldn't dare attempt to assassinate me unless Adán and Raúl, especially, were safely out of the picture. So either they are already dead or will be soon, or perhaps Güero has botched that as well. Let us hope so, he thinks, and makes a mental note to contact his nephews at the first opportunity, as soon as this *triste* business is concluded.

"Méndez offered you a fortune, didn't he?" Miguel Ángel asks the girl. "A new life for you, for your whole family?"

She nods.

"You have younger sisters, do you not?" Tío asks. "Your drunk of a father abuses them? With Méndez's money you could get them out, make them a home?"

"Yes."

"I understand," Tío says.

She looks up at him hopefully.

"Eat," he says. "It is a merciful death, isn't it? I know you wouldn't have wanted me to die slowly and in pain."

She balks at putting the bread in her mouth. Her hand trembles, leaving little crumbs sticking to her bright red lipstick. And now fat, heavy tears plop onto the bread, ruining the sugary frosting that she had so carefully applied.

"Eat."

She takes a bite of the bread but can't seem to swallow it, so he pours a glass of red wine and puts it in her hand. She sips it, and that seems to help, and she washes the bread down with it, then takes another bite and another sip.

He leans across the table and strokes her hair with the back of his hand. And softly murmurs, "I know. I know," as with his other hand he places another piece of the bread to her lips. She opens her mouth and takes it on her tongue, then a sip of wine, and then the strychnine hits and her head snaps back, her eyes open wide and her death rattle gurgles moistly between her parted lips.

He has her body thrown over the fence to the dogs.

Parada lights a cigarette.

Sucks on it as he bends over, putting on his shoes, and wonders why he's being awakened in the small hours of the morning, and what is this "urgent personal business" that could not wait until the sun came up. He tells his housekeeper to make the minister of education at home in the study and that he'll be right down.

Parada has known Cerro for years. He was bishop in Culiacán when Cerro was the Sinaloa governor, and even baptized two of the man's legitimate children. And hadn't Miguel Ángel Barrera stood as godfather on both occasions? Parada asks himself. Certainly it was Barrera who had come to him to make arrangements, both spiritual and temporal, for Cerro's illegitimate offspring, when the governor had taken advantage of some young girl from one of the villages. Oh, well, at least they came to me as opposed to an abortionist, and that is something in the man's favor.

But, he thinks as he pulls an old wool sweater over his head, if this is another teenage girl in an interesting circumstance, I am prepared to be seriously annoyed. Cerro should know better at his age. Certainly, he might have learned from experience if nothing else, and in any case, why does it have to be at—he glances at the clock—four in the morning?

He rings for the housekeeper.

"Coffee, please," Parada tells her. "For two. In the study."

Recently his relationship with Cerro has been one of alternate arguing and cajoling, begging and threatening, as he has petitioned the minister of education for new schools, books, lunch programs and more teachers. It has been a constant negotiation in which Parada has tiptoed on the edge of blackmail, once protesting to Cerro that the rural villages were not going to be treated like "bastard children"—a remark that was apparently worth two primary schools and a dozen new teachers.

Perhaps this is Cerro's revenge, Parada thinks as he goes downstairs. But when he opens the door to his study and sees Cerro's face, he knows it's far more serious.

Cerro gets right to it. "I'm dying of cancer."

Parada is stunned. "I am terribly sorry to hear this. Is there nothing . . ."

"No. There is no hope."

"Would you like for me to hear your confession?"

"I have a priest for that," Cerro says.

He hands Parada the briefcase.

"I brought you this," Cerro says. "I didn't know who else to bring it to."

Parada opens it, looks at the papers and the tapes and says, "I don't understand."

"I have been a conspirator," Cerro says, "in a massive crime. I cannot die . . . I am afraid to die . . . with this on my soul. I need to at least try to make restitution."

"Certainly if you confess you will receive absolution," Parada answers. "But if this is all evidence of some sort, why bring it to me? Why not to the attorney general, or . . ."

"His voice is on those tapes."

Well, that would be a reason, Parada thinks.

Cerro leans forward and whispers, "The attorney general, the secretary of the interior, the chairman of the PRI. The president. All of them. All of *us.*"

Good God, Parada thinks.

What is on these tapes?

He goes through a pack and a half listening to them.

Lighting one cigarette from another, he listens to the tapes and pores through the documents. Memos of meetings, Cerro's notes. Names, dates and places. A fifteen-year record of corruption—no, not just corruption. That would be the sad norm, and this is extraordinary. More than extraordinary—language fails.

What they did, in the simplest possible terms: They sold the country to the *narcotraficantes.*

He wouldn't have believed it if he hadn't heard it himself: Tapes from a dinner—$25 million per plate—to help elect this president. The murders of election officials and the theft of the election itself. The voices of the president's brother and the attorney general planning these outrages. And soliciting the narcos to pay for it all. And to commit the murders. And to torture and murder the American agent Hidalgo.

And then there was Operation Cerberus, the conspiracy to fund, equip and train the Contras through the sale of cocaine.

And Operation Red Mist, the right-wing murders funded in part by the drug cartels in Colombia and Mexico and supported by the PRI.

Small wonder Cerro is afraid of hell—he's helped to build it here.

And now I understand why he brought this evidence to me. The voices on the tapes, the names on the memos—the president, his brother, the secretary of state, Miguel Ángel Barrera, García Abrego, Güero Méndez, Adán Barrera, the literally scores of police, army and intelligence officers, PRI officials—there is no one in Mexico who can or will act on this.

So Cerro brings it to me. Wanting me to give it to . . .

Whom?

He goes to light another cigarette but finds to his surprise that he's sick of smoking—his mouth tastes filthy. He goes upstairs and brushes his teeth, then takes an almost scalding shower and, as he lets the water pound the back of his neck, thinks that perhaps he should give this evidence to Arthur Keller.

He's maintained frequent correspondence with the American, now unfortunately persona non grata in Mexico, and the man is still obsessed with bringing down the drug cartels. But think it through, he tells himself: If you give this to Arthur, what will happen to it, given the shocking revelation of Operation Cerberus and the CIA's complicity with the Barreras in exchange for Contra funding? Does Arthur have the power to act on this, or will it be suppressed by the current administration? Or any American administration, as focused as they are on NAFTA?

NAFTA, Parada thinks with disgust. The cliff we are marching toward in lockstep with the Americans. But there is hope. Presidential elections are coming up, and the PRI's candidate—who will, perforce, win—seems to be a good man. Luis Donaldo Colosio is a legitimate man of the left, who will listen to reason. Parada has sat down with him, and the man is sympathetic.

And if this stunning evidence that the dying Cerro brought me can discredit the dinosaurs in the PRI, that might give Colosio the leverage he needs to follow his true instincts. Should I give *him* the information?

No, Parada thinks, Colosio mustn't be *seen* to be going against his party—that would only rob him of the nomination.

So who, Parada wonders as he lathers his face and begins to shave, has the autonomy, the power, the sheer moral force to bring to light the fact that the entire government of a country has auctioned itself to a cartel of drug merchants? Who?

The answer occurs to him suddenly.

It's obvious.

He waits until a decent hour of the morning, and then phones Antonucci to tell him that he wants to relay important information to the Pope.

The order of Opus Dei was founded in 1928 by a wealthy Spanish lawyer-turned-priest named Josemaría Escrivá, who was concerned that the University of Madrid had become a hotbed of left-wing radicalism. He was so concerned that his new organization of Catholic elite fought on the side of the fascists in the Spanish Civil War and spent the next thirty years helping to entrench General Franco in power. The idea was to recruit talented, elite young lay conservatives who were headed into government, the press and big business, imbue them with "traditional" Catholic values—especially anti-Communism—and send them out to do the Church's work in their chosen spheres.

Salvatore Scachi—Special Forces colonel, CIA asset, Knight of Malta and made Mafia wise guy—is a tried-and-true member of Opus Dei. He met all the requirements—attended Mass daily, made his confessions only to an Opus Dei priest and made regular retreats at Opus Dei facilities.

And he's been a good soldier. He's fought the good fight against Communism in Vietnam, Cambodia and the Golden Triangle. He's fought the war in Mexico, in Central America through Cerberus, in South America through Red Mist—all operations that the liberation theologist Parada is now threatening to expose to the world. Now he sits in Antonucci's office considering what to do about the information that Cardinal Juan Parada wants to pass on to the Vatican.

"You say Cerro went to see him," Scachi says to Antonucci.

"That's what Parada told me."

"Cerro knows enough to bring down the entire government," Scachi says. And then some.

"We can't burden the Holy Father with this information," Antonucci says. This Pope has been a major supporter of Opus Dei, even to the point of recently beatifying Father Escrivá, the first step toward canonization. To force him to confront evidence of the Order's involvement in some of the harsher actions against the Communist world conspiracy would be, at the very least, embarrassing.

Worse yet would be the scandal that would erupt against the present government, just as negotiations are proceeding to return the Church to full legal status in Mexico. No, these revelations would scuttle the government, and with it the negotiations, and swing momentum toward the heretical liberation theologists—many of them well-meaning "useful idiots" who would help bring about Communist rule.

It's been the same story everywhere, Antonucci thinks—stupid, misled, liberal priests help bring the Communists to power, then the reds slaughter the priests. It was certainly true in Spain, which is why the blessed Escrivá founded the order in the first place.

As members of Opus Dei, both Antonucci and Scachi are well versed in the concept of the greater good, and for Sal Scachi the greater good of defeating Communism outweighs the evil of corruption. He also has something else on his mind—the NAFTA treaty, still under debate in Congress. If Parada's revelations were ever made public they would scuttle NAFTA. And without NAFTA, there will be no hope for the development of a Mexican middle class, which is the only long-term antidote for the poisonous spread of Communism.

Now Antonucci says, "We have an opportunity here to do something great for the souls of the millions of faithful—to return the true Church to the Mexican people by earning the gratitude of the Mexican government."

"If we suppress this information."

"Just so."

"But it's not that simple," Scachi says. "Parada apparently has certain knowledge, which he'll come forward with if he doesn't see—"

Antonucci gets up. "I must leave such worldly details to the lay brothers of the order. I don't understand such things."

But Scachi does.

Adán lies in bed at Rancho las Bardas, Raúl's large *estancia*-cum-fortress, off the road between Tijuana and Tecate.

The ranch's main living compound, composed of separate houses for Adán and Raúl, is surrounded by a ten-foot wall topped with razor wire and shards of broken glass bottles. There are two gates, each with massive, steel-reinforced doors. Spotlight towers are set in each corner, manned by guards with AK-47s, M-50 machine guns and Chinese rocket launchers.

And to even reach the place, you have to drive two long miles off the highway down a red-dirt road, but the chances are you're not even going to get on that road, because the junction with the highway is guarded twenty-four–seven by plainclothes Baja state policemen.

So this is where the brothers came as soon as possible after the attack on the La Sirena discó, and now the place is on high alert. Guards patrol the walls night and day, squads in jeeps patrol the surrounding countryside, technicians electronically sweep the area for radio transmissions and cell-phone calls.

And Manuel Sánchez sits outside Adán's bedroom window like a faithful dog. We're twins now, Adán thinks, with our identical limps. But mine is temporary and his is permanent, and this is why I have kept the man employed all these years as a bodyguard since the bad old days of Operation Condor.

Sánchez will not leave his post—not to eat, not to sleep.

Just props himself against the wall with his shotgun in his lap, or occasionally gets up and limps back and forth along the wall.

"I should have been there, *patrón*," he told Adán, with tears streaming down his face. "I should have been with you."

"Your job is to protect my home and my family," Adán answered. "And you have never let me down."

Nor is he likely to.

He won't leave Adán's window. The cooks bring him plates of warm flour tortillas with *refritas* and peppers, and bowls of hot *albóndigas,* and he sits outside the window eating. But he will not leave: Don Adán saved his life and his leg, and Don Adán and his wife and daughter are inside that house, and if Güero's *sicarios* somehow get inside the compound, they will have to come through Manuel Sánchez to get to them.

And no one is getting through Manuel.

Adán's glad he's there, if only to give Lucía and Gloria a feeling of security. They were already put through an upsetting ordeal, being woken in the middle of the night by the *pasador*'s *sicarios* and hustled off to the countryside without even a chance to pack. The upset had set off a major respiratory episode, and a doctor had to be flown in, blindfolded, then driven out to the ranch to see the sick girl. The expensive and delicate medical equipment—respirators, breathing tents, humidifiers—all had to be packed out of the house and moved in the middle of the night, and even now, weeks later, Gloria is still displaying symptoms.

And then when she had seen him limping, in pain, it was yet another shock and he had felt bad about lying to her, telling her that he had been in a motorcycle accident, and lying to her more, telling her they were staying out in the country for a while because the air is better for her.

But she's not stupid, Adán knows. She sees the towers, the guns, the guards, and she will soon see through their explanation that the family is very wealthy and needs protection.

And then she will ask harder questions.

And get harder answers.

About what Papa does for a living.

And will she understand? Adán wonders. He's restless, edgy, tired of being a convalescent. And be honest, he tells himself—you miss Nora. You miss her in your bed and at your table. It would be good to talk with her about this whole situation.

He'd managed to get a phone call off to her the day after the La Sirena attack. He knew that she'd have seen it on TV or read about it in the papers, and he wanted to tell her that he was all right. That it would be a few weeks before he could see her again, but more important, that she should stay out of Mexico until he tells her it's safe.

She'd responded just the way he'd imagined she would, just the way he'd hoped. She answered the phone on the first ring, and he could feel her relief when she heard his voice. Then she'd quickly started to joke with him, telling him that if he let himself be lured by any siren other than her, he got what he deserved.

"Call me," she'd said. "I'll come running."

I wish I could, he thinks as he painfully stretches his leg. You don't know how much I wish I could.

He's tired of being in bed and sits up, slowly swings his wounded leg out and gently eases himself to his feet. He takes his cane and hobbles over to the window. It's a beautiful day. The sun is bright and warm and the birds are warbling and it's good to be alive. And his leg is healing quickly and well—there has been no infection—and soon he will be up and around. Which is a good thing because there is much to do and not a lot of time to do it.

The truth is that he's worried. The attack on La Sirena, the fact that they used *federale* uniforms and identification—it must have cost hundreds of thousands in *mordida*. And the fact that Güero felt strong enough to violate the prohibition on violence in a resort town must mean that Güero's business is healthier than they had thought.

But how? Adán wonders. How is the man getting his product through La Plaza, which the Barrera *pasador* has all but shut down to him? And how has Güero won the support of Mexico City and its *federales*?

And has Abrego aligned himself with Güero? Would Güero ever have launched the La Sirena attack without the old man's approval? And if that is the case, Abrego's support would bring the president's brother, El Bagman, and the full weight of the federal government.

Even in Baja itself, there's a civil war going on between the local cops—the Barreras own the Baja State Police and Güero owns the *federales*. The

Tijuana city cops are more or less neutral, but there's a new player in town—
the Special Tactical Group, an elite group sort of like the Untouchables, run
by none other than the incorruptible Antonio Ramos. If he ever allies himself
with the *federales* . . .

Thank God there's an election coming up, Adán thinks. Adán's people
have made several discreet approaches to the PRI's handpicked candidate,
Colosio, only to be turned down flat. But Colosio at least gave assurances
that he is anti-narco across the board—when elected he will be coming after
the Barreras and Méndez with equal vigor.

But in the meantime it's us against the world, Adán thinks.

And this time, the world wins.

Callan don't like it one bit.

He's in the backseat of a stolen fire-engine red Suburban—the vehicle of
choice among the *narcotraficante* cowboys—sitting beside Raúl Barrera,
who's cruising around Tijuana like he's the fucking mayor. They're rolling
down Boulevard Díaz Ordaz, one of the busiest streets in the city. He has a
Baja State Police officer driving and another one in the front seat. And he's
tricked out in full Sinaloa cowboy gear, from the boots to the black pearl-
button shirt to the white cowboy hat.

This is no fucking way to fight a war, Callan thinks. What these guys
should be doing is what the old Sicilians would do—go to the mattresses, lay
low, pick your spots. But this apparently ain't the Mexican way, Callan has
learned. No, the Mexican way is macho—go out there and show the flag.

Like, Raúl *wants* to be seen.

So it ain't no surprise to Callan when two black Suburbans filled with
black-uniformed *federales* start to follow them down the boulevard. Which
ain't good news, Callan thinks. "Uh, Raúl . . ."

"I see them."

He tells the driver to take a right down a side street, alongside a gigantic
flea market.

Güero's in the second black Suburban. He looks out and sees this yuppie
fire engine take a right, and in the backseat he thinks he sees Raúl Barrera.

Actually, the first thing he sees is a clown.

A stupid laughing clown's face is painted on the wall of the enormous
flea market, which runs the length of two city blocks. Clown's got one of
those big red noses and the white face and the wig and the whole clown nine
yards and Güero sort of blinks at it and then focuses on the guy in the backseat of the red Suburban with California plates and it sure as hell looks like
Raúl.

"Pull him over," he tells his driver.

The lead black Suburban pulls ahead and forces the red Suburban to the curb. Güero's vehicle pulls up behind and wedges in the red SUV.

Oh, fuck, Callan thinks, as a *comandante federale* gets out of the lead car and comes toward them, pointing his M-16, two of his boys right behind him. This ain't no traffic ticket. He slides a little lower in his seat, gently pulls his .22 from his hip and lays it under his left forearm.

"We got it covered," Raúl says.

Callan's not so sure because rifle barrels poke out of the windows of the two black Suburbans like muskets out of wagons in one of them old Westerns, and Callan figures if the cavalry don't ride in soon there ain't gonna be much to bury here out on the old prairie.

Fuckin' Mexico.

Güero lowers the right back window, rests his AK on the sill, flicks the lever to "bush rake" and gets ready to hose Raúl.

The Baja state cop driver rolls down his window and asks, "Is there a problem?"

Yeah, apparently there is because the *comandante federale* spots Raúl from the corner of his eye and starts to pull the trigger on his M-16.

Callan shoots from his lap.

The two rounds smack the *comandante* in the forehead.

The M-16 hits the pavement a moment before he does.

The two Baja state cops in the front seat shoot right through their own windshield. Raúl sits in the back, zinging bullets past the ears of his two boys in the front and he's yelling and shooting because if this is the last *Arriba,* he's going out in style. He's going out in a way that the *narcocorridos* will be singing about for years.

Except he ain't going out.

Güero had spotted the bright red Suburban, but he didn't see the nondescript Ford Aerostar and the Volkswagen Jetta that were trailing it from a block behind, and now those two stolen vehicles roar in and trap the *federales.*

Fabián jumps out of the Aerostar and rakes a *federale* across the chest with an AK burst. The wounded *federale* tries to crawl for cover underneath the black Suburban, but one of his own boys sees how outgunned they are and makes a bid for survival by switching sides on the spot. He raises his own M-16 and as the man pleads for his life delivers the coup de grâce through his partner's upraised arms and into his face, then looks to Fabián for acceptance.

Fabián puts two rounds into his head.

Who needs a coward like that?

Callan pulls Raúl down onto the seat and shouts, "We have to get you the fuck outta here!"

Callan opens the car door and rolls out onto the sidewalk. He shoots from underneath the car at anything that has black pants on as Raúl climbs out over the top of them and then they start shooting their way out, backing down the street toward the main boulevard.

It's a major goat fuck, Callan thinks.

Cops are roaring in from all compass points, in cars, on motorcycles and on foot. Federal cops, state cops, Tijuana city cops, and they're not sure who's who—it is just a fucking free-for-all.

Everyone's trying to figure out who to shoot at the same time they're trying to work out how not to get shot. Fabián's shooters at least know who they're shooting at, though, as they methodically gun down the *federales* who pulled them over. But those guys are tough, they're shooting back, and there are bullets flying every which way and you have some moron across the street standing there with his Sony 8mm trying to videotape the whole goddamn mess, and through that grace given to idiots and drunks he lives through the whole ten-minute gun battle, but a lot of people don't.

Three *federales* are dead and three others wounded. Two Barrera *sicarios*—including one Baja state policeman—have checked out and two others are pretty badly shot up, as are the seven bystanders who are down with gunshot wounds. And in one of those surreal moments that seem to occur only in Mexico, you have the bishop of Tijuana, who just happened to be in the neighborhood, going from body to body giving last rites to the dead and spiritual comfort to the living. You got ambulances coming in, and cop cars and television trucks. You got everything except twenty midgets tumbling out of a little car.

The clown ain't laughing anymore.

The smile has literally been blasted off his face, his red nose is pockmarked with bullets and there are fresh holes drilled in the bottom inside corner of each pupil, so he's looking down at the scene cross-eyed.

Güero's done a walkaway—he spent most of the firefight lying on the floor of his Suburban and then he slid across to the opposite door and slunk away without anyone seeing him.

A lot of people see Raúl, though. He and Callan are backing down the street, shoulder to shoulder, Raúl just blasting away with his AK, Callan firing precise two-shot groupings with his .22.

Callan sees Fabián jump in the Aerostar and back it down the street even though the tires have been shot out. He's driving it on its rims—sparks are shooting out—and he pulls up alongside Callan and Raúl and yells, "Get in!"

Okay with me, Callan thinks. He's just in the fucking door when Fabián hits the gas again and they are flying backwards down the street and then crashing into *another* fucking Suburban that has blocked the intersection. The car is filled with plainclothes detectives, their M-16s leveled and ready.

Callan's relieved when Raúl drops his AK, puts his hands up and smiles.

Meanwhile, Ramos and his boys get there ready to kick ass, except most of the ass either is already bleeding on the pavement or is long gone. The whole street is buzzing like insects in Ramos' ear as he hears the rumor that the police have arrested one of the Barreras.

It was Adán.

No, it was Raúl.

Whichever the fuck Barrera, Ramos thinks, which cops arrested him, and where did they take him?! It matters, right, because if it was the *federales* they probably took him to the dump to shoot him, and if it was the Baja state boys they probably took him to a safe house and if it was the city police Ramos might still have a shot at bagging a Barrera brother.

Would be nice if it was Adán.

A close second if it's Raúl.

Ramos is grabbing one eyewitness after another until a uniformed city officer comes up to him and tells him that city homicide-squad detectives collared one of the Barreras and two other guys and drove off with them.

Ramos races back to the precinct house.

Cigar clamped in his mouth, Esposa at his hip, he storms into the homicide-squad room just in time to see the back of Raúl's head disappearing out the back door. Ramos raises his gun to put a bullet in the back of that head, but a homicide guy grabs the barrel.

"Take it easy," the detective says.

"Who the fuck was that?" Ramos asks.

"Who the fuck was who?"

"That guy who just gunned down a bunch of cops," Ramos says. "Or don't you care about that?"

Apparently not, because the homicide guys sort of bunch up in the doorway to let Raúl, Fabián and Callan get away clean, and if they're ashamed of themselves, Ramos can't see it in their faces.

. . .

Adán watches it on television.

The Sinaloa Swap Meet is all over the news.

He hears reporters breathlessly report that he's been arrested. Or his brother has, depending on which station he has on. But all the channels are commenting that for a second time in a few weeks innocent citizens have been caught in the cross fire between rival drug gangs right in the heart of a major city. And that something must be done to put an end to the violence between the rival Baja cartels.

Well, something will soon, Adán thinks. We were lucky to have survived the last two attacks, but how long before our luck runs out?

The bottom line is, we're finished.

And when I'm dead, Güero will hunt down Lucía and Gloria and slaughter them. Unless I can find—and stop—the source of Güero's newfound power.

Where is it coming from?

Ramos and his troops are ripping up a warehouse near the border, just on the Mexican side. The tip that led them there was a good one, and they're finding stacks of vacuum-wrapped cocaine. About a dozen of Güero Méndez's workers are tied up, and Ramos notices that they're all sneaking glances at a forklift parked in one corner.

"Where are the keys?" he asks the warehouse manager.

"Top desk drawer."

Ramos gets the keys, hops onto the forklift and backs it up. He can hardly believe what he sees.

The mouth of a tunnel.

"Are you shitting me?" Ramos asks aloud.

He hops off the forklift, grabs the manager and lifts him off his feet.

"Are there men down there?" he asks. "Booby traps?"

"No."

"If there are, I'll come back and kill you."

"I swear."

"Are there lights down there?"

"*Sí.*"

"Turn them on."

Five minutes later Ramos has Esposa in one hand as he uses the other to climb down the ladder bolted to the side of the tunnel's entrance.

Sixty-five feet deep.

The shaft is about six feet high and four feet wide, with reinforced concrete floors and walls. Fluorescent light fixtures are attached to the ceiling. An air-conditioning system pumps fresh air down the length of the tunnel. A narrow gauge track has been laid on the floor and carts have been set on the rails.

"Christ," Ramos thinks, "at least there's no locomotive. Yet."

He starts walking along the shaft, north, toward the United States. Then it occurs to him that he should probably contact someone on the other side before he crosses the border, even underground. He goes back to the surface and makes a few phone calls. Two hours later he's going down the ladder again, with Art Keller right behind him. And behind them, a troop of the Special Tactical Group and a flock of DEA agents.

On the American side, an army of DEA, INS, ATF, FBI and Customs agents are poised in the area across from the tunnel, waiting to rush the exact location as soon as the tunnel party radios in.

"Un-fucking-real," Shag Wallace says when they get down to the bottom. "Someone dumped a lot of money into this."

"Someone ran a lot of money *through* it," Art answers. He turns to Ramos. "We know this was Méndez, not the Barreras?"

"It's Güero's," Ramos says.

"What, someone show him a video of *The Great Escape*?" Shag asks.

"Let me know when we cross the border," Ramos says to Art.

"I'd just be guessing," Art answers. "Christ, how far does this thing go?"

Fourteen hundred feet, give or take, is how they pace it out before they get to the next vertical shaft. An iron ladder bolted to the concrete walls leads up to a bolted hatch.

Art punches in on a GPS system.

The troops will be rolling.

He looks up at the hatch.

"So," Art says, "who wants to be the first to go through that?"

"We're in your jurisdiction," Ramos answers.

Art goes up the ladder, with Shag at his feet, and they each balance with one hand on the rail as they twist open the hatch with the other.

It must take quite an operation, Art thinks, to hoist the dope up from the tunnel shaft. Probably a chain of men stationed on various rungs of the ladder. He wonders if they were planning to construct an elevator.

The hatch opens and light pours down the shaft.

Art firms his grip on his pistol and hauls himself up.

Chaos.

Men are running around like cockroaches when the lights come on, and the blue-jacketed task-force guys are sweeping them up, putting them on the floor and securing their wrists behind their backs with plastic telephone-cord ties.

It's a cannery, Art notices.

There are three neat, organized conveyor belts, stacks of empty cans, sealing machines, labeling machines. Art reads one of the labels: CALIENTE CHILI PEPPERS. And indeed, there are huge piles of red chili peppers ready to be fed onto the conveyor belts.

But there are also bricks of cocaine.

And Art thinks the coke is meant to be hand-canned.

Russ Dantzler comes up to him. "Güero Méndez—the Willy Wonka of nose candy."

"Who owns this building?" Art asks.

"You ready for this? The Fuentes brothers."

"No kidding."

"I shit you not."

Three Brothers Foods, Art thinks. Well, well, well—the Fuentes family is a prominent fixture in the Mexican-American community. Important businesspeople in southern California, and major contributors to the Democratic Party. The Fuentes trucks go from the canneries and warehouses in San Diego and Los Angeles to cities all over the country.

A ready-made distribution system for Güero Méndez's cocaine.

"Genius, isn't it?" Dantzler says. "They bring the coke in through the tunnel, can it as Caliente Chili Peppers and ship it anywhere they want. I wonder if they ever screw up—I mean, I wonder if someone in Detroit ever goes to buy himself a can of peppers and ends up with twelve ounces of blow instead. In which case, give me a bowl of *that* chili, you know what I mean? So what do you want to do about the Fuentes brothers?"

"Bust them," Art says.

Which is going to be interesting, he thinks. Not only are the Fuenteses major supporters of the Democratic Party, they're also big contributors to the presidential campaign of Luis Donaldo Colosio.

It takes about thirty-seven seconds for the news to reach Adán.

Now we know how Méndez has been getting his cocaine through La Plaza, Adán thinks. He's been going *under* it. And now we also know the source of his power in Mexico City. He's bought the heir apparent, Colosio.

So that's that.

Güero has bought himself Los Pinos, and we are finished.

Then the phone rings.

Sal Scachi wants to offer some help.

When he says what his offer entails, Adán instantly says no. Firmly, unalterably, absolutely, the answer is no.

It's unthinkable.

Unless . . .

Adán tells him what he wants in return.

The quid pro quo.

It takes days of covert negotiations, but Scachi finally agrees.

But Adán has to act quickly.

That's fine, Adán thinks.

But we'll need people to do it.

Kids.

That's what Callan is looking at—kids.

He's sitting in the basement of a house in Guadalajara. The place is a freaking armory. There's hardware all over the place, and not just the usual ARs and AKs, either.

This is the heavy stuff: machine guns, grenade launchers, Kevlar body armor. Callan sits on a metal folding chair looking at a bunch of teenage Chicano gangbangers from San Diego as *they* watch Raúl Barrera pin a photograph to a bulletin board.

"Memorize this face," Raúl tells them. "It's Güero Méndez."

The teenagers are rapt. Especially as Raúl slowly and dramatically takes bundles of cash out of a canvas bag and sets them on the table.

"Fifty thousand dollars American," Raúl says. "In cash. And it's going to go to the first one of you who . . ."

He pauses dramatically.

". . . puts the kill shot into Güero Méndez."

They're going on a "Güero hunt," Raúl announces. They're going to form convoys of armored vehicles until they find Méndez and then use their combined firepower to blow him to hell, where he belongs.

"Any questions?" Raúl asks.

Yeah, a few, Callan thinks. Starting with, How the hell you think you're going to take on Güero's professional hitters with the Kiddie Corps here. I mean, is this what we got left? This is the best that the Barrera *pasador,* with all its money and power, can come up with? A bunch of San Dog gangbangers?

They're a goddamn joke, with tags like Flaco, Dreamer, Poptop and—honest to Christ—Scooby Doo. Fabián recruited them from the barrio, says they're stone killers, claims they've all made their bones.

Yeah, maybe, Callan thinks. Maybe they have, but it's a big jump from doing a drive-by on some other banger smoking boo on his front porch to taking on a crew of professional killers.

A bunch of kids on a big-time hit? They'll be too busy pissing their pants and shooting each other—and hopefully not me—when they panic and start blasting anything that flashes by their peripheral vision. No, Callan still don't get it—what the fuck Raúl is thinking about with the Children's Crusade here. All it's going to be is one gigantic mess, and Callan is only hoping that (a) through the chaos he can find Méndez and take him off the count, and (b) he can do it before one of the kids guns him down by mistake.

Then he remembers that he was just seventeen when he took out Eddie Friel back in the Kitchen. Yeah, but that was different. You was different. These kids just don't look like killers to me.

So that's a question he wants to ask Raúl: Are you drunk? Are you out of your fucking mind? He doesn't ask that, though. He just settles for a more practical question.

"How do we know," Callan asks, "that Méndez is even in Guadalajara?"

Because Parada asked him to come.

Because Adán asked Parada to ask him.

"I want to stop the violence," he tells his old priest.

"That's easy," Parada answers. "Stop it."

"It isn't that easy," Adán argues. "That's why I'm asking for your help."

"My *help*? To do what?"

"Make peace with Güero."

Adán knows that he's rung the bell—hit the chord that no priest can resist.

Certainly it presents Parada with a difficult choice. He's no starry-eyed fool—he realizes that if, against the odds, he did succeed in brokering peace between the Barreras and Méndez, he would also be fostering a more efficient environment in which to operate the drug cartels. So in that sense, he would be helping to perpetuate an evil, which as a priest he has sworn not to do. On the other hand, he has also sworn to take every opportunity he can to mitigate evil, and peace between the two warring cartels would prevent God only knows how many killings. And if forced to choose between the evils of drug trafficking and murder, he has to judge murder the heavier evil, so he asks, "You want to sit down and talk with Güero?"

"Yes," Adán says, "but where? Güero wouldn't come to Tijuana, and I won't go to Culiacán."

"Would you come to Guadalajara?" Parada asks.

"If *you* guarantee my safety."

"But would you guarantee Güero's?"

"Yes," Adán says. "But he wouldn't accept that guarantee any more than I would accept his."

"That's not what I'm asking," Parada says impatiently. "I'm asking if you will promise not to attempt to harm Güero in any way."

"I swear on my soul."

"Your soul, Adán, is blacker than hell."

"One thing at a time, Father."

Parada hears this. If you can get a single shaft of light into the darkness, sometimes it is a wedge that will spread until it illuminates the entire void. If I didn't believe this, he thinks as he contemplates the soul of this multiple murderer, I couldn't get up in the morning. So if this man is asking for this one shaft of light, I can hardly refuse.

"I will try, Adán," he says. It won't be easy, he thinks as he hangs up. If even half of what I've heard about the war between these men is true, it will be virtually impossible to persuade Güero to come and talk to Adán Barrera about peace. Then again, perhaps he is also sick of killing and death.

It takes him three whole days just to get through to Méndez.

Parada contacts old friends in Culiacán and puts out the word that he wants to talk with Güero. Three days later, Güero calls.

Parada doesn't waste time with preliminaries. "Adán Barrera wants to talk peace."

"I'm not interested in peace."

"You should be."

"He killed my wife and children."

"All the more reason."

Güero doesn't quite see the logic of this, but what he does see is an opportunity. As Parada presses on about a meeting in Guadalajara, in a public place, with himself as a mediator and "the entire moral weight of the Church" guaranteeing his safety, Méndez sees a chance to finally lure the Barreras out of their Baja fortress. After all, his best chance to kill them failed, and now he is getting his ass kicked in San Diego.

So he listens, and as he listens to the priest rattle on about how his wife and children would have wanted it this way, he works up a few crocodile tears and then, in a choking voice, agrees to come to the meeting.

"I will try, Father," he says quietly. "I will take a chance for peace. Can we pray together, Father? Can we pray over the phone?"

And as Parada asks Jesus to help them find the light of peace, Güero is praying to Santo Jesús Malverde for something different.

Not to fuck it up this time.

. . .

They are going to *royally* fuck it up.

Is what Callan thinks.

Watching this Looney Toon spectacular that Raúl is staging in the city of Guadalajara. It's fucking ridiculous, making a big show of riding around town in this convoy, hoping to spot Güero so they can line up like battleships off an island and blast him.

Callan's done big-time hits. This is a man who personally took out the heads of two of the Five Families, and he tries to tell Raúl how it should be done. ("You find out where he's going to be at a specific time, then you get there first and set it up.") But Raúl won't listen—he's bullheaded; it's almost like he *wants* this to be a fiasco. He just smiles and tells Callan, "Chill out, man, and be ready when the shooting starts."

For a whole week the Barrera forces cruise the city, night and day, searching for Güero Méndez. And while they're looking, other men are listening. Raúl has technicians stationed in another safe house, using the most current high-tech equipment to scan cellular calls, trying to intercept messages that might be going back and forth between Güero and his lieutenants.

Güero's doing the same thing. He has his own techno-geeks in his own safe house monitoring the cellular traffic, trying to get a fix on the Barreras. Both sides are playing this game, switching cell phones constantly, moving safe houses, patrolling the streets and the airwaves, trying to find and kill each other with some kind of advantage before Parada sets up the peace meeting, which can only be a risky shoot-out.

And both sides are trying to get an edge on that, trying to glean any intelligence that could give them an advantage—what kind of car is the enemy driving, how many men do they have in town, who are they, what kind of weapons are they carrying, where are they staying and what route will they take? And they have their spies out working, trying to find out which cops are on which payroll, when they're on duty, will there be *federales* around, and if so, where?

Both sides are listening in on Parada's office phones, trying to get a fix on his schedule, his plans, anything that might provide a hint as to where he intends to hold the meeting and give them a head start on setting up an ambush. But the cardinal is holding his cards close to his chest, for that very reason, and neither Méndez nor the Barreras can find out when or where the meeting is going to be.

One of Raúl's techno-geeks does draw a bead on Güero.

"He's using a green Buick," the geek tells Raúl.

"Güero drives a *Buick*?" Raúl asks with some disdain. "How do you know?"

"One of his drivers phoned a garage," the geek explained. "Wanted to know when the Buick was going to be ready. It's a green Buick."

"What garage?" Raúl asks.

But by the time they get there, the Buick's been picked up.

So the search goes on, night and day.

Adán gets the call from Parada.

"Tomorrow at two-thirty at the Hidalgo airport hotel," Parada tells him. "Meet in the lobby."

Adán already knew this, having intercepted a call from the cardinal's driver to his wife discussing the next day's schedule. And it just confirms what Adán also already knew—that Cardinal Antonucci is flying in from Mexico City at 1:30 and Parada is picking him up at the airport. Then they'll go to a private conference room upstairs for a meeting, after which Parada's driver will take Antonucci back to the airport for his 3:00 flight and Parada will stay at the hotel for his peace summit with Méndez and Adán.

Adán has known this all along, but there was no point sharing any of it with Raúl until the last possible moment.

Adán is staying in a different safe house than the rest of them and now he goes down into the basement, where the real assassination squad is barracked. These *sicarios* were flown in on separate flights over the course of the last few days, quietly picked up at the airport and then sequestered in this basement. Meals have been brought in a few at a time from different restaurants, or cooked in the kitchen upstairs and then brought down. No one has gone cruising or nightclubbing. It's strictly professional. A dozen Jalisco State Police uniforms are neatly folded on tables. Flak jackets and AR-15s are neatly racked.

"I've just confirmed everything," Adán tells Fabián. "Are your men ready?"

"Yeah."

"This has to go right."

"It will."

Adán nods and hands him a cell phone that he knows has been compromised. Fabián dials a number and then says, "It's on. Be in place by one-forty-five."

Then he hangs up.

Güero gets the word ten minutes later. He's already gotten the call from

Parada, and now he knows that Adán intends to ambush him as he drives into the airport.

"I think we'll show up for the meeting a little early," Güero tells his head *sicario*.

And ambush the ambush, he thinks.

Raúl gets the call from Adán on a secure phone, then goes down into the dormitory and wakes up the sleeping gangbangers.

"It's off," he announces. "We're going home tomorrow."

The kids are pissed, disappointed, their dreams of a cool $50K having just gone down the shitter. They ask Raúl what happened.

"I don't know," Raúl says. "I guess he got word we were on his trail and ran back to Culiacán. Don't worry—there'll be other chances."

Raúl tries to make them feel better. "Tell you what, we'll leave early for our flight—you can go to the mall."

It's a small consolation, but it's something. The mall in downtown Guadalajara is one of the largest in the world. With the resilience of youth, the boys start to talk about what they'll shop for at the mall.

Raúl takes Fabián upstairs.

"You know what to do?" Raúl asks him.

"Sure."

"And you're good to do it?"

"I'm good," he says.

Raúl finds Callan in an upstairs bedroom.

"We're going back to TJ tomorrow," Raúl says.

Callan's relieved. This whole thing has been so fucked-up. Raúl gives him his airline ticket and the day's schedule then tells him, "Güero's going to try to hit us at the airport."

"What do you mean?"

"He thinks we're going there to make peace with him," Raúl says. "He thinks we're just protected by a bunch of kids. He's going to gun us down."

"He thinks right."

Raúl smiles and shakes his head. "We got you, and we got a whole crew of *sicarios* who'll be dressed as Jalisco State Police."

Well, Callan thinks, at least that answers my question about why the Barreras were using a crew of kids. The kids are bait.

And so are you.

Raúl tells Callan to keep his hand on his gun and his eyes open.

I always do, Callan thinks. Most of the dead guys he knows got that way because they didn't have their eyes open. They got careless, or they trusted somebody.

Callan don't get careless.

And he don't trust nobody.

Parada puts his faith in God.

Gets up earlier than usual, goes into the cathedral and says Mass. Then he kneels at the altar and asks God to give him the strength and wisdom to do what he has to do this day. Prays that he's doing the right thing, then ends with, "Thy will be done."

He goes back to his residence and shaves again, then chooses his clothes with more than particular care. What he wears will send an instant message to Antonucci, and Parada wants to send the right message.

In a strange way, he harbors hope for reconciliation between himself and the Church. And why not? If Adán and Güero can come together, so can Antonucci and Parada. And he is, for the first time in a long time, truly hopeful. If this administration goes out and a better one comes in, in this new environment perhaps the conservatives and liberation theologists can find a common ground. Work together again to seek justice on earth and the bliss of heaven.

He goes to light a cigarette, then snuffs it out.

I should quit smoking, he thinks, if only to make Nora happy.

And this is a good day to start.

A day of new beginnings.

He chooses a black soutane and drapes a large cross around his neck. Just religious enough, he thinks, to mollify Antonucci, but not so ceremonial that the nuncio will think he's gone completely conservative. Conciliatory but not obsequious, he thinks, pleased with his choice.

God, would I like a cigarette, he thinks. He's nervous about his tasks today—delivering Cerro's incriminating information to Antonucci, and then sitting down with Adán and Güero. What can I say, he thinks, to effect a peace between the two of them? How do you make peace between a man whose family has been killed and the man who—as rumor has it anyway—killed them?

Well, put your faith in God. He will give you the words.

But it would still be comforting to smoke.

But I'm not going to.

And I'm going to drop a few pounds.

He's going to Santa Fe for a bishops' conference in a month and plans to see Nora there. And it will be great fun, he thinks, to surprise her with a svelte, smoke-free me. All right, not svelte, maybe, but thinner.

He goes down to his office and occupies his mind with paperwork for a few hours, then calls his driver and asks him to get the car ready. Then he goes to his safe and takes out the briefcase filled with Cerro's incriminating notes and tapes.

It's time to go to the airport.

In Tijuana, Father Rivera prepares for a christening. He puts on his robes, blesses the holy water and carefully fills out the necessary paperwork. On the bottom of the form he lists as godparents Adán and Lucía Barrera.

When the new parents come with their blessed child, Rivera does something unusual.

He closes the doors of the church.

The Barrera crew arrives at the Guadalajara airport fresh from the mall.

They're loaded down with shopping bags, having basically tried to buy the freaking place. Raúl had tossed the kids some bonus money to soothe their disappointment over the cancellation of the Güero lottery, and they'd done what kids do in a mall with cash in their pockets.

They'd spent it.

Callan's watching all this with disbelief. .

Flaco bought a Chivas Rayadas del Guadalajara *fútbol* jersey—which he's wearing with the sales label still attached to the back collar—two pairs of Nikes, a new Nintendo GameBoy and half a dozen new games for it.

Dreamer went strictly the clothes route. Got himself three new lids, all of which he has jammed on his head at the same time, a suede jacket and a new suit—his first one ever—carefully folded in a wardrobe bag.

Scooby Doo is glassy-eyed from the video arcade. Hell, Callan thinks, the little glue-sniffer is usually glassy-eyed anyway, but now his pupils are glazed over from two solid hours of playing Tomb Raider and Mortal Kombat and Assassin 3 and now he's sipping the same giant Slurpee he's been hitting on the whole ride over from the mall.

Poptop is drunk.

While the others were shopping, Poptop went into a restaurant and hammered beers, and by the time they caught up with him it was too late, and it took Flaco and Dreamer and Scooby to wrestle him back in the van to go to the airport and they had to stop three times on the way so Poptop could throw up.

And now the little shit can't find his airline ticket, so him and his buddies are digging through his backpack looking for it.

Great, Callan thinks. If we're trying to convince Güero Méndez that we're sitting ducks, we're doing a damn fine job of it.

What you got out there is a bunch of kids with stacks of luggage and shopping bags on the sidewalk outside the terminal, and Raúl is trying to establish some kind of order, and Adán has just pulled up with a few of his people and it looks like nothing more than a high school field trip headed home on that last chaotic day. And the boys are laughing and hollering at each other, and Raúl is trying to figure out with the attendant at the outside counter whether they should check the bags at the curb or bring them inside, and Dreamer goes to find a couple of luggage carts and tells Flaco to come with him to help and Flaco's yelling at Poptop, "How could you lose your fucking ticket, *pendejo*?" and Poptop looks like he's going to puke again, but what comes out of his mouth isn't puke, it's blood, and then he crumples onto the curb.

Callan's already flat on the sidewalk, tracking a green Buick with gun barrels sticking out the side windows. He pulls out his .22 and fires two shots at the Buick. Then he rolls behind another parked car just as a burst from an AK blasts the sidewalk in front of where he just was, sending bullets bouncing off the concrete and into the terminal wall.

Stupid fucking Scooby Doo is standing there sucking on his Slurpee straw, watching like it's some video game with really radical graphics. He's trying to remember if they ever left the mall and exactly which game this is but it must have cost a ton of tokens because it's so lifelike. Callan dashes out from behind the relative safety of the van, grabs Scooby and throws him to the concrete, and the Slurpee spills all over the pavement and it's a raspberry Slurpee so it's hard to tell it from Poptop's blood, which is also spreading across the concrete.

Raúl, Fabián and Adán drop black equipment bags to the ground and pull AKs out of them, then lift the rifles to their shoulders and start shooting at the Buick.

The bullets bounce off the car—even the windshield—so Callan figures that the car is armored, but he squeezes off two shots, then drops down and can just see the opposite doors of the Buick opening and Güero and two other guys with rifles getting out, and then they lean against the car and rest their AKs on top and let loose.

Callan goes into that zone where he can't hear anything—it is just perfect silence in his head as he sees Güero, takes careful aim at his head and is about to squeeze him out of the world—when a white car pulls right into the line of fire. The driver seems oblivious to what's going on, like he's happened upon some on-location movie and is pissed off and determined to get to the airport anyway, so the car pulls past the Buick and over to the curb about twenty feet in front of it.

Which really seems to get Fabián going.

He spots the white Marquis and makes for it, running sideways past the Buick, blasting at it as he does, and Callan figures that Fabián has the white car lamped for a new carload of Güero's *sicarios,* and Fabián is fighting his way toward it so Callan tries to lay down some cover fire but the white car is in the line of fire and he doesn't want to shoot just in case these are civilians and not more of Güero's boys.

But now there are bullets hitting the Buick from the other side, and out of the corner of his eye Callan can make out some of the fake Jalisco cops training fire onto the car, which forces Güero and his hitters to squat down behind it, so Fabián survives his charge toward the white Marquis.

Parada doesn't even see him coming. He's too focused on the scene of bloodshed playing out in front of him. Bodies are splayed all over the sidewalk, some lying motionless, others crawling on their stomachs, dragging their legs behind them, and Parada can't tell if they're wounded or dead or just trying to take cover from the bullets that are flying everywhere. Then he looks out the window and sees a young man lying on his back with bubbles of blood gurgling out of his mouth and his eyes open in pain and terror, and Parada knows this young man is dying, so he starts to get out of the car to give him the last rites.

Pablo, his driver, tries to grab him and hold him back, but he's a small man and Parada easily shrugs him off and yells, "Get out of here!" But Pablo won't leave him there, so he huddles as far as he can under the steering wheel and puts his hands over his ears as Parada opens the door and gets out, just as Fabián gets there and points his gun into the priest's chest.

Callan sees him.

You dumb fuck, he thinks, that's the wrong guy. He watches as Parada squeezes his large body out of the car, straightens up and starts toward Poptop, and he watches as Fabián steps in the way and raises his AK. Callan stands straight up and yells, "NO!"

Leaps over the hood of the car and races toward Fabián, yelling, "FABIÁN, NO! THAT'S NOT HIM!"

Fabián glances over at Callan, and as he does Parada grabs the rifle and manages to turn the barrel down toward the ground, and now Fabián tries to lift it again and squeezes the trigger and the first shot hits Parada in the ankle and the next one in the knee but the adrenaline is coursing through Parada and he doesn't even feel it, never mind let go of the gun.

Because he wants to live. Feels it now more strongly, more urgently than ever in his life. Feels that life is good, the air is sweet and there is so much he still has to do, wants to do. Wants to get to that dying young man and soothe his soul before he goes. Wants to listen to more jazz. Wants to see Nora smile. Wants another cigarette, another good meal. Wants to kneel in sweet, soft prayer to his Lord. But not walk with Him, not yet, too much to do, so he *fights*. Holds on to the gun barrel with his whole life.

Fabián lowers his head and lifts his foot and plants it right on the crucifix on Parada's chest and kicks, sending the priest sprawling back against the car, and then Fabián lifts the gun's barrel again and sends fifteen bullets smashing into Parada's chest.

Parada feels his life draining out of him as his body slides down the side of the car.

Callan kneels down by the dying priest.

The man looks up at him and mumbles something Callan can't make out.

"What?" Callan asks. "What did you say?"

"I forgive you," Parada murmurs.

"What?"

"God forgives you."

The priest starts to make the sign of the cross, then his hand drops and his body jerks and he's gone.

Callan kneels there, looking down at the dead priest, as Fabián raises his rifle, aims and deliberately puts two more shots into the side of Parada's head.

Blood sprays onto the white paint of the car.

And hunks of Parada's white hair.

Callan turns around and says, "He was already dead."

Fabián ignores him, reaches into the front seat of the car, pulls out a briefcase and walks away with it. Callan sits down and cradles Parada's shattered head in his arms and, crying like a baby, asks over and over again, "What did you say? What did you say?"

He's oblivious to the battle going on around him.

Doesn't care.

Adán does.

He doesn't see Parada get killed; he's a little busy completing the execution of Güero Méndez, who's ducked behind the Buick, just realizing that he has fucked up. Two of his guys are already down and the car, even though it's armored, is vibrating with the number of bullets hitting it and isn't going to hold up much longer. A lot of the glass has finally shattered and the tires are shot out and it's only a matter of time before the gas tank explodes. He's badly outnumbered by the Barrera hit squad disguised as Jalisco cops, and this whole kiddie brigade bullshit was just that—bullshit. And now they've got him on three sides and if they can make it around to the fourth—behind the Buick—it's over. He's dead. And while he'd be perfectly happy to go if he could take Adán and Raúl with him, it's pretty clear now that isn't going to happen, so the thing is to boogie the fuck out of there and try again another time.

But getting out isn't going to be easy. He decides he has about one chance, and he takes it. He reaches into the backseat of the car and pulls out a tear-gas grenade and lofts it over the Buick toward the Barreras, then yells to his surviving four men to make a break for it, and they do, running parallel to the terminal, shooting as they go.

Adán's hit squad has a lot of hardware, but gas masks they don't have, and they start retching and coughing and Adán feels like his eyes are on fire and struggles to stay on his feet then decides that because he can't see and there are bullets zipping around, maybe that isn't such a good idea, so he lets himself drop to his knees.

Raúl doesn't.

Eyes on fire, nose burning, he charges toward the fleeing Méndez group, shooting from the hip. One of bursts takes Méndez's chief *sicario* in the spine and drops him, but Raúl watches in frustration as Méndez makes it to a parked taxi, throws the driver out on the pavement and gets behind the wheel, waiting just long enough for his three surviving *tiros* to jump in before he peels out.

Raúl fires at the car but can't hit the wheels and Güero speeds out of the parking lot, ducking low, his head just high enough to see, as the Jalisco cops who weren't hit by the tear gas fire away at the rapidly disappearing taxi.

"Son of a fucking bitch!" Raúl yells.

He turns to his right and sees Callan sitting there, holding Parada's body in his arms.

Raúl thinks that Callan has been hit. The man is crying and there's blood all over him and, whatever else Raúl is, he's not ungrateful, he remembers his debts, so he squats down to pick Callan up.

"Come on!" Raúl yells. " We have to get you out of here!"

Callan doesn't answer.

Raúl smacks him on the back of the head with his gun butt, hauls him to his feet and pulls him toward the terminal. Yelling as he does, "Come on, everyone! We have a plane to catch!"

Out on the tarmac, Aeromexico Flight 211 to Tijuana is already fifteen minutes late taking off.

But the flight waits.

The "Jalisco cops" peel off their uniforms to reveal civilian clothing underneath, toss their guns on the sidewalk and calmly walk toward the departure gate. Then the Barreras and the surviving gangbangers and the professional hit squad enter the terminal. They have to step over bodies to get there—not only Poptop's and Méndez's two shooters', but also six bystanders hit in the cross fire. The terminal is bedlam, people crying and screaming, medical personnel trying to sort out the wounded and Cardinal Antonucci standing in the middle of all this shouting, "Calm down! Calm down! What's happened? Will someone tell me what's happened?!"

He's afraid to go out and see for himself. He has a sick, sinking feeling in his stomach, and it isn't fair that he is in this position. All Scachi had asked him to do was to meet with Parada, that was all, and now there is this scene, and he feels a shamed relief when a young man strolls by him and answers his question.

"We gassed Güero Méndez!" Dreamer tells him. "El Tiburón gassed Méndez!"

The Barrera group walks calmly down the passageway toward their flight and lines up to hand the gate attendant their tickets, just like they would for any normal old flight. The attendant takes the tickets and hands them back their boarding passes and then they walk up the gangway and get on the plane. Adán Barrera is still carrying his equipment bag with the AK in it, but it's just like any carry-on, especially as he's in first class.

The only problem is when Raúl gets to the gate with the unconscious Callan draped over his shoulder.

The attendant's voice shakes as she says, "He can't get on like that."

"He has a ticket," Raúl says.

"But—"

"First class," Raúl says. He hands her their tickets and walks right past her up the gangway. Finds Callan's assigned seat and dumps him in it, then covers up his blood-soaked shirt with a blanket and says to the shocked flight attendant, "Too much partying."

Adán sits down next to Fabián, who looks at the pilot and asks, "What are you waiting for?"

The pilot closes the cabin door behind him.

When the plane lands, they're immediately met by airport police and escorted through a back entrance into waiting cars. And Raúl issues one order:

Scatter.

Callan don't need to be told that.

He gets dropped off at his house, where he stays long enough to shower, change out of his bloody clothes, pick up his money and go. Takes a taxi to the border crossing at San Ysidro and walks over the bridge, back into the United States. Just another drunk gringo coming back from a bender on Avenida Revolución.

He's been gone nine years.

Now he's back in the country where, as Sean Callan, he's wanted for conspiracy to distribute narcotics, racketeering, extortion and murder. He doesn't care. He'd rather take his chances here than spend another minute in Mexico. So he walks over the border and gets on the bright red trolley and rides it all the way into downtown San Diego.

It takes him about an hour and a half to find a gun shop, on the corner of Fourth and J, and buy a .22 in the back room without showing any papers. Then he finds a liquor store and buys a bottle of scotch, then walks over to an SRO hotel and takes a room for a week.

Locks himself in his room and starts drinking.

I forgive you, is what the priest had said.

God forgives you.

Nora's in her bedroom when she hears the news.

She's reading, with CNN on for background noise, when her ear catches the words, "When we come back, the tragic death of Mexico's highest-ranking cleric . . ."

Her heart stops, and there's a pounding in her head and she hits the speed dial for Juan's number as she sits through the endless commercials—hoping, praying that he'll answer the phone, that it's not him, that he'll pick up the phone—Please, God, don't let it be him—but when the news comes back on there's an old, posed photo of him on one half of the screen and the scene from the airport on the other and she sees him lying on the pavement and she doesn't scream.

Her mouth opens, but no sound comes out.

On a normal day, the Cross of Squares in Guadalajara is filled with tourists, lovers and locals out for a midday stroll. On a normal day, the walls of the cathedral are lined with stands where hawkers sell crosses, rosary cards, plaster models of saints, and *milagros,* tiny clay sculptures of knees, elbows and other body parts that people who feel they've been cured by prayer leave in the cathedral as a memorial.

But this isn't a normal day. Today is the funeral Mass for Cardinal

Parada, and now the twin yellow-tiled steeples of the cathedral loom over a *plaza* crowded with thousands of mourners, lined up in a serpentine formation, standing for hours to walk past the coffin of the martyred cardinal to pay their respects.

They've come from all over Mexico. Many are the sophisticated Tapatíos, in expensive suits and stylish, if subdued, dresses. Others have come from the countryside, *campesinos* in freshly cleaned white shirts and frocks. Others have made the trip from Culiacán and Badiraguato, and these men wear cowboy garb, and many of them were christened by Parada, received their First Communion from him, were married by him, watched their parents be buried by him when he was still just a rural priest. Then there are the government bureaucrats in gray and black suits, and priests and bishops in their clerical uniforms and hundreds of nuns in the varied habits of their particular orders.

On a normal day the *plaza* is alive with sound—the rapid-fire chatter of Mexican conversation, the shouts of hawkers, the music from busking mariachi groups—but today the *plaza* is strangely silent. All that can be heard are the murmurs of prayers, and darker mutterings about conspiracies.

Because few in the crowd believe what is now the government's explanation of Parada's death, that he was a victim of mistaken identity, that the Barreras' *sicarios* mistook Parada for Güero Méndez.

But the talk of conspiracy is subdued. Today is a day of mourning, and the thousands who wait patiently in the serpentine line and then move into the cathedral do so mostly in silence or in quiet prayer.

Art Keller is one of them.

The more he learns about Father Juan's death, the more troubled he is about it. Parada was riding in a white Marquis, Méndez in a green Buick; Parada was wearing a black sourtane with a prominent pectoral cross (now missing), Méndez was garbed in full Sinaloa cowboy chic.

How could anyone mistake a 6'4", sixty-two-year-old, white-haired man wearing a soutane and a crucifix for a 5'10" blond guy wearing narco-cowboy gear? At point-blank range? How could an experienced killer like Fabián Martínez do that? Why was an airplane waiting? How could Adán and Raúl and all their hitters get on board? How could they get off in Tijuana and get escorted right out of the airport?

And why, even though dozens of witnesses described a man identical to Adán Barrera at the airport and on the plane, did a Father Rivera in Tijuana—the Barreras' family priest—come forward to announce that Adán Barrera was the godfather at a christening performed at the exact time that Parada was gunned down?

The priest even displayed the baptismal records, with Adán's name and signature.

And who was the mysterious Yanqui a dozen witnesses saw cradling Parada's body? Who was carried on the plane with the Barreras and has since dropped out of sight?

Art says a quick prayer—there are people in line behind him—and finds a seat in the crowded cathedral.

The funeral Mass is long and moving. Person after person stands up to speak about what Father Juan had done in their lives, and the sound of weeping fills the large space. The atmosphere is quiet, mournful, respectful, subdued.

Until the president gets up to speak.

He had to be there, of course, the president and the entire cabinet and a score of other government officials, and as he gets up and walks to the pulpit an expectant silence falls over the crowd. And El Presidente clears his throat and begins, "A criminal act has taken the life of a good, clean and generous man—"

And that's as far as he gets because someone in the crowd shouts, "*¡Justicia!*"

Justice.

And then someone else picks it up, and then another and within seconds thousands of people in the cathedral and then thousands more outside start to chant—

"*Justicia, justicia, justicia—*"

—and El Presidente steps back from the microphone with an understanding smile as he waits for the chant to stop, but it doesn't stop—

"*Justicia, justicia, justicia—*" it just gets louder—

"*JUSTICIA, JUSTICIA, JUSTICIA—*"

—and the secret police start to get nervous, whispering to each other in their little microphones and earpieces, but it's hard to hear over the chant of—

"*JUSTICIA, JUSTICIA, JUSTICIA—*"

—which builds and builds until two of the police nervously hustle El Presidente away from the microphone and out a side door of the cathedral and into his armored limousine, but the shouts follow him as his car pulls out of the *plaza*—

"*JUSTICIA, JUSTICIA, JUSTICIA—*"

Most of the government men are gone by the time Parada is interred in the cathedral.

Art hadn't joined in the chanting, but sat there in amazement as the people in that church declared that they'd had enough of the corruption and faced the powerful leader of their country and *demanded* justice. And he thought, Well, you'll get it if I have anything to do with it.

Now he gets up to stand in line to file past the casket. He carefully maneuvers his place in line.

Nora Hayden's blond hair is covered with a black shawl, her body draped in a black dress. Even with all that she's still beautiful. He kneels beside her, puts his hands up in prayer and whispers, "Pray for his soul and sleep with his killer?"

She doesn't answer.

"How can you live with yourself?" Art says, then gets up.

He walks away from her soft crying.

By morning the national commander of the entire MJFP, General Rodolfo León, is flying to Tijuana with fifty specially selected elite agents, and by afternoon they've broken into heavily armed, combat-ready squads of six officers each, sweeping the streets of Colonia Chapultepec in armored Suburbans and Dodge Rams. By evening they've smashed into six Barrera safe houses, including Raúl's personal residence on Caco Sur, where they find a cache of AK-47s, pistols, fragmentation grenades and two thousand rounds of ammunition. In the enormous garage they find six armor-plated black Suburbans. By the end of the week they've arrested twenty-five Barrera associates, seized over eighty houses, warehouses and ranches belonging to either the Barreras or Güero Méndez and arrested ten of the airport security police who escorted the Barreras off Flight 211.

In Guadalajara, a squad of real Jalisco State Police stumbles on a pickup truck full of fake Jalisco police, and a chase through the city ends with two of the fake cops being trapped inside a house and shooting it out with over a hundred Jalisco cops all night and into the morning, when one is killed and the other surrenders, but not before they've killed two of the real police and wounded the commander of the state police force.

The following morning, El Presidente goes in front of the cameras to declare his determination to crush the drug cartels once and for all, and to announce that they've just exposed and fired and will criminally charge over seventy corrupt MJFP officers, and he offers a $5 million reward for information leading to the capture of Adán and Raúl Barrera and Güero Méndez, all of whom are still on the loose, whereabouts unknown.

Because even with the army, the *federales,* and every state police force scouring the country, they can't find Güero, Raúl or Adán.

Because they aren't there.

Güero's across the border in Guatemala.

And the Barreras have also crossed the border.

Into the United States.

They're living in La Jolla.

Fabián finds Flaco and Dreamer living under the Laurel Street Bridge in Balboa Park.

The cops couldn't find them, but Fabián hit the barrio and people told him stuff they weren't going to tell the cops. They tell him because they know if they stone the cops, the cops might harass them and shit, but if they stone Fabián, he'll fucking kill their asses, and that is the cold truth.

So Flaco and Dreamer are dozing one night under the bridge when Flaco feels a shoe dig into his ribs and he jumps, thinking it's a cop or a fag, but it's Fabián.

So he looks up at Fabián with big eyes because he's half-afraid the *tiro* is going to put a bullet into him, but Fabián smiles and says, "*Hermanitos,* it's time to show you have heart."

And he thumps his chest with the inside of his fist.

"What you want us to do?" Flaco asks.

"Adán is reaching out to you," Fabián answers. "He wants you to go back to Mexico."

He explains how the Barreras are taking all the heat from the death of that priest, how the *federales* are putting pressure on them, busting their safe houses, arresting people, and how it's not going to settle down until they get someone who was involved in the shooting.

"You go down and get yourselves arrested," Fabián says, "and you tell them the truth—we were going after Güero Méndez, he ambushed us instead, and Fabián mistook Parada for Güero and shot him by accident. Nobody ever meant for Parada to get hurt. One of those things."

"I don't know, man," Dreamer says.

"Look," Fabián answers, "you're kids. And you didn't do the shooting. You'll only get a few years, and while you're in, your families will be taken care of like royalty. And when you get out, you've had the appreciation and respect of Adán Barrera in the bank, earning interest for you. Flaco, your mother is a maid in a motel, right?"

"Yeah."

"Not anymore she isn't," Fabián says, "if you show heart."

"I don't know," Dreamer says. "Mexican cops . . ."

"Tell you what," Fabián says. "That reward for Güero? That fifty thousand. You two split it, tell us who to bring it to and it's done."

Both boys say they want the money to go to their mothers.

As they get near the border, Flaco's legs are shaking so hard he's afraid that Fabián can see them. His knees are literally knocking together and he can't seem to stop them, and his eyes are filled with tears and he can't stop the tears from spilling over. He's ashamed, even though he can hear Dreamer sniffling in the backseat.

When they get near the crossing, Fabián pulls over to let them out.

"You got heart," he tells them. "You're warriors."

They make it through Immigration and Customs with no problem and start walking south into the city. They get about two blocks when searchlights hit them in the face, blinding them, and the *federales* are yelling and telling them to get their hands up and Flaco throws his hands up high. Then a cop grabs him, throws him to the ground and cuffs his hands tight behind his back.

So Flaco's lying there in the dirt, his back arched painfully because his arms are pulled back so hard, but then that pain don't seem like nothing because the *federale* spits on his face then kicks him hard, right in the ear, with the toe of his combat boot, and Flaco feels like his eardrum has just exploded.

Pain goes off like fireworks inside Flaco's head.

Then, from a long way away, he hears a voice tell him—

It's just the beginning, *mi hijo*.

We're just getting started.

Nora's phone rings and she picks it up.

It's Adán.

"I want to see you."

"Go to hell."

"It was an accident," he says. "A mistake. Give me a chance to explain it to you. Please."

She wants to hang up, detests herself for not hanging up, but she doesn't hang up. Instead, she agrees to meet him that night on the beach at La Jolla Shores, by Lifeguard Tower 38.

Under the dim light of the tower he sees her coming. She looks like she's alone.

"You know I put my life in your hands," he says. "If you called the police . . ."

"He was your priest," she says. "Your *friend. My* friend. How could you—"

He shakes his head. "I wasn't even there. I was at a christening in Tijuana. It was an accident, a cross fire—"

"That's not what the police are saying."

"Méndez owns the police."

"I hate you, Adán."

"Don't say that, please."

He looks so sad, she thinks. Lonely, desperate. She wants to believe him.

"Swear," she says. "Swear to me you're telling the truth."

"I swear it."

"On your daughter's life."

He can't bear losing her.

He nods. "I swear."

She reaches her arms out and he holds her. "God, Adán, I'm so miserable."

"I know."

"I loved him."

"I know," Adán says. "So did I."

And the sad thing is, he thinks, that's the truth.

They must be at a dump because Flaco smells garbage.

And it must be morning because he can feel faint sunlight on his face, even through the black hood. One of his eardrums is ruptured, but he can hear Dreamer pleading, "Please, please, no, no, please . . ."

A gunshot explodes and Flaco don't hear Dreamer no more.

Then Flaco feels a gun barrel brush the side of his head, by his good ear. It makes little circles, like its holder wants to make sure Flaco knows what it is, then he hears the hammer click back.

Flaco screams.

A dry *click.*

Flaco loses it. His bladder lets go and he feels the hot urine run down his leg and his knees give out and he crumbles to the ground, squirming and twisting like a worm, trying to get away from the gun barrel at his head and then he hears the hammer go back and another dry *click* and then a voice says, "Maybe the next one, little *pendejo,* eh?"

Click.

Flaco messes his pants.

The *federales* whoop and holler. "God, what a stink! What you been eating, *mierdita*?"

Flaco hears the hammer click back again.

The gun roars.

The bullet plows into the dirt by his ear.

"Pick him up," the voice says.

But the *federales* balk at touching the filthy kid. They finally hit on a solution—they take the hood off Dreamer and the gag out of his mouth and make him pull off Flaco's soiled pants and underwear, and they give him a wet rag to wipe the shit off his friend.

Flaco murmurs to him, "I'm sorry. Sorry."

"It's okay."

Then they put both of them into the back of the van and take them back to their cell. Throw them on the bare concrete floor, slam the door shut and actually leave them alone for a while.

The boys lie on the floor and cry.

An hour later a *federale* comes back in and Flaco starts to tremble uncontrollably.

But the *federale* just tosses them each a pad of paper and a pencil and tells them to start writing.

Their stories hit the papers the next morning.

Confirmation of what the MJFP thought had happened in the Parada case—the cardinal was the victim of mistaken identity, killed because American gang members mistook him for Güero Méndez.

El Presidente gets back on television with General León at his side to announce that this news only strengthens his administration's resolve to wage a merciless war against the drug cartels. They will not stop until these thugs are punished and the *narcotraficantes* are destroyed.

Flaco's tongue lolls lazily from his mouth.

His face is dark blue.

He hangs by the neck from the steam pipe that runs across the ceiling in his cell.

Dreamer dangles next to him.

The coroner returns with a verdict of double suicide: The young men couldn't live with the guilt of killing Cardinal Parada. The coroner never deals with the unexplained blunt-trauma blows on the backs of their heads.

Art waits on the American side of the border.

The terrain looks strangely green through the night-vision scopes. It's a strange piece of ground anyway, he thinks. No-man's-land, the desolate stretch of dusty hills and deep canyons that lies between Tijuana and San Diego.

Every night a weird game is played out here. Just before dusk, the would-be *mojados* gather above the dry drainage canal that runs along the border, waiting for darkness. As if on a signal, they all rush across at once. It's a numbers game—the illegals know that the Border Patrol can stop only so many, so the rest will get through to find the sub–minimum wage jobs picking fruit, washing dishes, working on farms.

But this night's mad scramble is already over, and Art has made sure that the Border Patrol has been cleared from this sector. A defector is coming over from the other side, and even though he's going to be a guest of the United States government, he can't come across at any of the regular stations. It would be too dangerous—the Barreras have spotters who watch the checkpoints 24/7, and Art can't take the chance that his man might be spotted.

He checks his watch and doesn't like what he sees. It's 1:10 and his man is ten minutes late. It could just be the difficulty of negotiating the treacherous terrain at night. His guy could be lost in one of the numerous box canyons, or come up the wrong ridge, or . . .

Stop kidding yourself, he says. Ramos is with him, and Ramos knows this territory like it's his backyard, which it pretty much is.

Maybe Ramos didn't get to him, and the guy decided to keep his lot in with the Barreras. Maybe he just chickened out, changed his mind. Or maybe Ramos didn't get to him first, and he's lying in a ditch somewhere with a bullet in the back of his head. Or, more likely, shot in the mouth, as informers usually are.

Just then he sees a flashlight blink three times.

He blinks his own twice, flips the safety of his service revolver off and walks down into the canyon, the flashlight in one hand, the gun in the other. In a minute he can make out two figures, one tall and thick, the other shorter and much thinner.

The priest looks miserable. He's not wearing a soutane or collar, but a hooded Nike sweatshirt, jeans and running shoes. Which are, Art thinks, appropriate.

He looks cold and scared.

"Father Rivera?" Art asks.

Rivera nods.

Ramos slaps him on the back. "Cheer up, Father. You made a good choice. The Barreras would have killed you sooner or later."

Or at least that's what they'd wanted him to believe. It was Ramos, at Art's urging, who had made the approach. Found the priest out on his morning jog, trotted beside him and asked him if he liked the smell of fresh air and wanted to breathe more. Then showed him photos of some of the men Raúl had tortured to death, and added cheerfully that they would probably just shoot him, being a priest and all.

But they can't let you live, Padre, Ramos had told him. You know too much. You miserable, lying, ass-licking excuse for a holy man. I can save you, though, Ramos added when the man started to cry. But it has to be soon—tonight—and you'll have to trust me.

"He's right," Art says now. He nods to Ramos, and if a man's eyes can actually smirk, Ramos' are smirking.

"*Adiós, viejo,*" Ramos says to Art.

"*Adiós, my* old friend."

Art takes Rivera by the wrist and gently walks him back toward his vehicle. The priest allows himself to be led like a child.

Chalino Guzmán, aka El Verde, *patrón* of the Sonora cartel, arrives at his favorite restaurant in Ciudad Juárez for breakfast. He comes here every morning to have his *huevos rancheros* with flour tortillas, and if it weren't for the distinctive green lizard-skin boots, you'd think he was just another dry-country farmer scraping out a living from the hard, sun-baked red soil.

But the waiters know better. They usher him to his regular table on the patio and bring him his coffee and morning newspaper. And they take thermoses of hot coffee out to his *sicarios,* who sit in parked cars in front of the restaurant.

Just across the border is the Texas town of El Paso, through which El Verde ships tons of cocaine, marijuana and even a little heroin. Now he sits down and looks at the newspaper. He can't read, but he likes pretending that he can, and anyway, he enjoys looking at the pictures.

He glances over the top of the paper and watches one of his *sicarios* walk up to a Ford Bronco parked out in front to tell it to move along. El Verde is a trifle annoyed—most of the locals know the rules this time of the morning. This must be an out-of-towner, he thinks as the *sicario* taps on the window.

Then the bomb goes off and rips El Verde to pieces.

Don Francisco Uzueta—aka García Abrego, head of the Gulf cartel and *patrón* of the Federación—rides a palomino stallion at the head of the parade in the annual festival of his small village of Coquimatlán. He has the stallion in full parade trot, its hooves clapping on the cobblestones of the narrow street, and he's decked out in full *vaquero* costume, as befits the *patrón* of the village. He sweeps his bejeweled sombrero in acknowledgment of the cheers.

And well they should cheer—Don Francisco built the village clinic, the school, the playground. He even paid to air-condition the new police station.

So now he smiles at the people and graciously accepts their gratitude and love. He recognizes individuals in the crowd and makes a special point to wave to children. He doesn't see the barrel of the M-60 machine gun as it pokes out of a second-story window.

The first short burst of .50-caliber bullets takes the smile along with the rest of his face. The second burst rips his chest open. The palomino whinnies in terror, rears up and starts to buck.

Abrego's dead hand still clutches the reins.

Mario Aburto, a twenty-three-year-old mechanic, stands in the large crowd that day in the poor neighborhood of Lomas Taurinas, near the Tijuana airport.

Lomas Taurinas is a squatters' colony of improvised shacks and huts hidden in a ravine of the bare, muddy mountains that flank the east side of Tijuana. In Lomas Taurinas, when you're not choking on dust, you're slipping in the mud that pours down from the eroded hills, sometimes taking the shacks with it. Until recently, *running water* meant that you built your shack over one of the thousands of rivulets—water runs literally through your house—but the *colonia* recently received piped water and electricty as a reward for its loyalty to the PRI. But still, much of the muddy ground is an open sewer and slow-flowing garbage dump.

Luis Donaldo Colosio is flanked by fifteen plainclothes soldiers from the elite Estado Mayor, the presidential bodyguards. A special squad of ex–Tijuana cops, hired to provide security for the local campaign stops, are interspersed in the crowd. The candidate speaks from the bed of a pickup truck parked in a sort of natural amphitheater at the bottom of the ravine.

Ramos watches from the slope, his STG stationed at various points around the bowl of the amphitheater. It's a difficult task—the crowd is large and raucous and flowing like mud. The people had mobbed Colosio's red Chevy Blazer as it made slow progress up the one street into the neighborhood, and now Ramos is worried that the same thing will happen when Colosio goes to leave.

"It will be a goat fuck," he says to himself.

But Colosio doesn't get back in his car when the speech ends.

Instead, he decides to walk.

To "swim among the people," as he puts it.

"He's going to do what?" Ramos yells into his radio at General Reyes, the commander of the army guard.

"He's going to walk."

"That's crazy!"

"It's what he wants."

"If he does that," Ramos says, "we can't protect him!"

Reyes is a member of the Mexican general staff and second-in-command of the presidential bodyguard. He's not going to take orders from some grimy Tijuana cop. "It's not your job to protect him," he sniffs. "It's ours."

Colosio overhears the exchange.

"Since when," he asks, "do I need protection from the people?"

Ramos watches helplessly as Colosio dives into the sea of people.

"Heads up! Heads up!" he radios his men, but he knows there's little any of them can do. Although his men are fine marksmen, they can barely even see Colosio as he bobs in and out of the crowd, never mind get a shot at a potential assassin. Not only can they not see, they can barely hear, as speakers mounted on a truck start to blare the local Baja *cumbia* music.

So Ramos doesn't hear the shot.

He just barely sees Mario Aburto push his way through the bodyguards, grab Colosio's right shoulder, press the .38 pistol to the right side of his head and pull the trigger.

Ramos starts to fight his way down as chaos erupts.

Some people in the crowd grab Aburto and start to beat him.

General Reyes takes the fallen Colosio in his arms and starts to carry him to a car. One of his men, a plainclothes major, grabs Aburto by the shirt collar and pulls him through the crowd. Blood spatters on the major's collar as someone hits Aburto in the head with a rock, but now the Estado Mayor squad forms around the major like football linemen around a runner, bulldozes through the mob and shoves the assassin into a black Suburban.

As Ramos makes his way toward the Suburban, he sees that an ambulance has managed to drive in, and he sees Reyes and the EMTs lift Colosio into the back. That's when Ramos sees the second wound in Colosio's left side—the man was shot not once, but twice.

The ambulance howls and takes off.

The black Suburban starts to do the same, but Ramos raises Esposa and points it right at the army major sitting in the front seat.

"Tijuana police!" Ramos yells. "Identify yourself!"

"Estado Mayor! Get out of our way!" the major yells back.

He pulls his pistol.

It's a bad idea. Twelve STG rifles are aimed at his head.

Ramos approaches the car from the passenger side. Now he can see the alleged assassin on the floor of the backseat, between three plainclothes soldiers who are shoving him down and beating him.

Ramos looks at the major in the front seat. "Open the door, I'm getting in."

"The hell you are."

"I want that man to arrive at the police station alive!"

"It's none of your goddamn business! Get out of our way!"

Ramos turns to his men.

"If the car moves, kill them!"

He lifts Esposa and with the butt smashes through the passenger window. As the major ducks, Ramos reaches in, unlocks the door, opens it and gets in. Now he has Esposa's barrel pointed at the major's stomach; the major has his pistol pointed at Ramos' face.

"What?" the major asks. "Do you think I'm Jack Ruby?"

"I'm just making sure you're not. I want this man to make it to the station alive."

"We're taking him to federal police headquarters," the major says.

"As long as he gets there alive," Ramos repeats.

The major lowers his pistol and tells his driver, "Let's go."

A crowd arrives at Tijuana General before Colosio's ambulance does. The weeping, praying people have gathered on the front steps, shouting Colosio's name and holding up his picture. The ambulance brings Colosio around the back and into a waiting operating room. A helicopter has landed on the street, its rotors spinning, ready to fly the wounded man to a special trauma center across the border in San Diego.

It never makes the trip.

Colosio is already dead.

Bobby.

It's too much like Bobby, Art thinks.

The lone gunman—the alienated, isolated nut. The two wounds, one in the right side, the other on the left.

"How did this Aburto kid do that?" Art asks Shag. "He fires from point-blank range into the right side of Colosio's head, then shoots him again in the left side of his stomach? How?"

"Just like RFK," Shag answers. "The victim spins when the first bullet hits."

Shag demonstrates, snapping his head back and rotating to the left as he falls to the floor.

"That would work," Art says, "except the trajectory of the bullets have them coming from opposite directions."

"Oh, here we go."

"Okay," Art says. "We bust Güero's tunnel and it's connected to the Fuentes brothers, who are big supporters of Colosio. Then Colosio comes to Tijuana, the Barreras' turf, and gets killed. Call me crazy, Shag."

"I don't think you're crazy," Shag says. "But I think you have this Barrera obsession, ever since . . ."

He stops. Stares at the desk.

Art finishes the thought for him. "Ever since they killed Ernie."

"Yeah."

"And you don't?"

"I do," Shag says. "I want to get them all, the Barreras and Méndez. But, boss, at a certain level, I mean . . . at some point you have to let this go."

He's right, Art thinks.

Of course he's right. And I'd like to let it go. But wanting to and doing are two very different things, and letting go of this "Barrera obsession," as Shag puts it, is something I just can't do.

"I'm telling you," he says, "when all this shakes out, we're going to find out that the Barreras were behind this."

No doubt in my mind.

Güero Méndez lies on a gurney at a private hospital, where three of the best plastic surgeons in Mexico are getting ready to give him a new face. A new face, he thinks, dyed hair, a new name, and I can resume my war against the Barreras.

A war he will certainly win, with the new president on his side.

He settles back on his pillow as the nurse preps him.

"Are you ready to go to sleep?" she asks.

He nods. Ready to go to sleep, and wake up a new man.

She takes a syringe, removes the little rubber cap and places the needle against a vein in his arm, then pushes the plunger on the syringe. She strokes his face as the drug starts to take effect, then says softly, "Colosio is dead."

"What did you say?"

"I have a message from Adán Barrera—your man Colosio is dead."

Güero tries to get up but his body won't obey his mind.

"This is called Dormicum," the nurse says. "A massive dose—call it a 'lethal injection.' When your eyes close this time, they'll never open again."

He tries to scream, but no sound comes out of his mouth. He fights to stay awake, but he can feel it slipping away from him—his consciousness, his life. He struggles against the restraints, tries to get a hand free to rip off the mask and scream for help, but his muscles won't respond. Even his neck won't turn, to shake his head no, no, no, as he feels his life draining out of him.

As if from a tremendous distance he hears the nurse say, "The Barreras say to rot in hell."

Two guards roll a laundry cart, full of clean sheets and blankets, up to Miguel Ángel Barrera's suite of cells in Almoloya prison.

Tío climbs in and the guards throw a sheet over him and roll him out of the building, across the yards and out the gate.

That simple, that easy.

As promised.

Miguel Ángel climbs out of the cart and walks to a waiting van.

Twelve hours later he's living in retirement in Venezuela.

Three days before Christmas, Adán kneels before Cardinal Antonucci in his private study in Mexico City.

"The most wanted man in Mexico" listens to the papal nuncio chant, in Latin, absolution for him and Raúl for their unintentional role in the accidental killing of Cardinal Juan Ocampo Parada.

Antonucci doesn't give them absolution for the murders of El Verde, Abrego, Colosio and Méndez, Adán thinks, but the government has. In advance—it was all part of the quid pro quo for killing Parada.

If I kill your enemy, Adán had insisted, you must let me kill mine.

So it's done, Adán thinks. Méndez is dead, the war is over, Tío has been whisked out of prison.

And I am the new *patrón*.

The Mexican government has just restored the Holy Roman Catholic

Church to full legal status. A briefcase full of incriminating information has passed from Adán Barrera to certain government ministers.

Adán leaves the room with an officially shiny-clean new soul.

Quid pro quo.

New Year's Eve, Nora comes home from a dinner with Haley Saxon. She left even before they popped the corks on the champagne.

She's just not in a party mood. The holidays have been depressing. It was her first Christmas in nine years that she didn't spend with Juan.

She slips the key into her door and opens it, and as she steps inside, a hand clamps over her mouth. She digs into her purse and fumbles for the pepper spray but the bag is knocked out of her hand.

"I'm not going to hurt you," Art says. "Don't scream."

He slowly takes his hand off her mouth.

She turns and slaps him across the face, then says, "I'm calling the police."

"I am the police."

"I'm calling the real police."

She walks to her phone and starts to dial.

He says, "You have the right to remain silent. Anything you say can and will be used against you in a . . ."

She puts the phone down.

"That's better."

"What do you want?"

"I want you to see something."

"You have no idea how many times I've heard that."

He takes a videocassette from his jacket pocket. "Do you have a VCR?"

She laughs. "Amateur videos? Swell. Are they of you, to impress me? Or are they of me? First threats, now blackmail. Let me tell you something, honey—I've seen a hundred of them, and I look pretty good on tape."

She opens an armoire and shows him the TV and VCR. "Whatever turns you on."

He pops in the tape and says, "Sit down."

"I'm fine, thanks."

"I said sit down."

"Oh, it's the forceful thing." She sits on the sofa. "Happy now? Turned on?"

"Watch."

She's smirking as the tape starts to run, but she stops as the image of a young priest comes on the screen. He's sitting in a metal folding chair behind a metal table. A bar is displayed on the bottom of the screen, giving the date and time.

"Who's this?" she asks.

"Father Esteban Rivera," Keller answers. "Adán's parish priest."

She hears Art's voice in the background, asking questions.

Feels her heart drop as she listens.

May 24, 1994, do you remember where you were?

Yes.

You were performing a christening, is that right?

Yes.

In your church in Tijuana.

Yes.

Take a look at this document.

Nora sees a hand slide a paper across the table at the priest. He picks it up, looks at it and puts it back on the table.

Do you recognize that?

Yes.

What is it?

Baptismal records.

Adán Barrera is listed as the godfather. Do you see that?

Yes.

That's your handwriting, isn't it?

Yes.

You entered Adán Barrera as the godfather and indicated that he was present at the christening, is that right?

I did that, yes.

But that's not true, is it?

Nora can't breathe during the long pause as Rivera contemplates his response.

No.

She feels sick to her stomach.

You lied about that.

Yes. I'm ashamed.

Who asked you to say that Adán was there?

He did.

Is that his signature, there?

Yes, it is.

When did he actually sign that?

It was a week before.

Nora leans over and puts her head between her knees.

Do you know where Adán was that day?

No, I don't.

"But we do, don't we?" Art says to Nora. He gets up, pops the tape out of the machine and puts it back in his pocket. "Happy New Year, Ms. Hayden."

She doesn't look up as he leaves.

New Year's Day, Art wakes up to the sound of the television and a wicked hangover.

I must have left the damn thing on last night, he thinks. He shuts it off, goes into the bathroom, takes a couple of aspirin and chugs a large glass of water. Then he goes into the kitchen and puts on a pot of coffee.

He opens the door to the hallway while it brews and picks up his newspaper. Takes the paper and the coffee to the table in the living space of the sterile condo and sits down. It's a clear winter day outside, and he can see San Diego Harbor just a few blocks away, and beyond that, Mexico.

Good riddance to 1994, he thinks. A bastard of a year.

May '95 be better.

More guests at the gathering of the dead last night. The old regulars, and now Father Juan. Mowed down in the cross fire I created, trying to make peace in the war I started. He brought people with him, too. Kids. Two SD gangbangers, children of my own old barrio.

They all came to see the old year out.

Quite a party.

He looks at the front page of the paper and notes without much interest that NAFTA goes into effect today.

Well, congratulations, everybody, he thinks. Free trade shall bloom. Factories shall spring up like mushrooms just across the border, and underpaid Mexican labor shall make our tennis shoes, our designer clothes, our refrigerators and handy household appliances at prices we can afford.

We shall all be fat and happy, and what's one dead priest compared to that?

Well, I'm glad you all have your treaty, he thinks.

But I sure as hell didn't sign it.

PART FOUR

The Road to Ensenada

10

The Golden West

All the federales *say*
They could have had him any day.
They only let him go so long
Out of kindness, I suppose.

—Townes Van Zandt, "Pancho and Lefty"

San Diego
1996

The sunlight is filthy.

Filtered through a smudgy window and dirty, broken venetian blinds, it creeps into Callan's room like a noxious gas, sick and yellow. Sick and yellow also describes Callan—sick, yellow, sweaty, rank. He lies twisted in the unchanged-for-weeks sheets, his pores trying (unsuccessfully) to sweat out the alcohol, dried saliva caked at the edges of his half-open mouth, his brain trying feverishly to sort out the bits and pieces of nightmares from the emerging, waking reality.

The weak sun hits his eyelids and they open.

Another day in paradise.

Fuck.

Actually, he's almost glad to be awake—the dreams were bad, made worse by booze. He half-expects to see blood in the bed—his dreams are incarnadine; blood flows through them like a river, connecting one nightmare to another.

Not that reality is much better.

He blinks a few times, assures himself that he is awake, and slowly swings his legs, aching from the lactic-acid buildup, to the floor. He sits there for a second, considers lying back down, then reaches for a pack of cigarettes on the bedside table. He pops a cig in his mouth, finds his lighter and shakes the flame to the tip of the cigarette.

A deep inhale, a wracking cough, and he feels a little better.

What he needs now is a drink.

An eye-opener.

He looks down and sees the empty pint of Seagram's at his feet.

Hell's fuck—and it's happening more and more these days. More and more my aching ass, he thinks. It's happening every night now. You're finishing the whole bottle and leaving nothing for morning, not the thinnest ray of amber-liquid sunshine. Which means you'll have to get up. Get up and get dressed and go out to get a drink.

Used to be—doesn't seem like that long ago—he'd wake up with a hangover and what he'd want was a cup of coffee. In the earlier days of those earlier days, he'd go out to the little diner on Fourth Avenue and get that first headache-relieving cup and maybe ease into some breakfast—some greasy potatoes, eggs and toast, the "special." Then he stopped eating breakfast—the coffee was all he could handle—and then, somewhere in there, somewhere along the slow, drifting river trip that is an extended bender, it became not coffee he wanted in the first awful hour of the morning, but more liquor.

So now he gets to his feet.

His knees creak, his back hurts from sleeping so long in one position.

He shuffles into the bathroom, a sink, toilet and shower crammed into what had once been a closet. A thin, insufficient lip of metal separates the shower from the floor, so in the days when he was still taking regular showers (and he pays a considerable extra amount each week for the private bathroom because he didn't want to share the common one down the hall with the babbling psychos, the old syphilis cases, the drunken old queens), the water always overflowed onto the old, stained tile floor. Or sprayed through the thin, ripped plastic shower curtain with the faded peace flowers on it. He doesn't take many showers now. He thinks about it, but it just seems like too much work, and anyway the shampoo bottle is almost empty, the remaining shampoo dried up and stuck to the bottom of the bottle, and it's too much mental effort to go into Longs Drugs and buy another. And he don't like being around that many people—not that many civilians anyway.

A thin sliver of soap survives on the shower floor, and another shrinking bar of strong-smelling antiseptic soap—provided by the hotel along with the thin towel—sits on the sink.

He splashes some water on his face.

He don't look in the mirror but it stares back at him.

His face is puffy and jaundiced, his shoulder-length hair long and greasy, his beard matted.

I'm starting to look, Callan thinks, like every other wino, junkie and drunk in the Lamp. Well, shit, why not? Except that I can go to the ATM and always get money out, I *am* like every other wino, junkie and drunk in the Lamp.

He brushes his teeth.

That much he does. He can't stand the stale-whiskey-and-puke taste in his mouth—it makes him want to puke more. So he brushes his teeth and takes a piss. He don't have to get dressed—he's already dressed in what he passed out in, black jeans and a black T-shirt. But he does have get his shoes on, which means sitting back on the bed and bending over and by the time he finishes tying his black Chuck Taylor high-tops (no socks) he almost feels like going back to bed.

But it's eleven in the morning.

Time to get going.

Get that drink.

He reaches under the pillow, finds his .22 pistol, sticks it in the back of his waistband under the oversized, untucked T-shirt, finds his key and walks out the door.

The hallway stinks.

Mostly of Lysol, which the management pours around like fucking napalm to try to kill the stubborn scents of urine, vomit, shit and dying old man. Kill the germs anyway. It's a constant, losing battle—which is what this place is anyway, Callan thinks as he presses the button for the single, cranky elevator—a constant losing battle.

Which is why you chose it to live in.

Place to finally lose your own constant losing battle.

The Golden West Hotel.

SRO.

Single Room Occupancy.

Shit Right Out.

The last stop before the sheet of cardboard on the street, or the coroner's slab.

Because the Golden West Hotel converts welfare checks, Social (in)Security checks, unemployment checks, disability checks directly into room rent. But once the checks run out, you're Shit Right Out. Sorry, pops, hit the street, the cardboard, the slab. Some of the lucky ones die in their rooms. They haven't paid their rent, or the smell of the decomposition seeps under their door and finally overpowers the Lysol, and a reluctant desk clerk puts a handkerchief over his nose and turns the passkey. Then the call is made and the ambulance makes its slow, accustomed trip to the hotel, and another old guy is taken out on a gurney for the last ride, his sun at last setting over the Golden West.

It's not all old winos. The occasional Euro-tourist accidentally finds his way here, lured by the bargain price in otherwise expensive San Diego. Stays his week and checks out. Or the young American kid who thinks he's the next Jack Kerouac or the new Tom Waits is attracted by the down-and-out seediness—until his backpack gets stolen from his room with his Discman and all his money or he gets mugged in the street outside or one of the colorful old-timers tries to grope his joint in the common bathroom. Then the would-be dharma bum calls Mommy and she phones her credit card to the front desk to get sonny boy out of there, but he *has* seen a part of America he wouldn't have seen otherwise.

But mostly it's old drunks and ancient psychotics, gathered like crows in the torn chairs in front of the television set in the lobby. Babbling their own dialogue, arguing over the channel (there have been stabbings, actual fatalities, over *The Rockford Files* or *Gilligan's Island;* shit, there have been stabbings over Ginger versus Mary Ann) or just mumbling internal monologues from real or imagined scenes playing out in their own brains.

Constant losing battles.

Callan doesn't have to live here.

He has money, he could live better, but he chooses this place.

Call it penance, purgatory, anything you want—this is the place where he conducts his long self-punishment, pounds the booze in slowly fatal amounts (lethal self-injection?), sweats the night sweats, pukes blood, screams his dreams, dies every night, starts again in the morning.

I forgive you. God forgives you.

Why did the old priest have to say that?

After the fucked-up shootout in Guadalajara, Callan made his way to San Diego, checked into the Golden West and started drinking. A year and a half later he's still here.

This is a setting for self-hatred. He likes it here.

The elevator arrives, complaining like a tired old room-service waiter. Callan cranks the door open and hits the button below the faded L. The grille-door shuts, cell-like, and the elevator grinds its way down. Callan's relieved that he's its sole occupant—no French tourist jamming it up with duffel bags, no out-to-find-America college kid whapping him with his backpack, no smelly old drunk with BO. Shit, Callan thinks, I'm the smelly drunk with BO.

Doesn't care.

The desk clerk likes Callan.

Nothing not to like—the strange, young (for the Golden West) guy pays in cash, in advance. He's quiet and doesn't complain, and there was that one night when he was standing there waiting for his key and this mugger pulled a knife on the clerk and this guy looks over and then just *dropped* him. Drunk as a lord and he just dropped the mugger with one punch, then politely asked for his key again.

So the clerk likes Callan. Sure, the man is always drunk, but he's a *quiet* drunk who don't cause no trouble, and that's all you can ask for. So he says hi when Callan drops off his key, and Callan mumbles hi back and heads out the door.

The sun hits him like a punch in the chest.

Dimness to sunlight, just like that. Blinded, he stands and squints for a moment. He never gets used to this—they never had sun like this back in New York. Seems like it's always sunny in fucking San Diego. Sun Diego, they oughta call it. He'd give his left nut for one rainy day.

He adjusts his eyes to the light and walks into the Gaslamp District.

It used to be a tawdry, dangerous neighborhood filled with strip joints, porno places and SROs—your typical downtown in decline. Then the shabby hotels started to yield to condos as the process of gentrification set in and it became hip and trendy to live in the Lamp. So you have an upscale restaurant sitting next to a porn shop, a hip club across from an SRO, a condo building with a coffee shop on its ground floor playing neighbor to a derelict building with winos in the basement and junkies on the roof.

Gentrification is winning.

Of course it is—money always wins, and the Lamp is starting to become a yuppie theme park. A few of the SROs hold on, a couple of porn shops, a small handful of the seedier bars. But the process is irreversible as the chains start to move in—the Starbucks, the Gaps, the Edwards Cinemas. The Lamp starts to look pretty much like everywhere else, and the holdout porn places, alkie-bars and SRO hotels resemble aboriginal Indians drunkenly loitering in the parking lot of American commerce.

Callan ain't thinking about any of this.

He's just thinking about getting that drink, and his feet carry him into one of the old survivors, a dark narrow bar he doesn't know the name of—the sign faded long ago—wedged between the last of the neighborhood Laundromats and an art gallery.

It's dark, like all bars should be.

This is a serious drinkers' bar—no amateurs or dilettantes need apply—

and there are a dozen or so drinkers, mostly male, staggered around the bar and in the booths along the opposite wall. People don't come in here to socialize, or talk sports or politics, or to sample fine whiskeys. They come in here to get drunk and stay drunk for as long as their money and their livers last. A few of them glance up resentfully as Callan opens the door and lets a wedge of sunshine break into the darkness.

The door closes quickly enough, though, and they all go back to staring at their drinks as Callan walks in, takes a stool at the bar and orders.

Well, not all of them.

There's one guy at the end of the bar who keeps glancing surreptitiously over his whiskey. A little guy, an *old* guy with a cherub's face and a full head of perfectly silver hair. He looks a little like a leprechaun perched on a toadstool instead of a bar stool, and his eyes blink in surprise as he recognizes the man who just came into the bar, sat down and ordered two beers and a whiskey chaser.

It's been twenty years since he's last seen this man, twenty years ago in the Liffey Pub in Hell's Kitchen when this man—a boy then, really—pulled a gun from the small of his back and put two bullets into Eddie "The Butcher" Friel.

Mickey even remembers the music that was playing. Remembers that he had loaded the jukebox with replays of "Moon River" because he wanted to hear the song as many times as he could before starting on his next prison stretch. Remembers telling this man—no, it's clearly him, even down to the small bulge in the back where he still carries a pistol—to go toss the gun in the Hudson River.

Mickey never saw the boy again, not until this moment, but he heard the rest of the story. About how this boy—what is his name?—went on to overthrow Matty Sheehan and become one of the kings of Hell's Kitchen. How he and his friend made peace with the Cimino Family and became hit men for Big Paulie Calabrese, and how—if the rumors were true—he had gunned down Big Paulie outside Sparks Steak House just before Christmas.

Callan, the old man thinks.

Sean Callan.

Well, I recognize you, Sean Callan, but you don't seem to know me.

Which is good, which is good.

Mickey Haggerty finishes his drink, climbs off his stool and slips outside to a phone booth. He knows someone who'll be very interested to learn that Sean Callan is at a bar in the Gaslamp.

. . .

Must be the d.t.'s.

Callan reaches for his gun anyway.

But it's gotta be the d.t.'s—here at last—because there ain't no other explanation for Big Peaches and O-Bop standing over his bed in the Golden West Hotel, pointing their guns at him. He can see the bullets in their chambers, shiny and lethal, pretty and silver, reflected from the light of the street lamp outside, the fake gaslamp that the broken venetian blind can't block out.

The red neon from the porn shop across the street flashes like an alarm.

Too late.

If this ain't the d.t.'s, I'm already dead, Callan thinks. But he starts to pull the gun out from under his pillow anyway. Take them with him.

"Don't, you dumb fucking mick," he hears a voice growl.

Callan's hand freezes. Is this a drunk dream or reality? Are Big Peaches and O-Bop really standing in his room with their guns trained on him? And if they was going to shoot, why don't they shoot? They say if you die in your dreams you die in your life, but sometimes it's hard to tell the difference between dead and alive. Last thing he remembers is pounding beers and whiskeys at the bar. Now he wakes up (comes to) and he might be dead or he might be alive. Or is he back in the Kitchen, and the last nine years were a dream?

Big Peaches laughs. "What are you, some fucking hippie now? All that hair? The beard?"

"He's on a binge," O-Bop says. "An Irish sabbatical."

"You got that little .22 popgun under that pillow, don't you?" Peaches says. "I don't care how fucking drunk you are, you got that gun. Eeeeasy, there—we had come to whack you, you'd be dead before you woke up."

"Then why the guns?" Callan asks.

"Call it an abundance of caution," Peaches says. "You are Billy the Kid Callan. Who knows what brought you here? Maybe a contract on me. So bring the gun out slow."

Callan does.

Thinks for a half-second about popping them both, but what the hell.

Besides, his hand is shaking.

O-Bop gently takes the gun out of Callan's hand and tucks it into his own belt. Then he sits down beside him and wraps his arms around him. "Jesus, it's good to see you."

Peaches sits down on the foot of the bed. "Where the *fuck* you been? Jeez, we said go south, we didn't mean like the Antarctic. You fuckin' guy."

O-Bop says, "You look like shit."

"I *feel* like shit."

"Well, you look like it," Peaches says. "And what the fuck are you doing in this fucking toilet? Jesus, Callan."

"You got a drink?"

"Sure." O-Bop takes a half-pint of Seagram's out of his pocket and hands it to Callan.

He gulps down a heavy belt. "Thanks."

"You fucking Irish," Peaches says. "You're all drunks."

"How'd you find me?" Callan asks.

Peaches says, "Little Mickey Haggerty, speaking of drunks. He sees you at this shit-hole bar you been drinking at, he drops a dime, we find out you're living in the Golden West Hotel, we can't fucking believe it. The fuck happened to you?"

"A lot."

"No shit, huh," Peaches says.

"What'd you come for?"

"Get you the fuck out of here," Peaches says. "You're coming home with me."

"New York?"

"No, dumb fuck," Peaches says. "We live *here* now. Sun Diego, baby. It's beautiful. A beautiful thing."

"We got a crew going," O-Bop explains. "Me, Peaches, Little Peaches, Mickey. Now you."

Callan shakes his head. "No, I'm done with that shit."

"Yeah," Peaches says, "whatever you're doin' now is obviously working. Look, we'll talk about that later. Now we gotta get you sobered up, get some good food into you. A little fruit—you wouldn't believe the fruit out here. Not just the peaches, either. I'm talking pears, oranges, grapefruit so pink and juicy they're better than sex, I'm telling you. O-Bop, get your boy some clothes together, let's get him out of here."

Callan's drunk enough to be compliant.

O-Bop scoops some of his shit up and Peaches walks him out.

Tosses a c on the front desk and tells them the bill is settled, whatever the fuck it is. All the way out to the car—and Peaches got himself a new Mercedes—O-Bop and Peaches are telling Callan how great it is out here, what a sweet thing they got going.

How the streets are paved with gold, baby.

Gold.

.   .   .

The grapefruit sits like a fat sun in a bowl.

Fat, swollen, juicy sun.

"Eat it," Peaches says. "You need your vitamin C."

Peaches has become a health nut, like everyone else in California. He's still three bills and change, but now he's a *tan* three bills and change with a low cholesterol number and a high-fiber diet.

"I spend a lot of time on the can," he explains to Callan, "but I feel fucking great."

Callan doesn't.

Callan feels exactly like a man who's been on a years-long bender. He feels like death, if death feels really shitty. And now fat, tan Big Peaches sits there nagging him about eating his fucking grapefruit.

"You got a beer?" Callan asks.

"Yeah, I got a beer," Peaches says. "*You* ain't got a beer. And you ain't getting no beer, either, you fucking alcoholic. We're going to get you straightened out."

"How long have I been here?"

"Four fucking days," Peaches says. "And every moment a delight with you puking, crying, mumbling, hollering about shit."

What shit was I hollering about? Callan wonders. It's kind of worrisome because the dreams were bloody and bad. The goddamn ghosts—and there were a lot of them—just wouldn't go away.

And that fucking priest.

I forgive you. God forgives you.

No, He don't, Father.

"Man, I wouldn't want to see a picture of your fucking liver for anything," Peaches is saying. "Must look like an old tennis ball. I play tennis now, I tell you that? Play every morning, except the last four mornings I been playing nursemaid instead. Yeah, I play tennis, I Rollerblade."

Three hundred twenty pounds of Big Peaches on wheels? Callan thinks. Talk about your accidents waiting to happen . . .

"Yeah," O-Bop says, "we took the wheels off a Mack truck, put them on the blades for him."

"Fuck you, Brillo Pad," Peaches said. "I blade pretty good."

"People get the fuck out of his way, I'll tell you that," O-Bop says.

"You ought to get some exercise other than lifting your fucking elbow," Peaches says to O-Bop. "Yo, Lost Weekend, eat your goddamn grapefruit."

"What do you, peel it first?" Callan asks.

"Honest to God, fucking idiots. Gimme the thing."

Peaches gets a knife, cuts the grapefruit in half, then carefully slices it into sections and puts it back in Callan's bowl. "Now you eat it with your spoon, fucking barbarian. You know the word 'barbarian' came from the Romans? It meant 'redheaded.' They was talking about *you* people. I saw that on the—what do you call it?—the History Channel, last night. I love that shit."

The doorbell rings and Peaches gets up and goes to answer it.

O-Bop grins at Callan. "Peaches in that bathrobe, he looks like some old *mamma mia,* don't he? He's even getting tits. All he needs is them fuzzy pink slippers with the little pom-poms on 'em. Honest to God, you should see him on those Rollerblades. People like *run* out of the way. It's like some Japanese horror movie. Wopzilla."

They hear Peaches say, "Come in the kitchen, see what the cat dragged in."

Couple of seconds later, Callan's looking up at Little Peaches, who gives him a big hug.

"They told me about this," Little Peaches says, "but I didn't believe it until I saw it. Where have you been?"

"Mexico mostly."

"They don't got phones in Mexico?" Little Peaches asks. "You can't call people, let them know you're alive?"

"Where was I supposed to call you?" Callan asks. "You're in the Witness Fucking Protection Program. If I could find you, so could other people."

"All the other people are in Marion," Peaches said.

No shit, Callan thinks. You put them there. Old-school Big Peaches turned into the most spectacular songbird since Valachi. Put Johnny Boy in prison for life and then some. Not that life is going to be long—word is, Johnny Boy has throat cancer.

It's good, though, that Peaches flipped, because Callan don't have to worry about him calling Sal Scachi, who can't be happy that Callan has gone off the reservation. Callan knows too much about Scachi's work—all that Red Mist shit—to be out there in the wind, so it's a good thing that him and Peaches are disconnected.

Little Peaches turns to his brother. "Are you feeding this guy?"

"Yes, I'm feeding him."

"Not this grapefruit shit," Little Peaches says. "Jesus Christ, get him some *sausiche,* a little prosciutto, some raviolis. If you can find any. Callan, they got a Little Italy in this town, you couldn't get a cannoli with a machine gun. Italian restaurants here they serve sun-dried tomatoes. What is that? A couple years out here I *am* a sun-dried tomato. It's always eighty-three and sunny here, even at night. How do they do that, huh? Is anyone gonna get me some coffee, or do I have to order it like I'm in a fucking restaurant?"

"Here's your fucking coffee," Peaches says.

"Thank you." Little Peaches sets a box on the table and sits down. "Here, I brought doughnuts."

"Doughnuts?" Peaches says. "Why are you always sabotaging me?"

"Hey, Richard Simmons, don't fucking eat them if you don't want them. Nobody's putting a gun to your head."

"You fucking asshole."

"Because I don't come to my brother's house empty-handed," Little Peaches says to Callan. "Good manners make me a asshole."

"A *fucking* asshole," Peaches says as he grabs a doughnut.

"Callan, eat a doughnut," Little Peaches says. "Eat five. Every one you eat is one my brother doesn't, I don't have to listen to him whine about his figure. You're *fat,* Jimmy. You're a fat, greasy guinea. Get over it."

They go out on the patio because Peaches thinks Callan should get some sun. Actually, Peaches thinks that Peaches should get some sun, but he doesn't want to seem selfish. It's Peaches' opinion that there's no reason to live in San Diego if you're not going to go sit in the sun every chance you get.

So he leans back in the chaise, opens up his robe and starts to slather his body with Bain de Soleil.

"You don't want to fuck with skin cancer," he says.

Mickey sure doesn't. Now he puts on his Yankees cap and sits under the patio umbrella.

Peaches opens a chilled can of peaches and scoops a few into his mouth. Callan watches a drop of the juice plop on his fat chest, then merge with the sweat and suntan lotion and run down his belly.

"Anyway, it's good you showed up," Peaches says.

"Why's that?"

"How would you like," Peaches says, "to do a crime where the victims can't go to the cops?"

"Sounds okay."

"Sounds 'okay'?" Peaches asks. "Sounds like heaven to me."

He lays it out for Callan.

Drugs go north—Mexico to the States.

Money goes south—the States to Mexico.

"They just put the bones—six, sometimes seven figures—into cars and drive it across the border, into Mexico," Peaches says.

"Or not," Little Peaches adds.

They've done three of these jobs already, and now they got word that a narco safe house in Anaheim is bursting with cash and has to make the trip south. They got the address, they got names, they got the make of the car and the license plate. They even got an idea about when the couriers are going to make the run.

"Where are you getting the info?" Callan asks.

"A guy," Peaches answers.

Callan figured it was a guy.

"You don't need to know," Peaches says. "He takes thirty points."

"It's like being back in the dope business, except better," O-Bop says. "We get the profits but we never have to touch the stuff."

"It's just basic, honest crime," Peaches says. "Stick 'em up, give me the money."

"The way the Good Lord meant it to be," Mickey says.

"So, Callan," Little Peaches says. "You in?"

"I dunno," Callan answers. "Whose money are we taking?"

"The Barreras'," Peaches answers with this sly, questioning look in his eye, asking, *Is that a problem?*

I don't know, Callan thinks. Is it?

The Barreras are as dangerous as sharks, not people you fuck with thoughtlessly. That's one thing. Also, they're "friends of ours"—according to Sal Scachi anyway—so that's another thing.

But they murdered that priest, straight up. That was a hit, not an accident. A stone-pro killer like Fabián *"El Motherfucking Tiburón"* don't shoot nobody at point-blank range on accident. It just don't happen.

Callan don't know *why* they killed the priest, he just knows that they did.

And they made me part of it, he thinks.

So there's gotta be payback for that.

"Yeah," Callan says. "I'm in."

The West Side gang is back together again.

O-Bop watches the car pull out of the driveway.

It's three in the morning and he's tucked down in his own rig, half a block away. He has an important job to do: Follow the courier car without getting spotted and confirm that it goes onto the 5. He punches a number into his cell phone and says, "It's on."

"How many guys?"

"Three. Two in front, one in back."

He hangs up, waits a few seconds, then eases out.

As per plan, Little Peaches calls Peaches, who calls Callan, who calls Mickey. They start the chronometers on their watches and wait for the next call. Mickey has it timed, of course, the average drive time from the driveway to the on-ramp of the 5—six-point-five minutes. So they know within a minute or so when they should get the next call.

If they get the call, the plan is in place.

If they don't, they're going to have to improvise, and no one wants that. So it's a tense six minutes. Especially for O-Bop. He's the one doing the work right now, the one who can fuck it all up if he gets himself spotted, who has to stay where he can see them but they don't see him. He lays off at varying distances. A block, two blocks. He gives a left-turn signal and flips his headlights off for a second so he looks like a different car when he turns them back on.

O-Bop works it.

While Little Peaches sits, sweating, an hour and a half south on the 5.

For three minutes.

Four.

Big Peaches is in a booth at Denny's off the highway, just a little north of Little Peaches. He's scarfing down a cheese omelet, home fries, toast and coffee. Mickey don't like them eating before a job—a full stomach complicates things if you get shot—but Peaches is like, Fuck that. He don't want to jinx himself by taking precautions about what if he gets shot. He polishes off the greasy potatoes, takes two Rolaids out of his pocket and chews on them while he looks at the sports section.

Five minutes.

Callan tries not to look at his watch.

He's lying on the bed in a motel room at the Ortega Highway exit, off the 5. Got HBO on and he's watching some movie he don't even know what it is. No point in him sitting out there on a bike in the cold. If the couriers get on the 5 there'll be plenty of time. Looking at his watch ain't gonna change anything, it's just gonna make him nervous. But after what seems to be about ten minutes he gives in and looks.

Five and a half minutes.

Mickey don't look at his watch. The call will come when it comes. He's sitting in a car parked at the Oceanside Transportation Center. He smokes a cigarette and goes through in his head what happens if the couriers *don't* take the 5. Then what they *should* do is call it off, wait for the next time. But Peaches ain't gonna let them do that, so they'll have to scramble. Try to guess the route from the info that O-Bop's giving them and find a way to get ahead of the courier car and then figure out a place to take them down.

Cowboy-and-Indian stuff. He don't like it.

But he won't look at his watch.

Six minutes.

Little Peaches is about to yank.

A million in cash on the line and—

The phone rings.

"We're good," he hears O-Bop say.

He presses the restart button on his watch. One hour and twenty-eight minutes is the average drive time from the on-ramp to this exit. Then he calls Peaches, who picks the phone up without taking his eyes off the paper.

"We're good."

Peaches checks his watch, calls Callan and orders a piece of cherry pie.

Callan gets the call, coordinates his watch, phones Mickey, then gets up and takes a long, hot shower. There's no hurry and he wants to be loose and relaxed, so he stands in there awhile and lets the steaming water pound his shoulders and the back of his neck. He can feel the adrenaline start to build, but he don't want it to get too high too soon. So he makes himself take the time to shave slowly and carefully, and he feels good when he notices that his hand isn't shaking.

He also takes his time dressing. Slowly puts on black jeans, a black T-shirt and a black sweatshirt. Black socks, black biker boots, a Kevlar vest. Then the black leather jacket, tight black gloves. He heads out. He paid in cash the night before and signed in with a fake name, so he just leaves the key in the room and locks the door behind him.

O-Bop's job is easier now. Not easy, but easier, as he can lay back a good distance from the courier car and get closer only as they get near off-ramps. He has to make sure that they don't throw a curve and exit onto the 57 or the 22, or Laguna Beach Road or the Ortega Highway. But it seems like Peaches' hunch was right, these guys are headed straight up the gut—they're staying on the main road all the way down to Mexico. So O-Bop eases back, and now he can talk on the phone without fear of getting spotted, so he fills Little Peaches in on the details: "Blue BMW, UZ 1 832. Three guys. Brief-cases in the trunk." This last bit ain't great news, as it causes an extra step once they've taken the car down, but of course Mickey made them practice this option so O-Bop ain't too worried about it.

Mickey worries.

That's what Mickey does. He worries and waits until the Amtrak window opens, then he goes in and pays cash for a one-way fare to San Diego. Then he walks over to the Greyhound station and buys a ticket to Chula Vista. Then he goes back to his car and waits. And worries. They've practiced this dozens of times, but he still worries. Too many variables, too many what if's. What if there's a traffic jam, what if there's a state trooper parked nearby, what if there's a backup car and we don't see it? What if someone gets shot? What if, what if, what if . . .

"If my aunt had balls, she'd be my uncle," is what Peaches had said to all these worries. Now he finishes his pie, has another cup of coffee, leaves cash for the bill and tip (the tip just the right amount—not too small, not too large; he don't want to be remembered for any reason), and goes out to his car. Takes the gun out of the glove compartment, holds it low in his lap and checks the load. All the bullets are still there, like he thought they'd be, but it's a habit, a reflex. Peaches has this horror of going to pull the trigger some-day and hearing the dry click of an empty chamber. He straps the gun into his ankle holster and likes its comfortable weight as he starts the car and steps on the gas pedal.

Now they're all in place: Little Peaches off Calafia Road; Peaches on the Ortega Highway exit; Callan on his bike, waiting at the Beach Cities exit in Dana Point; Mickey at the Oceanside Transportation Center; O-Bop on the 5, following the courier car.

All in place.

Waiting for the stagecoach.

Which rolls right into the ambush.

O-Bop gets on the phone. "One half-mile out."

Little Peaches sees the car come past. Lowers his binoculars, hits the cell phone. "Now."

Callan pulls out onto the highway. "I'm on."

Peaches: "Got it."

Mickey starts a new chrono.

Callan sees the car in his rearview mirror and slows down a little and lets it pass him. No one in the car gives him so much as a glance. A lone biker headed south in the predawn darkness. It's twenty minutes to the empty stretch at Pendleton, where he wants to do it, so he drops back a little but keeps the car's taillights in sight. The commuter traffic is headed mostly north, not south, and the few cars that are headed their way will thin out even more as they leave the southernmost Orange County town of San Clemente.

They pass Basilone Road, then the famous surfing beaches called Tres-tles, then the two domes of the San Onofre Nuclear Generating Station, then the Border Patrol checkpoint that blocks off the northbound lanes of the 5 and then it gets empty and quiet. Nothing on their right except sand dunes and ocean, which are now beginning to emerge in the faint light as the rays of the sun start to appear on the left over Black Mountain, which dominates the Camp Pendleton landscape.

Callan has a mike and a headset inside his motorcycle helmet.

He utters a single word: "Go?"

Mickey answers, "Go."

Callan twists the accelerator, leans forward to cut down the wind resistance and speeds toward the courier car. Pulls beside almost exactly where he'd planned—on the long straightaway just short of the long right curve that sweeps toward the ocean.

The driver sees him at the last possible second. Callan sees his eyes widen in surprise, and then the car lurches forward as the driver steps on the gas. He's not worried about getting stopped by a cop now, he's worried about getting killed, and the Beamer surges ahead.

Momentarily.

This is why they got the Harley, right? This is why they bought the hog, basically an engine with two wheels and a seat attached to it. The fucking Harley ain't gonna lose to no yuppie-mobile. And it sure ain't gonna lose to no yuppie-mobile with two million dollars in cash for the taking.

So when the Beamer hits seventy, Callan hits seventy.

When it hits eighty, Callan hits eighty.

Ninety, ninety.

When it slides into the far right lane, Callan slides with it.

Back left, back left.

Back right, back right.

Beamer hits the hundred mph mark, Callan hits the century mark.

And now he lets his adrenaline loose. It's pumping through his veins like fuel through the bike's engine. Bike, engine, rider, adrenaline singing now, sailing, flying, Callan is in the zone now—pure adrenaline speed rush as he pulls even with the Beamer and the driver yanks the steering wheel to the left to try to ram him and almost does and Callan has to pull out and he almost loses it. Almost loses it at one hundred per, which would send him spinning out on the concrete, where he'd be just a smear of blood and tissue. But he rights the bike and pulls it behind the Beamer, which now has a ten-yard lead and then the back window opens and a Mac-10 peeks out and starts shooting like a tail gunner.

But maybe Peaches was right—even in a car you can't hit shit at that speed, and anyway Callan is leaning left and right, swaying the bike back and forth and the guys in the Beamer figure that ain't gonna work and they got a better chance with the gas pedal so they push it.

The Beamer hits 105, 110, and pulls ahead.

Even the Harley ain't gonna catch it.

Which is why Callan hit it where he did—because the straightaway ends in that gigantic sharp outside curve that the Beamer isn't going to handle at eighty, never mind a buck ten. That's the fucking thing about physics—it's uncompromising, so either the driver slows down and lets the shooter on the bike catch him or he goes flying off the road like a jet on a carrier deck, only this jet can't fly.

He decides to take his chances with the shooter.

Wrong choice.

Callan slides to the left, his foot nearly scraping the concrete. He comes out of the top side of the curve even with the driver's window and the driver freaks when he sees the .22 come up near his face. Callan fires one shot to spiderweb the window, then—

Pop pop.

Always two shots, right together, because the second shot automatically corrects the first. Not that it needs to in this instance; both shots go dead center.

The two .22 rounds are zipping around in the guy's brain like the balls in a pinball machine.

That's why the .22 is Callan's weapon of choice. It's not powerful enough to blast a round through a skull. Instead, it sends the bullet bouncing around inside the brainpan, frantically looking for an exit, lighting all the lights and then putting them out.

Game over.

No bonus play.

The Beamer whips into serial 360s and then goes off the road.

Stays on its feet, though—fine German engineering—but the two passengers are still in shock from whiplash as Callan pulls the bike over and—

Pop pop.

Pop pop.

Callan pulls back onto the highway.

Three seconds later, Little Peaches pulls in behind the Beamer. Gets out of his car with a shotgun in his left hand, just in case, walks up and opens the driver's door. Leans across the dead driver and takes the keys from the ignition. Walks to the back of the car, takes the briefcases from the trunk, gets back into his car and pulls out.

There must be a dozen cars spread out on the highway that see pieces of this scene, but none of them stop or pull over because Little Peaches is in a

California Highway Patrol car and a CHP uniform, so they have to figure he has it under control.

He does.

Gets back in the cruiser and calmly drives south. He ain't worried about getting stopped by a real cop, because moments before, right by Mickey's clock, Big Peaches hit a switch on a radio-control transmitter and in a vacant lot a half-block away an old Dodge van went up like an octogenarian's birthday cake and as Big Peaches pulls out for his next task he already hears the sirens screeching in his direction. He drives to the parking lot of a municipal golf course in north Oceanside and is sitting there when Little Peaches pulls in. Little Peaches takes the briefcases, gets out of the fake cop car and gets in with Peaches. As Little Peaches struggles out of his cop's uniform they drive toward the Oceanside Transportation Center.

O-Bop has passed the crashed Beamer, so he knows that at least part of the job has gone off, so he drives to the Highway 76 exit. There's a small dirt lot inside the cloverleaf and that's where Callan has pulled off. He leaves the Harley and gets in with O-Bop. They drive toward the transport center.

Where Mickey's waiting in his car.

Eyes on his watch, waiting.

The clock's running down.

Either the job's gone okay or his friends are hurt, dead, arrested.

Then he sees Little Peaches pull into the parking lot. They sit in the car until the train is announced and they can see it down the track, coming up from San Diego. Then they get out of their car, wearing conservative suits, each carrying a briefcase and a cardboard cup of coffee and an overnight bag slung over his shoulder, looking just like any other businessmen rushing to catch the train for a meeting in L.A. Mickey slips them their tickets as they walk past the car. They board moments before their trains pull out, and this is why they picked the Oceanside Transportation Center—because as the Amtrak train pulls up from the south, the local commuter train pulls out on a different track, headed south. Peaches takes one briefcase and gets on the L.A.–bound train. His brother takes the other case and heads south for San Diego.

As the trains depart the platforms, Callan and O-Bop pull into the parking lot and get out of the car. Their hair is cut short, Marine-style, and they're wearing the kind of bad clothes that Marines wear when they're off-duty. They sling their duffel bags over their shoulders, walk past Mickey's car and get their tickets and then walk over to the side of the transport station where the buses are parked. Just two more Marines out of Pendleton on leave. O-Bop gets on a bus bound for Escondido, Callan on one headed for Hemet.

Peaches has a ticket for L.A., but he doesn't take the whole ride. A few minutes south of the Santa Ana station, he goes into the lavatory and changes his clothes from the business geek's suit into California casual, and he doesn't come out until the train pulls into the station. Then he gets off at Santa Ana and checks into a motel. Little Peaches does a similar routine, only southbound, getting off in the funky surfing town of Encinitas and checking into one of those old roadside cottage motels across the PCH from the beach.

Mickey, he just drives back to his hotel. He hasn't been close to the action, and if the cops want to track him down and ask him any questions, he's got nothing to say anyway. He does his thirty-five per downtown and goes back to bed for a nap.

Callan and O-Bop take their full rides, O-Bop to a No-Tell Motel next to a porn shop, so he's happy and has things to do while he's lying low. He checks in, then walks over and buys twenty bucks' worth of tokens and spends most of the afternoon pumping the coins into the video machines.

Sitting on his bus, Callan tries to forget about having just killed three men, but he can't. He don't feel his usual nothin'; he feels something he can't put a name to.

I forgive you. God forgives you.

Can't get that shit out of his head.

He gets off his bus and checks into a Motel 6. The room ain't much, but it does have cable. Callan flops on the bed and watches movies on the television. The room smells of disinfectant, but it beats the Golden West.

The plan is to chill out for a few days, then if everything is cool—and there's no reason it shouldn't be—they're going to meet up at the Sea Lodge in La Jolla, chill out on the beach for a few days, call in some broads (Peaches actually says "broads") from Haley Saxon, have a party.

Callan remembers the girl he saw there, Nora. Remembers how much he wanted that girl, and how Big Peaches took her away from him. He remembers how beautiful she was, and thinking that if he could somehow touch that beauty it would make his own life less ugly. But that was a long time ago, a lot of blood's flowed under the bridge since then and it's not possible that the girl Nora is still in that house.

Is it?

He don't want to ask, though.

Three days later, Peaches is on the phone like he's ordering Chinese food: Whaddya want? A blonde, a brunette, how about a black chick? They're all hanging out in Peaches' room even though they all have adjoining rooms right on the beach. It's actually pretty cool, Callan thinks—you step right out of your room and you're on the beach, and he's getting off on watching the sun set over the ocean while Peaches is on the phone ordering pussy.

"Whatever," he tells Peaches.

"And a whatever," Peaches says into the phone, and then he chases them out because he's got business to do they don't need to be a part of. Take a swim, take a shower, have some dinner, get ready for the broads.

Peaches' business arrives about an hour later, after it's dark.

They don't talk a lot. Peaches just hands him a suitcase containing three hundred large in cash as his share for the information.

Art Keller takes the money and leaves.

Simple as that.

Haley Saxon has some business, too.

She decides on the five girls she's going to send to the Sea Lodge, then gets on the horn to Raúl Barrera.

Some wise guys from the old days are in town throwing around a lot of cash, and guess who they are. You remember Jimmy Peaches? Well, he suddenly came into a lot of money.

Raúl is very interested.

And sure, Haley knows exactly where they are.

Just leave my girls out of it.

Callan lies in bed watching the girl get dressed.

She's pretty, really pretty—long red hair, nice rack, nice ass—but she wasn't *her*. She got his rocks off, though, gave him his money's worth. Gave him head, then climbed on top of him and rode him until he came.

Now she stands in the bathroom fixing her makeup, and she sees him in the mirror, looking at her.

"We can go again if you want," she says.

"I'm good."

When she leaves he wraps a towel around himself and goes out onto the little terrace. Watches the small waves break silver in the moonlight. A nice-looking sports-fishing boat sits about a hundred yards out, its lights glowing golden.

It would be just goddamn tranquil, Callan thinks, if I couldn't hear Big Peaches going at it in the next room, still going at it. Fucking Peaches never changes—pulled his "I like your girl better" routine again, except this time it was his brother. Little Peaches didn't care—he'd already sent his girl to his room and he just said, "Take her," so they switched women and rooms and that's why Callan has to listen to Big Peaches huffing and puffing like an asthmatic bull.

They find Little Peaches' body in the morning.

Mickey knocks at Callan's door and when Callan answers it Mickey just grabs him and pulls him into Big Peaches' room and there's Little Peaches, tied to a chair with his hands in his pockets.

Except his hands aren't attached to his arms.

They're severed; the carpet is soaked in blood.

A washcloth is stuffed in Little Peaches' mouth and his eyes are bulging. You don't got to be Sherlock Holmes to figure out they chopped off his hands and left him to bleed out.

Callan can hear Big Peaches in the bathroom, crying and throwing up. O-Bop sits on the bed, holding his head in his hands.

The money is gone, of course.

What's in the closet instead is a note.

KEEP YOUR HANDS IN YOUR *OWN* POCKETS.

The Barreras.

Peaches comes out of the bathroom. His fat face is red and streaked with tears. Little bubbles of snot pop out of his nostrils. "We can't just leave him," he cries.

"We got to, Jimmy," Callan says.

"I'll get 'em," Peaches says. "Last thing I do, I'll pay these bastards back."

They don't pack or nothing. Just get into their separate vehicles and go. Callan drives all the way up past San Francisco, then finds a little motel near the beach and holes up.

Raúl Barrera has his money back, although it's three hundred thousand light.

Raúl knows that money went to whoever gave the Piccone brothers the tip.

But—and give Little Peaches credit, the man was tough—he never told them who it was.

Claimed he didn't know.

. . .

Callan goes into the basement in Seaside, California.

He finds one of them old cabin-style motels not far from the beach and pays in cash. He doesn't go out much at all the first few days. Then he starts taking long walks on the beach.

Where the surf whispers to him rhythmically.

I forgive you.

God . . .

11

Sleeping Beauty

His wonder was to find unwakened Eve
With tresses discomposed, and glowing cheek,
As through unquiet rest . . .

—John Milton, *Paradise Lost*

Rancho las Bardas
Baja, Mexico
March 1997

Nora sleeps with The Lord of the Skies.

That's Adán's new sobriquet among the narco-cognescenti—El Señor de los Cielos, The Lord of the Skies.

And if he's the Lord, Nora is his Lady.

Their relationship is in the open now. She's almost always with him. The narcos have tagged Nora, with intentional irony, La Güera, "The Blonde," Adán Barrera's golden-haired lady. His mistress, his adviser.

Güero was laid to rest in Guamuchilito.

The whole village attended the funeral.

So did Adán and Nora. He in a black suit, she in a black dress and veil, they walked in the cortege behind the flower-strewn hearse. A mariachi band played lachrymose *corridos* in praise of the deceased as the procession marched from the church Güero built, past the clinic and the soccer field he paid for, toward the mausoleum that held the remains of his wife and children.

People wept freely, ran up to the open casket and threw flowers on Güero's body.

His face in death was handsome, composed, almost serene. His blond hair was combed neatly straight back and he was dressed in an expensive charcoal-gray suit and conservative red tie instead of the black narco-cowboy garb he'd favored in life.

There were *sicarios* everywhere, both Adán's men and Güero's *veteranos,* but the guns were hidden under shirts and jackets out of respect for the occasion. And although Adán's men kept a sharp lookout, no one was too worried about the threat of an assassination. The war was over; Adán Barrera was the winner and, moreover, he was behaving with admirable respect and dignity.

It was Nora who had suggested not only that should he allow Güero to be buried in his hometown with his family, but that they attend the funeral, not just publicly but prominently. It was Nora who urged him to make large cash gifts to the local church, the local school and the clinic. Nora who led him into donating all the money for a new community center to be named after the late Héctor "Güero" Méndez Salazar. Nora who persuaded him to send emissaries in advance to assure Güero's *sicarios* and cops that the war was over, that no vengeance would be sought for past deeds and that operations would continue as before with the same personnel in place. So Adán marched in the funeral procession like a conquering lord, but a conquering lord who held the olive branch in one hand.

Adán walked into the little tomb and, again at Nora's urging, knelt beneath the little dome that held the pictures of Pilar, Claudia and Güerito and prayed to God for their souls. He lit a candle for each of them, then bowed his head and prayed in deep piety.

The shabby little piece of theater wasn't lost on the people outside. They understood it—they were used to death and murder and, in a strange way, reconciliation. By the time Adán emerged from the mausoleum they seemed to have almost forgotten that he was the one who'd filled it with bodies in the first place.

The memories were buried with Güero in his tomb.

This was a repeat of the process Adán and Nora had gone through for the funerals of El Verde and García Abrego, and everywhere they went it was the same. With Nora at his side, Adán endowed schools, clinics, playgrounds—all in the names of the deceased. Privately, he met with the dead men's former associates and offered them an extension of the Baja Revolution—peace, amnesty, protection and a lowered rate of taxation.

The word had gone out—you could meet with Adán or you could meet with Raúl. The wise majority met with Adán; the foolish few had funerals of their own.

The Federación was back, with Adán as its *patrón*.

Peace reigned, and with it, prosperity.

The new Mexican president took office on December 1, 1994. The very next day, two brokerage houses controlled by the Federación started to buy up *tesobonos*—government bonds. The next week, the drug cartels withdrew their capital from the Mexican national bank, forcing the new president to devalue the peso by 50 percent. Then the Federación cashed in its *tesobonos* and collapsed the Mexican economy.

Feliz Navidad.

As Christmas presents to themselves, the Federación bought up property, businesses, raw real estate and *pesos* and put them under the tree and waited.

The Mexican government didn't have the cash to honor the outstanding *tesobonos.* In fact, it was about $50 billion short. Capital was flying out of the country faster than preachers from a raided cathouse.

The country of Mexico was days away from declaring bankruptcy when the American cavalry rode in with $50 billion in loans to prop up the Mexican economy. The American president had no choice: He and every congressman on the Hill were getting frantic phone calls from major campaign contributors at Citicorp, and they came up with that $50 billion like it was lunch money.

The new Mexican president had to literally invite the narco lords back into the country with their millions of narco-dollars to reinvigorate the economy to pay back the loan. And the narcos now had billions more dollars than they did before the "*Peso* Crisis" because in the time between cashing in the *pesos* for dollars and the American bailout, they used the dollars to buy devalued *pesos,* which in turn rose again when the Americans issued the massive loan.

What the Federación basically did was buy the country, sell it back high, buy it again low, then reinvest in it and watch the investments grow.

Adán graciously accepted El Presidente's invitation. But the price he demanded for bringing his narco-dollars back into the country was a "favorable trade environment."

Meaning that El Presidente could shoot his mouth off all he wanted about "breaking the backs of the drug cartels," but he'd better not do anything about it. He could talk the talk but he couldn't walk the walk, because that stroll would be right off the gangplank.

The Americans knew it. They gave El Presidente a list of PRI bigwigs who were on the Federación's payroll, and suddenly three of these guys were appointed state governors. Another one became the transportation secretary, and another guy who made the list was appointed the drug czar himself—the head of the National Institute to Combat Drugs.

It was back to business as usual.

Better than usual because one thing Adán did with his windfall profits from the *Peso* Crisis was start buying Boeing 727s.

Within two years he has twenty-three of them, a fleet of jet aircraft larger than that of most Third World countries. He loads them full of cocaine in Cali and flies them to civilian airports, military airstrips and even highways that are closed down and guarded by the army until the plane is safely off-loaded.

The coke is packed into refrigerator trucks and driven to warehouses near the border, where it's broken down into smaller units and loaded into trucks and cars that are works of innovative genius. A whole new industry has been created in Baja, of "chop artists" who refit vehicles with hidden compartments called "stash holds." They have false roofs, fake floors and phony bumpers that are hollowed out and filled with dope. As in any industry, specialists have developed—you have guys who are known as great choppers and others who are sanders and painters. You have some guys who do things with Bondo that a Venetian plasterer could only dream of. Once the cars are prepared they're driven across the border into the United States and delivered to safe houses, usually in San Diego or Los Angeles, then earmarked for various destinations: L.A., Seattle, Chicago, Detroit, Cleveland, Philadelphia, Newark, New York and Boston.

The dope also goes by sea. It's delivered from its landing in Mexico to towns on the Baja coast, where it's vacuum-wrapped and then loaded into private and commercial fishing boats, which cruise up the coast to the waters off California and dump the dope into the water, where it floats until it's picked up by speedboats or sometimes even scuba divers who take it to shore and drive it to the safe houses.

It also goes by foot. Lower-end smugglers simply stuff it into packs and send it on the backs of *mujados* or coyotes who make the run across the border in the hope of making a fortune—say $5,000—for delivering it to a prearranged point somewhere in the countryside east of San Diego. Some of this countryside is remote desert or high mountains, and it's not unusual for the Border Patrol to find the corpse of a *mujado* who died from dehydration in the desert or exposure in the mountains because he wasn't carrying the water or blankets that might have saved his life, but was humping a load of dope instead.

The dope goes north and the money comes south. And both legs of this round-trip are a lot easier because border security has been relaxed by NAFTA, which assures, among other things, a smooth flow of traffic between Mexico and the United States. And with it, a smooth flow of drug traffic.

And the traffic is more profitable than ever because Adán uses his new power to leverage a better deal with the Colombians, which is basically "We'll buy your cocaine wholesale and do the retail ourselves, thank you." No more $1,000-a-kilo delivery charge; we're in business for ourselves.

The North American Free (Drug) Trade Agreement, Adán thinks.

God bless free trade.

Adán's making the old Mexican Trampoline look like a little kid bouncing on his bed. Hey, why bounce when you can fly?

And Adán can fly.

He's The Lord of the Skies.

Not that life has returned to the status quo ante bellum.

It hasn't; ever the realist, Adán knows that nothing can be the same after the murder of Parada. Technically he's still a wanted man: their new "friends" in Los Pinos have put a $5 million reward on the Barrera brothers, the American FBI has put them on the Most Wanted list, their photos hang on walls at border checkpoints and government offices.

It's a sham, of course. All lip service to the Americans. Mexican law enforcement is no more trying to hunt down the Barreras than it's trying to shut down the drug trade as a whole.

Still, the Barreras can't rub it in their faces, can't show them up. That's the unspoken understanding. So the old days are over—no more parties at big restaurants, no more discos, racetracks, ringside seats at big boxing matches. The Barreras have to give the government plausible deniability, allow them to shrug their shoulders to the Americans and claim that they would gladly arrest the Barreras if only they knew where to find them.

So Adán doesn't live in the big house in Colonia Hipódromo anymore, doesn't go to his restaurants, doesn't sit in a back booth doing the figures on his yellow manuscript pads. He doesn't miss the house, he doesn't miss the restaurants, but he does miss his daughter.

Lucía and Gloria are living back in America, in the quiet San Diego suburb of Bonita. Gloria goes to a local Catholic school, Lucía attends a new church. Once a week, a Barrera courier car meets her in a strip-mall parking lot and gives her a briefcase with $70,000 cash.

Once a month, Lucía brings Gloria down to Baja to see her father.

They meet at remote lodges in the country, or at a picnic spot by the side of the road near Tecate. Adán lives for these visits. Gloria is twelve now, and she's starting to understand why her father can't live with them, why he can't cross the border into the United States. He tries to explain to her that he's been falsely accused of many things, that the Americans take all the sins of the world and load them onto the backs of the Barreras.

But mostly they talk about more mundane things—how she's doing in school, what music she likes to listen to, movies she's seen, who her friends are and what they do together. She's getting bigger, of course, but as she grows so does her deformity, and the progress of the disease tends to accelerate in adolescence. The growth on her neck pulls her already heavy head down and to the left and makes it increasingly difficult for her to speak properly. Some of the kids at school—it is a cliché, he thinks, that children are cruel—tease her, call her the Elephant Girl.

He knows it hurts her, but she appears to shrug it off.

"They're idiots," she tells him. "Don't worry, I have my friends."

But he does worry—frets about her health, chides himself that he can't be with her more, agonizes about her long-term prognosis. He fights back tears when each visit comes to an end. As Gloria sits in the car, Adán argues with Lucía, trying to convince her to come back to Mexico, but she won't consider it.

"I won't live like a fugitive," she tells him. Besides that, she says she's afraid in Mexico, afraid of another war, afraid for herself and for her daughter.

These are reasons enough, but Adán knows the real reason—she has contempt for him now. She's ashamed of him, of what he does for a living, of what he's done for that living. She wants to keep it as far away from herself as possible, be a soccer mom, take care of their fragile daughter in the peace and tranquility of an American suburban life.

But she still takes the money, Adán thinks.

She never sends the courier car back.

He tries not to be bitter about it.

Nora helps.

"You have to understand how she feels," Nora tells him. "She wants a normal life for her daughter. It's tough on you, but you have to understand how she feels."

It's odd, Adán thinks, the mistress taking the side of the wife, but he respects her for it. She's told him many times that if he can get his family back together, he should, and that she would fade into the background.

But Nora is the comfort of his life.

When he's being honest with himself, he has to acknowledge that the bright side to his estrangement with his wife is that it's left him free to be with Nora.

No, The Lord of the Skies is flying high.
Until—

The supply of cocaine starts to dry up.

It doesn't happen suddenly. It's gradual, like a slow drought.

It's the fucking American DEA.

First they busted up the Medellín cartel (Fidel "Rambo" Cardona turned on his old friend Pablo Escobar and helped the Americans track him down and kill him), then they went after Cali. They picked off the Orejuela brothers as they were returning from a meeting in Cancún with Adán. Both the Medellín and Cali cartels fractured into small pieces—the "Baby Bells," Adán dubbed them.

It only makes sense, Adán thinks—a natural evolution in the face of ceaseless American pressure. Those who survive will be those who can stay small and low. Fly, as it were, under the American radar. It makes sense, but it also makes Adán's business more complicated and difficult—instead of dealing with one or two large entities, he now has to juggle dozens if not scores of small cells, and even individual entrepreneurs. And, with the demise of the vertically integrated cartels, Adán can no longer rely on the smooth and timely delivery of quality product. Say what you will about a monopoly, Adán thinks, it's efficient. It can deliver what it promises where and when it says it will, unlike the Baby Bells, with whom the prompt delivery of a quality product has become the exception rather than the rule.

So the production end of Adán's cocaine business is getting shaky, and this vibrates all the way down the line, from the wholesalers to whom the Barreras provided transportation and protection, to the new retail markets in Los Angeles, Chicago and New York that Adán took over after the Orejuelas' arrest. Increasingly, he has empty Boeing 727s—expensive to buy, maintain and staff—sitting on airstrips in Colombia, waiting for cocaine that's too often late or doesn't show up at all or, when it does get there, isn't of the promised quality and potency. So the customers on the street complain to the retailers, who complain to the wholesalers, who (politely) complain to the Barreras.

Then the flow of cocaine all but stops.

The flood becomes a stream, then a trickle, then a drip.

Then Adán finds out why:

Las Fuerzas Armadas Revolucionarias de Colombia.

Aka FARC.

The oldest and largest surviving Marxist insurgency movement in Latin America.

FARC controls the remote southwestern area of Colombia, along the critical borders with the cocaine-producing countries of Peru and Ecuador. From its stronghold there in the northwestern reaches of the Amazon jungle, FARC has waged a thirty-year-long guerrilla war against the Colombian government, the nation's wealthy landowners and the oil interests that operate from the petroleum-rich coastal districts.

And FARC's power is growing. Just last month, its guerrillas launched a daring attack on an army outpost in the town of Las Delicias. Using mortars and high-explosive charges, it took the fort, killed sixty soldiers and captured the rest. FARC cut off the critical highway connecting the southwestern districts to the rest of the country.

And not only does FARC control the cocaine-smuggling routes from Peru and Ecuador, it also has within its territory the Putumayo district, thick jungle and Amazonian rain forest and now also an important area for growing the coca plant. A domestic supply of coca was long a dream of the giant cartels, and they put millions of dollars of capital into coca plantations in the area. But just as their labors were coming to fruition, as it were, the cartels went out of business, leaving behind the chaotic Baby Bells and some 300,000 hectares under cultivation, and more being planted every day.

What Sinaloa was to the poppy, Putumayo is to the coca leaf—the source, the wellspring, the headwaters from which the drug traffic flows.

FARC cut it off, then reached out to him to offer to negotiate.

And I will have to do just that, Adán thinks now as he looks at Nora lying beside him.

She wakes up to see Adán looking at her.

Nora smiles, kisses him softly and says, "I'd like to go for a walk."

"I'll come with you."

They put on robes and step outside.

Manuel is there.

Manuel is always there, she thinks.

Adán has had a house built for him on the grounds. It's a small, simple house built in the Sinaloan *campesino* fashion. Except that Adán had the builder put it up in slightly outsized dimensions to allow for Manuel's stiff, dragging leg. Had special furniture built to make it easier for him to get up and down, and a little Jacuzzi put in the back to ease the aches in his leg, which get worse with age. Manuel doesn't like to use it, because he thinks it costs too much money to heat it, so Adán has a servant go over every night and turn it on.

Manuel gets up from a bench and follows them, his right leg dragging. At a discreet distance, he follows, with his distinctive limp. To Nora he is almost a caricature: an AK slung over his shoulder, a double loop of bandoliers over his shoulders like an old-time bandito, a pistol holstered at each hip, a huge knife tucked into his belt.

All he's missing, she thinks, are the big sombrero and the drooping mustache.

A maid comes scurrying out with a tray.

Two coffees: white and sweet for him; black, no sugar, for her.

Adán thanks the maid and she hurries back into the kitchen. She doesn't look at Nora, afraid that the *gringa*'s eyes will bewitch hers the way they did the *patrón*'s. It is the talk of the kitchen—look into the eyes of this *bruja* and you will come under her spell.

It was difficult at first, the staff's passive hostility and Raúl's active disapproval. Adán's brother thought it was fine to have mistresses but not to bring them into the family home. She heard the brothers quarrel about it and offered to leave, but Adán wouldn't hear of it. Now they've settled into a quiet domestic routine, which includes this morning walk.

The compound is beautiful. Nora loves it especially in the morning, before the sun reduces all the shapes to silhouettes and bleaches out all the colors. They start their stroll in the orchard because Adán knows that she loves the acrid smell of the fruit trees—orange and lemon and grapefruit—and the sweet smell of the mimosas and jacarandas, their blossoms dropping from their branches like lavender tears. They walk past the neatly ordered flower gardens—day lilies, calla lilies, poppies—and into the rose garden.

She looks at the flowers glistening with water, listens to the rhythmic *shoop-shoop-shoop* of the sprinkler system that sprays all the flowers before the sun makes watering an exercise in instant evaporation.

Adán shoos a peacock away from the garden.

Indeed, the compound is alive with birds: peacocks, pheasants, guinea fowl. One morning when Adán was away she went out early on her own and there was a peacock perched on the edge of the central fountain. It looked at her and spread its tail and it was a marvelous sight, all the colors spread out against the light khaki sand.

Other birds are in the trees. An amazing assortment of finches—Adán tries in vain to teach her their proper names, but she knows them only by colors: gold and yellow, purple and red. The warblers and the lazuli bunting, and the incredible western tanager that looks to her like a flying sunset. And the hummingbirds. Special flowers have been planted and sugar-water feeders hung to attract the hummingbirds—Anna's and Costa's and black-chinned, as Adán has tried to distinguish them for her. She knows them only as dazzling flights of jeweled colors, and that she would miss them very much if they no longer came to visit.

"You want to see the animals?" he says.

"Of course."

Adán is a practical, hardworking man and can't quite bring himself to approve of the time and money Raúl devotes to the menagerie. It's just another entertainment for Raúl, a sop to his ego that he has an ocelot, two kinds of camels, a cheetah, a pair of lions, a leopard, two giraffes, a herd of rare deer.

But no white tiger. Raúl sold it to some collector in Los Angeles, and the idiot tried to drive it across the border and got busted. Had to pay a big fine, and the tiger was confiscated. It lives in the San Diego Zoo now.

The whale he owned became a movie star. They busted out the amusement park for every penny it was worth then burned it down, and the whale ended up in a series of hit films. So the whale did pretty well for itself, although Adán hasn't seen it in any new movies lately.

So Adán and Nora walk through the private zoo in the morning, and one of the keepers is always ready with food for Nora to feed the giraffes. She loves their grace, their long necks and the way they walk.

She gets down from the little platform they use to feed the giraffes, picks up her coffee cup and moves ahead of Adán. Another keeper opens a gate to let her into the deer pen and hands her a plastic cup full of food.

"Good morning, Tomás."

"Señora."

The deer crowd around her, nuzzling her robe, pushing their noses out to get at the food.

Nora and Adán have breakfast on the east terrace, to catch the sun. She has grapefruit and coffee. That's all—grapefruit fresh from the orchard, picked literally moments before it is served to her, and coffee. He eats like one of Raúl's lions. An enormous plate of *huevos con machaca* with chunks of yellowtail and strands of hot chorizo. A stack of warm corn tortillas. At Nora's insistence, a bowl of fruit. And a small bowl of fresh salsa—the scent of its tomatoes and cilantro makes her mouth water, but she sticks with the slimming grapefruit.

He notices.

"It has no fat," he says.

"The tortilla I'd eat with it does."

"You have a few pounds to give."

"You're so gallant."

He smiles and goes back to his newspaper, knowing that he won't convince her. She's almost as obsessed with her body as he is. As soon as he showers and goes into his office for a day of work she'll spend the whole morning in the gym. He put in a stereo system and a television because she likes noise when she works out. And the gym has two of everything—two reclining cycles, two treadmills, two Universal weight machines, two sets of free weights—although she can rarely persuade him to work out with her.

On alternate days she runs on the long dirt road that winds up to the compound, which caused some complaint among the security staff until Adán found two *sicarios* who liked to run. Then she complained about it, said it made her self-conscious to have the men following her, but on this issue he put his foot down and there was no argument.

So when she runs two bodyguards trot behind her. At his specific instructions, they alternate running and trotting. He doesn't want them both out of breath at the same time. If it comes to shooting, he wants at least one of them to have a steady hand. And they have been told, "If anything happens to her, it's both your lives."

Her afternoons are long and slow. Because he works through lunch, she dines alone. Then she may take a short siesta, stretching out on the chaise under the umbrella, avoiding the sun. For the same reason, she spends most of the midafternoon indoors, reading magazines and books, idly watching Mexican television, basically waiting for Adán to show up before having a late dinner.

Now he says, "I have to go away on a business trip. I may be gone awhile."

"Where are you going?"

He shakes his head. "Colombia. FARC wants to negotiate."

"I'll come with you."

"It's too dangerous."

She tells him that she understands. She'll go to San Diego while he's gone—do some shopping, see a few movies, catch up with Haley.

"But I'll miss you," she says.

"I'll miss you, too."

"Let's go back to bed."

She fucks him with demonic energy. Grips him with her pussy, holds him tightly with her legs and feels him spurt deep inside her. Strokes his hair as he rests his face on her breasts and says, "I love you. *Tienes mi alma en tus manos.*"

You have my soul in your hands.

Putumayo, Colombia
1997

Adán sits in the back of a jeep bouncing slowly over a muddy, rutted road cut through the Amazonian jungle of southwestern Colombia. The air around him is hot and fetid, and he swats at the flies and mosquitoes that swarm around his head.

It's already been a difficult trip.

He rejected the idea of simply flying in on one of his 727s. No one can know that Adán is going to meet with Tirofio, the commander of FARC; anyway, the flight would have been too dangerous. If the American CIA or DEA intercepted the flight plan, the results would have been disastrous. And besides, there are *things* that Tirofio wants Adán to see en route.

So Adán first boarded a private sports-fishing yacht out of Cabo, then transferred to an old fishing boat for the long, slow trip for a landing on the southern Colombian coast at the mouth of the Coqueta River. This was the most dangerous part of the trip because the coastline is under control of the government and patrolled by the private militias hired by the oil companies to guard their drills and derricks.

From the fishing boat Adán climbed into a small, single-engine skiff. They went into the river at night, guided by the flames shooting out of the refinery towers like the signal fires of hell. The river mouth was silty and polluted, the air thick and dirty. They slipped up the river, past the oil-company properties, wrapped in ten-foot-high barbed-wire fences with guard towers at the corners.

It took them two days to get up the river, dodging army patrols and private security squads. Finally he'd got into the rain forest, and now he gets to make the rest of the trip by jeep. Their route takes them past the coca fields, and for the first time Adán sees the origins of the product that has made him millions.

Well, sometimes he does.

Other times he sees dead and wilted fields, poisoned by the helicopters that spray defoliants. The chemicals aren't particular—they kill the coca plants, but they also kill the beans, the tomatoes, the vegetables. Poison the water and the air. Adán walks through deserted villages that look like museum exhibits—perfect anthropological exhibits of a Colombian village, except no one's living there. They've fled the defoliants, they've fled the army, they've fled FARC, they've fled the war.

Other villages they pass have simply been burned out. Charred circles on the ground mark where huts once stood. "The army," his guide explains. "They burn the villages they think are in league with FARC."

And FARC burns the villages they think are in line with the army, Adán thinks.

They finally reach Tirofio's camp.

Tirofio's camouflage-clad guerrillas wear berets and carry AK-47s. A surprising number of them are women—Adán notices one particularly striking Amazon with long black hair flowing from beneath her beret. She meets his stare with one of her own, one of those what-are-you-looking-at glares that makes him turn his glance away.

Everywhere he looks he sees something going on—squads of guerrillas are training, others are cleaning weapons, doing laundry, cooking, policing the camp—and all the activity seems organized. The camp itself is large and orderly—neat rows of olive-green tents are set up under camouflage netting. Several kitchens have been constructed under thatched *ramadas*. He sees what appear to be a hospital tent and a dispensary. They even walk past a tent that houses a library of sorts. This is not a gang of bandits on the run, Adán thinks. It's a well-organized force in control of its territory. The camouflage nets—to disguise against airplane surveillance—are the only concession to a sense of danger.

The escort leads Adán to what looks like a headquarters area. The tents are larger, with canvas sunroofs attached to create porches, underneath which are washbasins, and chairs and tables made from rough-hewn lumber. A moment later the escort comes back out with an older, stocky man dressed in olive-green camouflage and a black beret.

Tirofio has a face like a frog, Adán thinks. Fatter than one expects from a guerrilla, with deep pouches under his eyes, heavy jowls and a wide mouth bent into what seems to be a permanent frown. His cheekbones are high and sharp, his eyes narrow, his arched eyebrows silver. Nevertheless, he looks younger than his almost seventy years. He walks toward Adán with vigor and strength—there is no shakiness in his short, heavy legs.

Tirofio looks at Adán for a moment, sizing him up, then points toward a thatched *ramada* under which are a table and some chairs. He sits down and gestures for Adán to do the same. Without any introduction he says, "I know that you help to support Operation Red Mist."

"It's not political," Adán says. "It's just business."

"You know that I could hold you for ransom," Tirofio says. "Or I could have you killed right now."

"And *you* know," Adán says, "that you would outlive me by perhaps a week."

Tirofio nods.

"So what do we have to talk about?" Adán asks.

Tirofio pulls a cigarette from his shirt pocket and offers one to Adán. When Adán shakes his head, Tirofio shrugs and lights the cigarette, then takes a long drag and asks, "When were you born?"

"Nineteen fifty-three."

"I started fighting in 1948," Tirofio says. "During a period they now call 'La Violencia.' Have you heard of that?"

"No."

Tirofio nods. "I was a woodcutter, living in a small village. In those days, *I* had no politics. Left wing, right wing—it made no difference to the wood I had to cut. I was up in the hills one morning, cutting wood, when the local right-wing militia came into our village, rounded up all the men, tied their elbows behind their backs and cut their throats. Left them bleeding to death like pigs in the village square while they raped their wives and daughters. Do you know why they did that?"

Adán shakes his head.

"Because the villagers had allowed a left-wing group to dig a well for them," Tirofio says. "That morning I came back to find the bodies lying in the dust. My neighbors, my friends, my family. I walked back into the hills, this time to join the guerrillas. Why do I tell you this story? Because you may say you have no politics, but the day you see your friends and family lying in the dirt, you will have politics."

Adán says, "There's money and the lack of money, and there's power and the lack of power. And that's all there is."

"You see?" Tirofio smiles. "You are half a Marxist already."

"What do you want from me?"

Guns.

Tirofio has twelve thousand fighters and plans to have thirty thousand more. But he has only eight thousand rifles. Adán Barrera has money and airplanes. If his planes can fly the cocaine out, they can fly the guns back in.

So if I want to protect my cocaine source, Adán realizes, I will have to do what this old warrior wants. I will have to get him guns to protect his territory from the right-wing militias and the army and, yes, the Americans. It is a practical necessity, but there is also a sweet measure of revenge in it. So he says, "Do you have an arrangement in mind?"

Tirofio does.

Keep it simple, he says.

One kilo equals one rifle.

For every rifle Adán flies in, FARC will allow one kilo of cocaine to be sold from its territory, at a price discounted to reflect the cost of the weapon. That's for a standard rifle—the AK-47 is the weapon of choice, but the American M-16 or M-2 is also acceptable, as FARC can get the right ammo from captured army troops or right-wing militias. For other weapons—and Tirofio desperately covets shoulder-held rocket launchers—they will allow a kilo and a half, or even two kilos.

Adán accepts without negotiating.

Somehow he feels it would be unseemly to bargain, almost unpatriotic. Besides, this deal will work. *If*—and it's a big *if*—he can get his hands on enough guns.

"So that's it, then," Adán says. "We have a deal?"

Tirofio shakes his hand. "One day you will come to see that everything is politics, and you will act from your heart instead of your pocket."

On that day, Tirofio tells him, you will find your soul.

Nora lays out clothes on the bed of their suite at a small hotel in Puerto Vallarta—shirts and suits she bought for Adán in La Jolla.

"You like?"

"I like."

"You've hardly looked at them," Nora says.

"I'm sorry."

"Don't be sorry," she says. She walks over and puts her arms around him. "Just tell me what's on your mind."

She listens attentively as Adán describes the logistical challenge he faces: where to get the quantity of military weapons he needs to fulfill his end of the deal with Tirofio. It's relatively easy to get a few weapons here and there—the United States is basically one big gun mart—but the thousands of rifles he'll need over the next few months, that's something even the American black market can't provide.

And yet the guns will have to come through America, not Mexico. As crazy as the Yanquis are about drugs coming across their border, the Mexicans are even more fanatic about guns. As much as Washington complains about narcotics coming across from Mexico, Los Pinos answers with complaints about guns coming in from the United States. It's a constant irritant in the relations between the two countries that the Mexicans seem to feel that firearms are more dangerous than dope. They don't understand why it is that, in America, you will get a longer jail sentence for dealing a little marijuana than you will for selling a lot of guns.

No, the Mexican government is sensitive about guns, as befits a country beset with a history of revolutions. Even more so now, with the insurgency in Chiapas. As Adán tells Nora, there is no way that he can import such a large amount of weaponry directly into Mexico, even if he can find a supplier. The guns will have to come into the States, then be smuggled by reverse route through Baja, loaded on a 727 and flown to Colombia.

"Can you even get that many guns?" Nora asks.

"I have to," Adán says.

"Where?"

Hong Kong
1997

The first glimpse of Hong Kong is always startling.

First there is the endless flight across the Pacific, with nothing but hours of blue water beneath, then suddenly the island pops up, a swatch of emerald green with tall towers glistening in the sun, and the dramatic hills behind.

He's never been there before. She has, several times, and points out landmarks through the window: Hong Kong itself, Victoria Peak, Kowloon, the harbor.

They check in to the Peninsula Hotel.

This is her idea, to stay on the mainland in Kowloon rather than in one of the modern businessmen's hotels on the island itself. She likes the colonial charm of the Peninsula, thinks that he'll like it, too, and besides, Kowloon is a far more interesting neighborhood, especially at night.

He does like the hotel—its old-style elegance appeals to him. They sit on the old veranda (now enclosed in glass) with its view of the harbor and the ferry landing, and have a full English tea (she orders) while they wait for their suite to be ready.

"This," she says, "is where the *old* opium lords used to hang out."

"Is that right?" he asks. He has very little knowledge of history, even of the drug trade.

"Sure," she says. "That's how the Brits got Hong Kong in the first place. They took it in the Opium War."

"The Opium War?"

"Back in the 1840s," Nora explains, "the British went to war against the Chinese to force them to allow the opium trade."

"You're kidding."

"No," Nora says. "As part of the peace treaty, the British opium traders got to sell their product in China, and the British crown got Hong Kong for a colony. So they'd have a port to keep the opium safe. The army and navy actually protected the dope."

"Nothing changes," Adán says. Then, "How do you know all these things?"

"I read," Nora says. "Anyway, I thought you might get a kick out of being here."

He does. He sits back, sips his Darjeeling, lathers his scone with clotted cream and jam, and feels as if he's one in a continuum of a long tradition.

When they get to their room, he collapses on the bed.

"You don't want to go to sleep," she tells him. "You'll never get over the jet lag."

"I can't stay awake," he murmurs.

"I can keep you awake."

"Oh yeah?"

Oh yeah.

Afterward, they shower and she tells him that she has the rest of the day and the evening planned, if he'll put himself in her hands.

"Didn't I just do that?" he asks.

"And did you enjoy it?"

"That was me screaming."

"Timing's critical," she says as he shaves. "Hurry up."

He hurries up.

"This is one of my favorite things in the world to do," she says as they walk down to the Star Ferry landing. She buys their tickets and they wait for a few minutes, then board the ferry. She chooses seats on the port side of the old, fire-engine-red boat, with the best view of downtown Hong Kong as they cross to the island. All around them, fishing boats, speedboats, junks and sampans ply the harbor.

When they land, she hustles him out of the terminal.

"What's the rush?" he asks as she grabs him by the elbow and pushes him ahead.

"You'll see, you'll see. Come *on*." She leads him down Garden Road to the base of Victoria Peak, where they hop the Tram. The Tram, a funicular, rattles up the steep grade.

"It's like an amusement-park ride," Adán says.

They get to the observatory just before the sun sets. This is what she wants him to see. They stand on the terrace as the sky grows pink and then red and then fades to darkness and the city's lights come on like a spray of diamonds against a black satin pillow.

"I've never seen anything like this," Adán says.

"I thought you'd like it," she answers.

He turns and kisses her.

"I love you," he says.

"I love you, too."

They meet the Chinese the next afternoon.

As arranged, a motor launch picks up Nora and Adán in Kowloon Harbor and takes them out into the bay, where they transfer to a waiting junk, on which they make the long trip to Silver Mine Bay on the east side of Lantau Island. Here the junk disappears into a fleet of thousands of other junks and sampans on which the "boat people" live. Their junk wends its way among the maze of docks, wharves and anchored boats before pulling alongside a large sampan. The captain sets a plank between his boat and the sampan, and Nora and Adán cross over.

Three men sit at a small table under the arch-shaped canopy that shelters the middle part of the boat. They get up when they see Adán and Nora come on board. Two of the men are older. One of them, Nora immediately sees, has the squared shoulders and rigid posture of a military officer; the other is more casual and a little stooped—he's the businessman. The third is a young man who is clearly nervous in the presence of high-ranking superiors. This, Nora thinks, must be the translator.

The young man introduces himself in English as Mr. Yu, and Nora translates this into Spanish even though Adán knows more than enough English to understand basic conversation. But it gives her a pretext for being here, and she's dressed for the role in a plain gray business suit with a high-collared ivory blouse and some simple jewelry.

Still, her beauty is not lost on the officer, Mr. Li, who bows when introduced, or on the businessman, Mr. Chen, who smiles and all but kisses her hand. The introductions having been performed, they sit down for tea and business.

Frustrating to Adán, the first part of the business is seemingly endless small talk and pleasantries, made all the more tedious by the double layer of translation from Mandarin to English, then English to Spanish, then back again. He'd like to cut to the chase, but Nora has warned him that this is a necessary part of doing business in China, and that he'd be considered a rude and therefore untrustworthy partner if he were to truncate the process. So he sits and smiles through the discussion of how beautiful Hong Kong is, then of the beauty of Mexico, of how wonderful its food, of how lovely and intelligent the Mexican people are. Then Nora praises the quality of the tea, and

Mr. Li responds that it is unworthy garbage, then Nora says that she wishes

—Of course, Li says, *given the modest volume, we would not be able to offer the same price as we can for larger orders.*

Adán answers, *Given as this order is just the beginning of what we hope will be a long business relationship, we were hoping that, as a good-faith gesture, you will offer us a price that will allow us to come to you for future needs.*

—Are you saying you cannot pay full price?

—No. I'm saying I won't *pay full price.*

Adán's done his homework, too. Knows that the PLA is as much a business as it is a national defense force, and that they are under great pressure from Beijing to produce revenue. They need this deal as much as I do, he thinks, maybe more, and the size of the order is nothing to sneeze at, nothing at all. So you are going to give me my price, General, especially if—

—Of course, Adán adds, *we would pay in American dollars. Cash.*

Because the PLA is not only under pressure to produce revenue, it's under pressure to produce foreign currency, and fast, and they don't want any unstable Mexican *pesos,* especially in the form of paper. They want the long Yanqui green. Adán likes the cycle: American dollars to China for guns, guns to Colombia for cocaine, cocaine to the United States for American dollars . . .

Works for me.

Works for the Chinese, too. They spend the next three hours haggling over the details—prices, delivery dates.

The general wants this deal. So does the businessman. So does Beijing. GOSCO is not only building facilities in San Pedro and Long Beach, it's also building them in Panama. And buying up huge tracts of land along the canal, which not only splits the American fleet in half but also sits astride the two emerging left-wing insurgencies in Central America—the FARC war in Colombia and the burgeoning Zapatista insurrection in southern Mexico. Keep the Americans busy in their own hemisphere for a change. Let them become more concerned about the straits of Panama than the straits of so-called Taiwan.

No, this arrangement with the Barrera cartel can only increase Chinese influence in the Americans' backyard, keep them busy putting out Communist brush-fires and also force them to spend resources on their War on Drugs.

A bottle of wine is procured and a toast made, to friendship.

"Wan swei," Nora says.

Ten thousand years.

In six weeks' time, a shipment of two thousand AK-47s and six dozen grenade launchers, with sufficient ammunition, will be shipped from Guang-zhou on a GOSCO freighter.

San Diego

A week after returning from Hong Kong, Nora crosses the border at Tecate, then takes the long, back-country drive through the desert and into San Diego. She checks into the Valencia Hotel and gets a suite with a view of La Jolla Cove and the ocean. Haley meets her and they have dinner at Top of the Cove. Business is good, Haley tells her.

Nora goes to bed early and gets up early. She changes into sweats and takes a long jog around La Jolla Cove, on the path that skirts the cliffs over-looking the ocean. She comes back tired and sweaty, orders her grapefruit and black coffee from room service and showers while she waits for her breakfast to be delivered.

Then she dresses and goes shopping in La Jolla Village. All the trendy shops are within walking distance, and she has a handful of bags before she hits her favorite boutique, where she selects three dresses and takes them into the changing room.

A few minutes later she comes out with two of the dresses, lays them on the counter and says, "I'll take these. I've left the red one in the dressing room."

"I'll hang it up," the owner says.

Nora thanks her, smiles and walks back out into the gorgeously sunny La Jolla afternoon. She decides on French cuisine for lunch and has no trouble getting a table at the Brasserie. She kills the rest of the afternoon with a movie and a long nap. She gets up, orders some consommé for dinner, then puts on one of her new black dresses and does her hair and makeup.

Art Keller parks three blocks away from the White House and walks the rest of the way.

He's lonely. He has his work and little else.

Cassie is eighteen now, soon to graduate from Parkman; Michael is six-teen, a freshman at the Bishop's School. Art goes to Cassie's volleyball matches and Michael's swim meets, and he takes the kids out afterward if they don't already have plans with their friends. They have awkward once-a-month weekends at his downtown condo—he makes extravagant efforts to entertain them, but they mostly just hang around the complex pool with the other "visitation daddies" and their kids. And his own kids increasingly resent the mandated visits, which interfere with their own social lives.

Art understands and usually lets them cancel with a fake-cheery "Next time."

He doesn't date. He's had a few short-term relationships with a couple of divorced women—convenience fucks scheduled between the demands of busy careers and the single parenthood of teenage kids—but they were more sad than satisfying, and pretty soon he quit trying.

So most nights he keeps company with the dead.

They're never too busy and there's no lack of them. Ernie Hidalgo, Pilar Talavera and her two kids. Juan Parada. All collateral casualties in Art's private war with the Barreras. They visit him at night, they chat with him, they ask him if it was worth it.

At least for now, the answer is no.

Art's losing the war.

The Barrera cartel now makes a profit of approximately $8 million a week. Fully one half of the cocaine and a third of the heroin that hits American streets comes through the Baja cartel. Virtually all the methamphetamine west of the Mississippi originates with Barrera.

Adán's power is unchallenged in Mexico. He's put his uncle's Federación together again, and he is the undisputed *patrón*. None of the other cartels can touch his influence. Furthermore, Barrera has established his own cocaine supply in Colombia. He's independent of Cali or Medellín. The Barrera drug operation is self-sustaining from the coca plant to the corner, from the poppy flower to the shooting gallery, from the sinsemilla seed to the brick that hits the streets, from the base ephedrine to the rock of crystal meth.

The Baja cartel is a vertically integrated polydrug operation.

And none of the above takes into account his "legitimate" businesses. Barrera money is heavily invested in the *maquiladoras* along the border, in real estate throughout Mexico—especially in the resort towns of Puerto Vallarta and Cabo San Lucas—and the southwest United States and in banking, including several banks and credit unions in the States. The cartel's financial mechanisms are fully enmeshed with those of Mexico's wealthiest and most powerful business concerns.

Now Art reaches the front door of the White House and rings the bell.

Haley Saxon comes into the foyer to meet him.

Smiles professionally and hands him the key to a room upstairs.

Nora's sitting on the bed.

She looks stunning in her black dress.

"Are you okay?" he asks.

The red dress was her signal that she had to see him personally. For over two years now, she's been leaving him messages in "dead drops" all over the city.

It was Nora who gave him the details of the Orejuela brothers' meeting with Adán, the info that allowed the DEA to arrest them as they flew back to Colombia.

Nora who has given him a rundown on the new organization of the Federación.

Nora who has provided him with hundreds of pieces of intelligence, from which he's been able to glean a thousand more. Thanks mostly to her, he has an organizational chart of the Barrera organization in Baja and in California. Delivery routes, safe houses, couriers. When drugs were coming in, money going out, who killed whom and why.

She's risked her life to bring him this information on her "shopping trips" to San Diego and Los Angeles, on her visits to spas, on any trip that she takes outside of Mexico and without Adán.

The method they use is surprisingly simple. The fact is that the drug cartels have a bigger budget and therefore better technology than Art does, and they don't have the constitutional restrictions. So the only way to beat the Barreras' superiority in high-tech is to go low-tech: Nora simply sits in her hotel room, writes down her information and mails it to Art at a post office box that he established under a false name.

No cell phones.

No Internet.

Just the good ol' U.S. Mail.

Unless there was an emergency; then she would leave the red dress in the changing room. The boutique owner was looking at a possession rap that could have sent her to prison for five years. Instead, she agreed to do this favor for The Border Lord.

"I'm fine," Nora says.

But she's angry.

No, angry doesn't describe it, she thinks as she looks at Art Keller. You said that with my help you would take Adán down quickly, but it's been two and a half years. Two and a half years of pretending to love Adán Barrera, of taking a man I *loathe* inside me, feeling him in my mouth, my pussy, my ass, and pretending to love it. Pretending to love this monster who killed the man I really loved, and then guiding him, molding him, helping him to get the power to commit more of his filth. You don't know what it's like—how could you?—to wake up in the morning with *that* beside you, to crawl between his legs, to open yours, to scream your phony orgasms, to smile and laugh and share talk and meals, all the time living a nightmare, waiting for you to act.

And so far, what have you done?

Besides the Orejuela arrest, nothing.

He's been sitting on this information for two and a half years, waiting for the right moment to act.

Now Art says, "This is too risky."

"I can trust Haley," she says. "I want you to take some action. *Now.*"

"Adán's still untouchable. I don't want to—"

She tells him about Adán's deal with FARC and the Chinese.

Art looks at her with awe. He knew she was smart—he's been tracking her as she's helped to steer Adán through the shoals—but he didn't know that she was *this* perceptive. She's thought it through.

Damn right I have, Nora thinks. She's been reading men all her life. She sees the change come over his face, his eyes are lit with excitement. Every man has his own turn-on. She's seen them all, and now she sees Keller's.

Revenge.

Same as mine.

Because Adán has made a serious mistake. He's doing the one thing that could bring him down.

And we both know it.

"Who else knows about the arms shipment?" he asks.

"Adán, Raúl and Fabián Martínez," she says. "And me. Now you."

Art shakes his head. "If I act on this, they'll know it was you. You can't go back."

"I'm going back," Nora says. "We know San Pedro and GOSCO. But we don't know which ship, which pier—"

And even if you can get that information, Art thinks, making the bust is the same as killing you.

When he's about to leave she asks, "Do you want to fuck me, Art? For the sake of realism, of course."

His loneliness is palpable, she thinks.

So easy to touch.

She opens her legs ever so slightly.

He hesitates.

It's a small measure of revenge for leaving her "asleep" for so long, but it feels good and she says, "I was joking, Art."

He gets it.

Payback.

He knows that leaving an undercover in place for as long as he has is unconscionable. Six months is a long time, a year is the max. They just can't last that long—their nerves unravel, they get burned, the information they provide gets tracked back to them, the clock just runs out.

And Nora Hayden isn't a professional. Strictly speaking, she isn't even an undercover, but a confidential informant. It doesn't matter—she's been under deep cover, and she's been under for too long.

But I couldn't have used any of the information she gave me in Mexico, because Barrera is under Mexican protection. And I couldn't have used any of her intelligence inside the States, because it might have compromised her before we could take Adán down once and for all.

The frustration has been awful. Nora has given him enough intelligence to virtually destroy the Barrera organization in one overnight coup, and he hasn't been able to use it. All he could do was wait and hope that The Lord of the Skies flew too close to the sun.

And now he has.

It's time to pull the trigger on him. And time to get Nora out.

I could just arrest her now, he thinks. God knows there are enough pretexts. Arrest her, compromise her and then she could never go back. Get her a new identity and a new life.

But he doesn't.

Because he still needs her close to Adán, for just a little while longer. He knows he's stretching her string to the breaking point, but he lets her walk out of the room.

"I need proof," John Hobbs says.

Solid, tangible evidence to show the Mexican government before he can even think about prodding them to launch an offensive against Adán Barrera.

"I have a source," Art says.

Hobbs nods—yes, go on.

Art answers, "I can't reveal it."

Hobbs smiles. "Aren't you the same man who rather famously created a source that didn't actually exist?"

And now Keller, with his well-known Barrera obsession, comes forward with a story about Adán Barrera making a deal with FARC to import Chinese arms in exchange for cocaine? Something that would get the CIA solidly on board in his war against the Barreras? It's a bit too convenient.

Art gets that. I'm the Boy Who Cried Wolf.

"What kind of proof?" he asks.

"The arms shipment would do nicely, for example."

But that's the dilemma, Art thinks. Busting the arms shipment would expose exactly what I'm trying to protect. If I could get Hobbs to pressure Mexico City into launching a preemptive strike against Barrera now, there'd be no need to put Nora in jeopardy. But to get them to launch the strike, I have to produce the arms shipment, and the only person who can get me that is Nora.

But if she does it, she's probably dead.

"Come on, John," he says, "you could mask this from the Chinese side. Intercepts of maritime radio signals, Internet traffic, satellite intelligence— just say you have a source in Beijing."

"You want me to compromise valuable sources in Asia to protect some *drug dealer* that you flipped? Please."

But he is tempted.

The Zapatistas in Chiapas are more active than ever, their ranks reportedly swelled by recent refugees from neighboring Guatemala, so the potential exists there for a Communist insurgency that could spread regionally.

And a new left-wing insurgent group, the EPR, the Ejército Popular Revolucionario, the Popular Revolutionary Army, emerged back in June at a memorial service for peasants in Guerrero killed by right-wing militias. Then, just weeks ago, EPR launched simultaneous attacks against police posts in Guerrero, Tabasco, Puebla and Mexico itself, killing sixteen police officers and wounding another twenty-three. The Vietcong started smaller than that, Hobbs thinks. He offered his Mexican intelligence counterparts assistance against the EPR, but the Mexicans, ever sensitive about Yanqui neo-imperialist interference, declined.

Stupidly, Hobbs thinks, because it takes only a quick glimpse at the map to see that the Communist insurgency is spreading north from Chiapas, fueled by the economic devastation of the *Peso* Crisis and the dislocations caused by NAFTA implementation.

Mexico is teetering on the brink of revolution, and everyone but the ostriches in State know it. Even Defense acknowledges the possibility— Hobbs has just finished reading the top-secret contingency plans for a U.S. invasion of Mexico in the event of a total social and economic breakdown. God, one Castro in Cuba is enough—can you imagine a Comandante Zero ruling from Los Pinos? A Marxist government sharing a two-thousand-mile border with the United States? And every state along that border soon to have a Hispanic majority? But God, wouldn't the Mexicans hemorrhage cats if they ever got wind of that report?

No, the Mexicans can accept American military aide only through the veil of the War on Drugs. Not unlike the American Congress, Hobbs thinks. The Vietnam Syndrome prevents Congress from authorizing a penny to wage covert wars against Communists, but they'll always open the vault to fight the drug war. So you don't go to Capitol Hill to tell them you're helping your allies and neighbors defend themselves against Marxist guerrillas; no, you send your supporters in the DEA to ask for money to keep drugs out of the hands of America's young people.

So Congress would never authorize, nor would the Mexicans openly accept, the offer of seventy-five Huey helicopters and a dozen C-26 airplanes to fight the Zapatistas and EPR, but Congress has funded the same package to help the Mexicans suppress the drug traffickers, and the equipment will be quietly transferred to the Mexican army for use in Chiapas and Guerrero.

And now you have the *patrón* of the Federación providing weapons to Communist insurgents in Colombia? That would get the Mexicans solidly on board.

Art plays his last card. "So you're just going to let a shipment of arms go through to Communist insurgents in Colombia? Not to mention the increase of Chinese influence in Panama?"

"No," Hobbs says calmly. "*You* are."

"Screw you, John," Art says. "If this goes down, the CIA gets *nothing*. I don't share intel, assets, credit, nothing."

"Give me the source, Arthur."

Art stares at him.

"Then get me the guns," Hobbs says.

But I can't, Art thinks. Not until Nora tells me where they are.

Mexico

There's a meeting going on at Rancho las Bardas, too.

Between Adán, Raúl and Fabián.

And Nora.

Adán insisted that she be included. The fact is that they wouldn't have the deal in place without her.

It doesn't sit well with Raúl.

"Since when do our *baturras* know our business?" he asks Fabián. "She should stay in the bedroom, where she belongs. Let her open her legs, not her mouth."

Fabián chuckles. He'd like to open La Güera's legs, *and* her mouth. She's the most delectable piece of *chocho* he's ever seen. You're wasting yourself with a wimp like Adán, he thinks. Come to me, *tragona*, I'll make you scream.

Nora sees the look on his face and thinks, Try it, asshole. Adán would have you skinned alive and roasted over a slow fire. And I'd bring the marshmallows.

The Chinese want cash on delivery, and will accept no other form of payment, not a wire transfer or a series of laundered payments through shell companies. They insist that the payment be absolutely untraceable, and the only way to do that is a hand-to-hand cash transferral.

And they want Nora to make it.

It's a guarantee for them, Adán sending his beloved mistress.

"Absolutely not," Adán and Raúl say simultaneously, albeit for completely different reasons.

"You first," Nora says to Raúl.

"You and Adán haven't exactly kept your relationship under wraps," Raúl says. "The DEA probably has more photographs of you than they do of me. If you are arrested, you have a lot of information inside that pretty head, and motivation to give it up."

"What would they arrest me for, sleeping with your brother?" Nora asks. She turns to Adán. "Your turn."

"It's too dangerous," he says. "If anything went wrong, you'd be looking at life in prison."

"Then let's make sure nothing goes wrong," she says.

She lays out her case—I go back and forth across the border all the time. I'm an American citizen with an address in San Diego. I'm an attractive blonde and can flirt my way through any checkpoint. And, most important, it's what the Chinese want.

"Why?" Raúl asks suddenly. "Why would you take the risk?"

"Because," she says, smiling, "in return, you'll make me rich."

She waits as her answer just hangs there.

Finally, Adán says, "I want the best chop-artist in Baja. Maximum security at both sides of the border. Fabián, get our best people in California to make the actual pickup. I want you there personally. If anything happens to her, I hold you *both* responsible."

He gets up and walks out.

Nora just sits and smiles.

Raúl follows Adán out into the garden.

"What are you thinking about, *hermano*?" he asks. "What's to stop her from turning on us? What's to stop her from just taking the money and never looking back?! She's a *whore,* for God's sake!"

Adán whirls around and grabs him by the front of his shirt. "You're my brother and I love you, Raúl. But if you ever talk about her that way again, we'll split the *pasador* and go our separate ways. Now please just do your job."

As Nora waits in the line at the San Ysidro border crossing, Baja's best chop-artist sits in a chair on the tenth floor of an apartment building overlooking the checkpoint. He's a little nervous because he's been asked to guarantee his work—if the car gets busted going across the border, Raúl Barrera is going to put a bullet in the back of his head.

"Just so you have a rooting interest," Raúl said.

He doesn't know where the car is going, he doesn't know who's taking it there, but he does know that it's unusual for cash to be heading north across the border instead of coming south. He's built stash-holds all over the non-descript Toyota Camry, and that little baby is loaded down with millions of American dollars. He only hopes that the Border Patrol doesn't decide to weigh the car.

So does Nora. She's not too concerned about a visual search, or even dogs, because the pooches have been trained to sniff for drugs, not cash. Even so, the bundles of hundred-dollar bills have been soaked in lemon juice to neutralize any smell. And the car itself is fresh—it's never been used to carry dope, so there can't be any residual scent.

There is residue of sand, however, carefully left on the driver's-side floor and in the backseat with some damp towels, a hooded sweatshirt and a pair of old flip-flops.

The wait at the border today is over an hour and a half, which is a pain in the ass. But Adán insisted that she cross on a late Sunday afternoon, when the crossing is the busiest, jammed up with thousands of Americans returning home from weekends at the cheap resorts in Ensenada and Rosarita. So she has ample time to work her way over into the third lane, where the Border Patrol agent coming on duty is on the Barrera payroll.

It hasn't been left to chance, though. Raúl stands at the window of the apartment and peers out through binoculars. There are three apartment towers overlooking the border from the Mexican side, and the Barreras own all three. Now Raúl watches his paid Border Patrol agent take his position and look up toward the apartment tower.

Raúl punches digits into his pager.

Nora's pager beeps and she looks to see the numbers 666 on the little display screen—the narco-code for "All clear." She nods to the driver in the Ford Explorer in front of her. The man is looking into his rearview mirror and now he turns right into the third lane, setting a pick for Nora to turn behind him. The Jeep Cherokee behind her does the same thing, making space for her. Horns honk, middle fingers are raised, but Nora is going to get into that third lane.

Now all she has to do is wait and fend off the squadrons of vendors who walk up and down the line of cars hawking sombreros, *milagros,* Styrofoam jigsaw-puzzle maps of Mexico, sodas, tacos, burritos, T-shirts, baseball caps, just about anything you can think of, to the bored people waiting to cross. The border wait is one long, narrow open-air marketplace, and she buys a cheap gaudy sombrero, a poncho and a MY GIRLFRIEND WENT TO TIJUANA AND ALL I GOT WAS THIS LOUSY T-SHIRT to fortify her tourist profile and also because she always feels bad for the street vendors, especially the kids.

She's three cars away from the checkpoint when Raúl looks through his binocs and yells, "Fuck!"

The chop-artist jumps up from his chair. "What?"

"They're switching. Look."

Raúl peers down. A Border Patrol supervisor is rotating the agents into different lines. It's a common practice, but the timing is awfully close to be just coincidence.

"Do they know something?" the chop-artist asks. "Should we abort?"

"Too late," Raúl answers. "She can't turn around."

Sweat pops on the chop-artist's forehead.

Nora sees the agent being changed out and thinks, Please God, no, not now, when I'm so close. She feels her heart start to race and makes a deliberate effort to breathe deeply and slow it down. Border agents are trained to look for signs of anxiety, she tells herself, and you want to be just one more blond chick coming back from a hard-partying weekend in Mexico.

The Ford Explorer pulls up to the checkpoint. It's "chock-full-o'-Chicanos," as Fabián had put it, again part of the plan. The agent will spend a lot of time checking this car out and be more likely to give her just a cursory look. Sure enough, the agent is asking a lot of questions, walking around the Explorer, looking in the windows, checking IDs. The golden retriever comes out and scurries around the vehicle, sniffing happily and wagging its tail.

It's good that it's taking time, Nora thinks, it's part of the plan. But it's also excruciating.

Finally, the Explorer clears the checkpoint and Nora pulls up. She pushes her sunglasses up on her forehead to give the agent the full benefit of her blue eyes. But she doesn't say hello or start the conversation—the agents look for people who are overly friendly or eager.

"ID?" the agent asks.

She shows him her California driver's license, but has her passport in plain sight in the passenger seat. The agent notices.

"What were you doing in Mexico, Ms. Hayden?"

"I came down for the weekend," she says. "You know, some sun, the beach, a few margaritas."

"Where did you stay?"

"At the Hotel Rosarita." She has receipts matching her Visa card in her purse.

The agent nods. "Do they know you took their towels?"

"Oops."

"Are you bringing anything back into the country?"

"Just this stuff," she says.

The agent looks at the tourist shit she bought in line.

This is the critical moment; he's going to wave her through, or search the car a little more, or pull her off into the inspection lane. Options one and two are acceptable, but option three could be a disaster, and Raúl's holding his breath as he watches the agent lean through the window and look into the backseat.

Nora just smiles. Taps her foot and hums along with the classic-rock station on the radio.

The agent leans back out.

"Drugs?"

"What?"

The agent smiles. "Welcome back, Ms. Hayden."

"She's through," Raúl says.

The chop-artist says he needs to take a piss.

"Don't get too relaxed!" Raúl yells to him. "She still has to get through San Onofre!"

The phone rings on Art Keller's desk.

"Keller."

"She's in."

Art stays on the line to get the make of the car, a description and the license-plate number. Then he phones the Border Patrol station at San Onofre.

. . .

Adán gets a similar call in his office.

"She's through," Raúl says.

Adán feels better but he's still worried. She still has to get through the checkpoint at San Onofre, and that's his fear—the San Onofre checkpoint sits on an empty stretch of Route 5 just north of the Marine base at Pendleton, and the area is rife with electronic surveillance and radio jammers. If the DEA were going to grab her, they would grab her there, far from the Barrera lookout towers or any possible help in Tijuana. It's entirely possible that Nora is driving straight into an ambush at San Onofre.

Nora drives north on the 5, the major north-south arterial that runs the length of California like a spine. She drives past downtown San Diego, past the airport and SeaWorld, past the big Mormon temple that looks like it's made from spun sugar and would melt in the rain. She drives past the exit to La Jolla, past the racetrack at Del Mar, and speeds past downtown Oceanside before she finally pulls over at a rest stop just south of the Marine base at Camp Pendleton.

She gets out and locks the car. She can't see the Barrera *sicarios* who are parked nearby, but she knows they're in one car or another, or maybe several, to guard her vehicle while she uses the bathroom. It's highly doubtful that anyone is going to steal a used Toyota Camry, but nobody's taking the chance with several million dollars in cash in the car.

She uses the toilet, then goes to a sink to wash her hands and freshens her makeup. The cleaning lady waits patiently while she finishes. Nora smiles, thanks her and gives her a dollar bill before going back out. She buys a Diet Pepsi from a vending machine, gets back in the car and starts driving north. She loves this stretch of highway that runs through the Marine base because once you get past the barracks it's mostly empty. Just the range of hills to the east and to the west, nothing but the lanes of southbound traffic and then blue Pacific.

She's been through the San Onofre checkpoint hundreds of times—most southern Californians have, if they make the trip from San Diego up to Orange County. It's always been kind of a joke, she thinks as the traffic in front of her slows, a "border" checkpoint seventy miles from the border. But the fact is that many illegals are on their way to the Los Angeles metro area, and most of them use the 5, so maybe it makes sense.

What usually happens is that you get to the checkpoint, tap your brakes, and, if you're white, the Border Patrol agent waves you through with a bored sweep of the hand. That's what usually happens, she thinks as she stops about a dozen cars before the checkpoint, and that's what she's expecting.

Except this time the Border Patrol guy signals her to stop.

Art looks at his watch—again. It should be going down now. He knows when she crossed the border, when she hit the rest stop. If she didn't turn around somewhere, if she didn't get hinky and change her mind, if . . . if . . . if . . .

Adán paces the office. He also has a timetable in mind, and Nora should be calling in soon. She wouldn't risk a call near the surveillance at Pendleton, and there's nothing for her to say until she's through San Onofre, but she should be through by now. She should be in San Clemente, she should be . . .

The agent signals for her to roll down the window.

Another agent walks over to the passenger side. She rolls that window down, too, then looks at the agent beside her, gives him her best beautiful look and asks, "Is there something wrong?"

"Do you have ID on you?"

"Sure."

She digs through her handbag for her wallet, then holds the wallet open for the agent to see her license. As she does, the agent on the passenger side pushes the tracking device between the headrest and the seat as he leans in to examine the back.

The first agent takes a long time looking at the license, then says, "Sorry for the inconvenience, ma'am," and waves her through.

Art grabs the phone before the first ring stops.

"Done."

He hangs up and blows out a long breath of relief. He has the aerial surveillance in place now, a mix of military-aircraft "traffic" helicopters and private planes, and can track her all the way.

And when she meets with the Chinese, we'll be there.

.   .   .

Nora waits until she's in San Clemente before she picks up the cell phone and punches in the number in Tijuana. When Fabián answers, she says, "I'm through," and hangs up.

Now it's just a matter of driving north until the Chinese give them a time and location for the meeting.

So that's what she does.

She just drives.

Adán gets the call from Raúl that Nora is through the San Onofre check-point, and goes outside for a walk. Now it's just a matter of waiting.

Yeah, he thinks, just waiting.

Fabián has trucks standing by in Los Angeles, waiting to take delivery of the arms and drive them to the border at an isolated spot in the desert, where they'll be transferred to different trucks, driven to several different airstrips and then flown to Colombia.

It's all in place—but first Nora has to make that first, all-important trans-action with the Chinese. And before she can do that, the Chinese have to tell them where and when.

Art also has men standing by—squadrons of heavily armed DEA agents, Federal Marshals, FBI—holed up in San Pedro waiting for the word. The San Pedro Harbor is huge, and the GOSCO facilities there are enormous—row after row of cargo warehouses, so they have to know, specifically, which one to hit. It's a tricky operation because they have to lay off until the deal is in place, but then get in there quickly.

Art's in a helicopter now, watching an electronic map of Orange County and a red blinking light that represents Nora. He debates with himself. Put a ground unit on her now, or wait? He decides to wait as she takes the 405 North exit off the 5 and heads for San Pedro.

No surprises there.

But he is surprised when the blinking red light gets off the 405 at MacArthur Boulevard in Irvine and turns west.

"What the fuck is she doing?" Art says out loud. He tells the pilot, "Pull in on her!"

The pilot shakes his head. "Can't! Air-traffic control!"

Then Art gets what the fuck she's doing.

"Goddamnit!"

He calls for ground units to hustle to John Wayne Airport. But the map tells him that there are five potential exits out of the airport, and he'll be lucky to cover even one of them.

She gets off MacArthur at the airport exit and pulls in to the parking structure.

Art's helicopter hovers over the 405, north of the airport. It's his best hope, that she pulled into the airport to block audio surveillance, is getting the location in San Pedro, and will shortly pull back onto the highway.

Or, Art thinks, she's taking millions of dollars in cash and getting on an airplane. He watches the screen but the blinking red light is just gone.

Nora gets on the cell phone.

"I'm here," she says.

Raúl gives her an address in nearby Costa Mesa, about two miles away. She pulls out of the structure and turns west on MacArthur, away from the 405, then turns onto Bear Street into the nondescript flat gridiron of Costa Mesa.

She finds it, a small garage on a street full of small warehouses. A man with a Mac-10 machine pistol slung over his arm opens the door and she pulls in. The door closes behind her, and then it's like the Formula 1 race she once went to with a client—a crew of men instantly jump the car with power tools, take it apart and put the money into Halliburton briefcases and then into the trunk of a black Lexus.

This, she thinks, would be the moment for a rip-off, but none of these men are even tempted. They're all illegals with family back in Baja and they know that Barrera *sicarios* are parked in front of their homes with orders to kill everyone inside if the money and the courier don't leave that garage quickly and safely.

Nora watches them work with the smooth, silent efficiency of a first-class pit crew. The only sound is the whine of power drills, and it takes only thirteen minutes to disassemble the car and reload the money in the Lexus.

The man with the machine pistol hands her a new cell phone.

She calls Raúl. "Done."

"Give me a color."

"Blue," she says. Any other color would mean that she's being held against her will.

"Go."

She gets into the Lexus. The garage door opens and she pulls out. Gets back on Bear and ten minutes later she's back on the 405, heading toward San Pedro. She drives right under a traffic helicopter circling the area.

Art stares at the empty screen.

Nora Hayden, he finally admits to himself, is in the wind.

She knows it, she gets it, she's driving north into God knows what and now she's doing it alone. Which is nothing new for Nora—except for her too few years with Parada, she's been doing it alone her whole life.

But she doesn't know how she's supposed to get this done now. Or what's going to happen. The easiest thing in the world would be to just take the money and keep going, but that won't get her what she wants.

It's nighttime as she passes through Carson, its natural-gas drills burning like signal towers in some sort of industrial version of hell. Working the plan, she gets off this time at the LAX exit and calls in.

They have the place for the meet.

An AARCO gas station heading west on the 110 exit.

On the way to San Pedro.

"Give me a color."

"Blue."

"Go."

For a second she thinks about just using the cell and calling Keller on the hotline number he gave her, but then the number would show up on phone records, and besides, the car might be bugged. So she just drives to the gas station and pulls up by the pump. A car flashes its lights. She pulls over by a row of phone booths (God, does anyone use pay phones anymore? she wonders) and sits there while an Asian man with a small briefcase in his hand gets out of the other car and walks over to the passenger side of her car.

She unlocks the door and he gets in.

He's a young man, probably mid-twenties, dressed in the black suit, white shirt and black tie that seem to be a uniform for young Asian businessmen these days.

"I'm Mr. Lee," he says.

"Yeah, I'm Ms. Smith."

"I'm sorry," Lee says, "but please turn around and put your hands on the door."

She does it and he frisks her for wires. Then he opens the briefcase, takes out a small electronic sweeper and checks the car for bugs. Satisfied it's clean, he says, "You will forgive me, I hope."

"No problem."

"Let's drive."

"Where to?"

"I'll tell you as we go."

He gives her directions and they head for the harbor.

Art has the GOSCO harbor facility under surveillance.

It's his last, best shot.

A DEA agent sits high atop a gigantic crane, his powerful night-vision glasses trained on the GOSCO entrance, and he sees the black Lexus coming down the street.

"Vehicle approaching."

"Can you ID the driver?" Art asks.

"Negative. Tinted windows."

It could be anyone, Art thinks. It could be Nora, it could be a GOSCO manager coming to check on a warehouse, it could be a john finding a dark spot for a quick blow job.

"Stay on it."

He doesn't want to be on the horn too much. If this is really going down, the narcos will have audio sweepers going, and even though his transmissions are encrypted, the sad fact is that the narcos have a bigger budget and better technology.

So now he sits in the back of a hippie van three miles from the harbor and waits.

It's all he can do.

Nora drives down a street between two rows of GOSCO warehouses that run perpendicular to their two loading wharves. Two huge GOSCO freighters are pulled up at the wharves. Sparks fly from welders doing repairs on the ships, and forklifts scurry back and forth between the wharf and the warehouses. She keeps driving until they're in a quieter area.

A warehouse door opens and Lee directs her inside.

"I lost them," the agent says to Art. "They went into a warehouse."

"*Which* goddamn warehouse?"

"Could be one of three," the agent answers. "D-1803, 1805 or 1807."

Art consults a plan of the GOSCO facility. He can have teams at the location inside ten minutes and cut the group of warehouses off from two sides. He switches channels and says, "All units, prepare to move in five."

Mr. Lee is polite.

He gets out, comes around and opens the car door for Nora. She gets out and looks around her.

If there's a huge shipment of weapons in here, it's cleverly disguised as a whole bunch of empty shelves and a black Lexus identical to the one she drove in.

She looks at Lee and raises her eyebrows.

"Do you have the money?" he asks.

She opens the trunk, then the briefcases. Lee flips through the stacks of used bills, then closes everything up again.

"Your turn," Nora says.

"We'll wait," he says.

"For what?"

"To see if the police arrive."

"This wasn't part of the plan," Nora says.

"It wasn't part of *your* plan," Lee says.

They stare at each other for a few long moments.

"This," she says, "is *really* boring."

She gets back in the car and sits down, thinking, Please God, don't let Keller come blasting through that door.

Shag Wallace's voice comes across the radio.

"On your signal, boss."

Art tightens his Kevlar vest, flips the safety of his M-16 off, takes a deep breath and says, "Go."

"Roger that."

"Hold!" he yells into the mike. It comes from his gut—something's wrong here, something's hinky. They've been too careful, too cute. Or maybe I'm just getting chicken in my old age. But he says, "Stand down."

Fifteen minutes.

Twenty.

Half an hour.

Nora reaches for her phone.

"What are you doing?" Lee asks.

"Calling my people," Nora says. "They're going to be wondering what the hell happened to me."

He hands her his own phone. "Use this one."

"Why?"

"Security."

She shrugs and takes the phone. "Where are we?"

"Don't send them here," Lee says.

"Why not?"

He has a little self-satisfied smile on his face. Nora's seen it on men a thousand times, usually after one of her spectacular fake orgasms. "The merchandise isn't here."

"Where is it?"

Now that no police have arrived at this location, he feels it's safe to tell her the real one. Besides, he has Adán Barrera's mistress as insurance.

"Long Beach."

The new GOSCO facility at Long Beach Harbor, he tells her.

Pier 4, Row D, Building 3323.

She calls Raúl and gives him the information. When she hangs up she says to Lee, "We have to call our boss and get the okay for this change of plans."

Art Keller is sweating bricks.

If that was Nora who went into the warehouse, she's been there for over half an hour. And nothing's happened. No one has gone in or come out, no trucks have arrived. Something's gone wrong.

"All units stand by," he says. "We're going on my signal."

Then his cell phone rings.

Lee listens anxiously as Nora tells Adán Barrera all about how they took her to an empty building and put a gun to her head as a test, and how the guns are really at Long Beach, "Pier 4, Row D, Building 3323."

"Pier 4, Row D, Building 3323," Art Keller says.

"You got it," Nora says.

She hangs up and hands the phone back to Lee.

"Let's get going," she says.

He shakes his head. "We're staying here."

"I don't understand."

She understands when he takes a .45 from beneath his black suit jacket and lays it on his lap. "When the transaction is safely completed," he says, "I will take the car with the money, and you will take the other car and drive away. But if something unfortunate should occur . . ."

Long Beach, Art thinks.

Fucking Long Beach. We have to get down there before Barrera's trucks can get there and load up. He gets on the radio and tells his people to scramble. We have to move this goddamn army down to Long Beach, and do it in a hurry.

Fabián Martínez is thinking pretty much the same thing. He has a freaking convoy on the road now, three semis painted as CALEXICO PRODUCE COMPANY that he had ready to go to San Pedro, and now they have to roll down the 405 to freaking Long Beach.

Pain in the ass.

He sits in the passenger seat of the lead truck with a Mac-10 under his coat.

Just in case.

Two of his best men are in a scout car about half a mile ahead. They'll go in first, and if they spot anything that shouldn't be there, they'll send him a beeper message to get the fuck out.

It's cold for a southern California night, even in March, and he pulls his collar up around his neck and tells the driver to turn on the fucking heat.

Nora sits in the front seat of the Lexus and waits.

"Do you mind if I turn on the radio?" she asks.

Lee doesn't mind.

Racing down to Long Beach, Art reformulates his plan.

What goddamn plan? he thinks. That's the problem. He *had* a tactical plan for the raid in San Pedro, but now it's just going to be a make-it-up-as-you-go cavalry charge into God knows what, and that makes him very goddamn nervous.

The best thing to do would be to let the Barrera trucks make the pickup and hit them on the road. But he has to make sure that Nora is all right. So the bust has to be at the warehouse, and now it just has to be smash-and-grab. Go in fast, go in hard.

All the agents have been briefed—they all know that The Border Lord wants La Güera bad, and he wants her alive because she can be pressured into giving up her boyfriend. They know that, Art thinks, but will they remember it in the chaos of a raid, especially if the Barrera people decide to shoot it out?

It has all the potential for a major-league goat fuck, and Nora could end up dead.

He radios back to Shag again to make sure he understands.

Fabián's scout cars don't see anything they don't like, and they give him the 666 signal.

It's one in the morning and the Long Beach complex is busy with trucks loading freight. Which is very good, Fabián thinks. What's three more?

He finds Pier 4, then Row D, then Building 3323, an enormous Quonset hut like all the rest. He hops out of the truck and knocks on the office door. He stands outside, stamping his feet, as two Chinese men inspect his trucks—the cabs and the trailers. Then the big metal door of the building slides open.

Fabián climbs back into the cab of the lead truck and leads them in.

Nora startles when Lee's cell phone rings.

She sees Lee's hand tighten on the pistol grip as he answers it. She sucks in a deep breath and readies herself to make a grab at his wrist as he hangs up, turns to her and says, "Your people are there. Everything's okay."

"Good," she says. "Let's get going."

He shakes his head.

"Not yet."

Fabián stands talking with the Chinese guy in charge.

"You got your money?"

"Yes."

"Where is she?"

"In another location," the man says. "As soon as this transaction is safely concluded, she will rejoin you."

Fabián doesn't like it. Not because he cares about Nora Hayden—other than wanting to fuck her in half, he wouldn't care if she *did* get smacked—but because Adán *does* care, and is holding him responsible for Nora's safety. And these slants are holding her hostage? Not good at all. So he says, "Get her on the line."

Lee hands Nora the phone. "They want to speak to you."

Nora takes the phone.

"Give me a color," Fabián says.

"Red."

Fabián gives the Chinese guy back his phone, then takes his Mac-10 from his jacket and sticks it in the guy's face.

"Call your boy back," he says. "Tell him it's cool."

Guns appear from everywhere. All Fabián's men pull, and all the Chinese guys. Except most of the Chinese are up in catwalks, aiming down, so they have a tactical advantage.

It's your basic stalemate.

Which disappears when the office door blows in.

It's just chaos.

Art's the first through the door, with a phalanx of agents behind him. He throws the switch and the metal cargo door opens again to reveal another platoon of DEA, FBI, and ATF, a whole lethal alphabet soup with automatic rifles, shotguns, Kevlar vests and bullet-resistant visors, nightlights shining from the tops of their helmets.

The agents are yelling at the top of their lungs.

"FREEZE!"

"DEA!"

"GET DOWN! GET DOWN!"

"FBI!"

"DROP YOUR WEAPONS!"

Weapons clatter on the metal catwalks and the concrete floor. Fabián thinks about trying to shoot it out but quickly sees that it's futile, lets his Mac-10 slide to the floor and puts his hands up.

Art looks around for Nora. It's hard to spot anything in the chaos, with men running, other men hitting the floor, agents grabbing people and throwing them down. He looks for her blond hair and doesn't see it, so he screams into his radio mike, "GO!" hoping Shag can hear him over the cacophony, praying it's not too late.

Beside him, a Chinese guy is yelling into a cell phone.

Art grabs him by the collar, throws him down and kicks the phone from his hand.

Lee hears his boss screaming over the phone.

Nora sees his eyes widen and then the gun comes up, pointed straight at her forehead.

She screams.

Over the dull *thump* of an explosion.

Blood and bone spray against the passenger window.

Lee's body slumps back into the seat and Nora turns to see the SWAT sniper standing in the doorway, the door hanging crooked off its blown hinges.

She's still screaming as Shag Wallace slowly approaches the car, opens her door and gently takes her by the elbow.

"It's all right," he's saying. "You're all right. Come on now, we have to get you out of here."

He takes her out of the car, walks her outside and puts her in the front seat of his own car. "Wait here for a minute."

Shag goes back into the warehouse, gets into the front seat of the Lexus and takes the .45 from Lee's dead hand. Then he holds it a few inches away from Lee's forehead, aims it at the entry wounds and pulls the trigger.

He wipes the gun and goes out to his car.

Sits next to Nora and tells her to hold the .45 for a second. Numb with shock, she does what he says. Then he takes the gun back and says, "Here's your story: Things went sick and wrong. He was going to shoot you. You grabbed the gun, you fought, you won. Do you understand that?"

She nods.

She thinks she understands. She's not sure. Her hands won't stop shaking.

"Are you okay?" Shag asks. "Look, it's all right if you're not. If you want to stop this right now, just say the word. We'll understand."

"Have they arrested Adán?" she asks.

"Not yet," Shag answers.

She shakes her head.

* * *

Art kneels on Fabián's neck and attaches the plastic telephone ties to his wrists.

"It was that cunt, wasn't it?" Fabián asks.

Art kneels down a little harder as he recites Fabián's rights.

"Fucking right I'm going to want a lawyer," Fabián says.

Art hauls him to his feet, shoves him into one of the DEA vans and walks over to inspect the two cargo containers—twenty feet long, eight feet wide and eight feet high—filled with crates.

His men take them out and bust them open.

Chinese-made AK-47s—two thousand of them—spill out of the boxes in pieces: barrels, magazines, stocks. Other tools include two dozen Chinese KPG-2 rocket launchers, which are considered especially valuable because they are handheld.

Two thousand rifles equals two thousand kilos of cocaine, Art thinks. God only knows how many kilos you get passed through for the rocket launchers, which are capable of shooting down helicopters.

Next they find six truckloads of M-2 rifles, converted M-1s, the standard army carbine. The difference between the original and the M-2 is that the latter can be flipped to full automatic by a single switch. He also finds a few LAWS, the American version of the KPG-2, not as effective against choppers but very good against armored vehicles. All of them perfect weapons for a guerrilla war.

And worth thousands of kilos of coke.

It's the largest arms bust in history.

But he's not done.

All of this is worthless if it doesn't lead to the demise of Adán Barrera.

Whatever the cost.

If Adán slips the noose, the only chance of finding him again is through Nora. You have a plan in place to extract her, but plans have a way of going wrong.

She wanted to go back in, he tells himself. You gave her the option of calling it quits and she made up her own mind. She's an adult, she can make her own choices.

Yeah, keep telling yourself that.

Nora drives the new Lexus down the highway to the first exit, pulls into a gas station, goes into the ladies' room and throws up. When her stomach is empty, she gets back in the car and drives to the Santa Ana train station, dumps the car in the parking lot, goes inside to a phone booth, shuts the door and calls Adán.

The crying is no problem. The tears come easily as she chokes back sobs and says, "Something went wrong . . . I don't know . . . He was going to kill me . . . I . . ."

"Come back."

"The police are probably looking for me."

"It's too soon," he says. Dump the car, get on the train, go to San Ysidro, walk across the pedestrian bridge.

"Adán, I'm scared."

"It's okay," he says. "Go to the city place. Wait there. I'll be in touch."

She knows what he means. It's a code they worked out a long time ago, for just such an emergency as this. The city place is a condo they keep in Colonia Hipódromo in Tijuana.

"I love you," she says.

"I love you, too."

She gets on the next southbound train to San Diego.

Plans have a way of going wrong.

In this case, the mechanics back in Costa Mesa are working on the tricked-out little Toyota Camry to get it ready for another run and they find something interesting jammed between the seat and the headrest on the passenger side.

Some sort of electronic device.

The crew chief makes a phone call.

Nora gets off the train in San Diego and grabs the trolley down to San Ysidro, gets off, climbs the steps to the pedestrian bridge and walks across the border.

12

Slipping into Darkness

Slippin' into darkness,
When I heard my mother say . . .
"You been slippin' into darkness, oh, oh, oh
Pretty soon you're going to pay."

—War, "Slippin' Into Darkness"

Tijuana
1997

Nora Hayden's in the wind.

That's the simple, brutal truth that Art's trying to deal with.

Ernie Hidalgo all over again.

Source Chupar redux.

These are the scariest times in the life of any person who handles under-covers. The missed check-in, the non-signal, the *silence.*

It's the silence that will make your stomach churn, your teeth grind, your jaws clench, the silence that will slowly extinguish the low flame of false hope. The dead silence as you launch one radar ping after another into the dark, into the depth and then wait for that returning ping. And wait and wait and get only silence.

She was supposed to have gone to the condo in Colonia Hipódromo to meet Adán. But she never showed up, and neither did The Lord of the Skies. Antonio Ramos did, in force—two platoons of his special troopers in armored cars sealed off the entire block and hit the condo like it was Normandy Beach.

Only it was empty.

No Adán Barrera, no Nora.

Now Ramos is tearing Baja to pieces looking for the Barrera brothers.

He's been waiting for this call for years. Convinced by John Hobbs that Adán Barrera is dealing arms to left-wing insurgents in Chiapas and elsewhere, Mexico City has taken the leash off Ramos, and he goes at it like a pit bull on steroids. A week into the operation, he's hit seven safe houses already, all in the exclusive neighborhoods of Colonia Chapultepec, Colonia Hipódromo and Colonia Cacho.

For an entire week Ramos' troopers storm through Tijuana's wealthy neighborhoods in armored trucks and Humvees, and they're none too gentle about it, blowing off expensive doors with explosive charges, ransacking homes, blocking traffic and disrupting businesses for hours. It's almost as if Ramos *wants* to alienate the city's elite, who, indeed, are torn between blaming Ramos or the Barreras for all the trouble.

Which, of course, has been a centerpiece of Adán Barrera's long-term strategy for years—to become so enmeshed with the Baja upper crust that an attack on him is an attack on them. And they do scream to Mexico City that Ramos is out of control, over the top, that he's trampling on their civil rights.

Ramos doesn't care if Tijuana's upper crust hates his guts. He hates them, too, thinks that they sold whatever souls they had to the Barrera brothers—taking them into society, into their homes, allowing their sons and nephews to dabble in the drug trade—in exchange for cheap thrills by association and quick, easy money. They acted, Ramos thinks, like a gaggle of narco-groupies, treating the Barrera scum like celebrities, rock musicians, movie stars.

And he *tells* them so, when they come to complain.

Look, Ramos tells the city fathers, the *narcotraficantes* murdered a Catholic cardinal and you welcomed them home. They gunned down *federales* on the streets in rush hour and you protected them. They murdered your own chief of police and you did nothing about it. So don't come to me and complain—you brought this on yourselves.

Ramos gets on television and calls the city out.

He looks straight into the camera and announces that within fourteen days he's going to have Adán and Raúl Barrera behind bars and their organization on the old ash heap of history. He stands beside stacks of captured weapons and piles of seized drugs and *names names*—Adán, Raúl and Fabián—and goes on to name the scions of several prominent Tijuana families as Juniors and promises to put them in jail as well.

Then he announces that he's fired five dozen Baja *federales* for lacking the "moral qualifications" to be policemen, saying, "It is a shame on the nation that in Baja, many of the police officers are not the enemies of the Barrera cartel, but their servants."

I'm not going away, he says. I'm taking on the Barreras—who will stand with me?

Well, not too many people.

One young prosecutor, a state investigator and Ramos' own men—and that's about it.

Art understands why the people of Tijuana aren't flocking to Ramos' banner.

They're scared.

And why shouldn't they be?

Two months ago, a Baja cop who exposed the names of crooked cops in the state police was found by the side of the road in a canvas bag. Every bone in his body had been broken—one of Raúl Barrera's trademark executions. Just three weeks ago, another prosecutor who had been investigating the Barreras was shot to death as he took his morning jog on the track of the city university. The gunmen had yet to be apprehended. And the warden of Tijuana's prison was killed in a drive-by shooting as he went out onto his porch to get his morning newspaper. The word on the street is that he had offended a Barrera associate who is incarcerated in his facility.

No, the Barreras might be on the run right now, but that doesn't mean their reign of terror is over, and people aren't going to stick their necks out until they see the two Barrera brothers on slabs.

The fact is, Art thinks a week into the operation, that we haven't produced. The people of Baja know that we took a swing at the Barreras' heads and missed.

Raúl is still at large.

Adán is still at large.

And Nora?

Well, the fact that Adán didn't walk into the trap in Colonia Hipódromo probably means that her cover was blown. Art still holds on to hope, but as the days go by in silence, he has to acknowledge the probability that he will have to search for her decomposed body.

So Art's not in a good mood when he goes into the interview room in the federal lockup in downtown San Diego to have a chat with Fabián Martínez, aka El Tiburón.

The little punk doesn't look so stylish now in his federal orange jumpsuit, handcuffed and in ankle bracelets. But he retains his smirk as he's led in and plopped into a folding chair across the metal table from Art.

"You went to Catholic school, didn't you?" Art begins.

"Augustine," Fabián answers. "Right here in San Dog."

"So you know the difference between purgatory and hell," Art says.

"Refresh my memory."

"Sure," Art says. "Basically, they're both painful. But your time in purgatory eventually ends, whereas hell lasts forever. I'm here to offer you the choice between hell and purgatory."

"I'm listening."

Art lays it out for him. How the weapons charge alone gets him thirty-to-life in federal prison, not to mention the drug trafficking charges, each of which carries fifteen-to-life. So that's hell. On the other hand, if Fabián becomes a government witness, he spends a few years painfully testifying against his old friends, followed by a short stretch in prison, then a new name and a new life. And that's purgatory.

"In the first place," Fabián answers, "I didn't know anything about those guns. I was there to pick up produce. In the second place, what trafficking charges? How did drugs get into this?"

"I have a witness," Art says, "that puts you at the center of a major narcotics network, Fabián. In fact, I kind of like you for 'kingpin status,' unless you have someone else in mind."

"You're bluffing."

"Hey," Art says, "if you want to pay thirty-to-life to see that card, call me. But basically, you're in a bidding war with my other witness, and whoever gives me a better shot at Barrera wins."

"I want a lawyer."

Good, Art thinks, and I want you to have one. But he says, "No, you don't, Fabián. A lawyer is just going to tell you to shut up and land you in prison for the rest of your life."

"I want a lawyer."

"So no deal?"

"No deal."

Art says, "I need to read you your rights."

"You already read them," Fabián says, slumping in his chair. He's bored now; he wants to go back to his cell and read magazines.

"Oh, that was on the weapons charge," Art says. "I have to do it all over again on the murder thing."

Fabián sits straight up. "What murder thing?"

"I'm arresting you for the murder of Juan Parada," Art says. "We've had a sealed indictment since '94. You have the right to remain silent. Anything you say—"

"You don't have jurisdiction," Fabián says, "on a killing that happened in Mexico."

Art leans over the table. "Parada's parents were wetbacks. He was born outside Laredo, Texas, so he's an American citizen, just like you. And that gives me jurisdiction. Hey, maybe we'll try you in Texas—the governor there really likes to hand out lethal injections. See you in court, asshole."

Now go talk to your lawyer.

Walk right into the shit.

If Adán had driven to his rendezvous with Nora in Colonia Hipódromo, the police would probably have nabbed him.

But he walked.

The cops would never expect Adán Barrera to be on foot, so when he saw the police vehicles start to pour into the neighborhood, he simply turned around and walked out. Strolled down the sidewalk, right past the roadblocks that had been set up in the streets.

It hasn't been that easy since.

He's been chased out of two more safe houses, getting warnings from Raúl just in time, and now he's in a safe house in the Río district, wondering when the storm troopers are going to come smashing in there. And the worst part is the communications—or the lack of them. Most of his cell phones aren't encrypted, so he is reluctant to use them. And the ones that are might have been compromised, so even if the police couldn't decipher what he was saying, they could still get a fix on his location just through the signal. So he doesn't know who's been arrested, what houses have been hit, what was found in those houses. He doesn't know who is conducting the raids, how long they are going to last, where they are going to hit, whether they know where he is.

What really concerns Adán is that the raids came without warning.

Not a word, not a whisper, from his well-paid friends in Mexico City.

And that scares him because if the PRI politicians have turned on him, *they* must be very scared. And they must know that if they strike at the Barrera head, they don't dare miss, which makes them dangerous.

They have to take me down, he thought.

They *have* to kill me.

So he's taking protective measures. First, he distributes most of his cell phones to his men, who disperse throughout the city and the state with the instructions to make calls and then dump the phones. (Sure enough, Ramos starts getting reports that Adán Barrera is in Hipódromo, Chapultepec, Rosarito, Ensenada, Tecate, even across the border in San Diego, Chula Vista, Otay Mesa.)

Raúl goes to Radio Shack, buys more phones and starts working them, reaching out and touching cops on the payroll—Baja *federales,* Baja State Police, Tijuana municipal cops.

The news isn't good. The state and local cops who do answer their phones don't know shit—nobody's told them anything, but the one thing they can say is that this is a federal effort, it's got nothing to do with them. And the local *federales*?

"Off the hook," Raúl tells Adán.

Now they've moved again—getting out of the "safe" house in the Río district just ten minutes before the police hit it. They're in a condo in Colonia Cacho, hoping to be able to hole up there for at least a few hours until they can find out what the fuck is going on. But the local police aren't going to be any help.

"They're not answering their phones," Raúl says.

"Get them at home," Adán snaps.

"They're not answering there, either."

Adán grabs a new phone and dials long-distance.

To Mexico City.

Nobody's home. None of his connections in PRI are available to take a phone call, but if he'd like to leave a number, they'd be happy to return . . .

It's the gun deal, Adán thinks. Fucking Art Keller has put together the guns and FARC, and used it to make Mexico City react. He feels like he wants to throw up. There were only four people in Mexico who knew about the arrangement with Tirofio—me, Raúl, Fabián . . .

And Nora.

Nora is missing.

She never showed up at Colonia Hipódromo.

But the police did.

She got there before me, he thinks. She got swept up in the raid and the police have her on ice somewhere.

Raúl gets hold of a laptop and then forces one of their resident computer geeks to come to this safe house, and the geek manages to get out encrypted e-mail messages to their network of computers. An encryption of the geek's own design—he was paid in the high six figures—so dense that even the DEA hasn't been able to crack it. This is what it's come to, Adán thinks, launching electronic messages into space. So they sit and watch for armored cars rolling up the street as they sit and watch the computer screen for messages. Within an hour Raúl manages to summon a few *sicarios* and a couple of clean work cars that can't be connected to the cartel. He also sets up a series of watching and listening posts to monitor the whereabouts of the police.

When the sun sets, Adán, dressed as a laborer, gets into the back of an '83 Dodge Dart with Raúl. In the front are a heavily armed driver and another *sicario*. The car makes its way through the hazardous maze that Tijuana has become, the scouts and listening posts electronically clearing paths until Adán finally makes his way out of the city and to Rancho las Bardas.

There, he and Raúl take a breath and try to figure things out.

Ramos helps.

The Barreras turn on the evening news and there he is, at a press conference, announcing that he's going to shut down the Baja cartel within two weeks.

"That explains why we didn't get a warning," Adán says.

"That explains *some* of it," says Raúl. Ramos has a virtual road map through the cartel. Locations of safe houses, names of associates. Where did he get his information?

"It's Fabián," Adán says. "He's giving everything up."

Raúl is incredulous. "It's not Fabián. It's your beloved Nora."

"I don't believe that," Adán says.

"You don't want to believe it," Raúl says. He tells Adán about finding the tracking device in the car.

"That could have been Fabián, too," Adán says.

"The police had an ambush set up at your little love nest!" Raúl yells. "Did Fabián know about that? Who knew about the arms deal? You, me, Fabián and Nora. Well, it wasn't me, I don't think it was you, Fabián's in an American prison, so . . ."

"We don't even know where she is," Adán says. Then a horrible thought occurs to him. He looks up at Raúl, who has pulled the blind aside and is looking out the window. "Raúl, did you do something to her?"

Raúl doesn't answer.

Adán jumps out of his chair. *"Raúl, did you* do *something to her?!"*

He grabs Raúl by the shirt. Raúl flicks him off easily and pushes him onto the bed. He says, "What if I did?"

"I want to see her."

"I don't think that's a good idea."

"*You're* in charge now?"

"Your obsession with that cunt has fucked up our business." Meaning, Yes, brother, until you come to your senses, I'm in charge.

"I want to see her!"

"I am *not* going to let you become another Tío!"

El chocho, Raúl thinks, the downfall of Barrera men.

Wasn't it Tío's obsession with young pussy that brought about his downfall? First with Pilar and then with that other cunt, whose name I can't even remember. Miguel Ángel Barrera, M-1—the man who built the Federación, the smartest, toughest, most levelheaded man I've ever known, except his brain shut down over some piece of ass and it did him in.

And Adán has inherited the same disease. Hell, Adán could have all the pussy he wants, but he has to have that *one.* He could have had mistress after mistress as long as he was discreet about it and didn't embarrass his wife. But not Adán—no, he falls in love with this *whore,* and is seen everywhere in public with her.

Giving Art Keller the perfect target.

And now look at us.

Adán stares at the floor. "Is she alive?"

Raúl doesn't answer.

"Raúl, just tell me if she's alive."

A guard bursts through the door.

"Go!" he yells. "Go!"

The animals in the menagerie scream as Ramos and his men come over the wall.

Ramos shoulders the grenade launcher, aims and pulls the trigger. One of the guard towers explodes in a flash of yellow light. He reloads, aims again, and there's another flash. He looks down and two deer are dashing themselves against the fence, trying to get out. He jumps into the pen and opens the door.

The two animals dash out into the night.

Birds are screeching and squawking, monkeys chattering madly, and Ramos remembers hearing rumors that Raúl has a couple of lions out here and then he hears their growls and it sounds just like it does in the movies and then he forgets about that because there's return fire coming in.

They'd come in by airplane after dark, a risky lights-out landing on an old drug-running strip, then done a night march across the desert and a long crawl for the last thousand yards to avoid the Barreras' patrol jeeps.

And now we're in it, Ramos thinks. He nestles his cheek into Esposa's comfortable old stock, squeezes off two rounds, gets up and moves forward, knowing that his men are laying cover fire for him. Then he drops and lays down cover for the men who leapfrog ahead of him, and this is the way they move forward toward Raúl's house.

One of his men gets hit in front of him. Is moving forward and then jumps like an antelope when he gets hit. Ramos crawls forward to help him, but the man's face is half blown away and he's past help. Ramos removes the ammo clips from the man's belt and rolls away as a burst of bullets stitches after him.

The fire is coming from the roof of a low building, and Ramos comes out of his roll into a kneeling position, flicks the rifle to bush-rake and strings the clip out along the roof line. Then he feels two hard thuds in his chest, realizes he's been hit in the Kevlar vest, unhooks a grenade from his belt and lofts it onto the roof.

There's a thud, then a flash and two bodies in the air, and the fire from that building stops.

But not the fire from the house.

Red, telltale muzzle flashes blaze from windows, roofs and doorways. Ramos keeps a close eye on the doors because apparently they've caught a few of Raúl's men inside the house and they'll be trying to get out to outflank their attackers. Sure enough, one of the mercenaries fires a clip from the doorway, then makes his break. Ramos' two shots take him in the stomach and he tumbles into the dirt and starts to scream. One of his mates comes out to drag him back in but gets hit half a dozen times himself and balls up by his buddy's feet.

"Get the cars!" Ramos yells.

There are vehicles everywhere—Land Rovers, the narco-favorite Suburban, a few Mercedeses. Ramos doesn't want any of the narcos—especially Raúl—to make it into one of the cars and drive away, and now, after a hail of bullets, none of these vehicles is going anywhere. They're all sitting on flat tires and shattered glass. Then a gas tank or two goes up and a couple of them are on fire.

Then things get weird.

Because someone has the brilliant idea that it would be a good diversionary tactic to open all the cages, and now there are animals running around all over the place. Running wild in all directions, panicked by the noise and the flames and the bullets whistling through the air, and Ramos blinks as a *condenado* giraffe runs in front of him, then two zebras, and antelope are zigzagging back and forth across the yard and Ramos thinks about the lions again and decides that this is going to be a very stupid way to die as he picks himself up and moves toward the house and ducks as some huge bird swoops low over his head and now the narcos bust out of the house and it is just the OK Corral out there.

Flickering silver moonlit images of men, animals, weapons—men standing, running, shooting, falling, ducking. It looks like some weird dream, but the bullets and death and pain are real as Ramos stands and snaps a shot here, then moves around some kind of wild donkey that's braying in terror, and then there's a narco to his left, then to his right—no, that's one of his men—and bullets are zipping, gun muzzles blazing, men yelling and animals screaming. Ramos pops off two shots and another narco falls and then Ramos sees—or thinks he sees, anyway—the tall form of Raúl running, firing pistols from his hips, and Ramos gets a momentary aim on his legs but Raúl disappears. Ramos runs toward where he saw him and then dives for the ground as he sees a narco raise his gun, and Ramos fires from his back and the man flies backward and hits the ground himself, a little cloud of dust poofing up against the moonlight.

The Barreras are gone.

As the firefight dies down—Ramos selects the word *dies* intentionally, because many of Raúl's mercenaries *are* dead, or at least down—he goes from corpse to corpse, wounded to wounded, prisoner to prisoner, looking for Raúl.

Rancho las Bardas is a mess. The main house looks like a gigantic folk-art colander. Cars are on fire. Rare birds perch in tree limbs, and some of the animals have actually crept back into their cages, where they cower and whimper.

Ramos sees a tall body lying by the fence on a bed of matilija poppies, the white blossoms flecked red with blood. Keeping Esposa trained on the body, Ramos kicks it over onto its back. It's not Raúl. Ramos is furious. We know, he thinks, that Raúl was here—we heard him. And I saw him, or thought I did, anyway. Maybe I didn't. Maybe the cell phone calls were fake, to throw us off the trail, and the brothers are sitting on the beach in Costa Rica or Honduras laughing at us over cold beers. Maybe they weren't here at all.

Then he spots it.

The trapdoor is covered with dirt and a little brush, but he can make out the rectangular shape on the ground. Looking closer, he can see the footprints.

You can run, Raúl, but you can't fly.

But a tunnel. That's very good.

He bends over and sees that the trapdoor has been opened recently. There's a narrow line at its edge where the dirt has fallen through. He tosses the brush aside and feels for the concave handle, digs his hand in and lifts the trapdoor.

He hears the tiny click and sees the explosive charge.

But it's too late.

"Me jodí."

I fucked myself.

The explosion blows him to pieces.

The silence that was once ominous is now funereal.

Art has tried everything he can think of to find Nora. Hobbs has turned over all his resources, even though Art has refused to divulge the identity of his source. So Art has had the benefit of satellite photographs, listening posts, Internet sweeps. They all turn up nothing.

His options are limited—he can't launch an Ernie Hidalgo–like search for her because that would blow her cover and kill her, if she's not already dead. And now he doesn't have Ramos waging his relentless campaign.

"It doesn't look good, boss," Shag says.

"When's our next satellite sweep?"

"Forty-five minutes."

Weather permitting, they'll get images of Rancho las Bardas, the Barreras' compound in the desert. They've had five of them already, and they've shown nothing. A few servants, but no one who looks like Adán or Raúl, and certainly no one who looks like Nora.

And no movement, either. No new vehicles, no fresh tire tracks, nothing coming in or going out. The same is the case with the other Barrera ranches and safe houses that Ramos hadn't yet hit. No people, no movement, no cell phone chatter.

Christ, Art thinks, Barrera has to be running out of places.

But so are we.

"Let me know," he says.

He has a meeting with Mexico's new drug czar, General Augusto Rebollo.

Ostensibly the purpose of the meeting is for Rebollo to brief him on the ongoing operations against the Barrera cartel as part of their recently rediscovered bilateralism.

The only problem is that Rebollo doesn't really know much about the operation. Ramos was keeping his activities close to his vest, and all Rebollo can really do is get on television, look fierce and determined, and announce his total support for everything that the deceased hero Ramos has done, even if he doesn't know what that is.

But the truth is that the support is wavering.

Mexico City is getting more nervous as days go by and the Barreras are still on the loose. The longer this war goes on, the more nervous they get, and they're looking, as John Hobbs carefully explains to Art before they go into the meeting, for a "reason for optimism."

In short, Rebollo purrs in his meeting with Art, his green army uniform pressed and neat as a pin, it is obvious that his DEA colleagues have an inside source of information as to the working of the Barrera cartel, and in the spirit of cooperation, his own office could be of much more assistance in the common struggle against drugs and terrorism if Señor Keller would share this source.

He smiles at Art.

Hobbs smiles at Art.

All the bureaucrats in the room smile at Art.

"No," he says.

He can see Tijuana from the picture windows of this office tower. She's out there somewhere.

Rebollo's smile has faded. He looks offended.

Hobbs says, "Arthur—"

"No."

Let him work a little harder for it.

The meeting ends unhappily.

Art goes back to the war room. The satellite photos of Rancho las Bardas should be in.

"Anything?" he asks Shag.

Shag shakes his head.

"Shit."

"They've gone under, boss," Shag says. "No cell traffic, e-mail, nothing."

Art looks at him. The old cowboy's face is weathered and lined, and he wears bifocals now. Christ, have I aged as much as he has? Art wonders. Two old drug warriors. What are the new guys calling us? Jurassic Narcs? And Shag's older than I am—he's looking at retirement soon.

"He'll call his kid," Art says suddenly.

"What?"

"The daughter, Gloria," Art says. "Adán's wife and the girl live in San Diego."

Shag winces. They both know that involving an innocent family is against the unspoken rules that govern the war between the narcos and themselves.

Art knows what he's thinking.

"Fuck it," he says. "Lucía Barrera knows what her husband does. She's no innocent."

"The little girl is."

"Ernie's kids live in San Diego, too," Art answers. "Except they *never* see *their* daddy. Set up a wiretap."

"Boss, no judge in the world—"

Art's stare cuts him off.

Raúl Barrera isn't happy, either.

They pay Rebollo $300,000 a month, and for that kind of money he should be able to come through for them.

But he didn't shut down Antonio Ramos before the attack on Rancho las Bardas, and now he can't confirm that Nora Hayden was the source of their troubles, something that Raúl needs to know badly, and in a hurry. He's holding his own brother virtual prisoner in this safe house, and if the *soplón wasn't* his brother's mistress there's going to be hell to pay.

So when Raúl gets the message from Rebollo—Gee, sorry—he sends word back. The word is simple—*Do better.* Because if you're no use to us, there's no loss in putting out the word that you're on the payroll. Then you can be sorry in prison.

Rebollo gets the word.

Fabián Martínez huddles with his lawyer and gets right down to business.

He knows the SOP in drug busts. The cartel sends an attorney and you tell the attorney what, if any, information you gave up. That way, it can usually be fixed before any harm is done. "I didn't give them anything," he says.

The attorney nods.

"They have an informant," Fabián continues, then drops his voice to a whisper. "It's Adán's *baturra,* Nora."

"Jesus, are you sure?"

"It can only be her," Fabián says. "You have to get me bail, man. I'm going crazy in this place."

"A weapons charge like that, Fabián, it's going to be tough."

"Fuck the weapons." He tells the lawyer about the murder charge.

That's messed up, the lawyer thinks. Unless Fabián Martínez makes a deal, he's looking at a long time in jail.

She's not exactly a prisoner, but she's not free to go.

Nora doesn't even know where she is, except that it's somewhere along Baja's eastern coast.

The cottage they keep her in is made of the same red stone as the beach around it. It has a thatched roof made of palm fronds, and heavy wooden doors. It isn't air-conditioned but the thick stone walls keep it cool inside. The cottage has three rooms—a small bedroom, a bathroom, and a front room facing the sea that is a living room combined with an open kitchen.

Electricity runs from a generator that hums noisily outside. So she has electric lights, hot running water and a flush toilet. She can choose between a hot shower and a hot bath. There's even a satellite dish outside, but the television has been removed and there is no radio. The clocks have also been taken away, and they confiscated her watch when they brought her in.

There is a little CD player but no CDs.

They want me alone with my silence, she thinks.

In a world with no time.

And, truly, she has started to lose track of the days since Raúl picked her up in Colonia Hipódromo and told her to get into the car, that all hell had broken loose and he'd take her to Adán. She didn't trust him but she didn't have a choice, and he was even apologetic when he explained that, for her own protection, she'd have to be blindfolded.

She knows they pulled south out of Tijuana. She knows they drove on the fairly smooth Ensenada Highway for quite a while. But then the road got bumpy, and then it got worse, and she could feel that they were slowly going uphill, rumbling along a rocky road in four-wheel drive, and then she could smell the ocean. It was dark by the time they walked her inside and took off the blindfold.

"Where's Adán?" she asked Raúl.

"He'll be here."

"When?"

"Soon," Raúl said. "Relax. Get some sleep. You've been through a lot."

He handed her a sleeping pill, a Tuinol.

"I don't need that."

"No, take it. You need sleep."

He stood there while she took it, and she did sleep hard and woke up in the morning a little groggy and with cottonmouth. She thought that she was on the beach somewhere south of Ensenada until the sun came up on the wrong side of the world and she worked out that she was on the inland side. When daylight came she recognized the distinctive, bright green water of the Sea of Cortez.

From the bedroom window she could make out a larger house just up the hill, and see that the entire area looked like a moonscape of red stone. A little while later, a young woman walked down from the larger house with a tray of breakfast—coffee, grapefruit and some warm flour tortillas.

And a spoon, Nora noticed.

No knife, no fork.

A glass of water with another Tuinol.

She resisted taking it until her nerves got the better of her, then she swallowed it and it did make her feel better. She napped the rest of the morning and woke up only when the same girl brought her a tray of lunch—freshly grilled yellowtail tuna, steamed vegetables, more tortillas.

More Tuinol.

They woke her out of a deep sleep in the middle of the night and started asking her questions. Her interrogator, a small man with an accent that wasn't quite Mexican, was gentle, polite and persistent—

What happened the night of the arms arrest?

Where did you go? Who did you see? Who did you talk to?

Your shopping trips to San Diego—what did you do? What did you buy? Who did you see?

Arthur Keller, do you know him? Does that name mean anything to you?

Were you ever arrested for prostitution? Drug charges? Income-tax evasion?

She asked her own questions in response—

What are you talking about?

Why are you asking me this stuff?

Who are you, anyway?

Where is Adán?

Does he know you're bothering me?

Can I go back to sleep now?

They let her go back to sleep, woke her fifteen minutes later and told her it was the next night. She knew better, barely, but pretended to believe them as the interrogator asked her the same set of questions, over and over again until she got indignant and said—

I want to go back to sleep.

I want to see Adán, and—

I want another Tuinol.

You can have one in a little while, the interrogator told her. He switched tactics.

Tell me about the day of the arms bust, please. Take me through it minute by minute. You got in the car and . . .

And, and, and . . .

She climbed back on the bed, put her head under the pillow and told him to shut up and go away, she's tired. He offered her another pill and she took it.

They let her sleep for twenty-four hours and then started again.

Questions, questions, questions.

Tell me about this, tell me about that.

Art Keller, Shag Wallace, Art Keller.

Tell me about shooting the Chinese man. What did you do? How did it feel? Where did you grab the gun? By the barrel? The handle?

Talk to me about Keller. How long have you known him? Did he approach you or did you approach him?

She answered, *What are you talking about?*

Because she knew if she gave him an answer she was going to mess up. In the fog of barbiturates, fatigue, fear, confusion, disorientation. She understood what they were doing, there was just nothing she could do to stop it.

He never touched her, never threatened her.

And that gave her hope because she knew it meant that they weren't sure it was her. If they were sure, they would torture her for the information, or just kill her. The "soft" interrogation meant that they had their doubts, and it meant something else—

That Adán was still on her side. They're not hurting me, she thought, because they still have Adán to worry about. So she held out. Gave evasive, confused answers, outright denials, indignant counter-assaults.

But she's wearing down.

It's getting to her.

Breakfast didn't come one morning—she asked for it and the girl looked confused and said that she'd just served it. But she hadn't. I know that—or do I? Nora wondered. And then there were two lunches, back to back, and then more sleep and then another Tuinol.

Now she wanders around outside the cottage. The doors aren't locked and nobody stops her. The compound is flanked by the sea on one side and endless desert on the other three. If she tried to walk out she would die of thirst or exposure.

She walks down to the ocean and goes in up to her ankles.

The water is warm and feels nice.

The sun sets behind her back.

Adán watches her from his bedroom window in the house up the hill.

He *is* a prisoner in the room, guarded by a rotation of *sicarios* whose loyalty is to Raúl. They take turns outside the door, round the clock, and Adán figures there must be at least twenty of them on the grounds.

He stands and watches her wade into the water. She wears an off-white sundress and a floppy white hat to keep the sun off her skin. Her hair hangs loose on her bare shoulders.

Was it you? he wonders.

Did you betray me?

No, he decides, I can't let myself believe that.

Raúl sure believes it, even though days of interrogation have failed to prove it. It's a soft interrogation, his brother has assured him. She hasn't been *touched,* never mind hurt.

She'd better not be, Adán has told him. One bruise, one scar, one scream of pain and I will find a way to have you killed, brother or no brother.

And if she's the *soplón*? Raúl asked.

Then, Adán thinks as he watches her sit down at the edge of the water, that is different.

That is a different thing altogether.

He and Raúl have come to an understanding: If Nora is not the traitor, then Raúl will step back down and Adán will resume his position as *patrón.* That's the understanding, Adán thinks, but experience tells him that no one who has assumed power ever gives it back again.

Not willingly, anyway.

Not easily.

And maybe that would be for the good, he thinks. Let Raúl have the *pasador,* cash out, take Nora and go somewhere for a quiet life. She's always wanted to live in Paris. Why not?

And the other half of the equation? If it turns out that Nora betrayed them, for whatever reason, then Raúl's little coup becomes permanent and Nora . . .

He doesn't want to think about it.

The example of Pilar Talavera is vivid in his mind.

If it comes to that I'll do it myself, he thinks. It's funny how you can still love someone who betrayed you. I'll walk her down to the ocean, let her watch the last rays of the sun fade on the water.

It will be quick and painless.

Then, if it weren't for Gloria, I'd put the pistol in my own mouth.

Children bind us to this life, don't they?

Especially this child, so fragile and needy.

And she must be worrying herself to death, Adán thinks. The news from Tijuana has surely hit the San Diego papers, and even though Lucía will try to shield her from it, Gloria will worry until she hears from me.

He takes another long look at Nora, then walks away from the window and bangs on the door.

The guard opens it.

"Get me a cell phone," Adán orders.

"Raúl said—"

"I don't give a rat's ass what Raúl said, *pendejo*," Adán snaps. "I am still the *patrón,* and if I tell you to get me something, then you go get it."

He gets the phone.

"Boss?"

"Yeah?"

"Heartbeat."

Shag hands Art the headset patched into the tap on Lucía Barrera's phone. He hears Lucía's voice—

Adán?

How's Gloria?

She's worried.

Let me speak to her.

Where are you?

Can I speak with her?

A long pause. Then Gloria's voice.

Papa?

How are you, baby?

I've been worried about you.

I'm okay. Don't worry.

Art hears the girl crying.

Where are you? The newspaper said—

The newspaper makes things up. I'm fine.

Can I come see you?

Not quite yet, darling. Soon. Listen, tell Mommy to give you a big kiss from me, okay?

Okay.

Bye, baby. I love you.

I love you, Papa.

Art looks to Shag.

"It's going to take a little while, boss."

It takes an hour but it feels like five, as the electronic data are sent to NSA and analyzed. Then they have an answer. The call came from a cell phone (we already knew that, Art thinks) so they can't provide an address, but they can specify the nearest transmittal tower.

San Felipe.

On the east coast of Baja, straight south from Mexicali.

A sixty-mile radius from the tower.

Art already has the map spread out on the table. San Felipe is a small town, maybe twenty thousand people, a lot of them American snowbirds. There's not much down there except the town, a lot of desert and a string of fishing camps to the north and south.

Even with a sixty-mile radius, it's the clichéd needle in the haystack, and Adán may have traveled to get into cell phone range and may even now be rushing back out.

But it gives us a target area, Art thinks.

Some hope.

"The call didn't come from the town," Shag says.

"How do you know that?"

"Listen to the tape again."

They rerun it, and in the background Art can hear a faint hum with rhythmic pulses. He looks at Shag, puzzled.

"You're a city boy, aren't you?" Shag asks. "I grew up on a ranch. That's a generator you're hearing. They're off the power grid."

Art calls for a satellite sweep. But it's night, and they won't have the images for hours.

The interrogator picks up the pace.

He wakes Nora out of a deep Tuinol slumber, sits her in a chair and sticks the tracking device in her face.

"What's this?"

"I dunno."

"Yes, you do," he insists. "You put it there."

"What where? What time is it? I wanna go back . . ."

He shakes her. It's the first time he's touched her. It's also the first time he yells. "Listen! I've been very nice to you so far, but I'm losing my patience with you! If you don't start to cooperate I'm going to hurt you! Very badly! Now tell me who gave you this to put in the car!"

She stares at the little device for a long time, as if it's some object from a distant past. She holds it between her thumb and forefinger and turns it around, examining it from different angles. Then she holds it up to the lamp and looks at it more closely. She turns back to her interrogator and says, "I've never seen this before."

Then he's in her face, screaming. She doesn't even understand what he's saying, but he's yelling—flecks of spit hit her face—and shaking her back and forth, and when he finally lets her go she just slumps in the chair, exhausted.

"I'm so tired," she says.

"I know you are," he says, all softness and sympathy now. "This can all be over very soon, you know."

"Then can I sleep?"

"Oh, yes."

Art's sitting there when the photos come across the computer screen.

His eyes stinging from fatigue, he wakes Shag, who's sleeping tilted back in his chair with his boots up on his desk.

They pore over the photos. Starting with a large weather-satellite image of the entire San Felipe area, they cross off the section that is on the power grid, then start working their way through the enlarged vectors north and south of town.

They rule out the inland areas. No water supply, few passable roads, and the few roads that do snake their way through the rocky desert would allow the Barreras only one avenue of escape and they would be unlikely to place themselves in that trap.

So they concentrate on the coast itself, to the east of the range of low mountains and the main road, which runs parallel to the coast, with spur roads going east to the fishing camps and other small settlements on the beach.

The coast north of San Felipe is a popular spot for off-roaders and is pretty crowded with tourist, fishing, and RV camps, so they don't give it much play. The immediate coast south of the town is similar, but then the road gets considerably worse and civilization becomes sparse until you get closer to the little fishing village of Puertocitos.

But there's a ten-kilometer stretch between the two towns—starting about forty clicks south of San Felipe—where there are no camps, just a few isolated beach houses. The range is consistent with the strength of Adán's cell phone signal, 4800 bps, so that's where they concentrate their efforts.

It's a perfect spot, Art thinks. There are only a few access roads—more like four-wheeler tracks—and the Barreras doubtless have lookouts posted on those roads and in San Felipe and Puertocitos as well. They would spot every single vehicle that came down the road, never mind the kind of armed convoy it would take to launch a raid. The Barreras would be long gone—by road or by boat—before we could get close.

But you can't think about that now. First, find the target, then worry about how to take it out.

A dozen houses are set on the isolated stretch of coast. A few sit on the beach itself, but most are up on the low ridge above. Three are plainly unoccupied; there are no vehicles or recent tire tracks. Among the remaining nine it's hard to choose. They all look normal—from space, anyway—although Art is hard-pressed to determine what abnormal would be in this case. All of them appear to have been built on lots cleared from the rocks and agave brush; most of them are plain, rectangular structures with either thatched or composite roofs; most of them—

Then he spots the anomaly.

He almost misses it, but something catches his eye. Something not quite right.

"Zoom in on that," he says.

"What?" Shag asks. He doesn't see anything where Art is pointing but rock and brush.

That is a shadow made by some rocks indistinguishable from the millions of others, but the shadow—the shadow is an even line.

"That's a structure," Art says.

They download the frame and enlarge it. It's grainy, hard to tell, but examined under a magnifying glass there is *depth* there.

"Are we looking at a square rock?" Art asks. "Or a square building with a rock roof?"

"Who puts a stone roof on a house?" Shag asks.

"Someone who wants it to blend in," Art answers.

They zoom back out, and now they start to spot other too-regular shadows, and pieces of brush that have even lines. It's difficult at first, but then a picture starts to emerge of two structures—one smaller than the other—and shapes that could disguise vehicles underneath.

They coordinate the frame onto the large map. The house sits off a track that turns off from the main road, such as it is, forty-eight kilometers south of San Felipe.

Five hours later, a fishing boat beats its way up from Puertocitos through a heavy headwind. It anchors two hundred yards from shore, puts out its lines and waits for dusk. Then one of the "fishermen" stretches out flat on the deck and trains an infrared telescope on the beach in front of two stone houses.

He spots a woman in a white dress walking unsteadily down to the water.

She has long blond hair.

Art hangs up the phone, drops his head into his hands and sighs. When he looks up again, he has a smile on his face. "We got her."

"Don't you mean 'him,' boss?" Shag asks. "Let's not lose focus here. Getting *Barrera* is the point, isn't it?"

. . .

Fabián Martínez is still in his cell, but he's feeling a little better about life in general.

He'd had a good meeting with his attorney, who had assured him that he didn't have to worry about the drug charges—the government's witness was *not* going to appear, and certain people had been given information about the *soplón*.

The arms charge is still a problem, but the attorney has a genius idea about that, too.

"We'll see if we can get you extradited to Mexico," he said. "On the Parada murder."

"Are you kidding me?"

"First of all," the lawyer said, "Mexico doesn't have a death penalty. Second, it will take years to bring you to trial and in the meantime . . ."

He let it hang. Fabián knew what he meant. In the meantime, things will get fixed. Technicalities will emerge, prosecutors will lose enthusiasm, judges will get vacation *ranchos*.

So Fabián lies back on his mattress and thinks he's in pretty good shape. Fuck you, Keller—without Nora you've got nothing. And fuck you, La Güera. I hope you're having a nice evening.

They won't let her sleep.

When she first got there, they wouldn't let her do anything *but* sleep, and now they won't let her shut her eyes. She can sit down, but if she starts to doze they pick her up and make her stand.

She *aches*.

Every part of her—her feet, her legs, her back, her head.

Her eyes.

Worst of all, her eyes. They burn, they throb, they feel raw. She'd give anything to lie down and close her eyes. Or sit, or stand—just close her eyes.

But they won't let her.

And they won't give her any Tuinol.

She doesn't want it; she needs it.

She has an awful pins-and-needles feeling in her skin, and her hands won't stop quivering. Add to that the slamming headache and the nausea and . . . "Just one," she whines.

"You want things, but you don't want to *give* anything," the interrogator says.

"I don't have anything to give."

Her legs feel like wood.

"I disagree," the interrogator says. Then he starts in *again,* about Arthur Keller, the DEA, the tracking device, her trips to San Diego . . .

They know, Nora thinks. They already know, so why not just tell them what they already know? Just tell them and let them do what they're going to do, but whatever it is I can get some sleep. Adán isn't coming, Keller isn't coming—just tell them something.

"If I tell you about San Diego, will you let me sleep?" she asks.

The interrogator agrees.

He takes her through it step by step.

Shag Wallace finally leaves the office.

Gets in his five-year-old Buick and drives to a parking lot outside the Ames supermarket in National City. He waits there for twenty minutes before a Lincoln Navigator pulls into the lot, slowly cruises around, then pulls up beside him.

A man gets out of the Lincoln and into the Buick with Shag.

He sets the briefcase on his lap. The latches open with a metallic snap, then he turns the briefcase so that Shag can see the stack of wrapped bills inside.

"Are police pensions any better in America than they are in Mexico?" the man asks.

"Not much," Shag says.

"Three hundred thousand dollars," the man says.

Shag hesitates.

"Take it," the man says. "It's not as if you're giving information to the narcos, after all. This is from one cop to another. General Rebollo needs to know."

Shag blows a long breath.

Then he tells the man what he wants to know.

"We need some proof," the man says.

Shag takes the proof from his jacket pocket and hands it over.

Then he takes the three hundred thousand dollars.

A south wind blows up the Baja Peninsula, pushing warmer air and a layer of clouds over the Sea of Cortez.

With no more satellite photos, Art's latest intelligence is now eighteen hours old, and a lot could have happened in those hours—the Barreras could have left, Nora could be dead. The cloud cover shows no sign of breaking up, so the intelligence is only going to get older.

So what he has is what he's going to get, and he has to act on it quickly or not at all.

But how?

Ramos, the one cop in Mexico he could trust, is dead. The head of the NCID is on the Barreras' payroll, and Los Pinos is backpedaling on the campaign against the Barreras in six gears of reverse.

Art has only one choice.

And he hates it.

He meets John Hobbs on Shelter Island, the sailing boat marina in the middle of San Diego Harbor. They meet at night, across from Humphreys by the Bay, and walk along the narrow stretch of park that flanks the water on the way out to the point.

"You know what you're asking me to do," Hobbs says.

Yeah, I do, Art thinks.

Hobbs tells him anyway. "Launch an illegal strike on the sovereign territory of a friendly country. It violates about every international law I can think of, plus a few hundred *national* laws, and could trigger—you'll forgive the unhappy phrase—a major diplomatic crisis with a neighboring state."

"It's our last chance at the Barreras," Art argues.

"We stopped the Chinese shipment."

"This one," Art says. "You think Adán will quit? If we don't get him now, he'll set up the arms-for-drugs deal and FARC will be fully equipped inside six months."

Hobbs is silent. Art walks beside him, trying to read his thoughts, listening to the sound of the water as it laps on the rocks beside them. In the distance, the lights of Tijuana sparkle and wink.

Art feels like he can't breathe. If Hobbs doesn't go for this, Nora Hayden is dead and the Barreras win.

Finally, Hobbs says, "I couldn't use any of our normal assets. We'll have to outsource this, double-blind."

Thank you, God, Art says to himself.

"And Arthur," Hobbs adds, turning to him. "This can't be a bag job. We could never explain to the Mexicans how we got the Barreras into custody. This will not be a law enforcement operation, it will be a covert intelligence action. This will not be an arrest, it will be an extreme sanction. Are you all right with that?"

Art nods.

"I need to hear you say it," Hobbs insists.

"It's a sanction," Art says. "That's what I want."

So far, so good, Art thinks. But he knows John Hobbs won't walk away from this without extracting his price. It doesn't take long.

"And I need to know your source," Hobbs says.

"Of course."

Art tells him.

Callan walks from the beach back toward the cottage he's renting. It's a cool, foggy day on the NoCal coast, and he likes it that way.

It feels good.

He opens the door to the cottage, pulls his .22 and points it.

"Eeeeezy," Sal says. "We're good."

"Are we?"

"You walked off the reservation, Sean," Sal says. "You should have talked to me first."

"You'd have let me go?"

"With the right precautions, yeah," Sal says.

"What about the hit on the Barreras?"

"Old news."

"So we're good," Callan says, not lowering his aim. "Thanks for telling me. Now leave."

"I got a job offer for you."

"Pass," Callan says. "I don't do that kind of work anymore."

That's okay, Scachi tells him, because we're not talking about taking any lives this time. We're talking about saving one.

They decide to go in from the water.

Art and Sal pore over detailed area maps and decide it's the only way to get in quickly. A fishing boat will go up from the south at night, and they'll embark on Zodiacs and land on the beach.

Now it's a matter of time and tide.

The Sea of Cortez has extreme tides—the low tide can ebb hundreds of yards, and that distance would make a quick raid impossible. They can't get across hundreds of yards of open beach. Even at night, they'd be spotted and mowed down before they got near the houses.

So the window for a successful raid is narrow—it has to be night, and high tide.

"We have to go between nine and nine-twenty," Sal says. "Tonight."

It's too soon, Art thinks.

And maybe too late.

Nora talks all about her last visit to San Diego.

How she went shopping, what she bought, where she stayed, how she had lunch with Haley, a nap, a run, dinner.

"What did you do that night?"

"Hung out in the room, ordered dinner, watched TV."

"You were in La Jolla and you just watched TV? Why?"

"Just felt like it. Being by myself, hanging out, vegging out in front of the tube."

"What did you watch?"

She knows she's going down the slippery slope. She knows it, but there's nothing she can do about it. That's the nature of slippery slopes, isn't it? she thinks. What I really did that night was go to the White House and meet with Keller, but I can't say that, can I? So . . .

"I dunno. I don't remember."

"It wasn't that long ago."

"Dumb stuff, you know. Some dumb movie. Maybe I fell asleep."

"Pay-per-view? HBO?"

She can't remember if the Valencia has pay-per-view movies or HBO or anything. She's not sure she ever even turned the TV on there. But if I say I watched a pay movie, then that would show up my bill, wouldn't it? she thinks. So she says, "I think it was HBO or Showtime, one of those."

The interrogator senses that he's moving in on the kill. She's an amateur; a professional liar is vague about everything. ("I don't remember—it might have been this, it might have been that.") But this woman had been certain and detailed about everything that she'd done. Up until her account of the evening, when she became uncertain and evasive.

A professional liar knows that the key is not to make his lies look like the truth, but to make his truth look like lies.

Well, her truth looks like truth, and her lies?

"But you don't remember what the movie was."

"I was, you know, channel surfing."

"Channel surfing."

"Yeah."

"What did you have for dinner?"

"Fish. I usually have fish."

"Watching your weight."

"Of course."

"I'll be back in a bit. While I'm gone, please think about what movie you watched."

"Can I sleep?"

"If you sleep, you can't think, can you?"

But I can't think if I don't sleep, Nora worries. That's the problem. I can't think of any more lies, I can't keep them straight, I'm not even sure myself what happened and didn't. What movie did I watch? What movie is *this*? How does it end?

"If you can remember what you watched that night, I'll let you sleep."

He knows the process. When put under enough pressure, the mind will create an answer. It doesn't matter if it's fact or fantasy in this case. He just wants her to commit to an answer.

In exchange for sleep, the woman's mind will "recall" the information. It might even seem real to her. If it turns out to be so, fine. But if it turns out to be false, she will have given him the crack from which everything else will splinter.

She will fall apart.

And then we will have the truth.

"She's lying," the interrogator tells Raúl. "Making things up."

"How can you tell?"

"Body language," the interrogator says. "Vague answers. If I put her on a polygraph and ask her about that particular evening, she fails."

Do I have enough to convince Adán? Raúl wonders. So that I can dispatch this lying bitch without starting a civil war with my brother? First Fabián sends a message through his lawyer saying that the woman is the *soplón*. Now the interrogator is on the edge of catching her in a lie.

But do I wait?

For Rebollo to get us a definitive answer? *If* he can get us an answer?

"How long before you break her?" Raúl asks.

The interrogator looks at his watch. "It's five o'clock now?" he says. "Eight-thirty, nine at the latest."

Now the clouds are on *our* side, Art thinks, as the fishing boat cuts through the choppy water. He listens to the rhythmic slapping of the hull against the small waves that break against the bow. The bad weather that had obscured their intelligence-gathering operations is now working *for* them, hiding them from the view of spotters on the coast as well as other boats, some of them doubtless loaded with Barrera security.

He looks at the men sitting silently on the deck. Their eyes shine bright against their blackened faces. Smoking has been forbidden, but most of the men have unlit cigarettes playing nervously in their lips. Others chew gum. A few talk quietly, but most just sit and stare out at the gray fog glimmering under the moonlight.

The men wear Kevlar vests over black jumpsuits, and each man is his own arsenal, carrying either a Mac-10 or an M-16, a .45 pistol on one side of his belt and a wicked, flat, palm-leaf-killing blade on the other. The vests are festooned with grenades.

So these are the "outside resources," Art thinks.

Where the fuck did Scachi get them?

Callan knows.

It's old-fucking-home week, sitting here with the Red Mist boys, some of them his old bunkmates from Las Tangas, waiting to do what they do.

"Interdict the terrorists' arms supply at its source," was the way Scachi had put it.

Three Zodiac boats covered with canvas tarps are lashed to the deck. There will be eight men to a boat and they'll land fifty yards apart. The men in the two northernmost boats will head toward the larger house. The crew of the third boat will make for the smaller cottage.

Whether or not we get there is a good question, Callan thinks.

If the Barreras have been tipped off we'll be walking into a cross fire coming from stone houses, pinned down on a bare beach with no cover but the fog. The beach will be littered with bodies.

But they won't stay there.

Sal's been clear about the spec: No one is to be left behind. Dead or alive or anywhere in between, they're getting back on the boat. Callan glances over at the pile of cinder blocks on the aft deck. "Headstones," Sal called them.

Burial at sea.

We ain't leaving no bodies in Mexico. Far as the world is concerned, this was a hit carried out by a rival narco looking to take advantage of the Barreras' current difficulties. If you get captured—and don't get captured—that's what you tell them. No matter what they do to you. Better idea? Swallow your gun. We ain't the Marines—we won't be coming to get you.

. . .

Art goes below.

The strong smell of diesel fuel makes his stomach lurch. Or maybe it's nerves, Art thinks.

Scachi's drinking a cup of coffee.

"Like old times, huh, Arthur?"

"Almost."

"Hey, Arthur, you don't want this to happen, say the word."

"I want it to happen."

"You got thirty minutes on that beach," Sal says. "In thirty minutes we're back on the boat and heading out. Last thing we need is to get stopped by a Mexican patrol boat."

"I got it," Art says. "How long until we get there?"

Scachi kicks the question to the boat's captain.

Two hours.

Art checks his watch.

They'll hit the beach around nine.

Nora makes her mistake at 8:15.

She starts to fall asleep standing up, but they shake her and walk her around the room. Then they sit her down again as the interrogator comes in and asks—

"Do you remember what you watched that night?"

"Yes."

Because I have to get some sleep. Have to sleep. If I can sleep I can think, and I can think my way out of this. So give him something, a little something, buy some sleep. Buy some time.

"Very good. What?"

"Amistad."

"The movie about slaves."

"That's right."

Go ahead and ask me about it, she thinks. I've seen it. I remember it. I can talk about it. Ask me your questions. Fuck you.

"There are no network movies on a weeknight, so it must have been pay-per-view or HBO."

"Or some other—"

"No, I checked. Your hotel has only HBO and pay-per-view."

"Oh."

"So which was it?"

How the hell should I know? Nora thinks.

"HBO."

The interrogator shakes his head sadly, like a teacher whose student has disappointed him.

"Nora, that hotel does not get HBO."

"But you just said—"

"I was testing you."

"Then it must have been pay-per-view."

"Was it?"

"Yes, I remember now. It was pay-per-view because I can remember looking at that little card they put on top of the television and wondering if the staff thought I was ordering porn. Yes, that's right, and I . . .what?"

"Nora, I have copies of your bill. You didn't order a movie."

"I didn't?"

"No. Now, why don't you tell me what you were really doing that night, Nora?"

"I did tell you."

"You lied to me, Nora. I'm very disappointed."

"I'm just confused. I'm so tired. If you let me get some sleep . . ."

"The only reason to lie is to cover something up. What are you covering up, Nora? What did you really do that night?"

She puts her face in her hands and sobs. She hasn't cried since Juan died, and it feels good. It's a relief.

"You were somewhere else that night, weren't you?"

She nods.

"You've been lying all this time."

She nods again.

"Can I sleep now, please?"

"Give her some Tuinol," the interrogator says. "And get Raúl."

Adán's door opens.

Raúl comes in and hands him a pistol.

"Can you do this, brother?"

She feels a hand on her shoulder.

Thinks it's a dream at first, then opens her eyes and sees Adán standing over her.

"My love," he says, "let's go for a walk."

"Now?"

He nods.

He looks so serious, she thinks. So serious.

He helps her get out of bed.

"I'm a mess," she says.

She is. Her hair is disheveled and her face is puffy from the drugs. It occurs to him that he's never seen her without makeup.

"You always look lovely," he answers. "Here, put a sweater on. It's chilly—I don't want you to get sick."

She walks out with him into the silver mist. She's groggy and has a hard time getting her footing on the large pebbles of the beach. He holds her by the elbow and gently walks her away from the cottage, toward the water's edge.

Raúl watches from the window.

He saw Adán and his woman leave the stone cottage and walk into the dark. Now he's lost sight of them in the fog.

Can he do it? Raúl wonders.

Can he put the barrel to the back of that pretty blond head and pull the trigger? Does it matter? If he doesn't, I will. And either way, I am the new *patrón,* and the new *patrón* will run things differently than the old one. Adán has gotten soft. Always the little accountant—good with the numbers, not so good with the blood.

A loud knock at the door interrupts his thoughts.

"What?!" he snaps.

One of his men comes in. He's out of breath, as if he's run up the stairs.

"The *soplón,*" he says. "We just got word from Rebollo. He got it straight from the DEA guy, Wallace—"

"It's Nora."

The man shakes his head. "No, *patrón.* It's Fabián."

The messenger lays out the evidence—the sealed murder indictment, the threat of capital punishment, then the smoking gun: copies of deposit slips, deposits made by Keller in Fabián's name in banks in Costa Rica, the Caymans and even Switzerland.

Hundreds of thousands of dollars—profits from the *tombes* pulled off by the Piccone brothers.

"They made him a deal," the man says. *"Plata o plomo."*

He took the silver.

"Let's sit down," Adán says.

He helps Nora down and sits beside her.

She says, "I'm cold."

He puts his arm around her.

"Do you remember that night in Hong Kong?" he asks. "When you took me up to Victoria Peak? Let's imagine we're there."

"I'd like that."

"Look out there," he says. "Can you imagine the lights?"

"Adán, are you crying?"

He slowly pulls the pistol from its place at the small of his back.

"Kiss me," Adán says.

He turns her chin to him and kisses her softly on the lips as he eases the gun barrel behind her head.

"You were the *sonrisa de mi alma*," he whispers into her lips as he pulls the hammer back.

The smile of my soul.

Brother, I'm sorry. By the time the information reached me, it was too late. Such a tragedy. But we will avenge ourselves on Fabián, you can be sure of that.

Raúl rehearses his lines.

Deal with La Güera now, Fabián later, he thinks. It will destroy Adán, killing this woman. He won't be able to resume control of the *pasador.*

He's your brother.

Está chingada, he thinks. It's fucked.

He pushes the messenger aside and runs down the stairs and outside into the night.

Yelling, "Adán! Adán!"

Adán hears the shouts, muffled in the fog.

He hears the footsteps running on the stones, coming closer. He tightens his finger on the trigger and thinks, I can't let it be him.

Over his shoulder, he can see Raúl's tall form loping toward them like a ghost in the mist.

I have to do it.

Do it.

Art jumps out of the boat before it reaches the beach.

He stumbles through the ankle-deep surf, trips and falls face-first onto the beach. He gets up and crouches down low as he moves up the slope and then he sees—

Raúl Barrera.

Running toward—

Adán.

And Nora.

It's a long shot, a hundred yards at least, and Art hasn't fired an M-16 in anger since Vietnam. He raises the rifle to his shoulder, presses the nightscope to his eye, leads Raúl by a few feet and squeezes the trigger.

The bullet takes Raúl in mid-stride.

Square in the stomach.

Art sees him tumble, roll and then start to crawl forward.

Then the night lights up.

Raúl crumples to the ground.

Rolling in agony on the rocks, shrieking in pain.

Adán runs to him. Drops to his knees and tries to hold him, but Raúl is too strong; his pain is too strong and he writhes out of Adán's grasp.

"*¡Dios mío!*" Adán yells.

His hands are drenched in blood. The front of his shirt and his pants are soaked with blood.

It's hot.

"Adán," Raúl groans. "It wasn't her. It was Fabián." Then he howls to God, "*¡Dios mío! ¡Dios mío! ¡Madre de Dios!*"

Adán tries to clear his head.

The world's exploding around him. Gunfire everywhere, and the sound of footsteps running toward them on the rocks. Then Raúl's bodyguards are there, some firing behind them, others trying to lift Raúl off the ground.

"Get a car!" Adán yells. "Bring it here. Raúl, we're going to get you to the hospital."

"Don't move me!"

"We have to."

They start to drag him up the beach, away from the attack.

Adán grabs Nora by the arms and starts to pull her up.

"Come on!"

A grenade lands a few feet away and bowls them both over.

Nora lies on the rocks, concussed, blood flowing from her nose. Adán is screaming something but she can't hear a thing. Manuel is pulling him away.

Adán's screaming and trying to pull his way back to her, but the *campesino* is too strong for him.

Two *sicarios* try to grab her, but two short bursts of gunfire cut them down.

There's another flash of light, and then darkness.

Art sees Raúl and Adán being dragged up the hill toward some Land Rovers at the top of the hill, near the main house.

He heads for them.

Bullets stitch around his feet.

A slight man with rimless glasses comes out the front door of the cottage and starts to run up the hill, but a short burst of bullets catches him as he runs, and he flies backwards like a silent-movie comic slipping on a banana peel.

The door slams shut behind him and gunfire starts to blaze from the windows. Art drops to the ground and crawls toward Nora. Callan moves beside him, rolls, shoots in bursts of two and then rolls again.

Then Callan yells behind him, "Rounds!"

A second later a grenade whooshes through a window of the cottage and explodes.

The shooting from the cottage stops.

Raúl shrieks with agony as his men lift him into the backseat. Adán gets in from the other side and cradles his brother's head in his lap.

Raúl grasps his hand and whimpers.

Manuel jumps behind the wheel. Raúl's men try to stop him, but Adán yells, "I want Manuel!" and they let him go. The car starts up the beach, every bump a jolt of agony for Raúl.

Adán feels as if his brother's grip is going to crush the bones in his hand but he doesn't care. He strokes Raúl's hair and tells him to hold on, everything is going to be okay.

"*Agua,*" Raúl mumbles.

Adán finds a plastic bottle of drinking water in the seat pouch, twists off the cap and holds the bottle to Raúl's mouth. Raúl gulps it down and Adán feels the water pour onto his own shoes.

Adán turns and looks back down the slope.

He sees Nora's limp body.

"Nora!" he screams. Then, to Manuel: "We have to go back!"

Manuel isn't having any of it. He has the car in first gear, four-wheel drive, and is moving slowly up the hill, another Rover falling in behind, the *sicarios* pouring cover fire out the back.

Tracer rounds arc through the night like lethal fireflies.

A rocket-propelled grenade hits the car behind Adán's and explodes, sending shards of heated metal spinning into the air. The driver tumbles from the car in flames and twirls like festival fireworks in the night. Another body slumps out the open side of the car and sizzles on the rocks.

Manuel hits the accelerator and Raúl screams.

Art sees one of the Rovers go up, tries to peer through the flames and sees the lead Rover chugging up the slope.

"Goddamn it!" he yells. He turns to Callan and orders, "Stay with her!" He shifts Nora's dead weight onto Callan and starts running toward the escaping Land Rover. Rounds from the main house buzz around his head like mosquitoes. He puts his head down and keeps moving, past the burning Rover and its charred bodies, toward the other Rover that's struggling up the slope in front of him.

Adán sees him, twists around and tries to get his pistol in position to get a shot, but every muscle he moves sends Raúl into a fresh paroxysm of pain. He sees Keller, still running, bring his rifle to his shoulder.

Adán shoots.

Both men miss.

The Rover crests the ridge. It slips into its downhill slide and Raúl screams. Adán holds him tight as the vehicle picks up speed.

Art stands on the edge of the ridge. He's hunched over, catching his breath, as he watches the Rover rumble away from him.

He takes three deep, gasping breaths, raises his rifle to his shoulder and sights in on the back left windshield, where he last saw Adán. He takes a long breath, then squeezes the trigger on the exhale.

The car keeps moving away.

Art trots back toward the main house.

· · ·

Scachi's men go about their jobs in a workman-like, unhurried fashion. One squad lays down cover fire in short, disciplined bursts, while the other squad moves forward; then they exchange roles. Three rotations of this tactic get one of the men to the side of the house. He presses flat against its stone walls as the others pour fire through the windows. Then, on a signal, they stop shooting and Scachi's guy attaches a charge to the door and throws himself to the ground as the door splinters.

The other mercenaries jump in.

Three quick bursts of gunfire, and then silence.

Art goes in.

It's a charnel house, a madhouse.

Blood everywhere, dead and wounded bodies, Scachi's mercenaries moving efficiently to dispatch the *sicarios* who linger between worlds.

Three dead *sicarios* are sprawled on the floor of the front room. One of them lies facedown with two entry wounds in the back of his head. Art steps over him to get into the bedroom.

There are eleven more bodies.

One wounded man, his shoulder a splotch of red, sits against the wall with his legs splayed in front of him. Scachi walks up to the wounded man and swings his foot like he's trying to make a fifty-yard field goal against the wind.

His boot hits the man's balls with a solid *thump*.

"Start talking," Art says.

The *sicario* does. Adán and Raúl were here, so was La Güera, and Raúl was badly hurt, gut-shot.

"Well, that's happy news anyway," Scachi says. He does the same calculation that Art does—if Raúl Barrera has been shot in the belly, he isn't going to make it. He's as good as dead—better, in fact.

"We can catch them," Art tells Scachi. "They're on the road. Not far ahead."

"Catch them with what?" Scachi asks. "You bring a jeep?" He looks at his watch, then yells, "Ten minutes!"

"We have to go after them!" Art yells.

"No time."

The man keeps spewing information—the Barrera brothers left in the Land Rover, headed for San Felipe to get help for Raúl.

Scachi believes him.

"Take him outside and shoot him," he orders.

Art doesn't blink.

Everyone knew the rules going in.

The Land Rover rattles over the busted road.

Raúl screams.

Adán doesn't know what to do. If he tells Manuel to slow down, Raúl will certainly bleed out before they can get him help. If he tells Manuel to speed up, Raúl's suffering is even worse.

The left front tire drops into a wash and Raúl shrieks.

"Por favor, hermano," he murmurs when he catches his breath. Please, brother.

"What, brother?"

Raúl looks up at him. "You know."

He turns his eyes to the pistol at his hip.

"No, Raúl. You're going to make it."

"I . . . can't . . . stand it . . . anymore . . ." Raúl gasps. "Please, Adán."

"I can't."

"I'm begging."

Adán looks at Manuel.

The old bodyguard shakes his head. He's not going to make it.

"Stop the car," Adán orders.

He takes the pistol from Raúl's belt, opens the car door, then gently slides out from under his brother's head and lays it back on the seat. The desert air is pungent with sage and *hermosillo*. Adán lifts the pistol and points it at the top of Raúl's head.

"Thank you, brother," Raúl whispers.

Adán pulls the trigger twice.

Art follows Scachi out onto the beach, where Sal makes the sign of the cross over two dead mercenaries. "Good men," he says to Art. Two of the other mercenaries carry the bodies back onto the Zodiacs.

Art trots up the beach, back to where he left Nora.

He stops when he sees Callan walking toward him, carrying Nora over his shoulder, her blond hair hanging down around her limp arms.

Art helps him heft her dead weight into the boat.

Adán doesn't go to San Felipe, but instead to a small fishing camp.

The owner knows who he is but feigns ignorance, which is the smart thing to do. He rents them two cabins in the back, one for Adán, the other for the driver.

Manuel knows what to do without being told.

He parks the Land Rover right next to his cabin and carries Raúl's body inside and into the bathroom. He lays the corpse in the bathtub, then goes out to get a knife like the fishermen use. He comes back in and butchers Raúl's body, severing his hands, arms, feet, legs and, finally, his head.

It's a shame that they cannot give him the funeral he deserves, but no one can know that Raúl Barrera is dead.

The rumors will start, of course, but as long as there is a chance that the Barrera *pasador*'s enforcer is still alive, no one will dare make a move against them. Once they know he's dead, the gates will be open and enemies will flood in to take their revenge against Adán.

Manuel takes a scaling knife and carefully strips the skin off Raúl's severed fingertips, then washes the skin down the bathtub drain. Then he puts the body parts in plastic shopping bags and rinses out the bathtub. He carries the bags out to a small motorboat, fills them with the lead shot fishermen use to weigh down skein nets and takes the boat deep into the Gulf. Then, every two or three hundred yards, he drops one of the bags into the water.

Each time he does, he says a quick prayer, addressing both the Virgin Mary and Santo Jesús Malverde.

Adán stands in the shower and cries.

His tears swirl down the drain with the dirty water.

Art and Shag go to the cemetery and leave flowers at Ernie's grave.

"Only one left," Art says to his headstone. "Just one left."

Then they drive down to La Jolla Shores and watch the sun go down from the bar at the Sea Lodge.

Art lifts his beer and says, "To Nora Hayden."

"To Nora Hayden."

They touch glasses and silently watch the sun go down over the ocean in a ball of flame that turns to a fiery gold on the water.

Fabián swaggers out of the Federal Court Building in San Diego. The federal judge has agreed to extradite him to Mexico.

He's still in his orange jumpsuit, his wrists shackled to his waist, his ankles chained, but still he manages to swagger and flash his drop-dead-killer movie-star smile at Art Keller.

"I'll be out in a month, loser," he says as he passes Art and steps into the waiting van.

I know you will, Art thinks. For a second he considers trying to stop him, then thinks, Fuck it.

General Rebollo personally takes custody of Fabián Martínez.

In the car on the way to the arraignment, he tells Fabián, "Don't worry about anything, but try not to be arrogant. Plead not guilty and keep your mouth shut."

"Did they take care of La Güera?"

"She's dead."

His parents are at the courthouse. His mother sobs and holds him; his father shakes his hand. An hour later, for a half-million dollars in assurance and as much in private payoff, the judge releases Junior Número Uno to his parents' recognizance.

They want to get him out of sight and out of Tijuana, so they take him to his uncle's compound in the country outside Ensenada, near the little village of El Sauzal.

He gets up early the next morning to take a piss.

He gets out of bed, really a mattress set out on the terrace, and walks downstairs to the bathroom. He's sleeping out there because all the bedrooms in his uncle's *estancia* are filled with relatives and because it's cooler out there at night with the breeze off the Pacific. And it's quieter—he can't hear bawling babies, or arguments, or lovemaking, or snoring or any of the other sounds that come with a large extended family reunion.

The sun is just up and already it's hot outside. It's going to be another long, hot day here in El Sauzal, another baking, boring Ensenada day full of nosy brothers and their imperious wives and their bratty children and his uncle who thinks he's a cowboy trying to get him on a horse.

He gets downstairs and something is wrong.

At first he can't put his finger on it, and then he does.

It's not something that's there, it's something that isn't.

Smoke.

There should be smoke from the servants' quarters outside the gates of the main house. The sun is up, and the women should already be making tortillas, and the smoke should be rising above the compound walls.

But it isn't.

And that's odd.

Is it some sort of holiday? he wonders. A feast day? Can't be, because his uncle would have been planning for it, his sisters-in-law arguing obsessively about some detail of menu or table setting, and he would already have been assigned his proper, tedious role in the arrangements.

So why aren't the servants up?

Then he sees why.

Federales coming through the gate.

There must be a dozen of them in their distinctive black jackets and ball caps and Fabián thinks, Oh, fuck, this is it, and he remembers what Adán always told him to do and he throws his hands up and knows this is going to be a major hassle but nothing that can't be fixed but then he sees that the lead *federale* is dragging one leg behind him.

It's Manuel Sánchez.

"No," Fabián mumbles. "No, no, no, no . . ."

He should have shot himself.

But they grab him up before he can find a gun, and force him to watch what they do to his family.

Then they tie him to a chair and one of the bigger men stands behind him and grabs him by his thick black hair so he can't move his head, even when Manuel shows him the knife.

"This is for Raúl," Manuel says.

He makes short, sharp cuts along the top of Fabián's forehead, then grabs each strip of skin and peels it down. Fabián's feet pound the stone floor as Manuel skins his face, leaving the strips hanging against his chest like the peels of a banana.

Manuel waits until the feet stop and then shoots him in the mouth.

The baby is dead in his mother's arms.

Art can tell from the way the bodies lie—her on top, the baby beneath her—that she tried to shield her child.

It's my fault, Art thinks.

I brought this on these people.

I'm sorry, Art thinks. I am so, so sorry. Bending over the mother and child, Art makes the sign of the cross and whispers, *"In nomine Patris et Filii et Spiritus Sancti."*

"El poder del perro," he hears one of the Mexican cops murmur.

The power of the dog.

PART FIVE

The Crossing

13

The Lives of Ghosts

When you're headin' for the border lord,
you're bound to cross the line.

—Kris Kristofferson, "Border Lord"

Putumayo District
Colombia
1998

A
rt walks into the ruined coca field and plucks a brown, wilted leaf from
its stem.

Dead plants or dead people, he thinks.

I'm a farmer in fields of the dead. The barren crop I cultivate with only a
scythe. My landscape of devastation.

Art's in Colombia on an information-gathering mission for the Vertical
Committee to make sure the DEA and CIA are singing to Congress from the
same hymnal. The two agencies and the White House are trying to whip up
congressional support for "Plan Colombia," a $1.7 billion aid package to
Colombia to destroy the cocaine trade at its source, the coca fields in the jungles of the Putumayo district of southern Colombia. The aid package calls
for more money for defoliants, more money for airplanes, more money for
helicopters.

They took one of those helicopters from Cartagena down to the town of
Puerto Asís on the Putumayo River, hard by the border with Ecuador. Art
wandered down to the river, a muddy brown ribbon running through the
intense, almost suffocating green of the jungle, and stood above a rickety
dock, where long, narrow canoes—the principal means of transportation in
an area with few roads—are loaded with plantains and bundles of firewood.

Javier, his escort, a young soldier of the Twenty-fourth Brigade, hustled down the bank to get him. Christ, Art thought, the kid can't be more than sixteen years old.

"You can't cross the river," Javier told him.

Art wasn't thinking of going across, but he asked, "Why not?"

Javier pointed across the river to the southern bank. "That's Puerto Vega. FARC owns it."

It was clear that Javier was anxious to get away from the riverbank, so Art walked back with him to "safe" territory. The government controls Puerto Asís and the north bank of the river around the town, but just west of here, even on the north side, is the FARC-controlled town of Puerto Caicedo.

But Puerto Asís is AUC country.

Art knows all about the Autodefensas Unidas de Colombia. The United Self-Defense Forces of Colombia was started by the old MAS cocaine lord Fidel Cardona, aka Rambo. Cardona used to operate a right-wing death squad from his Las Tangas ranch in northern Colombia, back in the days when everything was fat and happy in the Medellín cartel. Then Cardona turned against Pablo Escobar and helped the CIA track him down, a deed for which all his cocaine crimes were forgiven. Cardona took his shiny new soul and went into "politics" full-time.

AUC used to operate just in the northern part of the country; its move into the Putumayo district is a recent development. But when it came in, it came in strong, and Art sees evidence of that everywhere.

He saw the right-wing paramilitaries all over Puerto Asís—with their camouflage fatigues and red berets, cruising in pickup trucks, stopping peasants and searching them or just brandishing their M-16s and machetes.

Sending a message to the *campesinos,* Art thought: This is AUC turf and we can do what we want with you.

Javier was hustling him to a convoy of army vehicles on the main street. Art could see John Hobbs standing by one of the jeeps, tapping his foot impatiently. We need a military escort to go out into the countryside, Art thought.

"We need to hurry, Señor," Javier said.

"Sure," Art said. "I just need something to drink."

The heat was oppressive. Art's shirt was already soaked with sweat. The soldier led him to a little street-side stand where Art got two cans of warm Coke, one for himself and one for the soldier. The stand's owner, an old lady, asked him something in a rapid local dialect that Art didn't understand.

"She wants to know how you want to pay," Javier explained. "In cash or cocaine?"

"What?"

Cocaine is like money here, the soldier explained. The locals carry little bags of powder the way you would carry change. Most people pay with cocaine. Buying a soda with cocaine, Art thought as he pulled some rumpled, wet bills from his pocket. Coke for Coke—yeah, we're winning the War on Drugs here.

He handed the soldier one of the sodas and then joined the tour.

Now he stands in a ruined coca field and rubs the surface of a leaf with his thumb. It's sticky, and he turns to the Monsanto representative who's hovering around him like a mosquito and asks, "Are you mixing Cosmo-Flux with the Roundup?"

Roundup Ultra is the trade name for the defoliant glyphosate, which the Colombian army, with American advisers, sprays from low-flying airplanes protected by helicopter cover.

The more things change, Art thinks . . . first Vietnam, then Sinaloa, now Putumayo.

"Well, yes, it makes it stick to the plants better," the Monsanto rep says.

"Yeah, but it also increases the toxic risk to people, isn't that right?"

"Well—in large amounts, maybe," the flack says. "But we're using small dosages of Roundup here, and the Cosmo-Flux makes the small amount a lot more effective. A lot more bang for your buck."

"What amounts are they using here?"

The Monsanto guy doesn't know, but Art won't quit until he gets the answer. He holds the whole junket up while they stop one of the pilots, open up his tank and find out. After tenacious questioning and some browbeating of the guys who load the tanks, Art finds that they're using five liters per acre. The Monsanto literature recommends a liter per acre as the maximum safe dosage.

"Five times the safe dosage?" Art asks John Hobbs. *"Five times?"*

"We'll look into it," Hobbs says.

The man has aged. I guess I have, too, Art thinks, but Hobbs looks ancient. His white hair is finer, his skin almost translucent, his blue eyes still sharp even though it's plain that they can see the approach of sunset. And he's wearing a jacket, even though they're in the jungle and it's sweltering. He's perpetually cold, Art thinks, in the way that only the old and the dying are.

"No," Art says. *"I'll* look into it. Five times the recommended dose of glyphosate, and you're mixing in Cosmo-Flux? What are you trying to poison here, a crop or a whole environment?"

Because he has his suspicions that he's not looking at ground zero in the

War on Drugs so much as he's looking at ground zero in the war against Communist guerrillas—who live, hide and fight in the jungle.

So if you defoliate the jungle . . .

As his hosts show him their "successes," thousands of acres of wilted coca plants, Art peppers them with endless aggravating questions: Does it kill just coca, or does it poison other crops as well? Does it kill food crops—beans, bananas, maize, yucca? No? Well, what am I looking at in that field? It looks like it was maize to me. Isn't corn the mainstay of the local diet? What do they eat after their food crops are destroyed?

Because this isn't Sinaloa, Art thinks. There aren't any drug lords who own thousands of acres here. Most of the cocaine is grown by small *campesinos,* who plant an acre or two at most. FARC taxes them in its territory, AUC taxes them on the land it controls. Where the *campesinos* have it the worst, of course, is on territory that both sides actively claim—there they pay double the taxes on the cocaine they harvest.

As he watches the planes spray, he asks, How high are they flying? A hundred feet? Even Monsanto's own specs say that spraying from anything higher than ten feet isn't recommended. Doesn't that increase the risk of drift onto other crops? There's a stiff breeze today—aren't your defoliants being blown all over the place?

"You're way off base," Hobbs tells him.

"Am I?" Art asks. "I want you to get a biochemist out here and test the water in a dozen village wells."

He makes them take him to a refugee camp, where the *campesinos* have gone to flee the fumigation. It's little more than a clearing in the jungle with hastily built cinder-block buildings and tin-roof shacks. He demands to be taken to the clinic, where a missionary doctor shows him the kids with exactly the symptoms he was afraid he'd see—chronic diarrhea, skin rashes, respiratory problems.

"One-point-seven billion dollars to poison kids?" Art asks Hobbs as they get back into the jeep.

"We're in a war," Hobbs says. "This is no time to go wobbly, Arthur. It's your war, too. May I remind you that this is the cocaine that empowered such men as Adán Barrera? That money from this cocaine bought the bullets used at El Sauzal?"

I don't need a reminder, Art thinks.

And who knows where Adán is now? Six months after the raid in Baja and the subsequent massacre at El Sauzal, Adán is still in the wind. The U.S. government put a $2 million reward on his head, but so far, no one has stepped forward to collect.

Who wants money you'd never live to collect?

An hour's drive later they come to a village that's totally abandoned. Not a person, a pig, a chicken, a dog.

Nothing.

All the huts look untouched, save for a larger building—the communal storage bin by the looks of it—which has been totally gutted with flame from the inside.

A ghost town.

"Where are the people?" Art asks Javier.

The boy shrugs.

Art asks the officer in charge.

"Disappeared," he answers. "They must have run from FARC."

"Run where?"

Now the officer shrugs.

They spend the night at a small army base north of town. After a dinner of steaks grilled over a petrol-fueled fire, Art excuses himself from the party to get a little sleep, then slips off to take a look around the base.

You've been on one fire-base, you've been on them all, Art thinks. They're pretty much the same, Vietnam or Colombia—a clearing hacked out of the bush and leveled, then enclosed with barbed wire, then the perimeter around the base cleared to provide a field of fire.

This base is roughly bisected, Art finds out as he prowls around. Most of it is Twenty-fourth Brigade, but he comes to a gate that separates the main part of the base from what appears to be a section reserved for AUC.

He walks along the high barbed-wire fence and looks through.

It's a training camp—Art can make out the shooting range and the straw dummies hanging from trees for hand-to-hand practice. They're at it now, sneaking up behind the straw dummies with knives as if taking out enemy sentries.

Art watches for a while, then goes back to his quarters, a small room at the end of one of the barracks buildings, near the perimeter. The room has a window, open but screened with mosquito netting, a cot, a lamp run off the generator and, thankfully, an electric fan.

Art sits down on the cot and leans over. Sweat drips off his nose onto the concrete floor.

Jesus, Art thinks. Me and the AUC. We're the same guy.

He lies down on the bed but can't sleep.

It's hours later when he hears a soft knock outside on the edge of the window. It's the young soldier, Javier. Art goes to the window.

"What is it?"

"Would you come with me?"

"Where?"

"Would you come with me?" Javier repeats. "You asked where the people went?"

"Yeah?"

"Red Mist," Javier says.

Art slips his shoes back on and climbs out through the window. He ducks low behind Javier and the two of them sneak along the perimeter, ducking the searchlight, until they come to a small gate. The guard sees Javier and lets them through. They belly-crawl across the fire range and into the bush. Art follows the kid along a narrow trail that leads down toward the river.

This is stupid, Art thinks. This is beyond stupid. Javier could be leading you into a trap. He can see the headlines now: DEA BOSS KIDNAPPED BY FARC. But he keeps following the kid. There's something he has to find out.

A canoe is waiting on the riverbank.

Javier jumps in and beckons Art to do the same.

"We're crossing the river?" Art asks.

Javier nods and waves for him to hurry.

Art gets in.

It takes only a few minutes for them to row across. They land the canoe, and Art helps Javier drag it onto the shore. When he straightens he sees four masked men with guns standing there.

"Take him," Javier says.

"You little fuck," Art says, but the men don't grab him, just gesture for him to follow them west along the bank of the river. It's a hard slog—he keeps tripping on branches and thick vines—but finally they arrive at a small clearing and there, under the moonlight, he sees where the people went.

Headless bodies are washed up on the shore like fish waiting to be cleaned. Other decapitated trunks are stuck on branches that overhang the river. Schools of tiny fish are feeding on their bare feet. Farther up on shore, severed heads have been neatly lined up and someone has closed their eyes.

"The guerrillas did this?" Art asks.

One of the masked men shakes his head then tells him the story: AUC went to the village yesterday, shot the young men and raped the women. Then they locked most of the survivors inside the village's barn, set it on fire and made the rest watch and listen. Then they took these people to a bridge over the Putumayo, beheaded them with chain saws and threw their heads and bodies in the river to drift downstream as a warning to the villages below.

"We came to you," Javier says, "because we thought that if you could see the truth, you would go home and tell it. The people in America—if they knew the truth . . . they would not send their money and their soldiers to do this."

"What do you mean, our soldiers?" Art asks.

"The AUC here," the masked man says, "were trained by your Special Forces."

The man gestures to the corpses and says, in perfect English, "Your tax dollars at work."

Art says nothing on the trip back.

There's nothing to say.

Until he gets back to the base and finds Hobbs' room and bangs on the door. The old man is befuddled, sleepy. He has a thin white robe wrapped around him and looks like a patient in a hospital.

"Arthur, what time is it? Good Lord, where have you been?"

"Red Mist."

"What are you talking about?" Hobbs asked. "Are you drunk?"

But Art can see in his eyes that the man knows exactly what he's talking about. "Do you have an op in Colombia called Red Mist?"

"No."

"Don't you fucking lie to me," Art says. "It's the Phoenix Program, isn't it? For Latin America."

"Get off the grassy knoll, Arthur."

"Are we training AUC?" Art asks.

"That's on a need-to-know basis."

"I need to know!"

He tells Hobbs what he saw on the river. Hobbs opens a plastic bottle of water on his little side table, pours himself a glass and drinks it down. Art watches his hand tremble as he does it. Then Hobbs says, "You're very foolish, Arthur, and surprisingly naïve for a man of your experience. Obviously FARC committed that atrocity to blame it on AUC and further alienate the local population and arouse international sympathy. It was a common ploy with the Vietcong back in the—"

"Red Mist, John—what is it?"

"You should damn well know, Arthur," Hobbs snapped. "You used it on your little incursion into Mexico recently. In the eyes of the law, you're a mass murderer. You're as deeply into this as any of us."

Art sits on the bed and slumps over. It's true, he thinks. From that moment when we last stood in an army camp in a jungle and I sold my soul to you for revenge. When I lied and covered up, when I came to you for help in killing Adán Barrera.

He feels Hobbs sit down beside him. The man weighs practically nothing; he's like a dead, dry leaf.

"Don't think about straying off the reservation," Hobbs says.

Art nods.

"I expect your full support on Plan Colombia."

"You'll get it, John."

Art goes back to his room.

He peels down to his underwear, fixes himself a scotch, sits on the bed and sweats. The fan wheezes in its losing battle against the heat. But it's trying, Art thinks. It's fighting the good fight.

I'm just a shill for a covert war.

The War on Drugs. I've fought it my whole goddamn life, and for what?

Billions of dollars, trying unsuccessfully to keep drugs out of the world's most porous border? One-tenth of the anti-drug budget going into education and treatment, nine-tenths of those billions into interdiction? And not enough money from anywhere going into the root causes of the drug problem itself. And the billions spent keeping drug offenders locked up in prison, the cells now so crowded we have to give early release to murderers. Not to mention the fact that two-thirds of all the "non-drug" offenses in America are committed by people high on dope or alcohol. And our solutions are the same futile non-solutions—build more prisons, hire more police, spend more and more billions of dollars *not* curing the symptoms while we ignore the disease. Most people in my area who want to kick drugs can't afford to get into a treatment program unless they have blue-chip health insurance, which most of them don't. And there's a six-month-to-two-year waiting list to get a bed in a subsidized treatment program. We're spending almost $2 billion poisoning cocaine crops and kids over here, while there's no money at home to help someone who wants to get off drugs. It's insanity.

Art can't decide whether the War on Drugs is an obscene absurdity or an absurd obscenity. In either case, it's a tragic, bloody farce.

Emphasis on the *bloody*.

So much blood, so many bodies. So many more night visitors. The usual guests, plus the dead of El Sauzal. Now the ghosts of the Río Putumayo. The room is getting crowded.

He gets up and walks to the window to try to get a breath of fresh air.

Moonlight reflects off a rifle barrel.

Art drops to the floor.

Machine-gun fire rips the mosquito netting to shreds, shatters the window frame, pockmarks the wall above Art's bed. He presses himself to the floor and hears the wailing of an alarm horn, the sound of boots running, rifles cocked, shouting, confusion.

His door bursts open and the officer in charge comes in with his pistol drawn.

"Are you hurt, Señor Keller?!"

"I don't think so."

"Don't worry, we'll get them."

Twenty minutes later, Art sits with Hobbs in the mess tent, drinking coffee, letting his nerves come down from the adrenaline high.

"Are you still so fond of the humanitarian agrarian reformers of FARC?" Hobbs asks dryly.

A little while later the officer comes back with three of his soldiers and tosses a young man—scared, shaking and obviously beaten—at Art's feet. Art looks down at the kid—he could be Javier's twin brother. Shit, Art thinks, he could be my kid.

"This is one of them," the officer says, then kicks the kid in the face. "The others got away."

Art says, "Don't—"

"Tell him what you told me," the officer says, his boot pushing the kid's face into the floor. "Tell him."

The kid starts talking.

He's not a guerrilla, he's not from FARC. They wouldn't dare attack an army base.

"We were just trying to make the money," the kid says.

"What money?" Art asks.

The kid tells him.

Adán Barrera will pay over $2 million to the person who kills Arthur Keller.

"FARC and Barrera," Hobbs says. "Same thing."

Art's not so sure.

He's only sure that either he will kill Adán or Adán will kill him, and those are the only two ways this thing can end.

Sinaloa, Mexico
San Diego, California

Adán also lives with ghosts.

His brother's ghost, for instance, protects him. Most of Mexico believes that it was Raúl who conducted the massacre at El Sauzal, that the rumors of his death are a screen to protect him from the police, and most of Mexico is too scared of him to make a move against either Barrera brother.

But what Adán feels is the pain of his brother's death, and rage that it was

Art Keller who killed him. So his brother deserves vengeance, and his ghost cannot be laid to rest until Adán has settled with Keller.

So there's the ghost of Raúl, and then there's Nora's ghost.

When they told him that she was dead, he couldn't believe it at first. *Wouldn't* believe it. Then they showed him the obituary, the Americans claiming that she was killed in a car accident driving home from Ensenada. Her body brought back to California for burial. A closed casket to disguise the fact that they murdered her.

That Keller had murdered her.

Adán gave her a proper funeral in Badiraguato. A cross with her photo was carried through the village, while musicians sang *corridos* to her courage and beauty. He built a tomb of the finest marble with the inscription TIENES MI ALMA EN TUS MANOS.

You have my soul in your hands.

He has a Mass said for her every day, and money appears daily at the shrine of Santo Jesús Malverde in her name. And every day, flowers appear on her grave in La Jolla Cemetery, a standing order placed with a Mexican florist who knows only that he must bring the best and that the bill will be paid. It makes Adán feel a little better, but he won't be satisfied until he has avenged her.

He's put out a $2.1 million reward for the person who kills Art Keller, adding the extra hundred thousand so that the bounty is higher than the one the United States is offering for him. It's a foolish indulgence, he knows, but a matter of pride.

It doesn't matter; he has the money.

Adán has spent the past six months patiently and painstakingly reconstructing his entire organization. The irony is, after all the events of last year, that he's richer and more powerful than ever.

All his communications are on the Net now, scrambled and encoded with technology that even the Americans can't crack. He sends out orders through the Net, checks his accounts on the Net, sells his product on the Net and gets paid on the Net. He moves his money in the blink of an electronic eye, launders it literally faster than the speed of sound without ever touching a dollar bill or a *peso*.

He can, and does, kill over the Net. He just types a message and sends it, and someone leaves the physical world. There's no need to show up anywhere in real space or time anymore; in fact, it would be a foolish indulgence.

I've become a ghost myself, he thinks, existing only in cyberspace.

He physically lives in a modest house outside Badiraguato. It's good to be back in Sinaloa, back in the countryside among the *campesinos*. The fields have finally recovered from Operation Condor—the soil is refreshed and revitalized and the poppies bloom in splendid shades of red, orange and yellow.

Which is a good thing, because heroin is back.

To hell with the Colombians and FARC and the Chinese and all of that. The cocaine market is in sharp decline anyway. Good old Mexican Mud is in demand again in the States, and the poppies are weeping once more, this time with joy. The days of the *gomeros* are back, and I am the *patrón*.

He has a quiet life. Up early in the morning to a *café con leche* that his old *abuela* housekeeper has made for him, and then he's on the computer to check his investments, to oversee the business, to give orders. Then he has a lunch of cold meats and fruit and goes to the screened-in balcony upstairs for a short siesta. Then he gets up and takes a walk along the old dirt road that runs outside the house.

Manuel walks with him, still on guard as if there were any real danger. Certainly Manuel is happy to be back in Sinaloa, with his family and his friends, although he still insists on living in the little *casita* behind the main house.

After his walk, Adán goes back to the computer and works until dinnertime and then he might drink a beer or two and watch a *fútbol* or boxing match on television. Some evenings he will sit out on the lawn and the sound of guitars will drift down to him from the village. On still nights he can make out the words they're singing, of the exploits of Raúl and the treachery of El Tiburón and how Adán Barrera outfoxed the *federales* and the Yanquis and will never be caught.

He goes to bed early.

It's a quiet life, a good life, and it would be a perfect life if it were not for the ghosts.

Raúl's ghost.

Nora's ghost.

The ghosts of an estranged family.

He now communicates with Gloria only over the Net. It is the only secure way, but it pains him that his daughter is now only a configuration of electronic dots on a screen. They e-chat almost every night, though, and she sends him pictures. But it is hard not seeing her, or hearing her voice— terrible, really—and he blames Keller for this as well.

In truth, there are other ghosts.

They come when he lies down and shuts his eyes.

He sees the faces of Güero's children, sees them plunging down onto the rocks. He hears their voices in the wind. No one, he thinks, sings songs about that. No one puts that moment to music.

Nor do they sing of El Sauzal, but those ghosts come, too.

And Father Juan.

He comes most of all.

Gently chiding. But there's nothing I can do about that ghost, he thinks. I have to focus on what I *can* do.

What I have to do.

Kill Art Keller.

He's busy planning that and running his business when the world comes crashing down around him.

He sits down at the computer to get his message from Gloria. But it's not his daughter online saying hi, it's his wife, and if an instant message could scream this one would.

Adán—Gloria had a stroke. She's at Scripps Mercy Hospital.

My God, what happened?

Uncommon but by no means rare for someone with her condition. The pressure on the carotid artery simply became too much. Lucía had gone into her bedroom and found Gloria unconscious. The e-techs were unable to revive her. She's on life support, tests are being run, but the prognosis isn't hopeful.

Absent a miracle, Lucía will soon have to make a very difficult decision.

Don't take her off life support.

Adán—

Don't.

There's no hope. Even if she does make it, they say she'd be a—

Don't say it.

You're not here. I've talked to my priest, he says it's morally acceptable to—

I don't care what a priest says.

Adán.

I'll be there tonight. Tomorrow morning at the latest.

She won't know you, Adán. She wouldn't know if you were here or not.

I'll know.

All right, Adán. I'll wait for you. We'll make the decision together.

Twelve hours later Adán waits in the penthouse of the apartment building overlooking the border crossing at San Ysidro. He peers through a pair of nightscope binoculars, waiting for two things to come together—the bribed guard on the Mexican side has to come on duty at the same time as the bribed agent on the American side.

It's supposed to happen at ten, but if it doesn't, he's going to make the run anyway.

He just hopes it happens.

It will make it easier.

Still, he's not taking any chances he doesn't have to; he has to get to that hospital, so he waits for the change of shifts at the border stations and then the phone rings. The single number 7 appears on the little screen.

"Go."

Two minutes later he's downstairs in the parking structure, standing outside a Lincoln Navigator stolen that morning in Rosarito and fitted out with clean plates. A nervous young man holds the back door open for him. He can't be more than twenty-two or twenty-three, Adán thinks, and his hand is trembling and moist with sweat and for a second Adán wonders if it's just because the kid is nervous or because this is a trap, and he says, "You realize that if you betray me, your whole family will die."

"Yes."

Adán gets in the back, where another young man, probably the driver's brother, removes the cushion off the backseat to reveal a box. Adán gets in, lies down, fits the breathing apparatus over his nose and mouth and starts to take in oxygen as the seat is replaced over him. He lies in the dark and hears the whine of the electric screwdriver as it replaces the screws.

Adán is locked inside the box.

It's too much like a coffin.

He fights off the initial panic of claustrophobia and forces himself to breathe slowly and steadily. You can't waste air hyperventilating, he tells himself. The radio stations list the current wait at the border as forty-five minutes, but that estimate could be wrong, and they will still have to drive a few minutes beyond that to find a place isolated enough to stop and get him out.

And that's if everything goes well.

That's if this isn't a trap.

All they'd have to do, he thinks, to collect a huge reward is to drive you straight to a police station: Guess what we have in the box. Or worse, they could be in the employ of one of your enemies, and then all they'd have to do is drive to an isolated desert canyon and leave the truck there. Leave you to suffocate or bake in tomorrow's sun. Or just stick a rag in the gas tank, light it and . . .

Don't think that way, he tells himself.

Just think that it will go as all-too-hastily planned, that these boys are loyal (really, there's been too little time for them to plan a betrayal), that you'll breeze through the bribed border checks and that in three hours or so you'll be holding Gloria's hand.

And maybe her eyes will flutter open, maybe there will be a miracle.

So he slows his breathing and waits.

Time passes slowly in a coffin.

Lots of time to think.

About a dying daughter.

Children plunging from a bridge.

Hell.

A lot of time to think.

Then he hears muffled voices—the Border Patrol agent asking questions. How long have you been in Mexico? Why did you go down? Are you bringing anything back? Do you mind if I look in the back?

Adán hears the car door open and then close.

They're moving again.

Adán can tell by the subtle shift inside the box. Maybe it's his imagination, or maybe the air actually is suddenly a little cooler inside the fetid container, and he literally breathes a bit easier as the car speeds up.

Then it slows again and he's getting knocked around inside the box on the apparently bumpy road and then the car comes to a stop. Adán clutches the *pistola* in the waistband of his pants and waits. If they've betrayed him, this might be the moment when the box lid will come open and men with pistols or machine guns will be standing over him, waiting to blast away.

Or, he thinks with a shudder, they might just never open the box.

Or they might light a match.

Then he hears the electric whine of the screwdriver, the lid is lifted off and the young driver stands there, smiling at him. Adán rips the breathing apparatus off his nose and takes the proffered hand as the kid helps him out of the box.

He stands stiffly in the dust of the dirt road and sees a white Lexus parked to the side. Another smiling kid, his neck festooned with gang tattoos, hands him a set of keys.

"You start it," Adán says.

You go turn the key, *you* go up in a ball of flame and jagged metal when the bomb goes off beneath you.

The kid turns pale, but nods, gets into the Lexus and starts it up.

The motor purrs.

The gangbanger gets out of the car and giggles.

Adán gets in. "Where are we?"

They tell him. Give him directions to get off this dirt road and onto the freeway. Fifty minutes later, he pulls into the hospital's parking lot.

Adán crosses the parking lot, imagining dozens of eyes on him.

No one appears from a car, no men in blue Windbreakers with DEA on them come yelling and screaming and telling him to hit the ground. There is only the sad, eerie quiet of a hospital parking lot. He crosses to the entrance, goes inside and finds that his daughter's room is on the eighth floor.

The elevator doors slide open.

Lucía sits on a bench in the hallway, hunched over, tears streaming down her face. He puts his arms around her. "Am I too late?"

Unable to speak, she shakes her head.

"I want to see her," Adán says.

He opens the door to his daughter's room and goes inside.

Art Keller sticks a gun in his face.

"Hello, Adán."

"My daughter—"

"She's fine."

Adán feels something sharp stick through his shirt and sting him in the back.

Then the world goes black.

Art and Shag put Adán's unconscious body on a gurney and take him down to the morgue. Put him in a body bag, strap him back on the gurney and roll him out to a van painted with HIDALGO FUNERAL HOME. Forty-five minutes later they're at a secure location.

It was relatively easy to force Lucía to betray her husband, and maybe the lousiest thing Art had ever done in his life.

They'd been on her for months, keeping the house under surveillance, the land line tapped, the cell phone monitored, trying to break the cybercode that sent messages back and forth between Adán Barrera and his daughter.

Art had to appreciate the irony that it was numbers that eventually gave them the key.

Lucía's bank accounts.

No matter how they laundered their money, Lucía couldn't account for her assets. End of story. She didn't work, but had a lifestyle that showed considerable income.

Art had approached her and pointed this out when she came out of a gourmet deli near their home in an expensive part of Rancho Bernardo. She's still an attractive woman, Art thought when he watched her come out, rolling a grocery cart in front of her. Her body trim from her three-times-a-week Pilates class, her hair coiffed and skillfully tinted in shades of amber at José Eber up at La Costa.

"Mrs. Barrera?"

She looked startled, then almost tired.

"I use my maiden name," she said, looking at the badge he proffered. "I know nothing about my husband's business or his whereabouts. Now please excuse me, I have to pick up my daughter from—"

"She's an honor-roll student, right?" Art asked, smiling despite feeling like a piece of shit. "Glee club? Honors English and math? Let me ask you a question: How's she going to fare with you in prison?"

He laid it out for her right there in the strip-mall parking lot: At the very least, she goes for income-tax evasion, but the worst-case scenario—and I think I can make it stick, Art added—is that she gets nailed with receiving narcotics money, which puts her in the thirty-to-life ballpark.

"I'll take your house, your cars, your bank accounts," Art said. "You'll be in a federal lockup and Gloria will be on welfare. You think Medicaid will take care of her health needs? She can stand in line at the walk-in clinic, see the very best doctors . . ."

Attaboy, Art, he thought. Use a terminally ill kid as leverage. He made himself remember the baby's corpse at El Sauzal, gripped in his dead mother's arms.

She reaches into her purse for her phone. "I'm calling my lawyer."

"Have him meet you at the federal jail downtown," Art said, "because that's where we're going. Listen, I can send someone over to school to pick up Gloria, explain that Mom's in jail. They'll take her to the Polaski Center. She'll make a lot of nice new friends there."

"You are the lowest form of human life."

"No," Art said. "I'm the *second* lowest. You married the lowest. You still take his money, you don't care where it comes from. Would you like to see some photos of how Adán makes his child-support payments? I have some in my car."

Lucía starts to cry. "My daughter is very ill. She has many health issues that . . . She couldn't stand . . ."

"To be without her mother," Art said. "I understand."

He let her think about it for a minute or so, knowing the decision she had to make.

She dried her eyes.

"What," she asked, "do you want me to do?"

Now Art finishes typing something into his laptop computer and looks down at Adán, who is handcuffed to a bed. Adán opens his eyes, comes to and realizes that he's not going to wake up from this nightmare.

When Adán recognizes Art, he says, "I'm surprised I'm still alive."

"Me, too."

"Why didn't you kill me?"

Because I'm tired of all the killing, Art says to himself. I am sick to my soul of all the blood. But he answers, "I have better plans for you. Let me tell you about the federal prison in Marion, Illinois: You'll spend twenty-three hours a day alone in an eight-by-seven cell that you can't even see out of. You'll get one hour a day to walk back and forth, alone, between two cinder-block walls topped with razor wire and a tantalizing slice of blue sky. You'll get two ten-minute showers a week. You'll get your crappy meals pushed to you through a slot. You'll lie on a metal rack with a thin blanket, and the lights will be on twenty-four/seven. You'll squat like an animal over an open toilet with no seat and smell your own shit and piss, and I won't push for the death penalty, I'll push for life without parole. You're what, mid-forties? I hope you have a long life."

Adán starts to laugh. "*Now* you're going to play by the rules, Art? You're going to take me into court? Good luck, *viejo*. You don't have any *witnesses*."

He laughs and laughs and laughs, feeling only a little disconcerted when Art starts to laugh with him. Then Art sets the computer in front of Adán, flips the screen open and presses a couple of keys.

"Surprise, motherfucker."

Adán looks into the screen and sees a ghost.

Nora sits in a chair, looking impatiently at a magazine. Then she looks at her watch, frowns and then looks back at the magazine.

"Live feed," Art says, then shuts the screen.

"You think she won't flip on you?" Art asks Adán. "You think she won't testify against you because she *loves* you so much? You think she's going to spend the rest of her life in the hole so that *you* can walk?"

"I'd trade my life for hers."

"Yeah, you're so fucking noble."

Art can feel Adán thinking, that little computer inside his head whirring, reconfiguring the new situation, coming up with a solution.

"We can make a deal," Adán says.

"You have nothing to deal with," Art says. "That's the problem with being at the top, Adán—you can't trade up. You got nothing to trade."

"Red Mist."

"What?"

"Red Mist?" Adán says. "You don't know? No, Americans never do. It's not just the drugs you buy that are soaked in blood. It's your oil, your coffee, your security. The only difference between you and me is that I acknowledge what I do."

Adán had made copies of the contents of Parada's briefcase. Of course he did; only an idiot wouldn't have. The information is in a safe-deposit box in Grand Cayman, and contains evidence that could bring down two governments. It details Operation Cerberus and the Federación's cooperation with the Americans in the Contra drugs-for-arms operation; it talks about Operation Red Mist, about how Mexico City, Washington and the drug cartels sponsored assassinations of left-wing figures in Latin America. There's evidence of the assassinations of two officials to fix the Mexican presidential elections, and proof of Mexico City's active partnership with the Federación.

That's in the briefcase. He has more inside his head—specifically, knowledge of the Colosio assassination, as well as Keller's perjury to the congressional committee investigating Cerberus. So maybe Keller will have him put away for life, and maybe he won't.

Adán lays out the deal: If they don't reach a satisfactory arrangement within thirty-six hours, he'll have a package of tapes and documents delivered to the Senate Subcommittee.

"I may wind up in a federal prison," Adán says, "but we might be cell mates."

Nothing to trade up? Adán thinks.

How about the government of the United States?

"What do you want?" Art asks.

"A new life."

For me.

And for Nora.

Art looks at him for a long time. Adán smiles like the proverbial cat.

Then Art says, "Go fuck yourself."

He's *glad* that Adán has the evidence. He's glad it will come out. It's time to eat truth like bitter dirt.

You think I'm afraid of prison, Adán?

Where the hell do you think I am now?

· · · ·

Nora sets the magazine down and paces around the room. She's done a lot of that over the past few months. First when they were weaning her off the drugs, then, after she felt better, out of sheer tedium.

She's told them she wanted to leave a hundred times. A hundred times Brown Eyes has given her the same answer.

"It's not safe yet."

"What? I'm a prisoner?"

"You're not a prisoner."

"Then I want to leave."

"It's not safe yet."

His were the first eyes she'd seen when she came to, that horrible night back on the Sea of Cortez. She was lying in the bottom of a small boat, and she opened her eyes and saw his brown eyes staring down at her. Not cold, like a lot of men have stared at her, not filled with desire, but with concern.

A pair of brown eyes.

She was coming back to life.

She had started to say something but he shook his head and put his finger to his lips, like he was hushing a small child. She tried to move but couldn't—she was wrapped in something warm and tight, like a sleeping bag that was a little too small. Then he gently brushed the palm of his hand over her eyes, as if he were telling her to go back to sleep, and she did.

Even now her memories of that night are vague. She's heard people on goofy talk shows tell about alien abductions, and it was sort of like that, without the probes or the medical experiments. She does remember being stuck with a needle, though, and wrapped in this thing like a bag, and she doesn't recall being scared when they zipped it closed over her head, because there was a little black screen over her face and she could breathe all right.

She remembers being placed on another boat, a bigger one, then onto an airplane, and then there was another needle and when she woke up, she was in this room.

And he was there.

"I'm here to keep you safe," was about all he'd say. He wouldn't even tell her his name, so she just started calling him Brown Eyes. Later that first day he put her on the phone with Art Keller.

"It's just for a little while," Keller reassured her.

"Where's Adán?" she asked.

"We missed him," Keller said. "We got Raúl, though. We're pretty sure he's dead."

And so are you, Keller added. He explained the whole ruse to her. Even though they had set up Fabián Martínez as the *soplón*, it was still better if everyone, especially Adán, thought that she had died. Otherwise, Adán would never stop trying to get her back or, alternatively, to have her killed. We'll put out the word you died in a car accident, Keller said. Adán will know that you were "killed" in the raid, of course, and read the news as a cover-up.

And that's all right, too.

It was weird when Brown Eyes brought in her obituary to show her. It was brief, listed her profession as an event planner and gave a few details of the funeral—calling hours, all that shit. She wondered who attended; her father, probably, no doubt stoned; her mother, of course; and Haley.

And that was probably about it.

A little while turns into a long while.

Keller calls in about once a week, saying that he was still working on getting Adán, saying that he'd like to come see her, but it wouldn't be safe. The mantra, Nora thinks. It wouldn't be safe for her to go for a walk, it wouldn't be safe for her to go shopping, to a movie, to resume any kind of life.

Anytime she asks Brown Eyes about any of this, the answer is always the same. He looks at her with those puppy-dog eyes and says, "It wouldn't be safe."

"Just let me know what you need," Brown Eyes tells her. "I'll get it for you."

It becomes one of her few sources of entertainment, sending Brown Eyes out on increasingly complicated shopping missions. She gives him detailed requests for hard-to-find, expensive cosmetics; very particular instructions as to the particular shade of blouse she needs; fussy, impossible-for-a-man-to-understand requests for designer clothes from her favorite shops.

He does it all, except for her request for a dress from her favorite boutique in La Jolla. "Keller says I can't go there," he says apologetically. "It wouldn't—"

"—be safe," she says; then for revenge she sends him out to buy feminine products and lingerie. She hears him kick-start his motorcycle and roar off, and she spends the hours that he is gone enjoying the thought of him stumbling red-faced through Victoria's Secret and having to ask a saleslady for help.

But she doesn't really like it when he's gone, because it leaves her alone with the weird trio of the other bodyguards. She goes along with the silly charade that she doesn't know their names, although she can hear them talking to one another from her room. The old man, Mickey, is sweet enough, and brings her cups of tea. O-Bop, the one with the kinky red hair, is just strange, but looks at her as if he wants to fuck her, which she's used to. It's the other one who really disturbs her—the fat one who incessantly eats peaches straight from the can.

Big Peaches.

Jimmy Piccone.

They pretend not to remember each other.

But I remember you, she thinks.

My first professional fuck.

She remembers his brutality, his sheer ugliness, that he used her so that she felt like a rag that he jerked off into. She remembers that night well.

So she remembers Callan.

It took her a while, especially as she was still so whacked-out when they first brought her here. But it was Callan—Brown Eyes—who eased her off the pills, gave her ice chips to suck on when she was so thirsty but was still throwing up everything, stroked her hair while she hunched over the john, talked bullshit to her during the bad insomniac hours, played cards with her all night sometimes, cajoled her into eating again, made her dry toast and chicken broth and made a special trip out to get her tapioca pudding just because she mentioned that it sounded good.

It was when she had pretty much detoxed and was feeling better that she remembered where she'd seen him before.

My debut as a hooker, she thinks, my coming-out party to be introduced to john society. He was the one I wanted for my first, she remembers, because he looked gentle and sweet and I liked his brown eyes.

"I remember you," she said when he came into the room with her lunch, a banana and some wheat toast.

He looked surprised. Said, shyly, "I remember you, too."

"That was a long time ago."

"A long time."

"A lot's happened since then."

"Yeah."

So although it was boring in her "confinement," as she came to call it, she was really doing all right. They got her a television and a radio and a Walkman, a collection of CDs and a whole bunch of books and magazines, and they even created a little outdoor workout area for her, Callan and Mickey putting up a wooden fence even though there wasn't another house around for miles, then going out and getting her a treadmill and a stationary bicycle. So she could exercise and read and watch TV, and she was really doing all right until the night she settled into bed and PBS came on with a special hour about the War on Drugs and she saw footage of the massacre at El Sauzal.

She felt the breath catch in her throat as the narrator speculated that the entire family of Fabián Martínez—El Tiburón—had been executed in reprisal for his becoming an informer to the DEA. Her entire body trembled as she saw the footage of the corpses splayed around the courtyard.

She made Callan get Keller on the phone right then.

"Why didn't you tell me?!" she screamed into the phone.

"I thought it better that you didn't know."

"You shouldn't have done it," she cried. "You shouldn't have done it . . ."

She went into a tailspin after that, a lie-in-bed, fetal-position, not-get-up, not-eat depression.

Nineteen lives, she brooded.

Women, children.

A baby.

For me.

Her bodyguards were terrified. Callan would come into her room and sit at the foot of her bed like a dog, not talking or anything, just sitting, as if he could protect her from the pain that was slicing her up from the inside.

But he couldn't do anything.

Nobody could.

She would just lie there.

Then one day Callan, looking very serious, handed her the phone and it was Keller and he said simply, "We got him."

John Hobbs and Sal Scachi also react to the news of Adán's capture.

"I really thought that Arthur would simply kill him," Hobbs says. "It would have been simpler."

"Now we have a problem," Scachi says.

"We do, indeed," Hobbs says. "This has become something of a mess. We need to start cleaning it up."

Adán Barrera dead is one thing. Adán Barrera alive and talking, particularly in court, is another. And Arthur Keller . . . it's difficult to know what's on his mind these days. No, it's prudent to make other arrangements.

John Hobbs gets on the phone to do just that.

He makes a call to Venezuela.

Sal Scachi goes to clean things up.

. . . .

The teakettle whistles.

Harsh, loud.

"Will you shut that fucking thing off!?" Peaches yells. "You and your fucking tea!"

Mickey grabs the kettle off the stove.

"Leave him alone," Callan says.

"What?"

"I said don't talk to him like that."

"Hey," O-Bop says. "We're all a little tense here."

No shit, Peaches thinks. Locked up in this cabin in the barren hills north of the border for months with Adán Barrera's mistress in the back room. The fucking cunt. "Mickey, I'm sorry I yelled at you, okay?" Peaches turns to Callan. "Okay?"

Callan doesn't answer.

"I'm going to bring her tea in to her," Mickey says.

"The fuck are you? The butler?" Peaches asks. He don't want Mickey getting attached to this woman. Guys who've done heavy time are like that. They get sentimental, they get attached to any living thing that ain't actually trying to kill or cornhole them—mice, birds. Peaches has seen old cons get weepy over a cockroach died of natural causes in the cell. "Let someone else do room service. Let O-Bop—he looks like a waiter. No, second thought, Callan, *you* do it."

Callan knows what Peaches is thinking and says, "Why don't *you* bring it in?"

"I asked *you,*" Peaches says.

"It's getting cold," Mickey says.

"No, you didn't," Callan says. "You didn't ask, you *said.*"

"Mr. Callan," Peaches says, "would you pretty-please bring the young lady her tea?"

Callan picks up the mug off the counter.

"God, the shit I have to go through," Peaches says as Callan walks toward Nora's room.

"Knock first," Mickey says.

"She's a whore," Peaches says. "Nobody's ever seen her naked, right?"

He walks outside onto the porch, looks out yet again at the moonlight shining on the barren hills and wonders how the fuck his life came to this. Babysitting a whore.

Callan comes out. "The fuck is your problem?"

"Barrera's cunt," Peaches says. "We're just supposed to turn her over now? I should cut her fucking hands off, send her back to him."

"She didn't do nothin' to you."

"You just want to fuck her," Peaches says. "Tell you what, let's *all* do her."

Callan nods slowly. "Hey, Jimmy? Start to touch her, I'll put two between your eyes. Come to think, I should have done it years ago, first time I saw your fat ass."

"You wanna dance, Irish, it ain't too late."

Mickey comes out on the porch and gets between them. "Knock it off, you two jerks. This is going to be over soon."

No, Callan thinks.

It's going to be over *now.*

He knows Peaches, knows the way he is. He gets something in his head, he's going to do it, no matter what. And he knows how Peaches thinks—Barrera killed someone *I* loved, I kill someone *he* loves.

Callan goes inside, walks past O-Bop, knocks on Nora's door and walks in. "Come on," he says.

"Where are we going?" Nora asks.

"Come on," Callan says. "Get your shoes on. We're leaving."

She's puzzled by his attitude. He's not being sweet, or shy. He's angry, hard, bossing her around. She doesn't like it, so she takes her time getting her shoes on, just to show him he's not going to boss her around.

"Come on, hurry up."

"Chill."

"I'm ice," Callan says. "Just get your ass in gear, all right?"

She stands up, glares at him. "What gear would you like it in?"

She's shocked when he grabs her by the wrist and pulls her out. He's being a typical asshole male, and she doesn't like it.

"Hey!"

"I don't have time to fuck around," Callan says.

I just want to get this over with.

She tries to pull away but his grip is too strong so she has no choice but to follow him as he pulls her into the other room. "Stay right behind me."

He pulls his .22 and holds it in front of him.

"What's going on?" she asks.

He doesn't answer, just pulls her into the main room.

"The fuck you doing?" Peaches asks.

"Leaving."

Peaches reaches for the pistol tucked in his jacket pocket.

"*Uh*-uhn," Callan says.

Peaches thinks better of it.

O-Bop whines, "Callan, what are you doing?" He starts to ease his hand toward a shotgun lying on the old couch.

"Don't make me hurt you, Stevie," Callan says. That would be too bad, seeing as how all this, *all this,* started with him trying to save O-Bop's life. "I don't wanna hurt you."

O-Bop obviously decides he don't want to be hurt, either, because his hand stays where it is.

"Have you considered this carefully?" Mickey asks him.

No, Callan thinks, I ain't considered nothing carefully. Only that I'm not letting anybody kill this woman. He keeps himself in front of her and backs out the door, his gun trained on his old crew. "I see any of you, I kill you."

"Hop on," he tells her.

He gets on the bike.

"Hold on to my waist," Callan says.

Good thing she does, because he rabbit-starts the bike and it shoots like a missile out of there, sending up a thick cloud of dust behind it. She holds on tighter when he steers onto a dirt track up a steep hill, the back wheel fish-tailing around in the soft dirt. He stops the bike at the top of the hill, a shallow, dusty patch stripped bare by the fierce Santa Ana winds. Around it, nothing but thick chapparal.

He says, "Hold on."

Then she feels herself falling.

Plunging down the hill in a free-fall.

Gunshots chase them.

Callan ignores them, concentrates on driving the bike.

Past the shack, past some cars, past the men who scramble behind the cars, then reach for guns, then duck as the lead splatters into glass, but she can barely see any of this, it's a blur, and she can hardly hear the shots, the bullets zipping past her ears, the startled shouts. All she can really see now is the back of his helmet as she lays her head into his shoulder and *holds on.* It's as if she's in a wind tunnel, the force of the wind trying to rip her off the back of the bike, they're going *so fast, so fast, so fast.*

Down this dirt road, it's dark now, blackness closing in around her in this tunnel of speed. She's knows now they're running for their lives, racing toward their lives, throwing fate to the wind, *faith* to the wind, her faith on the back of this madman driving, the rough dirt road rattling her, bouncing her, suddenly they're in the air, airborne, air*born,* hurled at this speed into the night sky by a small bump. She's flying, flying with him, the stars, the stars are beautiful, they're going to crash, they're going to die, their blood will pool on this dirt road, their common blood, she can feel her blood pumping, she can feel his, their blood coursing as it soars through the night sky, then they land, the bike tipping over out of control into a long skid. She holds on tight, she doesn't want to die alone, she wants to die with him in this long slide to death, this long slow fast slide to oblivion, a moment of agony then nothing, then nothingness, then peace. She always thought you flew to heaven, but you fall, fall, fall, falling, she holds him, hugs him, embraces him, don't let me die alone I don't want to die alone and then he rights the bike, they're up again, racing, the air is cool around her ears the leather warm against her skin, against her face. He takes a deep gulp of the cold air and she swears she hears herself laugh over the engine's thunder—or is that her heart?—but she hears herself laugh and hears him laugh and then it's suddenly smooth under the wheels, smooth and black as they hit asphalt, beautiful slick black American road, American highway.

The highway lights are golden in the night.

Jimmy Peaches steps out onto the porch.

Got himself a freshly opened can of Doles, and a spoon, and there's a pretty sliver of a silver moon out and it's a good time to think.

Maybe this is what Callan had in mind the whole time, the scheming Irish fuck. Or maybe he and the chick were planning it together, all them times he was bringing her cups of tea. Just like Callan, always the lone wolf.

Sal ain't gonna be happy. Called with his instructions—I'm coming for a meeting, I want to make sure everyone is there. Well, Scachi will hunt Callan down and teach him a lesson about fucking his friends. He digs the spoon into the can.

A slice of peach somersaults into the air.

Juice splatters on Peaches' chest.

He looks down, surprised that it's golden red, the color of a fiery sunset. He didn't know they made those kind of peaches. His chest feels all sticky and warm, and he wonders why the sun is setting twice tonight.

The next round smacks him squarely in his broad forehead.

O-Bop sees this as he looks out the window, through the little octagonal wire screen. His mouth gapes into a perfect O as he sees Peaches' brains jet out the back of his head and hit the cabin wall, and that's all he sees as a bullet zips into his open mouth and explodes in his cerebral cortex.

Mickey sees him melt like spring snow and puts the kettle on. The water is just starting to roil at the bottom of the kettle when Scachi and two shooters come in the door, their rifles leveled at him.

"Sal."

"Mickey."

"I was just having tea," Mickey says.

Sal nods.

The kettle whistles.

Mickey pours the water into the chipped mug and dips the tea bag a few times. The bowl rattles as he spoons in some sugar and a little milk, and then the spoon knocks against the side of the mug as his shaking hand stirs the tea.

He lifts the mug to his mouth and takes a sip.

Then he smiles—it's good and it's hot—and nods to Sal.

Scachi takes him out quick and clean, then steps over his body to go into the bedroom.

She's not there.

And where's Callan?

His Harley's gone.

Fuck.

Callan's taken the woman and is doing a solo, Scachi thinks. And now I'm going to have to track him down.

But first there's cleanup to be done.

Within a couple of hours his men have set up a meth lab in the cabin. They drag Peaches' body back in and pour hydriodic acid around inside, then walk back to the facing hillside and shoot an incendiary round through the window.

The firefighters are lucky that night—there's little wind and the fire from the meth-lab explosion burns only about twelve acres of some old grass and chapparal up the hill. That's not so bad; in fact, it's good to have a fire like that every once in a while.

Burns off the old grass.

So the new grass can grow in its place.

14

Pastoral

Love is all we have, the only way that each can help the other.

—Euripides, *Orestes*

San Diego County
1998

They get up early and ride.

"There'll be people looking for us," Callan tells her.

No kidding, Nora thinks. When they finally stopped driving last night and pulled over, she'd demanded to know just what the hell was going on.

"They were going to kill you," Callan answered.

He found them a cheap motel a little ways off the highway and grabbed a few hours' sleep.

He shakes her awake at four and tells her they need to get going. But the bed is so nice and warm she pulls the blanket up over her mouth and settles in for just a few more minutes. Anyway, he's taking a shower—through the cheap, paneled walls she can hear the water running.

"I'll get up," she thinks, "when I hear the water stop."

Next thing she knows, his hand is on her shoulder, nudging her awake again.

"We gotta get going."

She gets up, finds her sweater and jeans where she tossed them over the room's one chair, and puts them on. "I'm going to need some new clothes."

"We'll get you some."

He looks at her sitting on the bed and can't believe she's really with him. Can't believe what he did, doesn't know what the consequences will be, doesn't care. She's so beautiful, even looking tired and rumpled in clothes that do smell. But they smell like her.

She finishes tying a shoe, looks up and catches him looking.

It's always cold at four in the morning.

Can be the middle of summer in the middle of the Amazon jungle—if you just got out of bed at four in the morning, it's still cold. He sees her shivering and gives her his leather jacket.

"What about you?" she asks.

"I'm okay."

She takes the jacket. It's too big but she wraps the sleeves around her and the old jacket is soft and warm and it feels as if his arms are holding her like they held her last night. Men have given her diamond necklaces, Versace dresses, furs. None of them ever felt as good as that jacket. She climbs on the back of the bike, and then has to push the sleeves up so she can hold on to him.

They head east on Interstate 8.

There are mostly just truck drivers on the road, and a few old pickups full of *mojado* fieldworkers headed for the farms out by Brawley. Callan drives until he sees a turn-off for something called Sunrise Highway. Sounds about right, he thinks, and turns north onto that. The road climbs in sharp switchbacks up the steep southern slope of Mount Laguna, past the little town of Descanso, then runs along the top of the mountain ridge, with deep pine forest to their left side and, hundreds of feet below the ridge to their right, a desert.

And the sunrise *is* spectacular.

They stop at a pull-off and watch the sun come up over the desert floor, lighting it in tones changing from red to orange and then into the subtle panoply of desert browns—tan, beige, dun and, of course, sand. Then they get back on the bike and ride some more, along the mountaintop, as the forest gives way to chaparral and then to long stretches of grasslands, and then they come to the edge of a lake near the junction with Highway 79.

Callan turns south on 79 and they drive around the edge of the lake until they come to a little restaurant sitting right by the water.

He pulls up in front.

They go inside.

The place is pretty quiet—a few fishermen, a couple of men who look like ranchers and who glance up from their plates as Callan and Nora come in. They pick a table by the window with a view of the small lake. Callan orders two fried eggs, bacon and hash browns. Nora orders tea and dry toast.

"Eat some real food," Callan says.

"I'm not hungry."

"Suit yourself."

She doesn't touch the tea or the toast. When Callan's done wolfing down his eggs they go outside and take a walk along the lakeshore.

"So what are we doing?" Nora asks.

"Taking a walk beside a lake."

"I'm serious."

"So am I," he says.

There are pine trees on the other side of the lake. Their needles shimmer in the breeze, which kicks up little whitecaps on the water.

"They're going to be looking for me."

"You want them to find you?" Callan asks.

"No," she says. "Not for a while, anyway."

"The way I feel," he says, "I just want to live for a while, you know? I don't know how all this is going to turn out, but I just want to live for a while. Are you good with that?"

"Yeah," she answers. "Yeah, I'm real good with that."

He does want to take some precautions, though. "We'll have to get rid of the bike," he says. "They'll be looking for it, and it sticks out too much."

They find a new vehicle a few miles south on 79. An old farmhouse sits down in a bowl off to the east of the highway. One of those classic white-trash front yards, with old cars and old car parts scattered around outside an old barn and a few dilapidated shacks that might have once been chicken coops. Callan steers down the dirt road and stops the bike outside the barn, inside of which a guy in the inevitable ball cap is working on a '68 Mustang. He's tall, skinny, maybe fifty years old, although it's hard to tell under the cap.

Callan looks at the Mustang. "What do you want for it?"

"Nothin'," the guy says. "Ain't sellin' this one."

"Sellin' any of them?"

The guy points to a lime-green '85 Grand Am sitting outside. "The passenger-side door don't open from the outside. You gotta open it from the inside."

They walk over to the car.

"But does the engine run?" Callan asks.

"Oh, yeah, the engine runs real good."

Callan gets in and turns the key.

The engine comes to life like Snow White after the kiss.

"How much?" Callan asks.

"I dunno. Eleven hundred?"

"Pink slip?"

"Pink slip, registration, plates. All that."

Callan walks back to the bike, takes twenty hundred-dollar bills out of the sidesaddle and hands them to the guy. "A thousand for the car. The rest for forgetting you ever saw us."

The guy takes the money. "Hey, anytime you don't want me to see you, come back."

Callan gives Nora the keys. "Follow me."

She follows him north on 79 to Julian, where they turn east on 78, down the long, curving grade to the desert, across a long flat stretch, until he finally pulls off on a dirt road and stops about a half-mile from where the road stops, at the mouth of a canyon.

"This should do," he says when she gets out of the car, meaning that the fire won't spread here in the sand and there probably won't be anyone around to notice the smoke. He siphons some gas from his spare tank, then pours it over the Harley.

"You want to say good-bye?" he asks her.

"Good-bye."

He tosses the match.

They watch the bike burn.

"A Viking funeral," she says.

"Except we're not in it." He walks back to the Grand Am, gets in the driver's seat and slides over to open the door for her. "Where do you want to go?"

"Somewhere nice, somewhere quiet."

He thinks about it. If anyone does discover the bike's skeleton and connects it to us, they'll probably think we headed east, across the desert, to catch a flight somewhere from Tucson or Phoenix or maybe Las Vegas. So when they get back to the highway he backtracks west.

"Where are we going?" Nora asks. She doesn't really care; she's just curious.

Which is a good thing, because he answers, "I don't know."

He doesn't, either. He doesn't have anything in mind except to drive. Enjoy the scenery, enjoy being with her. They climb back up the same road they came down, into the mountains, to the little town of Julian.

They drive right through—they don't want to be around other people— and then the road starts heading down again as the terrain slopes toward the coastal plain to the west, and the land flattens into broad fields and apple orchards and horse ranches and then they go down a long hill, from which they can see a beautiful valley below.

In the middle of the valley there's a crossroads with one highway going north and another going west. There are a few buildings scattered around the junction—a post office, a market, a diner, a bakery, an (unlikely) art gallery on the north side, an old general store and a few white cottages on the south side, and beyond that there's nothing on any side. Just the road cutting through the broad grassland with cattle grazing on it, and she says, "This is beautiful."

He pulls off on the gravel driveway beside the cabins. Goes into the old general store, which now sells books and gardening stuff, and comes out a few minutes later with a key. "We got one for a month," he says. "Unless you hate it. Then we can get our money back and go someplace else."

It has a small front room with an old sofa and a couple of chairs and a table, and a small kitchen with a gas stove and an old refrigerator and a sink with wooden cupboards above it. A single door leads to the tiny bedroom, which has an even tinier bathroom—shower, no bath—in back.

We're not going to lose each other in this place, she thinks.

He's still standing tentatively in the front doorway.

"It's fine with me," she says. "How about you?"

"It's good, it's fine." He lets the door shut behind him. "We're the Kellys, by the way. I'm Tom, you're Jean."

"I'm Jean Kelly?"

"I didn't think of that."

After she showers and gets dressed they drive the four miles back up the hill to Julian to shop for clothes. The one main street is flanked mostly by little restaurants selling the apple pie that is the local specialty, but there are a few boutiques, where she buys a couple of casual dresses and a sweater. But they buy most of their clothes at the hardware store, which sells denim shirts, jeans, socks and underwear.

Down the street Nora finds a bookstore that sells used paperbacks, and she buys copies of *Anna Karenina, Middlemarch, The Eustace Diamonds* and a couple of Nora Roberts romances—guilty pleasures.

Then they drive back down to the market across the highway from their cottage and buy groceries—bread, milk, coffee, tea, Raisin Bran (his favorite), Grape-Nuts (hers), bacon, eggs, sourdough bread, a couple of steaks, some chicken, potatoes, rice, asparagus, green beans, tomatoes, grapefruit, brown rice, an apple pie, some red wine and some beer—and sundries—paper towels, dish detergent, toilet paper, deodorant, toothpaste and toothbrushes, soap, shampoo, a razor and blades, shaving cream, a hair-color kit and a pair of scissors.

They've agreed to take some precautions—not to run, but not to be need-lessly foolhardy, either. So the Harley had to go, and so does her shoulder-length hair, because while Callan's looks are pretty ordinary, hers aren't, and the first thing their pursuers will ask people is if they've noticed a strikingly beautiful blond woman.

"I'm not so beautiful anymore," she tells him.

"Yeah you are."

So back at the cottage she cuts her hair.

Short.

Looks in the mirror when she's finished and says, "Joan of Arc."

"I like it."

"Liar."

But when she looks in the mirror she kind of likes it, too. Even more so after she dyes it red. Well, she thinks, it'll be easier to take care of anyway. So here I am, short, *short* red hair, a denim shirt and jeans. Who'd have thought it?

"Your turn," she says, snapping the scissors.

"Get outta here."

"It needs cutting anyway," she says. "You got that '70s look going on. Come on, just let me trim it."

"No."

"Chicken."

"That's me."

"Guys have paid a lot of money to have me do this."

"Cut their hair? You're kiddin'."

"Hey, it's a big world out there, Tommy."

"Your hands are shaking."

"Then you'd better hold still."

He lets her cut it. Sits perfectly still on the chair, looking at her image and his as she stands behind him and snips away, brown locks of his hair falling first on his shoulders and then on the floor. She finishes and they look at themselves in the mirror.

"I don't recognize us," she says. "Do you?"

No, he thinks, I don't.

That evening he makes chicken broth for her and steak and potatoes for himself and they sit down at the table and eat and watch television and when the news comes on about a meth lab blowing up and bodies found he don't say nothin' to her about it because it's clear she don't know.

He tries to feel bad about Peaches and O-Bop, but he can't. Them two ushered too many people into the next world, and you had to know it was always gonna end that way for them.

Like it's gonna end for me.

He feels bad about Mickey, though.

But the news also means that Scachi is tracking them down.

She has a rough night—she can't sleep, and she doesn't want to see what's on the inside of her eyes. He gets that—he owns a lot of the same pictures. Only maybe I'm more hardened to them, he thinks.

So he lies behind her and holds her and tells her Irish stories he remembers from when he was a kid. Well, he sort of remembers them, and he makes up what he don't, which isn't too hard because you just got to talk about fairies and leprechauns and shit like that.

Fairy tales and fables.

She finally nods off about four in the morning and he sleeps, too, with his hand gripped on the .22 under the pillow.

She wakes up hungry.

No shit, Callan thinks, and they walk across the highway to the restaurant and she orders a cheese omelet with link sausages on the side and rye toast with lots of butter.

The waitress asks, "You want American cheese, cheddar or Jack?"

"Yes."

She eats like the condemned.

The woman sucks down that omelet as if it's her last meal, as if they're waiting outside to walk her that last mile, down to Old Sparky. Callan suppresses a smile as he watches her wield her fork like it's a weapon—those link sausages don't have a chance—and he doesn't tell her about the small smear of butter at the corner of her mouth.

"Didn't like it?" he asks.

"It was *wonderful*."

"Get another one."

"No!"

"Cinnamon roll?"

"Okay."

"They were baked fresh this morning," the waitress says as she sets down the huge pastry and two forks. Nora goes outside and comes back with *The San Diego Union-Tribune* and scans the personal ads.

"Kim, from her Sister. Family Emergency. Looking for You Everywhere. Urgent You Contact." With a phone number. Typical Keller, she thinks, covering all the bases just in case, as *is* the case, I'm a free agent on the run of my own free will. So Arthur wants me to come in.

I'm not coming, Arthur. Not just yet.

If you want me, you'll have to find me.

He's trying.

Art's troops are out in force. At airports, train stations, bus stations, shipping ports. They check passenger manifests, reservations, passport control. Hobbs' guys check immigration records in France, England and Brazil. They know they're on a fool's errand, but by the end of the week one thing seems certain: Nora Hayden hasn't left the country—at least not on her own passport. Nor has she used any of her credit cards or her cell phone, tried to get a job, been stopped for a traffic offense or put her Social Security number down to rent an apartment.

Art puts the heat on Haley Saxon and has her threatened with everything from violating the Mann Act and running a disorderly house to being an accessory to attempted murder. So he believes her when she swears she hasn't heard from Nora and will call him the instant she does.

Neither his listening posts on the border nor Hobbs' across it pick up a trail. Not her talking, not anyone talking about her.

Art drags an accident reconstruction guy out to measure the depth of Callan's motorcycle tracks, and the guy does some mojo with the dirt and tells Art that there were definitely two people on that bike and that he hopes the passenger was holding on tight because it was moving *fast*.

Callan couldn't have taken her all that far, Art reasons. He couldn't have taken a prisoner on a plane, a train or a bus, and there are so many places a prisoner could get off the back of a bike—at a gas station, a red light, a junction.

So Art narrows the search to within one gas tank's radius of the junction of the dirt road and I-8. Look for a Harley-Davidson Electra Glide.

He finds it.

A Border Patrol helicopter flying over Anza-Borrego looking for *mojados* spots the scorch mark and lands to investigate it. The report comes to Art right away—his guys are monitoring all the BP radio traffic, so he has a guy out there two hours later in the company of a Harley dealer who has a meth-possession rap hanging over him. Dude looks at the charred remains of the hog and almost tearfully confirms that it's the same model they're looking for.

"Why would anyone do something like this?" he moans.

You don't have to be Sherlock Holmes—shit, you don't even have to be *Larry* Holmes—to see that a car followed the bike in there, someone got out of the car and then everyone took off in the car again and went back onto the highway.

So the reconstructionist goes out again. Measures the depth of the tire tracks and the width between tires, takes a cast of the tire marks, plays in the dirt for a while and tells Art that he's looking for a smaller-size, two-door sedan with an automatic transmission and old Firestones on it.

"Something else," a Border Patrol guy tells him. "The passenger door doesn't work."

"How the hell do you know that?" Art asks. Border Patrol agents are experts at "cutting sign," that is, reading tracks. Especially in the desert.

"The footprints outside the passenger door," the agent tells him. "She stepped backward to let the door open."

"How do you know it's a she?" his man asks.

"These marks are from a woman's shoes," the agent says. "The same woman was driving the car. She got out the driver's side, walked over to where the guy was standing, stood and watched. See how the heel is heavier where she stood for a few minutes? Then she walked around to the passenger side and he walked around to the driver's side and let her in."

"Can you tell what kind of shoes the woman was wearing?"

"Me? No," the agent says. "But I'll bet you've got guys who can."

Yes, he does, and the guy's on a chopper heading out there within half an hour. He takes a cast of the shoe and takes it back to the lab. Four hours later he calls Art with the results.

It's her.

She's with Callan.

Apparently of her own free will.

Which boggles Art's mind. What are we looking at here, he wonders, an advanced case of Stockholm syndrome, or something else? And while the good news is that she's alive, at least as of a couple of days ago, the bad news is that Callan has broken through the radius of containment. He was in a car headed east with a "prisoner" who at least appears to be cooperative, so now he could be anywhere.

And Nora with him.

"Let me take it from here," Sal Scachi says to Art. "I know the guy. I can deal with him if I find him."

"The guy killed three of his old partners and kidnapped a woman, and you can deal with him?" Art asks him.

"We go back," Scachi says.

Art reluctantly agrees. It makes sense—Scachi *does* have a prior relationship with Callan, and Art can't pursue this much further without drawing attention. And he needs Nora back. They all do; they can't make the deal with Adán Barrera without her.

.   .   .

Their days have settled into a pleasant routine.

Nora and Callan get up early and have breakfast, sometimes at home, sometimes at the place across the highway. He usually goes the high-cholesterol route, and she usually has unadorned oatmeal and dry toast because the place doesn't serve fruit for breakfast except at Sunday brunch. They don't talk much during breakfast; neither of them is a big talker early in the morning. Instead of conversing, they swap sections of the newspaper.

After breakfast they usually take a drive. They know it's not the smartest thing to do—the smart thing would be to park that car behind the cottage and leave it there—but they're still in their fatalistic mind-set and they like taking the drives. He's found a lake seven miles north on Highway 79—a beautiful drive through oak-studded grasslands and rolling hills, big ranches on the west side of the road, the Kumeyaay reservation on the other. Then the hills give way to a broad, flat plain of grazing land with hills in the background to the south (the Palomar Observatory sits like a giant golf ball on top of the highest summit) and a big lake in the middle.

It isn't much of a lake as lakes go—just a large oval of water sitting in the middle of a larger plain—but it's a lake, and they can walk around its south end and she enjoys that. And there's usually a large herd of black-and-white Holstein cattle grazing on the east side of the lake, and she likes looking at them.

So sometimes they drive up to the lake and walk around; other times they drive into the high desert out past Ranchita to Culp Valley, where huge round boulders are scattered around as if a giant had suddenly walked away from his game of marbles and never came back to reclaim them. Or sometimes they drive just up the hill to Inaja Peak, where they park and climb up the short trail to the lookout point from which you can see all the mountain ranges and, to the south, Mexico.

Then they come home and fix lunch—he has a turkey or ham sandwich, she has some fruit she bought at the market—and they take a long siesta. She never realized until now how tired she's been, how flat-out tired, and how much she must need sleep because her body seems to crave it, easily falling asleep anytime she lays her head down.

After their siesta they usually just hang out, either in the front room or, if it's warm, out on the small porch. She reads her books and he listens to the radio and looks at magazines. Late in the afternoon they walk over to the market to buy food for supper. She likes shopping for one meal at a time because it reminds her of Paris, and she quizzes the guy behind the meat counter about what's good that day.

"Cooking is ninety percent shopping," she tells Callan.

"Okay."

He thinks she enjoys the shopping and the cooking more than the eating because she'll spend twenty minutes picking out the best cut of steak and then will eat maybe two bites of it. Or three bites, if it's chicken or fish. And she's incredibly fussy about the vegetables, which she does eat massive quantities of. And while she buys potatoes for him ("I know you're Irish") she makes brown rice for herself.

They cook dinner together. It's become a ritual he really enjoys, shuffling around each other in the tiny kitchen, chopping vegetables, peeling potatoes, heating oil, sautéing the meat or boiling the pasta and talking. They talk about bullshit—about movies, about New York, about sports. She tells him a little bit about her childhood, he tells her a little about his, but they leave out the heavy shit. She tells him about Paris—about the food, the markets, the cafés, the river, the light.

They don't talk about the future.

They don't even talk about the present. What the hell they're doing, who they even are, what they are to each other. They haven't made love or even kissed, and neither one knows if that's a "yet" or what it is. She just knows that he's the second man in her whole life who doesn't want to just fuck her and maybe the first man she might really want. He just knows that he's with her, and it's enough.

Enough just to live.

Scachi's driving Sunrise Highway when he spots it—a run-down farm that looks like a used-car lot. What the fuck, Scachi thinks, and pulls in.

Your typical goober in the seed-grain cap ambles over. "Help you?"

"Maybe," Scachi says. "You sell these heaps?"

"I just like to work on them," Bud says.

But Scachi sees the flicker of alarm cross the guy's eyes and plays a hunch. "You sell one a while back, the passenger door don't work?"

Bud's eyes pop wide like those suckers in the TV ads for the Psychic Friends Network, like, *How did you know that?*

"Who are you?" Bud asks.

"Whatever he paid you to keep your mouth shut?" Scachi says. "I'm the guy who's going to pay you more to open it up again. Alternatively, I'll seize your house, your land, *all* your cars *and* your autographed picture of Richard Petty and then put you in prison until the Chargers win the Super Bowl, which is, like, forever."

He takes out his money clip and starts peeling off bills. "Say when."

"Are you a cop?"

"And then some," Scachi says, still peeling out bills. "We there yet?"

Fifteen hundred bucks.

"Close."

"You're one of them *sly* goobers, aren't you?" Scachi says. "Taking advantage of the city slicker. Sixteen hundred and that's as big as the carrot gets, my friend, and you don't *want* to see the stick."

"An eighty-five Grand Am," Bud says, shoving the money into his pocket. "Lime green."

"Plates?"

"4ADM045."

Scachi nods. "I'm going to tell you pretty much what the other guy told you—anyone asks, I wasn't here, you didn't see me. Here's the difference— you sell *me* to the highest bidder . . ." He pulls out a .38 revolver. "I'll come back, stick this up your ass and pull the trigger until it's empty. Do we have an understanding here?"

"Yes."

"Good," Scachi says, putting the gun away.

He gets back in his car and drives off.

Callan and Nora go to a church.

They're taking one of their afternoon drives and pull off Highway 79 at the Kumeyaay reservation, to the old Santa Ysabel Mission. It's a small church, little more than a chapel, built in the classic California Mission style.

"You wanna go in?" Callan asks.

"I'd like to."

They walk up to a small abstract statue beside the church. It's labeled THE ANGEL OF THE LOST BELLS, and a plaque beside it tells the story of how the mission's bells were stolen back in the '20s, and how the parishioners still pray for their safe return so that the church will regain its voice.

Someone stole the freaking church bells? Callan asks himself. Typical. People can't leave *nothin'* alone.

They go inside the church.

The whitewashed adobe walls stand in stark contrast to the dark hand-hewn wooden beams that support the peaked ceiling. Incongruous but inexpensive pine paneling lines the lower half of the walls, beneath stained-glass windows with depictions of saints and the Stations of the Cross. The oaken pews look new. The altar is colorfully decorated in the Mexican style, with brightly painted statues of Mary and the saints. It's bittersweet to her—she hasn't stepped foot in a church since Juan's funeral, and this reminds her of him.

They stand in front of the altar together.

She says, "I want to light a candle."

He goes with her, and they kneel together in front of the votive candles. A statue of the Baby Jesus stands behind the candle, and behind that is a painting of a beautiful young Kumeyaay woman looking reverentially up to heaven.

Nora lights a candle, bows her head and silently prays.

He kneels, waiting for her to finish, and looks at the mural that takes up the whole right-hand wall behind the altar. It's a vivid painting of Christ on the Cross, with the two thieves nailed up beside him.

Nora takes a long time.

When they're outside she says, "I feel better."

"You prayed for a long time."

She tells him about Juan Parada. About their friendship and her love for him. How it was the murder of Parada that led her to betray Adán.

"I hate Adán," she says. "I want to see him in hell."

Callan don't say nothing.

They're back in the car maybe ten minutes when she says, "Sean, I have to go back."

"Why?"

"To testify against Adán," she says. "He killed Juan."

Callan gets it. He hates hearing it, but he gets it. He still tries to talk her out if it. "Scachi and them, I don't think they want you to testify. I think they want to kill you."

"Sean, I have to go back."

He nods. "I'll take you to Keller."

"Tomorrow."

"Tomorrow."

That night they lie in bed in the dark, listening to the sound of crickets outside and to each other's breathing. In the distance a pack of coyotes launches into a cacophony of yips and howls, and then it's quiet again.

Callan says, "I was there."

"Where?"

"When they killed Parada," he says. "I was part of it."

He feels her body tense beside him. Her breathing stops. Then she says, "For God's sake, why?"

It's ten, fifteen minutes before he says a word. Then he starts with being seventeen years old in the Liffey Pub and pulling the trigger on Eddie Friel.

He talks for hours, murmuring softly into the warmth of her neck, and tells her about the men he killed. He tells her about the murders he did in New York, Colombia, Peru, Honduras, El Salvador, Mexico. When he gets to that day at the Guadalajara airport he says, "I didn't know it was supposed to be him. I tried to stop it, but I was too late. He died in my arms, Nora. He said he forgave me."

"But you don't."

He shakes his head. "I'm guilty as hell. For him. For all of them."

He's surprised when he feels her arms wrap around him and pull him tight. His tears fall on her neck.

When he stops crying she says, "When I was fourteen . . ."

She tells him about all the men. The johns, the jobs, the parties. All the men she took in her mouth, her ass, herself. She looks into his eyes for the revulsion she expects to see but she doesn't find it. Then she tells him about how she loved Parada, and how she wanted revenge, and how she went with Adán, and how it led to so much killing and how it hurts.

Their faces are close, their lips almost touching.

She takes his hand and puts it under her denim shirt and on her breast. His eyes open, he looks surprised, but she nods and he brushes her nipple with his palm and she feels it get hard and it feels good and when he lowers his mouth to her breast and licks and sucks it's like she blossoms in his mouth and she feels herself getting soft and moist.

He's hard. She reaches down and opens his jeans and feels him and his moan vibrates on her breast. She frees his cock from his pants and strokes him and he tentatively unzips her pants and reaches in and touches her pussy with one finger and she says *It's good* so he dips his finger into her wetness then rubs it gently on her bud and feels it swell and get hard and after a while her back arches and she groans and cries and he slides his mouth down and sucks her and licks her like he's healing a wound and her body tightens and arches and she grips his hand as she comes and he strokes her neck and her hair and says *It's okay, it's okay* and when she stops crying she bends down to take his cock in her mouth but he says *I want to be inside you, is that okay* and she says *Yes* and he asks again *Is that okay* and she says *I want you in me*.

She lies back and takes his cock and guides it to her and he gently pushes and she wraps her legs around him and pushes him in harder and then he's all the way in and he looks down at her beautiful face and her beautiful eyes and she's smiling and he says *God, that is so beautiful* and she nods and tilts her hips up to take him deeper and he feels this sweet place inside her and he slides out and then back in again and she is all sweet slippery heat to him, she is shimmering silvery wet, she strokes his back, his ass, his legs and moans

So good, so good and he reaches for that spot with his cock and touches it and there's sweat on her lips and he licks it off, sweat on her neck and he licks it off, he feels the sweat running between her breasts onto his chest, from her thighs onto his thighs, a sweet sticky wetness between her thighs she's wrapped around him so tight, he says *I'm going to come* and she says *Yes, baby. Come in me, come in me, come in me* and he pushes into her as deep as he can and holds himself there and then he feels her pussy squeeze him, grip him in place, and she pulses on him and he comes, screaming, and then screams again, and then crumples onto the warmth of her shoulder and she says *I love feeling you inside me.*

They fall asleep like that, with him on top of her.

He gets up early, while she's still asleep and goes into town to get groceries so that he can wake her up with the smell of blueberry pancakes, coffee and bacon.

When he comes back, she's gone.

15

The Crossing

This train carries saints and sinners.
This train carries losers and winners.
This train carries whores and gamblers.
This train carries lost souls . . .

—Traditional

San Diego
1999

rt meets Hobbs at the Organ Pavilion in Balboa Park. Rows and rows of white metal chairs in a broad semicircle inside the amphitheater slant down toward the stage. Hobbs sits reading a book in the second-to-last row. Sal Scachi sits above him, two seats to the left.

It's warm out. The beginning of spring.

Art sits down next to Hobbs.

"Any news on Nora Hayden?" Art asks.

"We've known each other a long time, Arthur," Hobbs says. "A lot of water has gone under the bridge."

"What are you telling me, John?"

Oh, Christ, is she dead?

"I'm sorry, Arthur," Hobbs says. "I can't let you take Adán Barrera to trial. You will hand him over to us immediately."

The same old, same old, Art thinks. First with Tío, now with Adán.

"He's a terrorist, John! You said so yourself! He's in bed with FARC and—"

"I have been given assurances," Hobbs says, "that the Barrera *pasador* will do no further business with FARC."

"Assurances?!" Art asks. "From *Adán Barrera*?!"

"No," Hobbs says calmly. "From Miguel Ángel Barrera."

Art can't say anything.

Hobbs can. "This was all getting out of hand, Arthur. Serious men had to step in before it got any worse."

" 'Serious men.' You and Tío."

"He was appalled at his nephew's dalliance with terrorists," Hobbs says. "Would have put a quick stop to it had he known about it. He knows about it now. This is a good solution, Arthur. Adán Barrera could be an invaluable source of intelligence, if given reason to cooperate."

It's bullshit, Art knows. They're terrified of what Adán might say on the stand. With good reason. I wouldn't take his deal, but they will. They've already figured it out. They'll give him a new face, a new identity, a new life.

The hell they will.

"You can't have him."

Hobbs's voice has some anger in it as he says, "May I remind you that we are in a war on terrorism."

Art tilts his face toward the sun and enjoys its heat on his skin. He says, "A war on terrorism, a war on Communism, a war on drugs. There's always a war on something."

"That is the human condition, I'm afraid."

"Not for me, not anymore," Art says. "I'm out of it."

He gets up.

"It has to *end*," Art says. "It has to end somewhere."

Hobbs says, "May I further remind you that we'll be pulling your fat out of the fire as well. Your sanctimonious air of moral superiority is frankly unbearable. And insupportable, I might add. You have been complicit in—"

Art holds his hand up. "He already offered me the deal. I turned him down. I'm going to take Adán Barrera to the DA and let justice take its course. Then I'm going to tell everything. About what happened in Condor, about Cerberus, about Red Mist."

Hobbs goes pale.

"You will *not* do that, Arthur."

"Watch me."

If Hobbs looked pale before, he looks ghostly now. "I thought you were a patriot."

"I am."

Art starts to walk away.

It really is spring—the gardens in the park are exploding with new color and the air is warm, with just enough of a residual trace of winter to still be refreshing. He looks down at the amphitheater, where little knots of schoolkids on field trips are gathered around their teachers, and young couples sit over sandwiches, and tourists with cameras draped around their necks study maps of the park and point, and old people walk slowly, enjoying the air and the new warmth of spring.

Just then an airliner flies low overhead to land at San Diego's short airstrip, and the noise is deafening and he can just hear John Hobbs say, "Nora Hayden."

"What?"

"We have her," Hobbs says. "We'll trade her."

Art turns around.

"You couldn't save Ernie Hidalgo," Hobbs says. "You can save Nora Hayden. It's very easy—bring me Barrera. Otherwise . . ."

He doesn't need to finish the threat.

They'll put a bullet in her head.

"The Cabrillo Bridge," Hobbs says. "Midnight is melodramatic. Let's say three a.m.? After the homosexual assignations are concluded but before the jogging commences. You bring Barrera from the west side, we'll bring Ms. Hayden from the east. And Arthur, if you still feel this pathetic urge to confess everything, may I suggest you go to a priest? If you think that anyone else will believe or even care about your 'truth,' you are sadly deluded."

Hobbs goes back to serenely reading his book.

Behind dark shades, Scachi stares off into infinite space.

Art walks away.

"You want me to set it up?" Scachi asks.

Hobbs nods. It's sad. Art Keller is a good man, but it's axiomatic, and true, that good men have to die in war.

Art goes back to the secure location where he has Adán.

"You got your deal," Art says.

One last job.

Is what Scachi tells Callan.

Yeah, it's always one last job.

But you got no choice but to believe him, Callan thinks as he walks through Balboa Park.

Do it, or they'll kill her.

He buys a ticket for a production of Harold Pinter's *Betrayal* at the Old Globe. At intermission, he steps outside to grab a smoke and walks around the back of the theater to an alley between it and the Zoological Hospital. He walks down the alley to a chain-link fence under some eucalyptus trees on the slope overlooking the highway and, to the left, Cabrillo Bridge. He's shielded from view by the back of the theater on one side and the back of the hospital on the other, and some storage trailers below the hospital mask him from the highway. He takes out the detached rifle scope and sights in on Scachi standing on the bridge, smoking a cigar. The range is .02 miles.

It'll be an easy shot, even at night.

He goes back and sits through the rest of the play.

Art stands on the front step and rings the doorbell.

Althea looks great.

Surprised to see him, but great.

"Arthur . . ."

"May I come in?"

"Of course."

She leads him to a sofa in the living room and sits beside him. This could have been my home, Art thinks, *should* have been my home. Except that I threw it away to chase something not worth catching.

I threw you away, too, he thinks, looking at Althea.

Some few women get prettier with age. Her laugh and smile lines complement her; even the worry lines are lovely. He notices that she's had some highlights put in her hair. She's wearing a black blouse over jeans and a gold chain around her neck. Art remembers that he gave her the chain but can't recall whether it was for her birthday or Valentine's Day. It might have been Christmas, he thinks.

"Michael's not home, I'm afraid," she says. "He went to the movies with some friends."

"I'll catch him next time."

"Art, are you okay?" she asks, suddenly looking concerned. "You're not sick or—"

"I'm fine."

"Because you look—"

"A long time ago," he said, "you wanted me to tell the truth. Do you remember that?"

She nods.

"I wish to hell I had," Art says. "I wish I hadn't thrown you away."

"Maybe it's not too late."

No, he thinks. It's way too late. He gets up from the couch. "I better be going."

"It was good to see you."

"You, too."

She hugs him at the door. Kisses him on the cheek.

"Take care of yourself, Art, okay?"

"Sure."

He goes out the door.

"Art?"

He turns around.

"I'm sorry."

It's okay, he thinks. I really only came to say good-bye.

He knows that he's walking into an ambush. That they're going to kill him and Nora on the Cabrillo Bridge.

They don't have a choice.

Nora gets into the backseat with John Hobbs.

He's very courtly to her—an old gentleman wearing a suit with a white shirt and a bow tie and an overcoat, even though the night is warm.

She looks beautiful tonight and she knows it. She's dyed her hair back to blond and they bought her a black dress that fits like a sheath. She wears diamond earrings and a diamond choker and heels. Her makeup is perfect, her eyes large, her lips glistening red.

She feels like a whore.

You play the part, she thinks, you dress the part.

Hobbs goes over everything with her again but she already understands it. Sal Scachi laid it all out for her. All she has to do is meet Adán in the middle of the bridge and walk back to the car with him.

Then she's free to go and so is Sean Callan.

New identities and new lives.

He's waiting for her back at the safe house, a hostage to her fulfilling her part of the deal. They needn't have bothered, she thinks. I've done my bit so far. What's a few more seconds of pretended love?

The only thing that bothers her is that Adán's going to get away with all of it. The CIA, as these men doubtless are, will keep him and hold him and take good care of him and he'll never be punished for Juan's murder.

It's wrong and she hates it but she'll do it for Sean.

And Juan will understand.

Won't you? she thinks, sending the thought to heaven. Tell me that you understand, tell me you want me to do this. Tell me you forgive me for the sins I've committed, and for the one I'm about to commit.

. . .

Sal Scachi looks at her in the rearview mirror and winks. He can easily understand how a man could become obsessed with her. Even Callan's in love with her now, and Sean Callan is the coldest motherfucker who ever walked.

Well, I hope you got her on your mind tonight, Callan. I'd prefer you a little distracted because I'm the one who's got to pop a cap in you. It's too bad, sonny boy, but you gotta go. Can't take the risk of you ever running your mouth about this.

It's all been set up. A drug shoot-out on the bridge tonight, then the media starts the official public mourning for the hero Art Keller and a day or so later they break the story that he was a dirty cop on the Barrera payroll who got greedy and got his. Shot by one of Barrera's hitmen.

The notorious Sean Callan.

You do get a new identity tonight, Sean boy.

This time you die for real.

John Hobbs inhales the woman's perfume.

Old men, he thinks, take their fading pleasures where they can. In days past, quite past, he might have tried to seduce her. If, indeed, one can be said to "seduce" a prostitute. Now, alas, all he requires of her is for her to fulfill her obligation.

Bring Adán Barrera peacefully into our hands.

Hobbs has no qualms about it, none of the regret that he feels for the unfortunate but necessary sanction of Arthur Keller.

Ah, well, the next world is perfect; this one, considerably less so.

He inhales the woman's perfume.

Art drives his own car to the rendezvous.

Adán sits beside him, his hands cuffed in front of him. There's no traffic on the streets at quarter to three in the morning. Art takes Harbor Drive because he likes to see the sailboats and the moon shining on the water and the downtown skyline.

Adán sits quietly, with a self-satisfied smirk on his face.

"You know something, Adán?" Art asks. "You're the reason I hope there's a hell."

"Don't think this is over," Adán says. "I still owe you for Raúl."

Art pulls over, gets out, yanks Adán out of the car and pushes him down on his knees. Art draws the .38 from his holster and enjoys the look of fear that comes into Adán's eyes. He raises the gun, then smashes it into Adán's face. The first blow cuts the cheek under his left eye, raising an ugly, bleeding welt. The second one breaks his nose. The third one splits his upper lip and breaks two teeth.

Adán topples over with a groan, spitting blood out of his broken mouth.

"That's just so you know I'm serious," Art says. "Fuck with me and I swear to God I'll beat you to death. You understand me?"

Adán nods.

"Who approached you about setting up Parada?"

"Nobody, it was an—"

Yeah, it was an accident, Art thinks. And it was an accident that Tío walked out of prison, an accident that Antonucci gave you absolution. Everything was a fucking accident. Art jerks him up by the hair and smashes the gun butt against his ear.

"Who approached you to set up Parada?"

What the hell? Adán thinks. It doesn't matter now.

"It was Scachi," he says.

Art nods. That's what I thought, he tells himself.

That's what I thought.

"Why?"

"He knew it all," Adán says. "Just like me."

"He knew about Cerberus?"

"Yes."

"How about Red Mist?"

"That, too."

Art hauls him back up, marches him to the car and shoves him back in.

It's time to go to the bridge.

Callan gets in position.

He takes the heavy sniper rifle from its bag, then attaches the tripod and the infrared scope and screws on the silencer. He lies down in the dead grass and sights in on the bridge.

There ain't gonna be nothing to it. As soon as Keller hands Barrera over, Sal will look up and nod and Callan will take out Keller.

Then just walk away.

Sal will swing by, pick him up on Park Boulevard and take him to Nora. Get their new passports, go to L.A., get on a plane to Paris.

A new life.

He settles in and gets himself ready to kill Art Keller.

Operation Red Mist comes home.

. . .

The Cabrillo Bridge spans Highway 63 where it bisects Balboa Park.

Art parks the car just to the west, by the bowling green where the old people come, dressed all in white, to play their slow game in the afternoon sun. He opens the car door and pulls Adán out by the elbow, shows him the .38 holstered on his hip and says, "Please make a run for it."

Then he pushes Adán out on the west end of the bridge and they start walking east toward the main part of Balboa Park.

The stone of the bridge glows softly gold under the amber lanterns.

To his right Art sees the downtown office towers and the huge red neon sign that reads HOTEL CORTEZ, which dominates the skyline.

Beyond that are the harbor and the ocean and the Coronado Bridge, rising up like a dream from its base in Chicano Park in Barrio Logan, where he grew up. To his left is the chasm of Palm Canyon, the redwoods and star pines looming above the west side of the highway behind him, the San Diego Zoo to the northeast.

Straight ahead is Balboa Park, with the California Tower rising above two tall palm trees like the top of a wedding cake. The bridge itself runs into the Prado, the long broad walkway between the museums and gardens, and at the end of the Prado a tower of water shoots into the night sky from the Balboa plaza.

He's taken this walk many times.

So they killed Father Juan as part of Red Mist, Art thinks.

And Hobbs ordered it.

For the first time in a long time, Art has perfect clarity.

He sees it all now.

Callan sights in on Keller's forehead, then his chest, then his forehead again. Make it a head shot, Scachi had told him. The narcos shoot turncoats in the head.

Art sees headlights swirl ahead of them as a car turns in the big circle in the middle of the Prado and then comes toward them. The car, a black Lincoln, stops at the east end of the bridge.

Art sees Scachi get out and open the back door. Hobbs gets out slowly, leaning heavily on his cane even as Scachi steadies him. Then Scachi walks around the back of the car and opens the other door and Nora gets out of the car gracefully, like a woman who's used to having doors opened for her.

He feels Adán's arm tense.

Then someone else gets out of the car and he blinks.

The man has aged. His hair is silver now, and so is his mustache. He's thinner, but he still carries himself like an Old World gentleman.

Ever gallant, Tío takes Nora by the arm.

Adán sees her and smiles.

She looks lovely, all the more so in the soft light. It's as if she's gained her vitality back, her femininity. He tries to run to her but Art holds him back. It doesn't really matter, though, because she's coming to him.

Don't get too close.

Is what Callan's thinking as Nora crosses the bridge. Just get Barrera and walk back to the car. She don't know what's going to happen. There's no reason to let her know. He hopes she's back in the car by the time he has to pull the trigger.

She don't need no more blood splattered on her.

They meet just west of the middle of the bridge.

Scachi walks ahead of the rest, comes up to Art and says, "No offense, Arthur. I need your weapon."

Art slides his jacket back and Scachi takes his .38 and tucks it into his own belt. Then he turns Art around, makes him lean against the bridge railing and frisks him. Finding nothing, he waves for the others to come ahead.

Art watches Tío come toward him with Nora on his arm. Like he's walking her down the aisle, Art thinks.

Hobbs lags behind.

Tío looks at Adán's bleeding, broken face and says to Art, "You haven't changed any, *mi sobrino.*"

"I should have put one in your head when I had the chance."

"You should have," Tío agrees. "But you didn't."

"What are you doing here?"

"I came so my nephew would know he was being delivered to safety," Tío says, "and not to be murdered. It looks as if I'm just in time."

He hugs Adán, both hands behind his head, being careful not to get blood on his suit. "*Mi sobrino,* Adán, what have they done to you?"

"Tío, it's good to see you."

"Take the handcuffs off him, please," Tío says.

Art steps behind Adán, takes the cuffs off and nudges him forward.

Hobbs looks at Art and says, "You're a man of your word, Arthur. You're a man of honor."

Art shakes his head. "Not really, no."

He grabs Hobbs and spins the old man in front of him as a shield, his left hand at Hobbs' neck, the other behind his head. One twist will kill him.

Scachi pulls his gun but is afraid to shoot.

"Put the guns down, Sal, or I'll break his fucking neck."

"You do and I'll kill you."

"Okay."

Sal lays his gun on the bridge.

"Now mine."

Sal lays Keller's .38 down beside his. Then he looks up at the ridge behind Keller and nods.

Callan sees it.

He puts the crosshairs squarely on the back of Keller's head and takes a deep breath.

Change your life.

Art says, "Nora, toss one gun over the bridge and give the other to me."

Adán laughs.

Until Nora goes and throws one of the guns over.

"What are you doing?!" Adán yells.

She looks him square in the eye.

"I was the *soplón*, Adán. It was *always* me."

Adán's head snaps back. "I loved you."

"You killed the man I loved," Nora says. "And I *never* loved you."

She hands Art the gun.

Sal looks over his shoulder and yells, *"Shoot!"*

Art spins to face the shooter.

Scachi pulls a second gun from his waistband and trains it on Art's back.

Callan puts the bullet square into Scachi's head.

Sal drops from the scope's sight.

Tío dives and grabs Scachi's gun.

Art turns.

Tío raises the gun.

Art puts two shots into his chest.

Tío's hand reflexively pulls the trigger.

The bullet goes through Hobbs' hip and into Art's leg.

They both go down.

Hobbs pulls himself up, grabs his cane and starts to stagger away on the bridge, wobbling crazily like a bad stage drunk.

Callan lays his sights on the man's frail chest.

Blood blossoms on Hobbs' back.

His cane clatters on the stone.

Adán crawls to Tío.

He takes the gun from his uncle's hand.

Callan tries to get a shot, but Nora's in the way.

Art struggles to his knees, sees Adán kneeling by Tío.

Adán's gun goes off once, twice, both bullets zinging past Art.

Dizzy, he aims his own gun and fires.

The bullet smacks into Tío's dead body.

Adán shoots again.

Art's head snaps back, a ribbon of blood swirls in the air, and he falls back into the bridge railing, his gun dropping to the highway below.

Adán turns his gun on Nora.

"GET DOWN!" Callan yells.

Nora drops to the ground.

So does Adán.

He drops to his stomach and crawls along the bridge, firing behind him as he goes.

Callan can't get a shot through the railings, can't even see Adán now. He drops his rifle and runs toward the bridge.

Adán gets up and runs.

. . .

The pain is ferocious. Blood flows from the deep cut on Art's forehead into his eyes so that he can barely see. He sways and fights the tunnel vision that's shrinking his brain, threatening to black him out. He looks up and can just make out the form of Adán running away. Adán looks like he's running in a fun house, with the floor slanting this way and that.

Art struggles to his feet, falls, then gets up again.

Then he starts to run.

Adán can hear the footsteps chasing him.

Keep running, he tells himself. He knows he doesn't have to make it across the border, he just has to get into the barrio and knock on the right door and the doors will open for Adán Barrera and close for Art Keller.

So he runs down the Prado, empty now in the small hours of the morning, the museum buildings looming like the walls of a lost city around him. If he can make it off the Prado and onto Park Boulevard he'll be all right. There'll be a thousand places he can duck into darkness, then work his way into the barrio.

He sees the fountain maybe fifty yards in front of him, marking the end of the Prado, its light shining on the tower of silver water.

Art sees it, too.

Knows what it means.

Adán gets past that and he's gone, probably for good. The Twenty-eighth Street boys will hide him, get him back across the border. He forces his legs to move faster, even though every fall of his foot sends a jolt of pain burning through his leg.

He hears sirens in the distance and wonders if they're real or in his head.

Adán hears them, too, and keeps running.

A few more yards and he'll be gone.

He turns to see where Keller is.

Art jumps.

Takes Adán high around the shoulders and drives him over the fountain's low wall and into the water.

Adán gets up and jams his hand into Art's face, clawing at his eyes.

Art's head explodes in pain, but he has a grip on Adán's shirt and won't let go. Just hold on, Art tells himself, just hold on. Adán's shirt rips free and he starts to pull away.

Art throws himself blindly, desperately, and feels Adán's body land under him and hears Adán grunt as the air is blown out of his lungs. Blood rises in the water where Adán struck his head. Art grabs him by his hair and forces his head under the water.

He lifts him up, hears him gasp and then pushes him down again, screaming over the sound of the fountain's cascade: "This is for Ernie, motherfucker! This is for Pilar Méndez and her children! This is for Ramos!"

He holds him down, loving the feel of the man's legs kicking helplessly beneath him, loving the feel of his body quivering, his suffering, his dying.

"This is for El Sauzal!"

Art presses down harder. Adán bucks beneath him, his back arching like it's going to snap. Art doesn't see that—he sees a baby dead in his mother's arms. He feels the power of the dog.

"This is for Father Juan!" Art yells.

He jerks Adán's head up and out of the water.

The two men kneel in the water, gasping for air, their blood swirling around them, water pouring down over their heads.

Art sees red lights flashing, then cops walking up on them, their guns out. He keeps one hand on Adán's neck and throws the other in the air.

"Don't shoot! Don't shoot!" he yells. "I'm a cop! This is my prisoner! This is *my prisoner*!"

In the distance, as if in a long tunnel, he sees Nora and Callan walking toward him.

Then he falls back into the water.

It feels cool and clean.

Epilogue

The poppies are in bloom.
  Bright orange, bright red.
  Art waters them carefully.
And savors the irony.

They didn't put him in prison, the judge having decided that the former Border Lord wouldn't have lasted a day in any federal institution. So it's been a series of safe houses between rounds of testimony, seemingly endless sessions before endless committees, then back to another refuge where he's relatively safe.

He's been at this one for three months now and soon it will be time to move again, but he takes it a day at a time, and today is sunny and warm and he's enjoying the garden in the enclosed courtyard.

He enjoys the solitude.

YOYO, he thinks as he sets down the watering can, sits on the little bench and leans back against the adobe wall.

But not really.

You have your ghosts.

Nora is gone now. She finished testifying and faded into her new life. Art likes to think that she's with Callan, who likewise disappeared. It's a pleasant thought.

Adán is serving twelve consecutive life sentences in a federal hole, also a pleasant thought. Art got to sit in the courtroom and watch him be led away in cuffs and ankle chains as Adán shouted back to tell him that the bounty on his head was still good.

And who knows, Art thinks, maybe someone will collect.

The drugs stopped flowing out of Mexico for about fifteen minutes after Adán's downfall, then new kids on the block stepped up to take his place. There are more drugs coming into the country than ever.

Based on Art's testimony, Congress launched an intensive investigation into Operation Cerberus and Red Mist and promised action. So far, nothing has been done. The government spends billions of dollars a year in aid to Colombia for drug interdiction. Most of it goes for helicopters to fight the insurgents. The war drags on.

The murder of Cardinal Juan Parada is still officially ruled an unfortunate accident.

Art supposes he should be bitter.

Sometimes he tries to be, but it feels like a slightly ridiculous parody of a former life, and he drops it. Althie and the kids—Hell, he thinks, they aren't kids anymore—are coming for a quick visit this afternoon, and he wants to be cheerful.

He doesn't know yet what will happen, how long he will have to spend in this limbo, whether he'll ever get out. He accepts it as penance. He still doesn't know if he believes in God, but he has hope of a God.

And maybe that's the best we can do in this world, he thinks as he gets up to resume watering the flowers—tend to the garden and maintain the hope of a God.

Against all evidence to the contrary.

He watches the water bead silver on the petals.

And mutters a snatch of an odd prayer he once heard, which he doesn't quite understand but that nevertheless sticks in his head—

Deliver my soul from the sword.

My love from the power of the dog.

The Cartel

Don Winslow

The fast-paced and thrilling sequel to Don Winslow's epic drug novel, *The Power of the Dog*.

It's 2004. DEA agent Art Keller has been fighting the war on drugs for thirty years in a blood feud against Adan Barrera, the head of El Federación, the world's most powerful cartel, and the man who brutally murdered Keller's partner. Putting Barrera away costs Keller dearly – the woman he loves, the beliefs he cherishes, the life he wants to lead.

Then Barrera gets out, determined to rebuild the empire that Keller shattered. Unwilling to live in a world with Barrera in it, Keller goes on a ten-year odyssey to take him down.

'Sensationally good, even after the near-perfection of *The Power of the Dog*. Less of a sequel than an integral part of a solid-gold whole'
Lee Child

'This is the *War and Peace* of dope-war books. Tense, brutal, wildly atmospheric, stunningly plotted, deeply etched. It's got the jazz-dog feel of a shot of pure meth'
James Ellroy

'Masterfully organised and teeming with memorable characters, it is unlikely to be bettered this year'
Sunday Times

arrow books

California Fire and Life

Don Winslow

The woman on the bed had died in the fire. Pamela Vale, aged 34. She was beautiful in life, and heavily insured. With her husband showing little grief, and her children seemingly terrified, insurance investigator Jack Wade is sure he knows what happened, and all he has to do is to gather the evidence to prove it. Wade is the best there is: fires talk to him, tell him exactly what happened, and how . . .

'A taut, well-plotted exhaustively researched thriller that takes hold like a torched warehouse and doesn't let up till the last embers are smoking . . . fascinating'
Maxim

arrow books

Isle of Joy

Don Winslow

Walter Withers is a CIA spy who has come in from the cold. After years as a honey-trap operative in Scandinavia (setting up blackmail traps for Soviet and other agents), he is back home in New York working as a private investigator with New York's leading security firm. He is assigned to look after up-and-coming Presidential hopeful Senator Jack Flynn, who is serially promiscuous. One of his assignations ends up with his sexy mistress dead. Withers is suspected of the crime.

As he fights to prove his innocence, it becomes clear that there's much more at stake than a crime of passion. Flynn may be over his head, and may be a target for Soviet (or FBI) blackmail. . .

Isle of Joy is a magnificent thriller that paints a complete (and sometimes bleak) portrait of the USA in the late 50s against a backdrop of the Cold War and anti-communist hysteria. . .

arrow books

The Death and Life of Bobby Z

Don Winslow

When Tim Kearney draws a license plate across the throat of a Hell's Angel, he's pretty much a dead man. It's his third crime and, according to California law, that gives him 'life without the possibility of parole.' Killing a Hell's Angel also makes him a dead man on any prison yard in California. That's when the DEA makes Kearney an offer: impersonate the late, legendary dope smuggler Bobby Z so that the agency can trade him to Don Huertero – northern Mexico's drug kingpin – for a captured DEA agent. Kearney bears an uncanny resemblance to Bobby Z, and with training, he might be able to pass.

Or not. But, really, what choice does he have?

'It has whiplash speed, deliciously sleazoid characters and a major attitude problem. What a blast' Carl Hiaasen

'Sparkling . . . genuine hardboiled American' *Time Out*

'Once you pick it up, you won't be able to put it down – the suspense is addictive . . . Punchy and action-packed, with a dash of raunchy sex thrown in, Winslow will have you totally hooked' *Company*

arrow books

ALSO AVAILABLE IN ARROW

The Winter of Frankie Machine

Don Winslow

Frank Machianno is the guy, a late-middle-aged ex-surf bum who runs a bait shack on the San Diego waterfront. That's when he's not juggling any of his other three part-time jobs or trying to get a quick set in on his long board. He's a beloved fixture of the community, a stand-up businessman, a devoted father to his daughter. Frank's also a hit man. Well, a retired hit man.

Back in the day, when he was one of the most feared members of the West Coast mob, he was known as Frankie Machine. Years ago, Frank consigned his mob ties to the past, which is where he wants them to stay. But a favour called in by the local boss is one Frank simply can't refuse, and before he knows it he's sucked back into the treacherous currents of his former life. Someone from his past wants him dead, and he has to figure out who, and why, and he has to do it fast. The problem is that the list of candidates is about the size of his local phone book and Frank's rapidly running out of time . . .

'Action sequences that put your heart into your mouth . . . Vegas nights, floating orgies, shakedowns and shootings galore all feature in this superb novel . . . The ending will blow you away'
Evening Standard

'Winslow is a sensational writer . . . Won't disappoint under any circumstances'
Independent on Sunday

arrow books

ALSO AVAILABLE IN ARROW

The Dawn Patrol

Don Winslow

Boone Daniels is a laid-back kind of private investigator. He has sleuthing skills to burn but is rarely out of his boardshorts, and with a huge Pacific storm approaching San Diego, Boone wants to be there to ride the once-in-a-lifetime waves with his buddies in the Dawn Patrol. Unfortunately he's just landed a case involving one dead and one missing stripper, but with the help – or hindrance, Boone thinks – of uptight lawyer Petra Hall, he's determined to wrap it up in time for the epic surf.

But all sorts of trouble follows with Hawaiian gangs and trafficked Mexican girls, as the case turns dark and personal, raising ghosts from Boone's troubled past and dragging in Sunny and the rest of the Dawn Patrol. The currents turn treachous on land and at sea as the big swell makes landfall, and Boone has to fight just to keep his head above water . . .

'Winslow is a sensational writer'
Independent on Sunday

'If you've never read Don Winslow, start now'
Val McDermid

'So good you almost want to keep him to yourself'
Ian Rankin

arrow books